PRAISE FOR M.M. KAYE

DEATH IN KENYA

". . . *Death in Kenya* offers not only a taut mystery, but a setting that is as lush and exciting as those created in romances like *The Far Pavilions*. . . . M.M. Kaye proves once again that she is a superlative storyteller in whatever she chooses to write."

—*The Chattanooga Times*

"*Death in Kenya* will delight and enthrall M.M. Kaye's hundreds of thousands of fans. It is consummate mystery, written by one of the finest storytellers of our time."

—*Mystery News*

". . . set in a gorgeously beautiful background. . . . M.M. Kaye outdoes Agatha Christie in palming the ace, and the solution of the many crimes is a stunner."

—*The San Diego Union*

"*Death in Kenya* is a small masterpiece in its genre—a mixture of historical novel, romance, gothicism, and suspense. . . . Reading *Death in Kenya*, you will waver from suspect to suspect, but you're not likely to anticipate the entirely logical and brilliant ending."

—*Hartford Courant*

DEATH IN ZANZIBAR

"If you like Agatha Christie's stories or Dorothy Sayers' elegant British mysteries, you will also enjoy this book."

—*South Bend* (Ind) *Tribune*

"A superb storyteller has taken over the classic mystery. Read M.M. Kaye's *Death in Zanzibar* and stop missing Christie."

—*Murder Ink*

"M.M. Kaye is a master at providing suspense. . . . Surprise twists mark the conclusion of this excellently written and conceived novel. The characters . . . are beautifully drawn. *Death in Zanzibar* is highly recommended."

—UPI

"*Death in Zanzibar* is an evocative, high-quality suspense tale of muted terror and romantic locale . . . scary enough to send a few delicious tingles up the spine."

—*Richmond Times-Dispatch*

DEATH IN CYPRUS

"The author of *The Far Pavilions* is also renowned for her superior mysteries: *Death in Zanzibar* and *Death in Kenya*. Kaye's new thriller is set in another exotic locale, Cyprus, when it was still unspoiled. . . . The island's ambience and the intriguing characters heighten the suspense and keep the reader turning the pages to find out what happens next."

—Publishers Weekly

"A superbly plotted tale enhanced by its exotic setting, Cyprus before the civil war. From beginning to end, Kaye has given us an I-can't-put-it-down-till-the-last-page mystery worthy of praise from Agatha Christie."

—Houston Chronicle

"*Death in Cyprus* is a superbly elegant tale of suspense, murder and romance set under the warm sun and mysterious moonlit skies of the picture-perfect island of Cyprus. . . . M.M. Kaye creates an aura of romance and menace that rivals anything created by the grand dames of the genre."

—Mystery News

". . . airy and entertaining . . . an agreeable Agatha Christie/Noel Coward hybrid."

—Kirkus Reviews

M·M·KAYE

THREE COMPLETE MYSTERIES

M·M·KAYE

THREE COMPLETE MYSTERIES

Death in Kenya

Death in Zanzibar

Death in Cyprus

WINGS BOOKS
NEW YORK · AVENEL, NEW JERSEY

This omnibus was originally published in separate volumes under the titles:

DEATH IN KENYA, originally LATER THAN YOU THINK,
copyright © 1958, 1983 by M.M. Kaye.
DEATH IN ZANZIBAR, originally THE HOUSE OF SHADE,
copyright © 1959, 1983 by M.M. Kaye.
DEATH IN CYPRUS, originally DEATH WALKED IN CYPRUS,
copyright © 1956, 1984 by M.M. Kaye.

This 1993 edition is published by Wings Books,
distributed by Outlet Book Company, Inc., a Random House Company,
40 Engelhard Avenue, Avenel, New Jersey 07001,
by arrangement with St. Martin's Press.

Random House
New York · Toronto · London · Sydney · Auckland

Printed and bound in the United States of America

Library of Congress Cataloging-in-Publication Data
Kaye, M.M. (Mary Margaret), 1911–
Three complete novels / M.M. Kaye.
p.   cm.
Contents: Death in Kenya — Death in Zanzibar — Death in Cyprus.
ISBN 0-517-10024-X
1. Detective and mystery stories, English. I. Title.
PR6061.A945A6   1994
823′.914—dc20   93-30395
                                                      CIP

8 7 6 5 4 3 2 1

CONTENTS

DEATH IN KENYA

Remembering TINA and JAY—
With Love

AUTHOR'S NOTE

Few people nowadays will remember the Mau Mau terrorist rising in Kenya, and millions more will never even have heard of it. But it was an unpleasant business while it lasted. I happened to be in Kenya towards the end of that period, because my husband's regiment had been sent there to deal with 'The Emergency'—which was the white settlers' name for it. And despite some hair-raising moments, I can truthfully say that I enjoyed practically every minute of my stay in that marvellous and exciting country.

The idea for this story came into my mind one evening when I was standing on our verandah in the dusk, and I heard birds calling down in the papyrus swamp that fringed the shores of Lake Naivasha. But the book itself, originally published under the prophetic title *Later Than You Think*, did not take shape until after we had left Kenya. Em's house, *Flamingo*, is an amalgam of several houses built by early settlers in the Rift or on the Kinangop, but I chose to site it on the same spot as the one we ourselves lived in. The opinions voiced by my characters were taken from life and at first hand. For though the Wind of Change was rising fast, very few of the Kenya-born settlers would believe that it could possibly blow strongly enough to uproot them from a country that every single one of them looked upon, and loved, as a '*Land where my fathers died, Land of the pilgrim's pride . . .*'

5

1

A flock of pelicans, their white wings dyed apricot by the setting sun, sailed low over the acacia trees of the garden with a sound like tearing silk, and the sudden swish of their passing sent Alice's heart into her throat and dried her mouth with panic. The shadows of the stately birds flicked across her and were gone, and she leaned weakly against the gate in the plumbago hedge and fought for control.

It was absurd and childish to allow herself to become so hag-ridden by fear that the mere passing of a flight of birds could set her flinching and cowering. But she could not help herself. She had fought fear for too long, and now at last she had reached the limits of endurance. She would have to leave Kenya: she and Eden. Surely he would see that she could not stand any more. For now, in addition to her fear of the country there was her terror of the house.

Alice had always been afraid of Kenya. It seemed to her a savage and uncivilized land full of brooding menace, in which only Em's luxurious house had provided a narrow oasis of safety and comfort. But now there was no longer any safety anywhere, for strange things had been happening in the house of late. Inexplicable, malicious, frightening things . . .

It was the cat, declared Zacharia, the old grey-headed Kikuyu who had served Em for almost forty years, explaining away the first appearance of the invisible vandal who had taken to haunting the house. Who else could have thrown down the K'ang Hsi vase from the top of the cabinet where it had stood for so many years? There had been no wind. As for the bottle of red ink that had rolled, unstoppered, across the carpet upon which the Memsahib set such store, there had been a bird in the room—see, here was a feather! Pusser must have pursued it, and in doing so knocked over both ink bottle and vase.

7

But Em had not believed it. She had stormed and raged and questioned the African servants, but to no avail. And later, when other things were broken or defaced, Zacharia had made no further mention of Pusser. He and the other house servants had gone about their duties with scared faces and starting, frightened eyes, and Em, too, had said nothing more. She had only become quieter—and looked grim and grey and very old.

Lady Emily DeBrett—Em DeBrett of *Flamingo*—had come to Kenya as a bride in the Colony's early days, and she and her husband, Gerald, had been among the first white settlers in the Rift Valley.

Gerald had never looked upon Kenya as anything more than a Tom Tiddlers Ground. But the seventeen-year-old Emily had taken one look at the great golden valley with its cold craters and savage lava falls, its lily-strewn lakes and its vast herds of game, and had fallen in love with it as some women fall in love with a man.

Gerald had staked out a claim on the shores of Lake Naivasha: acres and acres of virgin land on which he intended to raise sheep and cattle, and grow sisal and maize and lucerne. And on a rising slope of ground, overlooking the lake, he had built a crude mud and wattle hut that had in time given place to a small stone-built house; square, ugly and unpretentious. Em had named the farm *'Flamingo'* because a flight of those fantastic rose-coloured birds had flown across it on that first evening; and *Flamingo* it had remained.

Kendall, Em's son, had been born in the mud and wattle house and christened in the small stone building that had replaced it. There had been no other children, for when Kendall was three years old his father had been killed by a fall from his horse. But *Flamingo* had already begun to justify all Gerald's hopes, and Em had refused to go home. 'This is my home,' she had said, 'and I will never leave it.'

The estate had prospered, and she had pulled down the ugly stone house that Gerald had built, and raised in its stead a huge, sprawling single-storeyed house to her own design. A thatch-roofed house with wide verandahs and spacious rooms panelled in un-dressed cedar wood, that defied all architectural rules and yet blended with the wild beauty of the Rift Valley as though it had always been a part of it; and Em loved it as she had never loved Gerald or her son Kendall.

She had been a remarkably pretty woman, and she was barely twenty when her husband died; but she did not marry again. Partly because her absorption in the affairs of her estate left her little time for other interests, and partly because hard and unremitting toil soon dispelled that pink-and-white prettiness. She wore, from choice, trousers and shirt and a man's double-terai hat, and as her abundant hair was too much trouble to keep in order, she cropped it short. At thirty she might have been forty-five or fifty, and from forty onwards, though she became increasingly bulky, she was merely an elderly and eccentric woman whose age it would have been impossible to guess.

Kendall was sent home to Eton, and from there to Oxford. And it was from Oxford, on his twenty-second birthday, that he sent a cable telling of his marriage to pretty Clarissa Brook.

Clarissa had proved to be a girl after Em's own heart, and as Mr Rycett, Em's manager, had retired that year, Kendall had stepped into his place, and he and Clarissa had moved into the manager's house; a pleasant stone-built bungalow in the grounds of *Flamingo,* barely six hundred yards from the main house, and hidden from it by a grove of acacias and a plumbago hedge. But Eden DeBrett, Em's first grandson, was born at *Flamingo.*

Em had insisted on that. 'He must be born in this house. It will be his one day.' And looking at the baby she had thought with pride: I have founded a dynasty. A Kenya dynasty! A hundred years from now—two hundred—there will be DeBretts living in this house and farming this land when Kenya is no longer a raw new Colony, but a great and prosperous country . . .

She was as impatient for grandsons as though *Flamingo* had been a kingdom and the DeBretts a royal house whose succession must be assured.

But there were to be no more grandsons for Em. As there had been no more sons. Kendall and Clarissa had died in a car accident, and there was only Eden. Little Eden DeBrett who was such a beautiful child, and whom his grandmother spoiled and adored and loved only one degree less than she loved the land of her adoption.

After Kendall's death there had been another manager, Gus Abbott, who had lived in the bungalow beyond the plumbago hedge for over twenty years, and died in a Mau Mau raid on *Flamingo* in the first months of the Emergency. His place had been taken by a younger man, Mr Gilbraith Markham, and it was Mr Markham's wife Lisa whom Alice had come in search of on this quiet evening: poor, pretty, discontented Lisa, who loved cities and cinemas and gaiety, and who had been so bored by life at *Flamingo*—until the day when she had had the misfortune to fall in love with Eden DeBrett.

Alice pushed open the gate in the plumbago hedge and walked on down the dusty path that wound between clumps of bamboos and flowering shrubs, thinking of Lisa. Of Lisa and Eden . . .

It isn't his fault, thought Eden's wife loyally. It's because he's too good-looking. And just because women throw themselves at his head, and lose their own and make fools of themselves over him, it doesn't mean that he—She stopped suddenly, with a grimace of distaste. But it was a sound, and not her thoughts that had checked her.

The path had come out on the edge of a wide lawn in front of a green and white bungalow flanked by towering acacia trees, and someone inside the bungalow was playing the piano. Gilly, of course.

Gilly Markham was not a conspicuous success as a farm manager, and many people in the Rift Valley had attributed his appointment to his musical rather than his managerial abilities. For it was an unexpected facet of Lady Emily DeBrett's character that she was intensely and passionately musical, and there was probably some truth in the rumour that she had permitted Gilly Markham's musical talent to influence her judgement when Gus Abbott's death necessitated the appointment of a new manager at *Flamingo*.

But it was not Gilly's technique that had checked Alice and produced that grimace of distaste. It was the music itself. The Rift Concerto. As if it wasn't enough to hear Em playing it day after day! And now Gilly too——!

It had been an Italian prisoner-of-war who had written the Rift Valley Concerto. Guido Toroni. He had been sent to work at *Flamingo,* and Em had discovered by chance that he had once been a concert pianist. He had composed the concerto on Em's Bechstein grand, and later, when the war was over, he had gone to America where he had made a name for himself. There he had also made a single long-playing record of the concerto especially for Em, to whom he had sent it as a thank-offering and a memento. Em had been inordinately pleased, and had allowed no one to handle it except herself; but just two weeks previously it had been found smashed into a dozen pieces.

It could not possibly have been an accident. It had been a deliberate and ugly piece of spite that had frightened Alice and infuriated Em. But that had not been the worst of it, for Em had taken to playing the concerto from memory: 'so that I shall not forget it'. She had played it again and again during the last two weeks, until the wild, haunting cadences had plucked at Alice's taut nerves and worn them ragged. And now Gilly too was playing it. Playing it as Em played it, with passion and fury. But with a skill and magic that Em's gnarled, spatulate fingers, for all their love, did not possess.

Alice pushed between the canna lilies and ran across the lawn and up the stone steps that led on to the verandah. The door into the drawing-room stood open, and entering without ceremony she leant across Gilly's shoulder and thrust his hands off the keyboard in an ugly crash of sound.

Gilly spun round on the piano stool and stared at her contorted face.

'God! you startled me! What's up? You look all to pieces.' He rose hurriedly. 'Nothing the matter, is there?'

'No. No, nothing.' Alice groped behind her and catching at the arm of a chair, sat down rather suddenly. Her breathing steadied, and a little colour crept back into her pale cheeks. 'I'm sorry, Gilly. My nerves are on edge. It was only that tune. Em's been playing it and playing it until I can't endure the sound of it.'

'She has, has she?' said Gilly, mixing a stiff whisky and soda and handing it to Alice.

He poured out a second and larger one for himself, omitting the soda, and gulped it down: 'Then I'm not surprised your nerves are in ribbons. She's a bloody bad pianist. She takes that third movement as though she were an elephant charging an express train.'

He sat down again at the piano as though to illustrate, and Alice said in a taut voice: 'Gilly, if you play that again I shall scream. I mean it!'

Gilly dropped his hands and regarded her with some concern. 'I say, you are in a bad way! Have another drink?'

'I haven't started on this one yet,' said Alice with an attempt at a laugh. 'Oh, it isn't that. It's—well that record being broken. You heard about that, didn't you?'

'You mean the poltergeist? Of course I did.'

'It *isn't* a poltergeist! Don't *say* things like that! It must be some-one—a person. But Em swears by all her servants. She's had them for years and they're nearly all second-generation *Flamingo* ser-vants. Or even third! She won't believe it is one of them. But it's worrying her badly. I know it is.'

Gilly poured himself out another three fingers of whisky, and subsiding on to the sofa, sipped it moodily. He was a thin, untidy-looking man in the middle thirties with a pallid, discontented face and pale blue eyes that had a habit of sliding away from a direct look. His shock of fair hair was perpetually in need of cutting, and he wore a sweat-stained open-necked shirt, grubby khaki trousers and a sagging belt that supported a revolver in a well-worn holster. Altogether an incongruous figure in Lisa's over-decorated drawing-room. As incongruous as Alice DeBrett with her neat dark head, her neat dark expensive linen suit, her impeccable shoes and flawless pearls, and her pale, strained, Madonna face that was innocent of all but the barest trace of make-up.

'Won't do Em any harm to worry,' said Gilly, sipping whisky. 'Told her years ago she should throw out all her Kukes. Everyone's told her! But Em's always fancied she knew better than anyone else. "Treat 'em right and they'll be loyal." *Bah!* There's no such thing as a loyal Kuke. We've all learned that—the hard way!'

Alice said uncertainly: 'But she's fond of her Kikuyu servants, Gilly. And they did stay with her all through the Emergency, and now that it's over——'

'Who said it was over?' demanded Gilly. 'Over, my foot! What about this latest caper—the Kiama Kia Muingi? A *rose by any other name,* that's what! Secret ceremonies, extortion, intimidation—same old filthy familiar ingredients simmering away again and ready to boil over at the drop of a hat. And yet there are scores of little optimists running round in circles saying that it's all over! Don't let 'em fool you!'

He reached behind him, and groping for the bottle of whisky refilled his glass, slopping the liquid on to the rose-patterned chintz of the sofa in the process. 'Who's to say how many Mau Mau are still on the run in the forests, or Nairobi, or the Rift? Why, they haven't even caught "General Africa" yet—and they say it's over! Y'know—' Gilly's words were slurring together—'y'know Hector Brandon? Course you do! Well, Hector's been doin' a lot of interrogation of M.M. old lags, and he says one of 'em told him that there are still a gang of hard-core terrorists hidin' out in the *marula*—the papyrus swamp. Bein' fed by the African labour of the farms along the lake. And Greg Gilbert says he believes General Africa is still employed by a settler. Why, it might be any of Em's Kukes! Who's to tell? Nice quiet house boy or cook or cattleherd by day—Gen'l Africa in a lion skin hat at night. Might even be one of Hector's. In fact, only too likely if you ask me!'

'Oh no, Gilly! Why everyone knows that the Mau Mau swore

they'd get Hector because of his intelligence work. Yet they never did, and if General Africa had been one of his own men it would have been too easy.'

'Maybe,' said Gilly sceptically. 'But I'll tell you something that "everyone" doesn't know! And that is that once upon a time Drew Stratton's lot nearly got the "General"—he walked into one of their ambushes with five of his men, and though he managed to get away, he left something behind him: a hunting knife. It had been in a sort of holster at his belt, and by some infernal fluke a bullet chipped it off as clean as a whistle without harming him. But it was the next best thing to getting the man himself, because it had a set of his finger prints on it. The only clue to his identity the Security Forces had ever got their hands on. And what happened to them? Well, I'll tell you. Hector carefully cleaned 'em off! It's always been my belief that he recognized the knife, and that he wasn't taking any chances of one of his darling boys being accused. "Honour of the House", an' all that.'

'Gilly, no!' protested Alice. 'You shouldn't say things like that! It must have been a mistake—an accident.'

'That's what *he* said. Said he thought it belonged to Greg, and merely picked it up off Greg's desk to doodle with. Greg nearly hit the ceiling. It's no use, Alice. You just don't understand what some of these old Kenya hands are capable of; or how their own little patch of land can end by becoming the centre of the universe to them, just because they made it out of nothing by the sweat of their brow, and starved for it and gave up their youth for it, and sacrificed comfort and safety and civilization and a lot of other trivial little things for it. *Brandonmead* is Hector's pride. No—I'm wrong. Ken's his pride. *Brandonmead*'s his life; and he's always sworn by all his African labour. "Loyal to the core" and all that sort of stuff. It would have damned near killed him if it had turned out that one of his precious Kukes was a star Mau Mau thug. I believe he'd have done almost anything to cover it up, and salved his conscience by thinking he could deal with it himself. They're great ones for taking the law into their own hands out here. Haven't you noticed that yet?'

Alice said uncomfortably: 'But Em says——'

'Em!' interrupted Gilly rudely. 'Em's as bad as any of them. Worse! It was silly old bitches like her who caused half the trouble. "My Kukes are loyal. I'll stake my life on it." So they lose—*Bah!* You're not going, are you?'

Alice had put down her half finished glass and stood up. She said coldly: 'I'm afraid I must. I only came over with a message for Lisa, but if she's out perhaps you'd give it to her.'

'She isn't out. She's only gone down to the shamba with the Brandons and Drew Stratton. Here, don't go! Have the other half of that. I didn't mean to get your goat. I know how you feel about Em. You're fond of the old battle-axe. Well, so am I—when she isn't tearing a strip off me! So's all Kenya. Protected Monument—that's Em! Apologize, if I hurt your feelings.'

'That's all right, Gilly,' said Alice hurriedly. 'But I don't think I'll wait, all the same. It's getting late. And if Lisa has guests——'

There was an unexpected trace of embarrassment in her quiet voice, and Gilly's shrewd, pale eyes regarded her with observant interest. He said: 'Ken's not with them, if that's what's worrying you.'

His laugh held a trace of malice as he saw the colour rise in Alice DeBrett's pale cheeks. 'There's no need for you to blush like that, Alice. We all know that you've done your best to snub the poor boy. That is, all except Mabel. But you can't expect Mabel to believe that every woman isn't crazy about her darling son. He's her blind spot. Funny about Ken: I wouldn't have thought you were his type at all.'

'I'm not,' said Alice with a trace of a snap. 'Don't be ridiculous, Gilly. I'm old enough to be his mother!'

'Here! Give yourself a chance! You can't be much more than thirty-five!'

'I'm twenty-seven,' said Alice slowly. 'And Ken isn't twenty yet.'

'Oh well,' said Gilly, dismissing it, and unaware of the blow that he had dealt her. 'Chaps always fall in love with someone older than themselves to start with, and they always fall hard. He'll get over it. Hector ought to send him away. God, I only wish *I* could get the hell out of this Valley! Did you know that Jerry Coles is going to retire soon? You know—the chap who manages the DeBrett property out at Rumuruti. That's the job I'm after. But Em's being damned obstinate. Suit me down to the ground. Nice home, good pay and perks— and no Em looking over my shoulder the entire time, carping and criticizing. Heaven!'

Alice smiled a little wanly and said: 'Wouldn't you find it rather lonely? I shouldn't have thought Lisa would like living so far away.'

Gilly scowled, and his pale eyes were suddenly brooding and sombre. He said: 'That's another reason. It's far away. Over a hundred dusty, uncomfortable, glorious miles away. Far enough, perhaps, to keep her from making an infernal fool of herself over——'

Alice did not let him finish. She walked towards the door, her face white and pinched, and spoke over-loudly, as though to drown out words that she did not wish to hear: 'I really must go. It's getting late and I ought to get back. Will you tell Lisa that——'

Gilly said: 'You can tell her yourself. Here they are now.'

There were footsteps and voices in the verandah, and a moment later Gilly's wife and her guests were in the room. The Brandons, whose property touched the western borders of *Flamingo* and who were such a strangely assorted pair—small, soft-voiced Mabel with her kind, charming face and grey curls, and her choleric husband, Hector, who lived up to his name and was large, loud-voiced and ruddy-featured. Drew Stratton, whose farm lay five miles further along the shores of the lake. And Lisa herself, her bright brown hair bound by a satin ribbon and her wide-skirted dress patterned with roses.

Gilly rose unsteadily and dispensed drinks, and Lisa said: 'Why, hullo, Alice! Nice to see you.'

Her violet eyes slid past Alice with a quick eager look that turned to disappointment, and was neither lost nor misinterpreted by Eden's wife.

Lisa and Eden—! thought Alice. She pushed away the thought as though it had been a tangible thing and said a little stiffly: 'I only came over with a message from Em. She said that you'd asked for a lift next time she went into Nairobi, and to tell you that she'd be going in on Thursday to fetch her niece from the airport.'

'Great-niece, surely?' corrected Lisa.

'No,' said Mrs Brandon in her gentle voice. 'It's her sister's child. Good evening, Alice.' She dropped her knitting bag on the sofa and sat down beside it. 'Lady Helen was Em's half-sister, and a good deal younger than her. She came out to stay with Em during the first world war, and married Jack Caryll who used to own the Lumley place on the Kinangop: Victoria, the daughter, was born out here. I remember her quite well—a thin little girl who used to ride a zebra that Jack tamed for her. He was killed by a rhino while he was out shooting, and his wife took a dislike to the whole country in consequence. She sold the farm to the Lumleys, and went back to England; and now she's died. It's strange to think that she must have been about twenty years younger than Em, and yet Em's still so strong. But I am surprised that Em should have decided to bring Victoria out here. It seems rather an odd thing to do in—in the circumstances.'

For a moment her soft voice held a trace of embarrassment, and

Alice's slight figure stiffened. She said coldly: 'Lady Emily feels that it is time she had someone to take over the secretarial work and help with the milk records. She has always done those herself up to now, but she is getting old, and it tires her.'

'But then she has you,' said Mrs Brandon. 'And Eden.'

'I'm afraid I don't type; and Eden has never been fond of paperwork.'

'Eden,' said Hector Brandon roundly, 'is not fond of work in any form! And it's no use your lookin' at me like that, Alice! I've known your husband since he was in short pants, and if you ask me, it's a pity his grandmother didn't dust 'em more often—with a slipper!'

Mrs Brandon frowned reprovingly at her husband and said pacifically: 'You mustn't mind Hector, Alice. He always says what he thinks.'

'And proud of it!' boomed Hector.

Why? thought Alice with a spasm of nervous exasperation. Why should anyone consider it an admirable trait to speak their mind when it hurt other people's feelings?—when it was rude and unkind?

'Rugged individualism,' murmured Mr Stratton absently into his glass.

He caught Alice's eye and grinned at her, and some of her defensive hostility left her. Her taut nerves relaxed a little, and she returned the smile, but with a visible effort.

She liked Drew Stratton. He was one of the very few people with whom she felt entirely at ease. Perhaps because he took people as he found them and did not trouble to interest himself in their private affairs. Drew was tall and fair; as fair as Gilly but, unlike Gilly, very brown from the sun that had bleached his hair and brows. His blue eyes were deceptively bland, and if there was any rugged individualism in his make-up it did not take the form of blunt outspokenness. Nor did he find it necessary, in the manner of Hector, to dress in ill-fitting and sweat-stained clothes in order to emphasize the fact that he worked, and worked hard, in a new and raw land.

Gilly was talking again; his voice slurred and over-loud: 'Hear some of your cattle were stolen last night, Hector. Serve you right! Y'ought to keep 'em boma'd. Asking for trouble, leavin' 'em loose. It's men like you who play into the hands of the gangs. If I've heard the D.C. tell you that once, I've heard him tell you a thousand times! Invitation to help themselves—cattle all over the place.'

Hector's large red face showed signs of imminent apoplexy, and

Mabel Brandon said hurriedly: 'You know we always kept our cattle close boma'd during the Emergency, Gilly. But now that it's over there didn't seem to be any sense in it. And anyway, Drew has never boma'd his!'

'Drew happens to employ Masai,' retorted Gilly. 'Makes a difference. Makes a hell of a lot of difference! Who owned the Rift before the whites came? The Masai—that's who! And in those days if any Kikuyu had so much as put his nose into it, they'd have speared him! That's why chaps like Drew were left alone in the Emergency. But more than half your labour are Kukes. You're as bad as Em! Won't give them up, and won't hear a word against them.'

'There isn't one of our Kikuyu who I wouldn't trust with my life,' said Mrs Brandon, bristling slightly. 'Why, they've worked for us for twenty years and more. Samuel was with us before Ken was born!'

'Then why do you carry a gun in that knitting bag?' demanded Gilly. 'Tell me that! Think I don't know?'

Mrs Brandon flushed pinkly and looked as dismayed and conscience-stricken as a child who has been discovered in a fault, and Gilly laughed loudly.

'Pipe down, Gil,' requested Drew mildly. 'You're tight.'

'*A hit, a very palpable hit.* Of course I am!' admitted Gilly with unexpected candour. 'Only possible thing to be these days.'

Drew said softly: 'What are you afraid of, Gilly?'

The alcoholic truculence faded from Gilly's pale, puffy face, leaving it drawn and old beyond his years, and he said in a hoarse whisper that was suddenly and unbelievably shocking in that frilled and beruffled room: 'The same thing that Em is afraid of!'

He looked round the circle of still faces, his eyes flickering and darting as uneasily as trapped moths, and his voice rose sharply in the brief uncomfortable silence: 'There's something damned funny going on at *Flamingo,* and I don't like it. I don't like it at all! Know what I think? I think there's something brewing. Some—some funny business.'

'What d'you mean, "funny business"?' demanded Hector Brandon alertly. 'Em been having trouble with her labour? First I've heard of it.'

'No. I could take that. This is something different. Ever watched a thunderstorm coming up against the wind? S'like that! Waiting. I don't like it. Alice doesn't like it. Em don't like it either. She's stubborn as a mule—won't admit that anything could go wrong at

17

her precious *Flamingo*. But she's not been herself of late. It's getting her down.'

'Nonsense, Gilly!' Hector said firmly. 'Saw her myself only this morning. Top of her form! You're imagining things. Only trouble with Em is that she's getting old.' He allowed Lisa to refill his glass and added reflectively: 'Truth of the matter is, Em's never been her old self since Gus Abbott died. She never really got over that. Felt she'd murdered him.'

'So she did,' said Gilly. 'Murder—manslaughter—slip of the gun. What's it matter what you call it? She killed him.'

'Gilly, how *can* you!' protested Mabel indignantly. 'You know quite well that it happened in the middle of that dreadful attack. And it was largely Gus's fault. He saw one of the gang going for her with a panga, and jumped at him just as Em fired. She's never been quite the same since.'

'That's right,' said Hector. 'He'd been her manager since Kendall's day, and it broke her up. You didn't know her before— except by reputation. But we did. It did something to her. Not so much Gus's death, but the fact that she'd killed him. The whole thing must have been a pretty ghastly experience all round. She lost a couple of her servants that night, murdered by the gang, and two of her dogs were panga'd, and half the huts set on fire. But she shot three of the gang and wounded at least two more, and held off the rest until help came. It was a bloody fine show!'

'*I grant him bloody*—S-Shakespeare!' said Gilly with a bark of laughter. 'An' you're quite right, Hector. I didn't know her before. Mightn't have jumped at the job if I had! She's a difficult woman to work for. Too bloody efficient. That's her trouble. I don't like efficient women.'

He swallowed the contents of his glass at a gulp and Lisa seized the opportunity to return to a topic that was of more interest to her: 'Tell us about this niece of Em's, Alice. What's she like? Is she plain or pretty or middle-aged, or what?'

'I've never met her,' said Alice briefly. 'She must be quite young.'

Her tone did not encourage comment, but Lisa was impervious to tone. She had, moreover, the misfortune to be in love with Alice's husband, and was therefore interested, with an avid, jealous interest, in any other woman who entered his orbit—with the sole exception of his wife, whom she considered to be a colourless and negligible woman, obviously older than her handsome husband and possessing no attractions apart from money. But this new girl—this Victoria Caryll. She would be staying under the same roof as Eden, and be in daily contact with him, and she was young and might be pretty . . .

'I can't think why, if Em wanted a secretary, she couldn't have got a part-time one from among the local girls,' said Lisa discontentedly. 'Heaven knows there are enough of them, and some of them must be able to type.'

'Secretary, nuts!' said Gilly, weaving unsteadily across to the table that held the drinks, and refilling his glass. 'If you ask me, she's getting this girl out with the idea of handing over half the property to her one day. Dividing it up between her and Eden. After all, they're the only two blood-relations she's got. And there must be plenty to leave. Bags of loot—even if it's split fifty-fifty. Bet you Hector's right! Come to think of it, can't see why else she'd suddenly want to bring the girl out in such a hurry. Or why the girl was willing to come! Bet you it's that!'

'Perhaps,' said Mabel Brandon thoughtfully. 'But it's more likely to be what Alice says. Em's getting old, and when you're old there are times when you suddenly feel that the years are running out too quickly, and you begin to count them like a miser and to realize that you can't go on putting things off like you used to do—you must do them now, or you may not do them at all, because soon it may be too late.'

'For goodness sake, Mabel!' said Lisa with a nervous laugh. 'Anyone would think you were an old woman!'

'I'm not a young one,' said Mabel with a rueful smile. 'It's later than you think.'

'Don't!' said Alice with a shiver. The unexpected sharpness of her normally quiet voice evidently surprised her as much as it surprised Mabel Brandon, for she flushed painfully and said with a trace of confusion: 'I'm sorry. It's just that I've always hated that phrase. It was carved on a sundial that we had in the garden at home, and it always frightened me. I don't know why. I—I suppose it was the idea that everything would end sooner than you expected it to. The day—parties—fun—the years. Life! I used to make excuses not to go near the sundial. Silly, isn't it?'

'No!' said Gilly, harshly and abruptly. 'Do it myself. Make excuses to keep away from *Flamingo*. Same thing. Something that frightens me, but I don't know what. Don't mind a poltergeist that breaks things, but when it begins on creatures, that's different.

That's—that's damnable. Working up to something. A sighting shot. Makes you wonder where it will end. What it's got its eye on . . .'

His voice died out on a whisper and Mabel surveyed him with disapproval and said with unaccustomed severity: 'Really, Gilly, you are talking a great deal of nonsense this evening. And you're upsetting poor Lisa. What are you hinting at? That Mau Mau isn't dead yet and that Em's servants have taken the oath? Well suppose it isn't and they have? There's hardly a Kikuyu in the country who hasn't. But it doesn't mean anything any more. The whole thing has fallen to pieces and the few hard-core terrorists who are still on the run are far too busy just keeping alive to plan any more murders. And if it's the poisoning of that unfortunate ridgeback that's worrying you, I'm sure there's nothing sinister in that. It cannot be wise to keep dogs like Simba who attack strangers on sight, and I am not really surprised that someone took the law into their own hands. I might almost have felt tempted to do it myself, fond as I am of dogs, but——'

'But Simba didn't like Ken; that's it, isn't it?' said Alice, surprised to find herself so angry.

Mabel turned towards her, her gentle voice quivering with sudden emotion: 'That is not kind of you, Alice. We all know that Simba liked you, and of course Em is crazy on the subject of dogs. But considering that he once attacked your own husband——'

'Only because Eden was trying to take a book away from me. We were fooling, but Simba thought he was attacking me. He wouldn't let anyone touch me, and I suppose he thought that Ken——'

She bit the sentence off short, aghast at its implications. But it seemed to remain hanging in the air, its import embarrassingly clear to everyone in the room. As embarrassingly clear as the expression upon Mabel Brandon's stricken face, or Hector's stony tight-mouthed stare.

There was a moment of strained and painful silence which was broken by Drew Stratton, who glanced at his wrist watch and rose. He said in a leisurely voice: 'Afraid I must go, Lisa. It's getting late, and my headlights are not all they should be. Thanks for the drink. Can I drop you off at the house, Mrs DeBrett, or did you drive over?'

Alice threw him a grateful look. 'No, I came over by the short cut across the garden. And I really must walk back, because I promised Em I'd get some of the Mardan roses for the dining-room table.'

Drew said: 'Then I'll see you on your way. Eden shouldn't let you wander about alone of an evening.'

'Oh, it's safe enough now. Good night, Lisa. Shall I tell Em you'll go in with her on Thursday?'

'Yes, do. I want to get my hair done. I'll ring up tomorrow and fix an appointment. Drew, if your headlights aren't working you'd better not be long over seeing Alice back.'

'That's right,' said Gilly. 'Remember Alice's sundial. *"It is later than you think!"'*

He laughed again, and the sound of his laughter followed them out into the silent garden.

2

The sun had dipped behind the purple line of the Mau Escarpment, and the lake reflected a handful of rose-pink clouds and a single star that was as yet no more than a ghostly point of silver.

There had been very little rain during the past month, and the path that led between the canna lily beds and bamboos was thick with dust. Mr Stratton slowed his leisurely stride to Alice DeBrett's shorter step, but he did not talk, and Alice was grateful for his silence. There had been too much talk in the Markhams' drawing-room. Too many things had been said that had better have been left unsaid, and too many things had been uncovered that should have been kept decently in hiding. Things that Alice had never previously suspected, or been too preoccupied with her own problems to notice.

Was it, she wondered, the long strain of the Emergency, and the present relaxing of tension and alertness, that had brought these more petty and personal things to the surface and exposed them nakedly in Lisa's pink-and-white drawing-room? Had she, Alice, displayed her own fears and her own feelings as clearly as Lisa and Gilly and the Brandons had done? Had the brief coldness of her reply to Lisa's questions on the subject of Victoria Caryll been as illuminating as Lisa's own comments?

'Look out,' said Drew. He caught her arm, jerking her out of her abstraction just in time to prevent her treading full on a brown, moving band, four inches wide, that spanned the dusty track. A river of hurrying ants—the wicked safari ants whose bite is unbelievably painful.

'You ought to look where you're going,' remarked Mr Stratton mildly. 'That might have been a snake. And anyway you don't want a shoe-full of those creatures. They bite like the devil.'

'I know,' said Alice apologetically. 'I'm afraid I wasn't looking where I was going.'

'Dangerous thing to do in this country,' commented Drew. 'What's worrying you?'

Alice would have resented that question from anyone else, and would certainly not have answered it truthfully. But Drew Stratton was notoriously indifferent to gossip and she knew that it was kindness and not curiosity that had prompted the query. She turned to look at his brown, clear-cut profile, sharp against the quiet sky, and knew suddenly that she could talk to Drew. She had not been able to talk to anyone about Victoria. Not to Eden. Not even to Em, who had said so anxiously: 'You won't mind, dear? It's all over, you know —a long time ago. But she shan't come if you mind.' She had not been able to confess to Em that she minded. But, strangely, she could admit it to Drew.

'It's Victoria,' said Alice. 'Victoria Caryll. Eden and she— they've known each other for a long time. They're some sort of cousins. Em's her aunt and his grandmother, and he used to spend most of his holidays at her mother's house when he was home at school—and at Oxford. They—they were engaged to be married. I don't know what went wrong. I asked Eden once, but he—wouldn't talk about it. And—and her mother died a few months ago, so now she's coming out here . . .'

Alice made a small, helpless gesture with one hand, and Drew reached out and possessed himself of it. He tucked it companionably through his arm, but made no other comment, and once again Alice was conscious of a deep feeling of gratitude and a relief from strain. She could think of no one else who would not have probed and exclaimed, sympathized or uttered bracing platitudes in face of that disclosure. But Drew's silent acceptance of it, and that casual, comforting gesture, had reduced it to its proper proportions. There was really nothing to worry about. It was, in fact, a direct dispensation of Providence that Em's niece should be free to come out to Kenya, for it was going to make it so much easier to break the news to Em that they must leave her. It would have been impossible to leave her alone and old and lonely. But now she would have Victoria. And with luck, and in time, she might even grow to be almost as fond of Victoria as she was of Eden, and if that should happen perhaps she would leave her not only half of the estate, as Hector Brandon had suggested, but *Flamingo,* and the property at Rumuruti, whole and entire, so that she, Alice, would be free of it for ever, and need never come back to Kenya . . .

A huge horned owl, grey in the green twilight, rose up from the stump of a fallen tree and swooped silently across their path, and Alice caught her breath in an audible gasp and stopped suddenly, her fingers clutching frantically at Drew Stratton's sleeve.

'It's all right. It's only an owl,' said Drew pacifically.

'It was a death owl!' said Alice, shuddering. 'The servants say that if you see one of those it means that someone is going to die. They're terrified of them!'

'That's no reason why you should be,' said Drew reprovingly. 'You aren't a witchcraft-ridden Kikuyu.'

He frowned down at her, perturbed and a little impatient, and putting a hand over the cold fingers that clutched at his arm, held them in a hard and comforting grasp and said abruptly: 'Mrs DeBrett, I know it's none of my business, but don't you think it's time you gave yourself a holiday in England? You can't have had a very easy time during the last five years, but you mustn't let this country get you down. Why don't you get Eden to take you home for a few months? It will do you both good, and this niece of Em's will be company for her while you are away.'

'Yes,' said Alice a little breathlessly. 'I—we had thought . . .' Her colour was coming back and she breathed more easily. She stilled the nervous shivering of her body with a visible effort and said: 'I'm sorry, Drew. I'm behaving very stupidly. You're quite right; I should go home. I'm turning into a jumpy, hysterical wreck. Do you know what Gilly said to me this evening? He said, "You can't be more than thirty-five." And I'm twenty-seven. Eden's only twenty-nine. I can't look six or seven years older than Eden, can I?'

'Gilly was tight,' observed Drew dispassionately.

He studied her gravely, thinking that Gilly's estimate of Mrs DeBrett's age, though ungallant, was understandable. But Drew had seen nerves and shell-shock and sleeplessness before, and recognized the symptoms. He said: 'You look pretty good to me,' and smiled.

He possessed a slow and extraordinarily pleasant smile, and Alice found herself returning it. 'That's better,' approved Drew. 'You look about seventeen when you smile, not twenty-seven. You should do it more often. Are you and Eden going to this dance at Nakuru on Saturday?'

He talked trivialities until they reached the plumbago hedge that marked the boundary of the Markhams' garden, and Alice dismissed him at the gate:

'I'm not letting you come any further, or you won't get home before it's dark. And I'm perfectly safe, thank you. No one is likely to try and murder me between here and the house! Not now, anyway.'

'Probably not,' said Drew, 'but I imagine that it will be some years yet before half the women out here will feel safe without a gun.'

He watched her walk away across the garden and was conscious of a brief and unexpected flash of sympathy for Eden DeBrett. Not really the type for a settler's wife, thought Drew. She'll never stay the course.

A dry twig cracked in the soft carpet of dust behind him and he turned sharply. But it was only Gilly Markham.

'Came out for a breath of air,' explained Gilly morosely. 'Mabel's gone off to pick a lettuce or a pineapple or something, and Hector says he's going to walk home, so Lisa's locked up the booze. Women are hell.'

He leaned heavily on the gate, his eyes following the noiseless flight of a bat which swooped and flittered along the pale blossoms of the plumbago hedge, and said with sudden violence: 'God, what a country! What wouldn't I give to get out of this god-forsaken, uncivilized, gang-ridden hole! Can't think how you stand it.'

'No reason why you should stand it, Gilly,' observed Drew without heat.

'That's what *you* think!' said Gilly sourly. 'Easy enough for you. But I can't afford to up-sticks and get the hell out of it. D'you suppose I wouldn't if I could?'

Drew said dryly: 'If you're getting the same screw as Gus Abbott got, you can't be doing too badly. By all accounts, Gus left a packet.'

'Gus didn't have a wife!' retorted Gilly bitterly. 'You don't know Lisa. If I were making twenty times what I get, Lisa'd spend it. Thinks I don't know why she's always buying herself new clothes and having her face and hair fixed. Well I may be a fool, but I'm not such a fool as I look! Take my advice and don't ever get married, Drew.'

'I'll bear it in mind,' said Drew solemnly. 'So long, Gilly.'

'No, don't go!' said Gilly urgently. 'Stay around for a bit. Got the purple willies on me this evening and that's a fact. Know why people like talking to you, Drew? Well I'll tell you. It's because you're so bloody detached. You don't give a damn for any of it, do you? But tell anyone else anything, and before you know it it's all round the Colony. Why can't they mind their own business?'

'Why indeed?' said Drew. 'Sorry about it, Gilly, but I've got to go. It's late.'

Gilly ignored the interruption. 'Hector, fr'instance. Never forgiven Eden for marrying a woman who he doesn't consider is "The right type for Kenya". What's it got to do with him? Anyone would think he'd invented the place! Probably thinks that as soon as Em dies Alice'll persuade Eden to sell out to that syndicate of Afrikaners who offered a fortune for *Flamingo* last year. Wouldn't suit Hector one bit to have that sort of concern on his doorstep! Ruin the market for him. And the next thing you know they'd build a decent road round the lake, and how he'd hate that! Hector and his like may talk a lot of hot air about the Colony, but the one thing they're terrified of is development around their own little bit of it. They like it just as it is. Just exactly as it ruddy well——'

He broke off abruptly and lifted his head, listening intently.

There was no breath of wind that evening. The vast stretch of the lake lay glass-green in the twilight, and even the birds were silent at last. But someone in the big rambling house that lay beyond the pepper trees and jacarandas in Em's garden was playing the piano. The quiet evening lent clarity and a haunting, melancholy beauty to the distant sound, and Drew, who had turned away, paused involuntarily to listen, and said: 'What is she playing?'

'The Rift Valley Concerto,' said Gilly absently.

His thin, nervous, musician's fingers moved on the top bar of the gate as though it was the keyboard of a piano, and then clenched abruptly into fists, and he struck at the gate in a sudden fury of irritation and said savagely:

'Why the hell can't she play that third movement as it's meant to be played, instead of hammering it out as though it were a bloody pop tune? That woman 'ud make Bartok sound like "Two Eyes of Grey" and Debussy like "The British Grenadiers"! It's murder—that's what it is! Plain murder!'

He relapsed into glowering silence, slumping down on a square concrete block that stood among the grasses by the gate. His brief spurt of rage gave place to an alcoholic sullenness, and he took no note of Mr Stratton's departure.

Alice was half-way back to the house when she remembered the Mardan roses that Em had wanted for the dining-room table, and she turned off the path and walked across the parched grass, and through a sea of delphiniums that grew waist-high and half wild at the foot of a small knoll that was crowned by a tangle of bushes and the trunk of a fallen tree.

From the crest of the knoll, and between a break in the bushes, she could look out over the lush green of the shamba and the wide belt of grey-green vegetation, dark now in the fading light, which was the *marula*—the papyrus swamp that fringed the shores of the lake with a dense, feathery and almost impenetrable jungle, twice the height of a tall man.

A broken branch of the fallen tree supported a cascade of white roses that were not easy to pick even by day, for they were plentifully supplied with thorns. But Em loved them, and during their brief season she liked to arrange them in the Waterford glass bowls that had belonged to her grandmother. Was that why she asked for them now? So that she could fill other bowls with them and pretend that she did not care? For the Waterford glass bowls had gone. They had been found one afternoon almost a week ago, broken in pieces, though the house had been quiet that day, and the dogs had not barked . . .

'Don't touch them!' Alice had said, looking at Em's drawn, ravaged face. 'There may be finger prints on them. We can find out——'

'And have the police all over the house, trampling all over *Flamingo* and bullying my servants? No!' said Em. And she had gathered up the broken pieces with old, pitiful, shaking hands and given them to Zacharia, telling him to throw them away.

Em had refused from the first to send for the police. She had set a number of traps, but no one had fallen into them. The poltergeist seemed to be able to circumnavigate burglar alarms, trip-wires and similar booby traps, and to avoid by instinct objects smeared with a substance guaranteed to inflict an unpleasant sore on any hand that touched it. But the effects of its depredations had been more demoralizing to the whole household than anything achieved by the Mau Mau during the years of the Emergency. The servants were frankly terrified, Eden was angry and on edge, and Em grim and stubborn.

'If someone thinks that they can frighten me into leaving, they'll find they're wrong,' she said. 'The Mau Mau thought they could frighten us into leaving our farms, but we are still here. I don't know what anyone hopes to gain by destroying things I am fond of, but whatever it is, they won't get it!' And as if to emphasize her defiance she had sat down at the piano and played from memory Toroni's 'Rift Valley Concerto': playing it furiously and loudly and not very accurately.

That had been on the day that the recording of the concerto had been destroyed, and that same evening, looking tired and defeated and very old, she had told them she had sent for Victoria.

Victoria's mother had died that spring and Victoria was at present sharing a small flat in London with two friends, and working as private secretary to the assistant manager of a firm of importers.

'I have asked her to come out here and work for me,' said Em, not looking at Eden: looking at nothing but the candle flames on the dining-room table and, perhaps, the past. 'I am getting too old to deal with half the work I do. I need someone who can be a confidential secretary, and whom I can work hard. And at this time I would rather it were someone who—who belongs. It will also mean that I am doing something for Helen's child. Giving her a home as well as an adequate salary.'

She had looked at Alice for the first time, her eyes blank and unfocused from the dazzle of the candle flames, and said gently: 'You, who are an orphan too, will know what that must mean to her. But she shan't come if you would rather she did not, my dear.'

Perhaps Alice might have found it possible to protest if it had not suddenly seemed to offer a way of escape. She did not want to meet this girl whom Eden had once meant to marry and with whom he must once have been in love. And she did not want Eden to meet her again. But if Em's niece came to live at *Flamingo* perhaps she, Alice, could persuade Eden to leave Kenya: to take her back to England. It would not be as though they were leaving Em alone. She would have Victoria . . .

Alice looked down at the white roses that filled her hands, and letting them drop to the ground, sat down tiredly on the smooth trunk of the fallen tree and thought with affection and desperation and despair of Lady Emily DeBrett. Of Em and Eden. It was not going to be easy to tell Em that she could endure Kenya no longer. Em had a reputation for impatience, hard-headedness, shrewd business acumen, an iron nerve and a refusal to suffer fools gladly. Yet she had suffered Eden's wife, who according to all her lights must have seemed a fool. She had mothered her, protected her, encouraged her, and stood between her and danger.

Sitting in the dusk on the knoll at *Flamingo,* Alice recalled her first sight of Eden's grandmother, and the shock it had given her. Eden had mentioned casually that his grandmother was inclined to be eccentric in the matter of dress, but he had not prepared her for the grotesque figure that had appeared on the porch steps when the car that had brought them the fifty-odd miles from Nairobi Airport drew up before the big thatch-roofed house on the shores of Lake Naivasha.

The years had thickened Emily's stately figure to more than ample proportions, but had not eradicated her antipathy to skirts. She had never willingly worn feminine attire, but she had a fondness for bright colours and a leaning towards eccentricity. Em's scarlet dungarees and vivid blouses—both of which served to exaggerate her impressive bulk to a distressing extent—and the flamboyant wide-brimmed hats that she habitually wore crammed down upon her short cropped hair, had for more than thirty years been as familiar a sight to half Kenya as the roving zebra herds, the wandering, ochre-smeared Masai warriors, or the snows of Kilimanjaro. But they had done nothing to reassure Alice DeBrett, three weeks a bride and arriving at *Flamingo* dizzy from repeated attacks of airsickness and dusty and shaken from the last fifteen miles over an unmetalled road—a newcomer to a strange country torn with savagery and violence, where even the women carried guns and all men were afraid of the night, never knowing what darkness might bring.

It was odd, looking back on that day, to think that Em had been the only reassuring thing in all the months that had followed. She had been both mother and grandmother to Alice, who had never known either. It was Eden who had failed her. But then it could not be easy to be Eden, thought Eden's wife. To be so fatally good-looking that women looked once and fell desperately in love—as she herself had done. She had been married to Eden for almost five years now, and she still could not look at him without a contraction of the heart.

She loved him so much, and if he had loved *Flamingo* as Em loved it she would have forced herself to staying there for ever: to fighting her terror, her hatred of the land, and the ill health that constant fear, the height and the climate had inflicted upon her. But she did not believe that Eden's roots were too deep in the Kenya soil, or that the land meant to him what it meant to Em. And lately she had persuaded herself that he would be just as happy in England with an estate of his own. Happier! for it had always been a sore point with him that Em had not made him manager instead of Gilly. 'But *Flamingo* will be yours one day,' Em had said. 'You'll need a manager then, and it's better to have one who knows the ropes. Gilly's not much use at present, but managers are hard to get these days, and he'll learn. Besides, he needs the job.'

'I didn't know we were running a philanthropical society!' Eden had said crossly. 'You're losing your grip, Gran darling.'

'That's where you're wrong. You've got a hold over a man who needs a job. None over one who doesn't. And I like things done my way.'

Eden had laughed and kissed her. 'You do hate to have anyone accuse you of having a soft spot, don't you, darling? You gave Gilly the job because he was broke, and you know it—and because he knows the difference between Bach and Brahms!'

Em had made a face at him, but she had not denied it.

It was on Em's account more than Eden's that Alice had tried to reconcile herself to spending the rest of her days in Kenya, for although she had come to believe that she might be able to make up to Eden for the loss of *Flamingo,* she knew that she could never compensate Em for the loss of Eden. But now at last she had reached the breaking point. It had not been Victoria who had proved to be the last straw, but the things that had happened in the house during the last weeks: a situation that Eden had once referred to as 'this silly business'.

'It isn't silly,' Alice had said, and for the first time there had been hysteria in her gentle voice. 'It's horrible! Don't you see—everything that has been broken or spoiled has been something special and irreplaceable. It's as if someone who knew everything about Em, and wanted to hurt her specially, knew just the things to choose. Someone—someone *evil.'*

Eden had said sharply: 'That's nonsense! You mustn't be hysterical about this, Alice. Believe me, darling, it'll turn out to be some silly Kuke who fancies he has a grievance, or thinks he's had a spell put on him. You mustn't lose your sense of proportion. After all, even if the things are irreplaceable, they're still only things.'

But two days later it had not been a thing. It had been Simba.

Alice had not thought Em capable of tears, and the sight of her red and swollen eyes had been almost as shocking as the discovery of Simba's stiff, contorted body lying among the crushed geraniums below the verandah. She had been frightened before, but it had never been like this. The wanton destruction of Em's most cherished possessions had been horrible enough, but the poisoning of her favourite dog betrayed a cold-blooded malice that went deeper than mere spite.

Gilly was right, thought Alice, cold with foreboding. The 'things' were only a beginning. Simba was another step. Supposing—it is *someone* next? Someone Em loves. *Eden——! We must get away. We must!* While there is still time . . .

It had been a particularly trying day for Alice. Eden had gone to Nairobi and would not be back until late, and Em had been noticeably jumpy and on edge all day. She had apparently had a minor squabble with Mabel Brandon in the course of the morning, and had not been pleased when Ken Brandon had presented himself at the house in the afternoon and had to be asked to tea.

Alice had not been pleased either. She found young Ken Brandon's adolescent and unsnubbable infatuation for her more than a little trying, and had read him a stern lecture on the subject only the day before, which he had not taken well. He had ended by threatening to shoot himself—not for the first time—and Alice had lost all patience with him, and observed tartly that it would be no loss. She had hoped that this would put an end to his adoration, but Ken had turned up that afternoon asking to see her, and evidently intending to apologize for the dramatics of the previous day. Em had saved her from another scene by plying the boy with tea and arbitrarily taking Alice out shooting with her immediately afterwards.

Alice never went out shooting if she could help it, but on this occasion she had accepted gratefully, and they had taken Kamau, one of the boys, and driven out in the Land-Rover to shoot a buck for the dogs. Em had shot a kongoni out on the ranges, and helped Kamau to degut it and hoist the limp ungainly body into the back of the Land-Rover, where it lolled in a sticky pool of blood that smeared the seats, stained Em's hands and clothing with ugly dark splotches and filled Alice with shuddering revulsion. It was one of the many things about Kenya that she could never get used to. The casual attitude of most women towards firearms and the sight and smell of blood.

I haven't any courage, thought Alice drearily, staring into the green dusk. Perhaps I had some once, but it's gone. If only I can get away . . . If only I need not go back into that horrible house . . .

Em was still playing Toroni's concerto, and the too familiar cadences, muted by distance, plucked at Alice's taut nerves, demanding her attention and forcing her to listen.

She had never been able to understand Em's and Gilly's admiration for the concerto. It had seemed to her a tuneless noise, alternating from the discordant to the intolerably dreary. But tonight she seemed to be hearing it for the first time, and it was as if the Valley itself were speaking. The enormous golden Valley and the great yawning craters of extinct volcanoes—Longonot and Suswa and Menengai. The impassable falls of dead lava: the frowning gorge of Hell's Gate: the vast, shallow, flamingo-haunted lakes, and the long twin ramparts of the Mau and the Kinangop that were the walls of the Great Rift.

Em had told her that Toroni had loved the Valley. But Em was wrong, thought Alice, listening to the music. Toroni had not loved the Rift. He had been afraid of it. As she herself was afraid of it. She shivered convulsively, clutching her hands tightly together in her lap; and as she listened a little breath of wind whispered through the bushes and swayed the hanging trails of roses, and somewhere near her a twig cracked sharply.

Quite suddenly, with that sound, the garden was no longer a friendly place, but as full of menace as the house, and Alice stood up quickly and stooped to gather up the fallen flowers, aware that her heart was thumping painfully against her ribs. She had not realized that it had grown so dark.

Below the knoll and beyond the shamba, from the shadowy belt of the papyrus swamp, birds began to call; their clear piping cries mingling with the sweet clear notes of the distant piano. But the day had almost gone and the sky was already shimmering with pale stars, and there was as yet no moon. There should be no birds calling at this hour. Had something, or someone, startled them?

She remembered then what Gilly had said less than an hour ago. Something about General Africa—still at large despite the heavy price that the Government had set on his head, and suspected of being in the employment of one of the settlers in the Naivasha district. Something about a gang under his command who were rumoured to be still in hiding somewhere in the papyrus swamp, being fed by the African labour of the farms that bordered the Lake.

She had not paid much attention to it at the time, but now she remembered it with alarm, and remembered, too, Em's instructions that she should not stay out after sunset. But the sun had set long ago, and now it was almost dark, and the evening breeze had arisen and was stirring the leaves about her and filling the green dusk with soft, stealthy rustlings.

A twig cracked again immediately behind her, and turning quickly she caught a flicker of movement that was not caused by the wind. Her hands tightened about the roses, driving the thorns into her flesh, but caught in a sudden spider's web of panic she was almost unaware of the pain. Her brain told her to run for the house, but her muscles would not obey her. She could not even scream; and she knew that if she did so no one in the house would hear her, for the music of the piano would drown any sound from outside. But there was someone watching her from among the bushes; she was sure of it——

Alice stood quite still, as helpless and as paralysed with terror as the victim of a nightmare. And then, just as she thought that her heart must stop beating, a familiar figure materialized out of the dusk at the foot of the knoll, and the blood seemed to flow again through her numbed veins.

She dropped the roses, and with a choking sob of relief began to run, tripping and stumbling over the rough grass in the uncertain light. She was within a yard of that dimly seen figure when something checked her. A sound . . .

There was something wrong. Something crazily and impossibly wrong. She stopped suddenly, staring. Her eyes widened in her white face and her mouth opened in a soundless scream. For it was someone else. Someone suddenly and horribly unfamiliar.

3

'And as I was saying, what with Income Tax and strikes and the weather, well it's no wonder that so many people decide to live abroad. In fact, as I told Oswin—that's my present husband—I can't understand why more of them don't do it. Don't you agree?'

There was no answer, and Mrs Brocas-Gill, observing with annoyance that her neighbour had fallen asleep, turned her attention instead to the desolate green and brown expanse of Africa that lay far below her, across which the big B.O.A.C. Constellation trailed a tiny blue shadow no bigger than a toy aeroplane.

Miss Caryll, however, was not asleep. Only an exceptionally strong-minded woman, or one in need of a hearing-aid, could have slept in the company of that human long-playing record, Mrs Brocas-Gill. Victoria was neither; but she had endured Mrs Brocas-Gill's indefatigable monologue with barely a break since the aircraft had left London Airport, and as they had been delayed for twenty-four hours at Rome with engine trouble this meant that she had been compelled to listen to it for the best part of two days. Even the nights had not silenced Mrs Brocas-Gill, who had slept with her mouth open, and snored. And Victoria wanted to think.

She had not allowed herself much time for thought during the last three weeks. Once she had made her decision and cabled her acceptance of Aunt Emily's offer, there was little point in stopping to think; and little time in which to do so, for there had been a hundred things to see to. But there would be the flight to Kenya; twenty-four hours of sitting quietly in an aeroplane with nothing to do. There would be time then to think, and to sort out the turmoil in her mind and face the past—and the future. But she had not calculated on Mrs Brocas-Gill, and now they were flying over Africa, and the Dark Continent lay spread out below them with Nairobi Airport only half an hour ahead.

Half an hour! thought Victoria in a panic. Half an hour in which to sort out her thoughts and prepare herself for meeting Eden. To face all those things that she had cravenly refused to face during the past three weeks, and that she had forced herself not to think of for more than five years. Half an hour . . .

It was difficult to remember a time when she had not loved Eden DeBrett. She had been five on the day when she had tried to make Falda, the little zebra which her father had caught and tamed for her, jump the cattle gate by one of the waterholes. Falda had not taken kindly to the idea, and Victoria had pitched head-first into the sloshy churned-up mud by the drinking troughs where, in addition to winding herself badly, she ruined the clean cotton dress in which she was supposed to appear at a luncheon party.

It was Eden, nine years old and spending the weekend with his great-Aunt Helen, who had saved the situation. He had retrieved Victoria from the mud, dried her tears on a grubby pocket-handkerchief and suggested the immediate removal of clothes, shoes and socks, and their immersion—and Victoria's—in the clean water of the cattle troughs.

His suggestion had been followed, with such excellent results that when the gong had sounded she had been able to walk demurely up to the house in a crumpled but undoubtedly clean dress, and no one had noticed that her long brown plaits owed some of their sleekness to the fact that they were damp. Eden's superior male intelligence had saved her from disaster and from that day he was Victoria's hero.

She had been a plain little girl, with a tendency to stammer slightly when shy or upset; thin and leggy and very brown. Brown sunburnt skin, brown eyes and long, lank brown hair. But although her own lack of good looks had not interested her, she had been deeply impressed by Eden's beauty.

Even as a child Eden DeBrett was beautiful, and he did not outgrow that beauty as so many children do. It seemed, in fact, to increase as he grew older, and it had its effect on everyone he met, so that there were few people, if any, who were ever to know what he was really like, or to be quite fair to him: their judgement being invariably swung out of true by his amazing good looks.

He was ten when Em hardened her heart and sent him home to a famous preparatory school in England, and the six-year-old Victoria had wept bitterly and uncontrollably, and greatly to Eden's disgust and her own mortification, on the platform of Nairobi railway station where she had gone with her parents to see him off.

Her gay and charming father had died two months later, and the tragedy of his death, the sale of the farm and the misery of leaving Kenya—even the parting with her ponies and dear fat friendly Falda —had been mitigated by the thought that she would be seeing Eden again. For it had been arranged between Em and Helen that Eden should spend the Christmas and Easter holidays with the Carylls, and return to Kenya once a year to spend the two months of the summer holidays at *Flamingo*.

In actual fact he had spent all his holidays for the next six or seven years with them, and had seen nothing of Em and *Flamingo;* for tragedy on a Homeric scale had taken over the stage, and the war put an end to countless plans, as it was to put an end to countless lives.

Eden had missed active service, but he had done his National Service with the Occupation Forces in Germany, and followed it by three years at Oxford, during which time he had seen little or nothing of the Carylls, for he spent his vacations with Em in Kenya, flying between London and Nairobi. Victoria had not seen him for over a year when Em suddenly announced her intention of paying a visit to England and staying with her half-sister. She had not seen either for years, and she and Eden would spend July and August at Helen's instead of at *Flamingo*.

Victoria's Aunt Emily, who was Eden's grandmother, was exactly as Victoria remembered her, save for the fact that in deference to the post-war nerves of the Islanders she had refrained from wearing her favourite Kenya garb of scarlet dungarees, and was soberly and somewhat disappointingly clad in a brown coat-frock that whispered of moth balls and the Gay Twenties.

Eden had arrived two days later, and he had looked at Victoria as though he were seeing her for the first time: as though she were someone whom he had never seen before.

She had been picking roses and her arms were full of the lovely lavish honey-pinks of Betty Uprichards; but that had been an unrehearsed and entirely fortuitous circumstance, as Eden had not been expected for another two hours. She had blushed under Eden's startled gaze, and Eden had said foolishly: *'Vicky—! What have you been doing to yourself? You've—you've grown up.'*

And at that they had both laughed, and he had leaned forward and kissed her above the roses and they had fallen in love.

No, that was not true, thought Victoria. At least, it was not true of herself, for she had fallen in love with Eden years and years ago, when he had picked her up out of the mud by the cattle troughs and dried her tears with a handkerchief that smelt of Stockholm tar and chewing gum. And she had never stopped loving him.

It was Eden who had fallen in love that day. Or had he? Had it only been affection for someone he had known all his life? Sentiment and a summer evening, and a pretty girl in a yellow dress with her arms full of roses? *Any* pretty girl? No! thought Victoria. No. It isn't true. He did love me. He did! I couldn't have been mistaken.

It had been an enchanted summer. They had danced together, and dined together, and walked and talked and planned their lives together. Em had been pleased; but Victoria's mother had not approved of the cousins marrying, and she had been against it from the first.

'I might agree, if they were first cousins,' Em had said, 'but they are not.'

'Eden has Beaumartin blood in him,' said Helen unhappily.

'And Carteret and Brook and DeBrett blood too! It will be a great success.'

But Helen had counselled delay. Eden was only twenty-three, and Victoria four years younger. They could afford to wait. Eden was to do a year's course at an agricultural college so as to fit him for taking over *Flamingo*—as his years at Oxford would fit him, so his grandmother hoped, to hold political office one day in the country of his birth and her adoption.

'He is a second-generation Kenya-ite,' said Em, 'and there are not so many of them. The Colony needs men who love the country to run its affairs.'

By Helen's wish there had been no formal engagement, and no announcement to friends. Em had gone back to Kenya when the summer was over and Victoria had gone on with her secretarial course, because, she told Eden, it would be a help in the running of *Flamingo*.

They were to be married when Eden was twenty-four, and he had actually married when he was within a week of his twenty-fourth birthday. But it had not been to Victoria. It had been to Alice Laxton. Five years ago . . . Yet even now, to think of it brought back some of the suffocating, agonizing pain of those days.

It had happened suddenly and without warning. Eden had arrived one afternoon to see her mother, and left again without waiting to see Victoria, who was out. Helen had looked pale and upset but had said nothing more than that Eden had been unable to stay as he had to spend the weekend with friends in Sussex, but that he would be writing.

The letter had come three days later, and Victoria could still remember every line of it as though it had burned itself into her brain. They had made a mistake, wrote Eden, and confused cousinly affection and friendship for something deeper. Nothing could alter that fondness and friendship, and he knew her too well not to know that if she did not agree with him now, she would one day. One day she would fall in love with someone else, as he himself had done, and then her affection for him would fall into its proper place. And as they had never really been engaged, neither of them need suffer any public embarrassment.

As he himself had done . . . In the face of that statement there was nothing for Victoria to do but write an unhysterical letter accepting the inevitable and agreeing that his decision was the right one. She had saved her pride, and probably salved Eden's conscience, by doing so; if either of those things were worth doing.

Helen had been relieved and had not attempted to disguise the fact. 'I never think that marriages between cousins are a good idea,' she said. 'Inbreeding never did anyone any good.'

Em had written from Kenya. She had quite obviously accepted Eden's view that the break was mutual, and the letter had been charming and deeply regretful, and had ended with the hope that they might both think better of it. But on the same morning as its arrival *The Times* and the *Telegraph* had published the announcement of Eden's engagement to Alice Laxton, and less than a month later they had been married.

Oh, the agony of those days! The tearing, wrenching pain of loss. The shock of casually opening an illustrated paper at the hairdressers and being confronted with a full page photograph of Eden and his bride leaving St George's, Hanover Square. Eden, grave and unsmiling, and as heart-breakingly handsome as every woman's dream of Prince Charming. And Alice, an anonymous figure in white satin whose bridal veil had blown across her face and partially obscured it.

'Better looking than Robert Taylor or any of those,' said the hairdresser's assistant, peering over her shoulder. 'Ought to be on the films, he ought. It's a waste. Don't think much of her, do you? Can't think how she got him. Money, I expect. The papers say she's got any amount of it. Wish I had! What about just a touch of brillian-tine, Miss Caryll?'

Any amount of money . . . Had that been why Eden had mar-ried her? No, he *could* not be so despicable! Not Eden. But *Flamingo,* she knew, had been losing money of late, and Eden had expensive tastes. Em had spoilt him. It would be nice to be able to think that he only married Alice Laxton for her money, for then she could despise him and be sorry for his wife, and apply salve to her own hurt pride. But what did hurt pride matter in comparison to the pain in her heart? I won't think of him any more, decided Victoria. I won't let myself think of any of this again.

It had not been easy to keep that vow, but hard work had helped, and at last there came a time when memory did not rise and mock her whenever she was tired or off-guard. She had not thought of the past, or of Eden, for months before Helen died, and afterwards she had been able to read his letter of condolence, and reply to it, as though he had meant no more to her than the writers of a dozen other such letters. She had sold the house and taken a secretarial post in London. And then that unexpected letter had arrived from Kenya.

It was not the sort of letter that Em had ever written before, and there was an odd and disturbing suggestion of urgency about it. The same urgency that Helen had sometimes betrayed when she had wanted to do something, or to see someone, and had been afraid that she would not have time to do it before she died. A fear that was both harrowing and pitiful. But there was something else there too. Something that Victoria could not quite put her finger on, and which disturbed her even more.

The letter had contained only one reference to the past: 'You know that I would never have suggested your coming if I had not been quite sure that you and Eden could meet as friends. And I know that you will like his wife. Alice is such a dear girl, but we are neither of us strong, and I fear that I am getting old. I need help.'

Em had provisionally booked a passage for her on an air liner leaving for Nairobi on the twenty-third of the month. Which meant that she would have to decide at once, as the company would not keep the reservation for long. Was that why Em had done it? So that she would be forced to make up her mind quickly, and could not waver and hesitate? Was Em, too, afraid of dying too soon, and aware, as Helen had been, that it was later than she had thought?

England had been enduring an exceptionally cold and wet spell that year, and Victoria, clinging to a strap in a crowded bus on her way to work, the letter in her pocket, had looked out over the damp, bedraggled hat of a stout woman in a wet mackintosh, to the damp, bedraggled London streets that streamed past the rain-spotted windows, and thought of the Rift Valley——

The enormous sun-drenched spaces where the cattle grazed and the herds of zebra and gazelle roamed at will under the blue cloud shadows that drifted by as idly as sailing ships on a summer sea. It would be wonderful to see it again. It would be like going home. And *Flamingo* would be a home to her. Aunt Emily had said so. Aunt Emily needed her, and it was so comforting to be needed again. As for Eden, he was happily married, and Alice was 'such a dear girl'. The past was over and done with. She need not think of it.

◇   ◇   ◇

The stewardess of the air liner said: 'Fasten your safety belts please,' and Mrs Brocas-Gill said: 'Wake up, dear. We're going down to land. Are you feeling all right? You're looking very pale.'

'No,' said Victoria a trifle breathlessly. 'No. I'm all right thank you. It's just that——'

The plane tilted on one shining wing and the ground rushed up to meet it. And then they were skimming low over roof-tops and trees and grass and bumping down a long runway, and Victoria was thinking frantically and desperately and futilely: I shouldn't have come! I shouldn't have come! What shall I do when I see Eden? It isn't all over—it won't ever be all over! I shouldn't have come . . .

4

The sun was blindingly bright on the white walls of the Airport, and there seemed to be a great many people meeting the plane. But there was no sign of Lady Emily. Or of Eden.

A small stout man with a red face and bald head, wearing a singularly crumpled suit and, somewhat surprisingly, a revolver in an enormous leather holster, waved a white panama enthusiastically from beyond the barrier and yelled a welcome to someone called 'Pet'.

'There's Oswin,' said Mrs Brocas-Gill.

'You're late!' shouted Mr Brocas-Gill, stating the obvious. 'Expected you yesterday.'

He embraced his wife and was introduced to Victoria. 'Bless my soul!' said Mr Brocas-Gill. 'Jack Caryll's girl. I remember your father when——Why, dammit, I remember *you!* Skinny little thing in plaits. Used to ride a zebra. Glad to see you back.'

He relieved his wife of a dressing-case and an overnight bag and trotted beside them into the comparative coolness of the Airport building:

'Who are you stayin' with? Oh, Em. Hmm. Isn't here, is she? Can't understand it! Bad business. Just shows that it doesn't do to get too complacent. Who's meetin' you?'

'I don't know,' confessed Victoria uncertainly.

'Oh well, they're sure to send someone. We'll keep an eye on you for the moment. Hi! Pet——!' He plunged off in pursuit of his wife who had departed to greet a friend.

Left alone Victoria looked about her a little desperately, searching for a familiar face, until her attention was arrested by a man who had just entered the hall and was standing scanning the newly arrived passengers as though he were looking for someone.

He was a tall, slim, sunburnt man in the early thirties, who

carried his inches with a peculiar lounging grace that somehow suggested the popular conception of a cowboy. An effect that was
heightened by the fact that he, like Oswin Brocas-Gill, wore a belt
that supported a revolver. But there the cowboy resemblance ended,
for the cut of the carelessly careful coat, in contrast to Oswin's
crumpled attire, spoke almost offensively of Savile Row, while his
shoes were undoubtedly handmade—though not in Kenya.

It was not, however, his personal appearance that had caught
Victoria's attention, but the fact that he was now observing her with
interest and a distinct suggestion of distaste. Men were apt to look at
Victoria with interest. They had been doing so in increasing num-
bers since somewhere around her sixteenth birthday, so there was
nothing new in that. What was new was the distaste. No man had
ever previously regarded her with the coldly critical lack of approval
that was in the blue gaze of the gentleman by the doorway, and
Victoria involuntarily glanced down to assure herself that she was
not showing six inches of petticoat or wearing odd stockings. She
was engaged in this apprehensive survey when he crossed the hall
and spoke to her:

'Are you Miss Caryll?'

It was an agreeable voice—or would have been agreeable if it
had not been for her conviction that for some reason its owner
disapproved of her.

'Y-yes,' said Victoria, disconcerted by that disapproval and annoyed to find herself stammering.

The man reached out and calmly possessed himself of the small
suitcase she held. 'My name's Stratton. Lady Emily asked me to
meet you. You'd better give me your passport and entry permit and
all the rest of it, and I'll get someone to deal with it. Got any money
on you?'

'A little,' said Victoria.

'You'll have to get it changed into local currency.'

He held out his hand and Victoria found herself meekly surrendering her bag.

'Stay here. You'd better sit on that sofa,' said Mr Stratton, and
left her.

Victoria took his advice and sat staring after his retreating back
with a mixture of indignation and relief. She could not imagine why
Aunt Emily should have sent this disapproving stranger to meet her,
but at least it was not Eden.

She had not realized that she could feel like this. So shaken and unsure of herself and so afraid of being hurt. Well, it was entirely her own fault. She had refused to face facts while there was still time, and now it was too late. She leaned back on the sofa and rested her head against the wall behind it, unaware that she was looking exceedingly pale and shaken.

A stout figure bore down upon her, exuding an overpowering wave of expensive scent, and Mrs Brocas-Gill was with her once more, breathing heavily as though she had been running.

'Ah, I see you've heard,' said Mrs Brocas-Gill, panting a little. 'What an appalling reception for you. *Too* dreadful!'

Victoria struggled to her feet, endeavoring to collect her scattered thoughts, and said: 'Aunt Emily's sent someone to meet me. A Mr Stratton.'

'Oh, Drew,' said Mrs Brocas-Gill. 'I wonder she didn't send Gilly Markham. He's her manager, you know. I was telling you about him. I should have thought he was the obvious person to—but then I don't suppose any of the *Flamingo* people could get away today. Too ghastly for you, my dear. Oh, there you are, Oswin. Isn't it *too* dreadful?'

'Yes, yes, yes!' said Mr Brocas-Gill, thrusting passports and permits into his wife's hands. 'Don't let's go over all that again. Hullo, Drew. What are you doing here? Oh, you're collecting Jack's girl, are you? Splendid. Splendid! Was going to keep an eye on her myself until someone turned up. Knew Em wouldn't be here, of course. You'll be all right with Drew, m'dear. We shall be seeing you. Come *on*, Pet! Damned if I'm going to hang around here all day!'

He seized his wife's arm and hurried her away, and Mr Stratton piloted Victoria into the customs shed and said: 'Here's the rest of your luggage. Have you got the keys? You may have to open them.'

Five minutes later she was out in the bright sunlight again and being driven away from the Airport through an area of ugly slums and unattractive bazaars.

There was nothing in these mean, crowded streets that was in any way familiar to Victoria, or that struck any chord of memory. And as they left the town behind, and eucalyptus trees and vivid masses of bougainvillaea replaced the squalid huts and shop fronts, she caught glimpses between the green trees of neat, white, red-roofed houses—primly British and more suggestive of Welwyn Garden City than Darkest Africa—that could not have been here when she had last driven through Nairobi over sixteen years ago.

Mr Stratton spoke at last, breaking a silence that had lasted since they left the Airport:

'I take it that you didn't get your Aunt's cable? She was afraid you might not. That's why she asked me to call in at the Airport, in case you were on the plane.'

'In *case* I was? I don't understand. What cable?'

'I gather she sent one care of your bank, as she thought you might be spending the last few days with friends.'

'I was,' admitted Victoria, bewildered. 'But why did she cable? Didn't she want me to come?'

'Well, hardly, at a time like this. After all, it's a fairly nasty mess to land you into.'

'What mess?' demanded Victoria. 'Is Aunt Em ill?'

Mr Stratton's head came round with a jerk and the car swerved on the road as though his hands had twitched at the wheel. He said incredulously: 'Do you mean to say you don't know? But surely the Brocas-Gills——Look, wasn't it in the home papers?'

'Wasn't what in the home papers?' Victoria's eyes were wide with apprehension. 'Aunt Em . . . *Eden!* He isn't——'

'No,' said Mr Stratton shortly. 'He's all right. It's his wife. She was murdered three days ago. I'm sorry. I thought you'd know. It was on the B.B.C., and it must have been in the home papers.'

'No,' said Victoria unsteadily. 'I mean—I didn't listen to the news. There was so much to do. And I—I missed the papers. How did it happen? Tell me about it, please. I'd rather hear now. Before I meet . . . Aunt Emily.'

She had hesitated for a moment before speaking her aunt's name, as though she might have intended to use another one, and Mr Stratton, who was at no time unobservant, did not miss it. He turned his head and looked at her, and there was once again, and unmistakably, dislike in the hard line of his mouth and the cold glance of his normally bland blue eyes.

He looked away again and said curtly: 'Alice—Mrs DeBrett—was murdered in the garden of your aunt's house. Someone killed her with a panga—a heavy knife that the Africans use for chopping wood and cutting grass. Your aunt found her. It can't have been a pleasant sight, and though she's bearing up pretty well she was in no state to drive over a hundred miles into Nairobi and back in order to meet you. And neither was Eden. What with the shock, and the police and press swarming all over the place, they've both had a pretty bad time of it. And in any case the funeral's this morning.'

Victoria did not speak, and presently he glanced at her again and suffered a momentary pang of compunction at the sight of her white face. She looked a good deal younger than he had expected her to be, yet she must be at least twenty-four if she had been engaged to Eden DeBrett before he had married Alice. Quite old enough to appreciate the feelings of his wife, who could hardly be expected to welcome the idea of her husband's ex-fiancée as a permanent fixture in the home.

Drew had liked Alice, and he had been sorry for her. And remembering her haggard, defenceless face and haunted eyes, he took a poor view of Miss Caryll, whose arrival seemed to him vulgar and tactless, if not intentionally cruel.

Victoria spoke at last, and in a voice that was barely audible above the hum of the engine:

'I thought it was all over. The Emergency, I mean. Mrs Brocas-Gill said it was. But if the Mau Mau are still murdering people——'

'I see no reason to suppose that it was a Mau Mau killing,' said Drew shortly. 'It merely makes a better headline in the press that way.'

'Then who——?'

'God knows! A maniac. Or someone with a fancied grievance. You never can tell what goes on in an African's head. And there have apparently been a lot of odd and unpleasant happenings at *Flamingo* lately.'

'I knew there was something wrong,' said Victoria in a whisper, and once again Drew's head turned sharply.

'Why do you say that?'

'It—it was Aunt Em's letter. She wrote and asked me if I would come out. She said she was getting too old to do without someone to help her, and that Eden wasn't—and she would rather have someone who belonged, than a stranger. My mother was her only sister you see, and they were fond of each other. But there was something in the way she wrote. As if she had something on her mind that was —Oh, I don't know—But it was an odd letter. A rather frightening one.'

'Frightening in what way?'

'Well—perhaps not frightening. Uncomfortable. She sounded as though she really did need me. Badly. And she'd always been very good to me. My father didn't leave much money, and I know Aunt Em helped with the school bills. So I came.'

'Was that your only reason?'

'No,' said Victoria. She looked up at the blue sky and the blaze of sunlight, and thought of the London rain and fog, and of her longing to live once more under that hot sun and that wide sky. Her lovely mouth curved in the ghost of a smile, and she said softly: 'No. There were other reasons.'

'So I inferred,' said Mr Stratton unpleasantly.

Victoria turned to look at him in surprise, puzzled by his evident hostility, and after a moment or two she said a little diffidently: 'What did you mean about odd and unpleasant things happening at *Flamingo?* What sort of things?'

'Some person or persons unknown has been smashing up your aunt's possessions in a manner usually associated with poltergeists—or ham-handed housemaids.'

'A p-poltergeist! You can't believe that!'

'I don't. I'll start believing in evil spirits only when someone has eliminated all possibility of the evil human element; and not before! Your aunt must have been mad not to send for the police at once, but she's been fighting a rear-guard action with the authorities over her Kikuyu servants for the last five years, and I suppose she wasn't going to give Greg or the D.C. a chance of having them all up and grilling them again, and jailing a handful under suspicion. Trouble is, she's an obstinate old lady, and once she decides on a course of action she sticks to it. She says now that she realized it must be the work of one of her house servants, but that whoever it was must be acting under orders—or threats.'

'But why? Why should anyone do that?'

Mr Stratton shrugged. 'A Mau Mau gang attacked *Flamingo* during the Emergency, and your aunt stood them off and killed several. One of the dead men was rumored to be a relative of the man who calls himself "General Africa" and who is still at large; so it's just on the cards that this is a private vendetta on the part of the "General". He was always one of the more cunning of the Mau Mau leaders, and there has been a story in circulation for several years that he was and still is employed on one of the farms in the Naivasha area.'

'You mean—you *can't* mean that someone, a settler, is deliberately hiding him?' said Victoria incredulously.

'Good lord, no! If it's true, you may be quite sure that his employer hasn't a clue as to his identity, and that he is using that as a cover. Playing the part of a faithful and probably dull-witted retainer by day, and organizing prison breaks and thefts of cattle, and planning bloody murder by night.'

'Surely that isn't possible!'

'Why not? There is no photograph of him in existence and he wears a mask. A square of red silk with holes burned in it for eyes, nose and mouth. None of the men who have turned informer have ever seen his face, so that it's quite possible that he might be going about openly and quite unsuspected. It's also possible that he may have planned this poltergeist business at *Flamingo* as a prelude to murder, and intimidated someone into carrying it out. From all accounts he is intelligent enough to work out a really subtle revenge.'

Victoria shivered despite the hot sunlight, and said: 'I don't see anything subtle about murdering someone with a panga!'

'It isn't the method,' said Drew impatiently. 'It's the murder itself, coming as the climax of a series of petty outrages. If Mrs DeBrett had been murdered out of a blue sky, so to speak, it would have been ghastly enough. But it wouldn't have had half the impact that this has had. Especially on a woman of Lady Emily's temperament. Em can take a straight left to the jaw and survive it, but there's a kind of creeping, cumulative beastliness about this business that makes it all the more frightening for her. A sort of softening-up process. Starting in a small way and getting progressively crueller. She thought it was only an attempt to scare her into selling up and getting out, but when her dog was poisoned she ought to have been warned. That was what Gilly Markham called a "sighting shot". It seems to have scared *him* all right! He's manager at *Flamingo*.'

They were passing through the Kikuyu Reserve, and the scenery was at last vaguely familiar to Victoria: terraced hillsides and clusters of neat round beehive huts; fields of maize and small white patches of pyrethrum; the spiky foliage of pineapples and the vivid green of vegetables and banana palms. Mile upon mile of native shambas, bright against the red-ochre clay, and interspersed with plantations of eucalyptus. But Victoria had no eyes for the scenery. Even the sunlight had ceased to feel warm and gay, and she felt cold and a little sick. *'A sighting shot . . .'*

She turned sharply to look at her companion, and spoke a little breathlessly: 'Is it the end? Or——'

She found that she could not finish the sentence, but Mr Stratton appeared to have no difficulty in translating her confused utterance. He said:

'I imagine it's that thought that is getting Em down. Ever since it started it's been a case of "What next?" Now I should say it's "Who's next?"'

'Eden!' said Victoria in a whisper, unaware that she had spoken aloud.

Drew gave her a cold glance and said curtly: 'Why do you think that?'

'Who else would it be? Unless—unless it were Aunt Em herself.'

'Oh, I don't know,' said Drew with deliberate brutality. 'Anyone she liked—or who was useful to her. Or to *Flamingo.*'

'I don't believe it!' said Victoria suddenly and flatly. 'Things like that don't really happen. Not to real people.'

'They've happened this time,' said Drew dryly.

'Oh, I don't mean that Eden's wife hasn't been killed. That must be true. But the other things. There must be some quite ordinary explanation. After all, things get broken in everyone's houses. And the dog might have picked up poison that was meant for rats—or, something.'

'Have it your own way,' said Drew.

'But don't you think it could have been that?'

'No, I don't. I think someone was getting at your aunt. And very successfully, at that! This isn't merely a question of getting rid of a settler. Even the Mau Mau dupes didn't take long to drive up to the fact that if they killed one white settler another one—and not his Kikuyu servants!—would take over. If Em died tomorrow, and Eden the day after, another white settler would take over *Flamingo.*'

'I should,' said Victoria.

Drew's blond eyebrows twitched together in a sudden startled frown and he said slowly: 'Yes, I suppose so. I'd forgotten that you'd be the next-of-kin. Well, there you are, you see. That's why I don't believe that this poltergeist business was aimed at frightening a large landowner into doing a scuttle. In any case, anyone who knew the least thing about Em would know it wouldn't work; and whoever is at the back of this knows a great deal about her, and just how to hit her where it hurts most. Which is what makes me interested in this "General Africa" theory. The average African gets no pleasure out of just shooting an enemy. He prefers to kill him slowly, and watch him suffer.'

It can't be true! thought Victoria. And yet worse things had happened in this country; far worse things. And he was carrying a gun. He didn't look the sort of person who would carry a gun without a good reason for doing so. She said abruptly: 'What about the police? Surely they'll be able to find out who did it?'

'Smashed Em's bric-à-brac?' enquired Drew.

'No. Who killed Mrs DeBrett. People don't get away with murder!'

'You'd be surprised what they get away with in this country!' said Drew cynically.

'But didn't anyone hear anything? Surely she would have screamed?'

'I expect she did, poor girl. But as luck would have it your aunt was playing the piano, and so no one in the house would have heard her. I should never have left her.'

'You?' said Victoria. 'Were you there?'

'Yes,' said Drew bitterly. 'In fact I was the last person, bar the murderer, who saw her alive. I knew she never carried a gun, and it was getting dark; but it was only a short distance to the house and it seemed safe enough. I could even hear that damned piano! Oh well —what the hell's the use of making excuses for oneself now? It's done.'

He wrenched savagely at the wheel as they swerved to avoid a stray goat, and accelerated as though speed afforded him escape from his thoughts.

'But there must have been *some* clues,' persisted Victoria. 'Footmarks—tracks—bloodstains. *Something!'*

'You've been reading detective stories,' remarked Drew satirically. 'Possibly in books the body is not moved and no one mucks up the ground, but it's apt to happen differently in real life. Your aunt wasn't thinking of clues when she found her grandson's wife dead in the garden. All she could think of was that she might possibly be alive, and she tried to carry her to the house. She almost managed it, too! But she had to fetch one of the house boys in the end, and by the time the D.C. and the doctor and Greg Gilbert and various other people arrived, the "scene of the crime" had been pretty well messed up.'

Victoria said: 'Didn't they find anything, then?'

'Yes. They found a blood-stained cushion, belonging to one of the verandah chairs, in the long grass about twenty feet or so from where Mrs DeBrett's body was found. It looked as though it had been thrown there. And they found some marks amoung the bushes that seemed to suggest that someone had been standing there for quite a time, presumably watching her. There's a track that runs through the bushes and that links up at least three of the lakeside estates. It's an unofficial short cut that the labour use, and that the Mau Mau undoubtedly used during the Emergency.'

'So it was a gang murder after all!' said Victoria with a catch of the breath.

'Perhaps,' said Drew. 'But not on that evidence. Whoever had been watching from the bushes had never left them. The ground just there is pretty dusty, and it was obvious that he had merely turned and gone back the way he came.'

5

The car had been singing down a long straight stretch of road when it brought up suddenly with a screech of tortured tyres, and an abruptness that jerked Victoria forward and narrowly missed bringing her head into violent contact with the windscreen.

'Sorry,' said Mr Stratton, 'but I believe that was a friend of mine.'

He put the gear lever into reverse and backed some fifty yards through a dust cloud of his own making, to draw up alongside a stationary car that stood jacked up on the grassy verge where an African driver wrestled with a recalcitrant tyre.

A tall European in shirtsleeves and wearing a green pork-pie hat jammed on the back of his head appeared from the other side of it, wiping dust and sweat off his face with a handkerchief, and came to lean his elbows on the window of Mr Stratton's car:

'I might have known it,' he remarked bitterly. 'My God, Drew, the next time you do that I'll have you up for dangerous driving and get you sixty days without the option if it's the last thing I do! Didn't you see me flagging you?'

'No,' admitted Mr Stratton, unabashed. 'My mind was on other things. Greg, you won't have met Miss Caryll. Miss Caryll, this is Mr Gilbert, our local S.P.—Superintendent of Police, Naivasha.'

Mr Gilbert reached across him and shook hands with Victoria. He was a long, lean man who except for the fact that his hair was streaked with grey at the temples did not appear to be much older than Mr Stratton. His square, pleasant face was less deeply sunburnt than Drew's, and he possessed a pair of sleepy grey eyes that were anything but a true guide to his character and capabilities.

'You must be Lady Emily's niece,' said Mr Gilbert. 'She told me you were coming out, but I understood that she'd sent a cable to stop you.'

'Yes, I know. I didn't get it. I——'

'Do you want a lift, Greg?' cut in Mr Stratton, brusquely interrupting the sentence.

The S.P. threw him a quick look of surprise. 'Are you in a hurry?' he enquired.

'Not particularly, but Miss Caryll could probably do with something to eat. Her plane was late. Where do you want to be dropped?'

'Same place as Miss Caryll. *Flamingo.*'

'Oh. Anything new cropped up?'

'Not much,' admitted the S.P. climbing into the back of the car. He called out a few instructions to his driver and sat back, urging Mr Stratton to abstain from doing more than fifty: 'My nerves are shot to pieces. I thought we'd finished with this sort of thing for the time being, and I find it pretty exhausting when it crops up again. Old James has gone straight in off the deep end. I've never known him to be in such a bad temper. He bit my head off this morning for making some innocuous remark about the weather.'

'Where was this?' asked Drew, re-starting the car.

'Up at the Lab. They'd been doing a test on that ruddy verandah cushion.'

'Any results?'

'Oh, Alice's of course. Or same blood group, anyway. It was unlikely to be anyone else's. But it was just as well to make sure. Odd, though.'

He tilted his hat over his nose, and closed his eyes. Victoria twisted round in her seat to face him, and as though he were aware of the movement he opened them again and said: 'I must apologize for talking shop, but I'm afraid you're in for a lot of this. In fact you couldn't have chosen a worse time to arrive, and I wish I could suggest that you turn right round and go back again; though I can see that it is hardly practicable.'

'I wouldn't go if it was,' said Victoria with decision.

'Why not?' enquired Drew shortly.

Victoria turned her head to look at him, aware for the first time that his antagonism was personal and not a mere matter of irritation or bad temper. She said coldly: 'I should have thought it was obvious. If my aunt needed someone to help her before, she must need it even more now.'

She met his gaze with a hostility that equalled his own, and then deliberately turned her shoulder to him and gave her attention to the view.

The road wound and dipped through hot sunlight and chequered shadows, and swinging to the right came out abruptly on to the crest of a huge escarpment. And there below them, spread out at their feet like a map drawn upon yellowed parchment, lay the Great Rift. A vast golden valley of sun-bleached grass, speckled by scrub and flat-topped thorn trees, and seamed with dry gullies; hemmed in to left and right by the two great barriers of the Kinangop and the Mau, and dominated by the rolling lava falls and cold, gaping crater of Longonot, standing sentinel at its gate.

Nothing has changed! thought Victoria. But she knew that was not true. The passing of a handful of years might have made little difference, superficially, to the Rift, but everything else had changed. And looking out over that stupendous view she was dismayed to find that her eyes were full of tears.

At the foot of the escarpment the road ceased to wind and twist. The forests of cedar and wild olive fell away, and the car touched ninety miles an hour and held it on the long straight ribbon of tarmac that the Italian prisoners-of-war had built in the war years, until at last they could see the shining levels of Lake Naivasha.

'Might I suggest,' said Mr Gilbert gently, breaking a silence that had lasted for some considerable time, 'that you slow down to sixty before you take the turn? I have no wish to provide Naivasha with two funerals within twenty-four hours, and neither am I in any hurry to meet the mourners.'

Drew removed his foot from the accelerator, and as the car slowed down and swung left-handed into an unmade side road that branched off the tarmac of the main Nairobi road to circle the lake, Victoria said huskily: 'When is it—the funeral?'

'Eleven o'clock. Didn't Drew tell you? That's why none of them could meet you. But they'll have got back by now. How long is it since you last saw your aunt?'

'Six years,' said Victoria.

'Then I'm afraid you'll notice quite a change in her. This business has hit her pretty badly. She always seemed to me like a bit of the Kenya landscape—eternal and indestructible. But now she's suddenly an old lady. It's like seeing a landmark crumble. Poor old Em!'

'I can't see why you have to bother her, today of all days,' said Mr Stratton disagreeably. 'You might at least spare them a further grilling on the day of the funeral. It's going to be bad enough for them to have to—Oh, well. It's none of my business.'

'None,' agreed Mr Gilbert equably. 'For which you can be devoutly grateful. Asking personal questions on this sort of occasion, and of people who are your friends, is not exactly a pleasant task, I assure you. But the fact that we now know for certain whose blood was on the cushion opens up a new field of enquiry. It's an odd facet of the case, that cushion. What was it doing there, and why?'

Drew said: 'No one heard Alice screaming, and she must have screamed. I know that was probably because Em was playing the piano, but there might be another explanation.'

'You mean the cushion might have been used to smother her? I don't believe it. It would have been damned difficult to hold a cushion over the face of a struggling woman while hacking at her with a panga. Unless there were two people in it. But—No, somehow I don't think that it was that. I can't get it out of my head that that cushion ought to tell me something if I weren't too stupid to see it. It doesn't fit.'

'With what?' demanded Mr Stratton, swerving to avoid a pothole of unusually outrageous dimensions that added to the hazards of the dusty, unmetalled road.

'With any of the obvious theories. That cushion was removed from the verandah and carried to the spot where Alice was killed, and then thrown away into the long grass. Yet no one will admit to having touched it that day.'

Drew said: 'I suppose it hasn't occurred to you that Mrs DeBrett might have taken it down herself to sit on, and was merely carrying it back? Or is that a too simple solution for you and your sleuths to contemplate?'

'You should know the answer to that one,' said Mr Gilbert amiably. 'You were the last person to admit to seeing her alive. Was she carrying a brightly coloured cushion?'

'No,' said Drew, 'but——'

'But you think that despite the fact that the sun had set, and that it is apt to get a bit chilly around dusk, she went all the way back to the house in order to fetch one off the verandah? I doubt it! Yet someone took it out there, and I'd like to know why. If I did, I imagine we'd be a lot further on. But as it is, I don't know what to think, and all the things I do think of are decidedly unpleasant. I don't like anything about this case, and I wish to God I could wash my hands of it!'

'Why not hand it over to the C.I.D. squad from Nakuru?'

'I've tried that one, but this time it won't work. They happen to have rather a lot on their plate just now, what with the Hansford case and that Goldfarb business, and James says I can dam' well handle it myself—even though half my personal friends are involved.'

'You mean *because* half your personal friends are involved,' said Mr Stratton dryly. 'You know us all very well. Too well!'

The S.P. made no reply; which might have meant anything—or nothing.

The cold shadow of a cloud drifted across the sunlit scene, draining the colour from the grass and the flat-topped thorn trees and lending the landscape a fleeting suggestion of aloofness and hostility, and Victoria shivered again and was suddenly afraid: afraid of the valley and of Africa, and of arriving at *Flamingo,* the house that was Eden's home and where Eden's wife had died a horrible death.

What have I let myself in for? thought Victoria in a panic. What does he mean? That someone in the house is a murderer? Eden's wife—She's dead now. He's free. I should never have come . . .

The car ran out of the belt of shadow and past two tall Masai warriors, each carrying a serviceable spear; the red-gold of their lean, ochre-smeared bodies and elaborately plaited hair, and the clean-cut lines of their haughty aquiline features, reminiscent of ancient Egypt. Recognizing the car, they saluted gravely: a courteous salute tinged with gracious condescension, such as might have been accorded by the delegates of a powerful state to a member of a small and friendly nation.

'They don't change much either,' commented Mr Gilbert, following up a private train of thought. 'The Masai are the only ones who have looked at the things of the West and decided that they prefer their own ways, and have stuck to them. Who can say they are not right? The modern African youth with his European clothes and his inferiority complexes is not impressive, but it has never so much as crossed the minds of the Masai that they might be inferior to anyone.'

'Boot's on the other foot!' said Drew laconically, and Greg Gilbert laughed.

Victoria said: 'Father used to employ Mkamba. I can still remember most of them by name. They used to carry bows and arrows in those days—poisoned arrows, too!'

'They still do,' said Mr Gilbert with a grin. 'And that despite the fact that it is strictly against the law! I should say that at a conservative estimate several tons of arrow poison are manufactured yearly in this country. Talk about the "Secret Arrow Poison of the South American Indians!"—this has it licked into a cocked hat, for the simple reason that it's no secret. All you need is a saucepan, a box of matches and grandmother's recipe. The ingredients are growing all over the landscape, and——'

He broke off and hurriedly wound up the car windows as a black and grey sedan raced towards them and shot past, enveloping them in a choking cloud of dust.

'Ken Brandon,' said Drew briefly.

'Oh. How's he taken it?'

'On the chin,' said Drew.

'He's a spoilt brat. These conceited, mannerless young egoists bore me to distraction. Hector is pretty hot on the subject of motes in his neighbour's eye, but young Ken is the outstanding beam in his own.'

'You mean in Mabel's,' corrected Drew dryly. 'Ken is Mabel's sun, moon and stars, and always will be. She is devoted to Hector, but she'd probably have walked out on him if he'd laid a finger on her darling boy. She may be half Hector's size, and a dear, but she's quite capable of standing up to him.'

'I still don't think that excuses him,' grunted Mr Gilbert. 'Or his son! What Alice must have gone through with that boy is nobody's business!'

'It isn't ours, at any rate,' said Drew shortly.

'There,' corrected the S.P., 'you are wrong. It happens to be mine. Anyone or anything that had to do with Alice DeBrett is, at the moment, my business. And that,' he added gently, 'includes you.'

'Um,' said Mr Stratton thoughtfully, and refrained from further comment.

Five miles and eight minutes later a square, weather-beaten notice board bearing the single word *'Flamingo'* came in sight, and the car turned off the lake road on to a rough track that crossed a stretch of barren, rock-strewn ground bordered at the far side by a thick belt of trees and a glint of water. The wheels bumped in and out of deep dust-filled ruts and over and around boulders, roots and hummocks of parched grass, and leaving the hard sunlight, ran under the freckled shadows of pepper trees and giant acacias, to emerge on to a wide smooth sweep of ground before a long, rambling, thatch-roofed house whose bow windows and deep verandahs looked out on the glittering expanse of Lake Naivasha, blue and beautiful in the full blaze of the noonday.

What appeared at first sight to be half a dozen dogs of assorted shapes and sizes rushed out to greet them, barking vociferously, followed by two African houseboys wearing green robes and scarlet tarbooshes, who hurried out to remove suitcases and assist the travellers to alight. A door at the far end of the verandah opened, and an arresting figure walked towards them and stood waiting at the top of a shallow flight of stone steps. The Lady Emily DeBrett of *Flamingo*.

Em had worn a dark coat and skirt for the funeral, but she had discarded them immediately upon her return, and had changed back into the scarlet dungarees and vivid blouse that were her favoured wear. Her white closely cropped hair was adorned with a wide-brimmed hat of multi-coloured straw of the type that tourists buy in such places as Ceylon and Zanzibar, and there were diamonds in her ears and on her gnarled and capable hands and imposing bosom. She should have presented a grotesque appearance, but somehow she did not. She might, instead, have been the Queen of some barbaric kingdom. Hatshepsut of Egypt. Old Tzu-hsi, the Dowager Empress of China. Or Elizabeth the First, old and raddled and dying, but still indomitable: still royal.

Em had at no time been demonstrative, but she greeted Victoria with an unusual display of affection which contained, despite herself, a strong suggestion of relief.

'It's so good to see you, dear,' said Em, embracing her. 'And so good of you to come. I am sorry not to have been able to meet you at the Airport; but then Drew will have explained everything. We need not talk of that just now. How well you look. And how like your mother! You might be Helen all over again. Come along into the house. Drew will——'

She stopped as her gaze fell upon Greg Gilbert, and Victoria felt her stiffen. 'Greg! I didn't know you were here. Did you want to see me?'

'I'm afraid so,' said Mr Gilbert, leisurely mounting the verandah steps. 'I'm sorry about this, Em, but needs must. One or two things have cropped up. I won't keep you long. Eden here?'

'You are not,' announced Em with deliberation, 'going to worry Eden with any more questions today. And that is that! I like you, Greg, but there are some things I will not put up with, even from my friends. If you must worry the servants again, I suppose I can't stop you. But you can leave Eden alone. He can't tell you any more than he has already told you. None of us can!'

'I'm sorry, Em,' repeated Mr Gilbert quietly. 'I'm not doing this for choice.'

Lady Emily's bosom swelled alarmingly until the seams of her scarlet blouse appeared to be in imminent danger of parting. And then all at one she appeared to deflate, both physically and mentally. She stretched out a hand to him and spoke in a voice that was no longer measured and autocratic, but pleading:

'Greg, you can't! Not now. Not today. Surely it can wait?'

Mr Gilbert did not reply, and after a moment her hand dropped and she turned away and spoke to Victoria:

'Come dear, you will want to see your room. Drew, you will find drinks in the drawing-room. Help yourself. Greg had better stay to luncheon as he's here. He can ask his questions afterwards.'

The invitation could hardly have been less pressing, but Mr Gilbert said placidly: 'Thanks, I will,' and followed them into the house.

◇ ◇ ◇

The room that was to be Victoria's was large and comfortable, with windows that looked out on to a wide strip of lawn, a blaze of bougainvillaea and a view of the lake. Em sat down on the edge of the big old-fashioned bed as though she were very tired, and said: 'I hope you will be comfortable here, dear. And happy.'

Victoria said warmly: 'Of course I shall be, Aunt Em! It's so lovely to be back in Kenya. I can't tell you how grateful I am to you for all your kindness.'

'I have not been kind,' said Em heavily. 'I have been selfish. But I needed someone to help me, and I didn't want a stranger—some secretary who would spread gossip about *Flamingo* to half the Colony. I thought if I could only keep it to the family . . .' Her voice trailed away, and she shivered.

Victoria came quickly across the room and put her arms about her aunt's sagging shoulders and hugged her. 'It wasn't selfish of you, darling. It was wonderful of you to want me. If only you knew how nice it is to feel wanted again!'

Em patted her hand absently and was silent for a moment or two, and then her fingers tightened suddenly about Victoria's wrist and she looked up into her niece's face with eyes that were bright and intent and full of anxiety. She said harshly, and as though she were forcing herself to speak: 'You must choose for yourself, Victoria. I did not—I was not honest with you when I wrote. I did not tell you everything. Perhaps I was afraid that you might not come. But you are Helen's child, and you must have your chance to decide whether you will go or stay. No!—don't interrupt! Let me say what I want, and then it will be your turn——

'I shall not blame you if you decide not to stay. Remember that. I sent you a cable to try and stop you, but it must have missed you. I do not know how much Drew Stratton will have told you, but I suppose you know that Eden's wife was murdered. There is rumour that the remnant of a Mau Mau gang are hiding out somewhere near here, but the police cannot be certain that it is they who are responsible, because—because there have been strange things happening in this house for some weeks past. Not very serious things, but—but worrying, of course. It has meant that all my servants are under suspicion, which is not very pleasant. So if you would prefer not to stay, I shall quite understand.'

Victoria said: 'But of course I'm going to stay, Aunt Em. If you'll let me. Or even if you won't. Just try to get rid of me!'

Em's fingers relaxed their hold, and she said approvingly: 'Good girl.' The emotion and the strain vanished from her face and she stood up briskly and said: 'Luncheon will be ready as soon as you are. You will find us in the drawing-room.'

The door closed behind her, and Victoria turned to stare thoughtfully at her own reflection in the looking glass: a slim, remarkably pretty girl in a leaf-green frock.

'Yes of course I'm going to stay!' said Victoria, speaking aloud in the silence. 'I belong in Kenya. And as for Eden, that's all over and done with—so don't let's have any more nonsense about it!'

She nodded severely at her reflected face, and went off to the bathroom to remove the dust of the lake road.

$$6$$

There were four people waiting in the large, casual, beautiful drawing-room: Em, Greg Gilbert, Drew Stratton and Eden.

Eden had been standing by the window talking to Drew when Victoria entered, and he had turned when he heard the door open, and stopped in the middle of a sentence, looking at her.

There was a brief moment of silence, and it was Eden who spoke first; his voice an echo from a day six years ago when he had spoken to a girl in a yellow dress who held an armful of roses. *'Vicky——!'*

Victoria closed the door behind her and said lightly: 'Hullo, Eden. I hope I haven't kept you waiting, Aunt Em?'

Luncheon was an uncomfortable meal, full of odd, abrupt silences and patches of forced conversation. No mention was made of the funeral or any of the happenings of the last three days, and it was not until coffee had been drunk in the drawing-room and Zacharia had removed the empty cups, that Mr Gilbert at last referred to the errand that had brought him to *Flamingo*.

'I'm sorry about this,' apologized Greg, 'but owing to one thing and another I'm afraid I shall have to ask a few more questions.'

'I thought every African on the estate had already been questioned *ad nauseam,*' said Eden bitterly. 'What more do you think you'll get out of them?'

'Not much,' admitted Greg equably. 'But then I'm not really interested in them at the moment. I merely want to know a few more things about last Tuesday. Your movements, for instance.'

'My *what?*' Eden's handsome face was suddenly white with anger and he said furiously: 'Are you by any chance suggesting that I might have murdered my own wife? Because if you are——'

'Don't be ridiculous, Eden!' Em's voice was sharp and commanding. 'Of course he doesn't mean any such thing! We all know how you feel, but I presume that Greg has got to ask this sort of question, so at least let us get it over quickly, and without losing our tempers.'

Greg said pacifically: 'No one is accusing you of anything. But if we can tie up everyone's movements on that day it will at least help to fill in the background. So let's start with yours.'

The colour came back to Eden's face and he thrust his hands into his pockets and turned away to stare blindly out of the window at the sunlit garden. He said: 'You already know exactly where I was and what I was doing that day. You've heard it all before.'

'Roughly, yes. "Exactly"—no.' Gilbert broke off and looked at Drew Stratton. 'Thinking of going anywhere, Drew?'

'Yes,' said Mr Stratton, preparing to leave. 'I can't see that I am serving any useful purpose by staying. See you later, Em, and thanks for the luncheon.'

Mr Gilbert said: 'Just sit down again, will you? I was coming to see you later, but if I can get what I want now it will save me a ten mile drive. You too, Miss Caryll.'

Em said haughtily: 'There is no question that you need ask my niece. She was not even here, and she knows nothing about this.'

'There is one question at least that I think she can answer,' said Greg quietly, 'and I would like her to stay.'

He turned back to Eden before Em could speak, and said: 'You went to Nairobi on Tuesday, didn't you?'

'Yes. To see Jimmy Druce about a Land-Rover he wants to sell. We had luncheon at Muthaiga. You can check up with him if you like.'

'We have. And you left here about ten o'clock. Can you by any chance remember if all the verandah cushions were present and correct when you left?'

'Of course I can't! I don't even know how many there are.'

'Four, I believe,' said Greg. 'And they are fairly striking.'

'I still wouldn't have noticed if there were three or six or a dozen! It's not the sort of thing that anyone would notice.'

'Except Zacharia,' said Mr Gilbert thoughtfully. 'He should have known, but he insists that he can't remember.'

'He's getting old,' said Em in extenuation.

'Ye—s. All the same, you'd think he'd notice a thing like that. It's part of his job. And anything in Harlequin checks and primary colours is apt to be eye-catching. Which makes it look as though they were all there. He would probably have noticed if there was one short.'

Em said: 'So you think that someone removed it off the verandah sometime during the day, and you don't think it's likely to have
been done by a stray terrorist from some hide-out in the *marula.*'

'Do you?' enquired Mr Gilbert.

'No,' said Em bleakly. 'No.'

She had been sitting regally erect in a large wing-back chair by
the piano, but now she seemed to shrink and crumble and change
before their eyes from a vigorous and commanding figure into a
tired and anxious old woman. 'You are right, of course. It would
have had to be someone from this house.'

'Or someone who could come openly to this house,' amended
Mr Gilbert. 'And there is always, of course, the possibility that it was
taken out for some entirely unimportant and trivial reason. So trivial
that whoever did it has forgotten about it. Which is why, if we can
work out where everyone was at every moment of that day, it may
jolt someone's memory. What did you do after luncheon, Eden?'

Eden started slightly at the abruptness of the question, and said:
'Shopped in the town. Fetched a suit from the cleaners, collected a
clock that had been taken in to be mended, bought a couple of shirts
and took in a film to be developed. I think that was all.'

Mr Gilbert consulted a small notebook that he had removed
from his coat pocket, and nodded as if satisfied. It was obvious that
he had been doing quite a bit of checking on his own, and he made
no attempt to conceal the fact. He said: 'Where did you have tea,
and when?'

'I didn't. I skipped it.'

'When did you start back?'

'Oh—er—around about seven, I suppose. I'm not sure.'

Mr Gilbert said thoughtfully: 'The shops shut at five, and according to Jimmy Druce you left the Club just after two. Were you
really shopping for three hours?'

Eden flushed angrily and said: 'No, of course I wasn't. As a
matter of fact, I drove out to the Game Park.'

'When was that?'

'About four, I suppose. Might have been a little earlier. But you
won't be able to check that, because I didn't get there. I remembered that the Park is infernally crowded these days, so I pulled up
by the side of the road instead, and just sat there.'

'Why?'

'I had a few things I wanted to think about,' said Eden shortly.

'And none of them, Greg, if I may say so, are any of your dam' business!'

Mr Gilbert shrugged and consulted his notebook again. He said: 'Any idea as to how long you sat there? And did anyone you know pass you?'

'No. I wasn't paying attention to passing people, and I only pushed off at last because it was getting late. I'd told Alice I probably wouldn't be back until nine or ten, and I'd meant to dine in Nairobi or somewhere on the road. But I decided that I'd get back for a late meal here after all. I got back here about nine o'clock, and found——'

He did not finish the sentence, but turned once more to stare out of the window.

Mr Gilbert said briskly: 'Thanks very much. Now what about you, Em? First of all, have you remembered anything about that cushion? Moving it, or noticing that it was missing—or not missing?'

'No,' said Em doubtfully. 'I—I may have moved it. But I must admit that I don't remember doing so, and I don't think that there is anything I would have wanted it for. Perhaps Alice did.'

'When?' demanded Greg. 'Her day has been pretty well accounted for. She spent the morning shopping in Naivasha, the afternoon in her room, had tea with you on the verandah, and went out shooting with you immediately afterwards—in order to avoid, I gather, what looked like being an embarrassing *tête-à-tête* with young Ken Brandon. And as it was just after you got back that she went across to the Markhams with a message for Lisa, there doesn't seem to be any point during the day when she could have carried a cushion out to the knoll. Now, can you remember what you yourself did on Tuesday, Em? In detail?'

'I think so,' said Em, frowning. 'Let me see—I had breakfast in bed and didn't get up until just before Eden left. I asked him to fetch the clock and to ring up the Airport and check the time that Victoria would be arriving, and we discussed the purchase of Jimmy's Land-Rover. After Eden had gone I saw the cook and told Kamau what I wanted in the way of vegetables, and then Alice and I made out a list of things we wanted from the stores in Naivasha. As soon as she had gone I started on the milk records, and then Lisa came over to see Eden, but Zacharia told her he'd left. She said she wouldn't disturb me, and left a note asking if we'd give her a lift next time either of us went into Nairobi. I heard the dogs barking and went to see who it was, but she was already half-way across the garden by then, so I didn't stop her.'

Greg said: 'Do the dogs always bark when anyone comes to the house?'

'If they're around. But they stop at once if it's anyone they know.'

'What time was it when Lisa came over?'

'About twenty to eleven I should say: Alice had just left. Then at eleven Gilly came over on business and stayed for half an hour, and he'd only just gone when the Brandons dropped in. We had coffee, and Hector went off to see Kamau about some fodder we're selling him, while Mabel and I talked.'

'What about?'

The question was asked so casually that Em had started to answer it before she realized where it would lead her. 'She'd seen Alice's car in Naivasha and knew she wouldn't be here, and she wanted to see me alone because she was worried about——'

She stopped abruptly, her face flushing in the unbecoming and mottled manner of the old, while her lips folded into a tight hard line.

Eden gave a short and mirthless laugh, and finished the sentence for her. 'About Ken. You needn't worry, Gran darling. It's no secret. What did she want you to do? Ship Alice home, or slip some arsenic in her soup?'

'Eden!' Once again Em's voice was sharp and commanding, and this time it was edged with anger.

'I'm sorry,' said Eden impatiently. 'I quite see that under the present circumstances that was a bloody silly remark to make. But you must admit that Mabel's been making a complete cake of herself over her precious Ken. It wasn't Alice's fault that her kid had a hopeless crush on her. Heaven knows she did everything she could to choke him off! But it wasn't at all easy for her, what with Ken threatening suicide and generally behaving like an amateur actor getting his teeth into Hamlet. She ought to have let me deal with him.'

'She was quite right not to,' said Em tartly. 'She took the very sensible view that it was really only like measles or teething—something that everyone gets when young, though some children get it worse than others. He'd have got over it soon enough. But if you'd taken a hand and lectured him, we'd have had a first class Brandon-DeBrett feud on our hands, and we neither of us wanted that.

Hector and Mabel are good friends of mine, and good neighbors; but Ken is their Achilles heel.'

'Ken,' said Eden morosely, echoing sentiments recently expressed by Mr Gilbert, 'is a spoilt, egotistical pup who fancies himself as a cross between Byron and an Angry Young Man. For God's sake, what's he got to be crazy or mixed up about? He's only had to ask for something, to be given it!'

'Perhaps that's why,' said Em with a sigh. 'He's just finding out that now he is grown up there are a good many things he can't have for the asking, and he feels that someone is to blame for it. He'll grow out of it.'

'Returning to Mabel,' said Mr Gilbert firmly. 'How long did she stay on Tuesday morning, and could she have removed that cushion?'

'No, of course she didn't!' said Em with a snap. 'Why on earth should she?'

'That's not the point. The question was "could she?" Or was she with you the entire time?'

'Well, no,' said Em reluctantly. 'I—Well it was all rather stupid really. I suppose I wasn't very sympathetic, and Mabel was hurt. She said she'd wait in the garden until Hector was ready to leave, and I went back to the office. But if you think that Mabel had anything to do with Alice's murder, you must be going out of your mind! She was a bit upset about this infatuation of Ken's, but that was all. And of course she had nothing to do with that cushion. Unless——'

She paused, frowning, and Greg said: 'Unless what?'

'Well, I suppose she might have taken it up to the knoll and sat there to wait for Hector. I never thought of that. There you are—I expect that's all there is to it. A perfectly simple explanation.'

'Perfectly,' said Greg. 'But if so, why didn't she admit to it? We asked everyone about it the next day.'

'I expect she forgot,' said Em flatly.

'Perhaps. We can always try and jog her memory. What did you do for the rest of the day?'

'Nothing special. Alice got back around one, and after luncheon I rested, and as you already know we had tea on the verandah at half-past four. Ken arrived in the middle of it, so we had to offer him some. He said he wanted to discuss something with Alice, but I said he would have to postpone it as she was coming out in the Land-Rover with me. I was rather afraid that he'd still be there when we got back, but he wasn't.'

'What time did you get back?'

'About a quarter to six. It was only then that I remembered Lisa's note, and Alice said she'd walk over and tell her that I'd be going into Nairobi on the Thursday to meet Victoria, and she could come in then. I shouldn't have let her go. But—how was I to know?'

Em's voice cracked and Eden crossed the space between them in two strides and put an arm about his grandmother's shoulders. 'Don't, Gran! It wasn't your fault. You've nothing to blame yourself for.'

Em said almost inaudibly: 'Yes I have. If I hadn't sent her over— Or if I had only——'

Eden released her and said harshly: 'If!—if, if, if! Why worry yourself over ifs?—If I hadn't married Alice she wouldn't have come to Kenya. And if she hadn't come to Kenya she wouldn't have been murdered. But does that mean that I am responsible for her death?'

He flung away and dropped into another chair, his legs stretched out before him and his hands deep in his pockets, and Mr Gilbert regarded him thoughtfully for a moment or two, and then turned his attention to Drew Stratton.

'Now about you, Drew. I'd like an account—a detailed account, please—of your last meeting with Mrs DeBrett.'

'I'll try,' said Drew, and embarked on a reasonably accurate account of that evening. 'She was,' he ended deliberately, 'very much upset at the prospect of Miss Caryll's arrival.'

Victoria shrank back in her chair as though he had struck her, while Eden flushed a dull red and Em said indignantly: 'That is not true! You are imagining things. I told her that if she would rather Victoria did not come she had only to say so.'

Drew said: 'Lady Emily, I did not know your granddaughter-in-law very well. But I knew her well enough to know that she would not allow her own feelings in the matter to stand in the way of your wishes; and I cannot imagine any normal woman feeling much enthusiasm for having an ex-fiancée of her husband's installed as a permanent fixture in the home.'

'Is that true?' demanded Mr Gilbert of Victoria. 'Were you two engaged?'

'I——' began Victoria, but got no further. Eden was on his feet again, his handsome face ugly with anger.

'No it is not! There was at one time what I believe is termed an "understanding" between us, but it was a purely private matter, and still is. So you needn't think that you're going to wash a lot of dirty linen in public and drag Victoria into this beastly business. You can keep her out of it!'

'My dear Eden, no one is trying to drag Miss Caryll into anything,' said Greg pacifically. 'But, unfortunately, the personal relationships of people who are involved, however inadvertently, in a murder case, are always a matter of interest.'

'Victoria is not "involved" in any of this!'

'Only indirectly.'

Em straightened herself in the wing-back chair, and once again it was an autocrat who sat there, imperious, regal and accustomed to being obeyed. She said: 'I think we had better get this quite straight, Greg. I am not a fool, and I dislike beating about the bush. It wastes time. What you are attempting to discover is whether Eden, or possibly myself, murdered Alice—*be quiet, Eden!* That is it, isn't it?'

'As a matter of fact,' said Mr Gilbert, 'and speaking solely for myself—No. But that is because you are both personal friends of mine and I know you fairly well. Speaking officially, however, it is not outside the bounds of possibility, and therefore it is just as well to consider that angle so that it can be abandoned. Helps clear the decks, if you know what I mean.'

'I know exactly what you mean,' said Em tartly. 'And you will allow me to tell you that I consider the suggestion an impertinence.'

'Impertinence my foot!' blazed Eden. 'It's a damned insult!'

Em said wearily: 'Oh, *do* be quiet, Eden. To term it an insult is to take it seriously. I suppose that such a thing might just be possible, but it is in the highest degree improbable.'

Drew gave her an odd sideways look and said reprovingly: 'You ought to count up to ten before you make statements like that, Em. It was, I think, the late lamented Sherlock Holmes who announced that in any problem, if the impossible was eliminated, what remained, however improbable, was bound to be the answer. Or words to that effect.'

'If that is so, Greg had better arrest me at once!' retorted Em with spirit. 'Of course I *could* have done it! I was here, wasn't I? In fact I was the only person who *was* here. Eden was in Nairobi, and as far as I know no one else called at *Flamingo* that evening. However, I assure you that I did not do it. And now perhaps we can terminate this unpleasant interview. Unless of course there are any more questions that Greg wishes to ask?'

'A few,' said Greg placidly. 'These queer incidents in the house —the breakages. Can you remember exactly when they started?'

Em wrinkled her brow in thought and after a moment or two said slowly: 'Let me see—the first thing was the K'ang Hsi vase. We found it on the floor in bits when we came back from a luncheon party. And there was red ink all over the carpet.'

'The Langleys' party,' said Eden. 'Eleventh of last month.'

Greg jotted down the date and said: 'When was the next time?'

'Only a few days later,' said Em. 'It must have been a Saturday, because that's the day I give out the *posho,* and I'd just finished doing it when Zacharia came to say that something else had been broken. Mother's Rockingham plates.'

'Fourteenth,' said Greg, who had been checking the dates in a pocket diary. 'I gather you had a good many incidents of this kind. Any sort of pattern?'

'No. After that it was almost every day. Then nothing for several days, and we thought it had stopped, and then it started again. It—it began to get on my nerves.'

Greg said: 'You ought to have reported it to the police at once.'

'I know that—now. But at the time I—Well, you know quite well why I didn't, Greg! I won't have my servants taken away and held for questioning or jailed on suspicion. They couldn't all have been in it, and why should the rest suffer because one man had got some queer, twisted African idea into his head, and imagined himself to be paying off a grudge? I thought it would work itself out. If I'd realized——'

Em's voice failed, and Greg said: 'When did you decide to send for Miss Caryll? Before all this started? Or afterwards?'

'Afterwards. I think—I think on the day the record of the concerto was broken. That—upset me. I found that I couldn't concentrate any more on the things I usually did myself. And Alice was frightened. I felt I must have someone to help me, and I thought of Victoria.'

Greg turned an enquiring look on Victoria and she answered the unspoken question. 'Aunt Em's letter arrived about three weeks ago. It gave me just time to have all the inoculations and things done, and that was all.'

Mr Gilbert nodded absently and turned back to Lady Emily. 'Just one more question. After your dog was poisoned, were there any more acts of vandalism in the house?'

'No.' Em's voice was a hoarse whisper, and Eden spoke harshly, his back still to the room: 'Gilly was right: that was one step further and we ought to have realized it. It started with something quite trivial, and finished with—Alice.'

'If it has finished,' said Greg soberly.

Eden spun round. 'Why do you say that?'

Greg shrugged his shoulders and said: 'It has been fairly conclusively proved that someone who kills once, and gets away with it, will kill again. Either to cover the first killing, or because the snuffing out of a human life is like taking to drugs. Terrifying, but stimulating. That's why the initiation rites of any secret society of the Mau Mau description include a murder. Because it's only the first killing that is difficult. After that it becomes progressively easier and breeds a callousness towards human life and a frightening megalomania. There's no reason to suppose that your wife's death will put a stop to whatever ugly business has been going on here, and that is why we have got to find the murderer if we have to screen every African—and every European!—in the Rift. Which reminds me, Em, did the Brandons bring a driver with them when they came over here on Tuesday morning?'

'Yes. But Samuel has been with them for over twenty years. He would never——'

She was not allowed to finish. 'Why is it,' demanded Mr Gilbert bitterly, 'that none of you, in spite of all you have been through, can be brought to believe that a faithful servant can also be someone who has taken a binding oath to rid the country of all whites?'

He slammed his notebook shut, returned it to his pocket, and rose with a sigh. 'Well I think that's about all for the moment, though I'm afraid we're going to have to interview all your servants and the labour again tomorrow, Em. But Bill Hennessy will be dealing with that. Be gentle with him, won't you? He tells me that ever since you took a stick to him when you caught him playing toreadors in the bull paddock at the ripe age of ten, he's been scared stiff of you.'

'I wish I could believe that,' said Em bleakly. 'But I don't suppose that there is any more truth in it than in your inference that we ourselves shall not be called upon to endure any more of these inquisitions.'

There was the faintest possible suggestion of appeal in her voice, but Mr Gilbert disregarded it. He said: 'Until we find out who killed Mrs DeBrett, I'm afraid we shall have to go on asking questions. And I cannot believe that any of you would have it otherwise.'

He collected his hat, nodded amiably at them, and left.

7

Em leaned forward in her chair listening to the sound of his retreating footsteps, and a minute later, hearing a car start up and purr away down the dusty drive, she sighed gustily and relaxed.

'Thank heaven for that! I was afraid his driver would not have arrived and that he would fill in the next half-hour upsetting the servants. I am too old for this sort of thing.'

She turned to look at the French ormolu clock that stood on a lacquer cabinet at the far side of the room, and said: 'Four o'clock already! I suppose we had luncheon very late. Will you take tea with us, Drew?'

Mr Stratton declined the invitation, saying that he must get back, and Em heaved herself up out of her chair and accompanied him to the verandah, Victoria and Eden following.

There was someone on the path beyond the jacaranda trees, walking at a pace that suggested urgency, and Eden shaded his eyes with his hand and after a brief inspection announced with a trace of annoyance: 'It's Lisa. What do you suppose she wants?'

'You, I imagine,' said Em with some acerbity. 'Go and head her off, Eden. I don't want to see anyone else today. All I want is tea and peace!'

She turned to Drew with some query relating to a rumoured outbreak of swine fever on a neighbouring estate, and Eden went quickly down the verandah steps, and along the narrow path that led across the garden in the direction of the plumbago hedge and the manager's bungalow.

Victoria saw the woman break into a little run as he approached her, and reaching him, clutch at his coat sleeve. They were too far away for their voices to be audible above Em's plangent strictures on the inefficiency of quarantine precautions, but even from this dis-

70

tance it was possible to see from the woman's gestures and the very movement of her head that she was either excited or upset.

Victoria saw Eden throw a quick look over his shoulder in the direction of the house, and it seemed to her that his face was oddly colorless against the tree shadows. The woman tugged at his sleeve as though she were urging him to walk away with her, and Victoria caught the high-pitched urgency of her voice, pleading or arguing. Then suddenly Eden grasped her arm, and turning about came quickly back to the house, dragging her with him.

Em, immersed in farming shop, was not aware of them until they reached the foot of the verandah steps, and hearing the click of high heels on stone and the jingle of Mrs Markham's charm bracelets, she turned with a look of undisguised impatience.

'Well, Lisa? What is it?'

But it was Eden, and not Mrs Markham who replied. There was a white shade about his mouth and his voice was not quite steady:

'Lisa's got something to say that I think you should hear at once. She——'

Em threw up a hand in an imperious gesture and checked him. Her shrewd old eyes went from one face to the other, and then to the silent figures of Zacharia and a house-boy who were laying afternoon tea in a corner of the verandah. She said coldly: 'If it is important—and I take it that it is?—then we had better go back into the drawing-room. Goodbye Drew. Thank you for collecting my niece. It was kind of you. I'll send Eden over tomorrow to look at those calves.'

She nodded at him and turned away, and Victoria said a little stiffly: 'Goodbye, Mr Stratton. Thank you for all your trouble.'

'It wasn't any trouble,' Drew said shortly. 'I happened to be in Nairobi and this was on my way back.'

He went away down the steps to his car, leaving Victoria, who possessed a healthy temper of her own, with an itching palm and an unmaidenly desire to box his ears.

Em was speaking peremptorily to her grandson:

'My dear Eden, if this is something that concerns us, it must also concern Victoria, since she is now one of the household. By the way, Lisa, you will not have met my niece, Miss Caryll. Victoria, this is Mrs Markham——'

Victoria shook hands and found herself looking into a pair of large violet eyes, expertly enhanced with pencil and mascara and as unmistakably hostile as Drew Stratton's had been. And then Em

71

said: 'Lend me your arm, dear,' and led the way to the drawing-room with a firm step. But her weight pressed heavily upon Victoria's arm as though she really needed that support, and her bulky body was trembling with fatigue.

She lowered herself into the wing-chair once more, and Eden said: 'Look, Gran, Lisa didn't want to worry you with this, but it seems to me that it's something you should know. She says——'

His grandmother turned a quelling eye upon him and said firmly: 'Let her speak for herself, please. Well, Lisa?'

Lisa flumped down sulkily on to the window seat and rubbed resentfully at the marks that Eden's ungentle grip had left on her bare arm. 'I only thought that Eden ought to know, and then he could decide what to do about it. I wasn't going to tell anyone else. Not even Gilly! Though of course everyone's bound to know sooner or later, as Wambui's sure to tell someone else, and once the servants know it—well, you know how they can never keep anything to themselves.'

Em gave a short bark of laughter. 'How little you know this country, Lisa. They may not be able to keep a secret from their own people, but they can always keep it from us. Make no mistake about that! What is it that you have to tell me? If it is just some servant's gossip, you may be fairly sure that it is unimportant.'

'It wasn't gossip,' said Lisa angrily. 'It was serious.' There was a sudden flash of spite in her violet eyes: '*Very* serious! That's why I thought I ought to discuss it with Eden first. But if he prefers it this way, it's his own look out. It was Wambui, if you want to know. My *ndito.* She's been behaving very oddly the last day or two. Dropping things and forgetting things, and jumping as if she's been stung if anyone made a sudden noise. So this afternoon I tackled her about it, and it all came out. She's in a state about Kamau.'

'You mean *my* Kamau?' demanded Em.

'Yes. It seems he's been courting her, and they've been meeting every night in the bushes on the far side of the knoll.'

Em stiffened where she sat, and her expression was no longer one of bored patience. She said sharply and a little breathlessly: 'You mean they saw something? Is that it? They know who did it?'

Lisa shook her head. 'I don't know. You see Wambui couldn't get away on Tuesday evening, but it seems that Kamau waited for her for quite a time, and now he's hinting to her that he knows something about—Alice's murder.'

There was a sudden silence in the room, and in it Victoria heard a soft sound that was something like the click of a latch and seemed to come from the direction of the door that led out of the drawing-room into the hall. But the next moment her attention was distracted, for Em was speaking again:

'But the police questioned all the servants!' said Em. 'They've seen them half a dozen times already. Surely they would have told us if they'd got any information out of them? Why, Greg Gilbert has been here half the afternoon.'

'Wambui says Kamau told the police that he didn't know anything.'

Em made an angry, impatient gesture. 'Then I don't suppose he does. He's probably only showing off for Wambui's benefit.'

'But we know there was someone in the bushes that night,' insisted Eden. 'Why couldn't it have been Kamau? In fact why couldn't Kamau have been the poltergeist?—and the murderer, for that matter!'

'Don't talk nonsense, Eden,' said Em crossly. 'Kamau's father was one of your grandfather's first servants, and Zacharia is his uncle. He would no more harm me than—than Zacharia would! And you seem to forget that he was the one who killed Gitahi. If *that* isn't proof of loyalty, I'd like to know what is!'

'Oh, all right—all right. I know it's useless to try and persuade you that any of your darling Kukes might be anything but a hundred per cent loyal. But what about the man in the bushes? It squares with that, you know. *Someone* was there!'

'If it was Kamau, it is proof that he was not Alice's murderer,' said Em stiff with anger. 'Whoever was there had not approached the body. You know that quite well.'

'Of course I do. But he could have seen something, couldn't he? He could be telling the truth there.'

'If you think that,' snapped Em, 'I suggest you ring up Greg Gilbert immediately and tell him exactly what Lisa has told us. Then the police can deal with it—and with Wambui!'

'But you can't do that,' gasped Lisa leaping to her feet, her eyes wide with dismay. 'They'd take her away and hold her for questioning. You know what they're like. She might not be back for days, and I simply can't manage without her. Oh, I wish I hadn't said anything! I wish I hadn't.'

Her eyes filled with tears and she sat down abruptly and began to search blindly and without success in the inadequate pockets of her linen suit.

'Here,' said Eden, handing over a handkerchief. He patted her shoulder awkwardly and said: 'Don't cry, Lee.' Lisa dabbed at her tears, and groping for his hand, clung to it, looking up at him with eyes that were openly and helplessly adoring.

Eden withdrew his hand with more speed than gallantry, and Em said dryly: 'You would have done better to come straight to me, would you not, Lisa. Although I am aware that as a confidante I am likely to prove less sympathetic than my grandson! However, you are right in one thing. Unless they resort to violence the police will get nothing out of Kamau. And I will not have my servants intimidated. I will talk to him myself. He can do the rounds with me this evening after dinner. That will be the best way. I often take one of the boys with me, so it will arouse no suspicion; and he will talk better in the dark. They always do. And now let us have some tea.'

Lisa could not stay, but Eden did not offer to see her home, and after lingering for a few moments she turned from him with a petulant toss of the head and walked away down the long garden path, and he came back to his chair, and subsiding into it, stared moodily into space while his tea grew cold. He made no attempt at conversation, and Victoria sat silent, covertly studying him.

The passing of the years had not detracted from his spectacular good looks, and although he looked older and thinner, and there were frown lines on his forehead and fine lines at the corners of his eyes that had come from screwing them up against strong sunlight, there was no denying the fact that in appearance at least he was, if anything, more attractive now than he had been six years ago.

It's not fair! thought Victoria resentfully. How can anyone tell what he is really like when they can't get beyond what he looks like? What do I know about Eden? What did I ever know? Am I still in love with him . . . ?

Em too had been disinclined to talk, and now she pushed away her almost untasted cup and came to her feet with sudden decision, announcing that she for one did not intend to sit about all evening doing nothing, and that as they needed dog meat again she proposed to take out the Land-Rover and shoot a buck. Victoria and Eden had better come with her.

Eden said: 'You'll only tire yourself out, racketing round in the Land-Rover, Gran. Why don't you stay here and put your feet up for a change? I'll go. Victoria can come with me if she'd like to.'

Em shot a quick anxious look at her niece and said obstinately: 'I don't wish to put my feet up, thank you. I wish to get out of this house and into the fresh air.'

'What you mean,' said Eden, 'is that you're feeling upset. And whenever that happens you work it off by going out and driving round the countryside far too fast. Shooting for dog meat is just an excuse, and you know it.'

'It's nothing of the sort,' snapped Em. 'You know quite well that they get through a buck in about four days—what is left of it after the servants have had the best cuts. And fresh meat doesn't keep in this weather.'

She stumped off down the verandah and Eden turned to Victoria with a rueful grin. 'You'll have to make allowance for us, Vicky. We're all rather badly shaken up by this. It's a pity you had to arrive just now and get involved in it all. I wish I could have kept you out of it.'

Victoria said soberly: 'Eden, I haven't had time to tell you before how sorry I am about—your wife. But——'

'That's all right,' said Eden hastily. 'You don't have to say anything. Listen, Vicky——' He hesitated, flushed, and then said abruptly: 'I suppose this is quite the wrong time to mention it, but I know you must think I behaved pretty brutally to you in the past. I did, of course. There were reasons why—Oh well, there's no point in going into them now. But what I wanted to say is that I'm damned glad that you're here. I had no right to expect that you'd come, but we need a bit of sanity in this place. And you're right about Gran needing you. She's cracking up, and if we don't watch out she'll end up by having a stroke or running off the rails. Try to see if you can't get her to ease up a bit—on the work, if nothing else.'

Victoria said: 'I'll do what I can. You know that.'

'Yes, of course. But it isn't going to be easy. As you can see, you've landed right into the middle of a really nasty situation. Gran *will* have it that everything is over now, and I wish I could believe it. But I didn't like what Greg said about "only the first killing being difficult". Supposing he was right, and that Alice wasn't the end, but the beginning? Look here, Vicky, if you feel that you'd rather not stay, you—you don't have to, you know. I could always arrange a return passage for you.'

Victoria said: 'Aunt Em said that too. Are you trying to frighten me, Eden? Or merely get rid of me?'

'Good Lord, no! From what I know of you, you don't frighten easily, and thank God for it! Believe me, it's going to be a nice change to have someone about the house who doesn't jump every time a door opens or a leaf drops! But I don't want you to feel that you have to stay. That's all.'

He put out a hand and touched the tip of her nose lightly with one finger. It was a familiar, caressing gesture that he had used so often in the past, and which had been peculiarly their own, and Victoria stepped back as swiftly as though it had been a blow, and turning from him went quickly away.

Em and Eden were both waiting for her in the Land-Rover when she reappeared ten minutes later, and they had driven out on to the ranges, where Em had shot a kongoni and a Thomson's gazelle.

It had been dark by the time they returned, and Em had pronounced herself too tired to change for dinner that night, so they had dined as they were, in the candle-lit dining-room where portraits of dead and gone DeBretts and Beaumartins looked down from the walls. But afterwards, as Zacharia was leaving the drawing-room carrying the coffee tray, Em spoke briefly to him in Swahili.

Victoria did not understand what she said, but Eden turned sharply: 'Kamau? You aren't *really* going to see him tonight? You're far too done up! For goodness sake, Gran, leave it for the morning! He won't run away.'

'How do I know that?' enquired Em morosely, moving towards the door. 'Of course I'm going to see him. Besides, Zach says he told him after tea that he was to go round with me tonight, so he will be waiting. I said he was to bring a lamp and meet me at the gate into the shamba, as I wanted to make sure that the hippos haven't broken the wire again. It is too good an opportunity to miss: I have been told things after dark that I would never have heard by day, and I know these people better than you do—even though I'm not Kenya born!'

'For Pete's sake, Gran!' said Eden, exasperated. 'You're surely not going to do the rounds tonight?'

'Why not? I've never missed it yet.'

'But you're tired out! And anyway, it's not necessary any longer. Oh, you needn't remind me about what happened to Alice! Do you think I need reminding? But even Greg doesn't think that was anything more than an isolated attack, and if the Emergency is over— and we keep being told that it is—then what's the point of going round the place every night to see that the labour are all in and the place is properly locked up, and all the rest of this Commando nonsense? We can't keep it up for ever. Look here, I'll go instead. And what's more, I'll talk to Kamau for you.'

'No, dear,' said Em gently but quite definitely. 'He wouldn't talk to you as he will to me.'

'Then I'm going with you. You know I've never liked you wandering around alone after dark, but you would do it. It's quite time it was stopped. Victoria——'

He turned towards her as though for support, and Em said crisply: 'Victoria has nothing to do with this, and it's quite time she went to bed. Don't be silly, Eden. You've never tried to stop me doing it before, and I can't imagine why you are doing it now.'

'I did try, but——'

'But your wife wouldn't let you go instead of me, and she wouldn't allow you to go with me because she was afraid of being alone in the house. I know, dear. But you must see that this is no time to relax our precautions. If you really want to take over doing the rounds we'll discuss the matter tomorrow, but if we want to get anything out of Kamau it's important that I see him alone. So don't let's have any more argument about it. Victoria dear, go to bed. You must be tired out. And you too, Eden! There's no need for you to wait up for me. Good night, dear.'

The door closed behind her with decision, and Eden took a hasty step forward as though he would have followed her, and then looked at Victoria and shrugged his shoulders.

'Now you see what I meant when I said you wouldn't find it an easy job—helping Gran! You'd better do what she told you and get off to bed. I expect you could do with a bit of sleep. Good night.'

He turned and went out by the verandah door, leaving Victoria alone in the silent drawing-room.

8

Despite the anxieties and disturbances of the previous day—or perhaps because of them—Victoria slept soundly and dreamlessly, and awakened feeling refreshed and invigorated and capable of coping with any and every one of the problems that life at *Flamingo* might offer.

Breakfast had been laid on the verandah, and Eden, wearing riding breeches and a thin tweed coat, was sitting on the verandah rail and drinking black coffee. He was looking tired and heavy-eyed and as though he had not had enough sleep during the past night—or for several nights.

He slid off the verandah rail and said: 'Hullo, Vicky. No need to ask how you slept. You look offensively well. I hope the dogs didn't worry you? They're apt to be a bit noisy at intervals.'

'They did wake me a couple of times,' admitted Victoria, seating herself at the table, 'but I was too sleepy to bother. What was all the noise about?'

'Nothing. Or anything! Trouble is, they usually run loose about the grounds at night, but the Markhams' spaniel is in heat, and Lisa asked us if we'd keep 'em locked up for the duration, as apparently they sit under her window and serenade her all night. So they've been shut up in one of the spare godowns, and they hate it. Have some coffee. Gran's having her breakfast in bed. She said to tell you she'd like to see you as soon as you're through with yours. I should take your time if I were you. She's not in the best of tempers.'

'Why? Nothing else has happened, has it? I mean—nothing else has been broken, or——?'

'No, nothing like that. It's just that Kamau never turned up last night, and she hung about waiting for him and got chilled to the bone, and lost her temper into the bargain. She doesn't like being kept waiting and she doesn't take kindly to having her orders disobeyed. He probably had an assignation with his girlfriend. Or else he's lost his nerve and gone A.W.O.L. for a few days! Gran's livid, and I can clearly see that this is going to be one of those days when nothing goes right.'

Zacharia appeared with a dish of buttered eggs and bacon, and Victoria helped herself and enquired if Eden was going out riding.

'I've been,' said Eden briefly. He rejected the eggs with every appearance of loathing, and pouring out a second cup of black coffee, returned to his seat on the verandah rail. 'When you've finished I'll take you along to Gran's room. With any luck she may have simmered down a bit, and it mightn't be a bad idea if we ganged up on her and tried to see if we couldn't persuade her to spend the day in bed.'

But neither hope was to be realized. Em was already up, and in an exceedingly bad temper. They found her seated in front of her dressing-table, wearing a pair of grey corduroy trousers topped by what appeared to be a fisherman's jersey in a painful shade of orange.

'Oh, it's you,' said Em without turning, addressing their reflections in the glass. 'Good morning, Victoria. I trust you had a good night—it's more than I had!'

She turned to speak in trenchant Swahili to Zacharia, who was peering into one of the cupboards, and added crossly: 'He's getting too old for the work. That's what it is. I shall have to pension him off.'

'What's he been doing now?' enquired Eden perfunctorily.

'Lost a pair of my red dungarees. And as one pair hasn't been ironed yet and another is in the wash, and the pair I wore yesterday are filthy, I'm reduced to wearing a pair of your father's old corduroys. Sheer carelessness. Oh, do stop rootling round in that cupboard, Zach! If they weren't there five minutes ago they aren't there now. Here, take these ones away and get them washed at once. You'd better boil them. And see that they're dried and ironed by this evening.'

She reached down and picked up the discarded dungarees and blouse that she had worn on the previous day, and making a bundle of them, flung them at the old Kikuyu who caught them deftly and carried them away.

Eden put a coaxing arm around his grandmother's shoulders and said: 'Snap out of it, Gran. You can't tear a strip off everyone in the house on Victoria's first day here. It'll give her a wrong impression. Don't be cross, darling. It's bad for the blood pressure.'

'I'm not cross. I'm furious! Zach thinks that Kamau went off to meet that *ndito* of Lisa's last night instead of waiting for me. If he did, then of course she would have told him that she'd talked to Lisa, and naturally he wasn't going to face me after that. Just wait until I get my hands on him, that's all! I gather he's gone to help cut lucerne in the east field this morning; thinks he can keep out of my way, I suppose. I've told Zach I wish to see him the moment he gets back.'

Em pinned on a diamond brooch and catching sight of Victoria in the looking glass, turned about to study her approvingly.

'How nice you look, dear. I'd forgotten that you were so pretty. Have you had some breakfast? Good. Well now I'm going to show you the office and give you some idea of what there is to do, and then we'll do a tour of the house and the gardens, and after luncheon——'

'After luncheon,' cut in Eden firmly, 'I am taking her out in the launch. Unless you propose to keep her nose to the grindstone from the word "Go"?'

'No, of course not. I want her to enjoy herself. Certainly take her out on the lake. She will like that. And we must arrange a few expeditions—picnic parties, so that she can see something of the Rift. I see no reason why we should mope indoors. Let me see—you are going to take a look at the new bore hole this morning, aren't you? Then we shall see you at luncheon. Come along, dear.'

She swept Victoria out, and the remainder of the morning was devoted to the programme she had outlined. Eden had been delayed, so luncheon was late, and young Mr Hennessy of the police, accompanied by two police askaris, arrived halfway through the meal, and was kept waiting. 'It will do him no harm to cool his heels on the verandah,' observed Em tartly; and she had lingered over the coffee until the hands of the grandfather clock pointed at twenty minutes to three, before going out to see him.

'I wouldn't be in Bill Hennessy's shoes this afternoon for all the coffee in Brazil!' said Eden, taking Victoria's arm and hurrying her down a path that wound between a colourful wilderness of plumbago and wild lupins towards the lake. 'She can't forget that she knew him when he was a sticky little schoolboy, and to have him questioning her servants in the name of the Law is adding insult to injury. Look out for those thorns.'

He opened the gate into the shamba and ushered Victoria into a lush, green wilderness where the warm air was heavy with the scent of orange blossom and drowsy with the hum of bees, and the damp ground squelched under her sandalled feet.

'I suppose that's the trouble with Gran,' continued Eden. 'When you get to her age there's hardly anyone left whom you didn't know when they were children. Makes it difficult to take them seriously. She must feel like a governess in a schoolroom full of irresponsible brats. All the same, I get a bit tired of being treated as if I were still in the Lower Fourth. If Gran would only realize that I was now an adult she'd put me in as manager in place of that waster, Gilly. Damn it all, I may as well learn how to run it, considering that I shall own the place one day. That is, unless Gran cuts me out of her will and leaves it to you instead.'

'To *me?*' exclaimed Victoria, startled. 'What nonsense! Why should she do any such thing?'

Eden shrugged his shoulders and preceded her through another gate into a shadowy forest of banana palms. 'Ask me another. Why does Gran do anything? Because she wants to. Besides, she's a bit of a feminist, our Em. She may think you'd do more for *Flamingo*—and for Kenya—than I would. The female of the species being more deadly than the male—and all the rest of it.'

'Rubbish!' retorted Victoria. 'You know quite well that she adores you. She always has. She only snaps at you to try and disguise the fact; and fools nobody.'

Eden laughed. 'Perhaps. All the same, it's quite on the cards that she may have thought that I was taking my responsibilities as Heir to the Throne too lightly, and doesn't think it will do me any harm to realize that if I don't watch my step she can nominate another candidate. She's a Machiavellian old darling.'

'But *you* don't think that?' said Victoria, troubled. 'I mean, even supposing she did—and she wouldn't!—you don't think that I'd do you out of *Flamingo,* do you?'

Eden stopped, and turned to smile down at her, and her heart did a foolish check and leap. He said: 'Wouldn't you, darling? I wonder. You might think that it would serve me right.'

A tide of colour rose to the roots of Victoria's brown hair and she said confusedly: 'Don't be silly, Eden! I never thought—I mean —Well, we made a mistake. That was all. But we're still friends.'

'Are we?' asked Eden soberly. 'Are we really, Vicky?'

'Of course,' said Victoria, making a determined grab at lightness. 'I'm like Aunt Em. I can't forget that we were allies against Authority in the days when you were a beastly little boy with scratched knees and a dirty neck.'

But Eden refused to follow her lead. He said, unsmiling: 'Thank you, Vicky.' And reaching out he took her hand, and before she realized what he meant to do, he had lifted it and kissed it.

Victoria fought down a strong impulse to snatch it away and run, and an even stronger one to stroke his bent head with her free hand. Heroically resisting both, she said briskly: 'Do you think we could take some of these bananas on the boat with us? It's years since I picked one straight off the bunch.'

'They're not ripe,' said Eden a shade sulkily. He turned and walked on down the path, only to stop again a few minutes later with an impatient exclamation. 'Damn! The hippo have been in again. It's just ruddy idleness on Gilly's part; he won't see that the fences are properly made. What the hell's the use of a single strand of wire, even if you do run a mild electric current through it? It hasn't apparently even stopped the remnants of the Mau Mau gangs from keeping open an escape route round the lake!'

Victoria said: 'Do you think there's anything in it? Gangs hiding out in the *marula,* I mean?'

'No. Though I suppose it's just possible that the odd man who is still on the run spends a day or two there. There couldn't be a better hiding place, could there? Just look at it!'

He waved a hand in the general direction of the papyrus swamps that reared up like a solid grey-green wall between the shamba and the Lake. A weird, waving jungle, so dense that a man forcing his way through it, his ears filled by the noise of his own passage, might pass within a yard of another who stood still, and never know it. It stretched for miles along the lake shore, and during the Emergency the gangs had cut their own secret paths and built solidly constructed hides in it.

Years earlier Gerald DeBrett too had cut a wide pathway through the papyrus, and laid down a duckboard to the lake edge where he had built a wooden boat-house supported on piles and sheltered by the reeds. It was weather-beaten now, and ramshackle, but Em had kept the approach to it in tolerable repair, and it housed a small rowing boat, a battered punt and a neat white motor launch.

'We had to have a guard on this all through the Emergency,' said Eden, casting off and poling the launch down a narrow channel between shadowy walls of papyrus. 'Damned nuisance it was too.

Greg got pretty crisp about it. He wanted it pulled down and the boats holed or dragged up somewhere where they couldn't be used, to prevent the Mau Mau using them. But Gran wouldn't hear of it. She fixed up a roster of guards. Myself, Gus Abbott and half a dozen of the loyal Kikuyu. Even poor old Zach was pressed into service, but he was far more afraid of handling a gun—and of the hippo—than he was of being murdered. Kamau refused to take a gun at all. He pinned his faith to a panga; and got a chap with it, too! Caught him trying to cut a boat loose, and slashed at him in the dark. Cut his head clean off, and carried it triumphantly up to the house in the morning. Alice fainted all over the coffee cups, but Gran didn't turn a hair.'

Victoria said shuddering: 'You don't mean he actually *showed* it to them?'

'He certainly did. He was as pleased as Punch about it. And with reason! For it turned out to be one of the top Mau Mau brass, "Brigadier" Gitahi, no less. There was a nice fat price on his head too, which was duly handed over to Kamau, with the result that the entire labour force of *Flamingo* were beautifully tight for at least a week afterwards. Now let's see if we can get this engine to start.'

The launch glided free of the papyrus and the floating weed beds, and they were in hot sunlight again, with the wide expanse of the lake spread out before them. Bright blue lilies spangled the water, and there was a continuous quack and ruffle of birds: stately white pelicans, numerous as swans on the Liffey; spoonbills, dab-chicks, cormorants, wild duck and herons.

A huge head adorned by two wildly agitated ears rose up on the port bow, regarded them with austere disapproval, and sank again. 'Too many hippo in the lake,' observed Eden, frowning. 'It's quite time we shot some. One or two make rather pleasant local colour, but twenty or thirty of them can do as much damage to the lakeside shambas as a plague of locusts. Look—there are some flamingo. They must be on their way to Elmenteita. They don't often come to Naivasha. Beautiful, aren't they?'

'Lovely!' said Victoria on a breath of rapture. 'You know, I used to think of all this, and wonder if it could possibly be as beautiful as I remembered it to be. But it is. Every bit as beautiful!'

'So in spite of everything,' said Eden, 'you're glad you came back?'

'What do you mean? "In spite of everything",' demanded Victoria defensively.

'Me—Alice—Gran rapidly going off her rocker. A resident poltergeist, and the police almost permanently on the premises,' said Eden bitterly.

'Oh, Eden, I'm sorry!' Victoria lifted a flushed and contrite face. 'I keep on forgetting about Alice. I'm a selfish pig!'

'No you're not, dear. You're refreshingly normal. And thank God for it! To tell you the truth, Vicky, I can't quite believe it myself, and when I'm away from the house it all seems like a nightmare that I shall wake up from. It's only when I get back to the house that— Oh, hell! Let's talk about something else, shall we?'

'Yes, *let's!*' said Victoria gratefully. 'Where are we going, by the way? And whose is that house up on the hill over there?'

'Drew Stratton's. Chap who collected you from the Airport yesterday.'

'Oh,' said Victoria in a repressive voice, and after a moment or two of silence enquired: 'Do you mean his house, or where we are going?'

'Both.'

'Oh,' said Victoria again, betraying a marked lack of enthusiasm.

Eden threw her an amused glance. 'You don't sound wildly enthusiastic. Didn't you take to our Mr Stratton?'

'He didn't take to me. In fact I rather think that he went out of his way to be rude. Is he a confirmed misogynist, or something?'

'Not that I know of. And as everyone in Kenya knows everyone else's innermost secrets, you can take it that he is neither.'

'Merely mannerless, I suppose,' said Victoria with some acidity.

'You have got your knife into him, haven't you?'

'I have never,' said Victoria with dignity, 'taken kindly to being disliked and disapproved of at sight and for no reason.'

Eden laughed. 'Don't tell me it's ever happened to you before, because I won't believe it! You must have got hold of the wrong end of the stick. Everyone likes Drew.'

'I can't think why, when he's obviously conceited and egotistical, as well as being boorish and entirely lacking in manners, and——'

'Here! Hi!' said Eden. 'Give the poor chap a chance! You can't knock our local hero-boy, you know. He's one of our leading citizens. In fact we point to him with pride.'

'Why?' demanded Victoria frostily. 'Because he lounges around with a gun on his hip and drives too fast, I suppose?'

'Then you suppose wrong. To start off with he's Kenya-born, and his grandparents were two of the real pioneers—like Delamere and

Grogan and old Grandfather DeBrett—and in a young Colony that means something! He lost both his parents before he was twenty, and having copped a packet in the way of wounds and decorations during the Normandy landings, came back to find that his manager had let the place go to rack and ruin, and there was a load of debt instead of the fat profits that other farms had been making during the war years. A lot of men faced with that sort of mess would have sold up and got out, but Drew flatly refused to part with a single acre of his land. Said he knew he could pull it out of the red. And did. He must have lived on cattle food and *posho* for God knows how long, and he worked like ten men. And then just as things were really beginning to look up, the Mau Mau business broke . . .'

Eden looked broodingly out across the lake and was silent for so long that at last Victoria said impatiently: 'Go on. What happened to him then?'

'Who? Oh Drew. Nothing much, if you mean to his place. The Strattons have always employed Masai, and Drew was practically brought up in a *manyatta.* He's blood-brother to every ochre-painted *moran* in the Colony, and so the Mau Mau gave him a wide berth. But he's one of the *"My country, 'tis of thee",* brigade, and he handed over the management of the estate to old Ole Gachia, with instructions to keep it on an even keel, and offered his services to the Security Forces. He ended up by more or less running his own show, and used to go out with a pseudo gang, despite the fact that he's as blond as a chorus girl.'

'What's a "pseudo gang"?' asked Victoria, intrigued.

'Didn't you ever read your papers? They were the boys who pretended to be terrorists. Learnt all the jargon and dressed themselves up for the part—and blacked themselves all over, if they were British. They used to push off into the forests to make contact with the gangs. Drew had a hand-picked bunch of his own. Pukka devils, from all accounts. They pulled off some astonishing coups, and had a pleasant habit of cutting a notch in Drew's verandah rail for every kill. It made an impressive tally, and I am credibly informed that although the Emergency is officially a thing of the past, there is still an occasional new notch there. We'll take a look and see. Here we are. Stand by for the bump.'

He switched off the engine, and as the launch lost speed, manoeuvred it expertly alongside a small wooden jetty that thrust out into a narrow bay whose steep banks blazed with flamboyant and vivid cascades of bougainvillaea. A long flight of steps wound upwards from the jetty and passed between banks of roses and flowering shrubs, to come out on a gravel path which followed the curve of a stone wall buttressing a grassed terrace in front of a long, low, single-storeyed house whose wide verandah was shaded by flowering creepers.

Mr Stratton might employ Masai on his estate, but his house servants were coast Arabs, and a dignified white-robed figure, whose face might have been carved from a polished chunk of obsidian, greeted the visitors, and informed them that the Bwana should be immediately notified of their arrival.

'What a heavenly view!' said Victoria, leaning on the verandah rail and looking out across a vast panorama of lake and tree-clad hills and far rolling grassland ringed by blue ranges that shimmered like mirages in the afternoon sun. Her eye fell on a long row of notches cut into the wood of the rail, and she drew back sharply, the pleasure on her face giving place to disgust.

'What did I tell you?' said Eden, following the direction of her gaze. 'Quite a nice line-up.'

'*Nice!* You call that nice? Why, it's appalling! And—and barbaric! Chalking up a record of dead men!'

'Of dead murderers,' corrected a dry voice behind her.

Victoria whirled round, her cheeks flushing scarlet. Mr Stratton, dressed in impeccable riding clothes, was standing in the doorway of a room that opened on to the verandah. He was looking perfectly amiable, and his bland gaze travelled thoughtfully from Miss Caryll to her cousin.

'Courtesy call, Eden?'

'Business, I'm afraid. Those Herefords of yours. Gran wants me to have a look at them before we clinch the deal.'

'Of course. She said something about it yesterday. They're in the paddock just behind the house. You'll find Kekinai out there. He'll tell you anything you want to know. I'll entertain Miss Caryll until you're through.'

Eden looked doubtfully at Victoria, and then all at once a malicious smile leapt to life in his eyes, and he said: 'Good idea. I won't be long.' And left them.

Victoria made a swift movement as though she would have followed him, but Mr Stratton, either by accident or design, had moved forward in the same moment and barred her way. 'Cigarette?' he enquired, proffering his case.

'Thank you; I don't smoke,' said Victoria curtly.

'You won't mind if I do? Tea will be along in a minute. Or would you rather have a cold drink? It's quite a pull up from the lake on a hot day.'

Victoria disregarded the offer and said, stammering a little: 'I'm sorry that you should have heard w-what I said. About the notches. I didn't mean to be r-rude.'

'There's no need to apologize for your views,' said Drew gravely.

'I'm not. Only for letting you hear them.'

'My feelings,' said Drew, 'are not so easily wounded. So you think I'm appalling and barbaric because I allow the boys to cut a tally of their kills on my verandah rail, do you? You are not the only one. There are uncounted thousands of soft-hearted and fluffy-minded—and abysmally ignorant—people who would agree with you.'

'Thank you,' said Victoria sweetly.

'Don't mention it. Unlike you, I meant to be rude. You see, Miss Caryll, I get a little bored by people who broadcast views on something that is, to them, only a problem on paper, and one which does not touch them, personally, in any way. We each have something that we love deeply and are prepared to fight for and die for, and kill for! and I wonder just how many of the virtuous prosers, if it was the agony of their own child or wife or lover, or the safety of their own snug little surburban home that was in question, would not fight in their defence?'

Victoria said: 'I didn't mean that. I meant this sort of thing—cutting notches. Making a game of killing.'

'It wasn't a game. It was deadly serious. The men we were after had deliberately bestialized themselves by acts and oaths and ceremonies that were so unspeakably filthy and abominable that the half of them have never been printed, or believed by the outside world. If any of us were caught—and a good many of us were—we knew just how slowly and unpleasantly we should die. You cannot conduct a campaign against a bestial horror like the Mau Mau with gloves on. Or you can!—if you have no objection to digging up a grave in the forest and finding that it contains the body of your best friend, who has been roasted alive over a slow fire after having certain parts of him removed for use in Mau Mau ceremonials.'

Neither Drew's face nor his pleasant voice had altered, but his bland blue eyes were suddenly as hard and blank and cold as pebbles, and Victoria was aware with a sense of shock that he was speaking of something that he himself had seen—and could still see.

She said hesitantly and inadequately: 'I—I'm sorry.'

The blankness left Drew's eyes and he tossed the end of his cigarette over the verandah rail and said: 'Come here; I want to show you something.'

He took her arm in an ungentle grasp, and turning her about, walked her over to the far end of the verandah and stopped before the upright post that supported the corner of the roof. There were notches on that too. Each one cut deep into the flat of the wood pillar.

'Those are our losses,' said Drew, and touched them lightly. 'That one was Sendayo. We used to play together when we were kids. His father worked for mine when they were both young men. That was Mtua. One of the best men we had. They cut his hands and feet off and pegged him out where the safari ants would get him. That one was Tony Sherraway. They burnt him alive. This one was Barugu. He was a Kikuyu whose entire family—parents, grandparents, wife and children—were murdered in the Lari massacre, where the Mau Mau set all the huts in the village on fire and clubbed and panga'd the people as they ran out. Barugu worked for us for a year before they got him, and what they did to him is not repeatable.'

He released Victoria's arm with an impatient gesture and said: 'Why go on? They won't mean anything to you. Or to anyone else. But cutting a tally of kills helped the morale of the others. They also got a bit of satisfaction out of chalking up that score, and out of knowing that if one of them went, he would be amply avenged.'

Drew turned away and stood looking out across the beauty that lay below and around him, his eyes narrowed against the sun glare, and presently he said: 'It's no good trying to treat Africans as though their processes of thought were the same as Europeans. That is the way of madness—and politicians!'

Victoria said doubtfully: 'But it *is* their country.'

'Whose?' demanded Drew, without turning his head.

'The—the Africans.'

'Which Africans? All this that you can see here, the Rift and most of what is known as the White Highlands, belonged, if it belonged to anyone, to the Masai. But it is the Kikuyu who claim the land, though they never owned a foot of it—and would have been speared if they'd set a foot on it! The place was a no-man's-land when Delamere first came here, and the fact that cattle and sheep can now be raised here is entirely due to him and men like him. And even they didn't just grab the land. The handful of Masai then inhabiting it voluntarily exchanged it for the enormous territory that tribe now holds.'

'But——' began Victoria, and was interrupted.

'All the chatter about "It belongs to them",' said Drew, 'makes me tired. Sixty years ago Americans were still fighting Red Indians and Mexicans and grabbing *their* land; but I've never heard anyone suggesting that they should get the hell out of it and give it back to the original owners. Our grandfathers found a howling wilderness that no one wanted, and which, at the time, no one objected to their taking possession of. And with blood, toil, tears and sweat they turned it into a flourishing concern. At which point a yelping chorus is raised, demanding, in the name of "Nationalism", that it be handed over to them. Well, if they are capable of running this on their own, or of turning a howling wilderness into a rich and prosperous concern, let 'em prove it! There's a hell of a lot of Africa. They can find a bit and start right in to show us. But that won't do for them. It's the fruit of somebody else's labour that they are after.'

He flung out a hand in the direction of the green lawns and gardens, the orchards, outhouses and paddocks: 'There was nothing and nobody here when my grandfather first saw this. This is the fruit of his labour—and of my parents', and my own. I was born here, and this is as much my home as Sendayo's. I want to stay here, and if that is immoral and indefensible Colonialism, then every American whose pioneer forebears went in a covered wagon to open up the West is tarred with the same brush; and when U.N.O. orders them out, we may consider moving!'

He turned to face Victoria and for the first time since she had met him, he smiled. It was a disquietingly attractive smile, and despite herself she felt a considerable portion of her hostility towards him waning.

He said: 'I apologize for treating you to a grossly over-simplified lecture on the Settlers' point of view. Very tedious for you. Here's the tea at last. Come and pour out.'

He kept up an idly amiable flow of small-talk until Eden returned, and after that the conversation took a strictly technical turn, and Victoria allowed her attention to wander.

'An over-simplified viewpoint.' Perhaps. Yet she could still remember her father telling her tales of her grandfather's early days in the great valley. The gruelling toil under the burning sun. The laborious digging of wells and the struggle to grow grass and crops and to raise cattle. The first glorious signs of success—of the 'wilderness blossoming like a rose'. The years of drought when first the crops and then the cattle died, and ruin faced them—and was stared down and outfaced by men who refused to be beaten. The first roads. The first hospitals. The first railway. The first schools . . . It could not have been easy, but the sweat and the toil and the despair and determination that it had cost had made it doubly dear, and Victoria found herself remembering a line from the theme song of *Oklahoma!*—that exhilarating musical about another pioneer state which barely a century ago had also belonged to 'painted savages'.

'We belong to the land, and the land we belong to is grand.'

She was aroused from her abstraction by Eden saying: 'Look, Drew, if you're driving over to see Gilly, why not come back in the launch with us, and let your driver take the car round to *Flamingo?* Then you can have a word with Gran about the deal. Just as well to get it settled.'

Mr Stratton, having agreed to the suggestion, went off to change out of his riding clothes, and Eden cocked an interrogatory eyebrow at Victoria and said: 'How did you get on with the detestable Drew? Sorry I had to leave you like that, but you wouldn't have enjoyed inspecting cows and calves, and I took it that you wouldn't actually come to blows! Do you mind having him as a passenger on the way home? I want him to have a word with Gran, and this seems a good way of seeing that he gets it.'

'Of course I don't mind. Why should I?' enquired Victoria loftily. 'I'm not so prejudiced that I can't sit in a boat with him. And in any case you will be far too busy discussing milk yields and foot-and-mouth for either of you to notice whether I am there or not.'

Eden laughed and reached out to pull her to her feet. 'Did we bore you? Forgive me, darling. I promise to keep off shop in future whenever you're around.'

Something in Victoria flinched at his casual use of an endearment that had once meant so much but which now came so easily and so meaninglessly to his tongue. She removed the hand that he still held, and said lightly: 'If I'm to be of any use to Aunt Em, the more I know about milk yields and foot-and-mouth the better. So don't let me put you off. Do you suppose the police will have gone by the time we get back?'

'If they haven't, I don't suppose we shall get any supper,' said Eden with a laugh. 'The staff are apt to get a bit disorganized on these occasions. I can't tell you how many times during the Emergency we were reduced to bread and cheese because Greg's chaps had been asking questions and the cook was too upset to concentrate on such mundane matters as meals. Here's Drew. If you're ready, let's go.'

9

Day was withdrawing reluctantly from the valley, and the gardens of *Flamingo* were noisy with the chatter and chirrup of birds coming home to roost. But the house itself was silent, and the police had apparently gone.

Conversation during the return journey had been desultory, but now it had ceased altogether, and Victoria, looking round to see why Eden's steps had slowed, surprised an expression on his face that startled her. He was staring at the house as though he hated it, or was afraid of it, and was walking slowly to delay the moment when he must enter it again.

An unexpected and icy little shiver ran down Victoria's spine, and Mr Stratton, who had been strolling beside her with his hands in his pockets and his face blank and apparently unobservant, said: 'Are you cold? Or was that someone jumping over your grave?'

Victoria started as though she had been sleepwalking, and was suddenly angry with an unreasoning and defensive anger born of the sharp unease that had momentarily possessed her.

'Must you mention graves after what has happened here? I should have thought we could at least have kept off——' She stopped and bit her lip.

Drew's eyebrows lifted and his blue eyes were unpleasantly satirical, but his voice remained unruffled. 'I stand corrected. Very tactless of me. My apologies, Eden.'

'What's that?' said Eden, jerked out of abstraction as Victoria had been. 'I'm sorry. I didn't hear what you said.'

'Nothing of any importance. It doesn't look as though your grandmother is in, does it? Or else she's locked the dogs up.'

'More likely that the police have locked up all our labour!' said Eden bitterly. 'There don't seem to be any cars about, so at least Bill and his boys have pushed off—which is some comfort!'

At the top of the verandah steps he paused to listen, his head lifted and his face strained and intent. But no one moved in the silent house, and the normal cheerful noises from the kitchen and the back premises were conspicuous by their absence.

Something of his disquiet communicated itself to Drew Stratton, who said with unwonted sharpness: 'There's nothing wrong, is there?'

Eden's strained rigidity relaxed and he gave a short and rather uncertain laugh. 'No. No, of course not. I was only wondering where everyone had got to. Place seems a bit deserted this evening. I'll go and rout out Zacharia and some drinks.' But he made no move to go, and the hand that he had laid on the verandah rail tightened until the knuckles showed white through the tanned skin.

Somewhere in the house a door slammed and Victoria jumped at the suddenness of the sound.

'Somebody appears to be at home,' observed Mr Stratton dryly. 'Unless that was your poltergeist.'

Eden's hand dropped from the rail and he turned an appalled face. 'But it couldn't be!—not now. I mean——'

He whirled round and had started for the nearest door at a run when Em appeared at the far end of the verandah:

'Eden! Thank goodness you're back! I've been worried to death.' Her voice sharpened as she took in his expression. 'What's the matter? You haven't—heard anything have you?'

'No,' said Eden with a crack of laughter that held more than a trace of hysteria. 'Not a sound. That's what was worrying me. The whole place was as quiet as a tomb and I suddenly got the horrors, wondering if anything had happened to you. Where is everyone? Don't tell me that young Bill Hennessy has arrested the whole boiling—live stock included? What have you done with the dogs?'

'Locked them up,' said Em and sat down abruptly and heavily in one of the verandah chairs. 'They didn't take to the askaris.'

She appeared to notice Drew and Victoria for the first time and nodded absently at them. 'Good evening, Drew. Didn't see you. Eden brought you, I suppose? Well, I can't talk cattle with you today. It'll have to wait. I'm too upset. Did you have a nice trip on the lake, Victoria? Eden, go and tell Zacharia to bring the drinks. I need something. Brandy, for choice!'

'Bill been giving you a bad time, Gran?' enquired Eden. 'You should have let me stay and deal with him. Come on, tell me the worst. Are half our staff behind bars? Is that why the place is so quiet this evening?'

'No. Nothing like that. He only wanted to ask a lot of silly questions, and I let him get on with it. It isn't the police. It's Kamau.'

'Why? What about him? Don't tell me he really *does* know something after all?'

'I don't know,' said Em tiredly. 'Eden, *do* go and call Zach! I'm sure we could all do with a drink.'

Eden departed, and Drew said: 'Kamau? Isn't he the one who scuppered that Mau Mau "Brigadier" and scooped in a fat reward? Do the police think that he knows something about the murder?'

'No. I mean, yes, he's the one who killed Gitahi. Lisa thought he might know something . . .' Em recounted the tale, adding that Kamau had failed to meet her on the previous night. 'And when I sent for him this morning—Oh, *mzuri*, Zacharia. Put it down there. No, no, the Bwanas can help themselves.' She waved the old man away, and Eden dispensed drinks.

'Go on,' said Drew. 'You sent for him this morning?'

Em accepted an exceedingly stiff brandy and soda from her grandson and gulped down half of it before replying. 'They said they thought he'd gone off to cut lucerne, and now it doesn't look as if he did.'

'Bolted, I suppose,' said Eden succinctly.

Em lowered her glass and looked at him sharply. 'Why do you say that?'

'Well, it's the obvious conclusion, isn't it?'

'That's what the Police say. In fact they said just what you said yesterday: that he might have done the murder himself, and now that this girl, Wambui, has told on him, he's lost his nerve and run for it.'

'But you don't believe that,' said Drew slowly.

'No.'

Eden banged his glass down on the tray with such violence that the bottles jumped and rattled. 'Why not? The same old reason I suppose. "My Kukes are loyal!" My God, they ought to have that written up in letters of gold right across the Rift—and headed "Famous Last Words"! Why shouldn't it be the answer? *Someone* did it, and it all ties up with the other things that happened in the house— the poltergeist and the poisoning of Simba. Whoever was responsible for that must have been employed here, or working with an accomplice who was, and if Kamau had no hand in it why has he run away? Tell me that!'

'Because he may think he knows who did it, and is afraid.'

'Afraid of what?'

'Of his own life, of course! Really, Eden, you're being very stupid today. Suppose he *was* watching from the bushes and saw everything? Suppose he even recognized the murderer?'

'In the dusk? At that range?' said Eden scornfully. 'Don't you believe it, Gran! The distance between where he was standing and the spot where Alice was killed is well over fifty yards. And it was getting dark. For all we know, the marks he left may have been made hours earlier—or else they were made by an accomplice keeping *cave*. If Kamau really knows anything about this business it's either because he himself did the murder or connived at it!'

'I don't believe it,' said Em obstinately. 'That's just the sort of conclusion the police jump at—and Gilly and Hector and Mabel. Because it's the easiest one that offers. It's my opinion that Kamau *did* know something, and was sufficiently frightened by what he saw to keep his mouth shut, but couldn't resist throwing out hints to his girl. But I didn't think he'd run away, or that the police would immediately leap to the same silly conclusion that you appear to have leapt to!'

She sipped her drink and glared indignantly at her grandson over the rim of her glass. *'Men!'* said Em scornfully, and directed a speaking glance at her niece. But Victoria's attention had been momentarily distracted by the behaviour of Mr Stratton.

Drew had been sitting on the verandah rail within a foot of her, leaning back lazily against one of the pillars. He looked relaxed and at peace with the world, and appeared to be taking no more than a polite interest in the discussion, until something in Em's last sentence had jerked him to attention. Victoria did not know why she was so sure of this, for he had made no noticeable movement. Nevertheless she was aware that he was no longer relaxed but had abruptly stiffened into alertness, and that he was sitting very still.

She glanced sideways at him and saw that his eyes were wide and very bright and that they held a curious look of astonishment, as though some new and startling thought had suddenly presented itself to him. It was a look that for some reason disturbed Victoria, and she turned quickly to stare at her aunt as though she might find there some clue as to what had caused it. But Em's face was as aloof and sulky as an elderly bloodhound's, and there was nothing to be read there but her scornful impatience with the limited intelligence of all people who did not think as she did.

Eden said: 'Oh, all right, Gran. Don't let's argue about it. We shall always be on opposite sides of the fence over this. You are quite prepared to believe that everyone else's Kikuyu servants are untrustworthy, but never your own. Hector and Mabel are just as bad. Look at the way Hector behaved in '54 over that knife.'

Em said sharply: 'I will not have you talking scandal, Eden! It was an accident, and you know it. Hector and Mabel are old friends of mine, and——'

'And like Kamau can do no wrong,' finished Eden. 'I know, darling. Sorry I spoke. Have another drink. You've finished that one. What about you, Drew? Have the other half.'

'I've still got it, thanks,' said Drew. 'Have Hector and Mabel been over here this afternoon, Em?'

'Yes,' said Em, handing over her glass to be refilled. 'Mabel brought me a bottle of her chutney. A peace-offering, I think. Dear Mabel. She's such a kind-hearted, sensible person except when she gets on to the subject of Ken. Which reminds me, Eden; Ken was here just after you left. He wanted to know if that Luger of yours was still for sale.'

Eden looked slightly surprised. 'He must be mad. He knows quite well that I flogged it in Mays only about ten days ago. He was there! Besides, he wouldn't have been able to get any ammunition for it.'

'Oh well, perhaps I got it wrong. He may have wanted to know if Mays still had it. I'm afraid I was a bit sharp with him. I found him riding right across the lucerne patch behind the labour lines. He didn't expect to see me down there—let alone Hennessy!—and he stammered and stuttered like a schoolboy caught with his fist in the cake tin. Mabel ought to send him to the coast for a spell. Or better still, take him there herself. The boy is a bundle of nerves.'

Eden said shortly: 'The further away she takes him, and them, the better. I hope you were sufficiently sharp with him to discourage any more visits for the time being.'

'Ken is unsnubbable. You ought to know that by now. Lisa took him off my hands. She came over to borrow some sugar, and took him back with her. It's odd that two people like Hector and Mabel should have produced a child like Ken. He's not really the right type for Kenya.'

'Judging from his capacity for falling in love with other men's wives,' said Eden acidly, 'I should have thought he had at least one of the necessary qualifications.'

'Don't be cheap, dear,' said his grandmother severely. She selected a cigarette from a box on the table beside her, and Drew slid off the verandah rail and went over to light it for her.

'Gilly been around today?' he enquired idly, snapping on the lighter.

'I expect so. He's around so often that I don't notice any more. Thank you, Drew.'

Drew returned the lighter to his pocket and observed that he had not realized that Gilly was so hard-working.

'It's not always work,' said Em with a short laugh. 'My Bechstein is a good deal better than his own piano. He comes over to play.'

Eden muttered something under his breath that was uncomplimentary to Mr Gilbraith Markham, and a frown passed over Em's face. She said: 'I know you think I'm an old fool to keep him on, but God knows what would become of him if I didn't. He's very little use as a manager, and not really a good enough musician to keep himself in any sort of comfort—let alone Lisa!'

Eden said coldly: 'That's nonsense. He was offered a perfectly good job with a dance band. A more than adequate salary, with accommodation thrown in. What is more, Lisa was all for his taking it: Nairobi is far more her cup of tea than the Rift.'

Em looked at him with mingled affection and regret. 'You haven't inherited a particle of feeling for music, dear, have you? It's odd, when your father and all my mother's side of the family had such a love for it. All the Beaumartins have been musical, but it's missed you. If it hadn't, you couldn't talk like that. Gilly is enough of a musician to consider that playing in a dance band would rank with prostitution. He'd prefer to starve.'

'Don't you believe it! Gilly is far too fond of himself. He'd have taken it all right, if you hadn't fallen for all that high falutin' stuff and offered him Gus Abbott's job in order to save him from 'Prostituting his Art'. And if he'd put in as little work with the dance band as he has here, he'd have got the sack inside a week. Probably less! Yet he has the nerve to suggest that you put him in to manage the Rumuruti estates now that Jerry Coles wants to retire.'

Em said softly: 'Perhaps his reasons for wishing to remove to Rumuruti are domestic rather than financial.'

'*Domestic?* Why Lisa simply loathes the idea of going there.'

'Quite,' said Em dryly.

Eden stared at her for a moment, obviously puzzled by her tone, and then flushed hotly in sudden comprehension, and turning his back on her busied himself once more with the tray of drinks.

Em said placidly, but with a wicked twinkle in her eye: 'But I am unlikely to give it to him. You see, I should miss hearing him play.'

'Was he playing here today?' asked Drew.

'I don't think so. I didn't hear him. But then I went down to the labour lines with Bill Hennessy and his askaris, and I wouldn't have heard him from there. I'm getting too deaf.'

Em sighed and shook her head impatiently, as though the infirmities of old age were tormenting flies; and then all at once she stiffened in her chair, listening.

A car was coming up the long, rutted drive between the acacias and the spiky clusters of sisal, and Em rose hurriedly. 'If it's anyone else offering condolences, tell them I'm out. Or ill!'

'Don't worry,' said Eden, 'it'll only be Drew's car. His driver was bringing it round.'

But it was not Mr Stratton's car. It was Mr Gilbert's, and a moment later, accompanied by the Markhams, he walked on to the verandah; and at the sight of his face they all came quickly to their feet.

Greg dispensed with formalities and came straight to the point: 'Hennessy tells me that one of your Kikuyu boys has disappeared. Kamau.'

He ignored Drew, Eden and Victoria, and addressed himself solely to Em, while behind him Lisa fidgeted and twisted her fingers, her pretty face sulky and apprehensive, and Gilly leaned against a verandah pillar with a studied negligence that was belied by the avid interest that was plainly visible in his restless eyes.

Em said coldly and defiantly: 'Yes. And I presume, as you have brought Lisa and Gilly with you, that you know why.'

'Hennessey told me why. It seems that you told him of Mrs Markham's visit to you yesterday, and I came down to see what I could get out of this woman Wambui.'

Lisa gave a little whimpering sob. 'I wish I hadn't said anything to anyone! I *wish* I hadn't! I only thought that Lady Emily ought to know.'

Mr Gilbert ignored the interruption. He said: 'I got quite a lot out of her, but before we go any further I'd like to have your own account of exactly what happened yesterday; from Mrs Markham's arrival to the time you decided that Kamau wasn't going to turn up. Also what action, if any, you took about it this morning.'

Em looked at Greg Gilbert's grim unsmiling face, and her shrewd old eyes were puzzled and wary. She said slowly: 'Let me see ——' And for the second time that evening described Lisa's visit and the happenings of the hours that followed it, ending with her enquiries that morning as to Kamau's whereabouts, and her discovery, when Hennessy and his askaris had gone down to the labour lines to question the African employees and their families, that no one had seen him since Zacharia had delivered her message to him on the previous afternoon. Except, presumably, Wambui?

'No, she didn't,' said Lisa with an air of conscious virtue. 'I made a point of seeing that she couldn't get away last night. I thought that you should have every chance to speak to Kamau first, and as I said to Hector——'

She checked suddenly, her eyes and her mouth blank circles of dismay.

Greg turned with a swiftness that startled her, and said brusquely: 'You told me that you had not mentioned this to anyone else. Not even your husband.'

'Least of all her husband,' interpolated Gilly with an edge to his voice.

'Shut up, Gilly! Did you tell Hector Brandon, Lisa?'

Lisa's large violet eyes filled with tears and she said querulously: 'Don't bark at me, Greg! There's no need for you——'

'*Did* you?'

'Well—well, yes. But only in the strictest confidence. After all, I've known Hector for years, and I knew he wouldn't let it go any further. And I was very worried. You don't seem to realize——'

'When did you tell him? Before you'd been over here, or afterwards?'

'Oh, afterwards. Because of course by then I was sure that Lady Emily would get it all out of Kamau, and then everything would be all right. I mean, at least we'd all *know.*'

'Hmm,' said Greg disagreeably. He stared at her long and meditatively until she reddened under his gaze, and then turning away abruptly he addressed himself again to Em:

'We've got search parties out looking for Kamau, and with luck we should pick him up without much trouble. He's probably made for the Reserve. But even when we get him I doubt if we'll get much more out of him than we got out of Wambui.'

Em said tartly: 'You certainly won't if you start off by sending out your askaris to arrest him as though he'd done something criminal, when all he is guilty of is telling his girl-friend that he thinks he knows something about the murder.'

'I'm afraid he told her more than that,' said Greg quietly.

Em stiffened suddenly and once again her eyes moved from Greg to Lisa, and she said haltingly: 'But Lisa, you told me——' and stopped.

Lisa dragged at her handkerchief until the fabric tore, and her voice was high and hysterical: 'I didn't know there was any more! I tell you I didn't know! I had no idea—she just said that he—he knew something. But if I'd known what it was I wouldn't have said a word! Eden, you *know* I wouldn't——'

Eden said in an entirely expressionless voice: 'I'm afraid I don't know what you're talking about. Perhaps Greg will be good enough to explain.'

'Yes,' said Em harshly. 'If you have anything to say, Greg, let us hear it and get it over.'

Mr Gilbert surveyed her thoughtfully, and there was something in his expression that frightened Victoria. He said slowly and deliberately: 'Wambui told Mrs Markham that Kamau had hinted that he knew something about Mrs DeBrett's murder. That was not true. He had done a good deal more than hint, but she was afraid to admit to anything else because his story is too fantastic to be believed.'

He paused, as though collecting his thoughts, and Em said grimly: 'Go on.'

'Kamau's story,' said Greg, 'is that on Tuesday evening he waited for Wambui as usual among the bushes near the knoll, and that shortly after he got there he saw Mrs DeBrett arrive and start picking roses; so he lay low and waited for her to go away. But she sat down on the fallen tree and stayed there until it was nearly dark, and he began to get tired of waiting and must have made some movement in the bushes, for she jumped up as though she was alarmed and began to run away. And then, he said, he saw someone coming to meet her. Someone whom she knew, and ran to. And who killed her.'

'*No!*' cried Lisa, her voice shockingly shrill after Greg's quiet and unemotional tones. 'She made it up! She must have done! I don't believe it!' She burst into noisy sobs, but no one had any attention to spare for her, for they were looking with a fixed and fascinated intensity at Greg Gilbert.

Eden said loudly: 'If he saw who it was, why didn't he say so at once?—when he was questioned with the others? Why didn't——'

Em made a swift impatient gesture of the hand, silencing him, and Greg said slowly, frowning down at the matting as though he preferred not to meet the painfully intent stares that were fixed on him: 'Wambui says it was because he recognized the murderer, and was afraid.'

'Go on,' repeated Em, harshly and imperiously. 'Who did he say it was?'

Greg removed his gaze from the matting and looked up, meeting her gaze squarely.

He said softly: 'You, Em.'

10

There was a moment of complete and utter stillness, as though everyone on the verandah had been temporarily deprived of the power of speech or movement. The blood drained out of Em's face leaving it yellow and drawn and incredibly old, and she sat down heavily and abruptly as though her legs could no longer support her.

The protesting creak of the wicker-work chair broke the silence with the effect of a stone dropped into a quiet pool, and Eden said furiously: 'What the hell d'you mean by making accusations like that! By God, I've a good mind to——' He took a swift stride forward, and Drew said sharply and compellingly: 'Be quiet, Eden! You're only making matters worse.'

He reached out and caught Eden's arm, jerking him back, and Greg said: 'I am not making any accusations—at the moment. I am merely repeating something that I have heard at second hand. Well, Em? How about it?'

Eden shook off Drew's restraining hand and said: 'Don't answer him, Gran! If he's going to believe every silly fairy story cooked up by a half-witted African farm-hand, you'd better wait until you can see your lawyer!'

Em paid no attention to him. She looked at Greg with eyes that were blank with shock, and said slowly and as though it were an effort to speak: 'What do you want me to say? That I did not kill Alice? But telling you so is not proof, is it? And I was here in the house that evening, so I suppose from your point of view I could have done it.'

'Gran, for God's sake!' begged Eden.

'Oh, Eden dear, *do* stop being so silly! Drew is quite right. It really does not help at all to lose our heads and shout—or collapse into tears, like Lisa. Surely we can behave in a rational manner? Sit

102

down, Greg. You had better tell me what you propose to do about this—this extraordinary statement.'

Mr Gilbert drew up a chair and sat down facing her. He said: 'We can't do much about it until we pull in Kamau and get him to verify it. What I want you to do is to give me an exact account of what happened that evening. Yes, I know we've been into this before, but I want it once again. You'd been out shooting, and got back just before six. What did you do then?'

'I changed,' said Em patiently.

'Into what? That Japanese job with storks all over it that you were wearing when I arrived later that night?'

'No, of course not! That was a kimono. I changed into a house-coat. Yellow, if you want to know. But I had to take it off be-cause——' She stopped suddenly, and after a brief pause said: 'Be-cause it had blood all over it. Yes . . . I can see that that doesn't sound good. But I couldn't help it. I'd tried to carry her up to the house, and—well, you saw her.'

'Yes,' agreed Greg briefly. 'What did you do then? After you'd changed into the house-coat?'

'I came into the drawing-room for a drink, and saw Lisa's note asking for a lift into Nairobi—I'd left it on the piano—and Alice went over to tell her that I'd give her a lift when I went in to fetch Victoria.'

'What did you do when she'd gone?'

'Went out to tell Zach and Cookie about cutting up the kongoni, and after that I saw the dogs fed, and gave Majiri the curtains and covers from Victoria's room to wash—the water's always extra hot in the evenings, because of the baths. Zach came round just before half-past six and turned on the lights, and I told him to leave the drinks in the drawing-room. And then I played the piano.'

'Until when?'

'Until around eight o'clock, when he came in to say that Alice was still not back, and should he serve dinner? I hadn't realized it was so late, and I called the dogs and went off to fetch her. *Must* I go over all that part again?'

'No. That's not the really important time from your point of view, as she must have been killed around seven o'clock, and you say you were playing the piano from six thirty onwards. That in itself is a reasonably good alibi.'

'Why?' enquired Em with an attempt at a smile. 'You've only my word for it.'

Greg consulted the notebook they had seen on the previous day, and said: 'Not quite. Seven of your servants stated independently that the "Memsahib Mkubwa" had been playing during that time, and had not stopped for more than a minute or two at most. Certainly not long enough to murder Alice and then change into fresh clothes, as presumably even old Zacharia would have noticed blood-stains on a yellow house-coat! It couldn't have been done in under ten to fifteen minutes, and on a cross-check of the evidence you never stopped playing for anything like that.'

'You've forgotten something,' said Em dryly. 'I have an ex-tremely good radio-gramophone, and not one of my servants would know the difference.'

Eden said hoarsely: 'Gran, are you mad! Listen, Greg, she doesn't realize how serious this may be. She ought to have a lawyer. Drew, can't *you* stop this? Can't you make her see some sense?'

'Your grandmother,' said Drew, 'appears to me to be seeing it with extreme clarity. It would only be a question of time before someone else thought of that one, so she might just as well mention the radiogram herself.'

'Exactly!' said Em approvingly. 'Everyone knows about it—and about such things as long-playing records, too! I can see no point in laying claim to an alibi that is obviously as full of holes as a sieve. Besides I don't need one. I know quite enough about Kenya to know that no jury in this country is going to take such a charge seriously. And so does Greg! Because everyone knows me. If they did not, it might be possible to get a conviction on such evidence. After all, I am still tolerably strong—strong enough to kill a little weak defence-less creature like Alice who would have been too surprised to——'

Em's voice failed suddenly and she covered her face with her hands as though to blot out the horror that her own words had conjured up: the picture of Alice standing helpless and appalled in the dusk, too stunned with shock to scream or run. A strong shudder shook her bulky body and presently she lifted a ravaged face and staring, haunted eyes, and spoke in a voice that was barely more than a hoarse whisper:

'I've seen a lot of bad things in my time. Men who were mauled by lions or trampled by buffalo or rhino. And—and there was Gus Abbott too. But they were men. I suppose that made it different. It's silly to feel like this. But—but she couldn't bear wounds and blood. I used to tell her that she shouldn't mind. But when I saw her that night, I minded too. I minded . . .'

Eden said: 'Don't, Gran! Please——!' His face was as drawn and ravaged as her own, and, for a moment only, ugly with remembered horror. The sight of it seemed to act on Em like a douche of cold water, and she straightened her bowed shoulders with a palpable effort and said remorsefully: 'Forgive me, dear. I'm behaving very badly. But then this is all so absurd. I wish I knew why Kamau should have said such a thing. Perhaps Wambui made it up?'

'I don't think so,' said Greg. 'I can usually tell when I'm being spun a yarn. I'd say she was speaking the truth. But was Kamau?'

'Yes,' said Drew, abruptly and positively.

There was a simultaneous gasp from at least four throats, and Em shrank back in her chair and stared at him in horrified disbelief.

Mr Stratton viewed his audience with undisguised impatience and said: 'There's no need to look at me as though I'd gone off my head. The thing stands out a mile. Of *course* he was speaking the truth—or what he thought was the truth. Just take a look at Em. She's a nice, bright splash of colour, isn't she? And she's been dressing like that ever since I was in rompers! Eden has already pointed out that the distance between the bushes and the spot where Alice was killed is rather more than fifty yards, and it was getting dark. So all that Kamau saw was someone wearing the sort of hat and clothes she wears, and naturally he thought it was Em. Bet you any money you like I'm right!'

'No takers,' said Greg with a wry smile. 'I ought to have seen it myself.'

'But *why?*' demanded Eden vehemently. 'Why should anyone try and pin it on Gran, when she's the very last person who'd be likely to do it?'

Drew shrugged and said: 'Perhaps that was why. Because no one would credit it.'

'No,' said Greg slowly. 'I imagine that the reason was even simpler than that. Anyone, male or female, could wear that sort of outfit and get away with it, because no one would give them a second look. It also provided an excuse for being seen in the gardens at that hour, for if anyone happened to see the wearer, they'd take it for granted that it was Em. It was the perfect disguise. And that of course is the answer to the riddle of the verandah cushion!'

'How do you work that out?' demanded Em, thereby temporarily depriving Mr Gilbert of his composure.

'Well . . . er . . . I thought—padding?' he suggested cautiously.

Em looked bewildered but Lisa unexpectedly went off into a gale of giggles, and Em, turning to look at her, remarked coldly that they would all like to share in the joke: any joke.

'I'm s-sorry,' gasped Lisa, wavering helplessly between relief and hysteria. 'I suppose I shouldn't laugh, but it's so f-funny! He means your b-b-bosom! A man wouldn't have one, but you have! *Ha, ha, ha, ha!'*

Instinctively and simultaneously every eye was focused upon Em's imposing frontage, and the next minute they were all laughing as helplessly as Lisa—and for much the same reason. Only Em, like Queen Victoria, declined to be amused, and announced austerely that she saw nothing to laugh at.

'You wouldn't, darling. You're behind it!' said Eden, and collapsed into renewed mirth.

Em folded her hands in her lap and waited with a dignified display of patience for the laughter to subside.

'I apologize,' said Greg, mopping his streaming eyes and recovering himself. 'On behalf of us all. Extremely silly and unnecessary, but for some reason it's done me a power of good. Seriously, Em, that cushion worried me. But it's quite obvious that whoever impersonated you was too slim to be convincing, and needed a bit of— well, building up. Hence the cushion. Now what about those clothes? How many pairs of those red overalls have you got, and have you lost any recently?'

Victoria gave a startled gasp and Em said grimly: 'I never thought of that! I should have four pairs of them, but one can't be found.'

'Could it have been missing for some time?'

Em shrugged. 'Perhaps. I wouldn't have noticed, and I don't suppose Zacharia would have done either until an occasion like this morning, when three pairs happened to be in the wash at once.'

'Supposing someone wanted to steal a pair, would it have been easy or difficult? For an outsider, for instance.'

'I should say only too easy. All the washing is hung up on the lines behind the kitchen, and anyone could remove something from a line if they waited for the right moment. The odd thing does occasionally vanish—generally dish-cloths. But Zach ought to have noticed something like a pair of my dungarees. Except that he's getting old—like me.'

Mr Gilbert frowned thoughtfully at the small notebook that lay open on his knee, and presently said: 'By the way, in spite of what you said on the subject of alibis, I think you may turn out to have a cast-iron one after all. Can you remember what you were playing on the piano that evening?'

'Yes,' said Em, her face suddenly bleak. 'I was playing Toroni's concerto. *The Rift Valley Concerto.* There isn't any record of that. Not any longer.'

'So I understand. It was broken by the poltergeist, wasn't it? And I also seem to remember that there was only the one record, and that it isn't on sale, or available to the general public. Am I right?'

'Yes. He had it made for me in New York. But then none of my servants would know the difference between one tune and another, I'm afraid.'

Greg said: 'That's where you're wrong. The average African has a better ear for music than one would imagine, and that particular piece not only had a good many tribal tunes and rhythms incorporated into it, but I gather that Toroni composed it here at *Flamingo*, on your piano; and that you yourself have played it pretty frequently of late. Anyway, three of your servants say that you were playing "Bwana Toroni's songs". So you see it's not such a bad alibi after all. We shall have to check it of course, for form's sake: cable New York and make sure that you couldn't have got hold of a duplicate, and that sort of thing. And if their answer clears you, then the thing is buttoned as far as you are concerned.'

'I rather think that it's buttoned without that,' remarked Gilly unexpectedly. 'In fact you can save yourself the expense of a cable, and the F.B.I. a headache.'

'How's that?' demanded Greg, turning quickly to face him.

Gilly abandoned the pose of disinterested spectator, and strolled forward, his hands in his pockets.

He said: 'Drew'll tell you that I met him at the gate in the hedge just after he'd seen Alice off, and we both heard Em playing that thing. He pushed off, but I didn't. I sat on the concrete block just outside the gate for a goodish while. Until it was dark.'

'You *what?*' demanded Greg incredulously. 'Why the hell didn't you tell me this before? You mean that you were there after seven? Surely you must have heard *something*. A cry, or——'

Gilly cut him short. 'I didn't hear anything! You forget that the knoll is away to the right, and there are trees and bamboos and heaven knows what between it and the gate. But there is a fairly clear line between the gate and the house, and I could hear the piano. I sat there for quite a time, listening to Em tackling that piece. I know it a damn sight better than she does; every bar and every note of it! And you can take it from me that it wouldn't make any difference if you discovered that there were half a million of those records in existence, and all of them in Kenya!'

'Why?' demanded Greg tersely.

'Why? Because I'm enough of a musician to tell the difference between Em's rendering of the concerto, and Toroni's. That's why!'

Gilly transferred his gaze from Greg's relieved face to Em's tight-lipped, rigid mouth and basilisk stare, and laughed.

'I'm sorry, Em. I know that touches you on the raw. But let's face it, you're a pretty poor performer when it comes to the piano, while Toroni was in a class by himself. And if you think I couldn't go into the witness box and swear to the difference between your playing of the concerto and his—and be believed—you're even less of a musician than I take you for. Well?'

The fury died out of Em's face but she continued to eye him with considerable hauteur, and after staring at him in disdainful silence for a full minute, she said coldly: 'As both Greg and Eden seem to think that I could do with an alibi, I shall not argue with you.'

'It may be a useful thing to have handy,' observed Greg, and added briskly, 'And now the next thing is to go after that missing pair of overalls.'

'You are not going after them tonight,' snapped Em. 'At least, not in this house. I don't care what you do in the grounds. Or anywhere else! But I have had quite enough alarms and excursions for one day, and I propose to have an early supper and go to bed. Good night.'

She heaved herself up out of her chair and withdrew with the dignity of a Dowager Empress concluding an audience, leaving a somewhat conscience-stricken silence behind her. It was broken by Eden, who opened a bottle of soda water with an irritable violence that sent it frothing over the matting, and informed Gilly that this time he really had put his foot in it.

'If there is one thing that Gran is vain about,' said Eden, 'it's her playing. You may have given her a cast-iron alibi, but she won't thank you for it. She'd probably have preferred to stand trial! So if you find yourself queueing up at the Labour Exchange in the near future, you'll know why. You'd better get yourself a drink while the going's good. It's probably the last you'll get on the house.'

'Rot!' said Gilly. He giggled light-heartedly, and taking advantage of the offer, poured himself out a double whisky, gulped it down neat, and refilled his glass. 'Your grandmother may have been a tolerable amateur pianist in the days of her youth—though personally, I doubt it. But though her appreciation of good music is still Grade A, her performance, when compared to someone like Toroni's, is on a par with a pianola's. As for booting me out, *phooey!* Bet you she gives me a rise! After all, what's injured pride compared to a stretched neck?'

'Point is,' said Eden, 'that as she'll never believe in the possibility of the latter, she will have plenty of indignation to spare for the former.'

'You underrate her intelligence,' grinned Gilly. *'Skoal!* She may be a vain old peacock, but she's no fool. Sheerest stroke of luck that I didn't trot straight back to the house that evening. Very nearly did! But I'd had just about enough of Hector and Mabel for one day, and I didn't want to run into them; so I stayed where I was and listened to Em massacring that concerto. Stroke of luck!'

Greg slid the notebook into his pocket and said: 'Look, Eden, do you think I could have a word with Majiri and Zacharia without running into Em again—about those dungarees? I shall have to send Bill Hennessy down tomorrow to go into the question in more detail of course. That'll turn his hair white!'

'As long as you steer clear of the cook,' said Eden, 'I don't care who you see. But cheese and biscuits for supper on top of all this would be the last straw. All right, come on.' They departed, leaving Victoria to the society of the Markhams and Mr Stratton.

The sun had set and the gardens were no longer gaily coloured and noisy with bird song, but cool and green and quiet, and a bat swooped out from under the eaves and flitted along the silent verandah.

Lisa stood up and said in a bright, brittle voice: 'So it was all a storm in a teacup. I can't imagine why Greg should have insisted on our coming over with him. So embarrassing! And quite unnecessary, as it happened.'

Gilly poured himself out a third whisky and observed dispassionately that it provided an interesting and unexpected sidelight on his wife's character to find that she could refer to a brutal murder as a storm in a teacup, and that she knew quite well why Greg had brought them over. 'Or you should know. After all, you were the one who started this hare. Besides, you were quite prepared to believe that she'd done it. Don't tell me you weren't!'

Lisa said indignantly: 'Gilly, I do wish you wouldn't talk such arrant nonsense. Drew and I know you well enough to know when you're joking, but Miss Caryll might take you seriously.'

'And how right Miss Caryll would be! You also produced a very, very neat little theory as to *why* Em should have done it, didn't you?'

'Gilly, be quiet!' Lisa rounded on her husband, her eyes brilliant with anger.

'And a damned good theory, too, if I may say so,' said Gilly, ignoring her. 'Except for one small but vital point that you have overlooked.'

'*Gilly!*' Lisa's voice was imploring, and she dragged at his arm. 'It's getting late. Let's go home.'

'Pipe down, Lisa. Drew's interested; aren't you Drew? Interesting case—very. Drew doesn't believe that any stray Mau Mau thug did this, any more'n I do—or Greg, or Em. Much as they'd like to believe it, Lisa my love. But they don't know what I know.'

He began to giggle, and Drew said: 'What do you know, Gilly?' But the question had been asked too sharply, and the slightly vacuous expression that whisky had brought to Gilly's face was replaced by wariness and a trace of malice.

'We aren't discussing me,' said Gilly. 'Discussin' Lisa's theory about Em. Em and Alice. We all think that Em was fond of Alice—in a patronizing Protect-the-Weak the poor-kid-can't-help-it sort of way. But suppose we were wrong? Supposing that underneath all that surface affection she hated her guts? That it was all an act, and she was really jealous of her—because of Eden, or because one day she would be mistress of *Flamingo?* It's no secret that Em's nuts about Eden and dotty on the subject of *Flamingo*. She'd do anything for either of them—even murder! That was Lisa's theory. And mark you, granting the premise, perfectly feasible. I don't suppose that Em has ever heard that song about *You can't chop your momma up in Massachusetts,* but she'd be quite capable of chopping up a grand-daughter-in-law in Kenya if she judged it to be necessary. Law unto herself; that's Em! All the same, Lisa doesn't notice things . . .'

'What sort of things?' This time Drew's voice was deceptively casual.

'Oh—this and that. Or maybe she does? She's a sly little thing, Lisa. All women are sly. Ever noticed that, Drew? You will—you will! Take Mabel, for instance . . . asked if she could take a couple of pineapples home on Tuesday evening, just after Alice left, and went off to pick 'em. Lisa never noticed that she came back without any. And shall I tell you why? Because Lisa had been out too. Down to the shamba, *she* says, to get some tomatoes. Though what she wanted 'em for is anybody's guess—we had roast duck and cauliflower for supper. She thinks *I* don't notice things, but I do!'

Lisa made no comment, but Victoria saw her eyes widen in surprise and become fixed and intent. Gilly wagged his head sagely and helped himself to yet another drink, and Drew said curtly: 'Haven't you had enough of that?'

'Enough of what?' demanded Gilly. 'Women—or Em's whisky? If the former, certainly. But no one can have too much of Em's whisky. First because it's good, and secon'ly because it's Em's; on the house! *Prosit!*'

He took a deep gulp, and lowered his voice to a confidential undertone: 'Ever struck you, Drew, that all the time Greg was talking about alibis for Em, he hadn't noticed that no one else has one either? You, for instance. You say you went off home when you left me. Did you? Mabel says she was picking pineapples. Oh yeah? Hector walked home by the path that runs along the top of the shambas—so he says. Eden's supposed to have been driving around somewhere, and Lisa's wandering round the tomato patch. But is there an alibi in the bunch? Not on your life!'

Drew said amiably: 'That's quite a point. We might start with you. Can you prove one?'

Gilly looked startled. 'Prove what?'

'That you sat on that lump of concrete for half an hour or so and didn't hear a thing?'

Gilly put down his empty glass hurriedly. 'Here! Who says I didn't hear anything? I heard Em playing—I heard that damned concerto of Toroni's.'

'That's what *you* say. But Em had already told us what it was that she had been playing, and the evidence of three of her servants confirmed it. You might have decided to use that information as an alibi for yourself. Or you might still have heard it, but from a good deal nearer! See what I mean? So if I were you I'd lay off all these heavy hints that various people are in need of alibis. Because the obvious inference is that they must each have had a reason for wishing Alice dead, and that you know it. Which is dangerous bunkum.'

'But I do——' began Gilly. And stopped. He made a nervous grab at his glass, and then changed his mind and pushed it away so violently that it toppled off the table and splintered into pieces on the verandah floor.

Lisa said briskly and with a trace of satisfaction in her voice: 'Now look what you've done! That's one of Em's crystal set, and she won't be a bit pleased. Or do you think that if we just tiptoe away and leave her to find it she'll put it down to the poltergeist?'

She accompanied the remark with a high-pitched tinkling laugh; but her face as she bent to pick up the broken pieces was white and frightened, and Victoria, stooping to help her, saw that her hands were shaking uncontrollably.

A light clicked on in the dining-room behind them, and a warm yellow glow fell across the verandah from the windows and the open door. And instantly it was evening no longer, but dusk: the garden shadowy with nightfall and the sky already sprinkled with pale stars.

Lisa deposited the bits of broken glass on the tray and said: 'Would you tell your aunt that it was an accident, and that we're so sorry? Oh, and she did say something about a picnic on the twenty-ninth. It was arranged before—before anything happened of course, so it may not be on. Would you ask her to let me know about it, because I'm afraid we must rush. Drew, you're coming over to collect those papers, aren't you? You'd better stay to supper as it's so late. It's only ourselves and Ken Brandon. He's rather in a state, poor boy, and it might take his mind off things if we had some bridge.'

Drew said firmly: 'No thank you, Lisa. An evening spent coping with an adolescent who is "in a state" is not in my line. Besides, I must get back.'

'Don't blame you,' said Gilly feelingly. 'Good night, Victoria.' He nodded absently at her and followed his wife down the steps and out into the violet dusk.

Victoria watched them go, and then turned to look at Mr Stratton, who had not moved. She was unaware that at that moment her face was as white and as frightened as Lisa's had been—or Gilly's. But Drew, looking down at it, was unaccountably disturbed.

He said abruptly: 'You're scared, aren't you.'

'A—a little,' admitted Victoria. And having admitted it was immediately aware of a diminution of that fear.

'Of what?'

'I don't know. The house—the things that have happened in it. But you don't believe in ghosts, do you?'

'Not in this one,' said Drew grimly. 'That is, if you're referring to the poltergeist.'

'I don't either. It all sounds too——'

She hesitated, wrinkling her brows, and Drew said: 'Too un-ghostly?'

'I was going to say, "too planned"; as though someone had worked it all out very carefully to a—a sort of pattern. I think that is what is frightening.'

'Why? Because you think that no African would have planned something like this and carried it through? If that's what you think, you're wrong. It's just the sort of tortuous scheme that would appeal to them. But there's nothing to be afraid of now, for if there ever was a plan, or a pattern, Mrs DeBrett's death completed it. It's finished.'

He had spoken with complete confidence, but almost before the words were out of his mouth he realized with a sudden sense of shock that he did not believe them. How could anyone assert with confidence that Alice's death had put an end to the things that had happened at *Flamingo,* while her killer was still at large? *It is only the first killing that is difficult.* Greg had said that only yesterday . . .

A bird fluttered among the hanging creepers at the verandah edge, and Drew saw Victoria start at the sound and bite hard on her underlip; and was surprised to find himself suddenly and savagely angry. With Em for bringing the girl out here. With Eden for permitting it. With Greg and Gilly and Lisa for frightening her. And most of all with himself—for caring whether they did or not!

11

Breakfast was barely over on the following morning when young Mr Hennessy and his police askaris descended upon *Flamingo*.

Em interviewed them briefly on the verandah and dismissed them to the kitchen quarters and the labour lines in charge of Eden, there to pursue their enquiries into the disappearance of Kamau and a pair of scarlet dungarees.

An hour later Gilly had appeared with a batch of files, and she retired with him into the office, having refused her niece's offer of assistance.

Victoria, left to her own devices, fetched a hat and went out to explore the garden, and she had been following a narrow path that wound through bushes of bougainvillaea, plumbago and orange trumpet flower when she came suddenly upon a stranger. A middle-aged woman in a green cotton dress who wore a battered wide-brimmed double terai hat jammed down over a riot of grey curls, and who appeared to have lost something, for she was bending down and peering anxiously about her.

'Can I help?' enquired Victoria.

The woman jumped violently, and said in a breathless voice: 'Oh dear, how you startled me! I believe there's a puff adder in there. They are such dangerous creatures. You must be Victoria. I used to know your parents—oh, years ago. You wouldn't remember me. I'm Mabel Brandon. Our place, *Brandonmead,* is just over there——' She gestured vaguely to the west with one hand and began to move on down the path, still talking, so that Victoria had perforce to follow her:

'We have a sort of mutual right-of-way between *Flamingo* and our land,' said Mrs Brandon. 'It saves us going miles by road. There's a track that runs right round this side of the lake across at least a dozen estates. I believe it used to be a game track once.

There was any amount of big game in the valley when we first came here. Rhino and lion and buffalo, and even elephant. But of course they're gone now. Just as well really. It would have made farming impossible. Of course lions still come over sometimes from the Masai territory, though they get killed off very quickly. I believe one was seen at Crater Lake only last year. We must take you there. Em said something about a picnic. But she will have cancelled that of course.'

Mrs Brandon had quickened her steps as she talked and now she was walking quite briskly. Almost as though she did not want Victoria to linger among the bushes and was hurrying her away from them, talking trivialities to distract her attention from the fact.

The path took a sharp downward curve and came out upon a long belt of open ground, where a narrow trolley line ran parallel with the shamba and carried the heavy piles of maize and vegetables and bananas up to the higher ground where the *Flamingo* lorries were loaded. Mrs Brandon paused irresolutely and murmured something about running up to see Gilly.

'He won't be there,' volunteered Victoria. 'He's up at the house with Aunt Em.'

'Oh,' said Mrs Brandon doubtfully. 'Well perhaps I might call in there: just for a minute or two. No, don't let's go back that way——' She left the path and struck upwards again, following the trolley line, and they came out among a grove of acacias, one of which was being cut up and converted into charcoal.

Mrs Brandon sat down on the fallen trunk, and removing her hat, fanned her hot face with it and enquired conversationally if Victoria was glad to be back in Kenya, and how did she find Em? 'Personally,' said Mrs Brandon, 'I don't think that she is looking at all well. But then all this has been a terrible blow to her. And now I hear that one of her boys has run off. Kamau.' She paused expectantly, but receiving no reply went on to ask what Mr Gilbert had made of Wambui's story.

'What story?' asked Victoria innocently.

Mrs Brandon's pleasant face flushed and she shifted uncomfortably. But she was not to be deflected. 'The one she told Lisa. That it was Em who had killed Alice. Quite ridiculous of course, but—well, it does raise a question, doesn't it? I was never *quite* sure that Em really liked Alice. And Africans are so quick to spot these things. They're very observant. If Kamau thought that Em disliked her, that might have put the idea into his head—that Em killed her. It would have seemed quite natural to him. The wish being father to the thought. If—if you see what I mean.'

'No,' said Victoria, 'I'm afraid I don't. Mr Gilbert says it's quite obvious that Kamau thought he saw her do it.'

'But that's ridiculous!' protested Mrs Brandon.

'Of course it is,' said Victoria cheerfully. 'But Mr Gilbert thinks it was someone wearing the sort of clothes and hat that Aunt Em wears. He says it would have been the best possible disguise, as even a smaller person or a thinner one could have worn it, since no one would have looked twice.'

'A thin person,' repeated Mabel stupidly. And suddenly sat bolt upright, struck by the same thought that had struck Greg Gilbert. 'The cushion! So *that* was why—! Oh no, it isn't possible. It isn't!'

'What isn't possible?' enquired Victoria, puzzled.

'Prints,' said Mabel confusedly. 'It wasn't a plain one. It——' She seemed suddenly to recollect herself, and stopped short, biting her lip and presently smiled a little stiffly and said: 'It's difficult to know what to think, isn't it? One does not like to think that one's own servants may be under suspicion, and Em's have always been so staunch. It must be heartbreaking for her. For of course it must be one of the *Flamingo* servants. It could be no one else. What does Greg intend to do about it?'

'I don't know,' said Victoria with perfect truth, and firmly changing the subject, enquired: 'What are those odd looking mud heaps with smoke coming out of them?'

'Charcoal,' said Mabel briefly. 'Does Em think——'

'*Charcoal?* But it's mud and turf!'

'The charcoal is inside,' explained Mabel patiently. 'When a tree dies we cut it up into lengths and then put mud all over it in a huge mound—all those trenches are where the earth and turf were dug out—and when it's covered a slow fire is started at one end which burns away for weeks, and when that's out the charcoal is ready. They're really sort of home-made kilns. Does your aunt think that whoever murdered Alice was really wearing a pair of her dungarees? I mean, surely she must know if a pair is missing? It wouldn't be easy to steal them.'

Victoria gave it up. 'But there is a pair missing,' she said, resigning herself. 'And Aunt Em says it would have been quite easy for anyone who wanted a pair to take them off the washing line. I had a look this morning, and it would. In fact you could have had one

116

yourself today if you'd felt like it. That path you were on passes it quite close.'

'Oh,' said Mrs Brandon, momentarily disconcerted. 'Yes, I suppose it would be possible. It's very careless of Em to have her lines where she can't see them. It encourages pilfering. But the hat—is one of her hats missing too?'

'I don't think so. But one floppy hat would look exactly like another in the dusk, wouldn't it?'

Mrs Brandon's gaze fell on the wide-brimmed double terai she held, and she dropped it as though it had stung her, and then stooped hurriedly and picked it up. She jammed it back on her dishevelled curls and stood up, and said in a rather breathless voice: 'It's dreadfully hot here, isn't it? All those kilns—Shall we go back to the house? Em may have finished with the office work by now, and I should like some shandy.'

She led the way between the acacia trees, and across a waste of parched grass strewn with rough lava boulders towards a green belt of trees and bamboos that screened the gardens; and on arrival at the house went off to telephone her husband.

Victoria departed in search of cold drinks and discovered Eden in the dining-room similarly employed—though he appeared to favour something stronger than shandy.

'Hullo, Vicky. What'll you have? Scotch or rye. Or what about a gin and ginger? You'd better get down to some steady drinking, because the odds are once again heavily in favour of a bread-and-cheese luncheon. The entire household staff are having hysterics over the question of Gran's pants. What a party!'

Victoria laughed and said: 'I've got Mrs Brandon here. She's telephoning her husband to fetch her. She says she'd like some shandy, and I'll have some too. Is there any ice?'

'Lots. I've just collected a bowl from the 'fridge. Also some beer, so you're in luck. I presume Mabel is here with the object of collecting all the latest dope. Has she been cross-questioning you?'

'Yes,' admitted Victoria ruefully. 'I tried to dodge it, but it wasn't any use. She's madly curious.'

'She's scared stiff!' corrected Eden, mixing beer and ginger beer in a jug.

'Scared? But why?'

'Because her darling son had a juvenile crush on my wife,' said Eden.

'But that's no reason——' began Victoria, bewildered.

'No?' Eden added ice cubes, and filled a tankard, pushed it across to Victoria. 'You don't know Mabel! She's nuts about her ewe lamb, and it's my guess that she's been bitten with the crazy notion that Alice having repulsed him, he may have seen red and gone for her, preferring to see her dead rather than lost to him. All very dramatic and Othello-ish, and utterly ridiculous! I don't say that Ken mightn't have done that. In fact he's precisely the type of hysterical young ass who from time to time figures in the Sunday papers as having waylaid his ex-love, and bashed her with his own (and identifiable!) spanner, because she'd thrown him over. But what Mabel hasn't the sense to realize is that if he'd done it, he'd have shot himself five minutes later! Unless of course he had some totally different and entirely unsuspected reason for wanting Alice out of the way, which is absurd. If only one could put that to Mabel it would save her making an ass of herself. But of course one can't.'

'Why not?' demanded Victoria with some heat. 'Because "it's not done", I suppose!'

'No, darling. Because I, personally, do not fancy having my eyes scratched out. Just you try hinting to Mabel that she has even allowed such a possibility to cross her mind. She'd deny it with her last breath and never forgive you for having suggested it. But it's there all right—panicking about in her subconscious, if nowhere else. Nothing else will explain why she has taken to thinking up excuses for haunting the place and asking endless questions, and generally behaving like a flustered hen. Darling Mabel. The best thing we can do for her is to add a double brandy to her shandy.'

He mixed himself a stiff John Collins and lifted his glass to Victoria. 'Well, here's to you, darling. Don't let any of this get you down. You're too sweet to get involved in such a miserable business. Keep out of it, Vicky.'

Was there, or was there not, a note of warning in his voice? something more than the mere wish to save her from distress? The uncomfortable thought darted swiftly through Victoria's mind like a small fish glimpsed in deep water, and perhaps it had shown in her face, for Eden set down his glass, and crossing to her, put his hands on her shoulders and looked down into her eyes:

'I can't bear the idea of you getting mixed up in our troubles—in any troubles. And if only I were still strong-minded and self-sacrificing, instead of being weak-willed and abominably selfish, I'd insist on your leaving. But I'm not going to, because you are the one bright diamond in my present pile of coke.'

He smiled down at her, and once again, as it had on the previous day, Victoria's heart seemed to check and miss a beat. His hands tightened on her shoulders and the moment seemed to stretch out interminably.

'Oh, Vicky,' said Eden with a break in his voice, 'what a fool I've been!'

He released her abruptly, and picking up his glass and the jug of shandy, said: 'There's Mabel. Let's go and drink outside.'

He turned away and walked out on to the verandah, and Victoria, following more slowly, found Em and Gilly emerging from the hall door.

'Ah!' said Mr Markham enthusiastically, observing the tankard in her hand. 'Liquor! Just what I stand in need of after devoting an entire hour to the subject of milk (a dreary beverage and one I never touch). Would there be anything stronger than beer in the offing, Eden?'

'You'll find all the usual things on the sideboard in the dining-room,' said Eden. 'Help yourself.'

'Thanks, I will. What about you, Em?'

'Nothing, thank you. I dislike drinking at midday,' said Em grumpily, plumping herself down in a wicker chair.

'You don't know what you miss!' said Gilly blithely, and disappeared into the dining-room.

Mabel accepted a tankard of shandy and sat down on a long wicker divan that stood against the wall, its back formed by a row of three boldly patterned cushions—the fourth being presumably still in the possession of the police. She subjected her hostess to a worried scrutiny, and said anxiously: 'You don't look at all well, Em. You ought to get Dr North to give you a tonic.'

'Thank you, Mabel, I have no desire to fill my stomach with useless nostrums. I am merely tired, that is all. Tired of office work and silly questions and having the police permanently on the premises upsetting my servants. Is young Hennessy still here, Eden?'

'No,' said Eden. 'Having thrown the cook-house into hysterics he has retired to write up a report, and we shall probably have Greg here as soon as he's read it.'

'Did he get anything out of the servants?'

'Nothing but indignant denials and a suggestion that the dogs are responsible. Oh, and several missing dish-cloths that turned up in one of the huts. One of the *totos* had evidently been making a collection of them. No sign of your dungarees, however.'

'Where are the dogs today?' enquired Mabel, bending to peer along the verandah as though she expected to find them concealed under the chairs.

'Locked up,' said Eden. 'And they can stay there! They don't take to police on the premises, any more than Gran does.'

'Sensible animals,' observed Em morosely. 'Gilly, here's your wife. Get her a drink. Good morning, Lisa. What is it now?'

Gilly, who had emerged from the dining-room with a glass in one hand and a bottle of gin in the other, returned to fetch a second glass as Lisa came up the steps looking cool and spruce and pretty in a full skirted dress of pale blue poplin patterned with daisies. He returned with a gin and lime for his wife, and Lisa said: 'I only came over to ask about the picnic. I suppose you *are* postponing it?'

'What picnic?' enquired Em. 'Oh, yes. I remember. We were going to take an all-day picnic tomorrow to show Victoria something of the Valley. No, I see no reason why we should postpone it. It will do us all good to get away from the house for a day—and from the police! Mabel, you and Hector were coming, weren't you? And Ken. Then that's settled. Where shall we go?'

'Crater Lake,' suggested Mabel. 'I was telling Victoria about it just now. It's rather a fascinating spot, Victoria. A lake in the crater of an old volcano. They say it's bottomless, and——'

She was interrupted by the arrival of a Land-Rover containing Hector Brandon and a slim youth wearing the familiar garb of the Angry Young Men—a pair of exceedingly dirty grey flannels and a polo-necked sweater. A lock of his dark hair flopped artistically over a forehead not entirely innocent of the spots that adolescence is apt to inflict upon sensitive youth, and he possessed a pair of hot brown eyes, thin and passably attractive features, and the general air of a misunderstood minor poet.

So this, thought Victoria, was the boy she had caught a glimpse of driving furiously along the lake road on the morning of her arrival, and who had reportedly fallen so disastrously in love with Alice DeBrett.

She had been so intrigued by the unexpected arrival of Ken Brandon that she had not noticed that there had been a third man in the Land-Rover, and only became aware of it when Drew Stratton sat down beside her and observed amiably that it was a nice day.

Victoria started and bit her tongue. 'What? Oh, it's you. I didn't know you were here. What did you say?'

'I made the classic opening remark of the socially disposed Englishman. I said it was a nice day. It's your move now.'

Victoria eyed him with some misgiving and said: 'I didn't know you were coming here this morning.'

'Would you rather I hadn't? I'm afraid it's a bit late to do much about it now, but I shan't be staying long.'

Victoria flushed pinkly. 'You know quite well I didn't mean it like that. I was only surprised to see you.'

'Pleasantly, I hope?'

'No!' said Victoria, regarding him with a kindling eye. 'I don't think it's ever particularly pleasant to meet people who dislike you; and you don't like me at all, do you? You made that quite clear from the moment you first saw me. Why don't you like me?'

Drew returned her indignant gaze thoughtfully and without embarrassment, and paid her the compliment of disdaining polite denial. He said: 'Because of Alice DeBrett.'

'*Alice?* But I didn't even know her! I don't think I understand.'

'Don't you? I thought I'd been into this once already. You are a very pretty girl, Miss Caryll, and you were once engaged to her husband. I don't know why you broke it off, but whatever the reason, you cannot really have supposed that she would welcome your arrival as a permanent fixture in the household?'

Victoria stiffened and found that her hands were shaking with anger. She gripped them together in her lap and enquired in a deceptively innocent voice: 'And were Mrs DeBrett's feelings so important to you, Mr Stratton?'

She looked with intention at Ken Brandon, who was talking moodily to Lisa Markham, and Drew noted the look and interpreted it correctly. He said dryly: 'I wasn't in love with her, if that is what you mean. Can you say the same about her husband?'

The angry colour drained out of Victoria's face and once again, as on the previous night, she looked young and forlorn and defenceless—and frightened. The indignation and the rigidity left her, and she said in a voice that was so low that he barely caught the words: 'I don't know. I wish I did know. Did you think that I came out here to try and take Eden away from her?'

'No,' said Drew, considering the matter. 'She told me that your aunt had asked you to come. But I thought that knowing how she herself must feel about it, you might, perhaps, have refused.'

'You're quite right,' said Victoria, still in a half whisper that appeared to be addressed more to herself than to Drew. 'I should never have come. But—I wanted to come back to Kenya. Mother was dead and I had no one but Aunt Em. I wanted to—to belong again, and come home; and I wouldn't let myself think about Eden. He was married, and it was all over. I don't think I ever thought at all about Alice as a person. She was just something that proved it was all over, and made it safe to come. But now it's different . . .'

Drew looked away from her to where Eden's unstudied grace and startling handsome profile were outlined against the brilliant sunlight of the garden, and was startled to find himself wrenched by a physical spasm of jealousy and dislike. He said disagreeably: 'Because now he is free? Is that what you mean? But that should make everything pleasantly simple for you.'

Victoria shook her head without lifting it. It was only a very slight gesture, but somehow it revealed such a gulf of unhappiness and bewilderment that he was shocked out of his anger. He said: 'I'm sorry. That was rude and officious of me. And none of my business. Shall we talk about something else?'

He began to tell her about a film unit that had recently arrived in Nairobi, until Em interrupted him with an enquiry relative to the picnic and the rival merits of Thermos flasks and kettles.

'Not kettles,' said Hector. 'Don't care for lighting fires. Weather's been pretty dry, and we might do no end of damage. Are we going to do any shootin'? Have to bring a gun if we are. Just as well to bring one or two anyway, just in case. After all, one never knows. May be the odd hard-core terrorist hidin' out in those parts. There was always a rumour that the gangs had a hide somewhere near Crater Lake. Better to be on the safe side. And we might get a pot at a warthog or a guinea-fowl.'

'We must make a list,' announced Mabel, 'so that we don't leave anything behind. Has anyone got a pencil and paper?'

'Why worry,' enquired Eden lazily. 'As long as we take plenty of food and drink and enough rugs to go to sleep on afterwards, that's all we're likely to need.'

Mabel regarded him with friendly contempt and remarked that that was just like a man. There were dozens of things that must be taken on a picnic: a flit gun and a fly swatter, a first-aid kit, matches, snake serum——

Eden laughed and turned to Victoria. 'So now you know what you are in for, Vicky. Snakes in the grass and warthogs in the undergrowth, and the odd terrorist lurking on the skyline. A nice, peaceful, Kenya afternoon! You needn't bother with the first-aid kit, Mabel. We always keep one in the Land-Rover. Bandages, lint, bottle of iodine—the works! I don't think we run to morphia and forceps, but possibly you can provide those.'

'As a matter of fact, I can,' retorted Mabel, unruffled. 'I don't believe in being unprepared for emergencies in a country where emergencies are apt to arise, and I always carry a bottle of iodine with me in my pocket. You've no idea how easily a scratch can turn septic in this country. But so far neither Hector nor I have ever had blood-poisoning.'

'Well neither have I, if it comes to that,' said Eden with a grin. 'And without the benefit of iodine! Don't tell me that Hector and Ken carry round the stuff too?'

'Of course they do. It's an elementary precaution that I insist upon. One should really carry permanganate as well.'

'What for? Medicating the drinking water, or washing the salad?'

'Snake-bite, of course. Serum is a bit bulky to take around, syringe and all. But permanganate is better than nothing. If you cut the wound across and rub the crystals in at once it can be very effective.'

'Look, Mabel,' said Eden earnestly, 'let's call off this picnic and go to a cinema instead. The whole thing sounds far too hazardous to me. My idea of a picnic is a peaceful afternoon spent flat on my back in the shade, after eating heartily of cold chicken, stuffed eggs, sausage-rolls and salad, topped off with coffee cake and several pints of beer. I am prepared to put up with flies and ants, but not with having myself carved up with a penknife and doctored with permanganate of potash!'

'Not in the least likely to happen,' said Hector reassuringly. 'Hundred-to-one chance. Though I'm not saying that Crater Lake hasn't got a bad name for snakes. Saw a mamba there once when I was a youngster. Came at me like the wind. Ugly brute. Fortunately I had m'shot-gun. Blew it's head off. Very lucky shot.'

Eden covered his eyes and bowed his head on his knees, and Gilly burst into a roar of laughter to which Em added her rich chuckle, while even Ken Brandon momentarily, abandoned his Byronic gloom and permitted himself to smile.

Hector said huffily: 'It was not in the least amusing I assure you. If I'd missed it—well, that would have been the end of me. And it's a very painful way to die, let me tell you! Seen a chap do it. Blue in the face—writhing and twisting. Not at all funny.'

His son's reluctant smile broadened into a grin, and he said: 'Come off it, Dad! You're terrifying the girls. Lisa doesn't like snakes. Do you, Lisa?'

'No,' said Lisa with a shudder. 'Horrible things! Mbogo says that there are a pair of puff adders in a hole under the big acacia by the gate. He says he's seen their tracks in the dust. *Ugh!*'

Mabel gave a sympathetic shiver and said: 'There seems to be a plague of them this year. We're always passing dead ones on the road that have been run over by cars. It's the only thing I don't like about the Rift—the snakes. Hector and Ken don't seem to mind them. They collected them for the venom centre once. That place where they keep snakes and collect the poison for serums.'

'In that case,' said Gilly, 'any intelligent snake should give us a wide berth on Wednesday.' He waved his glass and chanted:

> *'You spotted snakes, with double tongue,*
> *Thorny hedge-hogs, be not seen;*
> *Newts, and blind-worms, do no wrong;*
> *Come not near*—there are Brandons about!'

'I can't see what you've got to be so cheerful about this morning,' said Lisa crossly.

'Can't you, my sweet? Well I'll let you into a secret. I've got a lovely surprise for you. Em's sending us off to Rumuruti when Jerry Coles leaves. How do you like that?'

There was a sudden startled silence. Eden sat bolt upright, while Lisa stared at her husband in open-mouthed, ludicrous dismay, and Drew's blond brows lifted in surprise. Even the Brandons seemed taken aback, and only Em remained tranquil.

The effect of his pronouncement appeared to afford Gilly considerable amusement, but Lisa's gaze had flown to Eden and she said involuntarily: 'Oh no! It isn't true! We can't——'

'Of course It's true,' said Gilly cheerfully. 'Why are you all looking so surprised? I've been trying to blarney Em into nominating me for the job for weeks, and she's seen reason at last. I received the accolade this morning. Manager of DeBrett Farms, Rumuruti. That's me. Or it will be. Aren't you going to congratulate me, Eden?'

Eden's mouth tightened into a narrow and ominous line and he stared at Gilly for a dangerous minute, and then turned to his grandmother. 'Is this true?' he demanded harshly. 'Have you really promised him Coles's job? *Have you?*'

'Come, come, my dear boy,' reproved Hector, intervening with all the tact of a charging rhinoceros. 'Must remember that you're speakin' to your grandmother!'

Drew said very softly: 'Ware wire, Hector!' but Eden did not appear to have heard the interruption. *'Have you?'* he insisted, his eyes on Em.

Em looked long and deliberately from Eden to Lisa, and back again, and said calmly: 'Certainly, dear. On consideration it seemed to me an excellent idea. I admit that I once thought otherwise, but circumstances alter cases. And in the present circumstances I consider that it may prove to be a very satisfactory arrangement after all. To *everyone.* Victoria dear, you have not yet told us if there is any particular spot that you would prefer to visit rather than Crater Lake?'

Victoria, disconcerted at finding herself suddenly drawn into the conversation, disclaimed any preferences, and was perhaps the only person present who interpreted Em's apparently inconsequent query as an attempt to change the conversation. Eden glanced quickly at her, and then at Lisa, whose desperate gaze was still fixed on him, and there was, suddenly, comprehension and something that might almost have been relief in his face.

The rigidity went out of his slim figure and he relaxed in his chair, and Gilly, who had been watching his wife with bright observant eyes and a smile that was tinged with malice, said: 'Aren't you pleased, dear? I thought you'd be delighted! Promotion. More pay. Nice house. New faces—I hope. You'll love it!'

Lisa said nothing. She looked away from Eden at last, her face white and wooden and her mouth a tight scarlet line, and it was Hector who spoke.

'Must say,' said Hector judicially, 'I'm surprised. Shouldn't have said you were up to it, Gilly. If you don't mind my speakin' frankly.'

'But I do mind,' said Gilly. 'And, speaking frankly, I don't consider that it is any of your dam' business. Which reminds me——' He turned his back on Hector, and addressing Ken said conversationally: 'I've been meaning to ask you, Ken. Was that Kerry Lad you were riding on Tuesday evening? Because if so, you really should enter him for the open jumping at the Royal Show. There can't be many hunters who can clear that hedge and the wire on the boundary side of my garden without coming to grief. You should have a walkover.'

Ken Brandon did not reply, and for the second time that morning a stricken silence descended upon the verandah. But now it was the boy's face that was as white and still as Lisa's had been, and the affectation and the Byronic pose fell away from him. He stared at Gilly like a hypnotized rabbit and licked his dry lips, and then Mabel had risen swiftly and was standing between them, her cheeks pink and her grey curls quivering:

'I don't know what you're talking about, Gilly,' she said in a calmly cheerful voice. 'Ken was riding White Lady on Tuesday. Wasn't he, Em? And she's no good over the sticks.'

'I didn't mean when he came over the first time,' said Gilly softly. 'I meant later on.'

'He wasn't out later on,' said Mabel positively, and turned to Lady Emily: 'We really must be going, Em. Thank you for the shandy. It was delicious. Where are we going to meet tomorrow? I suggest you all come along to us about eleven, as we're on your way, and then we can sort ourselves out and go on from there. Drew, you'll come won't you? Yes, of course you must. We won't take no for an answer. We fixed up who brings what food, didn't we? Then that's all right. Come on, Ken dear. Goodbye, Victoria. It's nice to have met Jack's girl. Can we give you a lift, Drew? Oh—but that's *your* Land-Rover, isn't it?'

'Yes,' said Drew, rising and stubbing out his cigarette. 'I am an uninvited guest at this party. I would appear to have the only transport that does not break down at awkward moments. Which has its disadvantages.'

His smile robbed the words of any offence, and the tension in the atmosphere decreased almost visibly. 'That's right,' confirmed Hector. 'Afraid we broke down. That damned clutch again. Drew picked us up. Wasted his morning, I'm afraid. Hope you won't mind givin' us a lift back, Drew?'

'Not at all, sir. Delighted. Goodbye, Em. Are you really expecting me to turn up at this picnic tomorrow?'

'You heard what Mabel said,' retorted Em with something that in anyone else would have been described as a sniff. 'She "won't take no for an answer". So naturally I shall expect to see you there.'

'All right,' said Drew resignedly, 'though frankly—if I may borrow a favourite word of Hector's—if I had any sense I'd remove myself to Nyali or the Northern Frontier until the situation here was less electric.'

'Greg wouldn't let you go,' announced Em a trifle grimly. '*You* haven't got an alibi either!'

126

The Land-Rover departed in a cloud of dust, and Eden, who had been watching the Markhams as they walked away across the garden, said slowly: 'What was Gilly getting at—about Ken riding across our land on Tuesday evening? Do you suppose he was here?'

'Yes,' said Em shortly. 'I imagine he did it fairly frequently, and for no better reason than the time-honoured one of passing the house in which his lady lived. Infatuated youth has done that sort of thing—and will go on doing it!—for centuries. But Ken is young enough and foolish enough to try and hide the fact, and Gilly is trading on that to tease him—and Mabel. It's a very silly thing to do, and I shall have to speak to Gilly. Drew is quite right. Too much electricity. I don't like it. I don't like it at all!'

She sighed heavily, and rising from her chair walked away down the verandah, muttering to herself after the manner of the old.

The remainder of the day had passed peacefully enough, but Victoria slept little that night. She lay awake hour after hour, worried at first by personal problems, but later by fear. For as the slow hours ticked away, the house that had seemed so silent began to fill with innumerable small stealthy sounds, until at times she could have sworn that someone was creeping about the darkened rooms—tip-toeing across the floors and easing open doors very softly so that the hinges should not creak.

She had locked her own door when she went to bed, and had been ashamed of herself for doing so. But as she lay awake in the darkness, straining her ears to listen, it occurred to her that it was no use locking your door against a ghost, and that if there were such things as poltergeists it might be in her room at the moment, watching her and chuckling at her fear.

Beyond her window the garden had been white with moonlight, but even there it had not been silent, for down in the papyrus swamps birds were calling; crying like gulls on a windy day; though there was no wind, and it was night.

Were there really still remnants of the Mau Mau gangs hiding in the swamp?—desperate, hunted, hungry men who were being fed in secret by those who were, by daylight, faithful and trusted servants of the settlers whose estates bordered the lake?

Several times during that long night the dogs had growled and barked and scratched at the door of the disused storehouse in which they were locked, and though there might be a trivial reason for that —a rat scuttling in the roof, or a prowling cat—might they not be barking at a man creeping out from the labour lines with food in his hands, to meet a shadow who had come up through the darkness of the shamba and the papyrus swamp? A shadow who had perhaps killed Alice DeBrett——?

12

The Land-Rovers bumped and bounced and jolted over the unmade lake road, trailing the inevitable dust clouds behind them like smoke from an express train, and the morning was hot and blue and brilliant.

The country was more rugged here, near the foothills of the Mau, and oddly shaped hillocks that had once been the cones of volcanoes jutted up out of the plain, turning from green to darkest midnight blue as an idling cloud shadow would engulf one and silhouette it blackly against the surrounding blaze of sunlight.

There was little game to be seen at this hour of the day, for in the hot noonday the great herds of zebra and gazelle that grazed across the open ranges in the early morning and the late afternoon had retired to the shade of the trees. But in a grove of acacias outside a small village a troop of baboons howled and leapt and danced among the branches as the Land-Rovers passed.

The picnic party had arrived separately at the Brandons' farm, and had there sorted themselves out into three Land-Rovers. Ken Brandon and Lisa in Drew Stratton's, Em with Mabel and Hector, and Victoria and Gilly with Eden.

Eden's complement had also included Thuku, Em's African driver, and old Zacharia who had been brought along to deal with such tedious but necessary chores as the cleaning of dirty knives and dishes, the disposal of debris and the repacking of depleted baskets. The Brandons had also brought their driver, Samuel, for it was still not considered safe to leave a vehicle unguarded in the remoter parts of the Rift, and both Samuel and Thuku carried loaded shotguns.

'There's Crater Lake,' announced Gilly, breaking a silence that had lasted for several miles. 'Or rather, there's the rim of the crater. Over on the right——'

129

'But there's no road,' objected Victoria.

'Lor' bless you, we don't need roads in this country,' said Gilly. 'What do you take us for? Sissies? I admit that this appalling chain of rocks and potholes that we have been bouncing along for the last umpteen miles or so calls itself a road, but you won't notice any appreciable difference when we take to the open range. Here we go!'

As he spoke, Eden drove the Land-Rover off the dust-laden road and across a long stretch of open country that sloped upward towards high ground crowned with rocks, candelabrum trees, thorn scrub and thickets of wild olive.

'See what I mean?' demanded Gilly, returning violently to his seat from hitting his head on the canvas roof. Victoria, who had inadvertently bitten her tongue, nodded dumbly and braced herself to withstand a sharp list to starboard as they roared up a steep cattle track that climbed over rocks and roots, and came at last to a stop in a small clearing where the two Land-Rovers that had preceded them were already parked.

'Well, that's as far as we can go,' said Eden, applying the brake and wiping the dust out of his eyes. 'We walk from here.'

Gilly descended and went round to the back of the car to super-intend the removal of the beer, and Eden jumped out and reached up to lift Victoria down.

He held her for a full half-minute before he released her, and Victoria, looking into the grey eyes that were so near her own, was astonished to realize that her pulse had not quickened nor her heart missed a beat, and that for the first time in her life she was looking at him as though he were a friend, or a cousin, instead of the glamour-gilded Hero of all Romance that he had been to her for so many years.

Her feet touched the ground, and feeling it rough and solid under her shoes it was as if she had touched reality at long last and relinquished her grasp upon illusion.

Eden released her, but she did not move away. She stood in the hot sunlight looking at him gravely and intently, and he smiled his charming quizzical smile and said lightly: 'What is it, Vicky? Learn-ing me by heart?'

'No,' said Victoria slowly. 'I know you by heart. I think that's always been my trouble. I've never known you any other way.'

'You mean, never with your head? Then don't start now, darling.

You mightn't like me with your hard little head, and I couldn't bear that.'

He lifted her hand and kissed it, and then suddenly his face changed. The warmth went out of his eyes and he dropped her hand, and Victoria, turning, saw that Lisa and Drew had walked back to the cars and were standing within a few yards of them, having obviously witnessed the brief scene. It was also equally obvious that neither of them was pleased. Drew looked blank and bored and thoroughly disagreeable, and Lisa looked frankly furious.

It was, somehow, a deeply embarrassing moment out of all proportion to the triviality of the occasion, and facing Lisa's white-faced, tight-lipped jealousy and Drew's cold eyes, Victoria found herself blushing as hotly as though she had been guilty of some gross impropriety. She looked away and became aware that Gilly too was an interested spectator. He had come round from the back of the car and was leaning against it, studying his wife with detached interest as though she had been some stranger whom he had not previously met. His gaze took in her ultra-feminine and un-picnic-like garb, and once again there was comprehension and malice in his face, as though he were perfectly aware for whose approval she had dressed.

His glance slid past her and came to rest on Victoria, neat and slim in slacks and shirt, and he said meditatively and in the manner of one speaking a thought aloud: 'You know, she's good, this girl: she uses her head. Lisa'll have to work fast. Very fast!'

Eden said coldly: 'What are you babbling about, Gilly? Have you got the stuff unloaded?'

'I was musing, like Polonius, on the frailty of human nature,' said Gilly. *Whose violent property fordoes itself, and leads the will to desperate undertakings, as oft as any passion under heaven*—and if you were referring to the beer, yes. I have unloaded it and it is on its way up. Hadn't somebody better stay and keep an eye on our transport, just in case the odd terrorist is still using this salubrious spot as a hide-out?'

Drew said briefly: 'Thuku can stay around.' And taking Lisa by the arm he turned her about and started back up the steep slope, the others following in single file behind him.

Lisa had not spoken, but Drew, holding her arm, could feel that she was shivering as though with ague, and he said sharply: 'Hold up, Lisa! If you don't look where you're going you'll end up with a broken ankle. Here we are——'

They had come out on a bare expanse of broken rock, and below them, ringed by the steep sides of the crater and bordered by a jungle of scrub and acacias, lay a little green lake. The eeriest place, thought Victoria, looking down on it, that she had ever seen. And the most silent.

The sky overhead was clear and blue, but the lake did not reflect it, and the whole cup of the crater was as green and dark and still as though a cold cloud shadow had fallen directly upon it. Victoria shivered, and drawing back from the edge of the cliff, said doubtfully: 'It looks rather an unfriendly place, doesn't it?'

'*A Daniel come to judgement!*' said Gilly. 'My opinion exactly. A morgue. However, don't worry, a few drinks will brighten your viewpoint considerably—and mine. And if you're worrying about the dangers of the African bush, Hector, Eden and Ken are all Grade A marksmen, while Drew has Annie Oakley beat to a frazzle. Anything she could do, he can do better. You are as safe as houses—except for the flies. And Mabel and her flit gun will probably be able to repel those. Let's go.'

Victoria laughed a little shamefacedly, and Drew, after favouring her with a brief, frowning glance, turned and led the way along the rim of the crater to a point where there was a fairly easy route down the cliff to the trees and the lake edge.

They met the Brandons' driver, Samuel, coming up the narrow track having helped carry down the baskets, and found Em, Mabel and Hector comfortably ensconced on rugs and ground sheets in the shade while Zacharia unpacked the luncheon.

Ken Brandon, who had been on a solitary ramble, reported that he had seen the pug marks of a leopard in a patch of wet mud at the far side of the lake, and that there was the skeleton of a big warthog among the bushes. He exhibited one of the enormous curved tusks, and said: 'Look at that! Must have been the great-grandfather of all warthogs. I've never seen tusks that size before.'

The air of embittered gloom had temporarily left him, and he looked boyish and refreshingly normal as he handled the yellowed chunk of ivory.

'Leopard kill?' enquired Drew.

Ken shook his head. 'No. The bones are complete. Old age probably. Or perhaps he was wounded somewhere on Conville's range, and came here to die.'

'Or got bitten by a snake?' suggested Gilly.

Ken dropped the tusk on to the ground and the animation went out of his face. He said: 'Perhaps,' in a colourless voice, and went to sit beside Lisa, who moved over to make room for him.

◇ ◇ ◇

It was well past two o'clock by the time Zacharia had washed up in the scummy water of the lake, and assisted by Samuel had carried the picnic baskets back up the cliff path to the cars.

Hector departed to inspect the leopard's spoor and the skeleton of the warthog, while his wife produced a voluminous cretonne bag and settled down to some knitting, and Em, who had thoughtfully provided herself with a cushion, announced her intention of resting for at least an hour.

The remaining members of the party had gone off to explore the crater—with the exception of Gilly who, having drunk two bottles of beer on top of seven pink gins, had quarrelled with Hector, been offensive to Ken Brandon and been spoken to sharply by Em, and had retired with a rug and a flit gun to sleep it off behind a clump of bushes. Lisa's sandals, however, were not made for exploring, and she had clung to Eden's arm and they had fallen back and got separated from the others, so that Victoria found herself left with Drew Stratton and young Mr Brandon. Neither of her companions evinced the slightest desire to talk, and Victoria only noticed that Ken had removed himself elsewhere when they had made an almost complete circuit of the crater and she had turned to ask him where he had seen the leopard's pug marks.

'He left us about ten minutes ago,' said Mr Stratton, bored. 'Is there anything else you want to see?'

'Not here,' said Victoria with a shiver. 'I don't think I like this place. And I don't think it likes us. It's too quiet.'

She turned her head, listening, and in the silence they could hear faintly but distinctly, and coming from somewhere twenty or thirty yards ahead and out of sight, a sound that after a moment or two she identified as snores. That would be Gilly Markham—or Em! The snores ended on a loud snort, and after an interval of silence began again, and Victoria turned back to Mr Stratton and enquired uneasily if he really thought that there might be a leopard in the crater?

'Possibly,' said Drew, without interest. 'There are hundreds of hiding places among the rocks, and those pug marks were fairly new. Which is one reason why you can't be left to wander round here on your own.'

Victoria stood still and stared at him for a fulminating moment. 'If that means that you feel that you have to stay around in order to protect me, you needn't bother. I shall be quite safe, and I don't want to explore any more.' She sat down on a convenient boulder, with chin in the air, and added coldly: 'Don't let me keep you.'

Drew looked at her thoughtfully for a full half-minute, and then he shrugged his shoulders slightly and turned away.

Victoria watched him go with a mixture of resentment and apprehension, and was strongly tempted to call him back. Not because she anticipated any danger from leopards or terrorists, but because she did not like being left alone in this eerie and disquieting spot, even though she knew that nine other people were presumably within call, and at least three of them—Aunt Emily, Mrs Brandon and Mr Markham—less than thirty yards away. But Drew had disappeared among the thick belt of trees and she could no longer hear the bushes rustling as he moved. She sat quite still, listening; but no one seemed to be moving anywhere in the crater, and the silence flowed back into it, filling it as a cup is filled with water.

It was not in any way a peaceful silence, but a stealthy, all-pervading stillness that contained a disturbing quality of awareness. And suddenly, and for no reason, she was afraid. Where had everyone else got to? Had they all stolen away and left her alone in this horrible place? She must find them again. She would walk over to the trees where they had picnicked, and sit beside Aunt Em and Mrs Brandon and listen to the comforting click of Mrs Brandon's knitting needles.

But she found that she could not make the first move to break that brooding silence, and when at last she heard movements among the trees the sounds were as frightening as the silence had been, for there was about them the same disquieting suggestion of stealth; as though someone—or perhaps several people?—were moving within the crater with infinite caution and the minimum of noise.

Once a stone rattled down from the cliffs with a small metallic clatter that was uncomfortably reminiscent of the chatter of teeth, and then a twig cracked, and Victoria turned quickly: but there was no one there. Only the trees and the shadows and the rank grass—and a flicker of movement that might have been imagination or a bird flitting between the leaves.

'Who's there?' called Victoria, astonished at the huskiness of her own voice. 'Is anyone there?'

The words seemed astonishingly loud in the silence, but no one answered her, and a minute or two later the undergrowth rustled as though something or someone was moving stealthily away. The soft sound grew fainter until it was submerged at last by the silence, and though there were no more sounds Victoria did not move. She sat quite still, listening intently, while the sun moved slowly down the sky and the deep blue shadow of the cliff crept forward across the cup of the crater. Only when it touched her did she give herself a mental shake and stand up.

I'm behaving like an idiot, thought Victoria with disgust: sitting here working myself into a panic over nothing, just because everyone else has very sensibly done what Aunt Em and Mrs Brandon have—gone to sleep! And with that thought courage flowed back and her fears seemed childish, and she began to walk along the marshy margin of the lake towards the spot where they had picnicked. She had almost reached it when a sound that was painfully associated with her recent flight out from England assaulted her ears, and she stopped in sudden distaste. Mr Markham, having awoken from sleep, was obviously—and regrettably—engaged in parting with his lunch and the excess of alcohol with which he had insulted his long-suffering stomach.

Victoria turned and tiptoed away again, feeling for the first time deeply sorry for Gilly's wife, and she was halfway round the far side of the lake when Hector Brandon came out of the bushes a few yards ahead of her and waved cheerfully, and a moment later Lisa Markham joined them. They found Ken Brandon taking photographs with a large box camera, and as they reached the little clearing where they had picnicked, Drew came down the cliff path and Eden strolled out from between the tree trunks.

Em was asleep—her hat tilted well over her nose—and Mabel's busy needles were silent while their owner snored gently.

'A pretty and peaceful picture,' commented Eden. 'But unless we're going to have tea here, it's time we moved on. Wake up, Gran darling!'

Em grunted like a startled warthog, and sitting up with a jerk that dislodged her hat, glared at her grandson.

'I wish,' she said crossly, 'that you would all go away and let me have a short rest. Surely you can amuse yourselves somewhere else for half an hour?'

'You've been resting, darling. And for well over an hour! It's getting on for half-past three.'

'That's right,' confirmed Hector, who had been rousing his

sleeping wife. 'Time we were makin' tracks. Here are Zach and Samuel to carry up the rugs. Better let 'em take your cushion too. Hope we haven't left any bottles about. Where's Gilly?'

'Still sleeping it off, I expect,' said Eden. He raised his voice and called out: 'Hi, Gilly, wake up! We're off! Ken, go and rout him out.'

'Rout him out yourself,' said Ken sulkily.

Eden raised his brows, and the boy coloured hotly and said: 'Oh, all right,' and plunged round the clump of bushes behind which Gilly had retired for his afternoon nap. They heard him give an exclamation of disgust and mutter in an undertone, 'Tight again!' and then, loudly: 'Hi, Gilly—we're going: wake up! *Gilly——!*'

There followed an indescribable gasp, and the next minute he was back again, his face sickly white and his eyes wide and staring. 'I —I can't wake him! I think he's having a fit.'

Drew departed at a run, closely followed by Hector, and the remainder of the party, rounding the bushes, found him on his knees beside Gilly's recumbent body.

Gilly was shivering violently, and Drew looked up and said curtly: 'It looks like an attack of fever. Has he ever had malaria, Lisa?'

'No,' said Lisa, staring in white-faced distaste at her husband's shuddering body. 'I don't think so. But he did once have——' She checked herself abruptly and bit her lip.

'D.T.'s,' finished Hector bluntly. 'Yes, we know. Perhaps you're right.'

'Nonsense!' said Em crisply. 'He may have had too much to drink, but he certainly wasn't *that* drunk. Must be malaria.'

'He's not hot,' said Drew, laying a hand on Gilly's sweating forehead.

Em bent down to touch him, and drawing back with a gasp, struck with her stick at something that had lain concealed by a fold of the rug.

'Look out!' shouted Hector, leaping forward. *'Snake!'* He snatched the stick from her hand and beat at the puff adder that had been curled up near Gilly's arm, and Ken Brandon ran in with a broken branch, and lifting the limp, battered thing, flung it far out so that it fell with a splash into the silent lake.

Mabel said: 'He's been bitten—*look!*' And plumping down on her knees she pointed a trembling finger at two small purplish punctures on Gilly's bare forearm, from one of which hung a small drop of blood, already congealed. 'Get the serum, Ken! Run——! It's in the pocket of the car. Quickly!'

Ken turned and ran, stumbling through the bushes and panting up the cliff path, and Drew, who had not spoken, pulled back the lid from Gilly's eye, and after a quick look, thrust his hand inside the open-necked shirt, feeling for the heart beat. He said: 'Have we any brandy?'

Hector jerked a small silver flask from his pocket and handed it over without a word, and Drew forced the liquid between Gilly's quivering lips while Em, who had torn the chiffon scarf from her hat, wound it tightly above the puncture marks in a tourniquet, and demanding a sharp knife, made a deep cross-cut from which the blood welled sluggishly.

Gilly made no sound beyond the shuddering breaths that another attack of shivering forced from him, and Em dropped the knife into the grass and said frantically: 'What on earth is Ken doing? Mabel, where's that permanganate you talked about? He'll die before Ken gets back with the serum! Do something, can't you!'

'It's in the car,' gulped Mabel. 'With the rest of the first-aid kit. But I've got some iodine——' She fumbled in the pocket of her skirt and produced a small bottle.

'It may be better than nothing,' said Em, and poured the contents over the cut.

The minutes ticked by, and except for Gilly's laboured breathing the afternoon was so quiet that it seemed to Victoria that those who watched him must be holding their breaths; and in the silence she heard someone's teeth chatter.

Em burst out desperately: 'Eden, for goodness sake go and see what's keeping Ken. He must have——' And then Ken slithered down the cliff path bringing a young avalanche of stones with him, and crashed through the bushes to arrive hot and panting.

Em snatched the syringe from him, and filling it, plunged it into Gilly's arm above the wound, and they waited breathlessly, watching the pallid face, while Mabel chafed his limp hands and the shivering lessened until at last he lay still. His colourless face twitched, and the brandy that Drew had been forcing down his throat trickled from the corners of his mouth.

Drew put down the flask and felt for Gilly's heart again, and after a full minute he stood up and brushed the broken grass from his knees.

'He's dead,' said Drew curtly.

Mabel gave a hoarse cry and Lisa broke into shrill hysterical laughter that was somehow worse than any screaming or tears would have been.

Em stood up swiftly and slapped her across the face with the flat of her palm, and the laughter broke off in a choking gasp.

'Take her away, Mabel!' said Em sharply. 'Take her back to the car.' She turned on Drew and said: 'Don't talk nonsense! Of course he isn't dead. It's only the reaction from the serum.'

'Yes, I should say that was probably the last straw. His heart couldn't stand any more. He's dead all right.'

'No!' said Em hoarsely. 'No!' She looked dazedly at the syringe that she still held, and then threw it from her in a sudden convulsion of horror, while Eden, pushing her aside, went down on his knees beside Gilly, feeling for his heart as Drew had done.

After a minute or two he lifted a drawn and ravaged face, and Lisa, seeing it, said hysterically: 'He is dead, isn't he? *Isn't he!* Oh God, what a fool I've been! Gilly!—Gilly!'

Em said angrily: 'Mabel, I asked you to take her away! *Is* he dead, Eden?'

'Yes,' said Eden briefly, and got slowly to his feet.

They stood looking down at Gilly's thin, bony face with its clever forehead and weak chin, and it seemed to sneer up at them; the mouth half open and pulled down at one corner, and the pale eyes glinting through their lashes as maliciously as they had in life.

Lisa said in a sobbing whisper: 'He isn't dead. He's laughing at us! He's laughing——'

Mabel put an arm about Lisa's waist. Her pleasant gentle face was grey and shrunken, and she looked as though she were going to be sick. She said in a quavering voice: 'Come away, dear. Drew, give me that brandy.'

Drew picked up the flask and handed it over, but Lisa refused to drink from it. She wrenched herself free, gasping and panting. 'No— no, I won't! How do I know it isn't poisoned? Drew gave it to him and he died! How do I know it didn't kill him?'

'Oh, for God's sake, Lisa!' said Eden, exasperated. 'Pull yourself together! Here, Vicky, give Mabel a hand and get her away from here.'

But Victoria was not listening to him. She was watching Drew who was looking at Gilly as he had once looked at Em on the verandah at *Flamingo*. As though some new and startling thought had suddenly presented itself to him. It was a look that had disturbed her then; but coming on top of the shock of Gilly Markham's death it frightened her as Gilly's death had not done, and she backed away from him, and groping for support, found a tree trunk behind her and leant against it, cold and shivering.

Drew turned abruptly away and stooped to search among the grasses, and when he straightened up again they saw that he was holding the syringe that Em had thrown away. The needle was broken and the glass appeared to be smashed, but he handled it with the extreme caution of a man who holds a live bomb, and wrapping it in his handkerchief, put it very carefully into his pocket and bent again to hunt very carefully in the tangled undergrowth.

Em said tersely: 'What is it, Drew? What are you looking for?'

'The needle,' said Drew. 'We may need it.'

'What for?' demanded Hector impatiently. 'Can't use that thing with a broken needle! Stands to reason. Come on, let's get out of here. How are we going to get him up the cliff?'

Drew paid no attention and continued his search, and Em said heavily: 'Eden and Ken should be able to manage it. The rest of us had better get back to the cars.'

She turned away, and pushing Mabel and the sobbing Lisa ahead of her, moved off through the bushes, walking very slowly and as though she were feeling for each step.

Victoria did not move. Partly because she felt incapable of movement, and partly because horrified curiosity had rooted her to the spot. Why should Drew think that it was important to find a useless thing like a broken piece of needle? And why were Hector and Eden watching him with such rigid apprehension? Why didn't they take Gilly back quickly to the cars? Surely they should get him to hospital as soon as possible? He *could* not be dead! Not just like that. There must be something that a doctor could do. Why didn't they do something—instead of watching Drew Stratton and looking so—so tense and strained and wary?

Something moved just behind her, and she whipped round, her heart in her mouth, but it was only old Zacharia calmly collecting the rugs and the ground sheets and various odds and ends that had not been taken away earlier with the picnic baskets.

Drew gave up at last, and turning to the three silent men who had watched him, he said curtly and incomprehensibly: 'They'll want that clasp knife, too. Where has it got to?'

The remark was meaningless to Victoria, but it was instantly obvious that it was clear to Eden, Hector and Ken. Eden's face took on a blankly wooden look that Victoria knew, and Ken gave an audible gasp, while Hector's bronzed features flushed darkly and he said explosively: 'Now look here, Stratton—you keep out of this! We don't want any more hysterical nonsense of that sort. I'll forgive it in Lisa. She's his wife—bound to be upset. But I'm damned if I'll stand it from you! Now, let's get the hell out of here.'

Drew said: 'I'm sorry, Hector, but it isn't as simple as that, and you know it. We must have that knife.'

But the knife was not there. They searched the grass and the bushes and shook out the rug on which Gilly had lain, but there was no sign of it.

'We're wasting our time,' said Hector angrily. 'It's probably in Em's pocket. Let's stop fooling about and get the body away. That's the most important thing to do.'

But when they at last arrived at the cars, after a slow and difficult ascent out of the crater, neither Em, Mabel nor Lisa knew anything of the clasp knife.

'I left it down there,' said Em. 'I think I dropped it on the grass. You can't have looked properly.'

'We looked everywhere,' said Drew. 'Who did it belong to? Was it yours?'

'No. I asked for a knife and someone handed me one.'

'Who?'

'I don't remember. And what does it matter, anyway? Why are they putting Gilly in your car?'

Drew said: 'We decided that Eden and I had better take him into Naivasha. You'll have your hands full with Lisa.'

He turned to Mabel and asked if she still had Hector's flask of brandy.

'Yes,' said Mabel, handing it over. 'Though I'm afraid there isn't much left. I think there's a bottle of whisky somewhere if you'd rather have that.'

Drew pocketed the flask without replying, and was turning away when Em spoke softly behind him.

'You've forgotten the iodine,' she said.

It was close on five o'clock by the time they arrived back at *Flamingo,* and Em had sent for Dr North and attempted to put Lisa to bed in one of the guest rooms.

But Lisa had refused flatly and with hysteria to sleep at *Flamingo.* The prospect of spending a night in a house that harboured a poltergeist appeared far worse to her than that of returning alone to her own empty bungalow, and eventually it was decided that Mabel should go back with her and stay the night.

Em and Victoria had eaten supper in the candle-lit dining-room, and it was towards the end of that silent meal that Victoria had asked a question that had been troubling her for several hours:

'Aunt Em, what did you mean when you told Drew—Mr Stratton—that he had forgotten the iodine?'

Em looked up from the food that she had barely touched, and her face in the soft light was grey and bleak. As grey and bleak as her voice:

'Because he does not happen to be a fool.'

She pushed her plate away and stared unseeingly at the candle flame that wavered in the faint draught made by Zacharia as he passed silently around the table, and Victoria said uncomfortably: 'I don't understand.'

'No,' said Em slowly. 'You wouldn't, of course. There are so few poisonous snakes in England. But I expect Drew had seen someone die of snake-bite, and that is why he thinks that Gilly Markham was murdered.'

She had spoken the word quite softly and casually into the quiet room, but it seemed to Victoria as though she had shouted it, and that the whole house must echo with it. *Murdered . . .*

Em waved away the dish that Zacharia was proffering, and selecting a cigarette from a box in front of her, lit it from the nearest candle and leant back in her chair, her bulky figure slumped and shapeless.

Victoria said with a catch in her voice: 'But why? How can he think that? It *was* a snake, wasn't it? We all saw it. Does he think that someone put it there? But no one could have— He didn't say so. He didn't say anything! I was there the whole time, and he never said anything about it being—being——'

'Murder,' said Em. And once again the word was like a stone dropped into a quiet pool. 'He may not have used that word; but all the same, that was what he meant.'

'No!' said Victoria breathlessly. 'I don't believe it. If anyone had put a snake there on purpose it might not have bitten him. Or it might have bitten *them!* No one would risk it.'

'Oh, I don't suppose Drew thinks it was put there on purpose,' said Em impatiently. 'I imagine he thinks that someone who happened to have the means was quick enough to seize the opportunity, and make quite sure that Gilly did die. Stupid, really, because if he had been bitten the chances are that he would have died anyway. Personally, I think Drew is wrong. I think Gilly had a heart attack, and that is why he didn't cry out. But if I'm right, then either I killed him, or Drew did. And—and that is not going to be a very pleasant thought for either of us to live with.'

'*You!* You mean he thinks— You think——' Victoria's voice stopped on a gasp and she pushed back her chair and stood up, gripping the edge of the table. 'Aunt Em, you can't think he did it! You *can't!*'

'No, of course I don't,' said Em with a return of impatience. 'Sit down, child. I will not have hysterics. They do not help at all, and after Lisa I have had enough of them to last me a good many years. Neither does Drew think I did it—on purpose. But only two people touched Gilly. Myself and Drew. I made two cuts in his arm and gave him a full strength dose of snake serum, and Drew gave him a great deal of brandy. You cannot do that sort of thing to a man who is having a heart attack without killing him. And then again, if someone did give him poison to ensure that he died, then it was given in one of four ways. It might have been on the blade of the knife, or in the iodine, or the syringe, or in the brandy. Though of course there is always a fifth possibility: that he was given something at luncheon. But Zacharia had washed up all the glasses in the lake. I asked.'

Victoria sat down again and stared at her aunt. She said imploringly: 'It isn't true. They'll find out that it was only snakebite, won't they? The doctors will know. It *must* have been snakebite.'

Em shook her head. 'People who have been bitten by poisonous snakes do not die like that. It's a pity Drew was there. Probably no one else would have noticed details. Or if they had, they'd have kept their mouths shut.'

'But if it was murder——'

'There are some things that are worse than murder,' said Em wearily. 'Trials, hanging, suspicion, miscarriage of justice.' She stubbed out her cigarette and quoted in an undertone: *'Duncan is in his grave; After life's fitful fever he sleeps well; Treason has done his worst: nor steel, nor poison, Malice domestic, foreign levy, nothing, Can touch him further.* Hmm. Gilly was fond of quoting Shakespeare. That would have appealed to him I imagine. *Malice domestic* . . . I wonder——'

She relapsed into brooding silence, looking exhausted and ill, and Victoria eyed her in some disquiet and wished fervently that Eden would return. But although it was by now well past nine o'clock there was still no sign of him, and when Em had gone to bed Victoria went out into the dark verandah to listen for the car.

The moon was already high and the lawns and the trees were silver-white and patched with black shadows, and once again from somewhere down by the shamba and the papyrus swamp, birds were calling.

A bat flickered along the verandah almost brushing Victoria's head, and something moved in the shadows and sent her heart into her mouth; but it was only Pusser, the *Flamingo* cat, who had evidently been asleep in one of the wicker chairs.

Victoria was annoyed to find that her heart was racing and that she was breathing as quickly as though she had been running. Why didn't Eden come back? What were they doing—he and Drew? It was hours since they had left Crater Lake with Gilly Markham's body.

Somewhere in the house a clock struck ten, and the light in the dining-room, where Zacharia had been putting away the silver, was turned out. Victoria heard his shuffling footsteps retreating down the hall and then the sound of a door closing. And all at once the house was deathly quiet and only the night outside was full of small sounds.

Victoria clutched at the sides of her chair and glanced quickly over her shoulder at the open doorway that led into the hall, but the

silent house seemed more frightening to her than the moonlit garden, and she stayed where she was, tense and listening, until at last
she heard the faint, far-away purr of a car.

The sound grew louder and nearer, and presently the yellow
glare of headlights lit up the pepper trees and threw long black
shadows across the sweep of the drive, and Eden walked up the
verandah steps and checked at the sight of Victoria.

'Vicky! What are you doing here! You ought to be in bed. Did
you wait up for us?'

'Us?' said Victoria. And saw then that Drew Stratton and young
Mr Hennessy of the police were with him.

'Drew brought me back. It was his car. And Bill has been sent
along to keep an eye on us and see that none of us makes a break for
the border. They're staying the night. We thought it would be more
convenient, as Greg wants to see us all in the morning. They can
share the double bed in the blue room, and I hope one of them
snores!'

He stopped by the hall door and said suddenly: 'There's nothing
wrong, is there? Is Gran all right?'

'No. I mean, there's nothing wrong. Aunt Em went to bed. I
stayed up because—because I didn't feel like going to sleep.'

'You look as though you could do with it, all the same,' said
Eden as the light from the hall fell on her face. 'How's Lisa?'

'All right, I think. Aunt Em wanted her to stay here, but she
wouldn't. Mrs Brandon is spending the night with her.'

'Good for Mabel. She won't enjoy it!'

There was a solitary table lamp burning in a corner of the drawing-room, and Eden switched on every other light and said: 'That's
better! Vicky, I suppose you couldn't be a darling and rustle us up
some coffee and sandwiches, could you? We've just driven back
from Nairobi. I ought to have 'phoned, but I didn't want Em asking
all sorts of awkward questions with half the Valley listening in on the
party line.'

Victoria said: 'There's both in the dining-room. Aunt Em said
you'd probably need something when you got back. Wait, and I'll
fetch it.'

'Bless you,' said Eden, sinking gratefully into an arm-chair, 'and
her. God, I'm tired!'

He lay back and shut his eyes, and looking down at him Victoria
felt protective and maternal and as though, in some strange way, she
had suddenly grown up.

She became aware that she herself was being watched, and turning her head met Drew Stratton's cool, level gaze. But tonight there was no hostility in his blue eyes; only interest and a faint trace of surprise. Victoria returned his look gravely, and then went away to fetch the Thermos flasks and the chicken sandwiches that Zacharia had left on the sideboard in the dining-room.

There was a light on in the hall, but the two long passages that led off it were full of shadows, and the house was as quiet as Crater Lake had been. Was it waiting for something to happen, as Crater Lake had waited? But that was absurd! thought Victoria impatiently. There was nothing wrong with the house; only with herself and her unruly imagination. *The fault, dear Brutus, is not in our stars, But in ourselves, that we are underlings*—Gilly . . . Gilly had been fond of quoting Shakespeare, and Gilly was dead. What was it that Em had said? *Nor steel, nor poison, Malice domestic . . . nothing, Can touch him further.* Yes, he was safe—if death were safety. But Eden and Aunt Em? and she herself, Victoria?—what about them?

Victoria shivered again, and setting her teeth, opened the dining-room door and groped for the light switches.

A single bulb in a red shade illuminated the sideboard but left the remainder of the room in shadow, and without waiting to turn on any more, Victoria collected a laden tray, and turned to see Drew Stratton standing behind her.

She had not heard him enter, and she was so startled that she would have dropped the tray if Drew had not taken it from her. He frowned at the sight of her white face and wide eyes, and said: 'What's the matter? Didn't you hear me?'

'No,' said Victoria breathlessly. 'You startled me.'

'I can see I did. You ought not to have stayed up. I suppose you've been sitting around alone, frightening yourself stiff?'

'Something like that,' admitted Victoria with a wan smile. 'What are you doing with that tray?'

'Making quite sure that the contents are as advertised,' said Drew. 'Though as I see that it wasn't only Eden who was expected, I imagine it's safe enough. Who made this? You?'

He had put the tray back on the sideboard and was unscrewing the cap of the Thermos.

'No. I suppose Zacharia did. Or the cook. Why?'

Drew did not reply. He removed the cork and poured a small quantity of coffee into one of the cups, smelt it suspiciously, and then put the tip of his finger into it and touched it cautiously to his tongue.

The import of the action was suddenly and horribly clear to Victoria, and she drew back with a gasp and put her hands to her throat: 'You c-can't— You can't think——' Once again she could not finish a sentence, for her breath appeared to have failed her.

Drew said: 'Seems all right.' He replaced the cork and turned his attention to the sandwiches, and after a moment or two said: 'How many people did Em order coffee for?'

'I—I don't know. She just said that Eden might want something when he came back, but she spoke to Zacharia in Swahili, so I don't know what she said.'

'Hmm,' said Drew thoughtfully. 'They all knew that as Eden had gone in my car, I'd probably be bringing him back. But there are four cups. If the extra two were Zacharia's idea, it shows that the old gentleman has more on the ball than one would imagine and had realized that someone from the police would come back with us. Which is interesting, to say the least of it.'

Victoria said huskily: 'Why have they sent a policeman here? Why not to the Markhams' bungalow? Why to us?'

'It isn't only to us. By this time there will not only be one at the Markhams' bungalow, but another at the Brandons.'

'Why? Is it— Was Gilly murdered?'

Drew replaced the sandwiches and looked up, frowning. 'Now what gave you that idea?'

'Aunt Em said you thought he h-had been. Was he?'

'Yes,' said Drew briefly, and picked up the tray.

Victoria had hardly slept at all during the previous night and had endured a harrowing day, and the effects were telling upon her. She began to shiver violently, and Drew put the tray down abruptly and took her into his arms.

It was an entirely unexpected action, but an astonishingly comforting one, and Victoria found herself clinging to him as frantically as though he had been a life line in a cold sea. His arms were warm and close and reassuring, and presently she stopped shivering and relaxed against him; feeling safe for perhaps the first time since her arrival at *Flamingo,* and suddenly and surprisingly sleepy. She turned her head against his shoulder and yawned, and Drew laughed and released her.

'You know,' he said, 'this is painfully like one of those detective novels in which just as the plot is getting littered with clues and corpses, the heroine holds up the action for three pages with a sentimental scene. Are you coming into the drawing-room to drink coffee with us, or would you rather go to bed?'

'Bed,' said Victoria; and yawned again.

Drew accompanied her down the dark passage to her room, and having turned on the light for her, subjected the room to a careful scrutiny.

'No one in the cupboards or under the bed. And Bill Hennessy and I will be in the next room, and Eden only a few doors off. So you've nothing to panic about. I must get back or I shall have the police after me. You all right now?'

'Yes,' said Victoria, and smiled sleepily at him.

Drew took her chin in his hand and bent his head and kissed her quite casually and gently, and went away down the long dark passage, leaving her looking blankly at the panels of the door that he had closed behind him.

◇   ◇   ◇

It was well past eight o'clock when Victoria awoke to the sound of knocking on her door, and unlocked it to admit an aggrieved Majiri who had apparently made several earlier attempts to rouse her.

The day, thought Victoria, blinking at the sunlight, could hardly be a pleasant one, but it was difficult to believe that horrible and frightening things could happen while the sun shone and the breeze smelt of geraniums and orange blossom, and the lake glittered like a vast aquamarine set in a ring of gold and emeralds. And yet Gilly was dead.

Duncan is in his grave . . .

She dressed hurriedly and went out to the verandah to find that Eden, Drew and the young policeman were already half-way through their breakfast, and that Em was having hers in bed.

Lisa and Mabel, both looking white and exhausted, arrived just as the breakfast things were being cleared away, escorted by a police officer who left them at the verandah steps and disappeared round the back of the house.

Mabel was wearing the same crumpled cotton frock that she had worn on the previous day, and she did not look as though she had slept at all, while for the first time in anyone's recollection Lisa Markham had paid little or no attention to her personal appearance. It was also equally evident that she was frightened.

Victoria had offered her some black coffee, and she had gulped it down thirstily, her teeth chattering against the rim of the cup, and replacing it clumsily on the table had let it fall to the ground, where it had smashed into half a dozen pieces.

It had been one of the Rockingham cups, but Lisa had offered no apology or even appeared to notice what she had done. Em, appearing on the verandah arrayed like Solomon in all his glory, had glanced at the broken fragments and made no comment. She had nodded at Mabel, Lisa and Drew, bestowed an affectionate kiss on Victoria and a more perfunctory one on Eden, and ignored Mr Bill Hennessy, who blushed pinkly and looked acutely uncomfortable. And then Hector and Ken had arrived with a third policeman who, after a brief colloquy with Mr Hennessy, also departed round the back of the house.

'I suppose you will all be staying to luncheon,' said Em morosely, surveying the assembled company without pleasure. 'If we are going to spend the entire morning being interrogated, we had better——'

She was interrupted by Lisa, who stood up abruptly and announced in quivering tones that she did not feel at all well: certainly not well enough to answer any questions today from Greg Gilbert or anyone else. That she had only come over because Mabel had said she must, but if she had known that Greg was going to be so inconsiderate and unfeeling as to expect her to undergo a police grilling when——

Her spate of words grew shriller and higher, but any idea of her returning home was forestalled by the arrival of Greg Gilbert, two CID officers from Nakuru, several police askaris and an anonymous individual in a brown suit.

Greg confined his greetings to a single comprehensive nod that embraced everyone in the verandah, but the two CID officers were more punctilious. And then the entire party, with the exception of Mr Hennessy and the askaris, moved into the drawing-room, preceded by Em who seated herself regally in the wing-chair.

Greg refused a chair and stationed himself with his back to the windows, facing the half circle of anxious faces. His own face was blankly impersonal and his voice as devoid of emotional content as though he were reading the minutes of a board meeting to an assembly of total strangers.

He said: 'I imagine that you all know why I am here. An autopsy has been performed on Markham's body, and the doctor's report is quite definite. Gilly was not bitten by a snake, and there is the possibility that he was murdered!'

'No!' Lisa leapt to her feet, white-faced and gasping. 'You can't say that! You can't! It *was* a snake—we saw it!'

Mabel put out a hand and pulled her down again on to the sofa, murmuring: 'Lisa, dear. *Please!* Let him speak.'

Greg said: 'You may have seen it, but it didn't bite him.'

'We saw the fang marks,' said Em quietly.

'So Drew says; and Eden.'

'And I say it—and Mabel, and Ken,' put in Hector. 'Plain as the nose on your face!'

Greg shrugged. 'You saw two punctures that may have been made by anything; one of those double thorns off a thorn tree, for instance. Or if they were made by a snake, it was a snake that had either outlived its poison or emptied its poison sac. The autopsy showed no trace of snake venom, and it's my opinion that the snake you saw was a dead one.'

'But——' began Em, and checked; biting her lip.

Greg turned on her swiftly; 'Can you swear to it being alive? Did you actually see it move?'

Em hesitated, frowning. 'I thought I did. It moved when I hit it, but that might have been—'

'Of course it was alive!' boomed Hector. 'Why, I killed it! Dammit, I've got eyes!'

'But you have to wear spectacles for reading, don't you? And strong ones,' said Greg. 'And so does your wife, and Lady Emily.'

'That's different! Look—I wouldn't have wasted my time bashing a dead snake. Broke its neck and smashed its head.'

'And then threw it into the lake. A pity. If we could have got our hands on it, it might have told us quite a lot.'

'But——' began Hector, and stopped, as Em had done.

There was a brief and painful interval of silence, and then Ken Brandon spoke, his voice a deliberate drawl: '*I* threw it away. And what of it? Are you by any chance suggesting that I did it to destroy evidence?'

'Ken, darling!' begged Mabel in a strangled whisper. 'Don't be silly. *Please* don't be silly, darling.'

Greg favoured the boy with a long cool critical look and said softly: 'No one is accusing you of anything—yet.'

Mabel caught her breath in a small sobbing gasp and Hector

took a swift stride forward, his chin jutting and his hands clenched into fists. 'Now look here, Greg,' he began belligerently.

Mr Gilbert turned a cold gaze upon him, and though he did not raise his voice it held a cutting quality that was as effective as the crack of a whip: '*I* am conducting this enquiry, Hector, and I will do it in my own way. All of you here are required to answer questions, not to ask them; and I would point out that there is a well-known saying to the effect that he who excuses himself, accuses himself. I have not, I repeat, accused anyone—yet. Will you sit down, please? No, not over there. Eden, give him a chair behind Mabel, will you. Thank you.'

Hector seated himself reluctantly, muttering under his breath, and Greg turned his attention back to Em:

'You were answering a question when Hector interrupted you. Are you quite certain that the snake was alive when you hit it?'

'No,' said Em heavily. 'It may have been, and it never occurred to me that it wasn't. I suppose we were all too worked up about Gilly to notice details, and puff adders are often sluggish creatures. But I wouldn't like to swear to it, because——' She hesitated for so long that Greg said: 'Because of what?'

Em sighed and the lines of her face sagged. 'Because I realized later that whatever he died of, it wasn't snake-bite.'

'Why?'

Em threw him a look of impatient contempt and said irritably: 'There is no need to treat me as though I were senile, Greg. You must know quite well that I have seen people die of snake-bite—and before you were born! It is, to say the least of it, an unpleasant death. Gilly didn't die that way; and if you want to know what I think, I think he had a heart attack; but because we saw the snake we jumped to the conclusion that it was snake-bite—and killed him.'

'By giving him that injection?'

Em nodded. 'Drew said it was probably the last straw, and he may have been right. If we'd left him alone he might have pulled through: people do survive heart attacks. But he didn't have a chance. It was seeing the snake—I didn't even think of it being anything else.'

'It wasn't your fault, Gran,' said Eden roughly. 'If you hadn't done it, someone else would. We all thought he'd been bitten. What did he die of, Greg?'

'Heart failure,' said Mr Gilbert calmly.

14

'What!' bellowed Hector, bounding to his feet and stuttering with wrath. 'Then what in thunder do you mean by interrogating us in this fashion? By God, Gilbert, I've a good mind to take this straight up to the Governor! You have the infernal impertinence to post one of your men in my house, and another to keep an eye on my wife and on poor Gilly's widow, when all the time Markham died a natural death from heart failure!'

Mr Gilbert waited patiently until he had quite finished, and for at least a minute afterwards, and his silence appeared to have a sobering effect upon Hector, for he said with considerably less truculence and a trace of uncertainty: 'Well? What have you got to say for yourself?'

'Quite a lot,' said Mr Gilbert gently. 'For one thing, most deaths are due to failure of the heart. What we do not know is *why* Markham's heart stopped beating. It is of course just possible that he was suffering from a heart attack when you found him. He drank fairly heavily—I'm sorry, Lisa, but that's true, isn't it?'

'Yes,' said Lisa. She had ceased to slump in a frightened heap in a corner of the sofa, and there was a look on her pale face that was curiously like eagerness. 'He always drank too much, but in the last few months he seemed to be much worse. I told him we couldn't afford it, and—and that it would kill him if he went on like this; but he only laughed.'

Greg nodded, but said: 'All the same, I don't believe he had a heart attack.'

'But surely—the doctors,' urged Mabel distressfully.

'The doctors say that his heart was flabby and full of blood, and that the symptoms described by Drew and Eden square with a heart attack. But they also square with something else—Acocanthera. *Msunguti.*'

151

Once again the words meant nothing whatever to Victoria, but in the sudden silence that followed them she became acutely aware that they held a meaning—and a singularly unpleasant one—for every other person in the room. Knowledge and shock—and wariness—was written plainly on six faces. Only Drew showed neither surprise nor wariness, but it was quite clear that he too knew the meaning of those two words.

Greg Gilbert looked round the room as though he expected someone to speak, but no one moved or spoke. They did not even look at one another. They looked at Greg as though they could not look away, and their bodies were still with a stillness that spoke of tensed muscles and held breath.

Greg said slowly: 'I see that you all know what that means. Except Miss Caryll; which is possibly a good thing for her. For your information, Miss Caryll, I am talking of arrow poison. Something that is only too easy to come by in this country and which produces death—by heart failure—in anything from twenty minutes to two hours. Unfortunately it also produces no detectable symptoms, so unless we can produce other evidence the autopsy verdict on Markham will have to stand as "heart failure due to unknown causes". A verdict with which I, personally, am not prepared to agree.'

'Why?' demanded Em harshly. 'He might well have had a heart attack. He'd been drinking far too much, and he was three parts drunk by lunch-time yesterday—the autopsy must have shown that, too! And he was too thin and too highly strung. He lived on his nerves. Why do you have to believe the worst, when there is no shadow of proof to support it?'

'But there is a shadow of proof,' said Greg gently. 'The fact that three things which might have proved that it was a heart attack are all missing. We had a squad of our men down at Crater Lake at first light, and they went all over the ground with a small tooth comb—and a magnet. But though they found the broken half of the needle, they didn't find the knife you slashed Markhams' arm with, or the bottle of iodine you doctored it with. Or the snake that may or may not have bitten him. Odd, to say the least of it.'

Ken Brandon leant forward, his hands gripping the arms of his chair so tightly that his knuckles showed white, and said in a high strained voice that had lost all traces of a drawl: 'Why do you keep harping on that snake? What would *you* have done with it? Put it in your pocket? I didn't even know that it would fall in the lake! It was a fluke, I tell you! I——'

Hector said brusquely: 'Shut up, Ken! I'm not letting you say anything more without a lawyer. And if the rest of you have any sense you won't answer any more questions either! If Gilbert is accusing one of us of murder—and it looks damned like it to me!—then he's got no right to expect us to answer questions until we have had legal advice.'

Greg surveyed him thoughtfully, and then turned to look at Em. 'That your opinion too, Em?'

'No, of course not,' said Em crossly. 'I'm no fool. Or at least, not so big a fool as Hector is making himself out to be. Lawyers! *Bah!* The only useful advice that any lawyer could give any of us is to speak the truth and stop behaving as though we had something to hide.'

'If that is to my address,' flared Hector, 'I have nothing to hide! *Nothing!* But I still say——'

'Be quiet, Hector.' Mabel had not raised her voice, but the three softly spoken words were drops of ice, and they froze Hector's torrent of words as ice will freeze Niagara.

No one had ever heard Mabel use that tone before; or had believed her capable of it. And Hector's instant and instinctive reaction to it was equally surprising. He stood for a moment with his mouth open, looking like some large and foolish fish, and then he shut it hurriedly and sat down, and thereafter only spoke when he was spoken to.

Mabel said composedly: 'You must forgive us, Greg. We are all a little upset. Of course we will answer any questions that we can. We all know that you are only here to help, and that it cannot be any less unpleasant for you than it is for us. I suppose you want to know all about the picnic? Why we went and how we went, and when. And what we ate, and things like that.'

Greg shook his head. 'I know that already. I heard it last night from both Drew and Eden. No. I want to know about the knife. And about the bottle of iodine. Em, you used the knife on Markham's arm, didn't you? Whose was it?'

Em met his gaze squarely and with composure, and replied without the least hesitation. 'My own.'

The two words were as coldly and quietly spoken as Mabel's had been, but they produced an even more startling effect. There was an audible and almost simultaneous gasp from several throats: a sound that might have been relief or apprehension or shock, and Eden spoke for the first time since they had entered the drawing-room:

'Gran, are you sure?'

'Of what?' enquired Em, continuing to look blandly at Greg Gilbert. 'That it was my knife, or that I know what I'm doing? The answer to both is "yes".'

For the first time that morning Mr Gilbert lost his calm. A flush of colour showed red in his tanned cheeks and his mouth and eyes opened in angry astonishment. 'Then why,' he demanded dangerously, 'did you say yesterday that you didn't know whose it was?'

'Did I?' enquired Em blandly. 'I can't have been thinking. We were all a bit——'

'*Upset!*' interrupted Greg savagely. 'So I have already heard. Now look here, Em, I'm not going to have any of this nonsense. That wasn't your knife, and you know it. Whose was it? You won't do any good to anyone by playing the heroine and telling lies to cover up for someone else.'

'You mean for Eden,' said Em calmly. 'But he never carries a knife. Only a silly little gold penknife arrangement on a chain that Alice gave him one Christmas. And I doubt if you'll find any bloodstains or arrow poison on that.'

For a moment it looked as though Mr Gilbert were about to lose his temper as explosively as Hector Brandon had done, but he controlled himself with a visible effort, and said quite quietly: 'I am not going to warn you of the consequences of deliberately obstructing the police, because you must be well aware of them. You also don't give a damn for the police or anyone else, do you? You're like too many of the Old Guard in that. You think that you can be a law unto yourselves. But that's where you're wrong. You can't have your cake and eat it too.'

He looked round at the ring of strained faces and added grimly: 'And that goes for all of you. You cannot let a murderer escape justice just because you happen to know him, or he is a relative or a friend. I do not believe that knife belonged to Lady Emily. The way I heard it, she asked for a knife and was handed one. Quite possibly she did not notice at the time who handed it to her, and she certainly told Stratton yesterday that she did not know whose it was. She has now, for reasons of her own, decided that it was hers. But there were half a dozen of you watching her, and one of you must remember where she was standing and who was next to her; and if the knife was not her own, one of you must have given it to her. That person had better speak up at once.'

No one spoke, and the silence lengthened out and filled with sullenness and strain and taut emotions, until suddenly and unexpectedly Eden laughed. It was an entirely genuine laugh and therefore the more startling. He leant back in his chair with his hands in his pockets, and said lightly:

' "Hands up the boy who broke that window!" It's no use Greg. This isn't the Fifth Form at St Custards, and you can't gate the entire class for a month if the culprit won't own up. Maybe that knife really was Gran's.'

'Maybe,' said Greg sceptically. 'Very well, then. If it was, let's have a description of it.'

'Certainly,' said Em briskly. 'It was a three-bladed knife that once belonged to Kendall. It had a horn handle with his initials cut on it, and the small blade had been broken off short. I often take it with me when I go picnicking or shooting. It's very useful. I had it in my pocket.'

'I see,' said Greg through shut teeth. 'Can you confirm that, Eden?'

Eden had been looking at his grandmother with an expression that was something between doubt and the effort to recall an elusive memory, and he started slightly on being addressed, and said hurriedly: 'Yes. Yes of course I can. It generally stays in the hall drawer. I've seen it a hundred times.'

'And it was the knife your grandmother cut Markham's arm with?'

Eden's face changed as though a mask had dropped over it, and he said in an entirely expressionless voice: 'I'm afraid I don't remember. If she says it was, then presumably it was. We were all looking at Gilly at the time.'

'Were you!' said Mr Gilbert grimly. And he turned again to Em: 'What did you do with it after that?'

'I put it down—or else I threw it on one side. I'm not sure.'

'And poured iodine on the wound? I'd like to hear about that.'

Em described the incident in some detail, but professed not to remember what she had done with the bottle.

'Then you didn't hand it back to Mrs Brandon?'

'I don't think so. I probably just dropped it too. It was empty.'

Mabel Brandon dabbed her eyes with a handkerchief and blew her nose with determination, and looking across at Em she smiled a little tremulously and said, 'Thank you, Em. I—I know you do remember, and that you're only saying that to keep me out of it. But I'm not going to hide behind you. She did give it back to me, Greg. I took it from her and put it down somewhere, and I didn't think of it again until Drew asked me what I'd done with it.'

Greg turned slowly and looked at Em, and it was noticeable that she returned his look with less assurance.

'Well, Em?' said Greg softly.

Em's mouth twisted into a wry and somewhat shamefaced smile.

'I'm sorry Greg. Yes, I knew Mabel had taken it. But I also know that she didn't kill Gilly, and I can't see that she need get mixed up in this horrible business just because she always carries around a bottle of iodine in case of accidents.'

'That,' said Greg, still softly, 'is the point. She always carries one, and everyone knows it. And that is why this may be a Mau Mau killing after all.'

'What!' The exclamation came loudly and simultaneously from half a dozen throats, and in a flash the atmosphere in the room changed as though a current of electricity had been switched off, and muscles that had been tense with strain and apprehension relaxed in sudden relief.

'I knew it!' cried Lisa; and began to sob loudly. 'I knew it would be all right!'

Em turned to gaze at her in disapproval, and observed coldly that she was glad that Lisa considered that everything was now all right: it was at least an original view of the case.

'I didn't mean Gilly being dead,' sobbed Lisa. 'Of course that's awful. It's just that I thought Greg might find out——'

'*Lisa!*' said Drew sharply and compellingly.

He had not spoken before, and his intervention checked Lisa, who gulped and turned to look at him.

'Whatever you were going to say—don't,' said Drew; and grinned at Greg Gilbert's furious face. 'Sorry, Greg, but I'm against shooting sitting birds. And in any case, from your last remark I gather we may all be out of the red, though I don't quite see how you can involve the Mau Mau in this one.'

Mr Gilbert said ominously: 'If you prompt anyone, or interrupt anyone again, Stratton, I shall get you ten days in the cells, if I get the sack for it!'

'And I'll go quiet,' promised Drew equably. 'What is this Mau Mau angle?'

'I should have thought it was obvious enough,' said Greg coldly. 'Hector is still doing a lot of useful interrogation work, and someone may have been laying for him—or for his wife or son. It would have been easy enough to substitute a solution of arrow poison for the iodine, and the next time any of them had a cut or a scratch Mabel would have doctored it from that bottle, and that would have been that. It's a possibility that we can't ignore.'

'And the knife?' enquired Em crisply.

'Same thing. Except—if it *was* your knife—it might conceivably have been a trap laid for either you or Eden.'

'No. Not for us,' said Em thoughtfully. 'The dogs. I have often used it to cauterize sores on the dogs, and it would have got one of them. Like—like Simba.'

Mabel said: 'So Gilly was killed by mistake. It should have been Hector or Ken—or me! Or one of Em's dogs.'

'Or the first person you happened to doctor with iodine or who happened to cut themselves on my knife—and who might just as well have been an African,' pointed out Em dryly. 'It sounds very farfetched to me, and it still doesn't explain the disappearance of the knife and the bottle. Where does that fit in?'

'It doesn't,' confessed Greg. 'It doesn't even fit in with my own theory of the crime.'

'And what is your theory? Or do you prefer to keep us in the dark?' enquired Em acidly.

Greg looked meditatively at the carpet for a minute or two without speaking, and then allowed his gaze to travel with deliberation along the half circle of intent faces that watched him so anxiously. And it is doubtful if he missed even the smallest change in any one of them.

He said slowly: 'No. There is no reason why I should not tell you, for although I believe that I am right, I can't prove it. I think that Gilly Markham died from the effects of arrow poison, and that his murder was carefully planned in advance. Everyone here, and everyone in the Rift for that matter, knew that he drank too much and could be trusted to drink too much even at a picnic, provided the drink was there; which it was. I believe that someone took a dead puff adder to Crater Lake yesterday, and sometime during the afternoon, while Gilly was asleep, placed it beside him and gave him a jab in the arm with some sort of pronged instrument that had been liberally coated with arrow poison. Something that would leave a wound similar to the mark of a snake's fangs.'

Lisa was the first person to speak. She said in a strained voice that was barely a whisper: 'But—why that way? The snake?'

'Because although arrow poison is not detectable in an autopsy, there might well have been some of it left outside the wound. Enough to prove that it had been used. But the first thing anyone does when dealing with a snake-bite is to make a deep cut on or just above it. That's why it had to be a snake; because the murderer could count on someone removing the evidence in double quick time. It would not matter who did it as long as it was done—and of course it was done. That disposed of any superfluous poison, and the snake was an equally easy bet. No one stops to see if a snake is alive if it is found lying curled up in a life-like attitude beside a sleeping person. They take a bash at it with the first thing that comes handy, and the blows would have made it appear to be moving. Also, no one is going to pay very close attention to it when there is a dying man to attend to. So you see, it would have been fairly foolproof.'

'But you said it could have been the knife,' whispered Lisa. 'Or the iodine. You *said* so!'

'It could have been. Because those two things have inexplicably disappeared. But it is far more likely that the poison was administered at least half an hour before either of those things were used. Acocanthera frequently produces vomiting, and your husband had been sick. He was also found in a state of coma just after three-thirty.'

Mabel's hands twisted together against the skirt of her crumpled cotton frock, and she said distressfully: 'Oh no!—Oh, I do hope not! I mean—I heard him. Being sick. If I had gone to him at once I might have been able to do something. But I thought—well, he *had* had too much to drink, and I thought it would be better to keep away. If *only* I had gone!'

'It wouldn't have done any good. Not if my theory is correct. There's no antidote.'

'But you can't be right!' said Mabel, suddenly sitting bolt upright. 'No, of course you can't be. You can't jab someone in the arm without waking them up. He would have cried out. I should have heard him. And,' she concluded triumphantly, 'I didn't! I didn't hear a *sound,* and neither did Em. Did you, Em?'

'I'm afraid I was asleep,' confessed Em reluctantly. 'I didn't even hear him being sick, and I certainly wouldn't have gone to him if I had.'

Greg said: 'Markham was sleeping off a fairly outsize dose of alcohol; and before the discovery of anaesthetics it was the accepted thing to give a man half a bottle of whisky to drink before an operation or an amputation—to deaden the pain. If the jab was a quick one it might have done no more than jerk him awake for a few seconds, and the chances are that he would have dozed off again at once. What is it, Miss Caryll?'

'N-nothing,' stammered Victoria, startled. 'I d-didn't say anything.'

'But you thought of something, didn't you?'

'Yes. I—it was nothing, really. It was only that while I was standing by the lake yesterday I heard someone snoring, and then they made a noise as though they had been woken up suddenly. You know. A—a sort of snort. I thought it was Gil—Mr Markham. But after a bit the snoring started again.'

'Hmm,' said Greg. 'What time was that?'

'I've no idea. Somewhere between half-past two and three I suppose.'

Greg turned to Mabel and asked her if she had also heard such a sound, and Mabel, looking a trifle conscience-striken, admitted to having dozed, though she had been woken later by hearing Gilly retching. 'But I didn't do anything about it. I remember thinking *"Really!* Poor Lisa." Or something like that, and the next thing I remember was Hector telling me to wake up because it was time we were going.'

'Hmm,' said Greg again, and was silent for so long that the tension became too much for Ken Brandon. His control cracked under the strain of that silence and his voice cracked with it:

'It's no good looking at me! I didn't go near him. I swear I didn't! I didn't even touch him. None of us did—only Stratton and Lady Emily. I'm not going to sit here and be accused of—of things, just because I threw away a dead snake! Dad was quite right. You haven't any right to do this. We aren't under arrest, and I'm going!'

He stood up clenching and unclenching his hands, and looking, for all his nineteen years, less like an Angry Young Man than a small boy who has flown into a temper to hide his fright.

'Oh *no,* Kennie darling!' moaned Mabel, wringing her hands. *'Don't* talk like that. Of course you didn't go near Gilly, darling. Greg knows that. We all know it. Stay here, darling. *Please!'*

Greg said patiently: 'Sit down, Ken. You're only making an ass of yourself, and I haven't accused anyone of anything.'

'Yet!' mimicked Ken savagely. 'That's what you said before, isn't it? *"Yet!"* But you will, won't you? Even though you haven't a shred of evidence! Even though you admit yourself that Gilly may have died of a heart attack. And what do you base your precious theory

on? The fact that a knife and an empty bottle have been lost or mislaid. Why, they're probably both still there, trodden into the grass by your flat-footed, bone-headed askaris!'

'Oh no, Kennie. Don't, dear,' sobbed Mabel in a monotonous moaning whisper. But Ken Brandon was beyond listening to reason or his mother's pleas, and the words poured out of him in a childish spate of nervous rage:

'What the hell does it matter if they aren't found? You've as good as admitted that there's nothing wrong with either of them, haven't you? *Haven't you?* And that if Gilly was poisoned, it was done half an hour before anyone used the knife or the iodine on him. And yet you can produce a footling thing like that and call it evidence of murder! If that's all the evidence you've got, then you haven't got a case at all. Not a shadow of a case!—and no right in the world to haul us in here and talk like this to us.'

He paused for breath, and Greg said mildly:

'I told you that the disappearance of those two things didn't square with any theory. But that is why I am interested in them: or rather, in why someone thought fit to remove them, and is now lying about it. There must be a reason for that, and it is my guess that whoever made away with them suspected murder—and the murderer—and having a shrewd idea as to how it had been done, jumped to the same conclusion that both Stratton and Lady Emily arrived at: that if it was Acocanthera, it was either on the knife or in the iodine bottle—and therefore hid them. But if it *was* murder, then the one person who would *not* have done that is the murderer; because such an action could only lead to suspicion of murder in what might possibly have passed as death from snake-bite, or, if questions were asked and an autopsy performed, from a heart attack due to heavy drinking. I am quite sure in my own mind that there was nothing wrong with either the knife or the iodine, and when we eventually find them we shall be able to prove it. That is why I am asking whoever made away with them to own up to it now. It must be one of you, and as it cannot possibly be the murderer, all that you are being asked to do is to clear yourself. And at the same time to help clear whoever it was that you suspected of doctoring either of those two things.'

Once again there was a strained silence in the room when he had finished speaking, but if anyone had intended to admit responsibility they were forestalled by Ken Brandon, who said loudly and scornfully:

'Oh no, you're not! You're not asking anything of the sort. We're not all fools, though you're treating us as though we were. What you're trying to do is to get one of us to implicate someone else. That's it, isn't it? Maybe there wasn't anything wrong with that knife or the iodine. But someone thought there might be, and they must have had a damned good reason for thinking it. You'd want to know that reason, wouldn't you? Well we're not falling for that one. You can do your own dirty work! I'm going, for one. Come on, Mother, let's get out of here.'

Mabel stood up, pale and trembling, and behind her Hector too had risen; but slowly and reluctantly.

Mr Gilbert moved deliberately and without haste, and placed himself between Ken and the door. He said quietly: 'I'm sorry, Ken, but you can't go just yet. Don't make this any more unpleasant than it need be. Because if you try and leave, I shall have to put you under arrest for obstructing the police.'

'*Try* and leave? I'm going to do more than try! I'm not putting up with this any longer, and that's all there is to it. And just *you* try and stop me!'

He whirled around and made a dive for the open window, and Drew rose swiftly and hit him once and scientifically.

Ken Brandon crumpled at the knees and collapsed upon the floor, his nose bleeding profusely and a foolish smile fixed upon his face. And peace reigned.

'Oh, thank you, Drew!' gasped Mabel with real gratitude.

The remainder of the morning was as unenjoyable as the beginning, though less full of unpleasant surprises, and although Mr
Gilbert and his entourage had departed shortly before one, the
respite had been brief, for they had returned an hour and a half
later.

This time the two C.I.D. officers as well as Mr Gilbert faced
their audience, while the unobtrusive gentleman in the brown suit
sat behind them, and judging from the soft and ceaseless scratching
of pen upon paper, occupied himself in taking down their replies
verbatim and in shorthand.

The questions that afternoon were mainly concerned with movements. They appeared to be merely routine ones, and often pointless, but one thing at least emerged from them. No one could produce an alibi that covered the period of time in which Gilly
Markham could have been murdered, for the entire party, with the
exception of Em and Mabel, had separated after luncheon. And
even Em and Mabel could not alibi each other, since both at different times had vanished into the bushes for, as Em observed frostily,
'obvious reasons', and later both had slept.

Eden and Lisa, who had departed together, had quarrelled and
separated. Not that either admitted to quarrelling, but it took very
little intuition on anyone's part to fill in the gap in their respective
stories. Lisa said she had 'just strolled about', and Eden said he had
sat on a fallen trunk and 'thought he might have dozed'.

Ken Brandon asserted that he had left the crater to explore the
far side of it, and had only returned just before the party reassem-
bled, while Hector said that he had spent the best part of an hour
searching among the rocks to see if he could pick up the track of the
leopard whose pug marks they had seen at the lake edge.

Drew also had left the crater and gone for a walk, and Victoria, answering endless questions as to the sounds she professed to have heard that afternoon, could only insist that she had seen no one for half an hour after his departure, and thought that they might have been caused by some animal.

No one appeared to have paid much attention to time until well after three o'clock, and though Greg went over and over the details of that last twenty-five minutes of Gilly's life, it had proved impossible to build up an accurate picture of exactly where everyone had stood, or who had been standing next to whom, for only Em, Victoria and Drew had remained in approximately the same position throughout, and they and everyone else had been far too intent on the life-and-death drama that was taking place under their eyes to note the movements or expressions of other people.

'Can't you understand?' said Em, her voice flat with exhaustion. 'He was dying! And we knew he was dying. It never occurred to any of us that it was murder. Why should it? Perhaps if it had we would have watched each other instead of him. But it didn't.'

'Oh, yes it did!' Greg contradicted grimly. 'Three of you at least thought that it might be murder. Otherwise Stratton would not have hunted for that broken needle, or Mrs Markham refused to drink the brandy. Even you knew that something was wrong!'

Em said wearily: 'But I didn't think of murder until much later. Not until Drew started asking questions about the knife and said we must go back and look for it. I'd thought it was a heart attack, and that I'd killed him.'

'I wasn't thinking of you when I said "three people". The third was whoever removed the knife and the iodine bottle. Or if two people were involved in that, then that makes it four. Four people out of seven suspected that Markham had been murdered, and I'd like to know why. Perhaps you can give me your reasons, Mrs Markham? Why did you think that your husband might have been murdered?'

Lisa clutched the arms of her chair and half rose from it. 'I didn't! You can't say I did. You're just trying to get me to admit things I never said. You're twisting things! I—I'd seen Gilly die. Drew gave him brandy, and he died. I wasn't thinking straight. I didn't mean it that way. I only didn't want to drink because—because Gilly had drunk from it—and—and died.'

Greg shrugged his shoulders, and somewhat unexpectedly did not press the question. He turned instead to Drew and demanded his reasons for suspecting murder, but was interrupted by Eden who observed with some asperity that considering Drew had, to his certain knowledge, already answered that question at length on the previous night, and had, moreover, been asked to sign a typed copy of his statement, it appeared to him to be a pointless question and a waste of time.

'I never ask pointless questions,' said Mr Gilbert without heat. 'Well, Drew?'

Drew said, 'I knew it couldn't be snake-bite for the same reasons that Em gave you. I've seen men die that way. I've also twice seen a man die from the effects of a poisoned arrow, and as I did not know that the symptoms of heart attack were similar, heart did not occur to me, but *msunguti* did. Gilly had been perfectly well, though a bit tight, an hour earlier, and now he was dying. That was all there was to it.'

'Thank you,' said Greg briefly.

The remainder of the afternoon was merely a repetition of the beginning, with the sole difference that the questions were asked again, and answered, individually and behind the closed door of the dining-room.

It was well after five when Greg had finished with Victoria, who had been questioned last. He looked tired and grim and driven, for excepting only Victoria, these were all his personal friends: people he had known for years, and had dined with and danced with, and suffered with during the harsh years of the Emergency. But he faced them now with the bleak impersonal gaze of a stranger, and his voice was as detached and unfriendly as his eyes:

'I shall probably have to see you all again during the next few days, and until this business is settled I'd be grateful if you'd arrange not to be out, or anywhere where I can't get in touch with you at short notice.'

And then he had gone.

'Well thank goodness that's over!' said Em with a gusty sigh. 'And at least he isn't likely to be back tomorrow, which means that with luck we should have one peaceful day.'

But the following day could hardly have been termed peaceful.

Gilly's body had been brought back for burial, and having notified Mr Gilbert of their intentions, they had all attended the funeral, which had been marred by the behaviour of Lisa and, in a lesser degree, Ken Brandon. Lisa had gone off into screaming, shrieking hysterics and had to be forcibly removed, and Ken Brandon had quietly and unobtrusively fainted.

Drew had caught him as he fell, and had driven him back to *Flamingo,* together with Mabel. And Em, Eden, Hector and Victoria had returned some twenty minutes later, with the information that Lisa was back in her own bungalow under the care of the doctor's wife, and had been given a strong injection of morphia.

'What was it all about?' demanded Mabel, pallid and shivering. 'You—you don't think she can possibly have . . . No! No, of course not! One should not even *think* such things!'

'That Lisa might have done it?' supplied Drew. 'Who is to say what anyone else is capable of under certain pressures? Or even where one's own breaking point lies? But personally I'd cross Lisa off any list of suspects, because unless she's a remarkably good actress, that performance of hers at Crater Lake was genuine. She thought someone had murdered her husband all right, whatever she says now, and she thought the stuff might be in the brandy. Q.E.D. —she didn't do the job herself!'

'My dear Drew,' said Em with asperity, *'all* women are excellent actresses when circumstances force them to it; and the sooner men realize that, the better! But of course Lisa did not murder her husband—though I have no doubt there were times when she wanted to. There were times when I myself felt like it, and I, let me point out, was not compelled to put up with Gilly's company as Lisa was. She could quite possibly have been another Mrs Thompson. Someone who might talk or dream about doing away with an unwanted husband, in the way a child will invent long and improbable stories, but who would never really *mean* it.'

Drew said softly: 'They hanged Mrs Thompson.'

He refused an invitation to stay to luncheon, and left, followed shortly afterwards by the Brandons; and Em, watching them go, had expressed a hope that they—and the police—would stay away from *Flamingo* for at least a week.

But it was a hope that was not to be realized.

Eden and Victoria had spent the afternoon out on the lake, and had returned in the peaceful, pearl-pink evening to find both Drew and the Brandons in the drawing-room again, and the house once more full of policemen. For Kamau, the lover of Wambui, had been found.

'It was the dogs,' said Em looking oddly shrunken in the depths of the big wing-chair, and hugging a woollen shawl about her shoulders as though she were cold. 'They've been kept shut up for days and only taken out on a leash, because of Lisa's bitch. But I—I couldn't keep them shut up for ever, could I? I suppose they smelt him . . .'

It had happened barely half an hour after Eden and Victoria had left. Em had heard the barking and had gone out with a whip and tried to beat them off. The dog boy had run out with the leashes, and Em had sent him for the askaris, and having left them on guard had returned to the house and telephoned Greg.

Mr Gilbert and several policemen had arrived within the hour, and what the ants had left of Kamau had been disinterred from a shallow grave among the charcoal kilns.

Greg's temper had not been improved by the discovery that Eden was out in the motor launch and could not be reached, and he had sent for the Brandons and for Drew, who had been questioned severally and separately as to their movements on the night of Kamau's disappearance.

'But why you and the Brandons?' demanded Victoria of Drew.

She had spent an unnerving half-hour in the dining-room answering endless questions, and had come out into the twilit verandah to discover Drew Stratton leaning against one of the creeper-covered pillars and smoking a cigarette.

Drew said sombrely: 'Because whoever killed Kamau presumably killed Alice DeBrett—and then killed Kamau because he had not only seen it done, but had talked about it.'

Victoria said in a small, shaken voice: 'But—but that's just what makes it so pointless. It would have been different if he'd been killed to stop him talking. But he'd talked already. He said it was Aunt Em!'

'I know. But we didn't hear that until the next day, did we? And by that time he was dead. If his girlfriend had only come clean straight away, instead of pretending that he'd merely hinted at knowing something, he might still be alive—though I doubt it. As it was, someone evidently thought it was worth while stopping his mouth permanently, and if it hadn't been for the fact that by a fluke, and because he was no mean pianist, Gilly was able to blow a hole through Wambui's story, your aunt would have been left in a very sticky position. She won't be in too good a one now. Not now that Gilly is dead.'

'Why not?' demanded Victoria anxiously.

'Because Gilly giving evidence on the one subject that he was really at home in would have been able to convince any jury that he knew what he was talking about. But the same evidence, given at second hand by Greg, isn't going to sound nearly so convincing. And now there's this business of Kamau. God, what a mess!'

Victoria said: 'But they couldn't think Aunt Em had killed Kamau! No one could!'

'Why not?' enquired Drew impatiently. 'She had the best opportunity of anyone. She was meeting him that night by the gate into the shamba.'

'How can you say that!' blazed Victoria, stiff with anger. 'You haven't any right to! You're just being s-stupid and—and——'

'*Shh!*' said Drew with the flicker of a grin. 'There's no need to fly off the handle. You're not looking at this from the police viewpoint, which is purely concerned with hard facts and is not swayed—or is trying not to be—by the personal angle. You are only thinking of your aunt as someone you know and are fond of. But they have got to think of her as "X", who allied to B, or minus Z, may equal Y.'

Victoria said scornfully: 'Then they're just being stupid too! Suppose she did meet Kamau that night, and kill him? All right, how did she carry him from the gate right up to the place where they found him? And when she got him there, how did she manage to dig a grave and bury him? She's over seventy!'

'Seventy-two, I believe—and as strong as a cart-horse. But that's beside the point. You're not using your head, Victoria. If Em had done it she wouldn't have needed to kill him by the gate. She could have invented a dozen excuses to get him to walk with her to the kilns, and dealt with him on the spot. And she wouldn't have needed to dig a grave. There were several there already. It must have been only too easy to topple a body into one of those trenches and cover it up with some of the loose earth that was lying around, and the fumes from the charcoal kilns would have interfered with the scent if tracker dogs were used.'

'But it was Aunt Em's dogs who found him!'

'Ah, that was different. He'd been underground for quite a few days by then.'

Victoria flinched, and Drew said quickly: 'I'm sorry. This is a beastly business for all of us, but the rest of us have at least seen or heard of worse things in our day. The Emergency wasn't a picnic!— though now I come to think of it, that's an unfortunate simile, isn't it? But you've been pitchforked into this from a safe and orderly existence, and it must be pretty unnerving for you. Wishing you hadn't come?'

'No—o,' said Victoria hesitantly. 'I don't think I could ever wish I hadn't come back to Kenya. But I wish I hadn't . . .'

She did not complete the sentence, but came to lean on the verandah rail beside him, looking out into the deepening dusk. There was something about Drew's mere physical presence that was reassuring, and as long as he was here the house seemed less frightening. She turned to look at him and said abruptly:

'Are you staying here tonight?'

'Yes. Greg wants all his suspects under one roof. Or rather, under two: the Brandons are reluctantly parking out at Lisa's. Just as well really, as he seems to have roped in our respective house servants for questioning, and turned all our labour lines into the nearest thing to a concentration camp that I've seen outside one.'

'Then he does think it may possibly be an African after all?'

'Of course he does. He's no fool. They've been getting a far stiffer grilling than we have. You mustn't think that just because Greg has been hauling us over the coals that he hasn't had a squad of his boys doing exactly the same thing to every single African who works on this estate, or on mine or Hector's. There were even two of them who might have pulled off that picnic business. Zach and Samuel were actually down in the crater. And there is still "General Africa"—who is still at large and still unidentified, and who may yet turn out to be the snake in the grass. I don't believe that Greg has lost sight of that possibility for a moment. In fact he's quite capable of making all this display of suspecting one of us with the sole object of confusing the issue and making it look as though the enquiries in the labour lines are merely routine, and that it is the Bwanas who are really under suspicion.'

Victoria gave a little sigh that was partly relief and partly weariness. 'I didn't think of that. You must be right. After all, we couldn't *really* be suspects. Not you or the Brandons, anyway.'

'Why not? We all happened to be here or hereabouts on the night Mrs DeBrett was killed. *And* on the night that Kamau disappeared.'

'But the Brandons weren't even here then!'

'No. But they called at the Markhams' bungalow that evening. Gilly was out, but Lisa had just got back from here, and it seems that she spilt the works. Which means that any one of them could have got over here in time to head off Kamau. It's no distance at all by the short cut between *Flamingo* and *Brandonmead,* and there was a moon that night.'

Victoria said: 'But they wouldn't have got him to go with them. You said that Aunt Em could have made an excuse to get him to walk to the kilns, but he might not have gone with one of the Brandons.'

'Ever noticed that there's a trolley arrangement that runs from the shamba to the road, and passes within a few yards of the kilns? No one would have needed to do any carrying of corpses. Even you could have managed it without much difficulty.'

'*Me!* But——'

'No, I'm not accusing you of running amok with a hatchet, so there's no need to glare at me. Though I daresay Greg has had to consider that possibility.'

'What possibility?'

'That you and Eden might have cooked this up between you.'

Victoria looked at him, meeting his bland blue gaze thoughtfully and without anger. Studying his face in the dusk as if it had been a letter held up for her to read: a very important letter.

She said at last: 'And what do you think?'

'Does it matter?'

Victoria did not answer, and presently Drew said slowly and as though he were thinking aloud:

'People who are desperately and deeply in love are probably capable of anything. There are endless examples in history and the newspapers to prove that love can be a debasing passion as well as the most ennobling one; and a stronger and more relentless force than either ambition or hate, because those can be cold-blooded things, but love is always a hot-blooded one. Men and women have died for it—or for the loss of it. They have committed crimes for it and given up thrones for it, started wars, deserted their families, betrayed their countries, stolen, lied and murdered for it. And they will probably go on doing so until the end of time!'

He stubbed out his cigarette against the rail and dropped it among the geraniums, and after a moment or two Victoria said meditatively and without turning her head:

'And you think I might be—capable of anything?'

Drew gave an odd, curt laugh. 'Not of murder. Or even of conniving at it. But of covering up for someone you were in love with, or even very fond of, yes.'

'Even if I knew they had committed a murder? A horrible murder?'

'No. Because you would never love anyone like that.'

Victoria turned to look at him. The last of the daylight was running out with the swiftness of sand in an hour glass, and now it was so dark that she could no longer see the lines in his face.

She said: 'Then at least you don't believe that Eden could have done it.'

'I didn't say that. For all I know, he may have done it; though I shouldn't say it was in the least likely. But then you aren't in love with Eden.'

Victoria did not say anything, but she did not turn away, and Drew said: 'Are you.'

It was an affirmation rather than a question, and as she still did not speak he took her chin in his hand, as he had done once before.

Victoria stood quite still, aware of a crisis in her life: of having reached the end of a road—or perhaps the beginning of one. And then a door at the far end of the verandah opened and the shadows retreated before a flood of warm amber light, and it was no longer dusk, but night.

Drew's hand dropped and he turned unhurriedly:

'Hullo, Eden. Has Greg finished with you at last? How much longer is he likely to be around?'

'God knows,' said Eden shortly. 'What on earth are you two doing out here in the dark?'

'Talking,' said Drew pleasantly. 'Any objection?'

'No, of course not! But there are drinks in the drawing-room if you want one. I've sent Gran to bed.'

'Did she go?'

'Yes, surprisingly enough. She's going to be the next person to have a heart attack if we don't watch it.'

'A genuine one?' enquired Drew. 'Or one of the kind that hit Gilly?'

'Oh, for Pete's sake!' said Eden angrily, and turning his back on Drew he took Victoria's arm. 'Come on, Vicky darling. You must be cold. Come and have a glass of sherry. Or let's finish off the vodka and get really tight.'

They found Mabel in the drawing-room, sipping a brandy and soda and watching the door. Hector, accompanied by Bill Hennessy, had returned to *Brandonmead* to collect various necessities for a night's stay at the Markham's bungalow, but Ken was still being questioned, and Mabel would not leave without him.

'What *are* they doing with Kennie?' she demanded unhappily. 'He's been in there for hours! They must know that he can't know anything at all about this. It isn't kind of Greg—and after all the years we've known him! Drew, don't you think you could go and tell him that we're all very tired, and couldn't he let us go home?'

'No, Mabel. I couldn't,' said Drew firmly, collecting himself a stiff whisky and soda and sinking into an arm-chair. 'It would not only be a pure waste of time, but I have no desire to receive a blistering snub. He'll stop when he feels like it, or when he's got what he wants, and not before.'

'But we shall all be here tomorrow, and the next day.'

'We hope,' said Drew dryly. 'Well, here's to crime.'

He lifted his glass and drank deeply, and Eden said furiously: '*Must* you make a joke of it?'

'Sorry,' said Drew mildly.

But Eden refused to be placated. His handsome face was taut with strain and his voice was rough with fatigue, anxiety and anger: 'In the present circumstances, that sort of remark is in bloody bad taste, besides being entirely un-funny!'

Drew raised his eyebrows and pulled a faint grimace, but forebore to take offence. He said amiably: 'You're quite right. I can't have been thinking. My apologies. Have an olive, Mabel; and stop watching that door. Ken will be along any minute now. Hullo, here's another car. Who do you suppose this is? the D.C.?'

But it was only Hector, returning from *Brandonmead* with an assortment of pyjamas, tooth brushes and bedroom slippers. He accepted a drink, and after a nervous glance at his wife said in a subdued voice that contained no echo of his former booming tones: 'Is Kennie still there? They're keeping him a long time. Surely they know the boy isn't feeling fit. Never known him to pass out like that before. He ought to be in bed, not being badgered with silly questions.'

'Then why don't you put a stop to it?' demanded Mabel, wavering on the verge of tears. 'You're his father. They're bullying him: I know they are. Oh, if *only* he'd never met her! Why did this have to happen just when it seemed that everything was going to be peaceful and happy again? I'll never forgive Greg for this—never!'

Hector said uncomfortably: 'He's only doing his duty, dear. Why don't you come over to Lisa's with me now? She won't have given any orders about supper, so we'd better go and see about it.'

Mabel burst into tears and said wildly that it was just like a man to think of his own stomach before the welfare of his son, and Drew got up and left the room.

He returned a few minutes later, looking particularly wooden and accompanied by a white and subdued Ken Brandon, and the reunited family removed themselves into the night.

'How did you work that?' enquired Eden with grudging respect.

'Stuck my neck out,' said Drew morosely, 'and was duly executed.' He drew his index finger across his throat in a brief expressive gesture. 'Greg is in no very pleasant temper, but at least it was preferable to having Mabel going on a crying jag.'

Mr Gilbert appeared in the drawing-room on the heels of this remark, and informed them curtly that he was leaving, but would be back at nine o'clock on the following morning. He would be obliged if they would all be in the house and available at that hour, and he was leaving Bill Hennessy to see to it.

He had refused a drink, and had left; and they had dined frugally on soup and sandwiches, for the majority of the house servants had spent the day being questioned at police headquarters, and Zacharia and Thuku, together with the cook, were being kept there overnight.

Victoria had retired to bed immediately afterwards, and had been accompanied to the door of her room by Eden. He had not searched her room as Drew had done, but he had asked her if she had any aspirins, and on hearing that she had, advised her to take two and get a good night's rest. And then he had kissed her. Not lightly, as Drew had done, but hard and hungrily, holding her close.

She had made no attempt to avoid his embrace; but neither had she returned it. And when he released her at last she had put up a hand and touched his cheek in a fleeting caress that was purely maternal, and there was relief and pity and sadness in her smile; as though she had been a much older woman who has found a page of a forgotten love letter, and is smiling a little ruefully at herself because she cannot remember the name of the boy who wrote it.

Mr Gilbert was not only true to his word, but regrettably punctual. It was exactly one minute past nine, and breakfast was still in progress, when the now familiar squad of police and C.I.D. men arrived at *Flamingo*.

But this time the proceedings were brief. Typewritten copies of statements made on the previous day were produced and they were asked to sign them, and that being done Mr Stratton and the Brandons were curtly informed that they could return to their own houses, with the proviso that they must stay within reach of a telephone and not leave the Rift until further notice.

'And that means that you can't suddenly decide to go off on safari to the Northern Frontier, Stratton. Or take a holiday to Malindi, Mrs Brandon. I want you where I can get in touch with you at short notice. I hope that is quite clear.'

'Painfully, thank you,' said Drew.

'Are we under arrest?' demanded Hector, who appeared to have recovered some of his former truculence.

Greg favoured him with a bleak stare and said: 'No,' and went away, armed with a stop watch and a pair of binoculars, to head what appeared to be a conducted tour of the grounds and the short cut between *Flamingo* and *Brandonmead*.

It had been decided after some discussion that Mabel would remain with Lisa for a few days, and Eden had escorted her back to the Markhams' bungalow. Em had gone off to deal with some domestic crisis, pausing only to say morosely: 'I won't ask you to stay to luncheon, Drew, because there probably won't be any. But you should find some beer in the dining-room—if the C.I.D. haven't removed it for analysis to make quite sure we haven't added arsenic to it!'

The door slammed behind her, and Drew laughed. But Victoria

did not. Victoria was standing by the bow window, watching Eden and Mabel Brandon as they walked away down the narrow dusty path that led across the garden towards the plumbago hedge and the Markham's bungalow, and presently Drew said: 'What are you thinking about?'

He had spoken very quietly, as though he did not wish to break her train of thought, and Victoria answered him as quietly:

'Eden.'

A bee flew into the room and buzzed about it, and when it flew out again into the sunlight the room seemed strangely silent.

Victoria said, still looking out the window: 'You said last night that Eden might have killed his wife; and Kamau. You don't really think that, do you?'

'No. In fact I should say that the betting is about a hundred to one against, despite the fact that the first question that is asked in a murder case is *cui bono?*—who benefits? and, financially at least, Eden does. But then I've known him, on and off, for a good many years, and this affair doesn't fit in with anything I know about him. Eden isn't a fool. He's got plenty of intelligence, and despite all that sunny surface charm, a cool brain and more stubborn determination than most people would give him credit for. He would have known quite well, for instance, that he was bound to be the number one suspect; and why. And that being so he would, if he were guilty, have provided himself with a reasonably cast-iron alibi. Whoever murdered Alice DeBrett planned it pretty carefully—the fact that Em's red trousers were stolen is proof enough of that!—and only someone who did not need an alibi would have failed to provide one. That, to my mind—and I think, to Greg's—washes Eden out. But I don't know what it leaves us with.'

Victoria said: 'Aunt Em, Mrs Markham, the Brandons, "General Africa"—and you.'

Drew laughed: a laugh that was singularly devoid of amusement. He said: 'I asked for that one, didn't I?'

And then the door opened and Em was back, looking tired and cross and harried, and addressing someone in the hall in vituperative Swahili.

She broke off on seeing Drew and Victoria, and shutting the door with a defiant bang, sank gratefully into the depths of the wing-chair and observed that had she but died an hour before this chance, she had lived a blessed time.

Drew turned his head rather quickly and looked at her with

frowning intentness, his blue eyes narrowed and his brows making a straight line across his forehead, as though he were trying to recall some tag-end of memory. Victoria, who had forgotten any Swahili she had ever known, said: 'Who were you talking to, Aunt Em?'

'Myself,' said Em. 'It's the privilege of the aged.'

'In Swahili?' enquired Victoria with a smile.

'Oh, that. That was only Samuel: Hector's gun-bearer-cum-driver-cum-general factotum. I found him wandering round the hall, hunting for Mabel's knitting bag that he seems to think she left here. I told him that it wouldn't be here, it would be over at Lisa's if anywhere. He must have misunderstood her. What are you scowling about, Drew?'

'Hmm?' said Drew in a preoccupied voice. 'Oh—nothing much. Just an idea. I must go. Thanks for your enforced hospitality, Em.'

He walked to the door, opened it, and then hesitated as though he were reluctant to leave, and turned to look back at them, the frown still in his eyes and a strange unreadable look on his face that was oddly disturbing. As though he were puzzled and disbelieving—and afraid.

He stood there for at least a minute, looking from one to the other of them; and then he had shrugged his shoulders and gone away without saying anything, and they heard his car start up and purr away down the drive.

Em said uneasily: 'Something's worrying Drew. I wonder— Oh, well, I suppose this wretched business is getting us all down.'

It was shortly after his departure that they heard Greg's car drive away, but it was almost two o'clock by the time Eden returned. He had replied to Em's questions in monosyllables, been uncommunicative on the subject of Lisa, and refusing the dishes that Zacharia proffered, had lunched frugally off a biscuit and several cups of black coffee.

Em had retired to her room to rest, having advised Victoria to do the same. But Victoria had seldom felt less like resting, and she had wandered into the drawing-room, and sitting down at the piano had played scraps of tunes: playing to keep herself from thinking, not of the frightening happenings of the last week, but of the past and her own personal problems. But when she lifted her hands from the keys the thoughts were there waiting for her, and even her hands betrayed her, for they turned from Bach and Debussy to the trite, sweet sentimental melodies of songs that she had once danced to with Eden: 'Some Enchanted Evening' . . . 'La Vie en Rose' . . .

'Hullo, Young Lovers' . . . And an older tune that an older genera-tion had danced to in the days before the war, and that Eden had taken a fancy to. *I get along without you very well . . .*

> *I get along without you very well;*
> *Of course I do.*
> *Except perhaps in spring——*

But she had not got along without him very well. Not in spring or summer, autumn or winter . . .

> *'What a fool am I . . . !'*

Her fingers stumbled on the yellowed keys in a jarring discord, for she had not heard Eden enter and she started violently when he touched her; spinning round on the piano stool so that she was in his arms.

He had not meant to touch her. He had been through a horrible and harrowing week, and had endured a recent interview with Lisa Markham that he did not want to think of ever again—and knew that he would never forget. He supposed that he deserved it, al-though all the initial advances had been made by her, and he had thought that she knew the rules and would keep to them. But it had been a mistake from the beginning, and now that he had seen Victo-ria again, it was a calamity.

He had not expected to see Victoria again, or wanted to. But he had not been able to protest against her coming, because to do so might have led to questions, and he had never discussed Victoria with either Alice or Em, and he would not do so now. He had tried to shut Victoria out of his mind and his heart, but it had not been easy. That sentimental song of the 'thirties, that they had discovered and played light-heartedly in the sober post-war years, had indeed proved prophetic. *I get along without you very well—of course I do— except perhaps in spring* . . . Or when a tune was played to which they had once danced. Or a girl wore a yellow dress. Or when a rose, or a scent, or a sound recalled Victoria . . .

And then Em had sent for her, and he had not had the moral courage to explain to Em why she must not come; though knowing that he would see her again he had realized at last, and with blinding clarity, that neither Alice nor any of the shallow, foolish affairs with which he had attempted to fill the void in his heart meant anything to him; that only Victoria mattered, and despite any barrier of blood he must have her. That he would risk anything to have her! If only he were free——

Victoria had arrived at *Flamingo,* and Alice was dead. He was free. But he knew that he must behave circumspectly. He could not court another woman, even one to whom he had once been engaged, within a few days or even a few months of his wife's death. He would have to wait. He would persuade Em to send him to Rumuruti, and when enough time had elapsed to blur the raw memory of Alice's death he would come back and ask Victoria to marry him, and take her away from the Rift and all its tragic associations until people had forgotten. Until then he would not even touch her again.

But he had walked into the drawing-room and found her playing the tune that had been peculiarly their own, and had touched her almost without meaning to. And she had whirled about and was in his arms, and he was holding her hard against him: decency, convention, common sense thrown to the winds and forgotten. Kissing her hair and whispering broken endearments; telling her that they would get married at once—they could keep it a secret and no one need know except Em. That he could not wait, and that nothing mattered now that they were together again.

He was not aware for several minutes that Victoria was struggling to free herself, and when he realized it at last, and released her, he thought that it was emotion that had driven the blood from her face, and shyness and surprise that made her jump up and back away from him.

Victoria said breathlessly: 'No, Eden! No, please don't! It's no good saying I don't care for you any more, because I suppose I always shall. But not in that way any more. It's all over, and I never realized it. Not even when someone told me so. I still didn't believe it. Until you kissed me last night. I wanted you to kiss me——'

Eden took a swift step towards her, his hands outstretched, and once again she backed away from him.

'No! Oh Eden, I'm so very sorry! But how was I to know that you meant it? You hadn't meant it before, and——'

Eden said: 'Darling, I don't know what you're talking about, and I don't care. But I always meant it—with you. Right from the beginning. And I mean it now.'

Victoria wrung her hands and her face crumpled like a child's when it is going to cry. She said pleadingly: 'No you don't. Please say you don't! You see, I thought you were only kissing me because—

because you like kissing girls. Because it was a sort of—of a game, and didn't mean anything. I knew that if you kissed me I'd know. And I did. He was quite right. It's all over. It's—it's as if I'd grown up at last. That's silly, at my age. I should have done it before. But I didn't. I'm so fond of you Eden, but I don't love you any more, and I'm not sure that I ever did, in—in the way that matters.'

'Who was right?' demanded Eden, white-lipped and seizing on only three words out of all those that she had said.

Victoria looked bewildered, and he repeated the question in a voice that startled her: *'Who was right!* Who have you been discussing me with? Drew?'

A tide of colour flooded Victoria's pale cheeks and her eyes widened in dismay. 'No—I mean—I ought not to have said that. I didn't mean to. Eden, don't look like that! I wasn't discussing you with him. Not in that way.'

'In what way, then? Since when have you been on such intimate terms with Drew Stratton that you can discuss your love affairs with him? No, I don't mean that! Don't let's quarrel, darling. I know I treated you abominably once—over Alice. But I had to do it. At least—I thought I had to, and that it would be the best thing for both of us. I can explain, if you'll let me. And I know that I can make you happy.'

Victoria shook her head and her eyes filled with tears.

'No you can't. Not now. I meant what I said, Eden. I don't love you any more. I'm free too. I realized it when you kissed me last night.'

Eden said harshly: 'Or when Stratton did? Has he kissed you?'

He saw the bright colour deepen in her cheeks and was aghast at the tide of sheer physical jealousy that rose and engulfed him, and over which he had no control. He had always had a quick temper and now he had to hit back: to hit blindly, and to hurt as badly as he himself had been hurt. He gave a curt, ugly laugh:

'So you've fallen for our Mr Stratton, have you? Very amusing! And after all those vows of deathless devotion you used to write me. Remember them? A letter a day—sometimes two. I kept them all. A whole box full. I couldn't bear to part with them, but I might as well send them to Stratton for a wedding present. Or you might like to send him a few? Any of the undated ones would do. It will save you time and paper, and the sentiments you addressed to me will do just as well for him, won't they? After all, if he's getting a second-hand love, he may as well get his love letters at second hand too!'

He laughed again, seeing the disgust and contempt in Victoria's white, frozen face and sparkling eyes, and having begun to laugh, found that he could not stop. He dropped into a chair and hid his face in his hands, pressing them over his eyes as though he could blot out the desperate weariness, the shamed despair and the savage jealousy; and shut out the horrifying sound of his own senseless mirth.

It stopped at last, and he said tonelessly: 'I'm sorry, Vicky. That was a filthy thing to say. I didn't mean it. I don't know what got into me. I'm going to pieces these days—not that that's any excuse. Forgive me, dear.'

He dropped his hands and lifted a haggard face, to find that he had been talking to himself. The room was empty and Victoria had gone.

◇　◇　◇

Fifteen minutes later, leaning against the window-sill of her bedroom, Victoria heard the sound of horses' hooves and saw Eden gallop past, heading for the open country and riding as recklessly as though he were in the last lap of a race. It was a relief to know that he was no longer in the house, and she hoped that he would stay away for an hour or two and give her time to think.

One thing at least was clear. She would have to tell Aunt Em that she could not remain at *Flamingo*. How *dared* Eden talk like that! How could he turn on her like a spoilt, vindictive character out of a third-rate novel? Had he really kept her letters? She had a momentary vision of Drew Stratton reading one, his blue eyes cold with scorn, and her face flamed at the thought.

'But Eden isn't like that!' said Victoria, speaking aloud in the empty bedroom.

He couldn't be like that! He couldn't have changed so much in just five years. She was used to his brief outbreaks of black rage. They had never lasted long and they had never meant anything; and when they were over he had always been desperately ashamed and deeply apologetic. No, he would never do such a cruel, vulgar thing as this.

But the thought of the letters persisted. Not so much because she was afraid that Eden would carry out his preposterous threat, but because of Greg Gilbert.

Who was to say that Mr Gilbert would not order another search of the house, and this time find her letters—and read them? There must be many undated ones, and he might well jump to the conclusion that she had continued to correspond with Eden long after his marriage. He might even think what Drew himself had suggested— that she and Eden had planned Alice's death between them. That Eden, and not Aunt Em, had sent for her.

Seized with sudden resolution, Victoria left the room and walked quickly down the corridor to pause outside the door that led into the wing that had been Alice's and Eden's, and where Eden now slept alone. But with her hand on the door knob, she hesitated.

These were the only rooms in the big, rambling house that she had not as yet seen. She thought fleetingly of Bluebeard's chamber, and found the thought a singularly unpleasant one. Supposing that there was something waiting for her on the other side of that door? The poltergeist, who had ceased its vandalistic pranks with the first taste of blood?

I mustn't go in, thought Victoria with sudden conviction. If I do, I shall be sorry. They are Eden's rooms. I haven't any right to search someone else's rooms. Not even for my own letters——

And yet Mrs Thompson had been convicted on the strength of her letters to her lover, and they had, as Drew had pointed out, hung Mrs Thompson . . .

Victoria set her teeth and turned the handle of the door.

17

Alice's bedroom was a long, blue-and-white room that looked out over the rose garden. An impersonal room: neat and cool and without emphasis. A room very like its owner.

There was a blue-and-white bathroom, a small writing room containing a roll-top desk in addition to a rosewood writing table, and finally, Eden's dressing-room, in which he apparently slept, for there was a camp bed made up in it. There were no photographs of Alice in the room, but a single small snapshot in a battered leather frame adorned the dressing-table. It was badly faded, for it had been taken many years before with a Box Brownie, and Eden had developed and printed it himself. A snapshot of a skinny little girl riding on a zebra.

Looking at it Victoria's resolution wavered. There was surely no need for her to hunt through Eden's belongings for her letters. She had only to ask for them, and he would give them to her. Unless Greg Gilbert found them first——

It was a sobering reflection, and Victoria abandoned hesitation. But fifteen minutes later she was compelled to admit that either Eden had lied about keeping her letters, or they were not here, and she was about to leave the room when her eye was caught by an inequality in the panelling on the wall behind the camp bed. She turned back, and pulling the bed away from the wall, saw for the first time that there was another cupboard in the room: a long low cupboard built into the wall, and probably intended as a toy cupboard for a small boy.

Victoria went down on her knees and opened it, to find that it ran back far farther than she had supposed, and was stacked with old boxes and suitcases. She regarded them with some dismay, for if they were full it was going to take her hours to go through them. But the first two or three that she pulled out were empty, and it seemed likely that the remainder would be.

A small cabin trunk, dragged out to the light of day, revealed a battered collection of birds' eggs and an old box camera that was undoubtedly the one with which Eden had taken the photograph of Victoria on Falda. Victoria shut it with a sigh and pulled out an incongruous and outmoded piece of luggage that could only have belonged to Eden's grandfather, Gerald DeBrett: a tin hat box of antediluvian design. It was empty except for a quantity of yellowing tissue paper, dead moths and D.D.T. powder, but Victoria regarded it with interest, remembering a similar relic of vanished days that had stood in a schoolfriend's attic: a hat box that had possessed a false bottom to it, in which, she had been told, ostrich plumes could be packed. This one too was made to the same pattern, and without thinking, she pressed the almost invisible catch that revealed the hidden space.

There were no ostrich plumes, but there was something else. A flat package wrapped very carefully in several folds of soft silk.

Victoria never knew why she should have unwrapped it, for it could not have been what she was looking for. The action was purely automatic, and for a moment the object that lay revealed merely surprised her, and she was about to replace it when her hands checked and her heart seemed to stop, and she sat back on her heels, staring at it, wide-eyed and rigid, while a hundred frantic thoughts whirled round in her brain, falling into fantastic patterns and breaking up into chaotic fragments that did not make sense.

The poltergeist . . . Who was it who had said: 'I'll start believing in evil spirits only when someone has eliminated all possibility of the evil human element.' Drew——! And Drew had said too, 'Who can say what anyone is capable of under certain pressures?'

A dozen things that she had seen or heard during the past week, isolated incidents that had seemed to have no connection with each other, took on shape and meaning: a horrible meaning. But it was the malice in it that frightened her most. Em must be made to suffer the loss of her dearest possessions, starting with the small but cherished things and working up to greater things. Her dog. Her grandson's wife. Her pride and her good name. And at the last there would still be blackmail.

But would Em allow herself to be blackmailed? From what Victoria knew of her, Lady Emily, faced with such a threat, would be just as likely to take the law into her own hands, and shoot the blackmailer and take the consequences, rather than submit. Had the 'poltergeist' thought of that? Or had that malicious brain over-reached itself?

Victoria re-wrapped the package in its folds of bright silk, her hands trembling so that she could barely hold it, and replacing it in its hiding place, closed the hat box and pushed it back into the cupboard. And as she did so she heard a faint sound outside the open window; a scrape and rustle that might have been a bird among the creepers. Or had someone been watching her? She started up, shaking with panic, and pushing the camp bed into place, ran from the room.

Em was walking slowly across the hall at the far end of the corridor, supporting herself on a stick and evidently on her way to the verandah and tea, but Victoria pretended not to have seen her and took refuge in her own room, banging the door behind her and locking it. She did not want to face Aunt Em's shrewd old eyes just yet.

She leant against the closed door, panting and shivering and fighting a panic desire to run out of the house and keep on running until she had put as much distance as possible between herself and *Flamingo*.

She must tell Drew. He would know what to do. Or Mr Gilbert. No, not Mr Gilbert!—he was a policeman first and he would not be able to remember that he was also a friend. She could not do it. She was as bad as Em or Mabel, or any other woman, when it came to that.

It was at least a quarter of an hour later that she went out on the verandah and found tea and her aunt waiting for her.

Em did not look as though her afternoon's rest had benefited her, but her old eyes were as sharply observant as ever, and she dismissed Zacharia with an imperious wave of the hand, and said: 'What has happened, dear? You look as though you had seen a ghost.'

'Not a ghost,' said Victoria with a shiver in her voice. 'A poltergeist.'

'What on earth do you mean!'

'N-nothing,' said Victoria. 'I didn't mean—Aunt Em, I have to tell you something. I can't stay here any longer. I'd like to go as soon as possible. I know I'm being ungrateful, and—and—ungrateful, but I must go!'

Em said gently: 'Sit down, dear. I can see that something has happened to upset you. Here—have some tea. No, drink it up first ·`. . That's better. Now tell me what is the matter. Is it Eden?'

The cup in Victoria's hand shook so badly that the tea slopped into the saucer, and she put it down hurriedly and said breathlessly: 'Why do you say that?'

Em sighed a little heavily and shrugged her shoulders: 'I don't know. You were engaged to him once, and though I thought that was all over, I have not been so sure during the last few days. I know him very well, you see, and I am not unobservant—even though I may be a silly old woman! Has he asked you to marry him? Is it that?'

'Y—yes,' said Victoria. 'But it isn't that. And I couldn't marry him. *Ever!* Not even if he were the—last person on earth!'

She shuddered so violently that her teeth chattered and she could not go on.

Em's brows drew together in a grimace of annoyance and she said tartly: 'Really, I had credited Eden with more intelligence! I am not surprised that you should feel disgusted. It can hardly be pleasant to receive a proposal from a man whose wife has just been murdered. In the worst *possible* taste! He must have taken leave of his senses. But he has been under a great deal of strain, and you must make allowances, dear. He is not himself just now. I will send him away for a month or so. To Rumuruti perhaps; just as soon as this dreadful business has been cleared up. There is no reason at all why *you* should leave.'

Victoria said desperately: 'You don't understand! It isn't that. It's—it's something else. I can't explain! But this afternoon I found out something that has—has made me realize that I must either go away, or go to the police. Th—that's all!'

She pushed back her chair and stood up, trembling with the effort not to burst into tears, and would not meet Em's shocked gaze.

Em said on a gasp: *'Victoria!'*

'I'm sorry,' said Victoria, her voice high and strained. 'I shouldn't have said that. I didn't mean to. I won't say anything else. But I must go away. I must! I know it's cowardly of me, but I can't help it.'

Em's face was grey and drawn and bleak with anger, but she spoke in a strictly controlled voice, as though she were some efficient governess dealing with a naughty and hysterical child:

'I do not know what you are talking about, but I can see that you are in no fit state to make any rational decisions at the moment. I am afraid it is quite out of the question for you to leave for Nairobi immediately. Greg Gilbert would never permit it, and we cannot reach him at the moment to explain that you refuse to stay here. If you are of the same opinion tomorrow morning you can talk to him yourself, and perhaps you will be able to persuade him to let you leave. But you will have to resign yourself to staying under my roof for at least one more night.'

Victoria's heart sank. She had forgotten Mr Gilbert. She found that she was staring at her aunt in helpless dismay, and she sat down again slowly, feeling weak and boneless and very frightened.

'No,' said Victoria in a whisper, 'I can't go away, can I? I had forgotten that. I shall have to stay.'

'For the moment, anyway,' said Em coldly. And went away, walking very stiffly and upright.

She returned some ten or fifteen minutes later, looking grim and implacable and inconceivably old, and ordered Zacharia to send Thuku round with the Land-Rover. Victoria had not moved. She was still sitting huddled in one of the verandah chairs, staring into vacancy.

'I'm going out to shoot something for the dogs,' said Em without condescending to look at her. 'I shall not be long. Zach tells me that Eden has gone up to see the new bore hole, so I will drive in that direction and tell him that you would prefer not to see him just now.'

She stumped off down the verandah as the Land-Rover drove up, and Victoria saw her climb in stiffly, hoisting her bulk into the driver's seat, and remembered Eden saying that Em invariably worked off her feelings in this manner when she was upset. Poor Aunt Em! However fast she drove, she would not be able to drive away from this!

The Land-Rover bucketed away at a dangerous pace and vanished in a whirling cloud of dust, and silence settled down on *Flamingo* like a grey cloud on a hilltop.

Em had taken the dogs with her, and Pusser, who had been lying on the wicker divan posed against the vivid background of the three harlequin-patterned cushions that Zacharia had arranged in a neat row, rose and stretched elaborately, and jumping down with a flump on to the matting, stalked away and vanished down the verandah steps into the garden.

The low sunlight painted the acacia trees a warm orange and the shadows began to stretch out long and blue across the rough Kikuyu grass of the lawns. Now was the time to telephone Drew, while the house was empty and there was no one to hear.

But Victoria had underestimated the difficulties of getting a number on a party line, and when at last she got the Stratton number Drew was out and the servant who answered the telephone spoke the minimum of English, so that after a brief but tangled conversation she was forced to abandon the attempt to make herself understood.

Returning to the verandah she was startled to find Zacharia there, patting the cushions into place, straightening chairs and emptying ash-trays. He must have been in the dining-room, and he gave Victoria the blank, disinterested glance of an elderly tortoise, and went away down the front steps and round the corner of the house.

Em returned just over half an hour later, but it was obvious that the exercise and exertion had not on this occasion produced a particularly mellowing effect upon her. She looked grim and exhausted and her clothes were stained and dirty and clotted with the dust of the ranges. She slapped it off in clouds, and having wiped her face with a handkerchief on which she obviously cleaned her hands after assisting to degut the gazelle that was being removed from the back of the Land-Rover, said shortly:

'Eden won't be back tonight. He's ridden over to Hector's and he'll put up there.'

She made no further mention of their previous conversation, but talked instead of the progress of the new bore hole and the unusual dryness of the season. It seemed that she had met Mabel and Lisa out on the ranges. They had driven out more for something to do than for any specific purpose, and Em reported that Lisa looked more her old self.

'She says that she has got some of the account books that Gilly had brought up to date, and she asked if I'd send you over for them, as she can show you which sections will have to be completed, and which ones only need to be checked. I'd appreciate your help with them, if you feel up to it; I'm afraid I don't.'

Victoria said gratefully: 'Of course I will. I'll go now. It will be nice to have something to do.'

'That's what I thought,' said Em. 'Work is a very useful thing in bad times: it has to go on, and so one goes on too. Don't stay too long. It gets dark very quickly once the sun is down. You might pick me some of those delphiniums if you're not too late. I've done nothing about the flowers for days. I haven't had the heart to. But I suppose one has got to start again sometime. You'll find a pair of secateurs somewhere on the bottom shelf of the bookcase in the office.'

Em's office was not noted for its tidiness, for she was in the habit of using it as a junk room, and Victoria discovered the secateurs among the welter of raffia and old seed catalogues; dislodging in the process a pyramid of dusty cardboard boxes that cascaded to the floor.

She was stacking these back again when one of them fell open, spilling out several dozen wooden slips of the type used for making seed beds, and, from beneath them, a heavier object that slid out with a dull thud.

It was a very ordinary object to find in such a place: a well-worn and somewhat old-fashioned clasp knife faced with horn. But Victoria, touching it with shrinking fingers, saw that the small blade had been broken off short, and that there were initials cut deep into the horn. K. D. B.

So Em knew! Or if she did not know, she had suspected. She had palmed the knife that Eden had given her—his father's knife—because she had realized that Gilly Markham had not died from snakebite, and she had been afraid. And later, when she had realized her mistake, she could not explain why she should have hidden it, so had blandly insisted that she herself had taken that knife to Crater Lake. She would not have done that for anyone but Eden.

Victoria lifted it with an unsteady hand and put it back quickly into the box, covering it again with the wooden slips and thrusting the box at the back of the shelf and at the bottom of the pile.

She stood up, breathing quickly as though she had been running, and taking up the secateurs, left the office; closing the door very carefully behind her as though it were vital that she should make no noise that might remind Em of where she had been.

But Em would not have heard anything, for she was sitting at the piano and drowning her troubled thoughts in a flood of melody. The music filled the room and flowed out through the open windows into the quiet garden, and Victoria paused on the verandah to listen to it, and being no more than an average performer herself was not critical of her aunt's execution, as Gilly would have been. Em was playing a Bach fugue, and playing it, in her niece's opinion, remarkably well. Victoria listened, soothed and enchanted.

She did not know at what point she began to be aware that there was something missing from the verandah, or why she should have noticed it at all—or been worried by it. But some elusive fragment of memory nagged at her brain; a sixth sense that whispered words she could not quite hear and drew her attention to something that she could not see.

She looked about her uneasily, but nothing had changed. The shabby wicker chairs and table stood where they had always stood, and Pusser's food and milk were still untouched. Why should she think there was something different about it? Something missing?

She gave an impatient shrug of her shoulders and turned away, and it was not until she had reached the gate in the plumbago hedge that the answer dropped into her mind as though it had been a dry leaf falling from the acacia trees above her—and with so little impact that she could smile at it, thinking only that it was a trivial thing after all . . .

One of the three remaining verandah cushions had been missing. There had been only two brightly patterned squares on the long wicker divan against the wall, though there had been three earlier in the day.

18

The Markhams' bungalow appeared to be empty, and Victoria could hear no voices, though from somewhere in the silent house there came a faint, intermittent sound that resolved itself into the plaintive whining of a dog.

There was no bell, and as no one answered her tentative calls Victoria went through an open doorway and found herself in Lisa's drawing-room.

It was an essentially feminine room. Pink and white and be-ruffled, with the accent on ribbons and roses. But at the present moment it bore a forlorn aspect, for the flowers in the white vases were fading or dead, there was a film of dust on the piano and the occasional tables, and the ash-trays did not look as though they had been emptied for days.

A familiar object lay upon the sofa and provided an incongruous note of colour against the chintzy prettiness: a large cretonne knit-ting bag in excruciating shades of blue and orange—the property of Mabel Brandon. But there was no sign of its owner, or of Lisa, and after a hesitant interval Victoria opened one of the doors leading out of the drawing-room and found herself on the threshold of an untidy office. If the account books were anywhere they should be here, and she was looking doubtfully about her when she became conscious of being under surveillance, and turned swiftly.

Lisa had entered the drawing-room by the verandah door and was standing quite still, watching her.

For a moment Victoria did not recognize her, for she had never seen Lisa dressed in this fashion before. She was wearing slacks and a shirt of faded khaki, both of which looked as though they might have belonged to her late husband, and in place of her usual high-heeled sandals she wore a shabby pair of tennis shoes, which ac-counted for the fact that Victoria had not heard her approach.

The room was already growing dark, and as Lisa was standing with her back to the windows Victoria could not see her face very clearly; but there was an expression on it that even in the uncertain light was sufficiently disconcerting to make Victoria regret that she had not waited until the morning before coming over to fetch Gilly's account books.

Lisa was smiling—but only with her red, rigid mouth: above it her violet eyes were fixed in a look that was as purely animal as that of a cat who is watching a bird, or a mousehole.

There was a curious moment of silence that had the effect of being loud with suppressed sound, and then Lisa laughed.

It was a gay sound, light and genuinely amused, and she moved forward and said: 'So you did come! I wondered if you would. Em sent you for the account books, I suppose? They're in there. On the table behind you.'

Victoria said confusedly, conscious that she was stammering badly: 'I-I'm sorry. About w-walking in like this. It was r-rude of me, b-but there didn't seem to be anyone about.'

Lisa walked past her into the office and picked up a pile of account books from one of the cluttered tables.

'I know. But the servants are all to pieces because of Greg and his boys, and I don't know where that little beast Wambui has got to. She's been in an awful state since her boy-friend was dug up. I shall have to sack her. Here you are—I suppose this is what you want? It'll do to go on with, anyway, *'Tis enough. 'Twill serve!'*

She laughed again, as though at some exquisite joke, and said in a surprised voice: 'You know, Gilly was always saying things like that. Bits of Shakespeare. It used to madden me. But it's odd how those silly remarks seem to fit in.'

She came back into the drawing-room and said: 'Would you like a drink? There's gin and sherry, and there should be some whisky if Hector and Ken haven't drunk it all.'

'N-no thank you,' said Victoria quickly. 'I must be getting back.'

'What's the hurry? It isn't dark yet.'

'It's not that, but Aunt Em's alone. Besides I said I'd cut some delphiniums. We haven't had any fresh flowers for days.'

'Neither have I,' said Lisa, looking vaguely round at the limp and faded stalks that lolled in the flower vases and made a faint, unpleasant smell in the room. 'The best delphiniums grow by the knoll. The tall pink ones——'

She embarked on a long and disjointed account of the difficulties of growing flowers in a dry year, and as she was standing between Victoria and the door it was not really possible to push past her and leave. And yet Victoria discovered that she wanted to get out of that room as badly as she had ever wanted to get away from *Flamingo:* as badly as she had ever wanted anything. But Lisa continued to talk in her light brittle voice, and to keep between her and the door . . .

'I do wish you'd have something to drink. I don't like drinking alone. Mabel will be sorry to have missed you. She thought you'd be along a bit later. She'll be back any minute now. She's taking Dinah for a walk.'

A faint whining sound disproved her words, but she did not seem to have heard it: 'It's so good of her. Mabel is the kindest person. She knows how I hate taking out Dinah when she's like this, because Em's dogs sometimes follow us. You aren't going, are you? I haven't explained about the account books yet.'

Victoria, who had forgotten that she was clasping them, cast them a startled glance, and Lisa said: 'Give them to me, and I'll show you.'

She took them and carried them over to the window seat, where she laid them out carefully and slowly as though she were deliberately wasting time, and after studying them for several minutes announced that the ones with green covers dealt with the sale of fodder and vegetables, the red ones with fruit—mostly oranges—and the black ones with cattle.

'Very simple and kindergarten, isn't it? Gilly's idea. I don't think you'll have any trouble.'

Victoria scooped them up hurriedly and said: 'No. I'm sure I won't. Thank you so much. I really must be getting back.'

Lisa glanced over her shoulder at the sky beyond the window and said: 'Yes. I think you should. Blue is a difficult colour to see in the dusk. The delphiniums, I mean.'

She laughed lightly and stood to one side, and Victoria said: 'Good night. And thank you.' And went quickly out of the room.

The sun had gone and there were bats flittering in an airy ballet among the trees as Victoria hurried down the dusty path that wound between feathery clumps of bamboo, pepper trees and jacaranda. She was out of sight of the bungalow and had begun to walk more slowly when a nightjar flew up with a harsh cry that startled her, and something rustled in the bushes as though an animal, perhaps an antelope, had slipped past her unseen.

She stopped and stood listening, but a vagrant breeze blew in from the lake and rustled the leaves and grasses, drowning all other sounds. And when it died away she could hear nothing but a distant crying of birds from the papyrus swamp, and the sound of Em's piano, sweet in the silence.

She began to hurry again, and turning a corner, reached the gate and found that she must have forgotten to latch it, for it stood open. She closed it carefully behind her and walked on quickly through a grove of acacias, listening to the music that drifted out across the garden from the open windows of Em's drawing-room.

Em had abandoned Bach and was playing something that was unfamiliar to Victoria. A strange, passionate, haunting piece of music that somehow fitted into the scene as though it were a tangible thing and an integral part of the Valley.

The Rift Valley Concerto! thought Victoria. It could not be anything else. Toroni must have loved the Rift—or hated it—to write like that.

She had almost forgotten the delphiniums, but the weight of the secateurs in her pocket reminded her of them, and she turned off the path and walked across the grass to the foot of the knoll, where they made a sea of blue and pink and purple.

She had begun to cut the flowers when another breath of wind blew across the garden, filling the green dusk with soft and stealthy rustlings, and she straightened up and stood alert and listening. Had it really been only the wind that had moved among the bushes?

The secateurs slid from her hand and were lost among the flowers, and she was aware that her heart was thumping painfully against her ribs. She had not realized that it was so late, or that the interval between sundown and darkness was so brief. Down in the papyrus swamp beyond the shamba birds were crying and calling. As though they had been alarmed by something . . .

Victoria stood quite still, held by the instinct that will make an animal freeze into immobility in the hope of being overlooked, rather than draw attention to itself by running. And as she stood there a familiar figure materialized out of the dusk, walking towards her, and her heart gave a great bound of relief.

She called out a little breathlessly: 'I'm sorry I'm so late. It was the flowers——' And bent to pick them up.

Her hands were full of them when something suddenly slid into her mind; icily and with a blinding impact. Something completely impossible.

The piano was still playing.

The flowers fell from her hands and she jerked upright, staring at the figure that stood facing her in the dusk: staring, paralysed, at a stranger, suddenly and horribly unfamiliar.

Her eyes widened in her white face and her mouth opened in a soundless scream—as Alice's had done. But Alice had not fought, or even flinched from the savage sweeping stroke of the sharpened panga.

Victoria saw it coming and flung herself to one side, and the blow missed its mark and grazed her right shoulder, shearing through the short linen sleeve.

She saw the blade flash in the dusk as it lifted again, and she was struggling and fighting, gripped to something that was soft and yielding and as suffocating as a feather bolster; her hands round a wrist that seemed made of iron, fending it off, and her ears full of the sound of grunting, panting breaths.

She made no attempt to cry out, for she needed her breath and her young strength to fight for her life. Her foot caught in a rough tangle of grass and she stumbled and fell to her knees, and saw the panga lift again. But it did not fall.

There was someone else there. A dark shape that appeared out of nowhere and sprang at her assailant with the silent savagery of a giant cat.

Victoria, crouched on the grass, heard a hoarse gasping cry, and saw the shapeless scarlet-clad figure crumple and fall sideways. And then the green sky and the purple dusk darkened and closed in on her, and she pitched forward on her face into merciful unconsciousness.

There was a light somewhere that was hurting her eyes, and she felt cold and very sick and aware of a burning pain in her right shoulder.

There were voices too, and someone was saying: 'She'll be all right. It's only a flesh wound.'

A hand touched her forehead and Victoria shuddered uncontrollably and opened her eyes to find that she was lying on her own bed and looking up into Drew Stratton's face.

She said in a gasping whisper: *'Drew!*— Oh, Drew!'

Drew said: 'It's all right, darling. It's all over. Drink this——'

He lifted her against his shoulder, and holding a glass to her mouth, forced her to swallow something that tasted exceedingly nasty. But when he would have laid her down again she turned and clung to him.

'Don't go. Please don't go.'

'I won't.' Drew's leisurely voice was quiet and level and completely reassuring. And all at once she knew that she was safe—for always.

Someone who had been standing just out of range of her vision went out of the room, closing the door, but she did not turn her head, and Drew did not move.

She could hear cars arriving and leaving, and the occasional shrilling of the telephone. The house was full of muffled voices and movement, and somewhere a woman was crying with a hysterical despairing persistency. But none of it had anything to do with her, and presently Drew lifted her head and kissed her, and time and death and violence ceased to have any meaning.

She said at last, with her head against his shoulder:

'It was Aunt Em.'

'I know, dear.'

'Why did she do it?'

'I'll tell you in the morning.'

Victoria said urgently: 'No! Tell me now. I couldn't sleep—not knowing.'

Drew smiled down at her. 'You won't be able to help yourself, darling. Not after that stuff you've just taken!'

'Then I shall dream about it, and that will be worse. Tell me now.'

But Drew only shook his head, and presently she fell asleep, and when she awoke the sun was high, and it was Mabel Brandon, red-eyed with weeping, who had brought her breakfast on a tray, and after putting a fresh bandage on her shoulder, helped her to dress.

But Mabel would not answer her questions. She had only said: 'She's dead. She died at three o'clock this morning. Eden was with her. One should not speak ill of the dead.' And she had gone away, blowing her nose vehemently and making no attempt to disguise her tears.

The drawing-room had been full of sunlight, and Drew had been standing by the window looking out across the garden. He turned and smiled at her, and Victoria said unsteadily:

'Mrs Brandon says she—she is dead.' Even now she could not bring herself to say that name, because to say it was to admit the impossible. 'Drew, what happened? I don't understand. I don't understand anything!'

Drew said: 'Greg knows more about it than I do. Ask him.' And Victoria turned quickly and saw for the first time that there was someone else in the room.

Greg Gilbert gave her a brief smile that did not reach his eyes and left his face as grim and drawn as it had been a moment before, and when he spoke it was to ask what appeared to be an entirely irrelevant question:

'Did you ever know why Eden broke off the engagement between you, and married Alice Laxton?'

'No,' said Victoria, considerably taken aback. 'I suppose he— What has it got to do with this?'

'More than you would think,' said Greg tiredly. 'He broke it off because your mother told him that there was insanity in the family.'

'*Insanity!* Do you mean that I——' Victoria's face was white.

'No. Not in yours. Your grandfather married twice. But both Lady Emily's mother and her grandfather died in lunatic asylums, and there was always some doubt about the manner in which Eden's father met his death.'

'But—but it was a car accident!'

'Yes. But an odd one. Odd enough for a rumour to get around that he might possibly have engineered it himself. There was no shadow of evidence that he was abnormal, or even highly strung. But your mother heard the rumours, and because she knew all about Em's family history she believed them. And in spite of everything that the doctors say about insanity not being hereditary, she was very much against your marrying Eden.'

'Yes,' said Victoria in a whisper. 'I remember.'

'In the end she told Eden, as the only way of stopping it. He was young and impressionable, and it came as an appalling shock to him. I gather he went off for a week by himself and drank himself silly, and decided on a heroic gesture. He wouldn't tell you, because you would insist on disregarding it, and he felt he must do something quite irrevocable—burn his boats before he could weaken. He had met Alice Laxton a few weeks before, and through a cousin of hers he knew her history. Alice had had a bad riding accident in her early teens, and she could never have children. That was the deciding factor. He married her in a haze of self-sacrifice, youthful heroics, desperation and alcohol—and pure selfishness! And woke up to the full stupidity of what he had done when it was too late.'

But Victoria had no interest and little sympathy to spare for Eden just then, and she brushed the information aside and demanded bluntly: 'Do you mean that Aunt Em was mad?'

Greg said: 'No; she was sane enough. But she loved *Flamingo* too much and made a god out of it, and she had meant to found a dynasty: a Kenya dynasty. When she realized that Alice could never have children it meant only one thing to her: that there would be no heir to *Flamingo*. She had a shrewd suspicion that Eden was still in love with you, and she thought you were the right kind of girl for Kenya—as Alice was not! I think the seeds of the idea must have been in her mind for a long time.'

Victoria said: 'But the—poltergeist. They were *her* things. The things she liked best. She *couldn't* have done that!'

'Oh, yes she could. Not the first time. That was the cat, who had chased a bird round the drawing-room. But it gave her an idea for an alibi—that and the rumour that "General Africa" was hiding somewhere in the Naivasha area—and she decided to use it as a smoke screen. I think too that it appealed to some twisted instinct in her. She seems to have looked upon it as a—a penance for what she intended to do. A sort of burnt offering upon the altar of *Flamingo*. There was too much of the fanatic in Em's make-up: and plenty of cunning too, for she knew that if the broken things were her own personal treasures she would be the last person to be suspected of destroying them. But it must have been a small martyrdom to do it.'

Victoria said: '*Things*, yes. But not her dog!'

'Ah! The dog was a different matter. It had been her favourite, and it had switched its allegiance to Alice. She couldn't forgive that.'

Victoria shivered and said in a whisper: 'You said once that the first killing was the hardest. Perhaps that was why she had to do it. To—to practise.'

'It wasn't her first killing. She'd killed her manager, Gus Abbott. We always thought that was an accident, but it seems we were wrong. Abbott lost his nerve, and when *Flamingo* was attacked he didn't want to stay and fight. He wanted to save himself, and he thought he could make a break for it and hide in the garden. But to run away, and from a gang of Mau Mau, was to Em an unforgivable sin, and she apparently shot him quite deliberately. I think that afterwards it gave her a sense of power. To have done that and got away with it. Perhaps it swung the balance, and made it possible for her to plan the murder of Eden's unsuitable wife. For she did plan it. She seized on that first accident, for which Pusser was responsible, and kept on with a series of faked ones; and at the psychological moment she sent for you. It had given her a good excuse for doing so.'

Victoria said: 'She sent for me because my mother had died!'

'No, she didn't. If it had been that, she would have sent for you six months earlier. She sent for you because her plans were working out, and she murdered Alice just as soon as you were due to leave England and could not turn back. If she'd done it earlier, you wouldn't have come, would you?'

'No,' said Victoria slowly.

'Because of Eden. Yes, she knew that. You thought it was safe to come because he was married. But by the time you arrived here he would be free, and she was banking on his marrying you.'

Victoria went over to the window seat and sat down on it, staring out at the green lawns and the placid lake, and presently she said without turning her head:

'There are so many things I don't understand. The piano. Gilly Markham. Were there two records of the concerto? I found one, you know. It was in the false bottom of a hat box in Eden's room. I—I thought it must mean that he was the poltergeist, and that he'd kept it to blackmail her with.'

'Did you? That's irony, if you like! Em didn't know that. She said you told her that you'd found something, and you must leave at once, or go to the police. She went straight to Eden's room and realized that you'd been at the cupboard, and knew what it was that you had found. She thought it meant that you knew everything. That was why you had to be killed. She told us a great deal before she died. I think she was afraid that we might suspect Eden, and she had to clear him.'

'Then there *were* two records!'

'No. Only one. She needed it to manufacture that alibi, and she couldn't bear to destroy it. She smashed another one instead. One long-playing record looks much like another when it's in bits, and no one bothered to piece it together to read the label. She had the whole thing worked out by then. She went off ostensibly to shoot a buck, but actually to ensure that she had a good excuse for getting bloodstained—which was a point that had escaped me. And when she came back she sent Alice over to the Markhams', put a house-coat over her stained clothes and started to play the piano. And when she'd got rid of Zacharia she put on the recording instead, removed the house-coat and went out to meet Alice . . .

197

'She killed Alice with a panga in order to bolster up the "General Africa" angle, and she came back to the house and dropped it, with a piece of twine round the handle, into the rainwater tank outside her window. Then she came back to her room, took off her stained clothes, put on the house-coat again, and went back to the drawing-room where she was found by Zacharia, still playing the piano, half an hour later. After that it was easy. She removed the record, took it back to its hiding place, stopped to pick up her stained clothes and see them put into the boiler—Majiri did most of the washing at night—and went out to search for Alice.'

Victoria said: 'But the cushion! Why should she have needed that?'

'She didn't. That was a mistake. Mine, as much as anyone's! That cushion threw me right off beam, and incidentally frightened the life out of Mabel! Apparently there had been six of those cushions sold at some charity bazaar, and Mabel had bought two; one of which had disappeared only about ten days ago. Ken says he took it on a picnic on the lake and lost it overboard, but Mabel began to add two and two together and make it eighteen.'

'Then why was it there?'

'Someone had left it on the verandah rail by the rainwater tank, and Em knocked it off and it fell against the panga and got badly stained. It couldn't be left there with the stain on it, so she ran back with it and threw it into the bushes. It was the best she could do, and as it turned out it provided her with an alibi that she had never even thought of—which is why she took another with her when she went out to meet you! She thought she'd covered everything, but she hadn't.'

Victoria said: 'You mean Kamau.'

'Kamau—and Gilly Markham.'

'*Gilly?* But he didn't see her! He only heard her playing. He said so.'

'No he didn't. We merely jumped to the conclusion that that was what he meant. But Gilly was doing a very stupid and dangerous thing. He was letting Em know that he knew the difference between her playing and Toroni's. Gilly knew quite well when Em put on the recording of the concerto. And he wanted that job at Rumuruti and thought he could blackmail her into giving it to him. He should have known better.'

Victoria said in a whisper: 'Then—then that was her too.'

'I'm afraid so. It was a fairly easy job I gather, and done in the way I had outlined—She carried a dead puff adder to the picnic inside her cushion. But Mabel threw a spanner into the works by hiding the clasp knife, and Hector by palming the iodine bottle.'

'But *why?*' demanded Victoria. 'Why should they have done that?'

'Because they both knew that Gilly hadn't died from snake-bite, and that Ken had been hanging about *Flamingo* on the evening that Alice was murdered, hoping to see her, and that Gilly knew it. They also knew that Ken had quite a collection of poisoned arrows—they are a dam' sight too easy to come by in this country! And the knife was Ken's. Hector had borrowed it earlier in the day. Mabel threw it into the lake, and Hector apparently did the same thing with the iodine bottle because it had come out of Mabel's pocket. They both seem to have acted on a silly spur-of-the-moment panic.'

'But it wasn't Ken's knife!' said Victoria. 'It was Eden's. Or rather, his father's. It's here. In the office. I found it.'

Greg did not show much interest. He said: 'Did you? Eden said it was somewhere around, but he couldn't remember what he'd done with it. It had been lost; which was why Em said she'd taken it to the picnic, and described it in detail. She thought it wouldn't turn up again, and she'd realized by then that no one thought Gilly's death was an accident, so that laying claim to it made it look as though she were shielding someone. It was quite a good line in double bluff, when you come to think of it. Em was a good poker player.'

'I suppose she killed Kamau too,' said Victoria, looking very white and sick. 'She went out shooting that evening too, after Mrs Markham had been over. Like—like she did that other time; and last night. Did she kill him?'

'Yes. And it was poetic justice, as it happened. Em thought she knew a lot; but she didn't know that she had killed the man who half the security forces in the country have been hunting for years. Kamau was "General Africa".'

'Good Lord!' said Drew, startled. 'Are you sure of that, Greg? How on earth do you know?'

'Wambui told us,' said Greg. 'She knew. And so did old Zacharia. In fact you'll probably find that there's hardly a Kikuyu from here to Nairobi who didn't know it, but they kept their mouths shut. They were frightened stiff of that man. Specially after he'd killed his only real rival, "Brigadier" Gitahi, and actually collected the Government reward for doing so!'

Greg looked from Victoria to Drew and back again, and said 'You don't know how lucky you are, Miss Caryll. If it hadn't been for Wambui, you'd probably have gone the same way as Alice. It was Wambui who knifed your aunt. She'd been laying for her. She said Kamau had told her that it was the "Memsahib Mkubwa" who had killed the small memsahib, and she was sure that she had also killed Kamau; and now he was avenged. I don't know what the hell we're going to do about that one. Technically, she ought to hang for murder; but actually she saved your life. We didn't hear until pretty late that you had tried to ring Drew, and we wouldn't have got there in time.'

'And—and if you hadn't, you would have thought it was someone else,' said Victoria in an almost inaudible voice. 'Eden, or Mrs Markham, or one of the Brandons. Or an African.'

Greg shook his head. 'Not this time. The pattern was becoming too plain and she wouldn't have got away with it again. Also I think Mrs Markham had tumbled to it at last. It seems that Em had told her that she was going to send you over to get some account books that were of no immediate interest. And Em had asked Alice to pick some flowers too: the knoll was out of sight of the house. I think Lisa guessed.'

Victoria nodded, remembering that curious interview in the Markhams' drawing-room and how it had seemed to her that Lisa was deliberately delaying her—until it got darker. Lisa who had loved Eden, and been driven frantic by jealousy.

A car drew up outside the house and they could hear voices on the verandah. Greg Gilbert looked at his watch and said: 'That will be for me. I must go.'

He turned to Victoria and said: 'I'm afraid you're going to find that there are a bad two or three days ahead of you, and a lot of police procedure to be got through before you can put all this behind you and try and forget it. But I've promised Drew that I'll leave you alone until tomorrow. Goodbye.'

He went out of the room, closing the door behind him, and Victoria was silent for a long time, twisting her hands in her lap and staring before her.

She said at last: 'You thought it might be her, didn't you.'

Drew did not answer for a moment or two, and she turned to look up at him.

'I—wondered,' said Drew slowly.

'Why?'

'I don't know. A lot of trivial things. But they added up. The first time was when Kamau had disappeared. Even Greg thought that he had just made a bolt for the Reserve, but when Em spoke of him she used the past tense. As though he were dead.'

'Was that all?'

'No. She couldn't stop talking about the things she had done. Remember the times she accused herself of killing Alice—and Gilly? She put it in such a way that we didn't take it seriously. But it was interesting. And then suddenly she said something that was more than merely interesting, and I began to wonder again. She quoted something from Macbeth; do you remember?'

'Yes,' said Victoria. 'Something about if she had died before, she would have lived long enough. I didn't know it was from Macbeth.'

Had I but died an hour before this chance, I had liv'd a blessed time', quoted Drew. 'Macbeth says that, when having murdered Duncan, the murder is discovered. I was interested in the workings of Em's mind; and I didn't like it. I was afraid for you then, and I began to consider seriously the possibility of Em being the murderer. I went to see Greg, which was why I was out when you telephoned. I was at his office until about six, and when I rang my house to say that I'd be back late I was told that the new memsahib from *Flamingo* had wanted to speak to me. I knew it must be you, and that you wouldn't have done that unless you had been frightened.'

Victoria nodded without speaking, and turned to look out of the window again; and presently Drew asked a question that he had asked her once before in that room: 'What are you thinking about?'

'Eden,' said Victoria, as she had said then. 'Drew, you don't mind about Eden, do you?'

'Do I have to?' asked Drew.

'No,' said Victoria, 'Not any more.'

She did not turn her head, but she groped for his hand, and finding it, held it to her cheek; and he felt the wetness of it and knew that she was crying: for Eden and Alice—and Em.

Outside on the drive a car started up and drove away with an impatient blare on the horn. Greg and the police had gone, and the house was quiet again. But there was no longer any awareness in its silence. The tension and the trouble that had filled it had departed from it at last. It had ceased to be a Graven Image demanding sacrifices, for its High Priestess was dead, and it was only a pleasant rambling house whose windows looked out across green gardens to the wide beauty of Lake Naivasha and all the glory of the Rift Valley.

DEATH IN ZANZIBAR

To
The Zanzibar I knew.
With love

FOREWORD

In the early years of the 1950s there used to be a B.B.C. Radio programme called 'Housewives' Choice', which consisted of popular records—in those days, presumably 78s?—that provided a pleasant accompaniment to tedious and repetitive chores. Any tune in the Top Twenty got played fairly frequently, and one in particular caught my fancy: the first line of the refrain being 'Then I'll go sailing far— off to Zanzibar!'

Since I myself was in the all-too-familiar position of a British Army wife—abandoned, with my two small daughters, in depressing Army quarters in a small garrison town while my husband and his regiment were on active service somewhere on the other side of the world (on this occasion, Korea!)—I would have given a great deal to go 'sailing far', to almost anywhere. But Zanzibar is one of those names that possess a peculiar, singing magic in every syllable; like Samarkand or Rajasthan, or Kilimanjaro; and when the radio was not playing that song I used to sing it to myself, and like Dany in this story, I read anything I could get hold of on the subject of Zanzibar: never dreaming that I would ever see it myself.

Then, when my husband was almost due back in England, his regiment, while *en route* for home, was suddenly diverted to Kenya. And since families were allowed to go out there to join their husbands and fathers, it was not long before the children and I were setting off to Nairobi on a flight that nowadays would only take a few hours, but which in those days, as in this story, took well over twenty-four.

It was during our time in Kenya that I got the chance to visit

Zanzibar. And I fell in love with it at first sight, for it turned out to be one of those rare places that live up to everything one has hoped and dreamed that they would be. I also had the honour of meeting its greatly respected and much-loved old Sultan, His Highness Seyyid Khalifa bin Harub: grandson of Thuwani of Muscat and Oman—who was a half-brother of the two successive Sultans of Zanzibar, Majid and Bargash, about whom I wrote in a historical novel, *Trade Wind,* which tells the story of Tyson Frost's grandfather, Rory—Emory Tyson Frost of *Kivulimi.*

Since my husband kept being posted to all sorts of novel and entertaining places, I wrote a 'whodunit' set in each of them. Because of this, I made detailed notes of things I was afraid I might forget. So that when, several years later, I got around to writing this story, all I had to do was to hunt up my Zanzibar notebook, and there it was. An exact description of everything I could possibly need, down to the advertisement painted on looking-glass in the Mombasa Airport, and the millipede crawling across the floor of the tiny, makeshift one on Pemba.

The Zanzibar I knew has gone for ever, and this book is already a 'period piece'—almost a historical novel, so much has changed. But at least I saw it, and lived in it for a brief while, and it is stored away in my mind for ever.

The heavy brocade curtains stirred as though they had been blown by a breath of wind, and a billowing fold touched the corner of the dressing-table and overset a small bottle of nail varnish.

It was a very slight sound, but it woke Dany; jerking her out of an uneasy dream in which she had been hurrying down a long lonely country road in the sad fog and drizzle of an early autumn, clutching a small sealed envelope and listening to the drip of rain off the unseen hedges and the footsteps of someone who followed close behind her.

She had caught brief glimpses of this person when she stopped and turned, and once it had been Mr Honeywood with his narrow, dry, solicitor's face and his small dry disapproving cough, and sometimes it had been a large hearty woman in tweeds, striding through the wet mist, or an Oriental; a dark-faced man wearing flowing white robes and a fez—or was it a turban? But none of them had any right to be following her, and she dare not let them overtake her. It was vitally important that they should not overtake her . . .

The bottle fell over and Dany awoke.

She sat up in bed shivering in the aftermath of nightmare, and was momentarily surprised to find herself in an unfamiliar room. Then the dream receded, and she remembered that she was no longer in her great-aunt's house, but at the Airlane Hotel in London.

Yesterday, in Market-Lydon, it had been misty and damp; as though autumn were already far advanced. But here in London on this September morning it still seemed to be high summer, and although it was very early and the city was as yet barely astir, the sky beyond the open window was clear and bright.

The curtains that had been closely drawn last night were now partially open, and the pale light of early morning, filtering into the room, showed a clutter of cardboard boxes, air-weight suitcases, tissue paper, and the new lizard-skin bag that was Great-aunt Harriet's parting present and which contained, among other things, a brand new passport.

Dany had checked over all the impedimenta of foreign travel late last night, and now all she had left to do was to buy a beach hat, a sun-suit and something for air sickness, and to introduce herself to her step-father's sister, Mrs Bingham, whom she had so far never met but who had been staying since yesterday in the same hotel and was also travelling out to Zanzibar on a Zero Zephyr of the Green Zero Line.

London, Naples, Khartoum, Nairobi. Mombasa, Tanga, Pemba, Zanzibar——

Dany shivered again. A shiver of pure delight that ended unexpectedly in a quiver of unease: a sense of disquiet so sharply urgent that she turned quickly, half expecting to find someone standing behind her. But nothing moved except the curtains billowing idly in the dawn wind, and of course there was no one there. And no one watching her! It was only the effect of that silly dream about people following her . . .

◇ ◇ ◇

Dany Ashton had left school almost a year ago, but this was her first taste of freedom, for despite the fact that, as her mother's daughter, she might have been expected to have led an erratic and entertaining existence, her life had hitherto been a remarkably sheltered one. Her mother, currently Lorraine Frost, was a notable beauty who collected and discarded husbands in a manner that would have done credit to a film star, and Dany, her only child, was the daughter of her first husband, Daniel Ashton.

Lorraine had never been maternally minded, and Daniel Ashton, explorer and big-game hunter, had been more interested in such things as the Lesser Kudu and the upper reaches of the Amazon than in fatherhood. He had met his death at the hands of an unenlightened and excitable tribe of South-American Indians when Dany was three years old, and Lorraine had promptly married Dwight Cleethorpe, an affable millionaire from Chicago, and handed her small daughter over to the care of a maiden aunt, Harriet Henderson.

Mr Cleethorpe, whose hobbies were golf and deep-sea fishing, had not lasted, and there had been three more step-fathers in rapid succession, the latest of whom was Tyson Frost, the novelist. But none of them had taken more than a passing interest in their step-daughter, and Lorraine's visits, though exhilarating, were always brief and did little to disturb the even tenor of life at *Glyndarrow*, the large red-brick house in Hampshire where Dany's Great-aunt Harriet lived in cosy Edwardian seclusion while the world passed her by.

Great-aunt Harriet disapproved of Progress and the Post-War World. She had also disapproved strongly of this visit to Zanzibar, but had been unable to prevent it since she was not the child's legal guardian, and moreover her great-niece had suddenly displayed an unsuspected streak of independence.

Dany had been wildly delighted at the prospect of going to this outlandish spot where Tyson Frost owned a house, and she had not only paid no attention at all to her great-aunt's warnings, but had flatly refused to spend the three nights in London under the roof of an elderly relative, or to be accompanied there by Twisdon, Great-aunt Harriet's austere and aged maid.

Chaperones, declared Dany, were as dead as the Dodo, and she was perfectly capable of looking after herself: or if she were not, the sooner she started learning, the better. In any case, Lorraine had advised her to stay at the Airlane, as there would be half a dozen other people there who were also bound for Zanzibar and the house-party at *Kivulimi*, and who would be travelling on the same plane. Her fellow-guests were Tyson's sister, Augusta Bingham and her friend and companion, Miss Bates; the Marchese di Chiago, who raced (but whether horses, dogs, cars or yachts was not disclosed); Amalfi Gordon, a close friend of Lorraine's, and her fiancé Mr Holden—American and something to do with publishing—who intended to get married on the eve of departure and thereby combine business (discussing terms for a new Tyson Frost novel) with pleasure in the form of a honeymoon in Zanzibar. And finally, Mr Holden's secretary, Miss Kitchell. One or any of these people, wrote Lorraine airily, would be sure to keep an eye on Dany.

'If she means Mrs Bingham or Miss Bates, then possibly they will do so,' said Aunt Harriet, frigid with disapproval. 'But what if it should be this Marchese? I cannot think what has come over your mother. It all comes from living abroad: foreigners are notoriously lax. And *no* one could approve of Mrs Gordon! There was an exceedingly unpleasant rumour going round that she had——Well, never mind. But she is not in my opinion a suitable companion for any young girl. Besides, she has been married and divorced several times already.'

'I don't see that you can hold that against her,' said Dany with a somewhat rueful smile. 'What about Lorraine?'

'That is *quite* different,' said Aunt Harriet firmly. 'She is your mother—and a Henderson. And I do wish you would not refer to her as "Lorraine". You know how much I dislike it.'

'Yes, Aunt. But you know how much she dislikes me calling her anything else.'

Aunt Harriet shifted her ground. 'It's a very complicated journey. I understand that the Green Zero Line only fly as far as Nairobi, and that you would have to spend a night in an hotel there, and take another aeroplane on the following day. Anything might happen. There have been race-riots in Nairobi.'

'Yes, Aunt. But Lorraine—I'm sorry; Mother—says that Tyson's secretary, Nigel Ponting, will be meeting the plane there, so I shall be quite safe.'

'Ponting . . . Yes. I have met him. He came here with your step-father two years ago. You were at school. A most affected man. More like a dancing master than a secretary. He minced and giggled. Not at all a reliable type, and I did not take to him.'

'I'm sorry, Aunt.'

Old Miss Henderson had been compelled to give up the unequal struggle, and Dany—naïve, romantic, eager—had left for London unchaperoned, taken a room with a private bath and balcony at the Airlane, and indulged in an orgy of theatres, shopping and freedom.

She had also had a commission to execute for Lorraine, who had asked her to call on Tyson's solicitor, Mr Honeywood, in Market-Lydon in Kent, to collect a document that Tyson would like her to bring out for him. *'This is the address,'* wrote Lorraine. *'It's his house, not his office, as he's more or less retired now. I do hope this won't be an awful bore for you, darling, and of course the person who should really be doing this is Gussie Bingham, or that hearty girl-friend of hers, as they live practically on his doorstep. But Tyson says Gussie is an unreliable gossip with a memory like a sieve, and so he would far rather you did it. I do hope you won't mind, baby? Tyson has written to Mr Honeywood and told him that you'll call for it on the afternoon of the twelfth, between three and four, and that he's to have it ready for you. You won't forget, darling, will you?'*

Dany had duly gone down to Kent, though as she had wanted to fit in a cinema in the afternoon as well as a theatre that night, she had rung up Mr Honeywood and changed the time to eleven-fifteen in the morning instead. That had been yesterday. And now it was the last day: really the last day. Tomorrow she would be flying eastward —to Zanzibar!

Ever since Lorraine had married Tyson Frost, Dany had dreamed of going to Zanzibar. She had ransacked the local library and spent her pocket-money on books about the island: *Princes of Zinj, Isle of Cloves,* and a dozen others. Books that told the saga of the great Seyyid Saïd, Imam of Muscat and first Sultan of Zanzibar. And of such things as the underground wells whose waters were said to come from far inland in Africa, the haunted palace of Dunga and the sacred drums of Zanzibar, the vast legendary treasure buried by Seyyid Saïd in Bet-el-Ras; the horrors of the slave trade and the pirate raids, and the witch-haunted island of Pemba, home of devils, djinns and warlocks.

Europeans were not permitted to hold land in Zanzibar, but long ago Tyson's grandfather—that rowdy, roving, colourful adventurer, Emory Frost—had done a service to the great Saïd, and his reward had been the lease of a house, *Kivulimi,* for a period of a hundred and fifty years. Tyson's visits there were irregular and brief, but as this year happened to be the seventieth anniversary of Emory's death, and he intended to write a book based upon the life and times of that fabulous character, he had descended upon *Kivulimi,* complete with wife, private secretary and an assortment of guests. And Dany's dream had at last come true.

'Then I'll go sailing far, off to Zanzibar—though my dream places seem—better than they really are . . .' Dany slid out of bed, crooning a snatch from a song that had been popular when she was in the fourth form; and as she did so something moved at the far side of the room and she started violently and bit her tongue. But it was only her own reflection in the looking-glass, and she made a face at it, and going to the dressing-table, picked up the new lizard-skin bag and rummaged through it for a slip of paper on which she had written down the time that the bus for the Airport left the Terminal. It did not seem to be there, and she was about to try one of the drawers when she remembered that it was in the pocket of the camel-hair coat that she had left in the ladies' room on the previous evening, and forgotten to retrieve. She would have to remember to fetch it after breakfast.

Once again something made her jump nervously; a soft slapping sound in the corridor outside that she identified a moment later as the morning papers, dropped by a page-boy whose feet had made no sound on the thick pile of the carpet. She could not understand why she should be so ridiculously on edge this morning; she had never previously been given to nerves. Perhaps this curious feeling of tension was something that everyone experienced when they first realized that they were entirely on their own? If so, she could only hope it did not last long! Giving the page-boy a minute or two to leave the corridor, she crossed to the door. Tea would not be arriving for at least another hour and a half, and she might as well fill in the time by reading the papers.

The corridor was silent and empty, its lushly carpeted length punctuated by white and gold doors, numerous pairs of freshly polished shoes and a varied assortment of daily newspapers. Dany stepped out cautiously and picked up her own selection, the *Daily Dawn*. And as she did so her eye was caught by the heading of a column: *'Man Murdered in Market-Lydon'*.

She opened the paper and stared at it, frowning. Market-Lydon . . . ? Why, that was where she had been yesterday! The little town where——

There was a sharp click immediately behind her and she whirled round. But it was too late. The draught had blown the door shut behind her and she was locked out in the corridor.

Dany dropped the paper and pushed futilely at the door. But it possessed a spring lock and remained blandly impervious to her efforts, and she turned from it to stare helplessly up and down the silent corridor. There was, fortunately, no one in sight, but she could see no sign of a bell either; and even if there had been one she could hardly use it when the chances were that it would be answered by a man.

For the first time Dany regretted the purchase of that diaphanous and far too expensive nightgown. Nylon and lace might be enchantingly frivolous, but its purpose appeared to be to reveal rather than conceal, and she was only too well aware that to all intents and purposes she might just as well be naked. Why, oh why had she flung away those sensible, high-necked and sacklike garments of white winceyette that Aunt Harriet had considered to be the only suitable and modest night wear? If only——

It was at this inopportune moment that footsteps sounded on the staircase that led into the corridor some twenty feet from her door.

Despite the heavy pile of the carpet the footsteps were clearly audible and noticeably uneven, and they were accompanied by a male voice singing in a blurred undertone the same song that had recently been running through Dany's head.

' "*I want to go away—be a stowaway,*" ' announced the gentleman on the staircase, ' "*Take a trip, on a ship, let my troubles——*" blast!' The singer stumbled noisily on the stairs, and something—possibly a hat?—bounced down them.

Inspiration born of despair descended upon Dany, and snatching up the fallen newspaper she retired hastily behind the front page of the *Daily Dawn* just as the owner of the voice reached the top of the stairs and turned into the corridor.

He proved to be a tall, dishevelled young man in formal evening dress, wearing his white tie several inches off centre, and carrying a gaily coloured balloon and a large and fluffy toy cat with a pink ribbon round its neck. His dark hair was in a state of considerable disorder, and quite apart from his undeniably festive appearance he possessed an indefinable air of what an earlier generation would have termed 'rakishness'.

He stood for a moment or two swaying slightly and looking vaguely about him, and then his gaze alighted upon Dany.

'Well, say!' said the young man, saying it in an unmistakably transatlantic voice: 'what do you know about that!'

He advanced until he was level with her, and then as the full beauty of her situation dawned upon him he gave way to immoderate mirth, and stood before her laughing his head off, while Dany glared back at him like an angry kitten, scarlet cheeked, helpless and infuriated.

'Be quiet!' hissed Dany, 'you'll wake everyone up! Do you know what time it is?'

' "*Three o'clock in the mor* . . . *ning, I've danced the whole night through!*" ' carolled the young man, throwing his head back and giving it everything he had got in a blurred but pleasing baritone.

'And you look like it!' said Dany in a furious whisper. 'But it's nearly six now, and I want to get back into my room. Don't just stand there laughing! *Do* something! Get me a pass key—anything! Can't you see I'm locked out?'

'I can,' said the young man. 'And let me tell you that I haven't seen anything better in days. No, sir! It's a pity that your taste in newspapers didn't run to a smaller sized sheet, but who am I to carp and c-cavil? Let's face it, it might have been *The Times.* Not, le' me

215

tell you, that you look like a dame who reads *The Times.* No, I sh'd say——'

'*Will* you be quiet?' demanded Dany frantically. 'And if you aren't going to help, go away! No—no, don't do that! For goodness sake get me a pass key.'

'Sure,' said the young man cordially. 'Any li'l thing you say. Here, hold the children.'

He handed over the balloon and the white cat, and Dany, making a rash attempt to accept them, came dangerously near to losing the front page of the *Daily Dawn* in the process. The balloon bounced out of reach and the white cat fell to the floor.

'Now look what you've done!' said the young man reproachfully. 'You've dropped Asbestos. Have you no compassion on dumb animals? He may be heat-resistant, but he doesn't like being kicked around.'

He retrieved the cat and hunted through his waistcoat pockets with his left hand. 'Don't rush me. I know I had it some place. Ah, here we are! Madam—no. No wedding ring. That's good. Miss—your key.'

He held out a door key with a courtly bow.

'But that *isn't* my key,' said Dany on the verge of shedding tears of sheer exasperation. 'It's yours!'

'Why, so it is! You know something? you're a very intelligent girl. You may even read *The Times.* A pity. Well, I'll tell you what. You can't stand there for everyone to take a look at; 'tisn't decent— besides being darned chilly. I'm parked in that room over there, and I guess you'd better go right in and wait while I fetch some gilded flunkey to batter down your door. O.K.? Don't mention it: my fam'ly motto has always been "Never Give a Sucker an Even Break". Let's go.'

He tacked across the corridor, humming gently, and after a couple of unsuccessful tries succeeded in opening the door of the room opposite Dany's.

'There you are,' he said in the self-congratulatory tone of the one who has performed an intricate conjuring trick: 'Move right in. We Holdens are nothing if not hospitable. Make yourself at home. And if there's any little thing you fancy, such as a blanket or a bath towel or a bathrobe, jus' go right ahead and wrap it up. The joint's yours. I'll be right back.'

He bowed again, sweeping the floor in an old-world gesture with the white cat, and removed himself.

Dany did not move until he was out of sight (the *Daily Dawn* did not meet round the back) but as soon as it was safe to do so she crossed the corridor at a run and took refuge in his room.

It was in darkness, for the curtains were still drawn, and she switched on the lights and saw that the bed had been neatly turned down and a pair of maroon-coloured pyjamas laid out upon it. There was also a bottle-green dressing-gown hanging over the back of a chair, and she reached for it thankfully. It was far too large, but all the more welcome for that; for Dany, though slim, was by no means short, and it covered her adequately from throat to ankle, allowing no more than a glimpse of bare feet.

A small travelling-clock on the bedside table informed her that it was already ten minutes to six, and from behind the heavily curtained windows she could hear the muted rumble of the early morning traffic. But there were as yet no sounds of movement from inside the hotel, and Dany sat down on the edge of the bed and prepared to wait.

The room was an almost exact counterpart of her own, though a good deal tidier, and it contained one slightly surprising object: a large photograph of an extraordinarily beautiful woman that stood on the dressing-table, expensively framed in silver and inscribed largely across one corner 'To Lash—with all my love for always— Elf'. It was not, however, the film-star features or the extravagant inscription that was surprising, but the fact that someone had draped the frame in a length of black crêpe, drawn a heavy line through the word 'always' and substituted tersely above it, and in red ink, 'September'.

Dany was engaged in studying these interesting additions when her eye was caught by something else: a familiar coloured label on a suitcase that stood on a chair by the dressing-table. Lashmer J. Holden, Jnr, it would appear, was also intending to fly to Zanzibar via Nairobi.

Holden . . . Why, of course! Lorraine had mentioned him. American and something to do with publishing. He was going to see Tyson about some book or other, and to spend his honeymoon in Zanzibar. Although if that photograph was anything to go by . . . A cold draught of air blew through the room and billowed the curtains, and a quantity of letters that had been carelessly propped against a china ornament on the writing-table fluttered to the ground and lay strewn across the carpet.

Dany rose and replaced them, noting as she did so that Mr

Holden's correspondents appeared to be numerous, but unexciting; the large majority of the envelopes being of the strictly utilitarian variety with the address typewritten on them, and having apparently come from various secretarial agencies.

She stacked them in a neat pile and put them back, and then stopped to retrieve the discarded sheet of newspaper. And as she did so her gaze fell on a word in black type: *'Murder'*.

'Man Murdered in Market-Lydon. Retired Solicitor Found Shot. Mr H. T. Honeywood . . .'

But it couldn't be. There must be some mistake. It couldn't possibly be Tyson's Mr Honeywood. That small, dried-up, disapproving solicitor. It must be someone with the same name. People one had met—people one knew—were never murdered. But there was no mistake. Here was his name. And his address: the prim greystone house standing back from the road behind a high wall and an ugly screen of wet laurels. Dany sat down slowly on the bed and read the incredible column of close print.

Mr Honeywood had been shot through the heart at close range, presumably by someone whom he had no reason to fear, for there were no signs of a struggle. The safe in his study had been open, and certain sums of money—the funds, apparently, of local societies of which he was treasurer—had vanished, though no one was in a position to say if anything else had been removed. Mr Honeywood had virtually retired from active work and seldom visited the office in the High Street, which was in the charge of a junior partner, Mr John Honeywood, a nephew; but he occasionally saw an old client at his house. It was this scarcity of visitors, allied to the absence of his housekeeper, that accounted for the fact that the crime was not discovered until so late . . .

The police were of the opinion that he had been killed some time during the morning, possibly between eleven-thirty and twelve, but his housekeeper, who was elderly and deaf, had asked for the day off to visit a cousin in Tunbridge Wells, and had left the house shortly before 10 a.m. She had not returned until late in the evening, and it was she who had eventually found the body. There was also a charlady who came every morning for two hours and who had left about the same time, but neither lady could say for certain if Mr Honeywood had been expecting a visitor, and the sole entry in his engagement pad for the day read 'D.A. between 3 and 4.' The police were anxious to interview a young woman who had been seen leaving the house shortly after half-past eleven that morning, and whom they thought could give them some information . . .

Why—they mean *me!* thought Dany, horrified. But I can't tell them anything! It can't be true——

She let the paper slide to the floor and sat staring down at it. She would have to go round to the nearest police station as soon as she was dressed. Or did one merely reach for a telephone and dial 999? They could not detain her for long, for there was very little that she could tell them. But all the same it would cut badly into her last day, and she had meant to——

Another and far more disturbing thought suddenly struck her. Wouldn't there be an inquest? And if there were, would she have to attend it and lose her seat on the plane? But if she did that she might not be able to get another one for days! Possibly for weeks——! Or even months, if the Nairobi run was a popular one. Tyson and Lorraine might have left Zanzibar and moved on to Spain or Cape Town or New York before she could get another passage, and she could not *bear* it if that were to happen!

Perhaps after all it would be better to say nothing, and do nothing. She had only to wait one more day and then she would be safely aboard the plane. And the police were not in the least likely to fetch her back from Zanzibar for any inquest. It wasn't as if she could give them any help, and anyway she could always write them a letter.

She straightened up with a sigh of relief as though a weight had fallen off her shoulders, and her gaze fell again on the travelling-clock. Twenty-five minutes past six! She had not realized that so much time had slipped by. What on earth was Mr Holden doing? Had he forgotten all about her? It could not possibly have taken him over half an hour to find a valet or a pageboy and collect a pass key.

She jumped up and had started for the door when it opened, and Mr Holden was back, still clutching the cat.

'Relax!' said Mr Holden buoyantly. 'Here come the United States Marines! One of those retired ambassadors in striped pants and ten dollars' worth of whiskers rustled up a spare key. The guy seemed to think he should stand by and personally usher you in, but I urged him to spare your blushes, and he reluctantly handed it over. I guess he fears the worst.'

He held out the key and Dany clutched it gratefully.

'Sorry to have kept you waiting,' pursued Mr Holden cheerfully, 'but I got side-tracked by an Alka-Seltzer. They certainly offer service in this gilded flop-house. Hey!—you're not going, are you? Stick around and be sociable.'

'I don't feel sociable,' said Dany. 'Not at this hour of the morning. Thank you for your help. And for the dressing-gown. I'll return it.'

'So I should hope,' said Mr Holden. 'It has sentimental associations. Say, if I can manage that one I must be in better shape than I thought. "Sentimental Associations". Not bad. Not bad at all. That bathrobe was a present from Elf. Embroidered that flashy great monogram on it with her own fair hands—so she says. But you don't have to believe a word of it. The truth is not in that girl. Jus' between you an' me, honey——'

The door shut with a decisive bang, and he was alone.

'No gratitude,' said Mr Holden sadly, addressing himself to Asbestos. 'That's what wrong with women. No—bloody—gratitude!'

2

The corridor was still silent and empty, and the entire hotel appeared to be still asleep: a fact for which Dany was profoundly grateful. She fitted the key into the lock, opened the door—and stood wide-eyed and aghast.

The room looked as though a tornado had struck it. Drawers had been pulled out and their contents emptied on to the floor, suitcases had been dragged out and opened, and tissue paper, cardboard boxes and bedclothes strewed the carpet.

'So *that's* what he was doing!' said Dany, breathing stormily. 'I suppose this is his idea of a screamingly funny joke! How dare he—how *dare* he!'

She whirled round and ran back across the corridor, and had reached out her hand to bang on his door when she changed her mind. Mr Holden was undoubtedly under the influence of alcohol—a condition that Dany had not previously encountered—and the chances were that he was at that very moment gleefully waiting for her to burst into his room in a fury so that he could enjoy his silly practical joke to the full. It would therefore be more dignified—and snubbing—to ignore the whole thing.

She went back to her own room and, shutting the door with a commendable lack of noise, spent the next half-hour restoring order, so that by the time the room-maid put in an appearance with a tray of morning tea, the place was tolerably tidy again.

Dany had gone down to breakfast at eight-thirty to find the vast dining-room sparsely populated, and had lost her appetite after one glance at the representative selection of the morning papers that had been thoughtfully placed at her table.

Yes, there it was again. 'Murder at Market-Lydon.' Every paper carried the story, and the accounts did not vary much, except as to detail. One paper mentioned that the 'fatal shot' had been fired from an automatic small enough to be carried easily in a coat pocket or a lady's handbag, and another said that the initials 'D. A.' on Mr Honeywood's engagement pad had been duplicated on a lace and cambric handkerchief that had been found under Mr Honeywood's desk. So that's where I lost it! thought Dany guiltily. It must have been when I was hunting through my bag for Lorraine's letter.

There was one point, however, on which every account agreed. The police wished to interview a young woman who had been seen leaving Mr Honeywood's house 'shortly after half-past eleven', and whom they hoped might be able to assist them in their inquiries.

Well, I won't! decided Dany stubbornly. I'm going to fly to Zanzibar tomorrow, and nothing and no one is going to stop me! I'm not going to help them. I'm not—I'm not!

She pushed the papers aside, and snatching up her bag, almost ran from the room, colliding *en route* with a slim man in a pepper-and-salt suit who had just entered the dining-room. Dany apologized breathlessly, the man said it didn't matter at all, and a stately waiter who, if he were not actually a retired ambassador, might well have been a retired ambassador's gentleman's gentleman, looked so gravely disapproving that Dany flushed hotly and returned to her room at a more decorous pace.

She found that in her absence the room had been swept and tidied and the bed made. And on the bed, laid out with some ostentation on the satin counterpane, was a large and unmistakably masculine dressing-gown.

It managed, somehow, to convey the same austere disapproval that the stately waiter had conveyed with a single cold glance, and Dany's flush deepened as she looked at it. She had meant to return it before going down to breakfast, but she had not trusted herself to be civil to Mr Holden, and it had not occurred to her to put it out of sight in a drawer or cupboard.

He'll have to wait for it, she thought. If he's been up all night he'll be sound asleep by now. I'll wrap it up and hand it in to the hall porter.

She sat down in front of the dressing-table and tried on a small cyclamen velvet hat that had been one of her first purchases in London. Her great-aunt would undoubtedly have disapproved of the colour and swooned at the price, but there was no doubt at all that it did things for her that Aunt Harriet's choice of hats did not.

Lorraine was dark haired and tiny, and Daniel Ashton had been tall and blond; but their daughter had struck out on a line of her own. Dany's hair was light brown: soft, shining and shoulder-length, and curling under in the traditional manner of a medieval page-boy's, while her eyes, a happy medium between Lorraine's blue and Daniel's hazel, were large and grey and lovely.

There was no doubt about it, thought Dany, studying herself in the looking-glass, hats and clothes did make a difference—an aston-ishing difference. She was never going to wear navy-blue serge again!

She pulled open a drawer that contained gloves, scarves and handkerchiefs—one of the few that had escaped Mr Holden's prankish attentions—and was rummaging through it in search of a pair of gloves that could be worn with a cyclamen velvet hat, when her fingers encountered something that had certainly not been there before. She felt it, frowning, and then took it out; wondering if this was another practical joke and if that was why he had not emptied the contents of this drawer on to the floor as he had the others. It was something hard and cold and heavy that had been rolled in one of her chiffon scarves and hidden at the back of the drawer. Dany unrolled it, and instantly dropped it.

It hit the edge of the open drawer and fell with a clatter to the floor, and she sat very still, staring at it, and after a minute or two stooped slowly and stiffly and picked it up. It was a small gun. 'Small enough to be carried in a coat pocket or a lady's handbag . . .'

Quite suddenly Dany was frightened. Her knees felt weak and her hands cold, and she seemed to be having some difficulty with her breathing. The looking-glass reflected a movement behind her and she gave a startled gasp and turned swiftly.

She had apparently left the door ajar, and now it swung open and Mr. Holden was with her once more: changed, and presumably in his right mind, though still accompanied by the cat.

He did not present the appearance of one who has spent the entire night on the tiles, and except for a slight heaviness about the eyes, no one would have suspected him of having had no sleep in the last twenty-four hours. But the sight of the weapon that Dany held clutched in her hand wiped the amiable smile from his handsome features.

'Hey!' said Mr Holden, considerably startled. 'Put that down! My intentions are strictly Grade A. All I want right now is my bathrobe—it's got a couple of letters I need in the pocket.'

Dany gasped and whipped the gun behind her.

'Tell me,' said Mr Holden, 'do you always hold up visitors in that dramatic fashion? Life in London must have gotten a lot brisker since I was last over.'

Something in Dany's white face and wide eyes suddenly struck him, and his own face changed. He came in quickly and shut the door behind him.

'What's up, kid? In trouble?'

Dany licked her dry lips and swallowed convulsively. She found it astonishingly difficult to speak. 'Yes . . . No . . . I don't know. Would you . . . ? There's your dressing-gown. On the bed. Please —take it and go away.'

Mr Holden favoured her with a long, penetrating look and ignored the suggestion. He deposited the cat on the nearest chair and said: 'I thought maybe I'd better bring Asbestos along to play propriety. *"When in Rome . . ."* you know. He may not be much of a chaperone, but he's better than none. Makes a third.'

He came across the room and stood in front of Dany, looking down at her, and then turning abruptly away he vanished into the bathroom; to reappear a moment later carrying a tooth-glass which he filled almost a third full from a silver flask that he produced from his pocket.

'Here, drink this,' ordered Mr Holden sharply, handing it to her. 'No, don't sip at it! Knock it back!'

Dany complied, and having done so, choked and coughed, and Mr Holden thumped her on the back and inquired with a trace of impatience if she had never come across rye before, and who the heck had been responsible for her upbringing?

'G-great-aunt Harriet,' gasped Dany, made literal by shock.

'She the one who taught you to tote a gun?' inquired Mr Holden, interested.

'No, of course not! I—it isn't mine.'

'Just borrowed it, I guess. Now, look, I know it's none of my business, but are you in some sort of a jam?'

'N-no,' said Dany uncertainly. 'There isn't anything—I mean . . .' She looked down at the gun that she still held clutched in her hand, and said: 'Is this an automatic?'

'Yes,' said Mr Holden.

Dany shuddered suddenly and uncontrollably, and he reached out, and taking it from her, jerked back the cocking-piece. She saw his eyebrows go up in surprise and he said in a startled voice: 'Loaded, by golly!'

He removed the magazine and counted the rounds, and finding

these one short, sniffed the barrel. 'And fired! Say, look sister—you haven't by any chance been taking a shot at someone, have you?'

Dany said: *'Has* it been fired? Are you sure?'

'Yep. And fairly recently, I'd say.'

He clicked the magazine back into place and, laying the little gun on the dressing-table, thrust his hands into his pockets and stood looking down at her with a crease between his brows. She looked, he thought, very young and scared and helpless, and he wished that his head felt a bit clearer. He had an uncomfortable suspicion that he was about to become involved in something that he would regret and that were he in full possession of his faculties he would collect his bathrobe and leave the room without loss of time. But he did not go. He picked up the empty tooth-glass instead, and having poured out a second and larger tot from the flask, swallowed it and felt better.

'Now,' said Mr Holden bracingly, drawing up a chair and disposing himself in comfort, 'let's get down to cases. Go ahead—tell me what's the trouble.'

Dany had not previously come into contact with anything stronger than cider cup, and four fingers of rye whisky were beginning to have their effect. The fact that Mr Holden was a stranger to her, and should therefore be treated with proper reserve, did not seem to be of the slightest importance. And anyway he knew her current step-father and was going to marry one of her mother's oldest friends, and perhaps he would be able to tell her what to do.

She said haltingly: 'I—I don't know where to start.'

'Try starting at the beginning,' suggested Mr Holden sensibly.

Dany looked at the gun, and shivered again. She said: 'I found this—the gun—in that drawer just now. Someone must have put it in there while I was at breakfast, or—some time. And I—know it's silly, but I suddenly wondered if it were *the* gun. The papers say it was a small automatic, and though I know it can't possibly be, I thought——'

'Hey, wait a minute,' intervened Mr Holden, pardonably confused. 'What gun, and what papers? You'll have to do better than that, sister. My wits are not all that sharp this morning. And by the way, what's your name? I can't keep calling you "hey" or "you" or "whatsername".'

'Aston. Dany Ashton.'

'Delighted to meet you, Miss Ashton. I'm Lash Holden, from——'

'I know,' said Dany, cutting him short. 'You're going to *Kivulimi* too, aren't you?'

'What's that?' Lash sat bolt upright, and the movement appeared to be painful, for he screwed up his eyes and winced. 'Say, do you know Tyson?'

'He's my step-father.'

'Well, whatdoyouknow?' demanded Lash in pleased surprise. 'That makes us practically relations. My Pop is a life-long pal of the old reprobate. They used to infest the speakeasies back in the old days when the States were technically dry and Tyson was over on some lend-lease college course. Well, well! It is, if I may coin a phrase, a small world. Yep, I'm off to Zanzibar.'

'On your honeymoon,' said Dany.

Mr Holden winced. 'Who told you that?'

'Lorraine. My mother. She said——'

'The wedding,' said Mr Holden, 'is off. Let's not discuss it, if you don't mind.'

'Oh,' said Dany confused. 'I'm sorry.'

'I'm not. Merciful escape. T'hell with women! Say——' He paused and frowned. 'Haven't we wandered off the point some place? You were telling me something. Yeah; I remember now. That gun. Someone stowed it away among your nylons. Now why would anyone do that?'

'Because of Mr Honeywood,' said Dany.

'Mr Who?'

'Honeywood. I don't suppose you've seen the papers this morning, but he was murdered yesterday, and it says that the police want to—to interview a young woman who was seen leaving his house not very long before it happened. And that was me.'

'*You?* Now listen, kid—let's get this straight. Are you trying to tell me that you shot this guy?'

'*No!*' said Dany furiously. 'Oh, what's the good of telling you anything? Of course I didn't shoot him!'

'O.K., O.K.,' said Lash pacifically. 'I just wanted to clear that point up before we went any further. What were you doing in this Honeywood's comb, I mean house?'

'He's Mr Frost's solicitor—the Frosts live near there. Tyson wanted me to bring a letter out with me, and Lorraine, my mother, asked me to call in and fetch it; and I did. I fetched it yesterday morning at eleven o'clock—no, it must have been nearly twenty past, because the train was late; there was some fog about.'

'Well, go on. What happened?'

'Nothing happened. We talked for a bit, and I left.'

'Meet anyone coming away?'

'No. I passed a few people, of course, but I didn't pay much attention. There was a woman with a walking-stick and one with a puppy on a lead, and an African—or an Indian—anyway an Oriental of sorts, in a white—no, that was in the dream. In a raincoat: one of those students. I can't remember any more. But it was rather misty, and I wasn't bothering.'

'And why are you bothering now?'

'Because the papers say that the police think Mr. Honeywood was—was murdered some time between eleven-thirty and twelve. And I was there until just after half-past eleven, and it seems that someone saw me leave.'

'The murderer, you mean?'

'No, of course not! He wouldn't have told the police. But someone told them; and—now someone else is trying to make it look as though I did it.'

'Baloney!' said Lash impatiently.

'It isn't baloney! It isn't! It was that kind of gun. It said so in the papers. A—a little gun. An automatic. And that horrid thing there isn't mine. I've never even *seen* one before! But it was wrapped up in my scarf, and it wasn't there yesterday because I wore that scarf yesterday——'

'O.K., sister!' said Lash. 'I get you. Yes, it's quite a point. You think someone planted this on you, so that when the police came around asking questions it would be found right here in your room? Well you don't have to worry. It won't have your fingerprints on it, and——Yes, by God, it will! Mine, too. *Hmm.* That's a fast one.'

He brooded for a few minutes, and then said abruptly: 'Know what I'd do if I were you? I'd drop that damned thing down the elevator shaft and think no more about it. The cops aren't likely to locate you before you get aboard the plane tomorrow, and once you're out of the country they can go ahead with tracing the guy who did the job. Simple.'

'But suppose they do find me?' said Dany, twisting her hands together distressfully. 'Mr Honeywood may have told someone I was coming down. And I telephoned him. I was going down in the afternoon, but I wanted to go to a film, so I telephoned and asked him if I could come in the morning instead. They might trace the call because I telephoned from here. And—and I left a handkerchief in Mr Honeywood's office. It had my initials on it.'

'You *what?*' said Mr Holden, unable to credit it. 'You're telling me that you actually pulled the corny old gag? Good grief! *Women!*'

'You don't suppose I did it on purpose, do you?' retorted Dany hotly. 'And anyway, how was I to know that this sort of—of awful thing was going to happen? How could *anyone* know? People oughtn't to keep valuable things in safes in their houses and then leave their safes open and—and——' Her lips began to tremble.

'Hey!' said Mr Holden, appalled. 'Don't cry. I can handle any-thing else—well, almost anything else. But not tears. Not at this hour of the day, there's a good girl. Here, let me lend you a handker-chief—unmonogrammed!'

He handed one over, and Dany accepted it with a dismal sniff. 'I'm sorry,' she apologized, blowing her nose. 'It was only because I'm so worried, and it's all so—so fantastic and impossible and horrid. Mr Honeywood being murdered, and then finding that gun wrapped up in one of my scarves, and—and not knowing what to do. What *am* I going to do?'

'Nothing!' said Mr Holden firmly. 'Masterly inactivity is my ad-vice. It may be regrettably short on Public Spirit, but right now it looks like saving you a helluva headache. We'll make a nice tidy parcel of that gun, address it to Scotland Yard and drop it in the nearest post box. And you can spend your air trip in writing them a full account of your visit to this guy Honeycomb, and post it in Nairobi: allowing it to be supposed that you missed reading the newspapers today on account of one little thing and another. Not strictly truthful, but a labour-saving device if ever there was one. That should satisfy both your conscience and cops. O.K.?'

'O.K.,' agreed Dany with a breath of relief and a somewhat watery smile.

'Good,' said Mr Holden briskly. 'Then that's fixed.'

He stood up, reached for the gun, and having carefully cleaned off all possible fingerprints with his handkerchief, wrapped it in the crumpled square of linen and stuffed it into his pocket.

'And now I'm afraid I must leave you. I have to go out gunning for a secretary-typist. Mine, believe it or not, has contracted mumps. *Mumps*—I ask you! There ought to be a law against it. See you at the airport, babe.'

He collected his dressing-gown and Asbestos, and departed.

3

Dany sighed and stood up. She still felt badly shaken, but at least she was no longer frightened, for Lash Holden's casual attitude toward the whole horrifying affair had reduced it to manageable proportions.

She was not, she assured herself, obstructing the course of justice by keeping silent. Any information that the gun might convey to the police would be theirs by tomorrow morning. And as far as the details of her visit to Mr Honeywood were concerned, she would tell them that too; but, as Lash Holden had sensibly suggested, by letter. Probably by the time they received it the murderer would have been caught; and if not, at least she would be with Lorraine and Tyson, who could support her story and deal adequately with the police.

Dany closed the drawer in which she had found the gun, and having repaired the ravages caused by tears and Mr Holden's handkerchief, reached for the lizard-skin bag. The unpleasant happenings of the morning had driven the day's programme out of her head, but she had made a list of the few things that she still had to buy, and she took it out of her bag and studied it.

Beach hat, sunsuit, something for air sickness? Ticket for matinee of 'Sun in Your Eye'. *Book for journey?* That should not take long.

It was only when she was replacing the list that she noticed that something was missing from the bag. Surely there ought to be more in it? Money, cheque book, powder compact, lipstick, a crumpled face tissue, a pocket comb, a bunch of keys, a leather pocket-book containing tickets, reservations permits and certificates, and——

With a sudden sickening sense of shock she realized that her passport was no longer there! The brand new passport that Aunt Harriet had impressed upon her that she must on no account let out of her keeping, and which she had carried about in the new lizard-skin bag for the last three days.

She hunted through the bag with desperate, shaking fingers, and finally emptied the entire contents on to the dressing-table. But there was no passport.

It must be there. It *must* be! thought Dany frantically. I couldn't have lost it. It's never been out of my sight, and it was there last thing last night—I saw it when I was checking the plane tickets. *The tickets!* Had those gone too?

She tore open the pocket-book with hands that were so unsteady that she could barely control them. But the tickets were still there. Everything else was there. And none of it was any use without a passport!

Dany dropped the pocket-book and began a frenzied search through the dressing-table drawers. But the action was purely a panic-stricken one, for she knew quite well that it had been in her bag when she had checked over all her various forms and tickets before turning out the light last night. She had taken the bag down with her to the dining-room at breakfast time, and it had never once been out of her sight except——

Dany straightened up suddenly and stood gripping the edge of the dressing-table. She had been locked out of her room for nearly three-quarters of an hour this morning, and during that time Lash Holden had entered it and turned all her things upside down for a practical joke. Had he taken her passport too, as part of it?

She gathered up the scattered contents of her bag in feverish haste, crammed them back into it, and ran out of the room and across the passage.

Mr Holden's door was shut and she hammered on it, terrified that he might already have left and that she might have to wait the best part of the day before catching him again. But Mr Holden was still at home.

The door opened and he regarded her with a trace of annoyance. 'What, again? Not another lethal weapon, I trust? I've only just finished packing up the first one. Here it is.'

Dany said breathlessly: 'Did you take my passport this morning? When you were ragging my room?'

'Rag——? Sorry; I no speaka-da English.'

'Turning it upside down. Did you? Because if you did I don't think it's in the least funny, and I want it back at once. How *could* you?'

Mr Holden stared, scowled, and then reaching out a hand and

grasping her by one arm he jerked her into his room and shut the door behind her.

'Say, what goes on here? I don't get it. No, I have not taken your passport. And just when am I supposed to have roughed up your room?'

'This morning. While I was waiting in here. It *must* have been you. It couldn't have been anyone else! You had the key and——'

Dany stopped: suddenly realizing that someone had got into her room without a key, and hidden a gun there. The balcony——? the fire-escape——?

Lash said: 'Now relax. Just sit right down and have another slug of rye. Looks like you could use one. No? Well I certainly could. You've got me all confused. Chicago was never like this!'

Dany said: 'Then—then it wasn't you. All that mess. I thought it was meant to be a joke, but it was someone looking for my passport. I—I don't understand. Why should anyone want to steal my passport?'

'Probably to use,' said Lash. 'Very useful things, passports. You can't go any place without 'em these days. Some dame may have needed one badly and thought yours would fill the bill. Or else someone wants to stop you catching this plane.'

He paused for a drink, and then said meditatively. 'You know, that's quite an idea—taking that gun into account. Know what I think? I think someone saw you leave this Honeyball's house, and decided that you'd make a very useful red-herring. Probably saw you coming away as he went in, and——Say, how did you get back to town yesterday?'

'By train. The 12.5.'

'Well, there you are. Simple! He bumps off this guy, takes what he wants from the safe, and beats it for the station. And who does he see on the platform but a dame who he knows was visiting this solicitor only a few minutes before he was there himself. If he can only play his trump card, it may keep the police dogs baying on the wrong trail for long enough to let him get clear. So he follows you up to town, works out a way of planting that gun among your undies to make the thing foolproof, and——Has that room of yours got a balcony?'

'Yes. But I don't think——'

'Too easy. The dam' things connect. And there's a fire-escape somewhere. He plants his little time bomb, and then suddenly notices that your bags are lying all over the place covered with air labels—seems you're lighting out for foreign parts. That washes you out as a red-herring, so where does he go from here? Easy: fixes it so you can't leave! No passport, no foreign parts; and there must be a passport around somewhere. He turns the joint upside down until he finds it, pockets the thing and lights out. You are now not only tied by the leg but, what with the newspaper accounts and the fact that you were in this Honeydew's house within the time limit—and that gun and no passport!—it's a cinch you'll panic and start behaving in a manner likely to arouse suspicion in a babe of three: which will be just dandy. How's that for a piece of masterly deduction? Brilliant, if you ask me. The F.B.I. don't know what they missed when father's boy followed him into the business!'

He put down his glass and sat down rather suddenly on the end of his bed, and Dany gazed back at him dazedly. She had taken in very little of what he had said, because her mind was filled with only one distracting thought: she could not catch the plane! She would have to stay here and face the police and questions and inquests and newspaper men, and the scandalized disapproval of Aunt Harriet who would, understandably, feel that all her dire predictions as to the fatal consequences of independence had been fully justified. She was caught!

'No!' said Dany on a sob. 'Oh *no!* I can't stay here. I won't. I *will* go to Zanzibar. They shan't stop me. But—but they can if I haven't got a passport! What am I going to do? Oh *why* did I ever telephone Mr Honeywood? Why did I ever change the times? If I'd only gone in the afternoon instead!'

'And found the body? You wouldn't have liked that.'

'It would have been better than this! Far, *far* better. Can't you do something?'

'Such as what?' demanded Lash reasonably. 'Call up the cops? That would be one helluva help! Now just shut up and let me think for a minute. I don't know how you expect anyone to think while you're carrying on in this uninhibited manner. Hush, now!'

He helped himself to another drink and relapsed into frowning silence while Dany struggled with an overwhelming desire to burst into tears, and was only restrained from this course by a strong suspicion that Mr Lashmer J. Holden, Jnr, was quite capable of boxing her ears should she try it.

She sat down weakly on the nearest chair, her brain feeling as numb and useless as wet cotton wool. The whole thing was impossible and horrible and fantastic: she must be dreaming and she would wake up suddenly and find herself back in her snug, safe bedroom at *Glyndarrow*. This could not be happening . . .

But it was Lashmer J. Holden, Jnr, who woke up.

'I've got it!' he announced. 'By God, what it is to have a brain! Can you type?'

'Yes,' said Dany, bewildered.

'What about shorthand?'

'A—a little.'

'Secretarial college?'

'No. Class at school. Why——'

'Never mind. It'll have to do. O.K. Consider yourself engaged.'

'W-*what!*' gasped Dany.

'Oh—in a purely secretarial capacity. Nothing personal. I'm through with women. Now listen, kid; here's the layout—and is it a lily! If someone thinks they're going to use you as a red-herring to cover up their own get-away, let's wreck the scheme. I've been travelling with a secretary—Miss Kitchell. But Ada has developed mumps, and I haven't so far been able to get hold of a suitable substitute who possesses a valid passport and the necessary visas and forms and whathaveyou to enable her to leave pronto. So what do we do? We take you!'

'Don't be ridiculous,' said Dany crossly. 'You know quite well that I haven't got a passport either! That's the whole point.'

Mr Holden made an impatient noise that is normally rendered in print as '*Tcha!*'

'Use your brain, girl! I'm not taking you as you. I shall take you as Miss Kitchell. You aren't too unlike her. Height about right. Eyes roughly the right colour. Shape a whole lot better, but they don't include that in the photograph. She's older of course, and her hair's red, but she wears glasses and a fringe and about a million curls. The thing's a gift! We dye your hair red—it's a pity, but one must suffer for one's art—get it fringed and frizzed à *la* Ada and buy you a pair of glasses. It's a cinch!'

'But—but . . . No! it isn't possible! She won't agree.'

'She won't be asked,' said Mr Holden firmly. 'I have all her documents right here in a briefcase with my own, and all the files and things we need. She sent 'em to me along with the bad news, and forgot to take her own stuff out. So there we are. Masterly, I think. And what's more it will enable me to put a long-cherished theory to the test.'

'What theory?' asked Dany faintly.

'That no one ever yet looked like the photograph on their passport, and that anyway no official ever really glances at the thing. Well, we shall know tomorrow.'

'We can't do it,' protested Dany, though with less conviction. 'We can't possibly do it!'

'Why not?'

'Well—there's this secretary of Tyson's—Nigel Ponting. He's meeting the plane at Nairobi, and he's bound to have seen photographs of me, and——'

'By the time I've finished with you,' said Mr Holden blithely, 'you will have ceased to resemble any photograph ever taken. Except possibly the libel that is pasted to Ada's passport, and that only remotely. And he will not be expecting you, because we will cover that contingency by sending your parents an express cable to say 'Sorry. Delayed—writing.' That'll hold 'em! As for this Ponting, he is an elegant tulip of the precious and scented variety that your great and glorious country has suddenly taken to breeding like rabbits. A pain—no kidding. I met him last time your step-father was in the States, and I can assure you he wouldn't know one girl from the next. One of those. So *phooey* to Ponting. You don't have to worry about him.'

'Well . . .' began Danny hesitantly; and was caught in another spasm of panic and doubt. 'No! No, I can't. We couldn't!'

'What's to stop us? They can't give us more than a two-year stretch at Sing-Sing—or Borstal, or wherever they send you in this country. And what are two years among so many? Haven't you British any guts?'

There was a sudden angry sparkle in Dany's grey eyes, and her chin lifted. 'All right. I'll do it.'

'That's the girl,' approved Mr Holden, and helped himself to another drink.

'I can't think,' he said, 'why I don't write for a living instead of publishing the puerile efforts of lesser minds. It's all here—brains, dash, fertility of invention and a frank approach to the problems of daily life. What are you just sitting there for? Get going, girl! Jump to it!'

'What am I supposed to do?' inquired Dany, startled.

'Well, pack I guess. You've got to get out of here before the cops catch up on you, so the sooner you check out the better. Get the girl at the desk to call up and cancel your seat on the plane and to send off that cable. That'll help. And tell the room girl and the hall porter and anyone else you meet that you've just heard that your bedridden old grandmother is dangerously ill in Manchester or Aberdeen or some place, and you're having to cancel your trip and rush to her side. Ask the hall porter to get you a taxi to go to whatever station it is where trains leave for the wilds of Caledonia.'

'King's Cross, I think,' said Dany.

'O.K. King's Cross. And when you get there, grab a porter and get him to put your bags in the checkroom, and I'll meet you in the booking hall in an hour and a half's time. Think you can make it?'

'I'll try.'

'Try, nothing! You'll make it or else. If there's one thing that makes me madder than a hornet it's women who keep one waiting around. I've put up with plenty of that in the past, but no more of it for L. J. Holden, Jnr. No sir! Not from now on. Besides, there won't be much time to waste. We have a stiff itinerary before us. Check you in at another hotel, change all your baggage labels, find an intelligent hairdresser and buy a pair of spectacles, for a start. So the sooner you get going the better. See you at King's Cross at 11 a.m. sharp. And mind, I'm not waiting there for ever! Ten minutes is my limit.'

It was, in actual fact, twenty. But he was still there, and in excellent spirits—in every meaning of the words.

'I'm sorry I'm late,' apologized Dany breathlessly, 'but as I was checking out I saw him again—at least it may not have been, but I thought——'

'Saw who?' demanded Lash, confused.

'The African—or whatever he is. I told you I passed one when I was leaving Mr Honeywood's. No, it couldn't possibly have been the same one I suppose. I'm being silly. But he was talking to the man at the desk about some letters, and it gave me such a jolt that I forgot I'd left a coat in the ladies' room, and so of course I had to go back and fetch it, and that made me late. I was afraid you would have left.'

'Another two minutes, and your fears would have proved well founded. But a mish ish as good as a—A miss ish—Oh, well; the hell with it! Let's go.'

He hailed a porter, retrieved Dany's suitcases from the left-luggage office where they had been deposited only a few minutes previously, and half an hour later she was sitting in front of a large looking-glass, swathed in a peach-coloured overall, while Mr

Holden explained breezily to a giggling blonde hairdresser's assistant the details of Miss Ada Kitchell's coiffure.

'He's a one, isn't he? Your gentleman friend,' said the blonde, dunking Dany's head into a basin. 'In films, are you dear? Must be ever so interesting. Ever been a red-head before? No? Well I expect it'll make a nice change. You won't know yourself.'

'Not bad,' said Lash, viewing the result some time later. 'Not bad at all. Though I can't say that it's an improvement. Definitely a retrograde step. Or is that because I'm seeing two of you? Never mind—you can't have too much of a good thing. Let's eat.'

They had eaten at a small restaurant in a side-street near the hairdresser's shop. Or rather Dany had eaten while Mr Holden had confined himself to drinking. And later that day he had deposited her at a sedate family hotel in Gloucester Road, with instructions to keep to her room and not to panic. He would, he said, call for her on the following morning on his way to the Air Terminal, and he regretted his inability to entertain her further, but he had a date that evening. In fact, several.

'You won't oversleep, or anything dreadful?' said Dany anxiously, suddenly terrified by a vision of being abandoned—alone, red-headed and masquerading as Miss Ada Kitchell—in darkest Gloucester Road.

'Certainly not,' said Mr Holden, shocked. 'You don't suppose that I intend to waste valuable time in going to sleep, do you? In the words of some poet or other, I am going to "cram the unforgiving minute with sixty seconds' worth of drinking done". Or know the reason why!'

'But you didn't have any sleep *last* night,' protested Dany, worried.

'What's that got to do with it? Tomorrow is another day. Be seeing you, sister.'

Dany passed the remainder of the day in solitude and acute anxiety, and crept out at dusk to buy the evening papers. But a fire in a large London store, a train crash in Italy, another revolution in South America and the fifth marriage of a well-known film star, had combined to push the murder of Mr Henry Honeywood off the front pages and into small type.

There were no further details, and with repetition the accounts lost much of their horror for Dany, and became more remote and impersonal. Which soothed her conscience somewhat, though not her fears, for there had been nothing either remote or impersonal about the gun that had been hidden in her room at the Airlane. Or in the fact that someone had stolen her passport! The whole thing might sound like an impossible nightmare, but it had happened. And to her—Dany Ashton. Oh, if only—if *only* she had gone to see Mr Honeywood at the proper time!

She had passed a sleepless night, and was looking white and worn when Lash collected her in a taxi at a comparatively early hour on the following morning. But a glimpse of herself in the large Victorian looking-glass that adorned the hall of the family hotel had at least served to convince her that no one would be likely to recognize her. She had not even recognized herself, and for a fleeting moment had imagined that the wan-faced young woman with the over-dressed red hair and wide-rimmed spectacles was some stranger who was standing in the narrow, chilly hall.

Lash, however, apart from noticeable pallor and the fact that his eyes were over-bright, showed no signs of fatigue. He exuded high-spirits and was accompanied by a strong smell of whisky and the cat Asbestos, and no one would have suspected for a moment that he had not been to bed or had any sleep at all for two consecutive nights.

He had dismissed with a single short word Dany's trembling assertion that she had changed her mind and couldn't possibly go through with it, and once in the taxi and *en route* to the Air Terminal had made her take several sea-sick pills and swallow them down with rye whisky.

She had been unable to eat any breakfast that morning, panic having deprived her of an appetite, and the raw spirit, coming on top of a sleepless night and an empty stomach, had quietened her post-operative nerves and filled her with a pleasant glow of confidence which had lasted until the passengers bound for Nairobi were marshalled in the departure lounge, and she found herself standing next to a slim, youngish-looking man with a thin, triangular, attractive face, observant brown eyes and a square, obstinate chin.

Catching Dany's eye he had smiled at her; a swift and singularly pleasant smile that she found it impossible to resent, and said: 'I see that we're both bound for Zanzibar. Have you ever been there before?'

His voice was as irresistibly friendly and good-humoured as his smile, and Dany smiled back at him and shook her head.

'No? That's a pity: I'd hoped to pick up a few pointers. This'll be my first visit too. As a matter of fact, I never expected to make it.

I've had my name down on half a dozen waiting lists for weeks on end, but all the Nairobi planes seemed to be booked solid. I'd almost given up hope when my luck turned—someone cancelled a seat only yesterday, and I got it.'

'Oh,' said Dany, jumping slightly. 'H-how lucky for you.'

'It was that all right! I'm a feature writer. Freelance. My name's Dowling—Larry Dowling.'

'Oh,' said Dany faintly. 'A—reporter.'

Mr Dowling looked pained. 'No. Feature writer. Have you ever heard of a novelist called Frost? Tyson Frost? But of course you have! Well, he's got a house in Zanzibar, and I've been commissioned by a newspaper and a couple of magazines to try and get a feature on him. That is, if he'll see me. He's not an easy man to get at, from all accounts. Still, I ought to be able to get something out of the trip, even if Frost won't play. Might be able to do something on the elections down there. There's a rumour that the local Moscow-Nasser stooges are making an all-out bid for control of the island.'

'Of *Zanzibar*? But it's quite an unimportant little place!' protested Dany, momentarily forgetting her own predicament in a sudden sense of outrage. Was there then no longer any lovely, romantic spot left in all the world that was free from squabbling political parties?

Mr Larry Dowling laughed. 'You know, there was a time when a good many people might have said the same of Sarajevo. But they learnt differently. I'm afraid you'll find that in a world that plays Power Politics there is no such thing any longer as "an unimportant little place".'

'Oh, no!' said Dany involuntarily. 'Why does everything have to be spoiled!'

Mr Dowling lifted a quizzical eyebrow, but his pleasant voice was sympathetic; 'That's Life, that is. I didn't mean to depress you. I'm sure you'll find Zanzibar every bit as attractive as you expect it to be. I believe it's a lovely place. Are you staying with friends there, or are you going to put up at the hotel like me? I hear there is——'

He broke off, his attention sharply arrested by the Vision at that moment entering the crowded lounge. A vision dressed by Dior and draped in mink, preceded, surrounded and followed by a heady waft of glamour and exceedingly expensive scent, and accompanied by a slim, dark Italianate young man and a tall, distinguished-looking gentleman with grey hair and cold pale eyes.

Her entrance created something of a stir, and Mr Holden, also turning to look, lost a considerable portion of his *bonhomie.*

'Here come some of your step-father's guests,' he observed sourly to Dany. 'The Latin type is Eduardo di Chiago. A Roman louse who races his own cars and is a friend of Tyson's—he would be! The one with white whiskers and Foreign Office written all over him (erroneously, he's oil) is Yardley. Sir Ambrose. He's been getting a lot too thick with Elf of late, and she'd better watch her step—there was a rumour around that his Company might be heading for the rocks; and not the kind of rocks she collects, either! It's a pity it isn't true. But at least we don't have to put up with him for long. He's only going as far as Khartoum.'

He did not identify the Vision, but he did not need to. It was, unmistakably, the original of the affectionately inscribed photograph that had adorned his dressing-table at the Airlane. His ex-fiancée and Lorraine's great friend, Amalfi Gordon.

'She's lovely, isn't she?' sighed Dany wistfully, speaking aloud without realizing it.

'Is she?' said Mr Holden coldly.

He directed a brief scowling glance at the Vision, and turned his back on it. But Mrs Gordon had seen him.

'Why—Lash!' Her warm, throaty voice was clearly audible even above the babble of the crowded lounge, but Mr Holden affected to be deaf.

It did him no good. Mrs Gordon descended upon him in a wave of scented sweetness. 'Lash, darling—it's lovely to see you! I was so afraid you'd decide not to come after all.'

'Why?' demanded Lash haughtily. 'This started out as a business trip, and it can stay that way. You surely didn't think that I'd cancel it just because you decided to transfer your affections to some gilded Italian gigolo, did you?'

Mrs Gordon tucked a slender, gloved hand under his arm and gazed up at him from a pair of enormous sea-green eyes; her long soft lashes fluttering appealingly.

No one had ever been able to stay seriously angry with Amalfi Gordon for any length of time. Exasperated, yes. But it was an accepted fact that dear, soft-hearted, feather-headed Elf simply couldn't help it. If she fell into love, or out of it, and hurt people thereby, it wasn't her fault. She never meant to hurt.

Mrs Gordon made a *moue* and said: 'Sweetie, you're not sulking, are you?'

'Of course I'm not!' snapped Lash, descending rapidly from the haughty to the frankly furious. 'What would I have to sulk about? I am, on the contrary, deeply thankful. And now run along back to your Mediterranean bar-fly, there's a good girl.'

Amalfi gave his arm a little coaxing tug. 'Darling, aren't you being just a *tiny* bit kindergarten? Eddie's marvellous!'

'You mean Eddie's a Marchese!' retorted Lash bitterly. 'That's the operative word, isn't it? And you're just another sucker for a title! Apart from that, what's he got that I haven't?'

'Manners,' said Amalfi sweetly. And withdrawing her hand she turned away and rejoined her two cavaliers without having even glanced at Dany.

'How d'you like that?' demanded Lash indignantly. *'Manners!* I suppose if I bowed and scraped and went about kissing women's hands——'

He broke off and subsided into deep gloom, from which he was presently aroused by another clutch at his arm. But this time it was Dany, and he saw that she was staring in wide-eyed alarm at a thin, boney, dark-skinned Oriental in a blue lounge suit, who carried a brief-case, a neatly rolled umbrella and very new burberry.

'It's him!' said Dany in a feverish, ungrammatical whisper.

'Who? The one you think you saw in Market-something, or the one you saw in the hotel?'

'In the hotel. But—but perhaps it's both!'

'Nuts! The world is full of Oriental gentlemen—they come in all sizes. And anyway, what of it? He was probably staying at the Airlane. You were. I was. And so, as it happens, were Elf and that slick owner-driver. And we're all flying to Nairobi. Why not him?'

'But suppose he recognizes me? I was standing right next to him!'

Lash turned and surveyed her with a distinctly jaundiced eye, and remarked caustically that it was extremely doubtful if her own mother would recognize her at the moment. To which he added a rider to the effect that if she was going to lose her nerve every twenty minutes she had better give up the whole idea after all and run off back to her Aunt Harriet, as he did not fancy the prospect of being saddled with a spineless and probably inefficient secretary who suffered from frequent attacks of the vapours. A trenchant observation that acted upon Dany's agitated nervous system with the bracing effect of a bucketful of cold water, and stiffened her wavering resolution. She cast Mr Lashmer Holden a look of active dislike, and preceded him into the aircraft in chilly silence.

No one had questioned her identity, and if there were any plain-clothes police among the crowds at the airport she did not identify them. The stewardess said: 'Will you please fasten your seat belts,' and then they were taxi-ing down the long runway. The propellors roared and the airport slipped away from them: tilted, levelled out and dwindled to the proportions of a child's toy. They were safely away.

'Well, it seems we made it,' remarked Lash affably, unfastening his seat belt and lighting a cigarette.

He accepted a cup of coffee from the stewardess and added the remains of his flask to it. He seemed surprised that there was no more.

'Why, hell—I only filled it half an hour ago! No—I guess it must have been earlier than that. Oh well, plenty more where it came from. Happy landings! How are you feeling, by the way?'

'Sleepy,' said Dany.

'That's odd. So'm I. A very good night to you.'

He settled himself comfortably and was instantly asleep, and Dany, looking at him resentfully, was annoyed to find that her own head was nodding. She had no intention of wasting her time in sleep. This was her very first flight, and although the circumstances under which she was making it were, to say the least of it, unusual, she was not going to miss a moment of it. Soon they would be passing over the Channel. France . . . Switzerland. Looking down on the snowy peaks of the Alps. On the Matterhorn and Mont Blanc. Over the mountains to Italy. No, of course she could not sleep . . .

D any awoke with a start to find the stewardess once again urging her to fasten her seat belt. 'We shall be coming in to land in a few minutes.'

'Land? Where?' inquired Dany dazedly.

'Naples. Do you think you could fasten your friend's belt? I don't seem to be able to wake him.'

Dany performed this task with some difficulty, Mr Holden remaining immobile throughout. He did not even wake when the plane touched down, and the stewardess gave up the unequal struggle, and in defiance of regulations, left him there.

Dany climbed over him to join the other passengers who were being ushered out into the dazzling sunlight of the Naples aerodrome, and feeling quite incapable of any conversation, affected not to see Larry Dowling, who had given her a friendly smile as she passed him.

A curious mixture of lunch and tea was served in the dining-room of the airport, but Dany was in no mood to be critical, and she ate everything that was placed before her, surprised to find herself so hungry. Prompted by caution she had selected a table as far as possible from her fellow passengers, and from this vantage point she studied them with interest; realizing that among them, still unidentified, were two more guests bound for *Kivulimi.* Tyson's sister, Augusta Bingham, and her friend Miss—Boots? No. Bates.

It was, she reflected, the greatest piece of luck that she should have been suffering from measles on the only occasion on which this new step-aunt had suggested coming to see her, and that she had selfishly put off calling on Mrs Bingham at the Airlane on Wednesday evening. She had so nearly done so. But there had been the film of *Blue Roses,* and then there had been the choice between doing her duty by introducing herself to her step-aunt, or going to the theatre that evening—and the theatre had won.

Glancing round the dining-room, Dany decided that the two women she was looking for were obviously the two who had seated themselves at Mrs Gordon's table, for the older one bore a distinct resemblance to Tyson. The same blunt nose and determined chin. Yes, that must be Augusta Bingham: a middle-aged woman whose greying hair had been given a deep-blue rinse and cut by an expert, and whose spare figure showed to advantage in an equally well-cut suit of lavender shantung.

Mrs Bingham wore a discreet diamond brooch and two rows of excellent pearls, and looked as though she played a good game of bridge, belonged to several clubs and took an interest in gossip and clothes. Her neighbour, in marked contrast, conveyed an instant impression of Girl Guides, No Nonsense and an efficiently-run parish. Undoubtedly, Miss Bates.

Miss Bates, who despite the heat wore a sensible coat and skirt and an uncompromisingly British felt hat of the pudding-basin variety, provided a most effective foil for Amalfi Gordon, who was sitting opposite her. Mrs Gordon had discarded her mink cape and was looking cool and incredibly lovely in lime-green linen. How does she do it? wondered Dany, studying her with a faintly resentful interest. She's old! She was at school with Mother, and she's been married almost as many times. Yet she can still look like that!

The Italian marquis—or was it marchese?—and Sir Ambrose someone (oil) were giving Mrs Gordon their full attention, and Amalfi was being charming to both of them, as well as to Mrs Bingham and Miss Bates and a couple of openly admiring waiters. Even Larry Dowling was finding it difficult to keep his eyes from straying and his attention on what his table companion was saying.

Mr Dowling was sitting two tables away with the dark-skinned man whom Dany had seen at the hotel, and who was talking earnestly and with much gesticulation. His voice came clearly to Dany's ears: 'You do not understand! You are not Arab. It is the iniquity of it! The flagrant injustice! Why should a suffering minority be exploited for the benefit of cru-el and blood-sucking imperialists of a dying pow-ah, who mercilessly snatch their profits from the very mouths of the starving poo-er? Now I, as an Arab——'

So people really *did* talk like that! And, presumably, others listened. Mr Dowling was certainly listening, though perhaps not quite as earnestly as he should. But then he hoped to write a feature, whatever that was, on the elections in Zanzibar, and——. With a sudden sense of acute alarm Dany remembered something far more important. He wanted to interview Tyson! She would have to warn her step-father, and she would have to keep out of sight. It would be disastrous if this Larry Dowling, who wrote for the newspapers, were to find out that she was Tyson Frost's step-daughter, masquerading as the secretary of a visiting American publisher in order to escape giving evidence at an inquest on murder. It would make an excellent front page story for the newspapers, and Dany shuddered at the thought. Supposing—just supposing—someone were to recognize her? The man whom he was talking to——

Once again panic snatched at Dany. Even if the Arab was not the man she had passed in the mist near Mr Honeywood's house, he was certainly the man who had stood almost at her elbow in the hall of the Airlane, and if he should recognize her, and ask questions, she might be stopped at Nairobi and sent back.

What were the penalties for travelling on a false passport? Why hadn't she thought of that before? Lash Holden had made some flippant reference to it, but she had not stopped to think. She should have thought . . .

Mr Dowling's companion was talking again, even more audibly, but on a more topical subject. 'I feel always sick—most sick—in these aeroplanes. It is my stomach. Everything, I take it. It is no good. The height—I do not know. Yes, we do not move, but still I am feeling bad always. But worse over the sea. I am most bad over the sea. For if the engines fail over the sea, what will happen then? We will all drown! It is terrible!'

He's not airsick, thought Dany. He's only frightened! Well, so am I . . .

Larry Dowling caught her eye and grinned, and unaccountably some of the panic left her. He might be a reporter, and dangerous to know, but he was a dependable sort of person, and she had a sudden, strong conviction that Aunt Harriet would have approved of him. Which was odd . . .

She became aware that passengers for Nairobi were being requested to return to their aircraft and rising hurriedly she snatched up her coat and bag and hastened out in the wake of her fellow passengers.

Lashmer J. Holden Jnr had not moved, and he did not stir as she squeezed past him to regain her seat. He was, in technical parlance, out for the count; and Dany, vaguely recognizing the fact, was conscious of feeling lost and friendless and very much alone. Until this moment she had felt herself to be a mere member of the crew with Lash in charge and steering the ship, and provided she did what she was told he would bring her safely into port. Now she was not so sure. Viewed dispassionately in the bright Mediterranean sunlight, Lashmer Holden looked a good deal younger. His hair was dishevelled and he looked pallid and unshaven and she studied him with a critical and disapproving eye, and then—her maternal instincts getting the better of her—leant over and loosened his tie, which had worked round somewhere in the neighbourhood of his right ear, and drew down the blind so that his face was shielded from the sun.

The two red-faced gentlemen of unmistakably Colonial appearance who occupied the seats immediately behind her began to snore in gentle and rhythmic chorus, and she wished she were able to follow their example and fall asleep again herself, in order to avoid having to think. But she was by now far too anxious and far too wide awake; and in any case there was that letter to be written. The letter that she must post in Nairobi, explaining herself to the police.

Dany stood up cautiously and removed her attaché case from the rack above her head, noting, with a renewed sense of surprise, the label that proclaimed it to be the property of Miss Ada Kitchell. But with the writing paper in front of her and a Biro in her hand, she found that it was not going to be as easy as she had thought.

Looking back over the last twenty-four hours she wondered if she had temporarily taken leave of her senses. Or had Lash Holden's alcoholic exuberance exerted a hypnotic influence over her? She had been frightened and confused, and stubbornly determined that nothing should cheat her out of this long-looked-for-ward-to visit to Zanzibar. And in that state of mind she had been only too ready to grasp at the preposterous line of escape that he had offered. But now that she had plenty of time for thought, the folly of her behaviour was becoming increasingly clear.

She had done precisely what someone had hoped that she would do. Panicked and behaved in a foolish and suspicious manner, and allowed herself to be used as a red-herring to confuse the trail of a murderer. She was an 'Accessory After the Fact'; and that, too, was a punishable offence. If she had kept her head and rung up the police at once, even though it meant postponing this visit or perhaps sacrificing it altogether, then it would have been the police who would have found that gun—and without her fingerprints on it. And if she had given them what little information she could, it might have helped them to get on the track of the real criminal at once, instead of wasting time trying to trace her.

She had, thought Dany with bleak honesty, been selfish and cowardly and deplorably gullible. She had obstructed justice and played a murderer's game for him, and she wondered how long it would take the police to find out that Mr Honeywood's visitor had been a Miss Dany Ashton if she did not write and tell them so herself? Perhaps they would never find out. Perhaps, after all, it would be better to say nothing at all—having let things get this far. Could she get a jail sentence for having obstructed justice? Yet she had only wanted to see Zanzibar. Zanzibar and *Kivulimi* . . .

Lorraine had sent her some photographs of *Kivulimi* two years ago. They had arrived on a cold, wet, depressing afternoon in November, and brought a breath of magic into Aunt Harriet's stolidly unromantic house. *'There are jacarandas in the garden,'* Lorraine had written, *'and mangoes and frangi-pani and flamboyants, and any amount of orange trees, and they smell heavenly and keep the place nice and cool. I suppose that's where it gets its name from. "Kivulimi" means "The House of Shade".'*

Dany put away the writing paper and pen and returned the attaché case to the rack. It was all too difficult, and she would wait until she could make a clean breast of it to Lorraine and Tyson. Lorraine would think it was all thrilling, and Tyson would probably be furious. But they would take charge of the whole problem, and know what to do.

She sat down again, feeling cold and forlorn and more than a little ashamed of herself. If only Lash would wake up! But Mr Holden did not look as though he intended to wake up for anything short of the Last Trump, and Dany found herself regarding him with increasing hostility.

It was, she decided suddenly, all Lash's fault. If it had not been for him—him and that ridiculous stuffed cat! 'Asbestos' indeed!

A fragrant breath of *Diorissimo* competed triumphantly with the smell of cigarette smoke, antiseptics and upholstery, and Dany became aware that Mr Holden's pleasant profile was silhouetted against a background of lime-green linen.

Amalfi Gordon was standing beside him in the aisle, looking down at his unconscious form with a faint frown and an expression that was a curious mixture of speculation, doubt and annoyance. In the shadow of the drawn blind, and with the light behind her, she looked blonder and lovelier than ever, and it was impossible to believe that she must be a good deal nearer forty than thirty, and had been at school with one's own mother.

She lifted a pair of long, gilt-tipped lashes that were undoubtedly genuine, and glanced at Dany with the unseeing and entirely uninterested look that some women bestow on servants, and the majority of beautiful women accord to their plain or unattractive sisters.

It was a look that aroused a sudden sharp antagonism in Dany, and perhaps it showed in her face, for Mrs Gordon's sea-green eyes lost their abstraction and became startlingly observant. She looked Dany up and down, noting her youth and missing no detail of her dress or appearance, and the frown on her white brow deepened. She said without troubling to lower her voice:

'You must be Lash's—Mr Holden's—secretary. I thought he was bringing Ada.'

'She couldn't come,' said Dany shortly, disturbed to find that she was blushing hotly.

'Oh?' It was obvious, and in the circumstances fortunate, that Mrs Gordon was not in the least interested in Lash's secretaries, for she made no further inquiries. But something in Dany's gaze had evidently annoyed her, for she looked down again at the sleeping Lash, and then lightly, but very deliberately, stretched out one slender white hand and smoothed back an errant lock of hair that had fallen across his forehead.

It was a sweetly possessive gesture that spoke volumes—and was intended to. And having made her point, Mrs Gordon smiled charmingly and went on down the aisle to the ladies' room.

Dany subsided, feeling shaken and unreasonably angry, and unnerved by the narrowness of her escape. What if Mrs Gordon had asked her name, and she had said 'Kitchell'? What would have happened then? *But you aren't Ada Kitchell. I know her.* How would she have answered that? Two red-headed secretaries, both with the same name, would have been difficult to explain away. Unless they were sisters——? If Mrs Gordon questioned her again she would have to be Ada's sister. Lash should have remembered that Mrs Gordon had met his ex-secretary, and warned her of it.

She turned to look at him again, and apprehension gave place to that entirely illogical anger. She reached out and pushed the lock of hair over his forehead again. That, thought Dany, will show her!

The stewardess dispensed tea, and the two Colonial gentlemen in the seat behind woke up and embarked upon a long and dogmatic discussion of the race problems in Kenya. The thin Arab whom Dany had first seen in the hall of the Airlane—or possibly in Market-Lydon?—passed down the aisle, and one of the men behind her lowered his voice and said: 'See who that was? Salim Abeid—the chap they call "Jembe".'

'Believe you're right. Wonder what he's been doing over in London?'

'Being made much of by our messy little Pro-Reds and Pink Intellectuals, I suppose. Can't think why we allow that type of chap to go there. They're never up to any good, and they never get any good—the Reds see to that! Swoop down on 'em like vultures the minute they land, and cherish 'em and fill 'em up with spleen, and educate 'em in subversion.'

'I've always heard,' said the other voice, 'that he's an able feller. They say he's getting quite a following in Zanzibar.'

'So I believe. Which is Zanzibar's bad luck! That place has always seemed to me a sort of peaceful oasis in a brawling desert of politicians and power-grabbers. But Jembe and his ilk are out to change all that if they can. Ever noticed how for all their bellowings about "Peace and Brotherly Love" the average Red is eaten up from nose to tail with envy, hatred, malice and all uncharitableness? Their gods and their gospel are hate and destruction, and Jembe is typical of the breed. At the moment his target is the British, because that is a sitting duck these days. But he's a Coast Arab, and if ever he should manage to get us out he'll turn his followers on the Indian community next; or the Parsees—and then the Omani Arabs—and so on. There must always be an enemy to kick, so that he can keep hate alive and profit by it. If Zanzibar is a little Eden, then Jembe is the serpent in it! Did I ever tell you . . . ?'

The speaker lowered his voice again as the subject of his remarks passed again on his way back to his seat, and thereafter made no further mention of Zanzibar or of the man he had referred to as 'Jembe'.

The daylight faded, and Dany drew up the blind and found that they were still flying over the sea. She wished that she had something to read. Or someone to talk to. Anything to soothe her jangled nerves and keep her from thinking of Mr Honeywood—and of murder. The couple behind her, having exhausted politics and settled the fate of Kenya, had advanced—loudly—to the unnerving subject of air disasters. A painfully audible anecdote about a settler who, while flying his family in to Nairobi for a week-end, made a forced landing in waterless country where they all died of thirst before help could reach them, was succeeded by another concerning a convivial gentleman called 'Blotto' Coots who 'pancaked' in the sea off Mombasa and was devoured by sharks, and a third relating to one 'Toots' Parbury-Basset who crashed into the crater of an extinct volcano, killing herself, two friends and her African houseboy in the process . . .

'Must have got caught in a down-draught: or else her engine cut out,' trumpeted the narrator light-heartedly. 'We didn't find 'em till the next day. Nasty mess. Bits all over the shop—no idea who was who. Did you hear about that airliner that broke up over the Mediterranean last Tuesday? Come to think of it, must have been just about where we are now. Forty-eight people on board and——'

The Arab, Jembe, rose abruptly and hurried down the aisle once more, casting the speaker a look of virulent dislike as he passed. It was obvious that he too had caught part of the conversation, and Dany remembered his recent assertion that he felt 'always most bad over the sea, for if the engines should fail then, we will all drown: it is terrible!' He had something there, she thought, peering down at the enormous empty leagues of sea so far below them, and wondering if there were sharks in the Mediterranean. She had it on good authority that there were plenty off the Mombasa coast, and it occurred to her that if the timorous Jembe had been tuned in on the fate of the late 'Blotto' Coots, he was likely to feel a lot worse once they left Mombasa on the last lap of their journey.

If he has any sense, thought Dany, he'll take a strong sedative! She was not sure that she couldn't do with one herself.

A star swam palely into the blue immensity above, to be followed by another and another, until at last it was dark. The chairs were tipped back to facilitate sleep, and the lights were dimmed to no more than a faint blue glow but it was not a restful night—although judging from the stentorian snores, a few people found it so.

In the yellow dawn they came down for breakfast at Khartoum, where the stewardess, assisted by the First Officer, made another unsuccessful attempt to arouse the slumbering Mr Holden. 'We're supposed to turn everyone out at these stops,' explained the First Officer, 'but short of carrying him out, and back in again, there doesn't seem to be much that we can do about this one. He must have been on one hell of a bender. Lucky chap! Oh well—let him lie. Are you with him, Miss—er——?'

'Kitchell,' supplied Dany hastily. 'Yes. I'm his secretary.'

'Tough luck! What are you going to do about him when we reach Nairobi?'

'I've no idea,' said Dany truthfully. 'But he's bound to wake up before then.'

'I wouldn't bet on it,' said the First Officer cheerfully, and went away followed by the stewardess.

Dany and the remainder of the passengers, looking heavy-eyed and somewhat creased, had eaten breakfast and exchanged wan, polite smiles as the sun rose over Ethiopia. Sir Ambrose Yardley had left, looking regretful, and his place had been taken by a stout Indian. But otherwise the passenger list was unchanged, and the weary, yawning faces were beginning to look as familiar to Dany as though she had known them all for several years.

Lash had woken shortly after they had taken off again. He had looked at Dany as though he had no idea at all who she was, and having informed his Maker that he felt terrible, had staggered off to the men's washroom where he had apparently drunk several quarts of richly chlorinated water, and returning to his seat had instantly fallen asleep again.

Dany peered anxiously down at Africa and did not think much of it. A vast, flat expanse of orange-brown, broken by splashes of livid green and dotted with clusters of pigmy beehives which she took to be native *kraals*. But at last there arose on the horizon a blue shadow topped by twin snow peaks.

'Mount Kenya,' announced an enthusiastic passenger who had been studying the flight card 'We should be coming down to land soon. We're due at Nairobi at eleven, and I make it a quarter to.'

'Will passengers please fasten their seat belts,' intoned the stewardess, and Dany turned her attention to the arduous task of rousing her employer.

5

'L'me alone,' mumbled Mr Holden thickly, and without opening his eyes.

'I can't,' said Dany, continuing to shake him. 'Wake up! You can't go on sleeping any longer. At least, not here. We'll be in Nairobi in a few minutes.'

'What of it?'

'We get out there,' explained Dany patiently. 'This particular plane goes no further. Remember? You've got to wake up. Lash, *please* wake up!'

'Go t'hell,' murmured Lash indistinctly.

Dany shook him viciously, and Lash moaned and attempted to sit upright. He forced open his eyes with a palpable effort and shut them again quickly.

'God! I feel terrible!'

'That's what you said before,' snapped Dany unsympathetically. 'And you look it!'

Lash opened his eyes again, but with caution, and scowled at her. 'Do I know you?' he inquired.

Oh dear God, he means it! thought Dany with desperation. He really means it! he doesn't remember——Panic threatened to rise and engulf her, but she fought it down.

'You should,' she observed briskly. 'I'm your new secretary.'

'Rubbish! What happened to Ada?'

'Mumps,' said Dany succinctly.

'Then how in hell——? Oh, let it go! Let it go! I'll sort it out later. God——! Have I got a hangover!'

The aircraft touched down on the runway with a light bump and Lash clutched his head and groaned aloud.

◇ ◇ ◇

Dany could never remember afterwards how she had got through the next half hour, but at least she had had no time in which to be frightened. There had been no sign of Tyson's secretary, Nigel Ponting, and somehow or other she had collected her luggage, and Lash Holden's, piloted him through a maze of official procedure, steered him through the customs and shepherded him into a taxi. Her passport—or more correctly, Ada Kitchell's—had received only the most cursory glance, and once in the taxi Lash had roused himself sufficiently to recall the name of the hotel where those passengers who were booked through to Zanzibar were to spend the night.

'Holden? said the receptionist, peering short-sightedly through rimless glasses. 'Mr L. J. Holden? Oh yes. Yes, of course. We were expecting you.' She beamed on them as though their safe arrival was a matter for congratulation. 'Your rooms are reserved. I hope you had a pleasant flight? There is a message from a Mr Ponting. He had to see the dentist—an emergency stopping, and he could get no other appointment. But he will be calling round later and hopes you will forgive him for not having been at the airport.'

'His loss, our gain,' said Lash sourly. 'Let's hope he gets a gumboil as well, and is hung up at the dentist's indefinitely. Suits me.'

'Er . . . um . . . quite,' said the receptionist with an uncertain smile. 'The boys will take your luggage along, madam. Sign here please, sir. Now is there anything you would like sent up——?'

'Black coffee,' said Lash. 'A bath of it. And some Alka-Seltzer.'

'Er—certainly. Of course. Will the other lady be arriving later?'

'No,' said Lash shortly. 'There isn't another lady. Where's this room? I can't stand here half the day.'

The receptionist left her desk in charge of an African clerk, and graciously accompanied the procession herself, ushering them at last into a sitting-room lavishly supplied with flowers. There was also, somewhat unexpectedly, a bottle of champagne in a bucket of ice, and two glasses.

'With the management's compliments,' beamed the receptionist, and withdrew.

'Wait a minute!' said Dany. 'What about me? Where do I——?' But the door had closed.

Lashmer Holden Jnr sat down heavily on the sofa, put his head in his hands and gave every indication of taking no further interest in the proceedings, and Dany looked at the flowers and the champagne, and struck by an unpleasant thought, crossed the room quickly and opened the only other door. It led into a bedroom where there were more flowers—orange blossom among them—and an impressive double bed.

'It's the honeymoon suite!' said Dany blankly. 'For heaven's sake——!'

She returned in haste to the sitting-room. 'You'll have to do something. There's been a mistake. They think we're married!'

Lash winced and said very distinctly: 'Would you mind not yelling at me?'

'But this is the Bridal Suite!'

'Yeah. I booked it.'

'You *what?*'

'Don't *shout!*' implored Lash testily.

'You mean to sit there and tell me that——? Is this your idea of a joke?'

'*Joke!*' said Lash bitterly. 'If you think that being jilted on the eve of your wedding, and all for the sake of a grinning, greasy-haired, hand-kissing son of a snake-in-the-grass who——Oh, go away! Be a good girl and get the hell out of here.'

'*Elf!*' said Dany, enlightened. 'I forgot. Oh, Lash, I *am* sorry. I didn't mean to . . . I mean, I . . .' She stopped, confused and remorseful.

'I'll take it as read,' said Lash. 'And now, if you don't mind fading away, I think I could do with some sleep. Thanks very much for your help. Good-bye.'

He dropped his head back into his hands again and Dany stood looking down at him with exasperation that was replaced, suddenly and entirely unexpectedly, by a strong desire to pillow his ruffled, aching head on her breast and whisper consolation and endearments. And this to a man whom she had met only forty-eight hours before, and who, having been instrumental in landing her in this intolerable and probably dangerous situation, could not now even bring himself to remember her!

I must be going out of my mind! thought Dany, astounded at herself. And anyway, he's in love with that Gordon woman, and he's been drinking himself silly because she threw him over. He doesn't care one bit what happens to me. All he wants to do is to get rid of me as soon as possible. He's selfish and stupid and spoiled and egotistical, and he drinks. *And* drinks!

But it was no use. She could not even feel indignant about it, and she still wanted to stroke his hair and comfort him. Oh dear, oh dear, oh *dear,* thought Dany. I suppose this is it!

In common with all young women she had dreamed of the time when she would fall in love. It would be a romantic and rapturous and altogether wonderful moment, and the hero of it would certainly not be a pallid and dishevelled stranger who was suffering from an imperial hangover, and who was himself hopelessly in love with a glamourous widow who had jilted him for an Italian marquis!

Nothing, it seemed, turned out as one had pictured it or planned it. Life was very disappointing. *'Damn!'* said Dany aloud and deliberately.

Lashmer Holden flinched. There was a rap on the door and a white-robed African entered with a tray that bore coffee, a jug of water, a glass and some Alka-Seltzer. Dany was relieved to find that he both spoke and understood English, and having given him several precise orders she dismissed him and turned her attention to the tray.

The coffee, though not supplied in the quantity originally suggested, was hot and very strong, and she poured out a cup of it and took it over to the sufferer. 'Try some of this,' she suggested. 'It'll probably make you feel a lot better.'

Lash lifted his head and scowled at her, but he took the coffee and drank it. Dany removed his empty cup, refilled it and handed it back, and went into the bedroom. She had already possessed herself of his keys in the Customs shed at the airport, and now she unlocked his dressing-case and dealt efficiently with the contents.

'I've run you a bath,' she announced, returning to the sitting-room. 'You look as though you could do with one. And you need a shave. You'll find your brushes and things in the dressing-room, and the room waiter will be along with something to eat in about twenty minutes. I'm not sure whether it's an early luncheon or a late breakfast, but I don't suppose it matters. Don't be too long, or it will be cold.'

She left him to it, and went away to sort out the room situation with the desk clerk and the receptionist, and returned sometime later looking thoughtful. A room-boy was waiting with a laden tray, and she told him to leave it on the table, and that he need not wait, and after he had gone she stood for several minutes staring thoughtfully at a forlorn white object that was lying upside down on the floor, displaying a neat satin label that guaranteed it to be washable and heat-proof.

'Poor Asbestos!' said Dany, stopping and picking him up. She dusted him off and replaced him, right-side-up, on the sofa: 'I suppose he's lost interest in you too. Never mind. I'll look after you. And him—if it kills me!'

There was a faint sound behind her and she turned to find Lash standing in the doorway.

He was looking exceedingly pale and there were dark circles under his eyes, but he had shaved, and his hair was wet and smooth. He had apparently found the effort to look out a change of clothes too much for him, for he was wearing pyjamas and the bottle-green dressing-gown, and he looked exhausted and ill and bad tempered.

'Do you make a habit of talking to yourself?' he inquired morosely.

Dany flushed, but ignored the question. She said, 'Your food's come. The soup looks rather good, and it's hot. I didn't think you'd like curry, so I ordered steak.'

Lash shuddered, but he drank the soup, and feeling slightly revived by it, managed to eat a reasonable quantity of steak, and topped it off with two more cups of black coffee. After which he lit a cigarette, and said grudgingly: 'Thanks. I feel slightly better. I guess I must have been pretty well plastered. The whole thing is a blur.'

'Including me,' said Dany.

'Yes—no. I seem to remember thinking it was a good idea to bring you along instead of Ada, though God alone knows why.'

Dany told him. At length and in detail.

'I don't believe it,' said Mr Holden hoarsely, breaking the long silence that had followed that recital. 'I—simply—do—not—believe —it!'

'Well it's true!' said Dany hotly. 'And if you think I'd take the trouble to invent such a—a nauseatingly improbable story, I can only say——'

'I *couldn't* be such a brainless, goddammed, half-witted moron,' continued Lash as though she had not spoken. 'I couldn't. No one could! Are you giving me a line? No—no, I suppose not. For the love of Mike, why did you pay any attention to me? Couldn't you see I was higher than a kite and not responsible for my actions? Hell! you *must* have known I was drunk!'

'I'm sorry,' said Dany, 'but you see I'd never met anyone who was drunk before. Aunt Harriet, you know,' she explained kindly.

'No, I don't know your Aunt Harriet! But——Now listen—you can't have thought that I was talking sense. You can't!'

'I thought you were just—cheerful and optimistic.'

'Cheerful and optimistic! God Almighty!' He pushed his chair

255

back violently, and rising from the table began to pace up and down the room like some caged tiger. 'Look—you must have been able to work it out for yourself. That the whole thing was crazy, I mean. Stark, raving crazy. And that I must have been crazy to suggest it! And anyway, how were you to know that I wasn't? You didn't even know me! For all you knew I might have escaped from the local asylum!'

'But you were a friend of Tyson's,' explained Dany patiently. 'You told me you were. And you were going to stay at *Kivulimi*—like me.'

'What's that got to do with it?' demanded Lash unfairly. 'You can't go two-timing the police and skipping out of the country on a stolen passport—well, a borrowed one, then!—just because I happen to know your step-father. Don't you understand? It's illegal! It's criminal! It's—it's—Good grief, it's sheer, shrieking lunacy! You can probably go to jail for it. And so can I!'

'Well, after all,' said Dany, 'it was your idea.'

Lash stood stock still and glared at her for a full minute in a silence that was loud with unprintable comment, and then he sat down very suddenly on the sofa and shut his eyes.

'I give up,' he said, 'I am just not strong enough to compete with you—or this situation. And to think,' he added bitterly, 'that this was to have been my honeymoon! My romantic, orchids-and-champagne-and-tropical-moonlight honeymoon! Dear God, what have I done to deserve this?'

'Drunk too much,' said Dany unkindly.

Lash opened one inflamed eye and regarded her with strong revulsion. 'One more crack like that out of you,' he said dangerously, '—just one! and I shall ring up the nearest police station and spill the whole dam' story, and let *them* deal with you!'

'And if you do,' said Dany sweetly, 'I shall tell them that you persuaded me into it; and then if anyone goes to jail it will be you. For kidnapping a minor!'

There was a brief silence.

'Why you little——!' said Lash very softly.

Dany rose briskly. 'I don't think I know what that means,' she said, 'but I can guess. And I'm afraid that calling me names isn't going to be any help. You got me into this, and you're going to get me out.'

'Am I, by God!'

'Yes, you are! So it's no use saying "Am I, by God!" Once we're in Zanzibar, and at *Kivulimi,* you can wash your hands of me, or tell the police, or do anything else you like. But until then I'm your secretary, Miss Kitchell. And I'm going to go on being Miss Kitchell —or else! Do you see?

'O.K. I get it,' said Lash grimly. 'All right, Miss Kitchell, you win. And now, as I am not in the habit of sharing a bedroom suite with my secretary, will you kindly get the hell out of here?'

Dany studied him with a faint smile. He was looking completely exhausted and exceedingly cross, and once again it occurred to her how pleasant it would be if she were able to put her arms about him and kiss away his tiredness and ill-temper. She felt, suddenly, a good deal older than him, and that it was unkind of her to confront him with any more problems. But it couldn't be helped.

'I'm afraid,' she said carefully, 'that I can't do that either. You see, there are no other rooms.'

'Oh yes there are. There was one booked for Ada.'

'Yes, I know. But they thought I was your wife, and when that receptionist asked you about the "other lady"—meaning your secretary—you said there wasn't one.'

'So what?'

'So I'm afraid they've given the other room to someone else.'

'Then they can dam' well give you another,' snapped Lash.

Dany shook her head regretfully. 'I'm afraid not. There aren't any more rooms. Not even mine! A Mr Dowling's got that. He told them I'd cancelled my passage, and he'd taken it, and could he have my room as well. There isn't a hole or corner to spare anywhere, though the manager was very kind when I explained that I was only the secretary and not the bride, and he rang up at least eight other hotels. But it seems we've chosen a bad time to arrive. There's some special week on at the moment, and the town is packed out. I said I was sure you wouldn't mind.'

Lash looked at her for a long moment, and then he rose and crossed the room, and planted his thumb firmly on the bell.

'What are you ringing for?' inquired Dany, a trifle anxiously.

'Rye,' said Lash grimly. 'I intend to get plastered again. And as quickly as possible!'

6

Dany ate a solitary luncheon in a corner of the cool dining-room, and drank coffee on the hotel verandah with Mr Larry Dowling, whose conversation she found both restful and entertaining. He appeared to be aware that she was feeling worried and distrait, and cheerfully took it upon himself to do all the talking: for which she was profoundly grateful, as it enabled her to relax and enjoy the view, while the necessity for paying some attention to what he was saying prevented her from brooding over her own problems.

'I must get me a suit of white drill and a panama hat,' said Larry Dowling. 'It's obviously that sort of climate. I suppose you wouldn't be really kind and come and help me do a bit of shopping would you, Miss—Miss——?'

'A—Kitchell,' supplied Dany, almost caught off guard. 'Yes. I'd like to very much, thank you. I want to see something of Nairobi, and I have to send off a cable.'

'That's grand,' said Larry gratefully. 'Let's go.'

They set out on foot in the bright African sunlight, and found the Telegraph Office without much difficulty. Dany had dispatched a brief affectionate message by deferred cable to Aunt Harriet, reporting her safe arrival (after first making quite sure that it could not be delivered in England before she herself reached Zanzibar) and Larry Dowling had cabled an even briefer one, express, to an address in Soho. After which they had visited several shops, and Mr Dowling had duly acquired a tropical suit, a panama hat and a pair of beach shoes. He had also bought Dany an outsize box of chocolates, as a small return, he explained, for her invaluable assistance. But Dany was becoming uncomfortably aware of pitfalls.

It was proving no easy matter to talk for any length of time, even to an attractive stranger, without finding oneself mentioning things that belonged to Miss Ashton rather than to Miss Kitchell. And

258

although Larry Dowling had no more than a friendly interest in Miss Kitchell, he was intensely interested in Tyson Frost and anything and everything to do with him, and the indignant Dany found herself being compelled to listen to a candid thumb-nail sketch of her step-father's careers and her mother's marriages, with a brief reference to herself.

'I've heard that there's a child somewhere,' said Larry, strolling beside her. 'Kept well in the background, it seems. Not Frost's—hers. But the Lorraine type don't like being bothered by brats: spoils their glamour. Besides, it makes people start doing sums. Difficult to go around looking barely thirty when you've a lumping great deb of eighteen or nineteen summers along in tow. Ever seen her? Mrs Frost, I mean?'

Dany blinked and opened her mouth, and then shut it again, but his question appeared to be purely rhetorical.

'She's a honey!' he said enthusiastically. 'I saw her in London last year at a Press reception for Frost. Tiny, with dark curly hair like a baby's and blue eyes the size of saucers. Looks as though you could pick her up with one hand. Married at least half a dozen times, and when you see her you aren't surprised. Like that friend of hers on the plane—Mrs Gordon. Now there's another charmer! Though for all her looks she's had a pretty tragic life, poor girl. Her last husband fell down their cellar steps in the dark and broke his neck. Tight of course. And as if that wasn't enough, the man she was going to marry last year, Douglas Rhett-Corrington, took a header out of a top-storey window on the eve of the wedding. Seems someone had been writing him anonymous letters, or else she threw him over at the last minute, or something like that. But whichever it was it must have been sheer hell for her, and she deserves a break with the next one. I wish I were in the running!'

'Are you rich?' inquired Dany, startled to find herself feeling so angry and uncharitable.

'Ah! but she's not one of those. They say she only marries for love—even if she doesn't love 'em for long! It just happened that the ones she married had money, because those are the only kind she meets. And if it was only money she was after, she'd have married your boss. A week ago there were rumours that they were going to stage a surprise wedding at Caxton Hall. But now it looks as though it was off. What went wrong?'

'I've no idea,' said Dany coldly. 'Mr Holden does not discuss his private life with me.'

Mr Dowling's attractive triangular face lit up with amusement. 'The perfect, loyal little secretary!' he said, and smiled his swift, disarming smile. 'I'm sorry. I didn't mean to pry. But there's no need for you to clam up on me. I'm not a gossip writer, you know. Young Holden isn't news as far as I'm concerned. It's men like Tyson Frost who are my bread and butter. Him and the Zanzibar elections! That was why I was so dam' pleased about getting on that plane: there were two people on it who might have been very useful to me. An Arab agitator who hopes to become a little Hitler one day, and Tyson Frost's step-daughter—a Miss Ashton. The one I was telling you about.'

'Oh . . . really?' said Dany, swallowing a lump in her throat.

'Yep. And I'd rather hoped I might be able to scrape an acquaintance with the girl,' confided Larry Dowling with rueful candour. 'It shouldn't have been all that difficult, and I might have got a lot of inside information, and even wangled an invitation to stay if I'd played my cards right. I did everything I could to get on that plane, but not a hope. And then at the last minute someone cancels a seat, and I get it. And then you know what?'

'No. I mean—what?' said Dany nervously.

'It's the Ashton girl who's cancelled it! Probably contracted whooping cough or measles or something. A pity. I'd like to have met her. Her step-daddy is news in any language just now.'

'Why just now?' inquired Dany, curiosity getting the better of a strong conviction that she ought to change the subject at once.

'Surely you know? Why, I thought that must be what your boss was after. It's his father who publishes Frost's books in the States, isn't it?'

'Yes. But——'

'Then you can take it from me that's what he's here for. The Emory Frost diaries. They were released this year. Emory was the old rolling stone who was deeded the house in Zanzibar by one of the Sultans. He seems to have been quite a lad by all accounts. There were a lot of curious stories about him—that he was mixed up in the Slave Trade or the smuggling racket, and went in for a bit of piracy on the side, with a spot of wrecking thrown in. He left a whole heap of papers and diaries that he said were not to be read until seventy years after his death, which was June this year. Tyson Frost has had 'em for a couple of months now, so he should have had time to go through them. The betting is that they make pretty racy reading, and that Frost'll publish them in book form. If I can only get him to talk about them I shall be sitting pretty. Is Holden out to get the exclusive rights?'

'Perhaps,' said Dany, trying the effect of a cautious answer.

'Ah!' said Larry Dowling. 'I thought so! It'll go down well in the States. The Yanks had a lot of influence in Zanzibar in the eighteen hundreds, and the first treaty the Sultanate ever made with a foreign country was with America. And then there's some story that Emory ran away with an American girl—rescued her from pirates who attacked Zanzibar, and blockaded the American Consulate in eighteen-sixty something, and ended up by marrying her. What a film that'd make! She must have been Frost's grandmother. They say she was a stunner, and that after she married him Emory become a reformed character and . . .'

He broke off. 'Wait a minute . . . Isn't that one of the women who were on the plane over there? Mrs Bingham? The manager of our hotel told me that she's Tyson Frost's sister. I wonder if——'

He caught Dany's arm, and hurrying her along the crowded pavement, dived into a shop that appeared to sell everything from shoes to sauce pans, and went up to a counter piled high with sponges which Mrs Bingham and Miss Bates were prodding speculatively under the bored gaze of an Indian saleslady. Two minutes later Dany realized that she had been quite right when she had decided that Aunt Harriet would have taken to Mr Dowling. Mrs Bingham had instantly done so, and in an astonishingly short space of time he was involved in an animated discussion on the rival merits of natural versus foam-rubber sponges.

Dany had attempted to beat an unobtrusive retreat, having no desire to make her step-aunt's acquaintance before it was absolutely necessary. But she had not been quick enough, and before she could prevent it, Larry was introducing her.

'This is Miss Kitchell, Mrs Bingham. Mr Holden's secretary and a fellow-traveller to Zanzibar. She will be staying with the Frosts. Tyson Frost, the novelist, you know. What's that? . . . Your *brother*? Now that really is a coincidence!'

He met Dany's accusing eye with a wicked twinkle in his own, and grinned at her, entirely unabashed. But the remainder of the afternoon proved to be trying in the extreme, for he had not permitted her to separate herself from the company, and her step-father's sister had turned out to be one of those exceedingly talkative women who delight in asking endless personal questions, and handing out endless personal information in exchange.

Mrs Bingham wished to know *all* about America; a country she had not yet visited but hoped to one day. Dany, who had not visited it either, did not come well out of this catechism, and could only pray that Larry Dowling and the brisk Miss Bates were equally ignorant.

To Mrs Bingham's loudly expressed surprise at her lack of a transatlantic accent she replied glibly that her parents had only emigrated to America within recent years, and that she herself had been partly educated in England.

'Ah!' said Gussie Bingham with the satisfaction of one who has solved a problem. 'Then that of course is why Mr Holden selected you to come to Europe with him. You would *understand* us. I don't think I ever met this Mr Holden, but his father stayed with me once —let me see, was it in '38 or '39? He is a *great* friend of Tyson's, my brother's. A very pleasant man—for an American. Oh, I beg your pardon, my dear! How very rude that sounds. Do forgive me.'

'It's all right,' said Dany bleakly, wondering how long it was going to be before she was asked something that was so impossible to answer that discovery was inevitable. What a fool she had been to talk to people: any people! She should have kept well out of sight and out of danger. Lash was quite right: she had no sense. All she had thought of was that a stroll round Nairobi with Larry Dowling would be a pleasant way to spend the long afternoon, and that it would be quite easy to keep off dangerous topics. And now look where it landed her!

Gussie Bingham said: 'Do you suppose this is all there is of Nairobi? Perhaps I should have accepted Mr Ponting's offer to show us round. My brother's secretary, you know. He was here to meet me, and he took us out to luncheon at some club. It was really very pleasant. But as the poor man had spent half the morning in a dentist's chair I insisted that he take a couple of aspirins and lie down this afternoon, and that Millicent and I would look after ourselves. I feel sure he was grateful. You must have met him, of course, when he was in the States with my brother. What do you think of him?'

Dany's heart appeared to jump six inches and then sink at least twice that distance. *Had* Ada Kitchell met this Mr Ponting when Tyson had been over in the States? Certainly Lash had met him, and therefore probably Ada. Why hadn't Lash warned her? Why hadn't she thought of asking him? Why had they both forgotten that angle, and what on earth was she going to do when she did see this man, and he refused to recognize her as Ada Kitchell?

Fortunately Gussie Bingham did not wait for an answer: 'He has been with my brother for several years, but I had not met him before —though he has been to the house, of course. But that was when Tyson was in England a year or two ago and Millicent and I were having a little holiday in Jersey. Still, it was thoughtful of Tyson to arrange for him to meet me. Though I suspect he is really here on Dany Ashton's account—my brother's step-daughter, you know. She was to have been on the plane, but she was not at the airport, and when we made inquiries they told us that she had cancelled her seat. Very odd. Chicken-pox or mumps or something, I suppose.'

It was clear that in this matter Augusta Bingham's mind moved in much the same grooves as Larry Dowling's: school-girl diseases. But fortunately for Dany's nervous system, Mrs Bingham abandoned the subject of the missing Miss Ashton and turned to a less dangerous topic:

'We shall be quite a party at *Kivulimi,* shall we not? You know, I haven't stayed there since Father died. That seems a very long time ago. We spent almost a year there, as children. But Father never really took to the place. Not like his eldest brother, old Uncle Barclay, who was completely besotted with the house. He had a *thing* about it—and about Zanzibar. He loved the place, and hardly ever left it. I suppose that was why he never married.'

'Was he the eldest son of Emory—the first Frost?' inquired Larry Dowling.

'The first Frost to visit *Zanzibar,'* corrected Mrs Bingham gently. 'Yes. The family place is in Kent, of course. I live there now, because Tyson is so seldom in England. Millicent and I keep it warm for him, we say. I don't know what I should do without Millicent. She came to stay with me when my husband died, and she simply runs everything.'

'Does your brother live much in Zanzibar?' asked Larry, steering the conversation firmly back to Tyson Frost.

'Not really. He's such a restless person. Always on the move. He only lives in it by fits and starts. Asks some of his friends there, and then off he goes again. I've always thought it was such a *romantic* thing to have a house in Zanzibar, but Tyson never really stays in it very long.'

'Probably finds it jolly uncivilized,' said Miss Bates. 'Romance is all very well, but give me H. and C. every time! I always say there's absolutely nothing to beat "All Mod. Cons".'

'I'm afraid Millicent doesn't care for foreign travel,' confided Gussie Bingham in an undertone to Dany. 'She detests the East. And she misses the Institute and the Girl Guides and things like that. She has so many interests: a tower of strength. Our vicar often says that he doesn't know how Market-Lydon would get on without her, and I'm sure she agrees with him. Oh! I didn't mean—that sounds unkind of me. What I meant——'

But Dany had ceased to pay attention, for the words 'Market-Lydon' had brought a chill to the hot day. *Man Murdered at Market-Lydon* . . . But it wasn't just 'a man.' It was elderly, pedantic, disapproving Mr Honeywood. And since Mr Honeywood had been the Frost family's solicitor for at least two generations, he was almost certainly Mrs Bingham's too. She would have known him well. Did she know he was now dead? Even if she did, the news of his death could not possibly have shocked her half as badly as it had shocked Dany, who had only met him once and very briefly.

Larry Dowling was saying: 'Does your brother often entertain like this when he is in Zanzibar, Mrs Bingham? Or is this a special occasion?'

'Oh, I don't think it was my brother's idea at all. He's not really very sociable when he's writing, and I believe he is supposed to be working on a book just now. But his wife likes to have the house full of guests. I suppose she gets bored when he's writing all day. And then of course . . .'

Mrs Bingham's voice went on and on, and Larry Dowling listened with flattering attention, interjecting interested, incredulous or congratulatory noises whenever the flow showed signs of drying up. He was evidently as good a listener as he was a talker thought Dany uneasily. A very likeable man—but a dangerous one . . .

She said with forced lightness, breaking into the bubbling stream of confidences: 'Mr Dowling is a newspaper man, you know.'

But if she had intended this as a warning, it missed its mark.

Larry Dowling threw her a brief, quizzical grin that was strangely disconcerting, and although Miss Bates turned sharply and regarded him as though he were something she had unexpectedly turned up with a garden spade, Gussie Bingham, far from being taken aback, was enchanted.

'A *reporter*? But how interesting!'

'Feature writer,' corrected Mr Dowling patiently.

'The same sort of thing, surely?' said Gussie Bingham blithely. 'You must live such an exciting life. Fires and murders and film stars. Paris today and Bangkok tomorrow. How I envy you! Of course Tyson—my brother—knows a great many newspapermen. He says they are the lowest form of human——Oh, I *am* sorry. That was *very* rude of me. I really didn't mean . . . I am quite sure he would like *you,* Mr Dowling.'

Miss Bates sniffed audibly and muttered something about carrion crows and snooping nosey-parkers, and Mrs Bingham frowned repressively at her, and taking Mr Dowling's arm, walked on ahead, chatting energetically and leaving Miss Bates to fall in beside Dany.

'I'm sure I've seen that chap before somewhere,' said Miss Bates, directing a scowl at Mr Dowling's unconscious back. 'I never forget a face. Probably in the papers, being sentenced for libel and defamation, if you ask me. It'll come back to me. I know the type. All charm and good humour, and thoroughly untrustworthy. Only out for what they can get. No better than confidence tricksters. In fact that's probably what he is! We've only his own word for it that he's a feature writer—whatever that is!'

Miss Bates sniffed again, expressively. 'You know,' she confided, 'Gussie's a good sort, and she's got plenty of brains in her head. But there are times when you'd never suspect it. Look at the way she's letting that reporter pump her about Tyson. Anyone could see that he's up to no good. If he's not a crook, then he's after an article—preferably one with a lot of dirty linen involved. Newspapers are a menace. Garbage—that's all they're interested in. Garbage and Murder.'

Murder! . . . Yes, murder was only something that you read about in a newspaper. It wasn't real. People one knew died; but they were never murdered . . .

Dany had tea on the hotel verandah, still in the company of Augusta Bingham and Millicent Bates, and the Press, as represented by Larry Dowling. Larry had issued an unexpectedly diffident invitation, which she had been about to refuse when the sight of Lash Holden had made her change her mind. For Lash was also taking afternoon tea on the verandah—with Amalfi Gordon. He was wearing a grey suit and showed no signs of a hangover, and Amalfi was looking soft and sweet and appealingly lovely in something that had undoubtedly run someone into three figures in a cheque book, and whose simplicity of line made every other woman within range look (and feel) like a back number of *Home Chat.*

There was no sign of the Marchese Eduardo di Chiago, and Amalfi was talking earnestly and inaudibly, with an expression on her lovely face that admirably combined a sweetly sorrowing archangel and a child begging forgiveness for some minor peccadillo.

Lash was looking a little sulky, but at the same time bedazzled, and Dany wondered if the Marchese had been sent off on some errand that would keep him out of the way for an hour or two and allow Mrs Gordon to eat her cake and have it. The anxieties of the afternoon, together with the murder of Mr Honeywood and half a dozen pressing and unpleasant problems, retired abruptly from the forefront of her mind, to be replaced by indignation on the score of the predatory Mrs Gordon and the spinelessness of that gullible, besotted and hypnotized rabbit, Mr Lashmer J. Holden, Jnr.

What can he *see* in her! thought Dany indignantly. And instantly realized just exactly what he saw in her. Amalfi Gordon appeared to have everything.

Well she isn't going to have Lash! decided Dany fiercely, and sat down in a chair from which she could keep an eye upon that feckless and intransigent young man without appearing to do so.

Lash did not become aware of her for at least twenty minutes, but when he did, he reacted promptly; though in a manner that could hardly be termed gratifying. Suddenly catching sight of her, he remained for a moment transfixed, as though he could hardly believe his eyes, and then rising abruptly and excusing himself to Amalfi, he came quickly towards her, threading his way between the intervening tea-drinkers on the crowded verandah.

'I've been looking for you, Miss Kitchell,' said Lash ominously. 'There are several things that need your attention, and I'd be glad if you'd deal with them immediately. And another time, just let me know when you intend to take the afternoon off.'

Dany bit her lip and blushed painfully, but fortified by a sense of humour, and even more by the spectacle of the golden Mrs Gordon left abandoned at the far end of the verandah, she rose meekly.

'I'm so sorry, Mr Holden. I had no idea that you would be needing me this afternoon. Will you excuse me Mrs Bingham? It seems that I have some work to do. Thank you for the tea, Larry.'

She introduced Lash to the assembled company, and left. But she had been back in the bridal suite for less than five minutes when the door opened violently to disclose her employer.

He banged it shut behind him and said furiously: 'Say, have you taken leave of your senses? What the heck do you mean by flaunting yourself all over Nairobi and letting yourself get picked up by any Tom, Dick or Harry? Hell! d'you know who you've been getting off with? A newspaperman! Of all people to pick—of *all* people! And that blue-haired dame is Tyson Frost's sister. Your step-aunt, by God! Do you suppose she hasn't recognized you? You'll probably wake up tomorrow to find the whole thing splashed right across the front page. You ought to have your head examined!'

'Don't worry,' said Dany soothingly. 'I've never met her before, so of course she can't recognize me. And I'm very sorry about Larry Dowling. I didn't think—'

'You never do!' interrupted Lash bitterly. ' *"Larry"* indeed!' Her use of Mr Dowling's Christian name appeared to infuriate him further. 'Has it ever occurred to you to take a look at the passport you are travelling on? No? Well let me tell you that Ada comes from Milwaukee—and they don't talk with a British Broadcasting accent there!'

'Oh dear,' said Dany guiltily, 'that reminds me. Did I ever meet this Mr Ponting? Tyson's secretary?—I mean, did Ada Kitchell ever meet him? Because Mrs Bingham asked me about him, and I didn't know if I should know anything or not.'

Lash raised a couple of clenched fists to heaven while his lips moved soundlessly, and then, lowering them, said in a strictly controlled voice: 'No, by the mercy of Providence you did not meet him. Otherwise we'd have been in a worse jam than we're in right now. What did you tell her?'

'Nothing. Luckily she didn't wait for an answer.'

'Lucky is right! And I hope that's taught you a lesson. Can't you see that your only chance is to lie low and keep out of sight, and not to talk to anybody—*anybody!*—until you get to Zanzibar? Once you get there it's your step-father's headache. And if he has any sense, he'll give you six with a slipper where it hurts most!'

Lash went across to the table by the window and helped himself to a drink from a tray that had not been there when she left. But she was relieved to see that the bottle appeared to be far more than three parts full, and that the amount he took was unquestionably modest.

'This,' said Lash, intercepting her look and interpreting it correctly, 'is merely to take the taste of that godammed tea out of my mouth. Much as I should like to duck the whole situation by getting roaring drunk, I shall lay off it until I've got rid of you. Going on a bender is a luxury I can't afford while there are people like you around loose.'

Dany remarked pleasantly that it was kind of him to worry so much about her welfare.

'I'm not,' said Lash shortly. 'You can disabuse yourself of that idea right away. It's myself I'm worrying about. Which is why, Miss Kitchell, you will stay right here in this room and keep your mouth shut until we leave for the airport tomorrow morning. And you will continue to keep your charming trap shut until we are safely inside your unfortunate step-father's front door. After that, I shall, myself, take the first plane out again, with Ada's passport in my pants' pocket, and leave you to it.'

He finished his drink and moved to the door: 'You'll find the draft copies of several letters on that writing table. I guess you may as well fill in the time by typing them. Three carbons. And spell them correctly—in American.'

'Yes, sir,' said Dany meekly.

Lash laughed for the first time in twenty-four hours. 'You know, you're not a bad kid,' he conceded. 'Your I.Q. is probably the lowest on record, and I can't figure out how the Welfare State ever allowed you to go around without a keeper. But you have your moments. Don't let this lick you, honey. I'll see you through.'

Dany was aware of a sudden prickle of tears behind her eyes, and she turned away quickly so that he should not see them. 'Thank you,' she said in a small voice.

Lash said: 'The typewriter is in that square maroon-coloured case. I'm not sure where the paper and carbons are. Look around. Oh, and by the way, just for the look of the thing, you are occupying this suite on your own. I fixed it with the management. Officially, I am down as sleeping in Room 72, during the absence of the owner. Actually, as he's put a padlock on it, I shall be spending the night on this sofa. But as long as no one else knows it, the decencies will be preserved. And there's a lock on that door over there, in case you feel anxious.'

He opened the door into the passage, and added over his shoulder: 'I'll see that they send along some dinner for you. Safer than turning you loose in the dining-room, with wolves like that guy Dowling prowling around.'

'You, I suppose,' said Dany crossly, 'will be dining out. I should have thought you'd have more pride!'

'Take a letter, Miss Kitchell,' said Lash austerely, and shut the door with a bang.

7

I t was just on two o'clock in the morning when Dany awoke suddenly and lay still; listening.

She did not know what had awakened her, except that it was a sound. Perhaps it was Lash coming back. No, it could not be that. She had heard Lash come back before she fell asleep; and that was over an hour ago, for she could make out the position of the hands on the luminous dial of the travelling-clock that stood facing her on the dressing-table. Besides, the sound had not come from the next room. It had been nearer than that, she felt sure . . .

Dany had slept little and uneasily in the hotel in Gloucester Road, and worse on the plane last night, so she had confidently expected to make up for it here. But sleep had eluded her, and for hour after hour she had tossed and turned in the wide bed, worrying over her parlous predicament and listening for Lash's return.

He had come back at last, shortly before one o'clock. And presumably sober, for he had made so little noise that but for the fact that she was awake and listening for him, she would not have known that he had returned. She had heard a switch click, and a narrow thread of light had appeared under the door between the two rooms, and Dany had sat up in bed hugging her knees and wishing fervently that the conventions did not forbid her going in to the next room to talk to him.

She was feeling lonely and forlorn and frightened, and much in need of comfort, and Lash had not improved matters by starting to whistle very softly between his teeth as he undressed. It was only the ghost of a melody, but the song was familiar. Too familiar. *'Then I'll go sailing far, off to Zanzibar . . .'* He sounded light-hearted enough.

He's made it up with her, thought Dany desolately. What fools men are. She's old enough to be his mother! Well, not his mother

270

perhaps—but his aunt. And she doesn't care a button for him. Not really. She'd rather be a *Marchesa*—or a millionairess—or . . . Perhaps he *is* a millionaire? No, he can't be! He mustn't be. That Sir Somebody . . . Ambrose Something who got off at Khartoum. Oil. *He's* probably a millionaire, and old enough for her. Perhaps she will marry him instead. Or the Italian. But please, not Lash . . .

The light under the door vanished, and Dany had fallen asleep at last. To be awakened very suddenly an hour later by a sound that she could not identify.

She listened for it to be repeated, but it did not come again, and presently she relaxed once more and lay staring sleepily into the darkness. An hour earlier there had been a moon: a bright, white, African moon that had shone in at her window and made the room so light that she had got out of bed and pulled the heavy inner curtains over the muslin ones that were intended to keep out such things as flies and dust during the daytime. But now the moon had set and the lights in the hotel had winked out, and the streets of Nairobi were dark and silent. As dark and as silent as her room.

Dany's eyelids had begun to droop when suddenly and horribly she was aware that there was someone in the room with her.

She had been lying looking idly at the faint green dial of the travelling-clock, and she had heard no sound. But she did not need to. Something—someone—had moved between her bed and the dressing-table, and blotted out that small luminous circle. She could still hear the clock ticking quite clearly. But she could no longer see it.

Dany sat up very slowly, inch by terrified inch; moving as noiselessly as that other presence in the room, until at last she was sitting upright, pressed hard back against the pillows and the padded bedhead. Her hands were clenched on the sheets and every muscle in her body seemed atrophied by fear. She could move no further. She could only sit rigidly and stare into the darkness with dilated eyes, while her breath seemed to fail her and her heartbeats sounded as swift and as audible in the silence as hoof-beats on a hard road.

Nothing moved in the blackness, but there was an odd smell in the room. A queer sickly smell that was somehow familiar and yet very frightening. As frightening as the unseen thing that was in the room with her.

Then all at once the clock face was visible again. The blackness that had obscured it had moved from left to right, and that meant that it—whatever it was—was moving towards her.

Dany opened her mouth to scream and found that her throat was dry and stiff and so constricted by terror that the only sound that emerged from it was a foolish croaking little gasp. But it had been a mistake to make that sound.

There was a sudden sharp sense of movement in the darkness and something touched the side of the bed. And suddenly, born of a desperate instinct of self-preservation, courage and the power of connected thought returned to her. That foolish croak had only served to guide someone to her; and if she screamed, though she might wake Lash, he could not get to her for she had locked the door. And she might not have time for more than one scream . . .

Dany gathered her strength, and flinging herself suddenly to one side, rolled over to the far side of the bed and was on the floor and on her feet.

The suddenness of the movement evidently took the intruder by surprise, for she heard a sharp intake of breath and a quick movement that was followed by an involuntary gasp of pain. At least it was human, for it had stubbed a bare or a stockinged foot on the leg of the bed. The sound betrayed its position as her own effort to scream had betrayed hers, and that much at least helped her. But only for a moment.

Dany backed away into the darkness, and it was only then that she realized that whoever was in the room with her was not an ordinary thief. A thief, with the window behind him and realizing that she was awake, would have escaped into the night without loss of time. But this was someone who meant to get *her*—Dany Ashton! To kill her . . . For a swift sickening moment the pinched, prim face of Mr Honeywood seemed to float in the air before her.

Murder . . . That was no longer merely an arresting word in a newspaper headline. It was real. It was here in the room with her. Murder. When she moved, it moved. When she stood still, straining to listen, it stood still—listening too. Waiting to pounce . . .

She was shivering so badly that she could hardly stand and she felt as though she would go mad with fear. She had lost her bearings, and though her cold hands were against the wall and she felt along it, she no longer knew in which direction she was moving. Was she going towards the door into the sitting-room or moving away from it? Where was the bed? Where was the window?

And then, for a brief moment, she saw the clock dial again and knew where she was. But in the next instant there was a clatter and the ghost of a chuckle—a horrifying sound in the darkness—and it had vanished. The clock had been deliberately overturned so that it could no longer guide her, or betray a movement.

But she was within a yard of the door now. She must be. Another three steps and she would reach it.

Something struck the wall beside her with a sharp *plop* and almost succeeded in forcing a scream from her. The effort to restrain it and make no sudden movement beaded her forehead with a cold sweat and wet the palms of her hands, but with the next step she knew that she had saved herself; and what had made that sound.

The intruder had thrown one of her heelless velvet slippers at random across the room to trap her into a scream or an audible movement that would betray her position. Her foot touched the slipper and she stooped cautiously and silently, and picking it up threw it in the direction of the bathroom door.

It hit the wall with a soft thump, and once again she heard a harsh, quick-drawn breath, and then a rush of stockinged feet towards the sound. But she had reached the door of the sitting-room and the key was cold between her fingers. She turned it, and twisted the door-handle with hands that were so wet with terror that for a moment the knob slipped sickeningly and would not turn. And then the door was open and she was through; stumbling into unseen furniture and screaming for Lash.

She heard her pursuer cannon into the half open door behind her, but she had reached the sofa and Lash had woken up. 'What the hell——!' he demanded. And at the sound of his voice there came a quick incredulous gasp and a flurry of sound that ended with the slam of a door. And they were alone.

Lash groped his way blasphemously to the nearest switch, his progress grossly impeded by Dany who was clinging to him with the desperate tenacity of a limpet and then the lights snapped on and he blinked dazedly, mechanically patting her shuddering shoulders.

'*Lash . . . Lash . . . Oh, Lash!*' wept Dany, dissolved in tears and terror.

'It's all right,' said Lash awkwardly. 'I'm here. Everything's all right. Was it a real bad nightmare, honey?'

'It wasn't a nightmare,' sobbed Dany. 'It was a m-murderer! A *murderer!*'

'Don't think about it, bambina,' advised Lash kindly. 'It's no use letting all this get you down. Stop crying, honey.'

But Dany merely tightened her terrified clutch on him. 'You don't understand—I wasn't dreaming. It was real. It was *real*——'

'O.K., it was real,' said Lash soothingly. 'But you don't have to strangle me. Look, what about a little drink and a couple of aspirins?'

Getting no response to this suggestion, and finding that Dany had no intention of letting go of him, he picked her up bodily, and returning to the sofa sat down on it, holding her, and reached over her head for the tray of drinks that he had thoughtfully placed within range of his temporary bed.

'Now see here, for Pete's sake sit up and get a grip on yourself. Here, drink this—it's only water . . . That's a good child. You know, right now what you need most is a handkerchief. Or let's say six handkerchiefs. Come on, honey. Snap out of it! You're soaking me, and I shall catch one hell of a cold.'

Dany lifted her head from his damp shoulder and sat up, displaying a tear-streaked and terrified face, and gazed helplessly about her.

'What are you looking for?' inquired Lash.

'H-handkerchief, of course.'

'If you'll let go of me, I'll get you one.'

He freed himself from Dany's clutching fingers, and setting her down on one end of the sofa, collected a clean handkerchief from the pocket of his discarded dinner jacket, and handed it over.

'I seem to remember that nightgown,' he remarked, lighting himself a cigarette and smiling at her through the smoke. 'You were wearing that and a sheet of newspaper when we first met. This is quite like old times. I'll admit that right now your face isn't looking up to much, but if it's any consolation to you, the rest is a treat to the eye.'

This observation produced no reaction whatever, and the smile died out of Lash's grey eyes, to be replaced by concern. 'You have had a bad time of it, haven't you, brat? But everything will be all right now. You'll see. Come on, you're awake now.'

Dany dropped the handkerchief and stared up at him with shocked tear-blurred eyes. 'You still think it was a dream, don't you? But it wasn't. There was someone in my room. I heard a noise and woke up, and—then I . . . then I saw the clock. It's—I could see it in the dark. It's luminous. And then . . . then suddenly I couldn't see it any more, because someone was standing in front of it——'

The sentence ran out into a violent shudder that made her teeth chatter, and Lash's face changed suddenly and startlingly. He flung his cigarette away and was at the bedroom door in two swift strides, feeling for the light switch. It clicked on, revealing the tumbled bed and the curtains stirring idly in the soft dawn wind. But there was no one there.

The room was empty and the light twinkled on the little pearl and diamond brooch and the narrow gold wristwatch that Dany had worn. She had left them on the dressing-table, and near them, face downwards, lay the gilt travelling-clock.

'Nuts!' said Lash brusquely, relief giving place to irritation. 'You dreamt it. If there'd been a thief in here he'd have taken care of that stuff, and——' He stopped. There was something lying on the floor by the dressing-room door, and the door itself was ajar.

He crossed the room quickly and stooping, picked it up. It was a torch, of a type that is cased in heavy black rubber and capable of being focused.

Lash turned to find Dany at his elbow, white-faced and shivering. 'This yours?'

'No. Of course not.'

'Umm,' said Lash thoughtfully, and vanished into the dressing-room. He did not return for several minutes, and Dany sat down on the edge of the bed, still trembling violently and wondering if she were going to disgrace herself by being sick. It seemed only too likely.

Presently Lash returned, looking puzzled. He said: 'Nothing seems to have gone. It looks screwy to me. Why didn't he grab what he could, and scram?'

'Because he didn't w-want anything like that,' quavered Dany, shivering. 'He didn't come for t-that. He was looking for m-me. He was going to m-murder me.'

'Oh, baloney!' snapped Lash exasperated. 'Will you just lay off carrying on like a character out of a soap-opera? It was obviously only some little African sneak-thief. A town like this is probably full of them! It may even have been one of the hotel staff trying a bit of light burglary.'

'It wasn't,' insisted Dany, obstinately. 'It *wasn't*. B-burglars don't want to murder people, and he meant to murder me. I know he did!'

'Now see here,' began Lash patiently. 'You haven't a shred of evidence that he intended to do you any harm at all—beyond relieving you of any cash or jewellery you'd left lying about. He probably hadn't gotten around to that when you woke up, and the chances are that you scared him worse that he scared you: which is plenty! Now why don't you just——'

He broke off and looked about him, wrinkling his nose. 'What's that smell?'

'I d-don't know. It was in here before. *He* brought it——'

'*Chloroform, by God!*' said Lash in a whisper. 'That's what it is! Chloroform——!'

He swept the bedclothes to one side with a single savage jerk, and the smell was suddenly stronger and more clearly identifiable as something fell to the carpet with an almost inaudible plop.

It was an ordinary polythene bag of a size and type frequently used to pack sandwiches in for a picnic, and it appeared to contain nothing more than a pad of cotton wool and gauze.

Lash stooped rather slowly and picked it up, and opening it, jerked his head back sharply with a grimace of distaste as a strong waft of anaesthetic flowed out from it.

He rolled it up again swiftly and pushed it into an empty drawer of the dressing-table, and Dany said, also speaking in a whisper: 'I told you. I *told* you! That was m-meant for me, wasn't it?'

'Maybe,' said Lash curtly.

'Well then why don't you do something? Why are you just s-s-standing there?'

'What do you suggest I do?' inquired Lash coldly.

'Call someone! Wake up the manager. Telephone the police. Something—anything!'

Lash turned away and walked towards the open door into the sitting-room. He said: 'Don't be a fool, Dany. You know damned well that we are in no position to go bawling for the cops.'

He held the door open for her, and having shut it again behind her, went across to the armchair that contained his discarded clothes and picked up his dressing-gown.

'You'd better borrow this again. In fact, if this sort of thing is going to become a part of the daily round, I guess you'd better keep it. Your need would appear to be greater than mine.'

Dany said tonelessly: 'No. You have it. I can use this.'

She wrapped herself in a blanket off his makeshift bed, and sat down in a shivering huddle on the nearest chair, feeling limp and boneless from shock and fatigue and the aftermath of abject panic.

Lash put on his dressing-gown and helped himself to a drink, and sat silent for a time, staring ahead of him in frowning concentration while Dany watched him and did not speak. Presently he stood up abruptly, finished his drink at a gulp, and putting down the empty glass went back into the bedroom.

He was away for perhaps ten minutes, and though Dany would have liked to follow him, merely from terror of being left alone, she found that she was too exhausted to move. She kept her frightened gaze on the open door instead, and presently saw his shadow move once more across the wall.

He came back into the sitting-room, frowning blackly, and mixed another drink which he handed to Dany. 'You'd better take that. You look as though you could do with something stronger than water, and you can't fold up now. I want to talk to you.'

He poured out a second and considerably stronger one for himself, and then sat down on the sofa, facing her.

'I'm coming round to the idea,' said Lash, 'that there is more in this than meets the eye. It looks as though that guy in there had gone to quite a bit of trouble. And he wasn't after cash.'

'I *told* you——' began Dany again.

'*Ssh!* Now I'm telling you. He didn't come in by the bedroom window. He broke the one in the bathroom, and came in that way. There was quite a bit of my stuff, and most of yours in the dressing-room, and he's had a darned good look at it. Forced every lock on the ones that weren't open, and gone through every little thing. But as far as I can see he hasn't taken anything. Unless, of course, you were carrying a clutch of diamonds or something? Did you have much money in your bags? Or jewellery?'

'No,' said Dany in a hoarse whisper. 'I haven't much jewellery. Only that brooch and the watch, and a pearl necklace, a diamond bar pin and some costume stuff that were in my dressing-case.'

'And still are,' said Lash. 'They haven't been touched. And neither have my pearl studs and a rather flashy assortment of cufflinks, or a gold and platinum cigarette case and lighter, and one or two more far-from-inexpensive trifles. Not to mention a good few traveller's cheques. All, or any, of those things are just the size to go comfortably into any guy's pants' pocket. Yet he didn't take 'em. Now why?'

'I told you,' said Dany for the fourth time.

'Look, just quit talking will you? This is a soliloquy, not a dialogue. I'm sorting out the facts. That dressing-room and everything in it has had a real going over. The sort of frisking that it would only get if someone were looking for just one thing: one special thing. And it's my guess that if it had been found, your visitor would have got out the way he came in and there'd have been no more trouble. But because he didn't get what he was after, he came into your bedroom; and as you can't search a bedroom thoroughly while the owner is occupying the bed, that's where the chloroform was going to come in. If you hadn't woken up just then you wouldn't have known a thing about it: you'd have passed out cold, and when you woke up you might have felt a little sickish—but that'd have been all. Except that while you were out for the count your bedroom would have gotten the same treatment as the dressing-room. Now am I right, or aren't I?'

Dany merely shivered and drew the blanket more closely about her, and Lash answered his own question: 'I'll bet I am! But where do we go from here? that's the six-hundred-thousand-dollar question. Well, I'll tell you. Backwards!'

He drank deeply, and Dany said morosely, her gaze on the glass in his hands. 'Yes. I can see that!'

Lash grinned at her. 'The point is taken, honey. But you don't have to worry. I intend to stay strictly sober. This is merely medicinal: an aid to thought. And right now we're going to have to do some fast and fancy thinking, because I see I was way off the line in my first assessment of the situation.'

'I don't know what you mean,' said Dany. The whisky Lash had given her was beginning to make her head swim a little, and she felt better. But not much.

'You're not concentrating,' said Lash. 'Remember how I met you? You'd gotten yourself locked out of your room, and while you were out of it someone took it to bits. But they didn't take your money or your jewellery, which shows that they were after something else.'

'My passport,' said Dany impatiently.

'I don't believe it. Not now; though I admit I did once. It seemed the obvious answer at the time, and that, I guess, is where we tripped up. Why should anyone take a room to pieces looking for something that is exactly where they'd expect to find it? in your handbag and right under their nose. We ought to have seen that one: it stands out a mile. Those balcony rooms at the Airlane were a darned sight too easy to get into—always provided one was a resident. Someone probably meant to try that chloroform trick around six in the morning. Easier than poking about in the dark, and most people are dead asleep at that hour. They were probably already on the balcony or behind a curtain when you saved them a lot of trouble by going to fetch that newspaper, and getting locked out. Taking your passport and planting that gun was probably merely an afterthought, when they couldn't find what they were after. To stop you leaving the country with something that you've got and they want.'

'But I haven't got anything!' protested Dany, beginning to shiver again.

'You must have. And I'm willing to bet you five grand to a stick of bubble-gum that I know what it is! What have you done with the letter that Tyson's solicitor gave you?—that guy who got shot?'

Dany's eyes widened until they were enormous in her white face, and she stood shakily, clutching the blanket about her. 'No! No, it couldn't possibly be that. It was just a letter. It couldn't possibly——'

'Of course it is. It couldn't possibly be anything else! The question is, have you still got it?'

'Yes. I—I think so.' Dany's voice was hoarse and breathless.

'Where?'

'I think it's still in the pocket of my coat. The camel-hair one that's hanging in the cupboard.'

Lash got up and went into the bedroom, and returned carrying a light-coloured loose overcoat. 'This it?'

Dany nodded, and he thrust a hand into one of the deep silk-lined slit pockets and unearthed a crumpled slip of paper, two pink bus tickets, a receipted bill and three ha'-pennies. The other pocket was more productive. It contained, along with a face tissue and a card of bobby pins, a plain envelope addressed to *Tyson Frost, Esq. By hand*. Lash dropped the coat onto the floor, and slitting open the flap, drew out the contents.

It was another envelope, but of a different variety. This one was a piece of hand-made paper, yellowed with age and folded and sealed in the manner of a day when there were still a few people who did not use manufactured envelopes. There was no address on it. Only the heavy seal bearing the crest of the Frosts over the arrogant motto *'I Tayke Wat I Wyll'*, a number, 74389, and the initials E.T.F. written in faded ink.

'Women!' said Lash. 'And you had it in your pocket the whole time!'

He sat down on the sofa and gazed at her, shaking his head, and then looked down at the sealed envelope again. 'What beats me is why he didn't find it when he went through your things at the Airlane. I guess he can't know anything about women, or you'd have thought——Say, wait a minute! Didn't you say something about leaving some coat in a powder room! Was this it?'

'Yes,' said Dany, still having some difficulty with her voice. 'I—I forgot it. It was there all night.'

'So that's why. Then it all ties up.'

He stared at the small sealed packet that he held, and was silent for what seemed a very long time.

The room was so quiet that Dany could hear the tiny tick of his wrist-watch and the slow bubbles breaking at the rim of the glass that she still held clutched in one hand. Lash was looking tired and grim and oddly unfamiliar, and as though he had suddenly become a stranger; someone about whom she knew nothing at all.

The silence began to get on her nerves and she found herself watching the bedroom door again, and listening with strained attention for any faint sounds from the night outside. Was the broken window in the bathroom still open? Had Lash thought to lock the door between it and the dressing-room. Suppose the man were to come back—and with a gun or a knife instead of a pad soaked in chloroform?

Lash spoke at last: slowly and in an undertone, as though he were talking to himself rather than to Dany.

'Yes . . . that would be it, of course. It's the only way it fits. I remember now. You said something about telephoning. You phoned this solicitor of Tyson's and asked if you could see him in the morning instead of that afternoon. Which means that you should have gone there in the afternoon, and someone who knew that, but not that you had changed the time, meant to get there first—to get their hands on this!' He tossed the small envelope in the air and caught it again. 'That's why the safe was opened, of course.'

'But Mr Honeywood . . . Why should anyone murder Mr Honeywood?'

'Because you can't open a safe without keys. Unless you're a professional cracksman. And whoever was after this, and didn't realize that you'd got in ahead of him, expected to find it in the safe.'

'But—but he had a gun. He could have *made* Mr Honeywood open it. He didn't have to kill him!'

'Suppose your Mr Honeywood knew the guy? I'd sure like to know what's in this bit of paper.' Lash balanced it in his hand thoughtfully and said: 'I'm not sure we oughtn't to take a look at it.'

'But you can't. It's Tyson's! And it's sealed. You can't go breaking the seal.'

'Can't I? What makes you think that? There's something inside this that was worth a man's life. Someone was prepared to murder Honeywood in cold blood in order to get it and you don't get many people risking the death penalty for peanuts.'

'It's Tyson's letter,' said Dany stubbornly, and held out her hand for it.

Lash shrugged his shoulders and passed it over. 'I won't say "Take better care of it this time", because it seems to me that in your own cock-eyed fashion you haven't done too badly. But for Pete's sake don't leave it lying around, because whoever was after it has got a shrewd idea who's got it.'

Dany gazed at him appalled. 'I—didn't think of that. That means——' Her voice trailed away and she shuddered uncontrollably.

'Exactly!' said Lash dryly. 'It's someone who followed you from London and must have been on the plane with us. And what is more, it's someone who knows quite well that you are not Miss Ada Kitchell from Milwaukee!'

8

The alarm clock rang shrilly, notifying the fact that it was now 5 a.m., and Dany awoke for the second time that morning; to find herself in possession of a bad headache and sharing not only the bridal suite but the bridal bed.

The proprieties had been observed by the slenderest of margins, and one which would hardly have been recognized as such by even the most broad-minded: Miss Ashton being inside the bedclothes while Mr Lashmer J. Holden Jnr, still wearing his dressing-gown, was disposed gracefully outside them.

Blinking at him in the pale light of early morning Dany recalled with painful clarity that it had been her own hysterical and un-maidenly insistence that was responsible for this scandalous state of affairs. She had, she recalled, refused frantically and flatly to be left alone. A combination of panic and whisky had drastically altered her sense of values, and the ethics involved had ceased to have any meaning for her when compared with the terrifying prospect of being left alone once more in that darkened bedroom.

Lash yawned and stretched, and having propped himself on one elbow, regarded her flushed cheeks and appalled eyes with comprehension and some amusement.

'All in all, a very cosy and domestic scene,' he remarked pleasantly: 'I can't think what the younger generation is coming to. Or what your dear Aunt Harriet would say if she could see you now!'

'Or your dear "Elf"!' snapped Dany. And instantly regretted the retort.

'Puss, Puss, Puss!' said Lash, unruffled; and rolled off the bed.

He stood up yawning largely and rubbing his unshaven chin, and announced that she had better stay where she was while he had the first bath and shaved: 'And don't go ringing for the roomwaiter until I'm out of the way. The less publicity we get, the better.'

Dany occupied the time in wrapping the sealed envelope in a chiffon head scarf and then putting it back into her coat pocket as far down as it would go, and pinning the chiffon wrapping firmly to the lining with a large safety pin. That at least would ensure that no one could possibly pick her pocket without her knowledge.

Time being short, she took over the bathroom while Lash dressed, and as soon as she was in a fit state to answer any knock on the door he went away, leaving her to pack.

He had finished breakfast by the time Dany appeared in the dining-room, and had gone out into the verandah, where she could see him through an open door talking to Mrs Bingham, Millicent Bates and a pallid willowy man whose face was vaguely familiar to her. Amalfi, the Marchese, Larry Dowling and the Arab, Salim Abeid, were also on the verandah, standing together in a bored group just beyond them, yawning at intervals and making desultory conversation, while presumably waiting for a taxi, or taxis.

The sight of Salim Abeid was a shock to Dany. She had not realized that he too had been staying at the hotel, and she was digesting this fact, and its possible implications, when Lash came quickly back into the dining-room and over to her table.

'That out there,' said Lash without preamble, 'is your dear step-father's secretary, Ponting. So just watch your step, will you, and keep your mouth shut. He may look like the popular idea of an underdone Interior Decorator—and choose to talk like one—but there's nothing much the matter with his little grey cells, and don't you forget it!'

'So *that's* who it is!' said Dany, relieved. 'I knew I'd seen him somewhere.'

'Holy Mackerel——! Say, I thought you said——'

'Oh, I haven't ever met him before,' said Dany hastily. 'I've only seen his photograph. He was in some snapshots that Lorraine sent me.'

Lash exhaled noisily. 'Thank God for that! For a moment I thought we were going to run into more trouble. Well, if you've seen photographs of him, it's an even bet he's seen plenty of you, so for Pete's sake be careful. His hobby is ferreting out information and gossiping about it, and in that line he can give points to any women ever born! He was being infernally inquisitive last night. It seems that there should have been a Miss Ashton on that plane, and he can't figure out why she hasn't come.'

'Oh dear!' said Dany guiltily. 'He hasn't done anything about it, has he?'

'Nothing much he *can* do, is there? Apart from ringing the Green Zero office, and he did that yesterday. They came right through with it and said that Miss Ashton had cancelled her passage only twenty-four hours before the flight, so he had to be satisfied with that. But he's still making quite a song and dance about it, and but for that providential goddam tooth of his he'd have fetched up at the airport yesterday when I was in no condition to deal with the situation. It's a pity his dentist didn't give him an overdose of gas while he was at it, and save us his company this morning as well. But I suppose one can't have everything. Don't be too long over that coffee. We leave in ten minutes.'

They drove through Nairobi in the cool of the early morning, and once again there was the ordeal of passports and officials to be faced. But at last they were in the departure lounge, and the worst was over. The last lap——

Larry Dowling appeared at Dany's elbow, and relieving her of her typewriter, asked with some concern if she were feeling all right. Larry's eyes, thought Dany, were like a Kentish trout stream with the sun on it. Clear and cool—and friendly. Looking at them, she felt again that he was a dependable person—in a way that Lash was not. And yet . . .

Gussie Bingham, smart in a suit of lilac-blue linen that toned admirably with her blue-rinsed hair, said briskly: 'You look tired, my dear. I hope you don't allow Mr Holden to keep you working too late. Personally, I had an excellent night. But then I am thankful to say that I always sleep well wherever I am. It's all a matter of *control.* I don't think you have met Mr Ponting yet, my brother's secretary? Mr Ponting——!'

'Dear lady?' said Mr Ponting, hastening to obey that imperious beckoning finger.

Dany turned quickly so that her back was to the light, and shook hands with Mr Ponting. His hand felt limp and boneless and as soft as a woman's, and his voice was high and light and affected.

'Ah!' said Nigel Ponting gaily. 'A fellow wage-slave! A toiler at the oar! You and I, Miss Kitchell—mere downtrodden secretaries: hardworking honey-gatherers among this decorative swarm of holidaying drones. They toil not, neither do they spin, while we are compelled to do both. Gross injustice, is it not? We must form ourselves into a Trades Union. Ah——! Eduardo. *Buon giorno!* I didn't see you at the hotel. How are you? You look *deliriously* fit. I suppose you all know each other madly well by now——No? Oh dear! I'm so sorry. Miss Kitchell, this is the Signor Marchese di Chiago, a fellow guest bound for *Kivulimi*. Miss Kitchell is Holden's confidential secretary, Eduardo, so we are Birds of a Feather.'

The Marchese bowed over Dany's hand and gave her a long observant look that tabulated her admirable physical assets, added the spectacles, fringe and curls, and subtracted the number he had first thought of.

He was a slim, dark man, handsome in a typically Italianate manner, and although he was not much taller than Nigel Ponting, he gave the impression of being twice the size. The willowy Mr Ponting, thought Dany, would have made quite a pretty girl. And possibly he thought so himself, for he wore his butter-coloured hair far too long, and allowed a single artistic lock to fall carelessly across his white forehead—apparently as an excuse for a frequent graceful tossing of the head that would temporarily return it to place. His eyes were a limpid and unblinking blue like the china eyes of a Victorian doll, but nevertheless they conveyed a disturbing impression that very little escaped them, and Dany was more than relieved when he took the Marchese affectionately by the arm and walked away, talking animatedly of mutual friends in Rome.

Gussie Bingham, hailed by Miss Bates, hurried off to see to some question of luggage, taking Larry Dowling with her, and Dany returned to a seat near the window and struggled with another attack of panic. Officials came and went, appearing suddenly in doorways and glancing keenly about the room, and each time she was sure that she was the one they were looking for. Every stranger was, or might be, a plain-clothes detective, and every idle glance that came her way turned her cold with apprehension. They *could* not stop her now! Not now, when she was almost within reach of safety. Her head ached and she felt chilled and sick and taut with the strain of trying not to think of the happenings of the last few days, or the dreadful thing that Lash had said last night: 'It's someone who must have been on the plane with us.'

But that was absurd and impossible. It was out of the question that it could be anyone who had travelled out from London with them. Dany turned restlessly to look out across the vast, dun, dusty expanse of the aerodrome, and as she did so a man passed by on the other side of the window. It was the Arab, 'Jembe'—Salim Abeid— who had been on the plane from London. She saw him stop not far away in the shadow of an adjoining building to speak to a man who seemed to have been waiting there. An olive-skinned Arab in a well-cut white suit.

Salim Abeid seemed to be speaking with the same fervour that he had displayed at Naples, and Dany wondered if his conversation was still confined to politics. His hands waved, his shoulders shrugged and his eyes flashed, but his companion showed little interest, and apart from an occasional surreptitious glance at his wrist-watch, remained gravely impassive.

Salim Abeid turned and gestured in the direction of the glass-fronted departure lounge, and for a moment it seemed to Dany as though the Arab in the white suit looked straight at her, and once again panic attacked her. Perhaps he was a policeman. An Arab policeman. Perhaps this man 'Jembe' was telling him about her: that he had seen her in the hall of the Airlane in London. Or worse—far worse!—was *he* the one who had murdered Mr Honeywood, and searched her room at the Airlane—and meant to chloroform her last night?

Dany felt her heart begin to pound and race again, and she looked wildly round for Lash—or for Larry. But Lash was at the far side of the room being monopolized by Amalfi Gordon, and Larry, looking faintly resigned, was collecting a cup of coffee for Mrs Bing-ham. He smiled at her across the crowded room, and her panic unexpectedly diminished. She was imagining things and behaving, as Lash had said, like some hysterical heroine in a soap opera. Surely her situation was parlous enough without her manufacturing turnip-lanterns with which to scare herself further. And yet . . .

'Will passengers on flight zero three four, proceeding to Mom-basa, Tanga, Pemba, Zanzibar and Dar-es-Salaam, please take their seats in the plane,' announced a sepulchral and disembodied voice.

◇　◇　◇

The orange earth of Africa slid away beneath them. A waste of sun-baked earth and flat-topped thorn trees, dotted with slow-moving specks that were giraffe and zebra, wilde-beeste, lion, and drifting, grazing herds of antelope—for this was the Nairobi Game Park.

A lone white cloud, faintly tinged with pink, lay in the cool blue of the early morning sky, and as they neared it Dany saw that it was not a cloud, but a mountain. A solitary snow-capped mountain faintly reminiscent of a Japanese print of Fuji-Yama. Kilimanjaro, the 'Mountain of Cold Devils', looming lonely above the enormous, dust brown plains: a gaunt, burnt-out volcano whose snows defied the burning African sun.

A voice from the seat behind Dany's, a man's voice, fluting, high-pitched and seemingly a deliberate parody of an announcer on the B.B.C.'s Third Programme, said: 'Yes—*rather* spectacular, isn't it? And they say that there is the corpse of a leopard in the crater, frozen into the ice. No one knows how it got there, or why. Deliciously intriguing, don't you think? I *adore* mysteries!'

Dany made a movement as though she would have turned to look at the speaker, but Lash's hand shot out and closed warningly on her wrist. *'Ponting,'* he said soundlessly and Dany turned hurriedly back to her contemplation of the view.

Nigel Ponting's neighbour was apparently Mrs Bingham, and with the object of instructing the ignorant—or possibly because he was addicted to the sound of his own voice—he embarked on a lengthy verbal tour of Kenya.

'And you have simply no idea how primitive those up-country roads are,' fluted Mr Ponting. 'Mere tracks, I assure you. *Torture* to the tyres! Not, of course, to mention one's *spine!* Though actually, when one gets there, it is quite deliciously stark. The natives—the animals—the scenery! Intoxicatingly primitive. Such an improvement on down-country Kenya and the Settler Belt, which is so *painfully* Pre-World-War-One, I always think. *Too* Poona, don't you agree? But the Northern Frontier now . . .'

His voice tinkled on and on like water trickling from a faulty tap, interspersed at intervals by vague noises from Gussie Bingham (herself no mean monologist but at present patently outclassed) and it would have been a soothing enough sound had he not changed to the subject of Dany.

'I can't understand it,' said Nigel Ponting fretfully. 'I simply *cannot* understand it. No word at the hotel, and her room reservation not even cancelled. One hopes that the Frosts have had a cable, but really—one didn't know whether to go or stay! I suppose the wretched girl has been smitten with some form of spots. Measles, or some similar schoolgirl affliction.'

Lash turned his head and grinned maliciously at Dany, but she did not share his amusement. She was getting tired of hearing herself referred to as though she were a school-age adolescent, and in any case she could see nothing comic, in the present circumstances, in having to listen to this particular form of conversation.

'*Actually,*' said Nigel, 'it was on Miss Ashton's account that I was over here at all. Your brother thought that it would be a graceful gesture to have her met at Nairobi, and probably save you trouble if I could see to her and show her the town. So he kindly arranged for me to take a little holiday at about this time to fit in with the date, and now the wretched girl has not arrived! *Too* tiresome of her, as I fully expect to be sent back to meet her when she finally does so. And I *detest* air travel. I may not show it, but I'm always simply terrified in a plane. Aren't you?'

'No,' said Gussie Bingham, firmly seizing her chance. 'I can't say I am. But then I am a fatalist. I feel that if fate intends me to die in an air-crash, I shall die in an air-crash: and that is all there is to it. And if it does not then there is nothing to worry about. Everything, dear Mr Ponting, is pre-destined. Everything! There is no such thing as chance. Once one has grasped that simple but essential truth, life becomes far less complicated. One ceases to worry.'

Mr Ponting uttered a sharp cry of disagreement. 'Oh no, no, no, no *No,* Mrs Bingham! I cannot agree with you. The doctrine of pre-destination, even if it were proved right, *must* be wrong. So spineless. Surely one should grasp opportunity and *mould* it to one's will?'

'That's what Millicent says. We have *such* arguments. But it is my contention that when we think we are grasping an opportunity we are merely doing something that we were ordained to do, and cannot avoid doing. For instance, when we left Lydon Gables for London we were halfway to the station when I remembered that I had taken my passport out of Millicent's bag to show to a friend (a really laughable photograph!) and left it on the piano. So of course we had to hurry back, and what do you think! We found that a live coal had fallen out of the drawing-room fire, and the carpet was already smouldering! Mrs Hagby might not have had occasion to come in for several hours, and had we not returned the house might well have burned down!'

'Very lucky,' conceded Nigel Ponting.

'Lucky? No such thing. We were *meant* to return. I was meant to leave that passport behind, and so could not have avoided doing so.'

Nigel gave a little tittering laugh. 'And supposing you had missed your train and had not been able to reach London, and the airport, in time? Would that also have been *meant?*'

'Oh, but we were not meant to miss it! It was fortunately running late. Though even if it had not been we should not have missed the plane, because we came up to London two days early, on the afternoon of the twelfth, and stayed at the Airlane, as Millicent had some shopping to do and——'

Dany was aware of a slight movement beside her, and she saw that Lash's hands had tightened suddenly on the newspaper he held so that it's outer columns were crumpled and unreadable. But surely he had known that Mrs Bingham and Miss Bates had been at the Airlane? And surely he could not think—*Someone on the plane* . . . Gussie Bingham . . . No, that at least was not possible!

Nigel was saying pettishly: 'But really, Mrs Bingham, one cannot bring oneself to believe that Providence is interested in such matters as a coal falling out of your drawing-room fire or a fog to delay your train, or the fact that passport photographs always make one look so painfully improbable that you were impelled to share the joke with some friend. Now I myself am more interested in psychology, and it is my contention that when you left that passport on the piano——'

Dany rose abruptly. She did not want to listen to any more talk of passports, or the Airlane, or anything else that forced her to think of frightening and horrible things, and she handed her folded coat to Lash and said briefly: 'I'll be back in a minute.'

'Feeling all right?' inquired Lash, half standing to let her pass. 'You're looking a bit green.'

'No. I'm quite all right, thank you.'

She went quickly down the aisle and took refuge in the ladies' room, where she stood staring out of the window at the wide blue sky and the little idling clouds. But her thoughts had only come with her, and she could not hold them at bay.

Gussie Bingham . . . Millicent Bates . . . Jembe . . . Mr Honeywood. *Murder in Market-Lydon* . . .

Dany gave it up and returned to her seat.

The tiny, dragon-fly shadow of the aeroplane flitted across muddy green water, mangrove swamps and forests of palm trees . . . Mombasa. 'May I have your attention please? The indicator will tell you when to fasten your seat belts. In a few minutes we shall be coming in to land——'

The passengers trooped out dutifully into hard sunlight and a salty smell of the sea, and among them Dany noticed the slim Arab in the white suit whom she had seen Salim Abeid talking to so excitedly at Nairobi that morning.

Apparently there were others on the plane who also knew him, for Nigel Ponting, catching sight of him, left Mrs Bingham's side and hurried after him. They shook hands and stood talking together for a few minutes on the hot, sandy tarmac, and Dany, passing them, heard Tyson's secretary say: 'I do hope you had a lovely time? Frankly, Nairobi is *not* my cup of tea. But of course it's different for you—you've friends there. Now *I* went up to the Northern Frontier with Bunny, and——' The words 'deliciously stark' pursued her as she reached the shade of the airport entrance.

Salim Abeid—'Jembe', pushed past her, looking far from well, and making for the opposite side of the room he sat down at a small table, ordered himself a cup of black coffee, and began to read an Arabic newspaper which he held in noticeably trembling hands.

The waiting-room of the airport was hot and crowded, and Lash having left her to her own devices, Dany bought a magazine at random off the bookstall and retired with it to a comparatively secluded seat near a pillar. But she did not read it. She sat staring unseeingly at the printed page and listening absently to the medley of accents about her, until her attention was attracted by a large framed advertisement for a local airline that hung on one side of the pillar a little to her left.

The advertisement, she discovered, was painted on looking-glass and in it she could see the reflection of Gussie Bingham's blue curls, Millicent Bates' pudding-basin hat, and Amalfi Gordon's flower-like face.

Amalfi, thought Dany, was not looking her best this morning. She looked as though she were hot and rather cross, and the conversation of Eduardo di Chiago, whose handsome hawk-like profile was just visible at the extreme edge of the looking-glass, appeared to be boring her, for she was replying to it in monosyllables and allowing her gaze to wander. Mrs Bingham, on the other hand, seemed to be enjoying herself. She was laughing at something that someone had said, and all at once the wild idea that she might have had anything to do with the murder of Mr Honeywood was exposed as utterly ridiculous.

Perhaps it had been the Arab, Jembe, after all. Or else it was some stranger on the London plane whom she had taken no note of. Or even Sir Ambrose Yardley! The complete absurdity of that last thought drew a wan smile from Dany: she was letting her imagination run away with her with a vengeance! And anyway, Sir Ambrose had not been in Nairobi last night. It *must* be some stranger . . .

The group in the looking-glass broke up and moved away, and she could no longer see the reflection of anyone she knew. Passengers on other flights arrived and left again, and the waiting-room became noisier and more crowded. Dany's head began to ache intolerably, and every separate sound in the medley of sounds became an added irritation: a fretful Indian child wailing with dismal persistence, the crash of an overturned cup and the trickle of spilt liquid, the shrill giggling chatter of a covey of Arab matrons, and the loud laughter of a group of young planters round the bar.

'You never told me you could read Arabic,' remarked Lash's voice behind her.

Dany started violently and bit her tongue, and focusing for the first time on the magazine that she held, discovered that it was indeed printed in a totally unfamiliar script.

Lash reached across her shoulder, and twitching the magazine out of her hands, reversed it and handed it back. He said: 'You'll forgive me for mentioning it, Miss Kitchell, but there's nothing quite so conspicuous as someone pretending to read a paper that they're holding upside down. And that fresh boy-friend of yours, the newspaper guy, has been watching your reflection in that slice of glass with considerable interest. It's a game that two can play. Maybe he just likes red-heads—but then again he might have other ideas.'

Dany said breathlessly: 'Larry Dowling? What ideas? He—he couldn't know anything. And anyway he's only interested in people like Tyson. And politics.'

'That's a buyer's estimate,' said Lash dryly. 'Murder is news any place. So just try and stop acting like you had a ton-load of guilt on your conscience. It shows.'

'I'm sorry,' said Dany in a small voice.

'That's O.K. It's not much longer. We're almost there.'

'But not quite,' said Dany unsteadily.

'Where's your fighting spirit?'

'I haven't any—Not at present.'

Lash said: 'Poor baby.' But without sarcasm. And then once again a quacking, disembodied voice from the amplifier cut through the fog of babel in the crowded room:

'Passengers on flight zero three four, proceeding to Tanga, Pemba, Zanzibar and Dar-es-Sa-laam . . .'

9

They walked out into the glaring sunlight and a sea wind that sang through the casuarinas and whipped hot grains of sand against their legs, and took their places in the waiting plane; dutifully fastening their seat belts and stubbing out cigarettes. Larry Dowling, from a seat just behind Dany and across the aisle, called out: 'Hi——Stewardess! we're one short. Don't shut that door. My neighbour isn't here yet. Mr Salim Abeid.'

The stewardess smiled in the tolerant manner of a school teacher coping with a backward new boy, and said sweetly: 'Thank you, I have the list. There is no need to worry. He will be along in a minute.'

But five minutes ticked by, and then ten, and though the plane vibrated to the roar of the engines it did not move, and the passengers began to fidget restlessly, turning to peer over their shoulders at the open door or to look anxiously at their watches.

'What's holding us up?' demanded a stout man from a seat near the front. He rose and looked down the aisle, his red face purpling with indignation. 'We shall be late at this rate, and I've got a conference on at Tanga at 10.15. Hey! Stewardess—Miss!'

The stewardess turned and smiled a bright official smile. 'Just a moment, sir.' She leaned out and spoke to someone through the open door, and then came quickly down the aisle and vanished into the pilot's cabin. Two more minutes passed, and then she reappeared accompanied by the captain and the First Officer, and all three left the plane.

'*Now* what?' demanded the gentleman who had a conference in Tanga. 'This is the ruddy limit! How much longer do they intend to keep us hanging about?' He lumbered wrathfully down the aisle and peered out into the sunlight, and they could hear him shouting down to someone on the tarmac.

'*Really,*' said Nigel Ponting in a fading voice, 'these business types and their *hustle!* As if half an hour one way or another *mattered!*'

'There I don't agree at all,' said Gussie Bingham tartly. 'Delay is always maddening. And it will probably be most inconvenient for Tyson, who is sure to be meeting us. What do you suppose is holding us up?'

'Whatever it is, dear lady, it is surely a comfort to know that it is *Meant,*' said Nigel with malice. 'But let us trust that it is not some vital fault in the engines, or we shall be pre-destined to wait here for *hours!*'

Mrs Bingham was saved the necessity of finding an adequate retort to this shrewd shot by the return of the Tanga-bound passenger. 'Seems that one of the Zanzibar passengers has been taken ill,' he announced, and went angrily back to his seat. 'Can't think why we should all be held up for a thing like that. Do they expect us to wait until he feels better?'

At this point the stewardess returned, looking flushed and put out, and made a brief announcement: 'May I have your attention, please? I am afraid that we shall be delayed for a further—er—few minutes. We are so sorry that you should be put to this inconvenience, but we hope it will not be too long before we—er—take off. You may smoke if you wish, but will you all please keep your seats.'

Once again a buzz of conversation broke out; to die away as two airport officials and a young European police officer in a starched khaki uniform entered the plane. One of the officials spoke politely and briefly into the microphone: 'Sorry to trouble you, but we have to make another passport check. Will you have your passports ready, please?'

Dany threw a wild, terrified glance at Lash, but he did not return it. He drew out his own passport and held out a hand for hers, still without looking at her, and his complete lack of emotion brought her some measure of reassurance. She could hear the voices and footsteps and the rustle of paper as the officials passed up the aisle, examining every passport, checking it against a list and jotting down brief notes on a loose-leaf pad.

'Holden,' said Lash laconically, handing over his passport as they stopped beside him. 'My secretary, Miss Kitchell.'

Dany forced herself to meet the man's gaze and hold it calmly, and although it seemed to her that he stood there for an appalling length of time, it was, in fact, all over in under three minutes. They had only asked one question: the same question that they had put to everyone on the plane. 'Where can you be reached during the next ten days?'

Even the young police officer had heard of Tyson Frost, and had read his books. 'Another of you,' he said jotting down the address. 'Mr Frost seems to be throwing quite a party. He's a wonderful chap, isn't he? I saw him when he came through here a few months ago. Got his autograph, too!'

The boy grinned and passed on to the next passenger, and Dany relaxed again. It was all just some routine check after all. She turned to smile her relief at Lash, but Lash was not smiling. He was looking, on the contrary, remarkably grim and there was a curious suggestion of alertness about him: as though his nerves and muscles were tensed. It was the same look that he had worn during the previous night, and it frightened Dany.

The three men came back down the aisle, their check completed, and Larry Dowling said: 'How is he, officer?—Mr Abeid? Nothing infectious, I hope? He seemed all right when he got off just now. Is he really bad?'

'He's dead,' said the police officer shortly, and departed.

There was a brief shocked silence. The silence that must always greet such an announcement, whether it refers to a friend or a stranger. The ending of a life.

It was broken by Millicent Bates, who said loudly and incredulously: *'Dead?* D'you mean that Arab chap who was on the London plane with us? What rubbish! They must have made a mistake. Why, he was chatting away to Mr Dowling, on and off, all the way from Nairobi. I heard him. He can't possibly be dead!'

'Heart, I expect,' said Larry Dowling uncomfortably. 'He said he always felt bad in a plane. He looked a bit green. But he can't have been air-sick. We haven't bumped about at all. I think it was just nerves.'

'As long as it's not plague or cholera or one of those beastly Eastern diseases!' said Millicent with an audible shudder. 'I told you we should regret coming out East, Gussie!'

Dany heard Mrs Bingham turn sharply in her seat. 'Don't talk nonsense, Millicent! Of course it can't be anything infectious. If it were they'd quarantine the lot of us!'

'How do we know they haven't?' inquired Miss Bates. 'We're still here!'

The entire plane was silent again, digesting this. Presently the silence was broken by the return of the captain and the First Officer, and five minutes later Mombasa Airport was behind them—a dwindling speck among toy trees.

Dany turned to look at Lash again, and said in an anxious undertone: 'Would they really quarantine us if it was something infectious?'

'If it had been anything infectious they'd never have let us leave.'

'Oh. Yes. I didn't think of that. I suppose it must have been a heart attack. Or a heat stroke.'

'I doubt it,' said Lash curtly.

'Why?'

'They wouldn't have taken all that trouble to check up on the lot of us, and make certain of being able to get in touch with us again, if it were anything as simple as that. They think it's something else.'

Once again Dany was conscious of feeling oddly breathless. She said: 'I don't know what you mean.'

'Then you're lucky,' said Lash briefly, and put a stop to any further conversation by lying back and closing his eyes with deliberation.

Small puff-ball clouds lazed in the hot blue air and trailed their shadows far below across acres of pineapple plantations spiked with sisal, and thick, pale, leafless baobab trees . . .

Tanga, and another wait: shorter this time. An agonizing wait: but there were no police officers to meet the plane. The voice of the stewardess again: 'May I have your attention, please. The indicator will tell you when to fasten your seat belts . . .'

Now they were over the sea. A glassy sea that merged into a glassy sky with no line anywhere to show where one ended and the other began: blue and green, violet and amethyst, streaked with the pale ribbons of wandering currents; the colours shifting and changing as the shadow of the plane swept across deep water, coral beds, rock bottom or sandy shallows.

Pemba: the Green Island. Rich in cloves and dark with the legends of witches, demons and warlocks. A long, sandy runway and the sea wind rustling the palm-leaf thatch and matting sides of the little hut that did duty for airport office and waiting-room. Amalfi Gordon, looking as out of place as a diamond tiara in the one-and-nine-pennies, and gazing in horrified disbelief at an enormous slow-moving millepede that was crawling placidly across the dusty floor.

Millicent Bates, her worst fears realized and 'What Did I Tell You?' written all over her. Gussie Bingham, seated on the extreme edge of a wooden bench upon which she had first thoughtfully spread a clean handkerchief, and also watching the millepede with an expression of acute apprehension. Eduardo di Chiago, Nigel Ponting and the Arab in the white suit standing together in the open doorway, silhouetted against the hot empty expanse of sand and sky, talking together in Italian. And Larry Dowling fanning himself with his new panama hat and gazing absently at a framed poster that urged prospective travellers to 'Fly BOAC.'

There were eight other passengers of assorted nationalities in the hot little hut. A stout German business man, a Swedish tourist hung about with expensive cameras, two British army officers on leave, a Parsee, an elderly Indian couple and a citizen of the United States of America—Mr Lashmer J. Holden Jnr, who once again appeared to have fallen asleep.

How *can* he just doze off like that, thought Dany indignantly, when we shall be arriving in Zanzibar in no time at all, and if they've heard anything there we may find police waiting for us at the airport? And if Mother is there to meet us she'll know me at once, even in spectacles and with this hideous hair-fixing, and suppose she says something in front of the passport and customs people before we can stop her, and——Oh, I wish it were all over! How *can* he go to sleep!

Lash opened one eye, winked at her solemnly, and shut it again, and Dany blushed as hotly as though she had been caught speaking her thoughts aloud. She turned her back on him with deliberation as Nigel Ponting drifted in and introduced the Arab:

'Here's someone you simply *must* meet. Seyyid Omar-bin-Sultan. He has a simply heavenly, *heavenly* house in Zanzibar. In fact two—or is it three? Anyway, if you want to see the island you must lure him into taking you on a conducted tour. No one can tell you as much about it as he can. He practically *is* Zanzibar!'

Seyyid Omar smiled and bowed. His English was as fluent as his Italian had been and he spoke it with barely a trace of an accent. He in no way resembled his compatriot, the late Mr Salim Abeid, for his complexion was no darker than the Marchese di Chiago's, and he was a charming and entertaining conversationalist.

Lash did not open his eyes again until the passengers were summoned once more to take their seats in the plane, but as they left the little palm-thatched hut he took Dany's arm and delayed her, walking slowly until the others had drawn ahead.

'Now get this,' said Lash, speaking quickly and in an undertone. 'When we get there, waste as much time as you can before you leave the plane. Fuss over the baggage—anything. But get right at the end of the line. I've got to see your mother first—if she's at the airport. Or your step-father. Or both. Otherwise we're going to find ourselves in the can before we can blink twice. Got that?'

Dany nodded. And then they were back once more in their seats, facing an illuminated sign that was saying 'No Smoking. Fasten Seat Belts.'

Pemba dwindled in its turn to a little dark dot in a waste of blue, and ahead of them lay something that at first seemed no more substantial than the shadow of a cloud on the glittering sea. Zanzibar . . .

The blue of deep water gave place to the gorgeous greens of sandbars and shallows, and they were losing height and swooping in over acres of clove trees and groves of palms. Above orange orchards and the clustered roofs of houses.

Lash reached out a hand and closed it over one of Dany's, gripping it hard and encouragingly, and then there was a bump and a jolt and they were taxi-ing up the runway to stop at last before a long white building backed by innumerable trees.

Lash unfastened his seat belt for the last time and said 'Here we go!' And went.

Dany never knew what he had said to her mother and Tyson, both of whom were at the airport to meet the plane. He had had less than five clear minutes; certainly not more; but he had apparently made good use of them.

'*Darlings!*' called Lorraine, greeting her guests as they emerged from behind a barrier where they had queued to have their passports and permits inspected and stamped. 'How lovely to see you all. Elf——! What heaven to see you, darling. And Gussie! Gussie, you look *marvellous*. And madly smart. Hullo, Millicent. Eddie!——*years* since we saw you last! Oh well, months then, but it seems like years; and isn't that a lovely compliment?'

Lorraine never seemed to change, thought Dany, regarding her mother with indulgent affection. She was not beautiful in the way that Amalfi Gordon was beautiful, but she managed none the less to convey an impression of beauty, and that did equally well. Part of her appeal, thought her daughter dispassionately, undoubtedly lay in her lack of inches and that entirely deceptive appearance of fragility. It made even undersized men feel large and strong and protective.

Lorraine was wearing white linen and pearls, and she did not look like anyone's mother. Or, for that matter, like the wife of the burly, loud-voiced, bearded man in the salt-stained fisherman's slacks and faded blue T-shirt, who seemed slightly larger than life and was clearly recognizable to any reader of the Press of any country in the world as Tyson Frost, author of *Last Service for Lloyd, Clothe Them All in Green O, The Sacred Swine* and at least half a dozen other novels that had been filmed, televised, analysed, attacked, imitated, selected by Book Societies and Literary Guilds and sold by the million.

Lash said briefly: 'My secretary, Ada Kitchell; Mrs Frost,' and Dany, demurely shaking hands with her own mother, was seized with a sudden hysterical desire to burst into helpless giggles.

Lorraine had not blinked, but her small face had paled a little and her blue eyes had widened in dismay. She said faintly: 'So pleased——' And then in an anguished whisper: 'Darling—why *red?* and that *appalling* fringe!'

Tyson's large, sinewy hand descended on Dany's shoulder blades with a smack that made her stagger: 'Well, Miss Kitchell—delighted to meet you. Perhaps you and Bates won't mind going in the station wagon with the luggage. No, Lorrie! you'd better take Elf and Eddie and Nigel. Hiyah, Eddie? Back again like a bad lira? Didn't think we'd see you down this way again after giving you sandfly fever or whatever it was you caught last time you were here. No, by cripes—it was dysentery, wasn't it? Gussie, I'll take you and young Lash. Go on, pile in.'

He opened the door of the car, and suddenly caught sight of Seyyid Omar-bin-Sultan. 'Hullo, you old wolf. Didn't know you'd be back so soon. How was the night-life of Nairobi?'

He took Seyyid Omar by the arm and said: 'Gussie, this is a friend of mine. I'd like you to meet Seyyid—Oh, you've met? Good. Well get on into the car then. We don't want to hang around here all day.'

Gussie got in, followed by Lash. 'Come round and look us up as soon as you can,' bellowed Tyson as Seyyid Omar moved off towards a large white car bearing a Zanzibar number plate. 'Who the hell are you?' He turned to glare at Larry Dowling, who removed his hat and smiled amiably.

'Merely a fellow-traveller—in a strictly non-political sense,' said

Mr Dowling. 'As a matter of fact, I came here hoping to meet you, Mr Frost. If I may call sometime——'

'In what capacity? As a member of my public or the Press?'

'Both,' said Mr Dowling promptly.

'Then let me break it to you right away,' boomed Tyson, 'that I despise my public whole-heartedly, and I never talk to the Press. Good day.'

He dived into his car, slammed the door and drove off in a cloud of dust, followed by his wife in a second car, and Dany, Millicent and the luggage in a station wagon. Larry Dowling, who was not unused to this sort of thing, bestowed a brief, good-humoured grin on Dany, shrugged philosophically and hailed a taxi.

◇ ◇ ◇

At any other time or in any other circumstances, Dany would have found her first sight of Zanzibar fascinating and exciting. But now that she was here at last, all that she could feel was not so much relief as overwhelming exhaustion. She had, as Lash would have said, made it. But it did not seem to matter.

The station wagon, piled high with assorted suitcases and driven by a smiling African in a smart white uniform and a red tarboosh, whirled them along white, shadow-splashed roads, tree-lined or palm fringed. Past pastel-coloured houses and sudden glimpses of a sea that glittered blue as a broken sapphire.

Hibiscus, oleander, bignonia and wild coffee starred the roadside, and brilliant masses of bougainvillaea spilled over garden walls in an extravagant riot of colour. And then they had reached the town and were threading their way at a foot pace through streets so narrow that neighbours living on opposite sides of them could surely shake hands with each other from their upper windows. Tall, white-washed houses, so high that the streets were deep canyons and crevasses. Hot white walls, hot black shadows, and white-robed black-faced men. Huge, elaborately ornamental doors decorated with fantastic carving and great metal spikes. The smell of strange Eastern spices and hot dust; the scent of sandalwood and frangi-pani and cloves. A sound of laughter and music and drums . . .

On the far side of the town they passed through a fringe of squalid slums: an ugly shanty-town of rusty tin, corrugated iron, crumbling mud walls and decaying thatch, which gave Miss Bates an excuse for a dissertation on the subject of Oriental inefficiency and the inexcusable stupidity of Eastern races who were critical of the benign blessings of British rule.

The road crossed a bridge over a malodorous creek and skirted a shallow bay full of mud flats where the rotting hulks of ancient dhows lay stranded beyond the reach of the tide. And then they were among trees again: forests of coconut palms, thick groves of mango and orderly plantations of clove.

'How much farther do you suppose this place is?' inquired Millicent Bates restlessly. 'I should have thought Tyson would have had the sense to live nearer the airport.'

'There wasn't any airport a hundred years ago,' said Dany.

'What's that? Oh—Oh, I see. Well it's a bally nuisance all the same. I don't mind telling you that I could do with a strong cup of tea. Gussie and I always have one about eleven o'clock, and it's one of the things I miss. But at this rate it will be jolly nearly lunch-time by the time we get to this shady house of Tyson's. Shady house . . .'

Millicent threw back her head and laughed uproariously at her own joke. 'Not bad, that, you know. I must remember to tell Gussie. And I bet it's not far out, either! From all one hears about old Rory Frost, I'd say there'd been a good few shady goings-on in that house. And I wouldn't put much beyond Tyson, either! He's the kind who'd watch his grandmother carved up if he happened to need some first-hand information on dissection for a chapter in one of his books. All the Frosts have been hard nuts; or else crazy, like old Barclay. I can't think how Gussie——Ah, this looks like it at last.'

The car turned left off the main road and into a narrow side lane that was barely more than a track, and presently they were skirting a long, high wall of whitewashed stone. Bougainvillaea, flowering jasmine and orange trumpet flowers draped it with scent and colour, and from behind it rose the tops of many trees.

'Yes, this must be it,' said Millicent with relief. 'The road seems to end here. There's the sea.'

The station wagon had been the last to leave the airport, and the two other cars, having easily outpaced it, were already back in the garage. The road was empty as they drew up before an ancient, iron-studded door set deeply into the long wall, where a stately Somali servant in white robes and a wide, welcoming grin awaited their arrival.

A scent of orange blossom, frangi-pani and warm damp earth drifted out to meet them, and through the open doorway Dany could see a garden full of flowers and winding paths and freckled shadows, and a tall, square, three-storied Arab-style house whose windows looked out across the massed green of trees and a blaze of flowers towards the sparkling sea and the long blue horizon. *Kivulimi,* at last!

10

'And now,' said Tyson, closing the door of the guest-house behind him and depositing a bottle and a handful of glasses on the nearest table, 'for the love of Allah, let's get this sorted out. Have a drink, Junior. In fact, have several. You look as though you needed 'em—and by God, I do! What in the name of hell's delight is all this about?'

Lash had been allotted the small, three-roomed guest-house that was built on the seaward wall of the garden overlooking a curving bay which was part of the domain: a wall that had once been part of the outer defences of a small fort, and dated from the days of Portuguese domination. Half a dozen armed men could have walked abreast along its crenelated top, and Tyson's father, Aubrey Frost, had reinforced the crumbling stone, and converted a look-out and two guard rooms into a small but pleasant guest-house, shaded by a gigantic rain tree and overhung by a profusion of purple and crimson bougainvillaea.

Tyson had led the way there, followed by his wife, his stepdaughter and Lashmer Holden, after first seeing to it that his other guests were safely in their several rooms, unpacking suitcases and preparing for luncheon.

Lash accepted a drink and disposed of half of it before replying.

'You may well ask,' he said. 'And you aren't going to like the answer. We are, not to put too fine a point on it, in one helluva jam.'

'It was like this——' began Dany.

Lash said: 'Now look——! you keep out of it. Right now I'm doing the talking. You can take over when I'm through.'

He turned back to Tyson: 'There's just one question I'd like to ask before we get down to cases. Why did you send this kid here tracking all the way down to the country to fetch you a letter from a guy called Honeywood, when your sister's living right plunk on his doorstep? Don't think I'm inquisitive, but I'm interested. How is it you didn't ask Mrs Bingham to collect it for you?'

Tyson stared. 'What the hell's that got to do with this? Or you?'

'Plenty,' said Lash. 'How come?'

'I don't see that it's any affair of yours. But if you've travelled out in the company of my sister without learning that she is talkative, untrustworthy and bloody inquisitive, you must have brought lack of observation to a fine art!'

'Tyson, *darling!*' protested Lorraine faintly. 'Gussie isn't——'

'Yes, she is. And well you know it! And don't interrupt. Well, boy, having answered your question, let's have an answer to mine. What the hell is all this fantastic fandango about?'

'Have you,' said Lash, asking another one, 'by any chance heard that Honeywood was murdered a few days back?'

'*Honeywood!* Good God! When—how——' He turned sharply to face his step-daughter. 'Then you didn't see him after all? Does this mean that you didn't get that letter?'

'Yes, she did,' said Lash brusquely. 'That's the trouble. And it makes a long and screwy story.'

He finished his drink, and having replenished his glass sat down on the window seat and supplied the salient points of that story with terseness and economy.

'Is that all?' said Tyson Frost with dangerous restraint, breathing heavily.

'It'll do to go on with,' said Lash laconically.

'Then all I can say,' said Tyson, saying it, 'is that there must be insanity in your family! And, by heck, I always knew it! Were you out of your mind?'

Lash winced. 'To be frank with you, yes. I happened to be plastered at the time.'

'My God! So I should think! Why—it's sheer lunacy. It's criminal. It's——'

'I know, I know,' said Lash wryly. 'You aren't telling me anything. I seem to remember saying all that myself when I surfaced yesterday. And more! There isn't any angle you can put to me that I have not already come up against—hard. The point is, what do we do now?'

'Cut her hair,' said Lorraine in a fading voice. 'And wash it. Darling really——! It's quite *hideous*. Not the colour so much; I could bear that. But that awful fringe! The sort of thing film stars used to wear in the ghastly twenties. Too frightful. And darling, those spectacles! For goodness sake take them off at once. They make you look too dreadfully intelligent.'

'It's an illusion,' said Lash sourly.

Lorraine ignored him: 'That's right, darling. And don't put them on again. You look so much nicer without them.'

Tyson said: 'Your mother, thank the Lord, is utterly incapable of intelligent thought or of grasping the essential guts of any situation.'

'It would appear to run in the family,' commented Lash caustically. And added as a gloomy afterthought: 'And maybe they've got something there, at that. An inability to grasp the essential guts of this set-up is something I wouldn't mind having myself right now. And you're dead right about that hair-style. It's a pain. I never did go for red-heads, anyway.'

'No. You prefer blondes, don't you?' said Dany with a sudden flash of waspishness.

'Hell, who doesn't? Is there any more of that Scotch around?'

Tyson pushed across the bottle and said angrily: 'You're all mad! The whole lot of you! What the blue-asterisk-blank does it matter what Dany's hair looks like? It seems to me, young Lash, that you're taking a ruddy casual view of all this. What do *you* propose to do about it?'

'I?' Lash looked mildly surprised. 'Oh, that's dead easy. I propose to eat a hearty meal at your expense, and then I'm catching the next available plane out of here. And I don't give a damn which way it's headed! From now on this is your headache, brother!'

'Lash!' Dany's voice had a sudden break in it.

Lash got up quickly and going to her, took her face between his hands. 'Listen, babe, I know I got you into this, but you'll be all right now. All you've got to do is to make a clean breast of it. Lay all your cards on the table. I can't help you. You know that. All I've done is to give you a wrong steer, and make bad worse. I——'

Dany said in an imploring whisper: 'Lash, please don't go— please!'

'Look, honey; it isn't going to help one bit if I—Oh, hell!'

He released her abruptly and turned suddenly on Tyson Frost: 'What I want to know,' said Lash furiously, 'is why you ever let her get mixed up in this sort of thing in the first place! Couldn't you have got someone else to do your dirty work for you? You must have known darned well that there was dynamite in that letter. What was it?'

'Yes, dear,' said Lorraine, sitting suddenly upright. 'What was in it? Why should anyone else want it?'

Tyson said: 'Why does anyone want three million?'

'*W-what!*' Lorraine sprang to her feet. 'Tyson, darling! What are you talking about? You can't mean——'

'Sit down,' said Tyson. 'All of you. That's better.'

He crossed the room with a step that was curiously light for so big a man, and reaching the door, jerked it open and peered out; looking along the broad open top of the wall and down into the green shade of the garden below, as though to assure himself that there was no one within earshot. After a minute he closed it again carefully, and went over to the window to lean out and look down on the sun-baked slope of rock thirty feet below. At last, satisfied with the result of his survey, he came back to the low cushion-strewn divan that stood against one wall of the sitting-room and sat down on it; the wood creaking protestingly under his weight.

'I shall have to go back a bit,' said Tyson Frost, lighting himself a cigarette and inhaling deeply: 'As you probably know—it seems to be common property!—my revered grandfather, Rory—Emory Frost, who died way back in the eighteen-eighties—left a stack of papers and diaries with the family solicitors, Honeywood & Honeywood, with instructions that they were not to be opened or their contents made public for seventy years, which is reckoned to be man's permitted span. That time limit expired a few months ago, and the stuff duly arrived out here. And good ripe stuff it is! Roaring Rory must have been a hellraiser and a half in his day, and . . . But that's neither here nor there. The point is that it took me some time to go through it, and it wasn't until about three weeks ago that I came across a folded piece of paper that had been pushed in between the leather and the backing of one of the covers. And I wouldn't have found it at all if the backing hadn't split. It was interesting. It was very interesting . . .'

Tyson reached for the glass he had left on the floor and took a long pull at it.

'You know,' he said thoughtfully, 'it's astonishing how often life can give points to the movies. Have any of you ever heard the legend of the lost treasure buried by Seyyid Saïd?'

'Yes!' said Dany.

'No, *really,* darling,' protested Lorraine. 'You can't believe that story! I mean, it's *too* ridiculous. I know it's in one of the guide books, but——'

' "But me no buts",' said Tyson flapping an impatient hand, 'I too thought I was too old to fall for that one. But there was something mightily convincing about that bit of paper. If no one else believed in the treasure, Grandfather Emory certainly did. And for a very good reason.'

'I suppose he helped to bury it?' commented Lash with sarcasm.

'In a way,' said Tyson. 'And you can take that damned impertinent superior sneer off your face, young Holden!'

He glowered for a moment, refreshed himself from his glass, and then said: 'No. According to old Rory, when Seyyid Saïd died he left the secret with a witch doctor of Pemba, who promptly and rather meanly put a curse on it to the effect that anyone finding it could only use it to bring evil—something of that description. It was intended, one supposes, to discourage people from hunting around for it, but Saïd's successor, Majid, wasn't going to be put off by a thing like that. According to Grandfather Emory, he tortured the witch, collared the information, dug the stuff up with the enthusiastic assistance of my unregenerate ancestor, and generously went halves with him. Emory's share, if I have worked out its present-day value correctly, must have been close on three million sterling.'

There was a brief silence, and then Lash rose to replenish his glass. 'All this,' he said, 'if you will forgive my saying so, is the ripest slice of pure Gorgonzola that I have come across in an ill-spent life. Me, I don't believe a word of it! But it's obvious that someone else does. And I don't mean you or your grandfather, either!'

Lorraine's eyes were enormous and she spoke in little gasps: 'But Tyson! . . . but darling . . . three *million!* He can't have . . . What did he *do* with it?'

'Buried it,' said Tyson blandly. 'Or so he says.'

'But *where?*'

'Ah! that's the catch. He doesn't say. All he says is that he has deposited the key in a sealed envelope with old Honeywood (that would probably be our Honeywood's grandfather, or else his great-uncle) and that it is only to be handed over if and when someone asks for it, quoting, correctly, a number and some initials that were on the envelope. The number being seven four three eight nine, and the initials being his own, E.T.F.'

'I'll be damned!' ejaculated Lash, startled.

'I don't doubt it: not if this is your usual form,' commented Tyson unkindly. 'Well—there you are. It seemed a damned sight too good to be true, and I didn't believe a word of it. Life isn't *that* much like the movies! But it was worth investigating, and as a first step I wrote old Honeywood, asking if he had such a letter in his possession. He had—which shook me. Deposited with Honeywood & Honeywood in eighteen sixty one. I thought it was well worth looking at, and I didn't want to trust it to the post. *Or* to Gussie! Between you and me, I don't . . . Oh, well, let it go. The point is that as Dany was coming out, it seemed a good idea to ask her to call and collect it and bring it out with her. And that's all there is to it.'

'Except that you gave him a date and a time for that call,' said Lash.

'And why not? The thing was almost certainly in a safe deposit box in some bank, and he'd have to get it out and have it ready to hand over. It wouldn't have been at his house, and as I still correspond with him and not his junior partner, I said I'd send Dany to get it from him; which meant to his house. And if I know anything of old Honeywood, he wouldn't have had it there very much before he needed it. He's a careful guy. Or rather, he was, poor brute.'

'So that was it!' said Lash. 'Then I was right.' He got up and stood looking out of the window, his hands in his pockets. 'Someone knew, and meant to get there first. But Dany spoilt the game by going down in the morning instead of the afternoon.'

He turned abruptly: 'Who else knew?'

'No one,' said Tyson shortly.

'Oh, nuts! Of course someone else knew.'

'I apologize,' snarled Tyson. 'I should have said: "I myself did not tell anyone." Not even my wife.'

'What about Ponting?'

'Or my secretary!'

'But he could have found out.'

'Oh no, he couldn't. I took dam' good care of that! Curiosity is Nigel's besetting sin, and I had no intention of letting him get a look at the Frost papers—or my letters to Honeywood! I keep those papers in a locked box, and the key to it is round my neck. Some of that stuff could touch off quite a few explosions even now, and I'm taking no chances. Besides there's money in 'em.'

'And murder!' amended Lash grimly.

'So it would seem. All the same, I don't believe——'

'Belief is no good,' said Lash impatiently. 'Could you swear on oath that neither your secretary nor any servant or guest in this house, nor your wife, could possibly, under any circumstances, have seen that paper of Emory's?'

Lorraine gave a faint indignant cry: 'Well, *really* Lash! Why *me?* I mean, even if I had (and I didn't, I hadn't an idea) *would* I have been likely to tell anyone?'

'I don't know,' said Lash. 'Would you?'

Lorraine made a helpless fluttering gesture with her little hands and gazed appealingly at her husband.

'Of course she would,' said Tyson brutally. 'That's why I didn't tell her. I never tell any woman a secret unless I want it given the widest possible publicity in the shortest possible time.'

Lorraine gave a small sigh. 'You know, Tyson darling, I can't understand how it is that you write so well when you so often talk in clichés. Schizophrenia, I suppose. Not that you aren't quite right about me, as it happens. Whenever anyone tells me a secret I always think "Now who shall I tell first?" '

Tyson gave a short bark of laughter. 'I know. But to revert to your question, young Lash, the answer is "No". The key of that box has never been out of my possession, and just in case you are going to suggest that Lorrie might have removed it one night while I was asleep, I will add that I am a remarkably light sleeper. And anyway, I don't believe for one moment that anyone in this house was even aware of the existence of that paper.'

'And what about the letters you wrote this guy Honeywood? They must have contained quite a few relevant details. Enough, anyway, to arouse a considerable slice of curiosity as to the contents of that sealed envelope! The number and the initials, and roughly the date when it was deposited with the firm. Who mails your letters?'

'Abdurahman, when he goes into town. And he can't read English.'

'But he could have shown 'em to some of the local boys who could.'

'Why? My purely personal correspondence is pretty voluminous —quite apart from the stuff that Nigel deals with for me, which is vast. Any house-servant or local snooper who was interested in it would have had his work cut out for months, steaming open envelopes in the hope of stumbling across something of interest. So you can wash that one right out.'

But Tyson had forgotten, thought Dany, that there was at least one other person who had not only read his letters, but who possibly knew something—perhaps not much, but enough—of the contents of that time-yellowed envelope.

She said: 'Mr Honeywood knew something, I think. He didn't seem to approve of my taking the letter. He said something about letting sleeping dogs lie, and that no good would come of it. Perhaps he knew what was in it. His grandfather may have told him.'

'Of course! And *he* may have talked!' said Lorraine.

Tyson let out another crack of laughter. 'What, old Henry Honeywood? That desiccated clam? You didn't know him like Gussie and I did!'

'Perhaps not; but I do know that it isn't only women who talk,' retorted Lorraine. 'Any dried-up old-maid bachelor can usually leave them at the post when it comes to gossip. And he had a housekeeper: that stout old lady with the hearing-aid. She was probably eaten up with curiosity. It's an occupational disease with housekeepers. I expect she read all his letters and gossiped over the contents with all her friends at the Women's Institute!'

'Not Mrs Broughty,' said Tyson, looking thoughtful. 'She's another clam. But that char of his, Mrs Porson, is quite a different proposition. She often does odd jobs for Gussie, and she talks her head off. Why, once when Elf was staying down there she told her the most staggering details of a case that——. Oh well, that's neither here nor there. But as she could only have got hold of them by taking an unauthorized interest in old Henry's correspondence, I suppose we shall have to take it that there may have been a leak. In fact there must have been! So I think that our next move is to notify Scotland Yard—and see that the letter goes by hand. I'll write it first thing after luncheon, and take it round myself to the Residency and ask the Resident as a personal favour to send it in the next diplomatic bag—they must have one. Thank God I happen to know the Commissioner of Metropolitan Police. That may help. I'll write direct to him, and if he wants to set the local cops on to us, he can. But as it will be at least three days, and possibly four, before he can get a letter, it'll give us time to see if there's anything in this fantastic Buried Treasure yarn. Where's the key, Dany? Let's have it.'

'But it isn't a key,' said Dany. 'At least, not an ordinary key—a metal one. I would have felt it if it was. I think it's only a folded piece of paper.'

'Probably a map,' said Tyson.

'Or clues, like a crossword!' Lorraine's face flushed as charmingly as an excited child's.

Lash said dampingly: 'Far more likely to be one of those rambling bits of abracadabra that say *Walk fifty paces due south from the back porch of Ali Baba's house, and when you reach the blasted fig tree, wait until the sun be overhead, and dig where the shadow of the fig tree joins the ditch.* A fascinating document that fails to take into account that by this time Ali Baba's house has been pulled down and replaced by a fish-glue factory, the blasted fig passed out of the picture seventy years back and someone's drained the ditch in the course of an irrigation scheme! That's all we need yet!'

But Lorraine refused to be damped. 'But the treasure would still be there—*somewhere!* Oh, Tyson, just think if it should turn out to be true! It's the most thrilling thing. Will there be jewels? There ought to be. Carved emeralds and pigeon's blood rubies and diamond hilted daggers and ropes and ropes of pearls. *Marvellous!'*

'It depends on how Emory and his Sultan pal split the loot,' said Tyson, finishing his drink. 'But being a citizen on whom remarkably few flies appear to have rested, I bet he played safe and took the gold. Anyway, that's what it sounds like—if, of course, he took anything, and this isn't the old reprobate's idea of a belly-laugh at the expense of his posterity. I wouldn't put it past him!'

'Oh *no,* darling!' protested Lorraine. 'I won't believe it. It's got to true. I *want* it to be true. We shall solve the crossword, and creep out at night with spades and dig up buckets and buckets full of gold.'

'And find ourselves in the local lock-up for attempting to steal what is undoubtedly the property of the Sultan of Zanzibar,' said Lash morosely.

'Ah, that's just where you're wrong, boy,' said Tyson, heaving himself up and fetching another drink. 'There was no green in Grandfather Emory's eye. His half was a gift, for services rendered. Duly attested, too. There is a document to prove it. It was inside the opposite cover; and there's a nice clear thumb print attached, as well as the donor's seal and signature. It would probably stand in a court of law even today. However, we haven't got the stuff yet. Where's old Honeywood's letter, Dany?'

'In my coat pocket,' said Dany, and smiled a little wanly. 'It seemed the safest place, and I did fix it so that it couldn't be pick-pocketed!'

She reached for the camel-hair coat that she had carried over to the guest-house with her and hung over the back of her chair, and after struggling with the safety-pin, drew out a soft square of chiffon that was folded about a small yellow envelope with five numerals and three initials written on it in faded ink.

She stood staring at it wide-eyed, feeling it: horror and incredulity dawning in her face. Then she turned it over quickly.

The heavy seal that had closed the flap was broken, and the envelope was empty.

11

'It's preposterous!' bellowed Tyson for the fourth if not the fifth time. 'It's just plain bloody impossible!'

'Oh, darling,' moaned Lorraine, 'don't go on and on and *on* saying that. Besides, it's so *silly!* How can it be impossible when it's *happened?*'

'It can't have happened; that's why! Not the way she said anyway. You can see for yourself the way that bit of stuff was folded and pinned. I tell you it was humanly impossible for anyone—anyone outside of an astral body!—to do the job unless that coat was out of Dany's possession for at least five minutes. Great suffering snakes— I've tried it! You saw me. No one could unpin it from the lining, take it out, get at the envelope and remove the letter, and then put the whole shooting-match back again just exactly as it was, at the bottom of a deep slit pocket. Not even Houdini! She must have left the coat lying about.'

'But I didn't,' protested Dany, on the verge of tears. 'I had it under my pillow for the rest of the night, and it was perfectly all right when I wrapped it in the scarf this morning. The seal wasn't touched. I tell you, I *know!* I would have felt at once if it was empty. Like I did just now.'

Tyson said: 'You must have washed, I suppose? Or had a bath!'

'Of course I did, but——'

'And you took it with you?'

'No, but——'

'Well, there you are! Someone must have got into the room.'

Lorraine said plaintively: 'Tyson darling, don't keep on interrupting the child. Do let her finish a sentence.'

'Lash was there,' said Dany. 'He was dressing while I had a bath.'

'It all sounds very intimate and domestic,' growled Tyson.

Lash said pleasantly: 'It was. Though quite unavoidable, as I

312

have already explained. But if you make any further cracks like that you are going to find that life is even more like the movies than you had supposed.'

'Meaning that you'll knock me down?' inquired Tyson. 'You couldn't do it, boy.'

'It would give me the greatest pleasure to try,' snapped Lash.

'I daresay it would. But I do not intend to let the sons of my college friends use me as a punching-bag to work off their spleen.'

'Then stop bullying the kid!' said Lash. 'Can't you see that she's had just about all she can take? Lay off her, will you?'

Tyson cocked an eye at him, and said meditatively: 'I well remember your Aunt Maimie describing you once—accurately I have no doubt—as a rakish heel who could hook the average woman with the ease of a confidence trickster getting to work on a frustrated small-town spinster. That was when you were getting into trouble over the Van Hoyden girl—or was it girls? So let us have less of the Galahad attitude from you, boy, and fewer back-answers! Were you really in that suite the entire time that Dany was in the bathroom?'

'I was.'

'Did you know where the letter was?'

'I did. Are you by any chance suggesting that I took it?'

'*Bah!* Don't be tedious,' said Tyson crossly. 'Can you be quite certain that no one else came into the room during that time? No hotel servant, for instance?'

'No one. Repeat—no one.'

Tyson turned back to Dany. 'I presume he didn't stick around while you were dressing?'

Dany flushed pinkly. "No, he didn't. He went off to have breakfast.'

'And no one else came in?'

'No. I locked both doors. And I took the coat with me when I went in to breakfast, and I've never let go of it since, until I came in here and put it on that chair. No one could have taken that letter. No one but myself or Lash. It isn't possible!'

"Did you take it?'

Lash took a swift step forward and Tyson said: 'Let her answer for herself, boy! Well, Dany?'

Dany looked at him; her cheeks flushed and her eyes wide and sparkling. 'I think,' she said stormily, 'that you are the most odious, selfish, egotistical, *impossible* man I have ever met, and I'm sorry I ever came here!'

'Yes, isn't he?' said Lorraine, giving her husband a fond glance. 'I remember saying just the same thing to him the first day I ever met him. And he gets worse. But baby, you didn't really take it, did you?'

Dany rounded on her, anger giving away to exasperation. 'Mother, you cannot really think——'

'*Darling,*' protested Lorraine plaintively, '*how* many times have I asked you not to call me that? It makes me feel a *hundred.* No, of course I don't think you stole it or anything like that—nor does Tyson. Just that you may have thought that—what with the murder, and everything being so foul for you—that it would be better if you simply tore the horrid thing up and got rid of it.'

'Well I didn't!' said Dany tersely. 'And perhaps it's a pity I didn't think of it—now that someone else has got it.'

'Meaning me?' inquired Lash gently.

'Why do you have to say that?' demanded Dany resentfully. 'You know quite well I don't mean anything of the sort!'

'But you've just said that only you or I could possibly have taken it. And if *you* didn't, that leaves me, doesn't it? Or is there something wrong with my arithmetic?'

'Don't bully the girl!' boomed Tyson. 'Can't you see she's had all she can take? Lay off her, will you?'

Lash laughed and threw up a hand in the gesture of a fencer acknowledging a hit. '*Touché!* I'm sorry, Dany. Well, what do you suggest we do now?'

'Eat,' said Lorraine firmly, and rose to her feet. 'It must be nearly one o'clock, and everyone else will be wondering what on earth has happened to us, and getting hungrier and hungrier. Come on, darling, let's go and see what they're doing. And Dany will want to wash.'

'Just a minute,' said Tyson. 'Let's get this straight. If we are to subscribe to this theory that whoever was after that letter was also on the London to Nairobi plane, it follows that whoever has got it now was on the Nairobi to Zanzibar one this morning. Am I right?'

Lash said: 'It certainly looks that way, doesn't it? If it weren't for one outstanding snag, on which the whole thing snarls up.'

'And what would that be?'

'What the hell is the use of three million—or three hundred million if it comes to that—if you can't get it out of the island? O.K. for you perhaps, or for anyone who lives right here. But how would anyone else start in shifting it? Me, for the sake of argument?'

'I, boy. *I!* Don't be so sloppy with your grammar!'

'Okay; I. Me, Lashmer J. Holden, Jnr. What do I do with a coupla hundredweight of bullion? Load it into my bags and smuggle it through the Customs just like that, I suppose?'

'Then you suppose wrong,' snapped Tyson. 'Use your head! Do you *really* imagine that anyone who is after that much money, and prepared to kill in order to get it, hasn't worked that one out? Good God, boy, there are literally dozens of ways of getting in and out of countries illegally in these days, if you've money behind you—or the prospect of money. And don't start yapping that "It isn't possible!" Of course it is! A bloody sight too possible! What do you suppose there is to prevent you going for a sail or out fishing one fine evening, and being picked up a mile or so offshore by a dhow or a motor-boat? Or a private yacht?—damn it all, your own father's got one of those! There are hundreds of miles of empty coast-line and little creeks or beaches where you could be landed on a dark night, and be picked up by a plane. Good grief, this is the Air Age! There are any amount of privately owned planes around—and any amount of empty Africa for 'em to land on! You wouldn't be your father's son if you couldn't work out that one, and we can take it someone else has. The problem is, who?'

Lash shrugged his shoulders: 'Someone who was on both plane rides, I guess. I checked up on that, and apart from your personal guests there were only two. That newspaper guy you were so charming to outside the airport——'

'What newspaper guy?' interrupted Tyson, sitting up sharply. 'I don't remember any——Yes, by God, I do! Some blasted squirt in a panama hat who asked if he could call. Was he on the London plane?'

'I just told you so. And staying at the same hotel in Nairobi.'

'He was, was he?' said Tyson meditating. 'Perhaps I shouldn't have been so hasty. Well we can fix that. As there's only one hotel in this salubrious spot, we know where he is. Lorrie darling, ring up the hotel will you, and ask for——What's his blasted name?'

'Dowling,' supplied Dany. 'Larry Dowling.'

'Mr Dowling; and when you get him on the line, tell him I'll be delighted to give him an interview, and would he like to come and stay here. Run along and do it now.'

'But Tyson——!' Lorraine's gentian-blue eyes were wide with dismay. 'We can't. Darling—a reporter!'

'He isn't a reporter,' said Dany, but was ignored.

'Everything will be all over the front page of every newspaper before we know where we are,' wailed Lorraine. 'Think of Dany—and all of us. Just *think!*'

'I am,' said Tyson impatiently. 'And I appear to be the only one who is capable of doing so. It's a dam' sight safer to have all the suspects under one roof.'

'With an eye, of course,' said Lash, 'to the cash deposit.'

'If that was meant for sarcasm, boy, you'll have to do better. Naturally with an eye to the cash deposit. What do you take me for?'

Lorraine's hands made their familiar fluttering gesture, and she said: 'I don't understand. I don't understand anything.'

'He means,' translated Lash, 'that one of a reasonably narrow field of suspects has just got hold of the key to grandpop's bank vault. It is therefore quite an idea to keep 'em all right here, where he can watch 'em, and the first guy who is caught borrowing a spade and sneaking out to do a bit of digging is it. See?'

'But of *course!*' exclaimed Lorraine happily. 'Tyson darling, how clever of you. I'll ring up this Mr—Mr Dowling at once.'

'You do that,' said Tyson. 'Get going. No—wait a minute. There were two of them. Didn't you say there were two?'

'Were,' said Lash, 'is right. There's only one now.'

'I don't get you.'

'The other one,' said Lash, 'was an Arab. A shining light in the local Zanzibar-for-Mother-Russia movement, I gather. One Salim Abeid.'

'Oh, Jembe—"*the thin man*".'

'That's the guy. Or to be accurate, that was the guy.'

'What do you mean by that?' demanded Tyson sharply.

'I mean he's dead. He died rather suddenly this morning at Mombasa Airport, which is why our plane was held up. I thought maybe they'd have told you that one: you must have had to wait quite a while for us.'

'*Dead?*' said Tyson, his bull voice almost a whisper. 'You don't mean . . . What did he die of?'

'They didn't say. He walked off the plane and into the airport with the rest of us, apparently a sound insurance risk, and when we were herded back on, he failed to turn up. There was a certain amount of delay and flurry, and first the stewardess told us he'd been taken ill, and then a squad of cops and officials turned up and took another look at our passports and re-checked our visas—and for all I know got our fingerprints as well. They seemed anxious to know where they could get in touch with us during the next few days.'

'What do you suppose they'd want to do that for?'

'Your guess,' said Lash dryly, 'is as good as mine.'

Lorraine looked anxiously from Lash's face to her husband's, and came back from the door to clutch at Tyson's arm. There was a sudden trace of panic in her light, lilting voice: 'What guess, Tyson? What does he mean? What are you both hinting at?'

'Nothing,' said Tyson brusquely. 'Only that Jembe had a lot of political enemies. There's no need for us to start visualizing burglars under every blasted bed in the island. And anyway he probably died of heart failure.'

'Almost certainly,' said Lash pleasantly. 'Few of us die from anything else.'

'Be quiet, boy!' blared Tyson. 'The young should be seen and not heard! It's all right, Lorrie. You run along now and phone that infernal reporter. And be nice to him.'

Lorraine sighed and relaxed. 'I'm always nice to people, darling.'

She turned from him and directed an appealing smile at Lash. 'I do hope you don't mind being in the guest-house by yourself, Lash?'

'Why should I mind? It's charming.'

'Now that *is* sweet of you! I was afraid you might feel sore about it. Being put up in a sort of honeymoon cottage when——'

'Oh, not again!' groaned Lash. 'Once was enough. I get you— you mean this was the cosy little hideaway that you'd gotten all fixed up for the newly-weds, was it? Well, it was a swell idea and I shall not feel any qualms about occupying it—provided I'm allowed to do so strictly solo. You don't have to worry about it. It wasn't your fault.'

'But it *was*. That's what's so *awful*,' Lorraine's voice was tragic. 'I feel that it's so much my fault: Elf wrote to me, you know. You see it was I who asked Eddie—Eduardo—to look her up when he was in London, because he'd suggested that he might come down here again, so I thought it would be nice for them to know each other, and of course I never dreamed——But I don't expect it will come to anything: so much that Elf starts doesn't, you know. She's so vague and soft-hearted and irresponsible, and she never means any harm. She's like a sweet, spoilt child who just picks things up and then drops them.'

Lorraine illustrated with a graceful, expressive gesture, and Lash winced. 'I get you.'

'Oh, but I didn't mean *you*, Lash!' Lorraine's eyes were wide with dismay. 'I meant Eddie. He's only a new toy. And rather a novel one. But when that's over, everything will be all right again, won't it?'

'Sure. Just dandy,' said Lash bitterly. 'And now if you don't mind, could we just cut the whole question of my love-life off the agenda? I prefer murder.'

'Yes of course, dear,' said Lorraine hastily. 'I *do* feel for you. And I'm sure it will all come out right in the end. Come on, Dany darling, let's go and get tidy. And you *will* get rid of that awful fringe, won't you sweetie?'

'No she won't!' declared Tyson unexpectedly. 'Here, Dany——' he picked up the discarded spectacles and replaced them firmly on her nose. 'I'm sorry if it worries your mother and fails to please the United States Marines, but it seems to me that you'd better stick to that fancy dress and go on being Miss Kitchell for the next few days. It'll save a lot of explaining. And the less explaining we have to do once that scribbling journalist is on the premises, the better.'

'Are you really going to ask him over?' inquired Lash.

'Certainly,' said Tyson, bristling. 'Any objections?'

'None at all. It's your funeral. But it seems to me that your sense of proportion has slipped a disc. If you import this Dowling guy you can watch to see that he doesn't start in digging up grandpop's dollars, but if he starts digging any of this dirt instead, how are you going to stop him splashing it all over the tabloids?'

'Murder him!' said Tyson succinctly. 'Now let's get on up to the house and have some food.'

12

The House of Shade stood three storeys high on a wide stone terrace that was approached from the garden by short flights of steps set at regular intervals about it. Each of its storeys was of a different height, for the ground floor had once been a colonnade surrounding an open central courtyard about which the house was built, and the rooms on the first floor had been large and long, and were abnormally high. It had been Tyson's father—who had a mania for improvements—who had divided them into bedrooms, bathrooms and dressing-rooms.

The top storey, by comparison, appeared unduly low, and the rooms were hotter than those on the floor below, for the sun beat down strongly on the flat Eastern roof and the shade of the trees did not reach them. But the breeze did, and by night they were cool.

There was a lily pool in the courtyard, where lethargic goldfish idled in the shade of the flat green leaves, and on each floor the rooms led out on to pillared verandahs that faced each other across it, in a manner vaguely reminiscent of a courtyard in Seville.

Curious, curving stone staircases with shallow, disproportionally wide treads, their heavy banisters of hammered iron wrought in an odd geometrical design and barely a foot and a half in height, rose from each corner of the courtyard, inside the verandahs and leading up on to the next. Dangerous looking things, depending for their support only on the stout metal and the proportion of stone that had been built into the thickness of the wall, and proof that some long-dead Arab builder had known his trade as well as Adams or John Nash.

At the edge of each verandah, stone jars filled with sweet-scented creepers and flowering shrubs stood between the tall supporting pillars, and gave an entrancing impression of hanging gardens. But from the outside the house looked far less decorative and unusual: a square, white, very high building with a flat crenelated roof and rows of green-painted shutters.

It was sometime during the afternoon, and shortly before Tyson left to take a letter in to the Residency, that Mr Cardew, the Police Superintendent of the Zanzibar Division, called briefly at the House of Shade.

His car came and went again, making so little sound on the white coral dust of the palm-shaded road that no member of the house-party heard it, and apart from Tyson, only a Somali servant, a somnolent gardener's boy, and a drowsing cat on the wall above the main gate, had seen him.

He had stayed less than a quarter of an hour, and it was not until much later in the day, when night had fallen and the house-party were seated at the dining-room table in a glow of candlelight, that Tyson had chosen to bring up the subject of his visit.

The dining-room at *Kivulimi* was a long narrow room, with a row of arches along one side that had once been open, but which Tyson's father, Aubrey, had converted into french windows. They stood wide tonight, letting in a heady scent of flowers and luring moths and other nocturnal insects to a fiery death in the candle flames, and from her seat between Nigel and Larry Dowling, Dany could see out into the garden where the tree shadows and the moonlight formed a complicated mosaic patched with gold from the lighted windows.

She had plenty of leisure to enjoy the sight, for Lorraine, in the interests of playing safe, was keeping Larry Dowling engaged in conversation, while Nigel was hotly defending a modern master-piece, recently purchased for the nation, in the face of Gussie Bingham's assertion that it was a shocking waste of the taxpayers' money (by which she meant her own) and indistinguishable from a pool of spilt ink and a squashed tomato—which would have come cheaper.

Larry Dowling had arrived in a taxi shortly after luncheon, and much to her surprise Dany had found herself not only pleased, but more than a little relieved to see him. Which was foolish of her, she knew, since Larry's profession made him a danger to all of them. But for some indefinable reason she felt a greater sense of safety and a lessening of tension while he was within reach. Larry, she thought, would not let one down.

Lash Holden had greeted Mr Dowling with a marked lack of enthusiasm, and having commandeered his taxi had returned in it to the airport to inquire into the possibility of reserving a seat for himself in a Nairobi-bound plane on the following day. He had not been back by four-thirty, when Lorraine's guests had assembled for tea on the shaded terrace outside the drawing-room windows, but he had joined them later when they had gone down to explore the sea shore and exclaim over the weird, windworn shapes of the coral rocks, and watch the sun go down in a blaze of rose-tinted splendour.

He had not spoken to Dany, and had in fact appeared to avoid her, and she looked at him now across the width of the wide table in the glow of the candles, and wondered if she would ever see him again. I suppose I could always get a job in America, she thought. Tyson or Lorraine could fix that; they've got loads of friends there, and Lash's father is Tyson's best friend. I'd be able to see him. But if Mrs Gordon decides that she likes him better than Eduardo after all . . .

Dany turned to look at Amalfi, who was being charming to Tyson and prettily petulant to Eduardo, and her heart sank. She knew that she herself had little to complain of in the way of looks, for she had inherited them from her father who had been an outstandingly handsome man. But Ada Kitchell's unfortunate hair-style did not suit her, and neither did Ada Kitchell's spectacles. They combined to reduce her from a pretty girl to a nondescript one, and even the dress she had chosen to wear did not help, though once she had thought it entrancing—a short, smoke-grey dress whose wide skirt, ornamented with two enormous patch pockets appliquéd with white magnolias, reduced her slim waist to hand-span proportions. She had been charmed with it when she bought it; but now it only appeared rather ordinary, and what Aunt Harriet would have termed 'suitable for a young girl'.

Amalfi, looking anything but ordinary, was wearing pale gold chiffon that exactly matched her pale gold hair, and her jewels were an antique set of topazes set in gold filigree. It was a colour that did charming and complimentary things to her sea-green, mermaid's eyes, and she was using them now with dazzling effect on Tyson.

I don't know how Mother stands it! thought Dany resentfully: and turning to look at Lorraine was instantly answered.

Lorraine, wearing a fragile confection of black spider-lace, with diamonds that were a magnificent reminder of the brief reign of Dwight P. Cleethorpe, was, in her own and entirely different way, as entrancing as Amalfi, and she was engaged in employing all her charms on Larry Dowling; who was looking equally dazzled.

They can't help it, thought Dany, feeling depressed and deplorably gauche. They were born with charm. They just turn it on like a tap, and half the time it doesn't mean a thing. They can't help having it, or using it, any more than Millicent Bates can help being— Millicent Bates!

Millicent was sitting opposite her between Lash and Eduardo di Chiago, and 'Dressing for Dinner' meant only one thing to Miss Bates. A long dress, and she was wearing one. An undatable garment in solid blue marocain that made no concessions to frivolity and did nothing for her flat-chested, square-shouldered figure. She was engaged in giving Lash, as an unenlightened Colonial, a lecture on the advantages of a National Health system, when she was interrupted by Tyson who at last elected to broach the subject of the Superintendent of the Zanzibar Division's afternoon call. His voice boomed down the length of the table and successfully terminated an anecdote concerning scheming foreigners in search of free false teeth.

'By the way, Lash, about that plane reservation you wanted for tomorrow, I'm afraid you'll——'

Amalfi turned sharply: 'What plane reservation? Lash, you aren't leaving? Not when you've only just arrived! Darling, don't be silly!'

Nigel gave his little giggling laugh. 'It's all this American passion for hustle. Here today and gone tomorrow! So enervating.'

'Darling, I'm not all *that* dangerous,' cooed Amalfi dulcetly. 'Are you frightened?'

'Terrified!' said Lash promptly. 'But apart from that, as I find that the business side of this trip can be dealt with in half an hour— provided our host will sit still that long—I don't feel justified in wasting too much time idling; however pleasantly. I have a lot of commitments.'

Mrs Bingham said: 'Poor Miss Kitchell! And I feel sure that you were so looking forward to seeing something of Zanzibar. What a slave-driver your Mr Holden is!'

She beamed sympathetically at Dany, and Lash looked startled. It was a point that had somehow escaped him. If Dany had to continue masquerading as his secretary he could hardly leave without her. Or with her.

Blast! thought Mr Holden with quiet and concentrated bitterness. And was visited by inspiration. He half rose and bowed at Mrs Bingham. 'Ma'am, you put me to shame. You're dead right. I'm a slave-driver, and Miss Kitchell certainly needs a rest. But she's going to get one. I don't happen to need her for the next week or so, and she's going to stay right here, grab herself a nice long vacation, and join me later when I'm due back in the States.'

And now, thought Lash with some satisfaction, just try and gum up that one!

Tyson did so.

'It looks,' he said blandly, 'as though you will be spending it right here with her, my boy.'

'Oh no, I shan't,' began Lash firmly. 'I intend——'

Tyson said crossly: 'If you will all have the goodness to lay off interrupting me every time I open my mouth, perhaps I can get on with what I was saying? . . . Thanks! About that plane reservation. I'm afraid you'll have to cancel it, boy. In fact, I have already done so on your behalf. The police have requested that you all remain *in situ* for a day or two.'

'The *police?*' Amalfi dropped the glass she was holding, and it fell with a little splintering crash, sending a red stream of claret across the table. 'What police? Why?'

'Josh Cardew. He was over this afternoon. He says it's just a routine matter, but that they've been asked to check up on everyone who was on the Nairobi-Zanzibar plane this morning, and more particularly, on the London-Nairobi one. So it would help if you'd all stay around for a bit. It's that chap Jembe.'

'Salim Abeid?' inquired Larry Dowling. 'You mean the man who died in the airport at Mombasa this morning?'

'I mean the man who was murdered in the airport at Mombasa this morning,' corrected Tyson. 'It would appear that someone added a good-sized slug of cyanide to his coffee, and they somehow don't think he did it himself.'

Gussie gave her glass of wine a horrified look and put it down hurriedly. 'But how dreadful, Tyson! I remember him quite well. He was on the London plane too. But why on earth should the police want to question any of us? Too ridiculous, when it must have been someone in the airport. The barman who gave him the coffee, I expect.'

'They're checking up on all that. Needle-in-a-haystack job, I'd say. I gather the airport was pretty crowded.'

'Packed,' said Gussie Bingham, and shuddered. 'Besides being abominably hot, in spite of all those fans and things.'

Larry Dowling said reflectively: 'It can't have been all that easy to drop something in a man's drink without being spotted; even in a crowded room. Bit of a risk. It must have been someone he knew.'

'I don't see why,' said Nigel, mopping up claret with a clean handkerchief. 'Anyone—simply *anyone*—could have jogged his elbow or distracted his attention as they went past. *Too* simple. You knock the man's newspaper on to the floor, or stumble over his briefcase, and while he's picking them up and you're apologizing— *plop!*'

He dropped an imaginary pellet into an imaginary glass, and Eduardo di Chiago said: *'Brr—!* this is a most unpleasant conversation. For myself, I do not like to talk of death. It is unlucky.'

'Oh, I do so agree with you,' said Lorraine earnestly. *'Dreadfully* unlucky. And now I suppose there's *bound* to be a third.'

'A third what?' demanded Gussie Bingham, startled.

'Murder of course, darling. Things always go in threes. Haven't you noticed that?'

'But there's only been one murder so far,' objected Millicent Bates.

'My dear—but haven't you *heard?* Why, I thought we only hadn't because we don't get the English papers for days, but I thought you two must have seen all about it.'

Tyson cast his eyes up to heaven, and thereafter, realizing it was too late to intervene, shrugged his shoulders and circulated the port.

'Seen all about what?' demanded Millicent sharply.

'Why, about Mr Honeywood. Tyson's solicitor. He's been murdered.'

'Honeywood—old Henry Honeywood?' The thin stem of Gussie Bingham's wine-glass snapped between her fingers, and once more there was a dark pool of wine winking in the candlelight. But she did not appear to have noticed it. She leant forward to stare down the table at Lorraine, and her voice was suddenly strident: 'Where did you get that story?'

But Lorraine was not paying attention. She reached out, and picking up an empty tumbler, lifted it and dropped it deliberately on to the floor, where it shivered into fragments.

'That's the third one,' she said reassuringly. 'And it was an odd one anyway, so it means we needn't bother losing any more of the set. I do apologize, Gussie darling—what were you saying?'

Gussie turned towards her brother with a rustle of lilac satin and a clash of bracelets.

'Tyson, what is this preposterous nonsense that Lorraine has got hold of?'

'It isn't nonsense,' said Tyson, helping himself liberally to port. 'Only heard it myself today. The poor old boy's been murdered. Shot in his study on the morning of the day you left for London. I daresay you missed seeing it in the papers because of the move—last minute shopping and all that sort of flap. And it wouldn't have been front page stuff.'

'No, I didn't see it. And I still can't believe——What would anyone want to murder old Henry for?'

Tyson shrugged. 'Ask me another. Theft, I suppose. The safe was opened. I don't really know any details.'

'And where,' demanded Millicent, 'did you get all this from? If you've got the home papers, I'd like to see them.'

Tyson looked disconcerted, and Lash thought with a trace of malice: That'll teach him to watch his step!

'They'll be around somewhere,' said Tyson, rallying. 'But as a matter of fact, I had a letter by the afternoon post. Have some port, Gussie.'

'Who from?' inquired Millicent Bates.

'Oh—a man you wouldn't know,' said Tyson hastily.

'What did he say? When did it happen? How . . .'

Tyson rolled a wild eye in the direction of Lash, who refused to meet it, and found himself enduring a lengthy catechism which he replied to as well as he could.

'Why are you so interested anyway?' he inquired irritably. 'He wasn't *your* family solicitor.'

'He happened to be both honorary treasurer of our Wednesday Women's Guild and treasurer to the Market-Lydon Lads of Britain League, and as such was a personal friend of mine,' snapped Millicent. 'What time did you say it happened?'

'For Pete's sake, how am I expected to know? It'll be in the papers.'

'Eleven forty-eight, precisely,' put in Larry Dowling gently. 'They know the time because the murderer evidently pressed the muzzle of the gun against the victim's body—it would have helped to muffle the shot—and the shock of the explosion damaged a repeater watch the old gentleman carried in his breast pocket, and stopped it.'

'Good God,' said Tyson heavily. 'The Press! I'd forgotten we had a newshound in our midst.' He glared at Larry Dowling as though he

325

had found a slug in his salad. 'Did you by any chance cover this case, Mr Dowling? You appear to know a hell of a lot about it.'

'No. Not in my line. But I read the papers. It was in most of them on the 13th. I must have seen five accounts of it at least.'

'Umm,' grunted Tyson, and returned to the port.

'Eleven forty-eight,' said Millicent Bates, and repeated it slowly. 'Eleven . . . forty . . . eight.'

'And what exactly does that mean?' inquired Nigel of the table at large. 'It sounds *just* like the Girl with the Golden Voice "*On the third stroke it will be eleven forty-eight and twelve seconds precisely*".'

Millicent Bates scowled at him across the table. 'If you really want to know,' she said tartly, 'I happened to pay a rush visit to a friend of mine on the morning of the 12th. I'd forgotten to give her the key of the Wolf Cubs' hut, and we were leaving that afternoon. She lives at the end of Mr Honeywood's road—it's a *cul de sac*—and I was wondering if I might not actually have passed the murderer. He must have come down that road.'

Nigel smiled with maddening tolerance. 'Do you know, I *hardly* think so, dear Miss Bates.'

'And why not?' demanded Millicent Bates, bristling.

'But surely it stands to reason that a murderer would not go *prancing* along a public highway and in at the front door by daylight? He'd be far more likely to *creep* in by a shrubbery or something.'

'Which just goes to show,' said Miss Bates, 'how little you know what you're talking about. You could possibly creep *out* of Mr Honeywood's house through a shrubbery, because you could use the kitchen-garden door. But it has a slip lock and you can't open it from the outside. And as there is a high wall around the house, the only way in, for anyone who didn't want to do some jolly conspicuous climbing, is through the front gate. And I *do* know what I'm talking about, because I happen to know the house well.'

'So well,' said Nigel gaily, 'that you will soon have us shivering in our little shoes, wondering if you couldn't have done it yourself!'

Millicent Bates's weather-beaten countenance flushed an unbecoming shade of puce, and Gussie rushed angrily to her defence.

'You appear to look upon murder as a joke, Mr Ponting. But the death of an old acquaintance is hardly a joking matter to us.'

'Oh dear! Oh-dear-oh-dear-oh-dear!' wailed Nigel. 'What can I say? I *do* apologize. *Dear* Miss Bates, you must know that I didn't mean it! My wretched, *distorted* sense of humour. *Do* say that you forgive me?'

Millicent made a flapping gesture with one large and capable hand, in the manner of one waving away an irritating insect, and said gruffly: 'Don't talk rot! My fault for harpin' on it. But I couldn't help being interested—realizing that I might well have passed the man.'

'Or woman,' put in Larry Dowling softly.

Millicent Bates turned swiftly to face him. 'Why do you say that?' she demanded sharply.

'No reason. Just that it may have been a woman. Nothing to show it wasn't—if the papers were anything to go by. You didn't read them, or you'd have seen that he had a female visitor that day. She even took the precaution of leaving a handkerchief behind her—complete with monogram.'

'Oh,' said Miss Bates doubtfully. 'I didn't think of that. Yes, I suppose . . . it could be.'

'Some winsome ornament of the Wednesday Women's Guild, stealing through the mist on the track of the funds!' tittered Nigel. 'Oh dear—there I go again! My *wretched* sense of humour. I won't say another *word!*'

Millicent made no retort, beyond staring at him long and malevolently. But there was suddenly something in her face—in her frown and her narrowed eyes, that suggested that his words had reminded her of something. Or suggested something. Something quite impossible, and yet . . .

No one spoke, and for the space of a full minute there was a curious, strained silence in the room; and then Millicent nodded at Mr Ponting. The brief, brisk nod of someone who has been presented with a fresh viewpoint and accepted it.

On the opposite side of the table Larry Dowling leant forward with a small, swift movement that somehow had the effect of a pounce, and said sharply: 'So you *do* think it might have been a woman—a woman he knew!'

But if he had expected to startle Miss Bates into any admission he was disappointed. Millicent turned to look at him, and having successfully conveyed the impression of not liking what she saw, inquired blandly: 'What did you say, Mr Dowling?'

Larry Dowling flushed and sat back. 'Er—nothing.'

'For which relief, much thanks!' boomed Tyson. 'I am getting bored with this murder. Let us talk about something else.'

'Yes, *do* let's,' said Nigel. 'Murders are *not* precisely one's idea of sparkling dinner-table chit-chat. So gruesomely proletarian. I can never *think* why anyone should want to hear about them.'

Amalfi laughed her lovely throaty laugh, and said: 'Don't be so affected, Nigel darling. Everyone *adores* a good murder. Look at the way they always get into all the headlines and fill the Sunday papers. And what about the way you've been going on about this one? No one else has had a chance to get a word in edgeways!'

She turned to her host and said: 'Tyson, you ought to be entertaining us. If you don't like murders, talk about something else. Anything. Tell us about this house.'

'What about it?' inquired Tyson. 'It was allegedly built about a century and a half ago by a harassed husband whose second wife couldn't get along with the first. But if you want to swot up on it, my late Uncle Barclay wrote an exceptionally tedious book about it which he published at his own expense in the late 1890s and inflicted on his friends. You probably saw one at Gussie's—she has it bound in red morocco and displayed on the piano, to atone for the fact that she's never read it. You'll find several copies lying around here. All the historical and architectural dope down to the last deadly detail. I do not advise it for light reading. But don't let that stop you if you're really interested.'

'I'm not,' said Amalfi. 'Not to that extent, anyway. You are all being very dull tonight, and I want to be flattered and entertained.'

She turned and smiled meltingly at Eduardo, who accepted the invitation with alacrity, and not long afterwards they had all left the dining-room and gone out to drink Turkish coffee on the terrace in front of the drawing-room windows, where Gussie had again demanded the home papers.

Tyson had departed in search of them, and had returned saying that he could not find them, but a few minutes later Nigel had drifted languidly across the terrace with a wrapped package in his hand which he had handed to his employer with an eloquent lift of the eyebrows that had not been lost on at least one member of the party.

The London newspapers had arrived on the same aircraft that had brought the Frosts' guests from Nairobi that morning, and had not been delivered at *Kivulimi* until the late afternoon. The wrapping was still unbroken. 'I thought you said you'd read them?' said Gussie Bingham accusingly.

Tyson affected not to hear her, and removed himself hurriedly to the far side of the terrace where Amalfi Gordon, temporarily deserted, was leaning on the stone balustrade and looking out between the trees to where the moon had laid a shimmering golden carpet across the quiet sea.

'Pleasant, isn't it?' said Tyson, coming to anchor beside her. 'And peaceful. There can't be many places like it left in the world. Or there won't be soon. Progress can be a loutish thing.'

'Don't be pompous and gloomy, darling,' chided Amalfi. 'There are thousands of places just as lovely as this. And as peaceful.'

'That's where you're wrong,' said Tyson, leaning his elbows on the warm stone. 'I've seen a lot of the world. A hell of a lot of it! But there's something special about this island. Something that I haven't met anywhere else. Do you know what is the most familiar sound in Zanzibar?—laughter! Walk through the streets of the little city almost any time of the day or night, and you'll hear it. People laughing. There is a gaiety and good humour about them that is strangely warming to even such a corrugated, corroded and eroded heart as mine, and this is the only place I have yet hit upon where black and white and every shade in between 'em appear to be able to live together in complete friendliness and harmony, with no colour bar. It's a living proof and a practical demonstration that it can be done. They are all, whatever their race or caste or religion, loyal subjects of His Highness the Sultan—may he live for ever!—and they get on together. But it won't last. In the end one of the Jembe kind will manage to destroy it. Yes—there are times when I am prepared to agree with the bigoted old bore, my late Uncle Barclay, that Progress is a lout!'

Amalfi had been picking jasmine buds and smelling them absently, wearing the abstracted smile of one who is not in the least interested in the conversation, but the name 'Jembe' caught her attention, and she dropped the flowers and turned quickly:

'Tyson darling, that reminds me. I'm sorry to go on about this sort of thing, but did you *really* mean that we can none of us leave this house until the police find out who gave that tedious little Arab agitator a dose of poison in Mombasa?'

'God forbid!' said Tyson piously. 'If that were so I might find myself permanently stuck with the lot of you, and I'm not sure that my constitution could stand it. Or yours! No, it's only a question of a day or two, while they make a few inquiries. They might want to ask if any of you by any chance remember seeing someone speaking to him at the airport. Or standing near him. Something like that. Why? Were you thinking of cutting short your visit? I thought you were supposed to be staying with us for at least three weeks.'

Amalfi smiled at him, and reaching up to pull his greying blond beard said: 'But you know quite well that I never do what I'm supposed to do, and I never know how long I shall stay anywhere. If I'm enjoying myself madly, I stay, and if I'm not, I move on. It's as simple as that!'

'It must become expensive,' said Tyson.

'Oh, frantically. But I don't *always* have to pay for it myself.'

Tyson bellowed with sudden laughter. 'That's what I like about you, Elf. No deception, is there?'

'*Masses,* darling. You've no idea how much! But not in that way. After all, money *is* rather madly important. Don't you agree?'

'I work for mine,' said Tyson dryly.

'Oh, but so do I. One has to sing for one's supper, you know; and I sing—charmingly!'

'I'll grant you that,' said Tyson with a grin. 'But hasn't it been a bit trying at times? Johnnie Leigh, for instance.'

Amalfi's mermaid eyes clouded. 'Oh but darling—I never can think of money when I marry them. It's always *love.* And it's only later that one——Oh . . . wakes up to reality.'

'And in the wrong bedroom, with a private inquiry agent hired by your husband taking notes through the transom,' said Tyson cynically. 'Still, you've been lucky in one way. The co-respondent was always noticeably solvent and well able—and more than willing!—to keep you in the mink.'

'Darling!' said Amalfi reproachfully. 'You make it sound as though I were a gold-digger. But I'm not. I'd have married Johnnie even if he hadn't a *sou!'*

'And Robin Gratton? And Chubby?'

'But of *course!* I'm like that. I suddenly feel I *must* have something—that it's the only thing in the world worth having and that once I've got it I shall be happy ever after. And then I'm not. But I adored Chubby. My heart broke when he was killed. It did, really Tyson!'

'Nonsense! You were hardly on speaking terms that last year. And you haven't got a heart, darling. Only a soft mass of emotions. Though I'm not so sure about your head!'

'I'm afraid that's just as soft,' sighed Amalfi regretfully.

'I wonder? Still, you seem to have had your fair share of romance during the last year or two, despite that alleged broken heart. Why don't you bite on the bullet and marry one of them?'

Amalfi laughed. 'What, again? It doesn't seem to take with me, does it?'

'It will one day.'

'Like it has for Lorrie? Perhaps. But how is one to know? I always think I know; and then I find I don't.'

'Try marrying a poor one for a change. You ought to be able to afford it.'

'I don't think I could. One can never really have enough money, can one? All the really heavenly things cost so much. Diamonds and Dior models and holidays in Bermuda.'

'But Chubby must have left you a packet.'

'Not a packet, darling. Unfortunately there turned out to be platoons of dreary aunts and other dim relations that I had never even *heard* of, and it seemed that Chubby was depressingly Clan-minded—worse luck. And then the death duties were *iniquitous*. And anyway, I'm hopeless over money. I always have been. It seems to melt!'

'I'm not surprised; what with diamonds and Dior models and holidays in Bermuda!'

'Yes,' said Amalfi, and sighed deeply. 'That's why it's simpler to fall in love with someone rich. But then I like them to be handsome and charming too, and there's no getting away from it, that kind are limited in number and dreadfully spoilt. They know that they aren't a drug on the market, and they can be difficult.'

'What you mean is that they bite back and won't let themselves be trampled on by any woman for long. And more power to 'em. You know, Elf, I propose to give you some sage advice. You won't be able to go on looking like a luscious slice of peach for ever, and it's time you settled down with a different type. The kind that'll let you play your favourite game of eating your cake and having it.'

'I don't think I know what you mean, darling.'

'Cut out these playboys with plenty of cash, like young Lash or that slick-smoothie, Eddie. They may be fun, but they'd be hell as husbands for a woman like you. They aren't good at turning the other cheek—or a blind eye! You ought to have learnt that at least by this time. What you need now is a nice kind sugar-daddy of the adoring door-mat type, who will let you get away with murder.'

Amalfi shivered suddenly. *'Ugh!* Darling! What a simile to choose after all that gruesome chatter at dinner!'

'Well, "Make a monkey out of him with impunity", if you like it put that way.'

'Is that what Lorraine did? I wouldn't have said that you were exactly a door-mat type. Or a sugar-daddy!'

'Lorrie,' said Tyson, 'isn't in the least your type. Or only superficially. She's merely incurably romantic. That's her trouble. She'd be perfectly happy married to someone who could offer her a semi-detached and a "daily"—as long as she loved him. You wouldn't be. Now, would you?'

Amalfi gave him a narrowed, slanting look under her long lashes, and there was, all at once, a trace of scorn in her lovely face and a shade of contempt in her voice. 'Darling Tyson. You read us all like a book! So clever.'

'Sarcasm doesn't suit you, Elf. Am I to take it that you are going to take a brief whirl at being a Marchesa? If so, I ought to warn you that Eddie is even more susceptible than you are, and the only reason that he has not totted up a long list of ex-wives, all drawing heavy alimony, is because his grandmother holds the purse strings, and can not only cut off supplies when she chooses, but frequently does. It's a great trial to him; though it doesn't seem to have persuaded him to try work yet. He——What's the matter? Surely you knew that?'

'No,' said Amalfi shortly. 'I thought——' she stopped and bit her lip, and Tyson laughed.

'Well, don't say later that no one ever warned you! If you've really reached the fatal stage of marrying them younger than yourself, you'd better take Lash Holden. American men put up with a lot more rough stuff from their wives than less idealistic races, and when it comes to the parting of the ways they'll break out into a rash of Old World chivalry and allow themselves to be sued as the erring partner, and milked like goats for iniquitous alimony with never a bleat. But with Eduardo you'd be the one who'd do the paying, if anyone did. His family might have accepted Chubby's widow— though considering the circumstances, I doubt it—but they're likely to kick like cows at those two divorces. And as for that unfortunate business of Douglas——Well if you'll take my advice, Elf, you'll scrub Eddie and settle for young Lash. That is, if it's not too late.'

Amalfi drew back and regarded him with sudden hostility. 'I don't think,' she said slowly, 'that I am amused any longer. In fact I'm quite sure that I'm not.'

'Because I've told you the truth about yourself and a couple of gilded playboys?'

'No. Because you begin to bore me, darling. And I cannot endure being bored.'

She smiled sweetly at him, her eyes cold, and turned and walked back across the terrace to join the others. And presently Nigel had gone in to switch on the radio-gramophone and turn back the carpet of the drawing-room, and they had all danced: with the exception of Tyson, who could not be bothered, and Millicent Bates, who could not.

Tyson and Millicent had sat side by side on the stone balustrade of the terrace, watching the dancers through the open doors, and Millicent had said moodily: 'I wish you would tell me where you got that secretary of yours, and why. I don't know how a man of your type can stand all that affectation and giggling.'

'He's good at his job,' said Tyson lazily, 'and don't let that affectation fool you. It's fooled a lot of hard-headed businessmen in the publishing line and film racket into thinking that they can pull a fast one, and they've all wound up with headaches, having paid over far more than their original top figure. He deals with all my contracts, and behind that tittering facade he's as cunning and inquisitive as a barrelful of monkeys, and as shrewd as a weasel.'

'I don't doubt it,' said Millicent grimly. 'A nasty type. We had an assistant cashier like that in Market-Lydon. An absolute rotter. I always said that there'd be an ugly scandal one day, and of course there was. You can't trust 'em a yard!'

Tyson chose to be amused, and letting out a roar of laughter he clapped Millicent on the back with a large and hairy hand.

'Bates, you're perfect! You're a collector's piece. But so is Nigel; and I like collector's pieces. From all pale, pink-blooded, pure-souled people, Good Lord, deliver me!'

'That's *your* pose!' snapped Millicent Bates.

'Maybe,' said Tyson, unruffled. 'We all have one. Smoke screens to fool people with. Gussie's is good-nature.'

Millicent stiffened indignantly: 'Pose my foot! Gussie's the kindest creature alive!'

Tyson laughed again, and drained his glass. 'Bates, my Bonnie Brown Owl, I applaud your loyalty while deploring your dishonesty. You cannot have lived with Gussie all these years without knowing that there is nothing she enjoys more than planting a feline barb where she hopes it will hurt most, and then, covered with pretty confusion, pretending that it was just an unfortunate slip of the tongue. It's her favourite parlour sport. You must have found out long ago that Gussie only loves herself. And to forestall you saying "So do you!" I will hasten to say it myself—"And so do I." That may be selfish, but by golly it's sense! Let's face it, Bates. We're not a really pleasant lot, we Frosts. The only one of us who doesn't appear to have had any vices was old Uncle Barclay, and he was a crank! Let's drink confusion to his ghost.'

He got up and walked over to the table with the drinks, and Millicent Bates, following him, put down her empty glass and shook her head. 'No thanks. No more for me. I think I shall go to bed.'

She turned to stare once more at the dancers revolving in the lighted drawing-room: Gussie and Nigel, Dany and Larry Dowling, Amalfi and Lash Holden, Eduardo and Lorraine . . .

She stood there for perhaps five minutes, watching them with a curious intentness.

'It's very odd,' mused Millicent Bates.

'What is?' inquired Tyson.

'Everything!' said Millicent, and left him.

13

Dany leant wearily against the window-sill of her bedroom and looked out across the treetops to the silver stretch of the sea.

She had come up to her room over an hour ago, intending to go to bed. But once there she found that she was not sleepy. Merely too tired to go to the trouble of undressing, and too dispirited to take any pleasure in the beauty of the night. For it had been neither a pleasant nor a peaceful evening.

Tyson and Millicent Bates had both vanished shortly after ten, and Gussie had quarrelled with Nigel, who had withdrawn in a huff, leaving Dany to deal with the radiogram. Gussie had flounced off in search of her brother, presumably to complain, and Lash, having danced a particularly soulful waltz with Amalfi, had taken her down into the garden—ostensibly to look at the nocturnal flowering Lady-of-the-Night which grew in profusion in a bed some distance from the house.

They had stayed away for so long that Eduardo's southern blood had obviously begun to rise dangerously, and although they had returned separately it was perhaps unfortunate that Lash had been the first to reappear. For there was, unmistakably, a distinct trace of lipstick on his chin.

The Marchese's jealous gaze had not missed it, and his eyes had flashed in a manner that would undoubtedly have brought the house down in the days of the late Rudolph Valentino—a gentleman whom he much resembled. He had spoken a short, hissing phrase in Italian, to which Lash had replied with an even shorter one of strictly Anglo-Saxon origin, and only the agitated intervention of Lorraine had prevented a stirring scene.

Amalfi had not reappeared for some time—part of which, at least, she must have devoted to repairing her make-up. She had pointedly ignored Lash and devoted her attention to soothing

Eduardo's lacerated feelings, but she did not appear to be in a good temper.

The only person present who had shown no sign of nerves or temperament was Larry Dowling, and Dany, whose own nerves were uncomfortably taut, was not only duly grateful for it, but despite the fact that there was something about Larry's lazily observant gaze that suggested very little escaped him, even more grateful for the impulse that had made her step-father add him to the house-party. She tried to remind herself that as a journalist—feature writer or no —news was his business, and that the present complicated situation would make entertaining reading for a sensation-hungry public. But it did not seem to weight against the undoubted fact that she felt safer when Larry was in the room, and more insecure whenever he left it.

She wished that she could bring herself to take the sensible course of retiring to bed, but a raw recollection of the terror of the previous night had made her disinclined for sleep or solitude, and the lights and music, and Larry's strangely reassuring presence, at least provided an illusion of safety. But the long hours spent in an aeroplane had begun to tell on all of them, and by eleven o'clock lethargy had descended on the dancers, and with it a spirit of tolerance.

Nigel came out of his huff and apologized to Gussie, who yawned and informed him that of course she wasn't annoyed with him. She was never annoyed with anyone: even with people who pretended to a knowledge of subjects with which they had only the most superficial acquaintance, and—Oh, dear! but of course she hadn't meant *Nigel* . . .

Amalfi had shed her hauteur and awarded Lash a forgiving smile, Eduardo had ceased to simmer, and Lorraine had stopped looking vague and distrait and had begun to sparkle and laugh, and dispense her own particular and potent brand of charm to such good effect that her guests, with the exception of her daughter, had finally departed to bed in the best of tempers.

A bat flitted past the open window and Dany flinched, and was startled to find that so trivial a thing could have the power to make her heart leap and her breath catch. Especially when there was nothing to be afraid of any longer—except the discovery of her identity, which was inevitable anyway. And yet she was still afraid . . .

The night was very quiet and the house very still, and now that the lights had gone out the garden was blue and black and silver only. There were no glints of gold except where the warm reflected glow from her own window touched the top of a jacaranda, and a small orange square, barely visible through the intervening trees, that showed that Lash Holden, in the little guest-house on the seaward corner of the boundary wall, was still awake.

A nightjar cried harshly in the garden below, and Dany's taut nerves leapt to the sudden sound, and she turned impatiently away from the window and looked about her at the strange white-walled room whose high ceiling was almost twenty feet above her head. A room built tall and cool for some lovely lady of the harem in the years before Sultan Saïd had deeded the House of Shade to his friend, Emory Frost—rover, adventurer, black-sheep and soldier-of-fortune.

What had the house seen during its long life? Had there been, as Millicent Bates suggested, 'shady doings' there, and did the rooms remember them? Dany found herself turning quickly to look behind her, as she had done once before in another bedroom in the Airlane in London. But there was nothing behind her except a small cream-and-gilt writing-table on which someone had placed Miss Ada Kitchell's portable typewriter and a solitary book: a solid tome of Victorian vintage that did not look as though it would make entertaining reading.

Dany reached out and picked it up, to discover that it was a musty volume bound in leather that heat and many monsoons had patched with mildew. But despite its age the title was still clearly legible: *The House of Shade* by Barclay Frost.

Dany smiled, remembering Tyson's strictures on the author's style, and dipping into it she found that her step-father's criticisms were fully justified. Barclay's prose was insufferably pedantic, and he had never used one word where half-a-dozen would do instead. Still, it was nice of Lorraine to put it in her room, and she must certainly find time to read some if not all of it.

She was laying it down when she noticed that some inquisitive or would-be helpful servant had opened the typewriter case and had not known how to shut it again. Dany removed the lid in order to set the catches straight, and saw that the machine had also been used for a fragment of torn cream-laid paper, taken from a shelf on the writing-table, was still in it.

One of the *Kivulimi* servants had obviously been playing with this new and fascinating toy, and Dany could only hope that he had not succeeded in damaging it. She rattled off a line of type that in time-honoured tradition informed all good men that now was the time to come to the aid of the party, and finding that the machine still appeared to function, removed the fragment of paper, dropped it into the waste-paper basket and replaced the cover.

Turning away, she looked at the neatly turned-down bed, but sleep seemed as far from her as ever, and she went instead to the dressing-table, and sitting down in front of it, stared at her face in the glass. Lorraine was right. It was an unattractive hair style and her skin was too warm a tone for red hair.

She removed the spectacles, and reaching for her hairbrush swept the fringe off her forehead, and having brushed out the neat rows of curls that were arranged in bunches on either side of her head, twisted the soft mass into a severe knot at the nape of her neck. Dany's bones were good—as Daniel Ashton's had been—and where a frizzed and fussy style of hair-dressing reduced her to mediocrity, a severe one lent her distinction and a sudden unexpected beauty.

An enormous green and white moth flew in through the open window and added itself to the halo of winged insects that were circling about the electric light, and Dany rose impatiently and, going to the door, snapped off the switch. That should give the tiresome things a chance to find their way out into the moonlight, and she would give them a few minutes to get clear, and then pull the curtains before turning on the light again.

Now that the room was in darkness the night outside seemed almost as bright as day, and she returned to the window to look out once more at the shadowy garden and the wide, shimmering expanse of sea.

Lash's light had vanished and he was presumably asleep. But now that Dany's own light was out she became aware that the window immediately above hers had not yet been darkened, for there was still a warm glow illuminating the jacaranda tree. So Millicent Bates was still awake. And so, it seemed, was somebody else . . .

A pin-point of light was moving through the shadows in the garden below and for a moment Dany thought it must be a firefly. Then her ear caught the faint crunch of the crushed shell and coral on the winding paths, and she realized that what she could see was the lighted end of a cigarette, and that someone was walking up through the garden towards the house.

The tiny orange spark was momentarily lost to view behind a

screen of hibiscus, to reappear again as a man in a dinner jacket came softly up the nearest flight of steps on to the terrace, and turning along it, vanished round the far corner of the house.

He had looked up at Dany's window as he reached the top of the steps, and as the moonlight fell on his face she had seen the anxious frown between his brows, and had resisted an impulse to lean out and assure him that she was all right. Though why she should suppose that Larry Dowling was in any way interested in her safety she did not know. It was far more likely that he had merely been strolling in the garden at this late hour because he, like herself, did not feel sleepy.

From somewhere down among the shadowy trees the nightjar cried again. But this time the harsh sound did not make her start, for the thought that Larry was somewhere nearby, and would be spending the night under the same roof, was an astonishingly comforting one. So comforting, that tension and disquiet fell away from her, and all at once she was pleasantly drowsy. She could go to bed now. And to sleep.

Dany's room was the end one on the first floor, above the dining-room and at the top of one of the four flights of stairs that curved upward from the courtyard. A door at one end of her bedroom led at right-angles into a small bathroom that faced west, with beyond it another and larger bathroom belonging to another and larger bedroom that had been given to Gussie Bingham. On the opposite side of her room, and looking out on the same view, was a morning room, and beyond that again a bedroom and a bathroom, the duplicate of her own, which was occupied by Amalfi Gordon.

All the remaining rooms on the first floor—those on the other two sides of the courtyard—were taken up by Tyson and Lorraine, while Nigel, Eduardo, Larry Dowling and Millicent Bates had rooms on the top floor.

'Perhaps not *quite* the thing to do, popping Bates up among all the bachelors,' Lorraine had said. 'But anyone who has ever seen Millicent arrayed for bed—or merely seen Millicent!—would realize that no bachelor is ever likely to cast her so much as a speculative glance, poor girl, so I expect it's all right. I was going to put Ada Kitchell up there—the real one. But that nice Dowling man can have her room instead. He's rather a pet, isn't he?'

Dany caught herself listening for the sound of Larry Dowling's feet on the stone staircase outside her room. But the walls of the House of Shade had been solidly constructed to withstand high

A.	Verandah overlooking courtyard	Gussie	1 Dressing-room
		Bingham's	2 Bedroom
			3 Bathroom
B.	Passage to servants' staircase	Danny's	4 Bathroom
			5 Bedroom
			6 Morning-room
C.	Courtyard	Amalfi's	7 Bedroom
			8 Bathroom
d.	Staircase leading up to top floor and down to courtyard		9 Rooms occupied 10 by Tyson and 11 Lorraine 12 13
o	Pillars at verandah edge		14 Servants' staircase

temperatures, marauding pirates and tropical hurricanes, and the heavy wooden doors were old and carved and almost sound-proof. She did not know if Larry had returned to his own room or not, but concluded that he must have done so by now, and realized that he would probably have gone up by the servants' staircase on the far side of the house.

A little breeze blew in from the sea, ruffling the leaves in the garden below, and she heard for the first time the song of tropic islands and coral coasts: a sound that is as haunting and as unforgettable as the sigh of wind through pine trees. The dry, whispering rustle of coconut palms.

It was a soothing and pleasant sound and a relief from the stillness and silence that had preceded it, and Dany leant out over the windowsill, listening to it, until another sound made her turn. A curious scraping sound that seemed to come either from the verandah or from the room above her. Probably Millicent dragging a suitcase out from under the bed. Or Larry Dowling, scraping his feet on the stone stair. The breeze blew coolly through the hot room, billowing the mosquito curtains and bringing with it all the lovely scents of the tropic night, and presently Dany heard the clock strike the half hour. Half past twelve. It really was quite time that she got to bed.

She pulled the curtains, shutting out the moonlight and the moths, and had turned to grope her way across the room towards the light-switches by the door when she heard another sound. A curious harsh cry that was followed by a dull thud, and that seemed to come from just outside her door.

Dany stood still, listening, all her drowsiness gone and her pulses once again leaping in panic; until an obvious explanation occurred to her, and she relaxed again. It had only been a nightjar crying in the courtyard, and the wind must have overturned a top-heavy creeper-filled urn at the verandah edge. She smiled ruefully at her own fears, and walking forward in the darkness, felt for the switch.

The light clicked on and the room became safe and bright and comfortable, and there were no shadows. But the breeze had passed and the night was still again, and in that stillness she heard once again, and more distinctly, the sound that she had previously thought might be Millicent moving a suitcase: a soft, slow, unidentified sound that suggested stone moving on stone, and that seemed to come not so much from the room above her as from the verandah outside. It did not last for more than ten counted seconds, but this time it brought a sudden picture into Dany's mind: a picture of someone who was hurt, trying to crawl up the stairs. That cry she had heard—it had not been made by a nightjar, and of course the breeze could not have knocked over one of those heavy stone urns! It had been someone crying out and falling. Larry! . . . Supposing it were Larry, tiptoeing up the stairs in the dark so as not to wake her, and losing his footing——

Dany listened at the door, but could hear no further sound. Had Larry been trying to drag himself up the stairs with a sprained ankle, or was he still lying out there in the dark verandah, winded or in pain?

Forgetting caution, she turned the key and jerked open the door.

The moon was not high enough to shine into the well of the courtyard, and Dany could see nothing but darkness except where the light streaming out from her open doorway made a narrow yellow pathway across the coconut matting, and silhouetted a flower-filled stone jar and a single slender pillar against the black emptiness beyond.

There was no chink of light from any other of the many doors that faced each other across the central courtyard, and the night was once again so still that the plop of a goldfish rising at a moth in the pool below was clearly audible in the silence.

Dany spoke in a whisper, afraid of rousing the sleeping house. 'Larry!—Larry, are you there? Is anyone there?'

The whisper made a soft sibilant echo under the high dark roof of the verandah, but no one answered her, and nothing moved. Not even the fish in the pool.

Then another breath of breeze stirred the creepers and flowering shrubs in the stone jars, and as Dany's eyes became accustomed to the darkness the tall lines of pillars with their rounded arches, the dark squares of the doors in the long white-washed wall and the outlines of the stone jars became visible, like a negative in a bath of developing solution. She could make out the long empty stretch of the verandah to her right, but to the left, where it turned sharply at right-angles, the stairs leading to the floor above made a pool of blackness.

She set the door wide and took a hesitant step forward, peering into the shadows. Surely there was something there . . . ? Someone. An untidy heap, sprawled in the dense shadow below the curve of the stone stairs and so nearly the colour of the matting as to be almost invisible.

Dany ran forward, and stooping above it touched a tousled head that appeared to be twisted at an odd angle. But it was not Larry Dowling. Who then? She caught at the slack shoulders, desperately tugging the heavy shape nearer to the light from the open doorway, and then remembered that the switches of the verandah lights were on the wall near the staircase, and ran to them.

A switch clicked under her shaking fingers, and a sixty-watt bulb enclosed in a hanging lamp of oriental design dispersed the shadows, throwing elaborate fretted patterns across the white wall and the coconut matting. And on Millicent Bates, dressed in pyjamas and an oatmeal-coloured dressing-gown, lying face downwards and very still on the verandah floor.

'Miss Bates!' implored Dany, kneeling beside her and endeavouring to turn her over. 'Miss Bates, are you hurt?'

The foolish question echoed hollowly along the silent verandahs as Millicent Bates's head lolled back from Dany's supporting arm. The breeze had set the lantern swaying, and the fretted lozenges of light shifted and swung and gave an illusion of movement to Millicent's wide, staring eyes. But there was no movement in the dead weight of her slack, heavy body. No movement anywhere except for the swinging, soundless lozenges of light and the flutter of a crumpled piece of paper that stirred in the breeze, flapping like a large pale-coloured moth on the matting.

She's hurt, thought Dany stupidly. Badly hurt . . . or she's knocked the wind out of herself. No . . . no it can't be just that . . . Concussion. Miss Bates had fallen and stunned herself. Those shallow steps with their low, decorative, ridiculously inadequate balustrades——She must have been coming down them in the dark to see if Gussie were settled in for the night, and slipped and fallen.

Of all the silly things to do, thought Dany frantically. In the *dark!*

The paper fluttered again with a small sound that made her start violently, and she snatched at it, and thrusting it into her pocket, laid Millicent's inert weight back on to the matting, and stood up: trembling but no longer frightened. She must fetch help at once—Gussie Bingham. Tyson——

She ran to Gussie's door and hammered on it, and receiving no answer tried the handle and found that Gussie too had taken the precaution of locking herself in that night. Dany beat on the door and called her by name, and the silent courtyard picked up the sound and echoed it along the lines of arches: 'Mrs Bingham—! *Mrs Bingham . . . Mrs Bingham . . .*'

A door opened on the adjoining verandah, framing Tyson in a bright square of light.

'What in the name of Beelzebub is the meaning of this infernal din?' roared Tyson, adding his quota to it. 'Who's there? What's up?'

'It's Miss Bates,' called Dany. 'Tyson, *do* come! She's fallen off the staircase, and I think she's concussed herself or—or something. And I can't lift her. She's too heavy.'

The door beside her was thrown open and Gussie Bingham was there, wrapped in a violet silk kimono patterned with wistaria, and with her curling pins inadequately concealed by a turban of lilac tulle.

'Miss Kitchell! Did you want me? What on earth is the matter? Why, Tyson——!'

Tyson charged past her, clad in nothing but a scanty loin cloth of some gaily patterned cotton material, and switching on lights as he went.

Other lights flooded the top-floor verandahs and other heads appeared, peering downwards: Nigel's, Eduardo's, Larry Dowling's . . .

Lorraine ran along the verandah, her little bare feet thrust into absurd feathered mules whose high heels clicked as she ran, and her diaphanous nightgown barely concealed by an equally diaphanous négligée.

But there was nothing that anyone could do. Millicent Bates was dead. She had fallen from somewhere near the top of the staircase on to the stone floor of the verandah, and broken her neck.

14

'I've always said those stairs were dangerous,' shuddered Lorraine, white-faced and shivering. 'Those silly little edges. They aren't rails at all! But I still don't see how she could have done it, even in the dark. You'd think anyone would be *extra* careful in the dark, wouldn't you?'

'I suppose she must have felt faint,' said Tyson. 'In fact that was probably what she was coming down for. To get some aspirin or something off Gussie. Gussie's got their medicine chest in her room.'

'But wouldn't you think she'd have had the sense to just sit down if she felt faint? Really, people are *too* stupid!'

It was obvious from Lorraine's tone that, horrified as she was, she considered Millicent Bates to have been guilty of thoroughly inconsiderate behaviour, and now that the first shock of discovery was over, her emotions leant more to anger than grief.

It was over an hour since Dany had aroused the sleeping household, and they were all in the drawing-room waiting for the arrival of the doctor, an ambulance and the police. All except Gussie—who had succumbed to a fit of hysterics and was now in bed having been given two sedatives and a hot-water bottle—and Nigel Ponting, who had driven in to the town to fetch the doctor and inform the police.

They had carried Millicent's body into Dany's room because it happened to be the nearest, and left it on Dany's bed, where it lay alone, clad in sternly utilitarian pyjamas and an elderly woollen dressing-gown, staring open-mouthed at the ceiling.

Lash had been awakened by the car being backed out of the garage and the flick of headlights across the wall of his room, and seeing the house ablaze with lights, he had put on a dressing-gown and come across to make inquiries.

Amalfi, who had slept through the initial uproar and had been aroused by Gussie's shrieks, had joined the horrified house-party just as Tyson and Larry Dowling were carrying Millicent's limp body into Dany's room. She had behaved with admirable calm, and it was she who had succeeded in putting a stop to Gussie's hysterics by the simple expedient of picking up the jug of drinking water that stood on Dany's bedside table, and flinging the contents in Mrs Bingham's scarlet, screaming face.

Amalfi was now sitting on the sofa, wearing a most becoming confection of peach-coloured satin and lace and looking as poised and sleek and *soignée* as though this was some normal social occasion. She was talking to Lash and sipping black coffee that Lorraine had made in a Cona, but if her composure was genuine, she appeared to be the only one in the room to possess it.

Lash was not even making a pretence of listening to her. He was looking troubled and out of temper, and was apparently more interested in the pattern of the carpet than in anything else, though he occasionally lifted his gaze from it to direct a look of active irritation at Tyson Frost, who was prowling restlessly about the room, looking like some strayed beachcomber from the South Pacific.

Lash, glancing at him and wishing he would stay still, decided that although hair on the chest might be the hallmark of a he-man, too much of it merely suggested that Darwin had been dead right when he attributed the origin of the human species to the ape. There was little to choose between Tyson's torso and a doormat, and his caged-lion prowl was beginning to get on Lash's nerves. If only the man would sit still for five minutes——! And if only Amalfi would stop talking for ten. His gaze shifted briefly to Dany, and he frowned.

Dany was the only one in the room who was fully dressed, and Lash, noting the fact, and the time, was unreasonably disturbed. Two a.m. And they had all gone off to their several rooms shortly before half past eleven. Yet Dany alone had obviously not been in bed, for she was not only wearing the dress she had worn earlier that evening, but she was still wearing stockings. Which made it seem unlikely that she had merely hurriedly pulled on the dress in preference to coming down in a bathrobe as the others had done. He noticed that she was surreptitiously studying Larry Dowling, and his frown became a scowl.

Dany herself, sitting huddled in the depths of a big armchair and feeling cold and very tired, was wondering how Larry had managed to get back into the house and up to his room in time to change into the pyjamas and dressing-gown he now wore, when she had seen him on the terrace below her window, wearing a dinner jacket, only a short time before she had heard Millicent fall. Or had the interval been longer than she had imagined? How long had she stood near the window looking out into the moonlight after he had left the terrace? Surely not more than ten minutes. Yet Larry certainly had the appearance of one who has been awakened out of a sound sleep, for his hair was rumpled and he yawned at intervals. But despite the yawns there was nothing sleepy about those quiet, observant eyes, and Dany did not believe that he felt in the least drowsy.

Eduardo di Chiago, darkly handsome in scarlet silk pyjamas and a spectacular monogrammed and coroneted dressing-gown, was gallantly assisting Lorraine with the coffee. But he too was noticeably distrait and apt to jump when spoken to, and, like Lash, was obviously finding his host's relentless pacing an acute nervous irritant.

Lorraine, noticing it, said appealingly: 'Tyson darling, *do* sit down! You're making us all nervous. Why don't we all go back to bed?'

'Speaking for myself,' said Tyson, 'because I should have to get up again the minute the doctor and the police arrive. However, there's no reason why the rest of you should stay around. The only people they're likely to want to see are myself and Miss—er—Miss——'

'Kitchell,' supplied Lash with something of a snap.

Tyson turned to scowl at him and said: 'At least there's nothing to stop *you* getting back to bed, so don't let us keep you up. You weren't even here when it happened, and I don't know what the hell you're doing over here anyway.'

'Neither do I,' said Lash morosely. But he made no attempt to move, and once again he looked at Dany. A long, thoughtful and faintly uneasy look.

Amalfi, observing it, turned to follow the direction of his gaze, and her eyes narrowed while her charming, curving mouth was suddenly less charming as the red lips tightened into a line that was almost hard. She had not looked at Dany directly during the last hour, but she looked now.

Dany was sitting in a huddled and childish attitude that should have been ungraceful, but was not, for it revealed the fact that her figure was slim and her legs were long and lovely. She had done something, too, to her hair. Brushed it back and got rid of those distressing curls—and discarded her spectacles. Without them she looked absurdly young. Young enough to make Amalfi disquietingly conscious of her own age, and a crease furrowed her white forehead. She turned back sharply to look at Lash, but Lash was studying the carpet again and appeared to be immersed in his own thoughts which, judging from his expression, were not pleasant.

Eduardo too had looked at Dany: and from Dany to Amalfi Gordon. And his dark eyes were all at once intensely alert and curiously wary. He said abruptly, as though replying to Tyson's question:

'Then I think I go to my bed. You are right. No one will wish to ask me questions, and I feel that it may be I intrude. This Miss Bates —she has been known to you for many years, perhaps? *Allora*—it is very sad for you. I feel for you so much. You excuse me, Lorraine?'

He kissed her hand, and then Amalfi's—though with less than his usual lover-like gallantry—and having conveyed his sympathy to Tyson in an eloquent look, returned to his own room. But no one else appeared to feel called upon to follow his example; not even Larry Dowling, who could certainly not have considered himself an old friend of the family: and they were all still there when at long last Nigel returned with the doctor and an Indian Chief Inspector of Police.

The proceedings after that had been mercifully brief. The doctor's verdict had confirmed their own, and it was only too easy to see how the accident had occurred.

Miss Bates, descending the staircase in the dark, had either felt faint or misjudged a step and stumbled, and falling over the edge of the balustrade on to the verandah below had broken her neck. It was as simple, and as shocking as that.

Tyson had done most of the talking and shown them where the body had lain, and Dany had not been called upon to say very much. The doctor had seen Gussie and prescribed rest and, if necessary, another sedative, and he and the Inspector, having assisted in carrying Millicent's body to the waiting ambulance, had expressed their sympathy and left.

The moon was down and in the east the sky was already beginning to grow pale with the first far-away hint of dawn when Dany climbed in under her mosquito-net at last. Her sheets were crumpled and her pillow still bore the impression of Millicent Bates' head. But no one had thought to suggest that she sleep anywhere else, and she was too tired to care very much that she must sleep where Millicent's dead body had lain. Too tired to care very much about anything . . .

She slept so soundly that she did not hear the gentle tap of the house-servant who attempted to bring her a tea tray at eight o'clock, or, an hour later, Lorraine's voice outside her locked door, inquiring if she were awake yet. And it was, finally, Lash who awakened her.

He banged on her bedroom door and went on banging with increasing loudness until she opened it, and when he saw her there, drowsy and bewildered, he said with inexplicable fervour: 'Thank God for that!'

'For what?' asked Dany, blinking at him. 'Is anything the matter?'

'Apparently not,' said Lash, who was looking oddly white and strained. 'But when you didn't come down, and Lorraine said your door was locked and she could get no answer out of you, I thought maybe I'd better come up and make sure.'

'Of what?' inquired Dany, puzzled.

'That you were really only asleep. I guess that lousy business last night was an accident all right, but all the same——'

'*Miss Bates*——!' gasped Dany, recollection hitting her like a blow in the face. 'I—I'd forgotten. She—Oh, Lash! Oh *poor* Miss Bates. Poor Mrs Bingham . . . Is she all right?'

'Mrs Bingham? I guess so. She seems to have recovered enough to eat a fairly hearty breakfast, judging from the tray that went up. How about you? Are you thinking of coming down any time?'

'Of course. Is it late?'

'Just after ten.'

'Ten! Good heavens!'

The door slammed in his face, and a silvery voice from halfway down the verandah said: 'Serenading your secretary, Lash darling?'

Amalfi walked towards him and smiled sweetly up into his face; but above the lovely laughing curve of her mouth her green eyes were cold and steady and held no trace of amusement, and looking down into them Lash was conscious of a sudden sharp sense of shock, as though he had walked unwarily into some solid object in the dark.

He had not known that Amalfi could look like that while smiling like that, and it left him feeling uneasy and strangely unsure of himself. He said defensively, answering her question: 'Strictly in the way of business.'

'Really?' Amalfi's voice was as warmly sweet as her smile. 'And is a lace and nylon wrap her normal working dress? What fun you business men must have!'

She laughed her lovely laugh, and Lash was startled to find himself angry in a way that he had never been angry before.

He looked at Amalfi for a long moment; seeing her as someone he did not know at all, and noticing many things that he had never noticed before: the years that had been so skilfully held at bay; the ice that could glitter in those cool, mermaid eyes and the malice that could speak in that warm caressing voice. The steel that lay concealed behind that charming, irresponsible, childish sweetness . . .

Amalfi's long lashes fluttered and dropped, and when they lifted again her eyes were softly appealing and her voice coaxed. 'I'm dreadfully jealous, darling!'

'Are you?' said Lash grimly. 'It must make a nice change.' He turned away from her and went down the curving stair to the courtyard without troubling to see whether she were following or not.

Mr Cardew of the police, his peaceful Sabbath rudely interrupted, called again that morning at the House of Shade, and Tyson took him up to see the scene of the accident.

Mr Cardew commented unfavourably on the extremely inadequate balustrades, pronounced the staircases to be dangerous and suggested that iron rails of a reasonable height should be added at the earliest possible moment, and returned to the city taking Tyson, Dany and Gussie Bingham with him, where there had been certain depressing formalities to be gone through in connection with the death of Millicent Bates.

His office was in a tall, square building, four storeys high and facing the sea, with magnificent carved doors and a clock tower. The Bet-el-Ajaib, the 'House of Wonders'; once a palace built by the famous Sultan, Seyyid Barghash-bin-Saïd, and now doing duty as the Secretariat.

The House of Wonders had been built many years later than the House of Shade, and though on a far larger scale, its design was similar: the rooms with their tiers of verandahs being built about a central courtyard. Except that here the courtyard was not open to the sky, but closed over with a glass roof in the manner of a railway station.

Dany had left Tyson and his sister talking to Mr Cardew, and had gone out to stand on the steps and look out towards the harbour where the clove ship for Pemba lay at anchor, and to gaze at the three ancient guns that stood before the Bet-el-Ajaib: cannon that were stamped with the arms of Portugal, and were part of the booty taken by the Persians at the fall of Ormuz.

She had been tracing the worn inscriptions on the old sun-baked metal when a shadow fell across the cannon, and she looked up to see the Arab who had been on the Nairobi plane with them on the previous day, and whom Nigel had introduced as Seyyid Omar-bin-Sultan.

Seyyid Omar's excellent teeth flashed white in his olive-skinned face, and he bowed and said: 'Good morning, Miss Kitchell. How pleasant to meet you again so soon. You have started your sight-seeing already, I see. Are you admiring our guns? They are very old. Perhaps four hundred years and more.'

'Yes, I know,' said Dany. 'I read about them before I came here. What does that inscription on them say? It's Arabic, isn't it?'

'Persian,' said Seyyid Omar; and traced the graceful characters with one slim brown finger . . .

'In the Name of God and by the Grace of Mahomed and Ali, convey to the True Believers who have assembled together for war, the Good Tiding of Success and Victory . . . During the reign of Shah Abbas, Sajawi, King of the Earth and of Time, whose Power is ever increasing . . .'

His finger slowed and stopped, and he did not read the rest of the long inscription, but looking down at it, repeated in a low voice that held a curious thrill of awe (and perhaps of envy?) that magnificent, arrogant title: *'King of the Earth and of Time . . .'*

'That's wonderful,' said Dany, charmed by the cadence of the words. 'Thank you.'

Seyyid Omar dropped his hand swiftly and smiled at her, and his voice was casual and polite again.

'Yes, that is a fine title, is it not? But there are none to hold it now. Our great days have gone—and our court poets—and who knows when they will return again? But what are you doing alone here, Miss Kitchell? Do you go sight-seeing by yourself?'

'No. I'm afraid I'm not sight-seeing this morning. We—that is Mr Frost and Mrs Bingham and myself, had to come in on—on business.'

'Oh?' Seyyid Omar's expressive brows lifted. 'That sounds dull. I had hoped that your first day in Zanzibar would be more entertaining. I wish that I might offer to show you something of the town, but I myself am also here to keep a business appointment. With the police.'

'The police?' Dany looked started. 'Why—why so are we. With Mr Cardew.'

'Ah! You too. It is because of the death of an acquaintance of mine, I think? Salim Abeid, who died at Mombasa Airport yesterday. Well, I do not expect that you can give them any more assistance than I can.'

Salim Abeid . . . Dany heard the name with a sense of shock, for Millicent's death had pushed that other tragedy into the back of her mind. But now she was reminded of it again: and reminded too that she had seen Salim Abeid talking to this man in the shadow of a wing of the Nairobi West Airport barely an hour before he had died.

'Probably a political murder,' Tyson had said. Jembe had made many enemies among the aristocracy and the rich land-owners—such men, presumably, as Seyyid Omar-bin-Sultan. And Seyyid Omar had been on the same plane . . .

The midday sun that beat down upon the entrance to the House of Wonders was very hot, but a little cold shiver prickled down Dany's spine, and she remembered innumerable stories that she had read of the cruelty of the East: stories stretching from the Arabian Nights down to the recent atrocities of the Mau Mau.

The Isle of Cloves, as its history showed, was not unacquainted with violence and cruelty, and the murder of a rabble-rouser would probably be considered as of little account today as the death of a dozen slaves in the days when the dhows of the slave traders had moored where the little Pemba-bound steamer now lay at anchor, and their crews had tossed out the corpses from among their human cargoes on to those same beaches.

Dany shivered, and Seyyid Omar, observing it, said solicitously: 'It has troubled you. I am sorry that your first morning in our island should be spoiled by such a thing: the death of a man you had probably not even met. Though I believe he was a fellow-passenger of yours from London, was he not?'

The question was asked quite casually and as though it were a matter of no account, but he waited for an answer.

Dany said: 'Yes. But I didn't actually meet him.'

'But Mr Dowling did,' said Seyyid Omar gently. 'And of course your—host's secretary had met him before. Mr Ponting. I am surprised that Mr Cardew should not have wished to see them, rather than you and Mrs Bingham.'

'Oh, but we aren't here about that,' Dany hastened to assure him. 'There was a dreadful accident at *Kivulimi* last night. Mrs Bingham's companion, Miss Bates, fell from one of the staircases in the dark, and broke her neck.'

'You mean—she is dead?' inquired Seyyid Omar sharply.

'Yes.'

The monosyllable had a flat finality, and suddenly Millicent was dead. Really dead. Until then it had been unreal: a tale that someone had told her and which she had not quite believed. But now it was true . . .

She heard Seyyid Omar draw in his breath with a little hiss between his teeth. 'That is terrible! I am sorry. I am most sorry. This has been a sad arrival for you indeed. An ill-omened one. I can only hope that it will not give you a dislike of our island and make you wish to leave.'

Dany had no time for a reply, for at that moment Tyson and his sister joined them, and Seyyid Omar offered condolences and sympathy.

They stood in the white glare of the sunlight against a tropical background of flame trees, hard shadows and sauntering white-robed men with ebony faces, and spoke of Millicent: Tyson, burly, bearded and frankly impatient; Gussie looking suddenly ten years older—a lined, shocked, shrunken shadow of the assured and talkative matron of yesterday; Dany with her dyed hair and spectacles, and Seyyid Omar-bin-Sultan, suitably concerned and gravely sympathetic. *Requiem for a British Spinster* . . .

Seyyid Omar refused an invitation to accompany them to the English Club for lunch, and Tyson, Gussie and Dany returned to the car, and were driven through the narrow streets to a tall old building that fronted the sea and managed to epitomize all that is conveyed by the words 'Outposts of Empire.'

'The doors of all these houses are so lovely,' said Dany, pausing to look back along the white-walled street down which they had come. 'All that carving, and those huge brass spikes.'

'Those were to keep the war elephants from battering in the doors,' said Tyson. 'Useful, as well as ornamental.'

'*Elephants?* What nonsense! You couldn't possibly squeeze an elephant into one of these streets, let alone turn it end on to a door!'

'Yes, there is that,' said Tyson. 'But it's a pretty story all the same. And that really is why Arab doors had those spikes on them once. The days of the war elephants have gone, but the design has persisted. And you're right about the streets. Hell to drive through. In most of 'em, if a car is coming one way and a kitten the other, one of them is going to have to stop. And as this is Zanzibar, it's the car that would give way to the kitten. A pleasant crowd. A very pleasant crowd.'

Nigel joined them at the Club, and they ate a sturdy British meal that made no concessions to the climate, sitting in a huge, echoing, sparsely populated dining-room under the ceaseless whirr of electric fans.

Neither Gussie nor Tyson had much to say, and it fell to Nigel and Dany to sustain some semblance of conversation. But as Nigel was as voluble as ever, Dany's share was mercifully limited to adding an occasional yes or no at reasonable intervals.

Her mind was on other things than Roman society scandals, and she did not perceive their trend until Nigel said: '——the old Marchesa, that's Eduardo's grandmother, pulled *every* string within reach—and has she a reach! And so of course that was *that* as far as poor Eddie was concerned. *Too* frustrating for him. And then darling Lorraine asks him to look up Elf in London, and *here* we go again! Another *grande passion* that is doomed to crack on the same old rocks. Too awful for *both* of them, when you come to think of it.'

'Why?' inquired Dany perfunctorily.

'Oh, but my *dear!* It's obvious. Poor, poor Elf—so romantic and unbusiness-like! Throwing away the substance for an *utter* shadow; did she but know. There she was, all set to bridge the dollar gap by rushing Holden Jnr to the nearest registrar, when who should happen along but Eduardo. All Latin charm, a Marquis to boot, and apparently *solid* with lire. *Naturally* the poor sweet began to waver. Well, I mean—there *is* a certain glamour about being able to embroider authentic little coronets on one's smalls, and plain "Mrs Holden" doesn't carry *quite* the same simple charm as "the Signora Marchesa di Chiago". Provided the lire and the lovely green-backs balance, of course! But then they don't. Someone really ought to break it to darling Elf.'

'Someone has,' said Tyson briefly, entering the conversation for the first time.

Nigel registered surprise. 'You? Now that *is* a relief—though I did begin to wonder last night if someone hadn't perhaps dropped the *merest* hint. I hope you mean to do the same for poor Eddie. Just a whisper of warning?'

'Eddie,' said Tyson shortly, 'can look after himself.'

Gussie helped herself to a solid wedge of suet pudding, and said; 'What are you two talking about? Warn who about what?'

'Eduardo;' said Nigel, 'about our dear Amalfi. That she may look *stimulatingly* solvent, but that it's all done by mirrors. Or should one be *really* catty, and say *paste?* Excellent imitations of course— she had them made in Paris. But I happen to know that she popped the diamonds and all Chubby's emeralds. The family were furious— my dear, *furious!* But of course there was nothing they could do about it. And after all, one *does* sympathize with the poor sweet. She had every reason to believe that she'd be left madly well off, and it must have been too infuriating to find an absolute regiment of as- sorted relatives all queueing up for their cut—and getting it! *Too* soul-curdling. One wonders if it was *worth* it? No thanks, I don't feel I could *face* suet pudding. I think I'll try the cheese——'

Millicent was buried late that afternoon, and the entire house- party attended, with the exception of Amalfi, who complained of a headache, and added that in any case she was allergic to funerals.

It was a brief enough service; and to Dany, at least, a tragic one. Not because she had taken any special liking to Miss Bates, who had been almost a stranger to her, but because she could not forget that Millicent Bates had despised all things Oriental and had so disliked the East. Yet now she would never leave it. Alien and alone she must lie in this hot foreign soil, within sound of the surf and the trade winds and the rustling palms, until the Day of Judgement. Poor Miss Bates, who had been so deeply rooted in the life of one small En- glish market town, and who had not wanted to come to Zanzibar.

15

It was a silent and distinctly subdued party who assembled for dinner that night and afterwards they had gone out to sit on the terrace and made desultory conversation, and no one had suggested dancing.

Amalfi appeared to have recovered from her headache, and in deference to the memory of Miss Bates she wore a deceptively simple dress of black chiffon which lent her a frail and wistful look and made her white skin appear even whiter by contrast.

Both Lorraine and Gussie also wore black. Presumably for the same reason. But as Dany did not possess a black dress (Aunt Harriet having held pronounced views on the unsuitability of black for the young), she had put on the same grey magnolia-appliquéd one that she had worn the previous evening. And it was while Abdurahman, the head houseboy, was clearing away the coffee cups and liqueur glasses, and Nigel was languidly inquiring whether anyone felt like a game of bridge, that she thrust an idle hand into one of the wide pockets that decorated the skirt and touched a crumpled piece of paper.

Dany drew it out and regarded it with faint surprise, wondering how it had got there. It was a half sheet of writing paper, roughly torn along one edge, and flattening out its creases she held it so that the moonlight fell full on it, and read the few typewritten words it bore without at first comprehending their meaning.

May I please speak to you. I am in great trouble, and need advice. Could you be very kind and make it after half-past twelve, as it is rather a private matter, and I do not want other people to know. My room is underneath yours, and I will wait up. Please come. A.K.

What on earth——? thought Dany, looking at it with wrinkled brows. She turned it over, but there was no more of it. The writer had presumably meant to add something else to it, but had thought

356

better of it and thrown it away. But how had it got into her pocket, and when?

And then, as suddenly and as shockingly as though someone had treated her as Amalfi had treated Gussie's hysterics and thrown a pint of ice-cold water in her face, she remembered——

It was the piece of paper that had fluttered against her skirt when she had knelt above Millicent's body last night, and which she had snatched up and stuffed into her pocket without thinking. But it was more than that. It was proof of murder.

A fragment of conversation from the previous evening repeated itself in her brain as though it were a gramophone playing a record: *'A third what?' 'Murder of course, darling. Things always go in threes . . .'* They had gone in threes. There had been a third murder. And an attempt at a fourth—her own. For the note was neither unfinished nor unsigned. It had been written on her typewriter—Miss Kitchell's typewriter—and signed with her initials: Miss Kitchell's initials. And if it had been found——

A clammy mixture of nausea and cold fear engulfed Dany, drowning out the moonlight and the sound of the casual, idle voices. She was caught in a horrible, clinging spider-web, and however much she twisted and turned she could not escape, because there would always be another strand waiting for her ready to wind softly and terrifyingly about her until at last she would be bound and helpless.

Hysteria rose in her, prompting her to leap to her feet and scream and scream, as Gussie had done. To run across the terrace and through the moonlight and out into the white dusty road, and to go on running until she dropped. She fought it down, driving her fingernails into her palms and biting her lip until the blood came. And then a hand came out of the fog and closed over hers. A flesh and blood hand that was firm and real in the midst of miasma and unreality, and that steadied the spinning world and brought it back to some sort of sanity.

The fog cleared and the moonlight was bright again and Lash was standing in front of her; his body a barrier between her and the seven other people on the terrace.

He said: 'Come and take a walk down to the beach. I haven't had the chance of a word with you all day, and there are one or two things that I'd like to go over. You'll excuse us, Lorraine?'

He did not wait for permission, but jerking Dany to her feet he drew her arm through his, and holding it hard against him walked her away across the terrace and down the steps into the ink-black shadows of the tree-filled garden, where he began to talk of business matters and of names that meant nothing to her; continuing to do so as they passed along the shadowy, flower-scented paths, and leaving the garden by a door in the seaward wall, walked down a steep, rocky path to the shore.

The beach was deserted, and nothing moved on it save the quiet tide and a host of ghostly little sand crabs that scuttled to and fro as silently as moths. There were rocks at each end of it: tall rocks of wind-carved, water-worn coral that stood dark against the moon-washed sky and threw sharp-edged shadows on the white sand. But Lash avoided them, and keeping to the open beach stopped near the edge of the tide, where no one could approach unseen and they could not be overheard.

Releasing his grip on Dany's arm he turned her so that she faced him, but he did not lower his voice, or make any attempt to change its pitch, and anyone watching him from the shadows would have supposed him to be merely continuing the conversation he had started in the garden.

'What happened, honey? What was on that paper? Someone write you an anonymous letter?'

Dany held it out to him without words, and saw his face set into harsh and unfamiliar lines as he read it.

After a moment or two he said quite softly: 'Did someone put this in your pocket?'

'No,' said Dany in a whisper. 'I found it last night. It was on the verandah . . . by . . . near Miss Bates. She must have been hold-ing it when . . . I put it in my pocket, and I didn't think of it again until—until just now when I felt it, and took it out, and . . . read it.'

Lash was silent for a long time, looking at the piece of paper in his hand, and at last Dany said: 'It does mean—what I think it means, doesn't it?'

'Yes,' said Lash, still softly, and without pretending to misunder-stand her: his voice strangely at variance with the ugly grimness of his face and his taut hands.

'What are we going to do? Are you—are you going to tell the police?'

'I don't know. I shall have to figure it out. What did you do with that typewriter? Where is it?'

'In my room.'

'Then this probably wasn't written on it; which may help.'

'But it was,' said Dany with a catch in her voice. 'I thought one of the servants must have been playing with it—the lid wasn't on properly, and there was a bit of paper in it: the other half of that.'

'When was this?' asked Lash sharply.

'Last night, when I went up to bed.'

'Did you touch it?'

'Yes. I tried the typewriter to see if it was all right, and it was, and I took the paper out. It's in the waste-paper basket.'

Lash let out his breath in a little sigh. 'So your fingerprints will be on it. And they're on this too. A nice, neat, slick little fool-proof frame-up! Dear God, what have I let you in for?'

He crushed the piece of paper savagely in one clenched hand and turned to stare blindly out at the shimmering sea, and Dany saw the muscles along his jaw twitch and tighten. He said, half under his breath and as though he were speaking to himself: 'I ought to have taken you straight to the police—back in London. It might have been a little sticky, but no more than that. Instead of which I have to let you in for a piece of crazy, drunken lunacy that——'

He made a violent despairing gesture, and Dany said quickly: 'Don't, Lash! It wasn't your fault. It was mine for not realizing that you——Oh, what does it matter? We can go to the police now.'

Lash turned quickly to face her, his eyes blank with bitterness. 'No, we can't. That's the hell of it. We shall have to let the Bates woman's death stay on the books as an accident. There's no other way out.'

'But Lash——'

'There's no "but" about it!' interrupted Lash savagely. 'I may have been behaving like a certifiable moron of late, but I'm still capable of adding two and two together and coming up with the correct answer. That dame was killed because she talked too much; and but for the mercy of Providence, this bit of paper would have been found on her or near her. You'd have been asked to explain it —and a few other things as well! Such as how did the other half of it get into your room if you didn't write it, and what the heck were you doing fully dressed at least an hour after everyone else was in bed? What *were* you doing, by the way? *Were* you waiting for her?'

'*Lash!*' Dany flinched as though he had struck her.

'I didn't mean "Did you kill her?" ' said Lash impatiently. 'Or even "Did you type that note?" Of course you didn't. But did she say anything about dropping in to see you?'

'No.'

'Then why hadn't you been to bed? What had you been doing?'

'Nothing. I just didn't feel sleepy; that was all. I suppose I didn't want to put the light out, and so I kept putting off going to bed. And then I heard a nightjar again, but it wasn't a nightjar—'

Dany shivered, remembering that sound, and said with an effort: 'It was Miss Bates. She must have cried out as she fell. And then I heard a thud . . .'

She told him about that, and about finding Millicent's body and the scrap of paper, and about Larry Dowling, who had been walking in the garden so short a time before.

'Dowling,' said Lash slowly.

He appeared to be turning something over in his mind, and then he shook his head, and abandoning Larry Dowling, said: 'Didn't you hear any other sound at all? No footsteps? Nothing? If someone waited for her to come down those stairs, and then pushed her off them, you'd surely have heard footsteps.'

'No, I didn't. I didn't hear anything else. Just a sort of screech and a thud: I told you. There wasn't any other . . . No. No, I'm wrong. There was another sound. A queer soft grating sort of noise like——' She wrinkled her brows, trying to recall what it was like and put it into words, but gave it up. 'I don't know. But it wasn't footsteps.'

Lash dismissed it with a shrug. 'Let it go. But the fact remains that you were up and dressed, and it wouldn't have looked too good if that note had been found, because it would have helped back up the theory that you wrote it. Which wouldn't have been a criminal thing to have done, and would only have meant that you'd asked Miss Bates to come to see you, and that she'd slipped and fallen while she was on her way down. But the moment you denied having written it the thing would have begun to look screwy, and the chances are that you wouldn't have been believed. They'd have wanted to know why you were denying it when all the evidence supported it; and the next thing you know they'd have found out that you are no more Miss Kitchell than I am, and that you'd skipped out of England on a false passport to avoid a murder rap. It wouldn't have sounded so good, and though maybe you could have talked your way out of one of those situations, I doubt if you could talk yourself out of both. Which is why that accident last night is going to have to stay just the way it is—an accident! Anything else is too darned dangerous. And now the sooner we get rid of this particular piece of poison, the better.'

He took a cigarette lighter out of his pocket, snapped it open and held one corner of the crumpled type-written note to the flame, and Dany said on a gasp: 'Lash you can't—it's evidence!'

'Sure. But it won't be in a minute. And without it that other bit of paper in your room won't mean a thing, and there'll be nothing to connect you with Miss Bates.'

He watched the small scrap of paper that had lured Millicent to her death blacken and curl and burst into flame, and when he could hold it no longer he dropped it and ground the burnt fragments into the sand with his heel. He was silent for a moment or two, scowling down at the small dark depression that his heel had made, and then he said slowly: 'I wish I could take you out of here, but I can't. If we make a break for it, it would only look worse. And yet it's a risk either way. Listen, Dany, I want you to promise me something.'

'What?' inquired Dany in an uncertain voice.

'That you won't ever leave your room at night, for any reason at all. That you'll lock yourself in, and if anyone taps on your door and pushes a note under it asking you to go anywhere, even if it's signed by your mother and written in her own handwriting, you won't even touch it. Give it to me in the morning. And don't go off on any *tête-à-tête* expeditions with anyone—unless it's me! Get it?'

He smiled at her, but it was a smile that did not reach his eyes, and Dany said with a catch in her voice: 'But why should anyone want to harm me? Or try to pin things on me? It was different before —when I had that map or clue or whatever it was. But now it's been stolen. Whoever wanted it has got it. Why doesn't it all stop? Why did anyone have to murder Miss Bates?'

Lash said: 'Because she insisted on telling us that she was in the neighbourhood of this solicitor's house around the time that the guy who rubbed him out would have been on his way in to do the job. That same guy happens to know that you were around too; and he's giving you a strong hint not to talk, or it will be the worse for you! Either that, or he's laying on a useful scapegoat in case he should ever need one. A hell of a lot of guys will do a hell of a lot of lousy things for the sake of three million—take it from me! That's why you're going to watch your step from now on. And I *mean* watch it! We ought to have the cops down on us in a day or two, and after that it's their headache.'

Dany twisted her hands together and said on a sob: 'Lash—I'm frightened.'

'You're not the only one!' retorted Lash with strong feeling. 'I've never been so scared in all my life. I do not relish the idea that one of that bunch back there on the terrace makes a hobby of murder, and I wish I had a gun.'

'But it can't be one of us! It can't be!'

'Don't be silly, Dany. It can't be anyone else. It's one of six people. You, me, Amalfi, Gussie Bingham, the Latin lover or Larry Dowling. Take your choice!'

Dany shivered and Lash reached out suddenly and pulled her into his arms, holding her against him and ruffling the outrageous red curls with his free hand. He said: 'I know, honey. But it'll all be the same in a hundred years.'

Dany made a sobbing and unintelligible remark into his shoulder, and he put his hand under her chin and lifted it. 'What was that one? I didn't get it.'

'I said "be c-careful of my s-spectacles".'

'I never liked them anyway,' said Lash, removing them and kissing her lightly. At least, that is what he had meant it to be, but it did not turn out like that. It began lightly enough, but ended very differently, and when at last he lifted his head he was astounded to find himself feeling breathless and shaken.

'That your first kiss?' he inquired, holding her away from him.

'Yes,' said Dany dazedly; her face bemused and beautiful in the white moonlight. 'How did you know?'

'I get around,' said Lash dryly. 'Well, it's going to be the last for tonight, because if I do that again there's no knowing where we'll end up.'

He stooped and retrieved the spectacles that had fallen unheeded to the ground, and having dusted the sand off them, replaced them carefully.

'And that'll be all for today, Miss Kitchell. I guess we'd better get back to the house and see you safely locked in for the night. And with reference to that last item on the agenda, you might consider letting me have a copy of it tomorrow—in triplicate.'

He walked her back towards the house across the white beach and through the door into the garden, where they encountered Larry Dowling loitering in the shadows by the edge of a shallow pool set about with stone birds and spider lilies. They might have passed without knowing that he was there, except that a reflection moved slightly in the water, and there was a faint smell of cigarette smoke.

Lash had stopped and said: 'di Chiago?' and Larry had moved out into the moonlight and said: 'No. But that was quick of you. It's one of his cigarettes. Can't say I like 'em much: give me gaspers every time. Nice on the beach?'

'Yes, thanks,' said Lash curtly. 'You on your way there?'

'No. Just strolling around,' said Larry. 'Just strolling around.'

Lash said: 'Don't let us stop you,' and went on up the path that led to the terrace.

There were only two people on the terrace. Amalfi and Eduardo, who appeared to be quarrelling. They broke off on hearing footsteps, and Amalfi said with an edge to her voice: 'Oh, it's you. I hope you had a nice brisk businesslike session and got everything straightened out?'

'We did,' said Lash amiably. 'Thanks for asking.'

Amalfi laughed. 'Gussie was right: you're nothing but an old slave-driver. I really do believe that "Business First" is your motto.'

'The Americans!' said Eduardo. 'So efficient, so ruthless—so eye-on-the-ball. It is wonderful.'

Amalfi said hastily: 'Lorrie said to say good night to you, Lash; she and Gussie both thought they could do with an early night. She wanted to know if you'd like to go along to the fish market tomorrow morning. Gussie wants to see it. She says if she mopes around here she'll go mad, and Lorrie said that if you'd like to tag along you'll have to have breakfast at eight, and there'll be a car going in immediately afterwards. However, I told her I didn't think it sounded at all in your line.'

'Then you thought wrong,' said Lash, still amiably. 'I like fish. Where's Tyson? Is he making an early night of it too?'

'No. He and Nigel are as bad as you. They're doing a bit of work for a change.'

'It won't hurt 'em,' said Lash, and turned to Dany. 'That reminds me: I've got one or two things to do myself. I guess I'd better borrow your typewriter, Ada. I'll go right on up with you now and get it, if that's all right with you?'

'Yes, of course,' said Dany.

She moved towards the door, and Lash was following her when Amalfi spoke softly, addressing no one in particular: 'I do hope this means that Ada's mumps are better?'

16

'I have always considered,' remarked Nigel, holding a delicately scented handkerchief to his nose, 'that a fishmonger's emporium ranks slightly above a morgue, and only a point below a butcher's shop and an abattoir. All those slippery white stomachs and cold coddy eyes glaring at one. *Utterly* emetic. But just look at these colours! *Pure* Roerich. *Do* let's have some of those turquoise-blue fish with coral spots—or what about these heavenly shocking pink ones? You know, this might almost reconcile one to doing the weekly shopping.'

'But can one really *eat* the things?' inquired Gussie, apprehensively eyeing the fish in question. 'Lorraine, you're *surely* not going to buy those pink creatures?'

'Changu, Gussie. They're delicious. Wait until you taste them!'

'Well, if you say so,' said Gussie in a fading voice.

The fish market was a riot of noise and colour, and the variegated and vividly patterned clothing worn by the housewives of a dozen different nationalities was rivalled in both colour and design by the wares they were bargaining for.

It was as though the exotic contents of a tropical aquarium had been emptied onto the crude trestle tables, the floor and the wooden-sided pens and tubs: fish of every conceivable shape and colour, the beautiful jostling the sinister—such things as sting rays, hammer-headed sharks, cuttle fish and octopuses.

Competing with it in the matter of colour, while greatly improving on it in the way of smell, were the stalls of the open market where fruit and grain and vegetables were sold. A glowing, aromatic medley of oranges, limes, bananas, coconuts, cloves and chillies; yams, pawpaws, sweet potatoes, piles of green vegetables and flat wicker baskets full of assorted grains.

'What's that you've been buying?' inquired Lash, coming across

Dany standing before a fruit stall with her hands full of greenish-yellow objects.

'Mangoes. I said I only wanted one—just to try. But it seems they don't sell them in ones. Only by the basket, and I couldn't possibly cope with that many. But luckily Seyyid Omar came along, and he——You do know each other, don't you? This is Seyyid Omar-bin-Sultan; he was on the plane with us.'

'Yeah, I remember,' said Lash, shaking hands. 'I'm very pleased to know you. I'm Lash Holden. I don't think we actually met.'

'You're an American?' said Seyyid Omar.

'That's right. The Country of the Future.'

'Of the present, surely?' corrected Seyyid Omar with a faint smile and a slight emphasis on the noun.

'Maybe,' said Lash lightly, and turned to regard Dany with some suspicion. 'Say, you aren't going to start in eating those things right here, are you?'

'Where else?'

'Well, in your bath, I guess. It looks a messy business. And anyway, you can't possibly eat six mangoes.'

'Just watch me.'

'Not on your sweet life!' said Lash; and arbitrarily confiscated her booty.

Seyyid Omar laughed and said: 'It is plain that Miss Kitchell has not yet tried to eat a mango. A plate and a knife are a help. Will you allow me to lend you one? My house is only a short way from here, and I know that my wife would be very pleased to meet you. If you would accompany me, you may eat your mangoes in more comfort.'

Dany threw a quick look at Lash, and Seyyid Omar, intercepting it, made him a slight smiling bow that included him in the invitation.

'Sure,' said Lash slowly. 'We'd be very pleased to. Here—would you mind holding these for a minute?'

He unloaded the mangoes on Seyyid Omar and strode off across between the stalls to where Nigel was assisting Lorraine in the selection of pineapples, and returned a minute or two later to say that that was O.K. and that the others would be going on to the English Club later in the morning, and would meet them there.

'I will drive you over,' promised Seyyid Omar, and led the way out of the market and towards the harbour.

Seyyid Omar's house was in a narrow street that was a cavern of cool shadows slashed by an occasional hot, hard shaft of sunlight: a huge old Arab house, four storeys high and colour-washed in saffron and blue.

A magnificent brass-studded door with elaborately carved lintels and architraves opened into a stone-paved hall and a central court-yard surrounded by rising tiers of pillared verandahs: a house that was almost a duplicate of Tyson's, though larger.

Seyyid Omar led the way up two flights of stairs to a room on the second floor, where there were latticed windows looking out over the old stone-built town of Zanzibar to where the open sea lay blue and dazzling in the morning sunlight.

A white-robed servant brought sherbet, fruit and cigarettes, and their host's pretty wife instructed Dany in the best way—or the least messy one—of eating a mango.

Seyyid Zuhra-binti-Salem was on first sight a character straight out of the Arabian Nights: Scheherazade herself, or one of Blue-beard's lovely wives. A slender, charming, dark-eyed young woman with blue-black hair and a complexion of pale ivory. It was some-thing of a shock to discover that this enchanting creature not only spoke six languages besides her own, but was entitled, if she so wished, to write the letters B.A. after her name.

It altered all Dany's preconceived notions on the subject of 'ladies of the harem' to find that the young wife of an Arab in Zanzibar was infinitely better educated than herself, or, for that matter, than the majority of European women with whom she had so far come into contact.

It proved to be an entertaining, stimulating and surprising visit; in more ways than one. Time slipped past unnoticed while Zuhra laughed and talked of Oxford and Paris and the Sorbonne, and her husband told them enthralling tales of the island, and volunteered to take them that very afternoon, in the cool of the day, to see the underground wells and the ruins of the haunted palace of Dunga.

Conversation was easy and animated until the subject of the two tragedies that had marred the arrival of Lorraine's guests was raised. It was Lash who had introduced it, and his inquiry as to whether there had been any further developments in relation to the death of Salim Abeid was greeted by an odd little pause. Not long enough to be uncomfortable, but nevertheless definite enough to break the pleasant ease that had prevailed during the last hour and a half.

'Ah,' said Seyyid Omar thoughtfully. 'Jembe—"the thin man".'

He did not reply to the question, but asked one of his own. 'Did you know him?'

'No,' said Lash. 'But he was on the same plane out from London. I understand he was kind of well known in your island. A public character.'

'He wished to be one,' said Seyyid Omar dryly. 'That is not quite the same thing.'

'I take it you knew him?'

'Yes. Slightly.'

Seyyid Omar's expressive brown hands sketched a small deprecatory gesture as though he would have preferred to end the conversation, but Lash did not choose to take the hint. He said: 'Tell us about him. Would you have said that he was a man who made enemies?'

'He was a hireling of Moscow—and of Egypt,' said Zuhra gently.

She disregarded another faint gesture of her husband's as Lash had done, and said: 'Oh, he did not call himself that. He called himself a Democrat—which is Soviet double-talk for the same thing. He wished to found a Single Party in Zanzibar. In other words, a dictatorship. With himself, of course, as the dictator. It was very simple. He had a certain following, for there are, everywhere, dissatisfied, embittered or envious people who get pleasure out of tearing down what they cannot build. And also poor people and unfortunate people and ignorant people, who should be pitied and helped, not exploited—but who are so easy to exploit. Here in Zanzibar we have, perhaps, less of such people than in other places; but enough to cause trouble. He will be no loss.'

Lash said casually, watching the smoke of his cigarette: 'I guess it must have been a political murder. Sounds that way.'

Seyyid Omar shrugged. 'Perhaps. It is always a possibility.'

'But you don't believe it,' said Lash. 'Now I wonder why?'

'I did not say so.'

Lash gave him a slanting look. 'Not in words. Why don't you believe it?'

Seyyid Omar laughed and threw up his hands. 'You are very persistent Mr Holden. Why does the death of Jembe interest you?'

'I guess because it interests your local police to such an extent that I have been requested to stay in Zanzibar for a few days. Just while they make some inquiries. I don't know what that suggests to you, but it suggests quite a few things to me.'

Seyyid Omar rose to replenish Dany's glass, and said lightly: 'Yes, I had heard. I too had an—interview with Mr Cardew yesterday. They seem to think that someone must have stopped to speak to Jembe at the airport, and dropped a pellet in his coffee. Myself, I think it would have taken a brave man or an exceedingly rash one, or else a very stupid one, to do such a thing. Think of the risks of being seen! I cannot believe it was as clumsy as that.' He paused to stub out his cigarette, and added: 'Mr Cardew also told me about the unfortunate tragedy that occurred on the night of your arrival. It must have been very distressing for all of you.'

His face expressed nothing more than polite concern, but there was something in the tone of his voice that made Dany wonder if his linking of those two deaths had been deliberate, and she was conscious of a sudden and urgent sense of unease: as though someone had whispered a warning that she had been unable to catch.

'Nigel Ponting told me in the market this morning,' said Seyyid Omar, 'that she had been with Mr Frost's sister for many years—this Miss Bates. That is sad for Mrs Bingham; to lose a friend and a confidante. Nigel has not been so long with Mr Frost; a few years only, I think; but he could probably tell you more about Jembe than I could. You should ask him. If he does not know he will at least invent something interesting.'

Lash grinned. 'Yeah. You're probably right there. Nigel's a mine of gossip. He ought to be run as a syndicated column. But it's your opinion I'm interested in, not his. You belong here.'

'But it is not one of your sayings that the onlooker sees most of the game?' said Seyyid Omar with a slight smile.

'Meaning that you yourself are right out there with the team?' inquired Lash.

Seyyid Omar laughed and helped himself to another cigarette. He said reflectively, reaching for the match box: 'If you really wish for my opinion, I do not think that Jembe's group were either large enough or important enough to put any other party to the trouble of poisoning him. His was merely a splinter group, and though noisy, a thing of no real weight.'

'Not even worth anyone's while to nip in the bud?' suggested Lash. 'Vested interests, large land-owners and the ruling classes are never very anxious to see the seeds of revolution get sprouting.'

'That is true, of course. But then they never believe it can come to anything. Never. And so they do not even trouble to reach for the weed-killer!'

'You're probably right there,' said Lash. 'Which leaves us with what?'

'For a possible motive for the murder of a man like Jembe?' said

Seyyid Omar, striking a match. 'Who can say? Except that as a grave risk was taken, it must have been a strong one. Hate possibly: if it were deep enough and sharp enough. Or money, if it were a large enough sum.'

'Say—three million?' suggested Lash gently.

Seyyid Omar was suddenly very still. So still that he did not seem to breathe, or be aware that he still held a lighted match between his fingers.

It burned down, and he dropped it with a quick gasp of pain and put his foot on the tiny glowing fragment, and Dany stood up hurriedly and said a little breathlessly: 'It must be getting very late. I'm sure we ought to go. What time is it?'

'Just on twelve,' said Lash, rising. 'Yes, I guess we'd better be going. Well, thanks a lot, both of you, for a most enjoyable morning. It's been a great pleasure meeting you, and I hope we'll see more of you. A lot more.'

'I shall call for you this afternoon,' said Seyyid Omar, recovering himself. 'To take you to the wells. And now, if you must go, my car will be waiting below, and the driver will take you to the Club. You will forgive me for not taking you there myself, but I have some things to attend to.'

They took their leave of Zuhra, promising to come again, and went out into the high, shadowed verandah, closing the door behind them. There were no stone jars full of shrubs and creepers here, but in the courtyard below there was a tulip tree and a fountain, and Dany looking down from the verandah edge said: 'Are all the big houses in Zanzibar built like this?'

'To this design?' asked Seyyid Omar. 'No. Very few of them. But it is not surprising that you should ask that, for this house and the one you are living in now were built for the same man, and almost certainly by the same builder. They are probably the oldest houses in Zanzibar. He was a bad character, that old gentleman, but plagued with many wives, so perhaps much may be forgiven him! He came to a bad end, but a richly deserved one—"hoist with his own petard", I think you would say.'

'How?' inquired Dany, intrigued. 'What happened to him?'

'He fell into a trap that he had often laid for others. I will show you. But you must not tell, for it is a secret that very few know. Is that agreed?'

'Yes, of course. It sounds very exciting.'

'I think you will find it so. And instructive.'

Seyyid Omar turned and looked over his shoulder down the length of the verandah, and then down over the balustrade at the storey below. But though they could hear voices and laughter, for the moment there was no one in sight, and he said: 'Quick—while there is no one here.'

He led the way swiftly to the top of the staircase that curved down to the verandah below—a duplicate of the stairs in the House of Shade—and telling them to watch, went to a nearby pillar and stooping down moved something near its base.

There was a slow, soft grating sound; the sound of stone moving on stone; and two of the wide, shallow steps drew back into the wall, leaving a gaping space below the first step so that they were looking down on the stone floor of the verandah, sixteen feet below.

Dany gave a long, helpless gasp that was almost a scream, and Lash caught her by the arm and jerked her back as though he were afraid that she might have walked forward.

Seyyid Omar stooped again, and once more they heard that soft, rasping scrape, and the yawning gap closed as smoothly as it had opened. The steps were in place once more: solid and seemingly safe, and with nothing to mark them from any other steps.

'It is very ingenious, is it not?' inquired Seyyid Omar softly. 'More so than you would think. Naturally I cannot show you, as it is too dangerous, but when it is open, the first step will tilt when a foot is placed upon it: to ensure that the victim will fall head first, you understand. When that happens the steps go back of their own accord—it is all an ingenious matter of weights and balances—and if it is not done, then one can replace it oneself, as I did. I was sure that you would be interested.'

Lash swung round to stare at him, his mouth a tight line and his grey eyes dangerous, but Seyyid Omar returned his look blandly; the pleasant host, drawing attention to an unusual feature of his house for the entertainment of his guests.

'You will understand,' he said with a smile and a shrug, 'why I do not show many people this. It is always so much safer to keep one's own counsel, do you not think? Shall we go down? You need not be afraid. It is quite safe now.'

He led the way, talking polite trivialities, down the curving stairs to the ground floor and out into the street where a huge white car and an ebony-coloured chauffeur waited to drive them to the English Club.

It was a short enough drive, and during it neither Lash nor Dany spoke, or even looked at each other, and it was not until they were standing in the cool deserted hall of the Club that Lash said tersely: 'Did you move her?'

'Yes. I—I didn't think of that before, but she must have been lying under the staircase when I found her. It was dark and I tried to drag her towards my room. That was why it looked as if—as if——'

'As if she'd fallen over the edge,' finished Lash. 'Well, there's the proof, if we needed it. But at least it couldn't have been pinned on you. You couldn't possibly have known about that devilish booby-trap.'

'Yes, I could,' said Dany, her voice a dry whisper. 'Because I'm Tyson Frost's step-daughter, and it would be difficult to prove what I didn't know. You see, it's sure to be in the book.'

'What book?'

'*The House of Shade.* The one Tyson's uncle wrote. Tyson was talking about it at dinner that night, and he said that there were several copies in the house. There's one in my room. It may have been put there on purpose, so that it would look——'

'Business again?' inquired a charming voice from the staircase, and Amalfi was there: wearing a preposterous rainbow-coloured hat of fringed straw, bought at some shop in Portuguese Street and looking, on Amalfi's golden head, as decorative and enchanting a piece of nonsense as ever came out of Paris.

'No,' said Lash shortly. 'Pleasure. I hope we haven't kept you all waiting?'

'For *hours,* darling! We've all been drinking pints and pints of Pimms. Except Larry, who is being all British-to-the-Backbone on luke-warm beer. Did your fascinating Arab friend introduce you to all the luscious lovelies of his harem? Or don't they have them any more? Nigel says he has a quite ravishing wife, and Eddie's simply pining to meet her. But as it seems that she'd got a classical degree, I feel he'd better keep away and keep his illusions.'

Amalfi turned and led the way up to a large high-ceilinged room where the rest of the *Kivulimi* house-party were sitting under whirling electric fans, moodily sipping iced drinks and making no attempt at conversation.

Gussie greeted them with a sombre look and Lorraine with a vague smile, and Nigel said crossly: 'Had I known that you intended to spend the *entire* morning "fraternizing with indigenous person-nel" as I believe it is termed among your countrymen, I should have gone home and sent the car back for you. *I* happen to have work to do, even though some people have not. I hope we can go now?'

He sulked the whole way home, but both Dany and Lash had too much on their minds to notice the fact, and Larry Dowling, who was the fourth passenger in their car, took one long reflective look at Dany and also relapsed into silence.

They found Tyson in good spirits but still as averse as ever to discussing any form of business, and on hearing that Lash and Dany were accompanying Seyyid Omar on a sight-seeing expedition that afternoon, he instantly announced that it was a damned good idea and that they could all go: it would give him a pleasant spell of peace and quiet.

'Working, darling?' inquired Lorraine solicitously.

'No. Sleeping! And I shall do it a damn sight better without people chattering and nattering all over the house. Last time Gussie was taken to the wells she was eight—and screamed the place down, as far as I remember! Time she saw 'em again.'

So they had all gone. Lash, Dany and Gussie Bingham in Seyyid Omar's great white car, and Nigel, Amalfi and Larry Dowling in one of the *Kivulimi* cars driven by Eduardo.

They stopped by the roadside in a forest of palms to drink coconut milk from the ripe nuts; explored a copra factory and saw a clove plantation; and leaving the cars in a small dusty side road, followed a narrow, winding track across a no-man's land of scrub and rocks and dried grasses, and came suddenly upon a hole in the ground where a flight of worn stone steps led down into darkness.

'I don't think I like the look of it all,' said Gussie, shuddering and clutching nervously at Dany's arm. 'Suppose we fall into the water and drown in the dark? Hasn't anyone got a torch?'

No one had. But there were matches and cigarette lighters, and Seyyid Omar assured them that there was not the least danger of anyone drowning, and that women from the little village where they had left the cars came here daily to draw water.

The steps led down into a huge underground cave where the light barely penetrated and smooth water-worn rocks sloped sharply downwards towards, not wells, but a spring of water or an underground stream that came up out of the darkness and disappeared again into a black rock tunnel.

Holding cautiously to each other so as not to slip and fall on the rocks, they ventured down to the edge of the spring, their voices echoing strangely through the shadowy vault, and Seyyid Omar told them that the water was supposed to be the continuation of a stream that fed one of the great lakes in Africa, and flowing on far under the sea bed, bubbled up briefly here in Zanzibar; to vanish again into the rock and the Indian Ocean.

'I'm sure it's wildly interesting,' said Amalfi, 'but let's go, shall we? I think it's dark and spooky and altogether rather gruesome, and personally, the sooner I get out of the place the better. What happens if the roof falls in?'

There was an unexpected note of shrillness in her voice, and instantly everyone looked up at the dark curve of rock overhead, and moved closer to each other, their feet slipping on the steep rock-face.

Eduardo said soothingly: 'The roof will not fall in, *cara*. It is only a big cave. There are thousands of such places all over the world. But if it does not please you, we will go at once.'

'Yes, do let's,' said Gussie, shuddering. 'It's giving me claustro-phobia.'

Within a few minutes they were out in the open air again. But it was not until two hours later, as the cars drew up before the gateway of the House of Shade, that Dany discovered that the white suede bag that she had carried had been neatly slit open with a sharp knife or a razor blade, and everything in it had gone.

17

'I will see that it is reported at once to the police,' said Seyyid Omar.

He had invited Dany, Lash and Gussie to dine with him at a restaurant in the town, but Gussie having refused on the plea of tiredness they had dropped her at the House of Shade, and driven back to Zanzibar city under a green and lavender sky that was already freckled with pale stars.

'No, for goodness sake, don't!' said Dany hastily. 'The police have had enough of us. Besides, it isn't worth making a fuss about. There was nothing of any value in it. Only a handkerchief and a pair of sunglasses, and a powder compact and a lipstick. That sort of thing. And possibly about eightpence in English pennies!'

'It must have been lifted by one of those picturesque characters in the village near the wells,' said Lash. 'Darned disappointing for him. Though I guess his lady friends will get a load of fun out of smearing themselves with lipstick. It's a shame about the bag, though. I'll get you another one tomorrow. Souvenir of Zanzibar.'

The city by night was very different from what it had been in the heat of the day, for the cooler air had brought all Zanzibar out of doors, and there were gay crowds strolling under the trees in the public gardens and along the sea front, while every rooftop and *baraza* appeared to have its family party.

Music and laughter, the tuneful cry of the coconut seller, and a continual rub-a-dub-dub of drums made a gay, enchanting medley of sound, mingled with the more normal noises of any Eastern city.

'Is it some special day?' asked Dany. 'A feast day, or something?'

'No. What makes you think that?'

'Everyone seems so gay. Listen—can't you hear them? They all sound very happy.'

'It is a happy island,' said Seyyid Omar, smiling. 'And when we feel gay we laugh—or sing; or play the *kinanda*—the mandolin. Or beat a drum. And, as you hear, we feel gay very often. It is a thing worth keeping, I think. Yes—very well worth keeping. But there are times when I become afraid.'

Lash turned his head and regarded him attentively. 'Afraid of what?'

Seyyid Omar slowed the car to a stop under the scented canopy of an Indian cork tree that leaned above a high, white-washed wall, and sat back, resting his slim brown hands upon the wheel: his face faintly illuminated by the dashboard lights.

He said slowly: 'I will be frank with you, Mr Holden. I think that you know something about a sum of money: a very large sum of money that many people have searched for for a great many years, though few have really believed in its existence. That vast legendary treasure that Seyyid Saïd, the first Sultan, was rumoured to have buried at Bet-el-Ras.'

Neither Lash nor Dany made any answer, and Seyyid Omar presumably translated that silence as admission, for after a momentary pause he said: 'I myself did not believe that it had ever existed or was more than a tale or legend. But not so long ago there arose a rumour; a whisper that it was fact and not fiction.'

He shifted a little; a small uneasy movement, and his hands tightened on the wheel. 'There are certain people in this island who need money, a large sum of money, to buy power at the next election. We have an old proverb that says "I will change my religion and the colour of my coat, but thou must pay," and there are, alas, always votes—too many votes!—that can be bought for cash where they cannot be acquired from conviction. For money will always speak with a louder voice than any politician. One of those who wished to buy power travelled out with you from London, and is now dead. Jembe. But there are others, and they still need money.'

He was silent for a moment or two, and then he gave a quick shrug of his shoulders and drew a cigarette-case from his pocket.

'You do not smoke, I think, Miss Kitchell? You will not mind if we do?'

He offered the case to Lash with a pleasant smile and as the car filled with the fragrant smell of Turkish tobacco, leant back against the seat as though the conversation had been concluded and he had no more to say.

Lash said lightly: 'Then I guess a lot of guys are all set for a sad let-down. Why are you telling us this?'

Seyyid Omar laughed. 'You are not really stupid, Mr Holden, are you.'

It was an assertion, and not a query, and Lash said: 'Not that stupid, anyway! But I don't see what this has got to do with me, or with Miss Kitchell.'

'Don't you? Well, perhaps you are right. All the same, it is just as well to be warned.'

'Warned?' Lash's voice had a sudden sharp edge to it, and Dany felt his lounging body stiffen. 'That's quite often a fighting word where I come from. What exactly are you warning us about? Or have I got it wrong and is this a threat?'

'Ah, no!' Seyyid Omar held up a deprecatory hand. 'You misunderstand me. Why should I threaten? I am merely offering advice.'

'O.K., let's have it.'

'If there is any truth in this legend of the hidden treasure, and should—anyone, have any knowledge of where it may be found, it would, I think, be wise for that person to take such knowledge to His Highness the Sultan, whom God preserves. Or to the police.'

'Why? Because to possess that knowledge is dangerous?'

'That, of course. To be the possessor of such knowledge might prove very dangerous indeed. But there is a much more important, though less personal reason for speaking of it. To prevent it falling into the wrong hands. Such a sum of money can be a dangerous thing when used for evil. And it would be used for evil. Of that you can be sure. There is a curse on it.'

Lash said impatiently: 'You don't mean to tell me that you believe that old wives' tale?'

Seyyid Omar looked at him and laughed. 'So you have heard of it? Yes, I believe it, though you will not. But then you are a young man, Mr Holden, and from a very young country. You still have a great many things to learn—particularly about the East. One of them can be summed up best in words that have been worn threadbare from use, but which cannot be improved upon: "There are more things in heaven and earth," Mr Holden, "than are dreamed of in your philosophy"!'

He turned to Dany with an apologetic smile and said: 'I am sorry, Miss Kitchell. This cannot interest you. We will go on to my Club, where we will talk and drink and you will meet my friends. They will be far more entertaining than I.'

He refused to say anything further on the subject or to answer any questions, and took them to the Arab Club, where they sat out under the stars and spent a pleasant hour. And afterwards they dined on strange foods in a little restaurant in a quiet back street, and then drove to the sea front outside the Sultan's palace, to listen, in company with a light-hearted collection of His Highness's subjects, to the Sultan's band playing—of all things—excerpts from Gilbert and Sullivan and *The Belle of New York.*

The lights were still on and the house-party still up when they arrived back at the House of Shade, for it was barely half past ten. But Seyyid Omar would not come in with them, and watching the tail-lights of his car dwindle and fade Lash had said thoughtfully: 'That guy knows a heck of a lot more than he's telling. A heck of a lot! The question is, who is he really pitching for? Is he on the side of the angels, as he makes out, or is that just a bluff? He wouldn't be the first well-heeled *aristo* to go back on his class and join the fellow-travellers!'

Dany said in a low voice: 'He was talking to that man Jembe at the airport in Nairobi. I saw them.'

'When? Where? You didn't tell me.'

'I didn't think of it. There have been so many other things. Worse things.'

She told him then, and Lash said meditatively: *'Hmm . . .* It sounds a screwy set-up all round. Maybe he did the job himself. Slipped this Jembe a slug of cyanide because he's after the number one spot in the Dictator Stakes himself. He may fancy himself as the local Hitler. The Führer of Zanzibar.'

' *"King of the Earth and of Time",'* quoted Dany under her breath.

'What's that?'

Dany flushed and apologized. 'I'm sorry. I was thinking of something. A Persian inscription that he translated for me yesterday. I can imagine him dreaming of being that sort of king—and of restoring that sort of kingdom.'

'And wanting the cash to start it off with. Maybe.'

'But it can't be him. At least, he can't be the one who stole that letter or map or whatever it was off me, because then he'd know where the stuff was, and he doesn't. But he may think I've still got it. Perhaps he even thought I might carry it about with me. I never thought of that!'

'Thought of what? What are you talking about?'

'My bag. You said it must have been slit open by one of the

Arabs in the village, but it wasn't. I've been thinking about it, and none of them came within yards of me.'

Lash gave a short laugh and said: 'Listen, honey. If you're thinking that anyone can drive a car with one hand, and at the speed that guy drove, while slitting a passenger's purse and abstracting its contents with the other, you're nuts! And anyway, you weren't even sitting next to him this afternoon. Gussie was.'

'I didn't mean it was done in the car,' said Dany impatiently. 'I told you, I've been thinking. It was all right just before we got to the cave, because I put my sunglasses into it, and I remember stuffing them down on one side of the handkerchief.'

'So what?'

'So there was only one place where anyone could have cut that bag open without my knowing it. In the cave. It was dark in there, and we were all huddled together and grabbing at each other to keep from falling. But there wasn't anyone else down there except— except us.'

Lash stopped abruptly in a patch of pale moonlight and said: 'Are you sure? That it couldn't have happened anywhere else?'

'Yes. Quite sure. That's why I didn't say anything more about it. I was sorry that I'd said anything at all, but I was so surprised when I saw it that the words jumped out. But when I'd thought a bit I realized that it could only have been done while we were in the cave, and that no one who was there would do it just to steal a compact and a lipstick and perhaps a little money. So it must have been someone who wanted something special, and thought that I might carry it with me. It *must* have been!'

'Yes,' said Lash slowly. 'The same bunch again. Six of us who were on the London to Nairobi run, and two who were on the last lap to Zanzibar. Gussie and Elf and Larry Dowling; Nigel and Eduardo and our smooth Arab pal. None of them in the least likely to go in for lifting lipsticks and petty cash. I guess you're right. Someone thinks you've still got it.'

It was a verdict that was to receive swift confirmation.

The remainder of the house-party were playing *vingt-et-un* in the dining-room, but Lash excused himself from joining them and went off to the guest-house, and Dany went up to bed—to discover that in her absence someone had searched her bedroom as thoroughly, though far less untidily, as her room as the Airlane.

Every drawer and cupboard had been gone through, and even the sheets and blankets had been taken off her bed and replaced;

though not very neatly. A box of face powder had been probed with a pair of nail scissors and a jar of cleansing cream with a nail file: face tissues had been pulled out of their container and roughly stuffed back again, stockings unrolled and a locked suitcase forced.

'But I haven't *got* it!' said Dany, speaking aloud into the silence as though she were addressing that unknown searcher. The sound of her own voice startled her even more than the evidence of her disarranged possessions, and she turned and ran from the room.

The lights were ablaze in every verandah and in the courtyard, and there were no shadows on the staircases: but she tested every step, her hand pressed to the wall and her heart in her mouth. She could hear voices and laughter from behind the closed door of the dining-room, and she tiptoed past it and out into the quiet garden.

The moonlight and black shadows were not as frightening as the house had been, and she ran lightly along the twisting paths between the flower-beds and the scented bushes of roses, jasmine and Lady-of-the-Night, and skirting the shallow pool with its stone birds, reached the steep flight of narrow steps that led up to the guest-house on the wall.

The lights were on but Lash did not answer her knock, and she opened the door and went in. The little sitting-room appeared to be empty, and supposing Lash to be in the bedroom she was about to call out to him when a sound made her turn sharply.

Lash was standing on the narrow stone window ledge, holding on by the frame, and she could only see his legs and part of his body. The rest of him was outside the window, and he appeared to be attempting to pick a spray of the purple bougainvillaea that hung down over the wall of the house.

He swung himself in again and jumped down on to the floor, brushing dead leaves out of his hair, and said: 'For the love of Mike! —what are you doing here?'

Dany, who had been about to ask almost the same question, abandoned it in favour of more urgent matters. She said breathlessly: 'My room's been searched again. Every bit of it. Like last time, only——'

'Same here,' said Lash briefly. 'Take a look around.'

Dany looked about her and became aware of much the same mild disorder as her own room had contained, and stooping with a cry of dismay she picked up a white fluffy ruin that lay half concealed under the edge of the divan. The late Asbestos; that washable and unburnable cat, his stuffing ruthlessly removed and his green glass eyes stonily reproachful.

'All flesh is grass,' said Lash. 'And all cat's too, judging from the look of it. Yes, someone's frisked this joint in a conscientious manner.'

'Did he get in by the window?'

'I don't know. All I know is that he hasn't missed much. Even my soap has been broken in half to make sure that I hadn't hidden anything in it. Most of the stuff has been put back in place; but not, as you see, very tidily. Here, stand yourself a slug of your step-father's Scotch. At least that has been left alone—I hope!'

He poured out some of the whisky from the bottle that Tyson had left there on the morning of their arrival, and having smelt it, tasted it with extreme caution.

'Seems O.K. No cyanide. At least, not noticeably so. I'd better try it out for effect first. Here's to the witch doctor, deceased, who put a curse on that cash deposit. He certainly knew his onions!'

He drank, and having put down the glass turned to look out through the open window for a moment or two, and then said: 'Well, I guess this puts one suspect out of court. Pal Omar couldn't have pulled this one. He was with us the whole evening, so he's out. It was one of the others. If only we could find out who knew the trick of that staircase it would help a lot, but there would appear to be at least four copies of that damned book in the house, and you were right about it. It's all there: tucked away back in a musty maze of architectural drawings. It took some finding, but I ran it to earth. Anyone could have stumbled across it and put it to good use.'

He sat down on the window-seat, his reflective gaze still on the moonlit seascape outside, and said slowly: 'I'd like to know more about this Larry Dowling. A lot more. And I'm willing to bet that the cops will too, just as soon as Tyson's letter turns up at Scotland Yard and they move in on us.'

Dany said flatly: 'It isn't Larry. It couldn't possibly be Larry.'

'Why not? There's something phoney about that guy. I've known a good few newspapermen in my time, and he doesn't ring true.'

'But he's not a newspaperman! He's a feature writer. And——'

'What's that got to do with it? He's after a story—Tyson's. So why doesn't he get on with it? If he's done any writing since he arrived, I'm Ernest Hemingway! Then there's Gussie . . .'

Dany subsided suddenly on the divan, nursing the wreck of Asbestos. She said tiredly: 'Yes. I thought of her too. Because she would have known so many things that—that whoever it is must have known. But I don't believe it. I just can't see her climbing fire-escapes and things like that. And she was fond of Millicent.'

'How do you know that? None of us can really know anything much about anyone else. We can only go by what we see. I guess I thought I knew plenty about Elf. I meant to marry her, heaven help me!—and me, I'm an Old World throw-back to my respected Scotch ancestors when it comes to saying "I do." It's not going to mean to me "Until Alimony and the Other Man doth us part". No, I thought I knew more about Elf than any of the other guys had done: that none of them had understood her as I did—all the old routine. That'll show you!'

His laugh held more than a trace of bitterness, and turning his shoulder to the window and the moonlight, he said: 'Millicent Bates may have been rubbed out because she was the active partner in some little scheme of Gussie's. She may have done that job in London, then caught on to it later that Gussie had shot the family lawyer, and taken a poor view of it. And then there's the Latin lover . . .'

Lash rose and poured himself another drink, and broke off to remark conversationally: 'Your step-father is one hell of a host. He thinks of everything. Gin, soda-water syphon, bitters, Scotch. Look at 'em all! Say, who does he think I am? It's a libel. Have one?'

Dany shook her head, and he brought his drink across and sat down in an arm-chair facing her; holding the glass between both hands and looking down into the golden liquid intently, as though it were a crystal ball in which he could see the future—or the past.

'The Signore Marchese di Chiago,' said Lash softly. 'Apart from racing cars he has quite a reputation as a fast guy. And a weakness for blondes. He's known Tyson, and your mother, for a good many years, and this isn't his first visit to Zanzibar. He's stayed in this house before. And if there's anything in gossip—largely Nigel's I'll admit!—he's had several affairs of the heart that his family have managed to bring to a grinding halt just short of the altar, and it's a cinch that they'll queer this one too if they can. But maybe this time it's gone deeper. Maybe he's got to have Elf, come hell or high water. She can have that effect on some people. There was one guy —Douglas something—who took a header out of a top storey window when Elf threw him over. But Eduardo isn't the kind that likes taking "No" for an answer. He comes from a country where a male with a title gets all the breaks, and if he wanted anything badly enough I guess he wouldn't stop at much to get it. But Elf is a strictly cash proposition—from both angles. His and hers. No lire—no Elf. Maybe we haven't paid enough attention to Eduardo and his fiery Southern blood.'

Lash gave the contents of his glass some more practical attention, and lit a cigarette, and Dany watched him anxiously. She wished that she did not feel so frightened, and that she could look at it all as Lash appeared to be doing: as an interesting problem of the 'Who's Got the Button?' variety. But looking about the small room with its silent evidence of an unknown searcher, she was aware of nothing but an acute sense of danger.

This was neither a game nor a nightmare from which she would awake. It was real. It was the springing of a trap that had been set over ninety years ago, and which had caught her when she had called on a prim, elderly, country solicitor to fetch a letter written by a man who had died back in the last century.

Lash said thoughtfully: 'It could be Tyson,' and she came back to the present with a sharp jerk.

'*Tyson?* What are you talking about?'

'This——' said Lash, gesturing with his cigarette at the ill-concealed disorder of the room. 'That——' he indicated the sad remains of Asbestos. 'And your room too. He may have wanted to satisfy himself that one of us hadn't double-crossed him. If you remember, he did once suggest that you might have held on to the contents of that envelope yourself. It could be Tyson. Or Ponting. In fact, why not Ponting? He was in Nairobi. You know, that's quite an idea—except that I guess he'd have made a far neater job of it if this had been his lily-fingered handiwork! He could have been pressed for time, of course, but somehow I can't see that elegant, willowy tulip leaving the place in this sort of mess. If dear Nigel had been conducting "Operation Frisk" I've a strong feeling that we wouldn't have known that anything had been touched. And yet it's got to be someone in the house, who knew that we wouldn't be back for quite a while, and——Say! Wait a minute!'

He put his glass down and came suddenly to his feet. 'Why didn't I think of that?'

'Of what?' demanded Dany, her voice sharp with anxiety.

'Seyyid Omar! He knew damned well just how long we'd be away. He could even be the original weevil in the woodwork. Yes . . . why not? He's a big shot in this island. He'd be the only one who could easily plant his servants—or even his relatives—in the house. And who would know?'

Lash took a quick turn about the room and came back to stand in front of Dany.

'Now look. Supposing he got all his information from a servant in this house—that silent, slippered guy who slides in and out with the coffee and takes the letters to the post. Suppose he can read English after all, and that he read Tyson's letters to this Honeywood, and possibly Lorraine's to you as well, and passed on the information? Omar doesn't go after Emory's letter himself, but he sends a stooge—Jembe—who gets rid of Honeywood but fails to get the goods. Jembe has another try at finding it when he frisks your room at the Airlane, and so he——'

'Steals my passport,' put in Dany. 'But that *can't* be right! What would be the point of stopping me leaving the country?'

'Ah, I've thought of that one: it occurred to me once before. So that you'd mail it. The letter. Who's to say they haven't got a pal planted in the post office here, as well as in the house? It wouldn't be difficult if you were Seyyid Omar. For anyone else, yes. But not for him.'

'I don't think——' began Dany doubtfully.

'No one's asking you to! I'm developing a theory. Now, this Jembe finds that you are on the plane after all—thinly disguised by dyed hair and glasses. So what does he do? He has another shot at stealing the thing in Nairobi, fluffs it, and has to report failure to the boss—our friend Omar, who meets him at Nairobi West. You actually saw 'em talking.'

Dany said: 'Yes. But why should Seyyid Omar want to poison him? It doesn't make sense!'

'I'm not so sure. After all, you've arrived and you've still got the goods. Jembe has shot his bolt and is of no further use—and probably knows too much anyway! So the best thing is to get rid of him and leave the rest to one of these poker-faced guys in white nightgowns who seem to be all over the house, and who would probably skin their grandmothers alive for ten dollars down and ten to follow. For all we know any one of them may easily turn out to have majored in modern languages and picked up a coupla degrees on the side. Who's to tell?'

Dany said: 'Yes . . . I suppose so. But you've forgotten something. There are two quite different people in all this. The one—or the ones—who are still trying to find that letter and who think I've still got it, and the one who *has* got it. If Seyyid Omar hasn't got it, who has?'

Lash's face changed and became wholly expressionless. He looked down at the cigarette he held, and after a moment he flipped it away through the open window and said lightly:

'Yes—who? Certainly not our friend the Seyyid, if he was the guy who picked your pocket in the cave and so neatly got us out of the way while one of his tarbooshed minions went through our rooms.'

Dany said: 'But if you really think he's the one behind all this, why did he show us how Miss Bates was killed?'

'To scare us, I guess. Make us lose our nerve—and our heads.'

Lash finished his drink and tossing the empty glass on the sofa, said: 'I think a short talk with your step-father is indicated. I don't think he's got any idea of what a hornet's nest he stirred up, and I intend to bring it home to him—if I have to use a sledge-hammer to do it!'

He looked down at Dany's white face and smiled a little crookedly. 'It's a helluva mess, honey, but you don't have to lose your nerve.'

'I haven't any left to lose!' admitted Dany ruefully. 'Not an atom!'

Lash laughed and reached down his hands to pull her to her feet.

'Nuts, Miss Kitchell! Momentarily mislaid, perhaps, but never lost. And I don't know if that aunt of yours ever warned you against visiting in bachelor's apartments at this hour of night, but I believe it is frowned upon in the more prudish circles of society. So in about two minutes time I am going to take you back to your room.'

Five minutes later he said reflectively: 'You know something?— This looks as though it might become a habit.'

It was, in fact, just over fifteen minutes later that he finally escorted Dany back to the house.

18

There had been no chance for any private talk with Tyson on the following day, for he had slept late, and then in response to a message delivered to the house, had gone off deep-sea fishing with a friend: a visiting peer who had arrived unexpectedly, and only that morning, in a private yacht.

'Really, *too* exasperating!' complained Nigel. 'We have a positive plethora of work on hand, but will he get down to it?—will he hell! The *rudest* wires from the publisher: one can only hope that the operators can't read English. And he *swore* he'd have a talk with Larry this morning. Have you been able to pin him down to anything yet, Holden?'

'Nope,' said Lash lazily, and turned over on his stomach.

They had all been bathing, and were now basking on the hot white sand on the beach below the house, acquiring what they hoped would be an even tan and not a savage case of sunburn.

'Who's been sending rude cables?' inquired Lash. 'Sounds like my respected Pop.'

'No. Our British publishers. So *testy,*' said Nigel.

Gussie looked up from anointing her legs with sun-tan oil and said: 'I thought you were supposed to be doing some sort of deal with Tyson about the Emory Frost papers, Mr Holden. A business-with-pleasure visit. Though I'm afraid it can't have been very pleasant to . . . Oh, dear, I didn't mean to be tactless.'

'You weren't,' Lash assured her. 'And you're dead right about those papers. I am hoping to persuade your brother to sign on the dotted line. If I can get him to sit still that long. But he's a difficult man to pin down, and right now I feel too idle to chase after him.'

'Where's your American hustle?' demanded Gussie with a bright smile.

Lash yawned. 'I guess I shed it somewhere short of Naples—

385

along with my raincoat. Right now I prefer basking to business. But don't worry: I'll get round to it sometime—no kidding. What are we doing the rest of today?'

'Nothing,' said Nigel firmly.

'Swell. That sounds right up my street.'

'Nonsense!' said Gussie briskly. 'We're all going shopping and sight-seeing in the town. It's all arranged. And then we're having tea at the hotel, and Lorraine said something about a moonlight picnic somewhere along the shore.'

'Holy Moses!' murmured Lash devoutly.

'Didn't you, Lorraine?' said Gussie, ignoring the interruption.

'Yes, Gussie dear. But only for anyone who wants to do any of it. You don't have to, you know.'

'I can see no point in coming to a place like Zanzibar if one is going to lie about and sleep all day. One can do that at home.'

'But not on lovely white beaches in the sun,' murmured Amalfi. 'Nigel, why is this sand white instead of yellow?'

'Coral, you pretty ignoramus. And pumice I expect. You know, I found out something totally fascinating the other day. Do you know where all those silly little pumice-stones that you find all along the beaches come from? Krakatoa!'

'And where,' said Eduardo, 'is Krakatoa?'

Nigel shuddered and put a hand over his eyes. 'The educational standards of the drinking classes would appear to be universally and *utterly* inadequate. Krakatoa, my decadent barbarian, was a volcano in the Sunda Straits—that's between Java and Sumatra in case you didn't know—which blew itself to bits in 1883 with a bang that no A-bomb will ever equal. And these are the bits. They bobbed along in the currents and got stranded here. I can't say I ever used pumice-stone before, but I do now. It *enchants* me to feel that I'm scraping off my ink stains with Krakatoa!'

Eduardo said: 'You ought to write a guide book, you clever little thing, you. Me, I never read them.'

'You, you never read anything if you can help it!' said Nigel crossly.

'Now that is really *very* unjust of you, Mr Ponting,' put in Gussie, wagging an admonitory finger at him. 'And the Marchese was only joking. Why, he was reading all about the house on the very first afternoon we were here. My grandfather's book: *The House of Shade.* Weren't you, now?'

'Was I?' said Eduardo with a shrug of his bronzed shoulders. 'I do not remember. Perhaps I may have picked it up to glance at it. If I did I am quite sure I must have put it down again very, very quickly!'

'Not at all! You are too modest. You were so absorbed in it that you did not even hear me come into the library; and I assure you that there is *nothing* to be ashamed of in being a bookworm. I love a good book myself.'

'The point,' said Nigel, 'is that *The House of Shade* is probably the worst book ever written, and certainly the dullest, and one doubts if any book-lover, worm or otherwise, could bore their way past page two.'

'Then why,' demanded Amalfi petulantly, 'are we boring on about it now? Are you by any chance conducting this shopping and sight-seeing tour this afternoon, Nigel?'

'I am happy to be able to answer promptly,' said Nigel. *'No!* Why? Were you intending to join it?'

'I think so. As long as we don't start until half-past three or fourish. There was a shop in Portuguese Street that had the most divine Indian jewellery, and the man said he'd get in some more to show us today. So Eddie and I rather thought that we'd go along and take another look.'

'Not forgetting Eddie's cheque book,' said Nigel waspishly.

'Nigel darling, you *are* being cross and catty this morning!' complained Lorraine plaintively. 'What's the matter? It's such a lovely day, yet everyone seems to be jumpy and on edge instead of just relaxing peacefully.'

'We are relaxing peacefully,' said Lash, with his eyes shut. 'Just take a look at us.'

'No, you're not. You may look as though you are, but I can feel the atmosphere simply buzzing with jangled nerve ends. I suppose it's all this business of Honeywood and Jembe. And then poor Millicent——'

Gussie Bingham rose abruptly, and snatching up towel, sun-tan oil and sunshade, walked quickly away across the beach and up the short rocky path that led to the door into the garden.

Amalfi sat up, and removing her sun-glasses, said: 'Now you've upset your dear sister-in-law. Too bad. Lorrie darling, be a sweetie and *don't* let's get back onto that subject again.'

'But why be ostriches,' demanded Lorraine, aggrieved.

'Why not? I've nothing against ostriches. In fact I'm all for them if they prefer burying their heads in the sand to poking their beaks into drearily depressing subjects. Are you really taking us in to Zanzibar this afternoon?'

'Yes, if you like. It's Gussie really. She seems to want to keep doing something: so as not to have to think about Millicent, I suppose. Gussie hates being upset. As we're going in, you can all go and sign your names in the vistors' book at the Palace and the Residency. It's rather the done thing.'

'You have my permission to forge mine,' said Lash.

'I shall do no such thing. You'll do it yourself—and like it!'

'O.K., O.K.,' said Lash pacifically. 'Anything you say. I'll go.'

They had all gone. With the exception of Nigel who insisted that he had work to do, and Dany, who had unexpectedly fallen asleep in a hammock in the garden.

'Let her sleep,' said Lorraine, restraining Lash who would have woken her. 'It will do her more good than trailing her around Zanzibar city in this heat, and she doesn't look as though she's had much sleep of late. Nigel can keep an eye on her. She'll be all right. No, Lash!—I won't have her wakened.'

She had spoken with unexpected decision, and taking Lash firmly by the arm, had gone out to the car.

Lorraine had had few opportunities to see her daughter in private after the day of her arrival, for Tyson had warned her against treating Dany with more intimacy than would be due to the secretary of one of her guests. But she had seen her alone in the earlier part of the afternoon, and in the garden: Dany having gone out after luncheon to sit in the hammock, and Lorraine happening to catch sight of her on her way to pick some roses as a peace-offering for Gussie.

'Darling how nice to get you by yourself for a bit,' said Lorraine, abandoning the roses and joining her daughter on the hammock. 'It's so tiresome, never being able to talk to you without looking over my shoulder. I'm afraid all this is being simply horrid for you, baby, but Tyson says it will only be for a day or two, and then the police will sort it all out and we needn't go on pretending that you are the Kitchell woman. Thank goodness!'

She sighed and swung the hammock with one foot, and after a silent interval began a little diffidently: 'Darling . . . about Lash—
—' And then did not seem to know how to go on.

Dany said, startled: 'What about him?'

'You rather like him, don't you, darling?'

Dany blushed to the roots of that distressing dyed hair, and

Lorraine, observing the unfortunate colour effect, said abstractedly: 'No—quite the wrong shade for you. It *is* a pity.'

'Mother, what are you talking about?' demanded Dany.

Lorraine threw a hunted look over her shoulder. 'Darling, *don't!* Suppose anyone were to hear you?'

'There isn't anyone anywhere near,' said Dany. 'What were you saying about Lash?'

'Well—I felt perhaps I ought to say something, because it did rather occur to me that you perhaps liked him more than—let's say, than a secretary should. And after all, he is rather an attractive creature, and . . .'

She made a slight helpless gesture with one hand, and once again did not finish the sentence.

'And what?' said Dany defensively.

'Well, darling. I happened to go out on to the terrace last night to fetch a magazine I'd left there, and I saw you two coming back to the house. You looked very—friendly.'

Dany said nothing, and Lorraine gave a small unhappy sigh. 'I'm afraid I'm a useless parent,' she said. 'The trouble is, I don't seem to know how to behave like one. But I do feel that as a parent I ought to say something. About Lash, I mean. You do know that he was to have married Elf—Mrs Gordon—don't you?'

'Yes. You told me in your letter. And so did he.'

'Oh, well; that's something.' Lorraine sounded relieved. 'But darling, you will be a little careful, won't you? You see, you've met so few men so far. That's been my fault, I suppose: I've been horribly selfish and not really remembered how quickly time goes. I was always going to be a good mother one day, but you always seemed such a baby. And now suddenly you've grown up. But you don't want to go losing your heart to the first attractive man you meet. In fact it's the greatest possible mistake! It's not that I've got anything against Lash, but . . .'

'Which means that you have,' said Dany coldly.

'No, I haven't, baby. Really. It's just that Tyson says he's had a lot of girls, and—well, he simply *adored* Elf, and men do do such silly things on the rebound: snatch at admiration from the nearest person who offers it, to bolster up their wounded egos. It doesn't mean anything. I like Lash, but he's as wild as a hawk and I'm not sure I'd trust him as far as I could throw a grand piano. Elf can manage that type; but when one is young and romantic and naïve, one is apt to take things—and people—at their face value. So—so you will just think a bit, won't you, darling? I mean, you don't have to believe everything he says, just because he's gay and good looking and has a fair share of charm. Take it all——'

'With a pinch of salt?' interrupted Dany bitterly. 'I know!'

'I was going to say "in your stride",' said Lorraine reproachfully. 'But salt will do. After all, it improves so many things, doesn't it darling? Oh—here comes Larry. He's rather a charmer, isn't he. I'm glad we asked him to stay—though Tyson's being a bit sour about him. He says we ought to watch out, because Larry's the type that all women trust on sight and end up falling for, and that all the best bigamists and confidence tricksters have been that kind of man. You know, it's astonishing how catty men can be about each other when —Hullo, Larry. Are you looking for anyone?'

'No,' said Larry, smiling. 'Just looking around. This is a fascinating old place you've got here, Mrs Frost. That wall at the end of the garden is a good ten feet thick if it's an inch. There must have been guard rooms or stables in it once. Were they bricked up?'

'I expect so,' said Lorraine vaguely. 'If you're interested, I'm sure you'll find all about it in old Barclay's book. Are you going to the city with us later on?'

'Certainly; if you'll take me. Is there any chance of your husband joining us?'

'He's meeting us at the hotel for tea,' said Lorraine, rising. She turned and smiled at Dany. 'I'll leave you in possession of the hammock, Miss Kitchell. You ought to put your feet up and have a rest. We shan't be leaving for at least an hour.'

She took Larry Dowling away with her down the winding path between the orange trees and the roses, and Dany watched them go and thought of Lash; and of what he had said only last night about Amalfi Gordon. He had not sounded as though he were still in love with her. But had it just been bitterness and sour grapes?

You don't have to believe everything he says . . .

Was she just 'young and romantic and naïve'? An inexperienced school-girl, taking things and people at their face value? How was one to know? How did one ever learn? The hard way? Had Lash only made love to her because he was snatching at the nearest bit of admiration to soothe his sore ego? Trying to show Amalfi that he did not care?

For the better part of an hour Dany lay in the hammock, staring up at the blue chips of sky through the thick scented canopy of leaves and flowers over her head, her mind so fully occupied with personal problems that she never once thought of Mr Honeywood, or of Jembe, or of Millicent Bates—or of murder. And then, without warning, sleep reached out a light finger and touched her eyes, and she did not even hear Lorraine and Lash when they came in search of her.

It was close on five o'clock when she awoke, and the shadows had lengthened in the garden and the heat had gone from the day. The house was very quiet, but she found Nigel in the drawingroom, sipping China tea and reading a week-old London newspaper.

He dropped the paper on the floor and came to his feet when he saw her, but Dany, glancing down, found her eye caught by familiar words: 'Man Murdered in Market-Lydon.'

Nigel, following the direction of her gaze, laughed and said: 'You have caught me red-handed, Miss Kitchell—soaking myself in crime on the sly. I blush for it. *Too* fish-and-chip. But to tell you the honest truth, after all that sordid chit-chat the other night I felt quite intrigued. That Bates woman went on and *on* about it, until one couldn't help wondering what she was getting at: if *anything,* of course! But one felt, somehow, that there *was* something . . . Do sit down and have some tea. Indian or China? The China is divine. Tyson has it sent direct from some aromatic old Mandarin friend in Canton.'

Dany accepted a cup of pale yellowish-green liquid that smelt of dried flowers, and listened a little abstractedly to Nigel's light, melodious voice lilting on and on in a nonstop monologue. It was, she discovered, quite easy to listen to Nigel and think of something else. And then, with shocking suddenness, she was jerked out of her detachment.

'Now *do* tell me,' said Nigel, 'who you *really* are? I won't tell a *soul*. Of course one can *guess*. But it *has* been intriguing me so. Deliciously mystifying!'

Dany gaped at him and dropped her cup.

'*Tiens! Tiens!*' said Mr Ponting, leaping gracefully to his feet and repairing the damage. 'I *am* sorry. Entirely my fault. But honestly, *dear* Miss Whoeveritis, you simply *couldn't* be Ada Kitchell—not by any stretch of the most *elastic* imagination. And you have no *idea* how flexible mine is!'

Dany said stonily: 'Why couldn't I be?'

'Well darling—your *voice!* Utterly Nancy Mitford. Not a whisper of the New World in it. And what woman *ever* wore spectacles if she didn't need them? Why, those are just plain glass! And—well, not to labour the point, a little blonde bird told me that *actually* there is a rumour flying about to the effect that poor Ada is at this moment incarcerated in the Islington Isolation Hospital with mumps.'

'Mrs Gordon!' said Dany involuntarily. 'I might have known it!'

'Well, frankly, darling, I *do* think that you might. However, don't let it worry you. It probably isn't true, and anyway I won't breathe a syllable. Now do tell me: I'm *dying* to know. *Why?* And of course, *Who?* . . . though of course one can make a very accurate little guess at *that* one, can't one?'

'I don't know. Can one?'

'But of course! There is really nothing subtle about our sweet Lorraine, and when she hurries about the house removing every single photograph of her darling daughter, one *does* tend to ask oneself a few shy little questions. Not that there were *many* photographs. Lorraine is not what one would term *madly* maternal. But there were just one or two. And where are they now? "Gone with the wind that blew through Georgia?" But she forgot that there is a liberally illustrated volume lying around, all about explorations in Central somewhere, which includes a handsome photograph of her first husband; and I fear I was inquisitive enough to take a tiny peek. You really are very like your father, you know. The resemblance was quite remarkable as *soon* as one saw you without those spectacles and that distressing fringe. You forgot them the other night.'

Dany got up and went over to the window, and stood with her back to the room, tugging nervously at the edge of the curtain and staring blindly out at the garden. Her first feeling of panic had subsided, and now she was only conscious of a lessening of tension and a certain degree of relief. Being Miss Kitchell was a strain, and it was going to be very restful to be Dany Ashton again, and to stop pretending—and being frightened. But she wished that Lorraine were here. Or Tyson, or Lash. Someone to advise her as to what she should say and how much she could say.

Had everyone seen through her? Had they all guessed? Not the passport officials at all events! and they were the only ones who really mattered—except for Larry Dowling, who must not guess.

She said: 'Has Mrs Gordon told everyone?'

'About Ada? Oh, I don't think so. She may have whispered something into Eduardo's lovely brown ear, but he won't be in the least interested; and I'm quite *sure* she wouldn't tell anyone else. Not Gussie anyway. And *certainly* not our intrusive Mr Dowling.'

Dany turned quickly. 'Why do you say that? Are you sure?'

'That she wouldn't have twittered to Larry? But my dear, of course not! the man writes for the newspapers, and if he got his predatory little pen on to this, Tyson and your lovely Mum would be distinctly testy, and Amalfi wouldn't like being shown the door at all. You're quite, *quite* safe there. At least, for the time being. I suppose it's all bound to come out sometime or other, but, with any luck, after our scribbling little friend has got his interview—and enough material to libel the lot of us—and left.'

The thought of Mr Larry Dowling appeared to divert Nigel's interest into other channels, for he frowned and said: 'I simply cannot understand what Tyson is playing at. Why doesn't he give the man an interview and a basin full of facts, and send him off? Why ask him to the house and keep him hanging about?—putting him off, and putting him off. Really, *very* vexing. I wish you'd tell me what he's up to. I suppose you know?'

'I don't know anything about Mr Dowling,' said Dany hastily, evading the question.

'And how much do you know about Mr Holden, I wonder?' said Nigel, and gave a malicious, knowing little giggle. His face was both mocking and sly, and Dany said hotly: 'What do you mean?'

Nigel looked at her with his head on one side like some large, sleek, wary bird—a secretary bird. Then he put a finger to his lips and rose swiftly and silently and went quickly and very quietly to the door that led into the hall, and jerked it open.

The whole manoeuvre bore such an exaggerated air of secrecy and stealth that Dany quite expected to see a crouching figure disclosed, kneeling with its ear to the keyhole. But the hall was empty, and having satisfied himself that there was no one there or in the courtyard, Nigel returned to his chair looking slightly self-conscious.

'Forgive the amateur theatricals, but I would *so* much prefer not to be overheard. I take it that you don't really know much about the merry Mr Holden? apart from the usual things—the fact that he was head over heels about the bewitching Amalfi, and got pipped at the post by Eduardo (there ought to be a law against these Latins, don't you agree?). But otherwise, has he spilled the beans? Are you, in the distressing jargon of the age, "hep"?'

Dany said uncertainly: 'I don't know what you mean.'

'Don't you? Hasn't it ever struck you that there is something a little—odd about Lash Holden?'

'No. Why "odd"?'

'Well, "peculiar" if you prefer the word. And don't start jumping down my throat, I beg! As you see, I have been the *soul* of tact, and refrained from probing into *why* you feel it necessary to masquerade as his secretary. But hasn't it ever struck you as odd how *very* conveniently he always turns up at just exactly the right moment? Just like one of those *painfully* competent G-men. Or would it be more accurate to say, like some really expert card-sharp at work? It all looks *so* casual and simple; "Hey presto!—and here's the Ace of Spades; now how on *earth* did it turn up there? *What* an astounding piece of luck!" But is it?'

Dany came back to her chair, but she did not sit down: she held on to the back of it and stared at Nigel, white-faced:

'What are you trying to say?'

'Nothing, darling. I'm merely trying to *hint*. So much safer I always think, don't you? You see, Lashmer Holden, Senior, is a very old friend of Tyson's—an intimate friend, one might say. There isn't anything about Tyson or his house or his affairs that he doesn't know, and he also has the reputation of being one of those forthright characters whose motto is "Never Give a Sucker an Even Break".'

He saw Dany start, and said: 'Why the surprise? What have I said?'

'N-nothing,' stammered Dany. 'It was just that——What were you saying about Lash's father?'

'Only that Pop Holden is what is technically termed a tough egg. He sticks at nothing and he has of late been edging on to queer street.'

'On to——?'

'Queer Street, darling. Don't be all *ingénue*. I believe he only just squeezed out of being indicted before some committee on a charge of un-American activities. Toying with the Commies. Nothing was ever *proved* you know, so of course one is being *dangerously* libellous even to whisper it. But everyone knew; and I believe it cost him simply thousands of dollars in bribes and what-have-you to keep it out of the courts. We were over there just when it was boiling up, and I believe he tried to borrow off Tyson. *Most* embarrassing. That was why one couldn't help wondering if Tyson hadn't rather naughtily refused to play, and so Junior decided to put the screw on. Very filial, if he did.'

Dany frowned and looked bewildered: 'I really don't know what you're talking about, Nigel, and I think you'd better stop.'

'Blackmail, darling,' explained Nigel, ignoring the request. 'Is that his little game? Has he involved the Daughter-of-the-House in some complicated piece of jiggery-pokery, and is he now telling Step-pop to pay up, or he spills it all to the Press? Tyson's really *very* well supplied with stocks and shares and lovely money, and quite *devoted* to your charming Mum. He'd probably pay and pay. Could it be that, I wonder?'

'No, it couldn't!' said Dany stormily. 'I've never heard such ridiculous nonsense! There isn't a word of truth in it!'

'Now, now, *now,* darling——! Don't get so excitable. You're as bad as Eduardo. Oh well—it was just an idea. But one couldn't help wondering if he didn't have *some* little game on. One is sorry for him, of course. The family name teetering on the edge of the dustbin, the family fortune down the drain, and the glamorous girl-friend (who between you and me must have got wind of the cash deficiency!) abandoning ship for a coroneted Italian cutter. But what is he here for? Just what is he after? That's what I'd like to know. Call me inquisitive if you like—and how right you will be!'

Dany said stiffly: 'You know quite well why he is here.'

'Oh, but you're wrong. I don't. Has he joined the G-men or the F.B.I. perhaps? Is he, if one may be forgiven a winsome little pun, playing International M.I. Fives? Americans are becoming *painfully* Middle-East conscious these days. They can think of nothing else but Spheres of Influence and Rocket Bases. (And women of course —there's still simply *nothing* like a dame! Especially if she looks like Elf!) Or is he playing some sly little game of his own, and if so, what?'

Dany's hands tightened on the chair-back and she said furiously: 'You know perfectly well why he came here! He came to discuss the publication of the Emory Frost papers—and—and for a honeymoon in Zanzibar.'

'That's what *he* says. But the whole question of the Frost papers was discussed *ad nauseam* with his dear Papa less than six months ago in the States. Of course they hadn't been released from the lock-up then, and they might not have been worth publishing. But a couple of letters would have settled the matter. He wasn't invited here, you know. He suggested it himself. And who ever heard of anyone combining a honeymoon with business? Even the most dollar-adoring Yank would shy like a steer at that one. They may worship cash (and who doesn't!) but they are also simply *saturated* with sentiment about such things as Momma and Marriage Bells. That's what makes it all *so* intriguing. Surely you can see that?'

'No!' said Dany stormily. 'I can't. I think you've just got a—a fertile imagination.'

'My dear, *too* right! And at the moment it is positively *fecund.* The wildest conjectures came sprouting out of the soil as soon as I saw the dear boy turning up here minus a honeymoon and plus the phoniest American secretary that it would be possible to conceive in a month of provincial repertory matinees! One was *instantly* reminded of Crippen.'

'*Crippen?* Why? How . . .' Dany suddenly discovered that the chair-back was an inadequate support, and releasing it, sat down in the chair instead with a feeling that her legs were made of something that closely resembled half-cooked macaroni.

'*Surely* you've heard of Dr Crippen, dear? He brought off quite a tidy little murder, and then lost his head and skipped out of the country with his secretary, who was faintly disguised as a boy. It popped into my head almost as soon as I saw you. Well, perhaps not *quite* as soon as that, but as soon as I began to feel curious. I confess I was *thrilled.* Delicious shivers all up and down the spine! I said to myself "Now is he escaping from the law, and *where* has he buried the body of poor Ada—the real one?" But that of course was before I'd read the papers.'

Dany said in a brittle, breathless voice: 'What do you mean by that?'

Nigel gave his little tittering laugh and looked down at the newspaper that lay on the floor beside his chair, and then up again at Dany:

'Suppose you tell me that one?'

Dany said jerkily: 'I don't see why I should, but—but I will. If you want to know, Mr Holden happened to be staying at the same hotel as I was in London——'

'So convenient,' murmured Nigel.

'Do you want me to go on?'

'But of course, darling. I am *enthralled.* And I promise I won't interrupt again.'

'His secretary, Miss Kitchell, had developed mumps, and I had —had lost my passport, and hadn't time to get another before the plane left. So he suggested I should use hers. For—for a lark.'

' "Ha-ha"!' said Nigel. '*What* a cut-up the boy is! He must have lots in common with those Northern 'varsity students who think up all the sparkling and sophisticated pranks for the installation of a new Rector. But seriously, darling—*did* she have mumps? Or was it just sleight of hand?'

'I don't——' began Dany.

'The Ace of Spades,' explained Mr Ponting with a trace of impatience. ' *"Hey presto—why,* what *a bit of luck!"* That sort of trick. So simple really; if you know how it's done.'

'But there wasn't any trick about it,' protested Dany. 'Of course she had mumps.'

'How do you know? Because you are a nice, unsophisticated Innocent who believes everything she is told?'

The words were an echo of something else that Dany had heard that day. Lorraine had said almost the same thing. And she too had been talking about Lash——

Nigel said: 'So easy to *say* something like that. And almost as easy, one imagines, to see that you lose your passport! You did say that you'd lost it, didn't you? How—if one may ask another intrusive little question? It isn't a thing one just casually drops on the nearest counter, or leaves in the loo.'

'Well, it was—I mean, I . . .'

Nigel tittered again. 'You seem confused. But it was probably all *too* simple. Like the card trick. You palm one passport, and Hey presto!—here's another! *What* a happy coincidence. See?'

'No, I don't! And I don't believe a word of it. And anyway, why should Lash—Mr Holden—do anything like that? Why bother to bring me here when I was coming anyway?'

Nigel shrugged his shoulders and flung out his hands in an affected gesture: 'Well, darling—I *did* advance a little theory about that, didn't I? But as you trampled on the poor thing *most* harshly, I won't risk making it again. Perhaps he just wanted to keep you under his eye. And why not, indeed? Though I must admit that as the honeymoon was off it was perhaps a *teeny* bit tactless of him to tag along after his ex-love and the new Italian model, and one would have imagined that he would cancel the trip. Oh, well, I expect it will all be as clear as Vichy water one of these days—and equally innocuous. It's much more fun wondering, isn't it? I *adore* mysteries! Have another cup of tea?'

He peered into the tea-pot, clicked his tongue regretfully and announced that there wasn't any and that the hot water was cold. 'Just as well, really, as it's almost drinking time. I'd no *idea* it was so late and I'm dining out tonight with some enchanting Parsees. They serve the most delicious curries, which one can never resist but which play havoc with the digestive juices. Still, better that than eating a picnic meal by moonlight, which is sheer hell. Sandy sausages and mosquito-repellent getting into every glass. I *do* pity you all.'

He rose gracefully. 'Will you forgive me if I leave you to entertain yourself a bit while I hurry off and change? And don't worry, dear Miss Kitchell. Your guilty secret is *quite* safe with me. I promise I won't even drop the teeniest hint to anyone. Cross my heart!'

He retrieved the fallen newspaper, folded it carefully, and tucking it under his arm, tripped away, leaving Dany alone in the empty drawing-room with the tea cups and some most unpleasant thoughts.

19

Lash. *No . . . It isn't possible!* But it was. Unthinkable, but not impossible.

Lash . . . She must speak to him. She would ask him . . .

You don't have to believe everything he says.

But she had believed everything. Why? . . . Because he was Lash, and she had fallen in love with him. Because he was almost the first attractive man she had ever met, and any girl in love for the first time is convinced that this is the real thing—this is for ever. And find that it is neither.

'That your first kiss?' 'Yes, how did you know?' *'I've been around.'*

She hadn't stopped to analyse the significance of that reply, but she did now. It meant that he had made love to a good many other girls: and kissed a good many women. He would know just how to handle them. How to string them along.

She would, she realized, have been perfectly prepared to believe that anyone else might commit murder: Gussie, Seyyid Omar, Eduardo di Chiago, Amalfi Gordon and perhaps even Larry. But not Lash.

She had worked out ways and means and theories, and had heard Lash do so, in the case of other suspects: but it had never occurred to her for one moment that Lash himself might be one. And yet he was surely the most obvious one. He had even pointed it out himself—and she had rejected it: brushed it aside instantly and with impatience.

Was that why he had done so? To ensure that she would reject it? A form of bluff? And yet—he could have done everything . . .

Dany dropped her head into her hands, pressing them over her eyes and trying to think back. To think clearly.

His father knew Tyson probably better than anyone else, and Tyson might well have written to him about the discovery he had made among the Frost papers, and also told him what he intended to do. Lash could have gone down to see Mr Honeywood, and been seen by Millicent, who would not have recognized him, or he her—until later.

He had booked a room at the same hotel as Dany, and the rest would have been easy enough to contrive. He might even have been on the fire-escape or the balcony outside her room, and seen her leave it, and walked quietly across the room, and shut the door behind her. Then, taking her own key off the dressing-table, left by the window and come up the stairs, pretending to be the worse for drink.

He would have had plenty of time to search her room while she was waiting in his, and, when he could not find what he was after, to remove her passport and plant that gun. And now that she came to think of it, he had turned up right on cue, when she found it. *'Hey presto and here's the Ace of Spades! now how on earth did it turn up here?' That sort of trick!* . . . And it had been Lash's idea that she come with him in the place of Miss Kitchell.

Had Miss Kitchell really had mumps? Or had she merely been informed at the eleventh hour that her presence was not required—because her passport was?

But there had been that night in Nairobi, and the man who had meant to chloroform her. That could not possibly have been Lash. He had been sound asleep on the sofa. No, the whole thing was nonsense! A wild figment of Nigel's jackdaw imagination, that did not stand up to a moment's sober examination.

But . . . but there were two people who wanted that letter. Or two groups of people. One who was still looking for it, and the one who had it. The sealed envelope that bore Emory Frost's initials had been taken out of her coat pocket, the seal broken and the letter abstracted. And it could only have been done by one person—Lash Holden.

'No—no—*no!'* said Dany, aloud and desperately. 'He wouldn't. He didn't. I don't believe it and I won't believe it!'

Who else? whispered a small, remorseless voice in her brain. How else? You don't have to believe everything he says . . .

Dany stood up quickly and began to walk up and down the darkening room, arguing with herself: trying to remember; trying to persuade herself that someone else could have taken it. But there was no way out. No loophole of escape. It had to be Lash.

It was just conceivably possible that a skilful pickpocket could have stolen the whole thing; chiffon scarf and all. But to take it out, remove the letter and return it, was utterly impossible. But Lash could have done it with ease. Either while she was in her bath that morning, or when she had given him her coat to hold on the plane.

'No!' said Dany again, speaking pleadingly into the unheeding silence. But even as she denied it she knew that the answer was 'yes', for she had remembered something else——

Lash standing on the window-sill of his room last night, reaching up into the mass of bougainvillaea that grew above it. Lash's face when she had said: 'If Seyyid Omar hasn't got it, who has?' His face had changed and become blank and expressionless, and he had looked away from her and would not meet her eyes. Yes, Lash had got the letter. She was suddenly and wearily sure of it. He had probably carried it in his pocket, and been startled by the realization that pockets can be picked, when he had seen her ruined handbag, and had decided to find a better hiding place for it.

What did he want it for? If, as Seyyid Omar had said, there were men in Zanzibar whose ultimate object was a dictatorship under Soviet domination, was Lash a Secret Service man whose task was to prevent this? Or did he want Seyyid Saïd's treasure for himself?

Jembe . . . Millicent Bates . . . It could have been Jembe, who had meant to search her room at Nairobi, and Lash could have known it, or guessed it. Millicent had said that she never forgot a face, and Lash had said that she had died because she talked too much. Lash's father almost certainly possessed a copy of *The House of Shade,* and the note that had lured Millicent to her death had been written on Ada Kitchell's typewriter.

'A rakish heel who could hook the average woman with the ease of a confidence trickster getting to work on a frustrated small-town spinster . . .' Someone had said that—about Lash. Was she, Dany, a frustrated small-town spinster? Lorraine too had suggested that she was young and inexperienced and naïve—and too romantic!— and Nigel had begged her not to be so *ingénue.* So perhaps she was all those things.

A tear crept down Dany's white cheek and she brushed it away impatiently. Crying would not help her, but there was at least one thing that would. She could make sure. She could go to the guest-house and look for Emory Frost's letter. Not now, because it was getting late and the others would be back soon. But as soon as another opportunity offered and she was certain of Lash being out of the way.

The cars returned not five minutes later, and as Dany had no desire to see or speak to anyone at the moment, she ran up to her room and locked the door, and only opened it when Lorraine knocked on it to ask if she were all right, and had she had a good sleep?

'You know, darling,' said Lorraine worriedly, observing her daughter with some anxiety, 'you're looking very washed out. Or perhaps it's that hair. I really do think we should——'

'Mother,' interrupted Dany tersely, 'did Tyson ever write to Lash's father about that letter of Emory Frost's? The one I fetched from Mr Honeywood?'

'Darling, I've no idea. He may have done—they've always been such bosom buddies. Why?'

'Nothing,' said Dany quickly. 'I only wondered if—if anyone else knew about it.'

'I don't think so. Except of course that someone must have known, mustn't they? Really, it's all very worrying and upsetting, and I often wish—Oh, well—don't let's talk about it.'

She sat down on the dressing-table stool, and looking at her charming reflection said: 'I look a mess. I wonder if there's time for a bath before we start off on this picnic? No, I suppose not. We didn't mean to be back so late, but Tyson brought a friend of Elf's along to the hotel. It seems he flew to Mombasa only the day after you, and joined George Wallingborne's yacht, and they got here late last night. Tyson's been out fishing with them. A man called Yardley, Sir Ambrose Yardley. And if you ask me, he's only come here because of Elf. He should have been doing something or other in Khartoum, but he only stayed there about a day and a half, and followed her down here. I suppose I should have asked him back to the house: he was angling for it. But Eduardo was being rather rude and silly about the whole thing, and I really felt that I could not cope with any more dramas. And anyway, we're all lunching with them tomorrow.'

She dabbed her face absently with some of Dany's powder, rubbed it off again, and rose with a sigh.

'Don't put on anything too nice darling, because we're having a picnic supper on the beach. Tyson's idea. He's gone all Boy Scout and wants to build a drift-wood fire and fry sausages. *Ugh!* I can't think of anything much less alluring, but he's feeling energetic and all hearty-and-outdoor. Don't be too long, will you baby?'

The sky was rose-pink and apricot with sunset and the house was full of shadows by the time Dany returned to the drawing-room. She had expected to find the entire house-party assembled there, but there were only two people in the room: two people standing so close together that for a moment, in the dim light, they had looked like one.

They moved quickly away from each other as they heard the soft sound of Dany's sandalled feet on the thin Oriental rugs, and Amalfi Gordon came towards her, her face and her slender figure dark against the wash of sunset that burned beyond the french windows. She passed Dany without speaking, and went out of the room and across the darkening hall, her high heels clicking on the polished stone.

Lash said: 'Why the old-fashioned look, bambina? Did you think you'd walked in on a Grand Reconciliation scene? Because if you did, you've got it wrong. I'm not as polygamous as I look.'

Dany said coldly: 'I can't see that it is anything to do with me if you feel like hugging Mrs Gordon.'

'Now wait a minute! I was not hugging her!'

'No? Well that's what it looked like to me. Where has everyone else got to?'

'I don't know, and I can't say I care. Tell me what you've been doing with yourself all the afternoon? I didn't like the idea of leaving you on your own, but Lorraine said to let you sleep, and that Nigel would keep an eye on you. Did he?'

'Yes,' said Dany briefly.

She turned to leave the room and Lash came quickly after her and caught her arm. 'What's the matter, honey? You aren't really sore at me, are you? Look, I can explain——'

'Can you?' said Dany bleakly. 'But then I don't have to believe your explanations, do I?'

Lash's fingers tightened painfully on her arm and he jerked her round to face him, and then released her abruptly as someone came quietly through the open door behind her.

'Hullo,' said Larry Dowling, his casual, pleasant voice in marked contrast to the quietness with which he had moved. 'Am I late? Where is everyone?'

'In the garden, I guess. Why don't you go and look for them?' snapped Lash.

'Yes, let's,' said Dany thankfully. 'I'll come with you, Larry.'

She caught at his arm and they went out past Lash through the french windows and on to the terrace, where they were joined a few minutes later by Gussie and Tyson.

Dany had hoped to find some opportunity to speak privately to her step-father, but it was obvious that she was not going to get it tonight. Tyson had spent a strenuous day fishing and drinking, but it did not appear to have exhausted his energy. He herded his guests down to the shore and along the wet sands in the last of the sunset, and having selected a suitable spot in a little bay less than a quarter of a mile from the *Kivulimi* beach, set them to collect drift-wood for a fire.

'He gets these hearty fits at intervals,' explained Lorraine in a resigned aside. 'Very exhausting while they last, but fortunately they don't last long. You shall all have a lovely smoked salmon and caviar meal tomorrow to make up for it. But I do think this view is rather heavenly, don't you? Look at those fantastic rocks. And that dhow out there—isn't it enchanting? I wonder where it's bound for? Hejaz or Samakhand . . .'

Gussie said tartly: 'They'd have some difficulty in navigating her there, unless she's amphibious!'

'Oh, I didn't mean literally. Her cargo, perhaps. But those are such lovely names.'

As the sunset faded and the sky turned from pink to lilac, lavender and green, the firelight gained strength and lit up the weird shapes of the coral rocks and the fronds of pandanus as though they had been stage scenery. And presently the moon rose, lifting into the quiet sky like some enchanted Chinese lantern and filling the night with magic.

The sausages, as Nigel had predicted, were both sandy and underdone; but honour and Tyson being satisfied, Lorraine had produced an excellent selection of cold foods that had been carried down to the beach by one of the house-servants. And later, when the remains had been carried back again, they played what she called 'suitable moonlight music' on a portable gramophone, and explored along the shore.

Tyson and Lash went off armed with flashlights and fish spears to peer into the rock pools further down the beach, and Dany, watching them go, suddenly made up her mind that this was as good an opportunity as any to visit the guest-house. They would obviously be occupied for at least half an hour, and it would not take her much more than ten minutes to get back to the house, where there would be only the servants, who at this hour would have retired to their own quarters. She would be back again before anyone had troubled to notice that she had gone, and she could not endure the thought of another night—or even another hour—without knowing.

Gussie was discussing cookery with Lorraine, while Larry Dowling was lying on his stomach on the sand and putting records on the gramophone, and Amalfi and Eduardo had strolled away along the beach in the wake of Lash and Tyson. It would be quite easy.

Dany stood up, brushing off sand, and went across to murmur in her mother's ear, and Lorraine said vaguely: 'Yes, of course. But why not just behind a rock, darling? There are lots about.'

Dany withdrew, flushed and indignant, and once out of range of the dying firelight began to walk quickly, hurrying without running, until at last she reached the rocks that bounded one end of the *Kivulimi* beach, where she paused briefly to look back. But she could no longer see the glow of the drift-wood fire or any of her fellow picnickers, and the only thing that moved in the moonlit world were the ghostly little crabs, the lazy, lapping tide, a soft breeze and the lateen sail of an idling dhow.

Once on the far side of the rocks the *Kivulimi* beach lay before her, quiet and deserted, and Dany ran across the white, open sand and up the short rock path to the door in the garden wall.

The heavy wooden door with its flaking paint and iron nail heads creaked as it opened, and the sound was suddenly daunting. Dany stood still under the stone archway, listening intently, but she could hear nothing more than the soft breathing of a little breeze that whispered among the leaves of the garden and rustled the palm fronds.

There were no lights on in the house, but the white-washed walls and the window-panes caught and reflected the moonlight so that it gave the impression of being brightly lit and awake and watchful. An impression so strong that for a moment Dany found herself wondering if it was still looking seaward, as it had in a past century, for the sails of ships—merchant ships, pirate ships, whaling ships, ships from Oman and the dhows of the slave traders. *Then I'll go sailing far, off to Zanzibar . . .*

Dany caught her breath in a small sob, and looking resolutely away, turned to follow a path between the orange trees, skirting the pool and keeping parallel to the wall until she reached the flight of steps that led up to the guest-house.

The top of the wall was bright with moonlight, but the steps were in black shadow, and Dany was half-way up them when she heard the gate creak again.

She froze where she stood; listening with every nerve strained and alert for the soft crunch of crushed shell and coral that would tell her that she had been followed. But it did not come, and as the gentle breeze lifted the fringe on her forehead she remembered that she had left the gate open, and the breeze would have swung it on its hinges. And turning again she ran up the remaining steps, careless of noise and only aware of the necessity for speed.

The guest-house too was in darkness, and Dany turned the handle of the door, and pushing it open, felt for the switch.

The light seemed startlingly garish after the cool white night outside, and she turned it off again; realizing that she did not need it, for it was not here that she meant to search. She did not even glance about the room, but went straight to the window and looked out and up.

The bougainvillaea swung down from the roof edge in a mass of blossom whose colour had been almost lost in the moonlight, and it was not going to be nearly as easy as she had thought to stand on the narrow window-ledge and reach up.

The wall itself was built up on a little rocky cliff, and there was a drop of at least thirty feet from the window-ledge on to more rocks. Looking down on them Dany felt a cold qualm of vertigo, but it was too late to draw back, and she might not get a chance like this again.

She set her teeth, and having climbed cautiously on to the narrow ledge, holding desperately to the wooden frame, found that the worst part was turning round to face the wall. But once that was accomplished the worst was over, and with her back to the horrifying drop below her she found that she could look up into the mass of creeper above her with comparative ease.

She reached up and felt among the leaves, but could find nothing; and then her wrist touched a round edge of stone. There was a gutter some distance above the window; a narrow curve of stone, choked with dust and dead leaves and jutting out a few inches from the wall in the shadow of the overhanging creeper.

Dany found that she could just reach into it, and probing with shrinking fingers, fearful of snakes or spiders, she touched something that was not a dead leaf. And knew with a dreadful, sinking despair that she had been right. It was Lash who had taken the letter.

She drew it out from its hiding place and looked at it in the moonlight. A man's white linen handkerchief wrapped neatly about something that could only be a small folded piece of paper.

She felt a little sick and oddly light-headed, and for a moment she swayed against the wall, pressing her cheek against the rough stone, and afraid of falling. Her left hand, gripping the windowpane, felt cramped and numb, and she knew that she must make the effort to get down and back into the room while she had the power to do so. She could not stand here, silhouetted against the lamp light, where anyone passing on the beach below could look up and see her.

She bent her head and her knees, and sliding her left hand down the frame, stepped down on to the low window-seat.

And it was only then, looking down at her scarlet linen sandals on the gaily coloured cretonne cover of the window-seat, that she remembered that she had turned out the light only a few minutes ago. But it was on now.

Dany stood quite still: unable to move or breathe. Unable even to lift her head.

Then someone had seen her leave, and had followed her. Someone had come up the steps and into the guest-house; but standing on the window-ledge with the rustling of the creeper in her ears she had not heard them. And in the shock of finding the thing that Lash had hidden she had not even noticed that the light had been switched on, or known that someone was standing in the doorway, watching her . . .

She lifted her head very slowly and stiffly, as though fear had frozen her muscles, and looked into the cold eyes that were watching her from across the room.

20

'There now! I *knew* you'd lead me to it if I gave you the chance,' said Nigel Ponting in a self-congratulatory tone. 'Really, *too* simple.'

He tripped across the room and held out a thin, elegant hand. A hand as curved and predatory as the claw of a bird of prey.

'That's a good girl.'

He twitched the handkerchief from between her nerveless fingers and unwrapped it, disclosing a small folded square of yellowed paper which he opened and favoured with a smiling, comprehensive glance. 'Yes, indeed. The goods—as advertised. How very satisfactory! And now, darling, if you'll just stay right where you are——'

Dany shrank back and clutched at the sides of the window as he came towards her. 'Nigel—what are you going to do? You can't tell them! Not yet. He—there must be some explanation. He must be—be in the F.B.I., or something like that. You said so yourself! He *couldn't* be a murderer. He couldn't! Don't tell anyone. Give him a chance to explain first. Or—or to get away . . .'

'What *are* you babbling about, dear girl?' inquired Nigel. 'Don't tell who what? Give who a chance to explain?'

'Lash. Oh, I know he took it, and I suppose it looks bad, but it can't be. And even if it were, I don't want the police to get him, whatever he's done! Nigel, please——!'

Nigel stared at her for a long moment, and then burst out laughing. 'My dear girl——! Oh, this is *too* delicious! Do you mean to say that you still haven't got it? Well, well! don't they teach you anything at these expensive schools? Perhaps it's a pity to disillusion you. But why not? It isn't your American dreamboat whom the police would want to interview. Alas, no. It would be yours truly—Nigel P.'

'*You?* But you can't—It couldn't be——'

'Oh, but it could. It was! I read that peculiar document of Emory

Forst's (your respected stepfather is not aware that I possess a duplicate key to his locked box!) and also the letters to Honeywood. Even —I blush for it—your mother's to you. It was all laughably simple. Then all I had to do was to ask for a holiday, slip off to Kenya, and get a dear friend to flip me across to Egypt where there are simply *dozens* of nasty men who will do anything to annoy the Great White Raj.'

'Egypt——' repeated Dany in a dazed, foolish whisper. 'But Mr Honeywood wasn't——'

'*Tch! Tch!*' said Nigel reprovingly. 'You don't really suppose I stayed there, do you? No, they merely fixed me up with the necessary papers and popped me on to the plane for Naples, where I was met by a fascinating character; quite unscrupulous and *madly* talented. He used to be top make-up man in a film company before the war—and *what* a loss to the trade! You simply wouldn't have recognized me boarding the London plane a couple of hours later. I made a ravishing Signora. Too *chic!* I wasn't *nearly* so alluring on the return journey; but perhaps just as well, as we had some *rather* impressionable Oriental potentates on board. Direct to Cairo that time: and by a different line of course—you've no idea how efficient the whole set-up is! The staff work was quite beyond praise. As slick as a Sputnik. One was *most* impressed.'

A sudden hysterical wave of relief swept over Dany, drowning all other considerations. 'Then it wasn't Lash! It was you—it was you!'

Her knees buckled under her and she collapsed on to the window-seat, weak with tears and laughter.

'Of course it was,' said Nigel with a trace of impatience. 'Who else would be likely to know everything that went on in this house? And the whole affair would have gone off swimmingly if only you'd done what you were told. Really, *very* tiresome of you! I had it all worked out. Honeywood knew me, and he'd have had the packet ready and handed it over like a lamb when I explained that Tyson had sent me for it because you couldn't come. But you had to change the time and go and see the old fool in the morning instead, and mess everything up. So vexing and unnecessary.'

He frowned at the recollection, and then his face cleared and he laughed. 'Ah well——!' "All's well that ends well". And now, darling, as we haven't got all night——'

Dany scrubbed her eyes with the back of her hand and looked up. And then, suddenly, terror was back. A crawling, icy terror that widened her eyes until they were dark pools in her white face.

She had been too stunned by shock and relief to take in more than a fraction of what Nigel had said, but now, staring up at him, she realized that he had been saying things that he would never have said unless . . . unless . . .

Her mouth was so dry that it was an effort to speak at all, and when the words came they were only a harsh whisper:

'What . . . are you going . . . to do?'

'Only give you one little push,' said Nigel gaily. 'It's a thirty-foot drop, and on to rocks, so it ought to do even better than that cunning little staircase trick. And Holden will be able to tell them just exactly how it happened. You were standing on the sill to reach into his private *cache* and you must have slipped and fallen. Like this——'

His hands caught her, forcing her back over the low sill, and then the dreadful numbness left her and she began to fight, twisting and clawing. But the ledge was low and her back was to the uncurtained window, and there was nothing to grasp at but wood and stone.

Her finger-nails scraped and broke and her screams were no more than harsh, gasping breaths: she was no match for Nigel's five-foot-nine of lean bone and muscle, and those thin white hands, that had once felt so limp, were astonishingly strong and curiously smooth—as though they were encased in silk. They gripped her shoulders, pulled her forward and then jerked her head back violently against one side of the window embrasure so that it hit the stone and stunned her.

A savage pain seemed to slice its way through her skull: coloured lights shot before her eyes, and the strength went out of her. She heard Nigel's little giggling laugh, but it seemed to come from a long way off, and to be cut off suddenly and sharply. And then the grip on her shoulders relaxed and she was falling . . . Falling down miles of echoing darkness from the window . . . No, not the window . . . Down a well. An underground well. Deep and cold and black, where there was black deep water in which she would drown . . .

The water filled her eyes and nose and mouth, choking her, and something burned her throat and choked her afresh. She struck out wildly, struggling to swim and to keep her head above water, and her hand touched something and clutched at it frantically.

A voice that hurt her head abominably said: '*Hi!*—look out! Let go of my ear!' And she opened her eyes with an enormous effort and found herself looking up at Larry Dowling.

Mr Dowling, who also appeared to have been in swimming, was

tenderly massaging the side of his head and holding a dripping water jug, the contents of which he had evidently poured lavishly over Dany.

She stared up at him, blinking the water out of her eyes and wondering why he was there and where she was. Nothing made any sense except that, somehow, he had saved her from drowning.

'Are you all right?' inquired Larry Dowling anxiously.

Dany attempted to give the matter her consideration, and after a moment said childishly: 'I'm wet.'

'I'll say you are!' said Mr Dowling fervently, taking the words in an uncomplimentary sense. 'You must be mad! Going off like that on your own when——'

'You're wet too. Did you jump in with all your clothes on?'

'I fell into that bloody bird-bath—that's why I didn't get here a lot sooner. I'm sorry about that. But at least you're not dead. It was a near thing though—*phew!*'

He took out a sopping handkerchief and mopped his wet forehead and Dany said: 'I think I'm going to be sick.'

'Here——! don't do that,' said Mr Dowling, alarmed. 'Try another swig of this.'

He reached for a bottle that had been standing on the floor beside him, and lifting Dany's head poured a liberal quantity of some fiery liquid down her throat.

Dany gasped and choked, but the stuff warmed her stomach and helped to dull the excruciating pain in her head. Larry Dowling, having laid her back, took a long pull at the bottle himself and said: 'Gosh, I needed that!'

He put it down, and lifting Dany, carried her over to the divan and lowered her on to it carefully. 'Are you feeling any better?'

'I don't know. What happened? Was I going to drown?'

'Drown? No. He was stuffing you through the window, and in one more minute——However, don't let's think of that. Can you stand up?'

'Who was stuffing me through a window? I don't know what you're—*Nigel!*'

Dany attempted to rise and once again a blinding wave of pain and nausea lashed out at her.

'Here, take it easy,' urged Larry Dowling anxiously. He sat down beside her and put a dripping arm about her, supporting her.

Dany leant against his wet shoulder and said without opening her eyes: 'Where is he?'

'Over there,' said Larry briefly. 'It's all right. He won't move for hours—if ever. I cracked him over the head with a bottle of gin.'

Dany forced open her eyes again and saw for the first time that Nigel's limp body was lying face downwards on the floor near the window. She could not see his face, but there was a lump on the back of his head the size of a healthy orange, and his hands were joined behind him by links of metal.

She said slowly and stupidly: 'Handcuffs. Where did you get them?'

Larry Dowling looked slightly embarrassed. 'As a matter of fact, I thought at one time I'd have to use them on you.'

'On *me?*'

'Yes. I've been tailing you for days, young woman. And a tedious dance you've led me. You actually bumped into me once in London —rushing out of the dining-room at the Airlane. I was afraid you might recognize me next day, but you didn't.'

'*Tailing* me. To get a story? But you're——'

'Only a simple cop, I'm afraid. I'm sorry if it's a disappointment to you. We were going to grab you in London, and then, what with one thing and another, it seemed a better scheme to see where you went and what you led us to. The M.I.5 boys had a few ideas of their own on the whole situation, and wanted us to play it their way. So we radioed all the proper people to let you through on that borrowed passport, and I was sent along to find out what I could.'

'Oh,' said Dany; and added after a pause for thought: 'Lash isn't going to like that.'

'Lash has got a lot of explaining to do,' said Larry Dowling.

'I have, have I?' said a furious voice from the doorway. 'Well let me tell you that it's nothing to the explaining you're going to have to do!'

Dany said: 'Lash——Oh, Lash!'

'I'll deal with you later,' said Lash savagely. 'When I've taken care of this double-crossing ten-cent Romeo of yours!'

He covered the distance between them in two hasty strides, and before the startled Mr Dowling had even grasped the implications of his remarks he had thrust Dany to one side, gripped her rescuer by the collar, jerked him to his feet and slugged him scientifically on the jaw.

Mr Dowling went down for the count and Dany started to laugh, burst into overwrought tears, and quite suddenly slid off the divan on to the floor in a dead faint. Making it three in all.

◇ ◇ ◇

Lorraine was saying: '. . . raw beef steak. It's the only thing. I put it on Tyson once when he got into an argument with some men in San Francisco, and it worked *wonders*. Didn't it, darling?'

'Yes,' said a resonant voice. 'I ate it. And where do you think you're going to get a raw beef steak at this hour of the night, I'd like to know?'

Dany winced and opened her eyes. She was lying in her own bedroom and there seemed to be a lot of people in it. Lorraine, Tyson, Gussie Bingham . . . She tried to turn her head, but finding that it was too painful, gave up the attempt and lay still.

At least she was not wet any longer, for someone had removed her drenched clothes and put her into a nightgown. She wondered if anyone had removed Larry's, which had been a good deal wetter, and she must have made an attempt to inquire, for suddenly they were all leaning over her, looking at her anxiously, and Lorraine was saying: 'Darling, how do you feel?'

Tyson said: 'Now don't go trying to sit up. Much better to lie still. Get some brandy into her.'

'I think Mr Holden gave her some,' said Gussie.

'Nonsense! How could he? She wasn't conscious. Here, Dany——'

Dany attempted a feeble protest, but to no avail, and Tyson, having dealt efficiently with the matter, laid her back on the pillows and said bracingly: 'Now you'll feel better!'

'Do you, baby?' inquired Lorraine anxiously, holding both her hands. 'Lash has taken one of the cars in to fetch a doctor and the police and medicines and things, and they'll be here soon, and then you'll be all right.'

Dany said: 'I'm all right now. Where's Larry? He saved me.'

'I know, darling. *Bless* him! If it hadn't been for him——Oh, don't let's think of it. It's too awful!'

'It was Nigel.'

'Yes, darling. We know.'

'Ought to have known from the beginning,' growled Tyson, sitting down moodily on the end of her bed. 'No one else could have possibly known every dam' thing there was to be known. I suppose he took the letters off Abdurahman and said he'd post 'em. And he'd met old Honeywood, so he thought it would be quite easy. Turn up just before you, get the letter and then shoot him. And while you were being held up and questioned he'd be off and away.'

'But *how?*' said Gussie. 'How could he possibly be in England? He was in Kenya!'

Tyson said: 'Obviously he flew out. If you're in that camp, nothing is too difficult.'

'In what camp? What are you talking about?'

'The Reds, of course. Dowling is being a bit cagey about it, but it's obvious that the police, or M.I.5, or some of those cloak-and-dagger boys, had a line on him. And on this Zanzibar business.'

'What Zanzibar business?'

'An under-cover revolutionary movement that has recently been started in this island. Dowling says that Nigel's always been in it up to his neck. He's one of the really fervent kind, and those are always more dangerous than the ones who are merely after the cash rewards. He was behind Jembe's party: working to turn the island into a hot little Soviet stronghold. Get rid of British influence, then the Sultan, start a "Democratic" republic—and up with the red flag! And the next step would have been to slap an iron curtain round it, and use it as a spring-board for all sorts of merry Russian ballets. But they needed money to buy votes and supporters and get the thing really moving, and when that paper of old Emory's turned up it seemed they'd got it.'

'But they hadn't got it!' protested Gussie.

'Don't be unintelligent, Gussie! They meant to get it. They thought it was more or less in the bag. All they had to do was to get that envelope off Honeywood. And since Nigel was the obvious person to get it, they arranged to send him home and get him back again—presumably by means of some flourishing and very well organized under-cover route. And then Dany spoilt the whole show by jumping the gun.'

Gussie said: 'It's all very confusing. And I still don't understand what this Jembe was doing in England, anyway.'

'At a guess, because the Reds have never learnt to trust one another a yard, and I imagine that he was sent to keep an eye on Nigel. But Nigel failed to get the goods off Honeywood, so he put Jembe on to trying to find it—that is the supposition, anyway—and to planting that gun and pinching her passport for good measure. To ensure that the police would be kept busy suspecting her for a bit, so that she'd probably end by posting off the letter.'

'*Too* silly,' said Lorraine. 'Once he knew she had it, he ought to have just let her bring it out with her, and found some way of getting it off her here.'

'Ah, but he couldn't travel out with her—and Jembe could! Nigel would have had to nip back to Kenya in order to meet the plane at Nairobi, and I imagine he didn't trust Jembe. Probably thought that if Jembe got his hooks on it, while on his own, he'd stick to it and leave the Revolution to chase itself round the block. Dowling says that Jembe was obviously trailing Dany too, and so knew quite well who she was, and it seems that either he or Nigel had another crack at getting the letter in Nairobi. As a result of which, that blasted young idiot, Lash, got the wind up and swiped it.'

'Why?' croaked Dany.

'Oh, hullo kid. You feeling better? Have some more brandy,' said Tyson. 'Do you good.'

'Do you really think she ought to, darling? inquired Lorraine anxiously.

'Why not? Look how much better she's looking already. Drink it up, child.'

Dany drank, blinked, and said: 'Why did Lash take it?'

'Because he's an interfering, impertinent, insolent young son-of-a——Well, let it go. He didn't like the set-up and thought it was a dangerous thing for you to have. Thought you'd be safer without it.'

'Why didn't . . . he . . . give it . . . you,' said Dany slowly and carefully.

'Says he wanted to know a hell of a lot more about things before he did. Didn't trust me or anyone else with a sum like that at stake. Blast his impertinence!'

Gussie said in a hard voice: 'And Millicent? Why does Mr Dowling think that Nigel did that?'

'Probably because he was afraid that she really might have spotted him. He was officially supposed to be in Kenya, so what had he been doing mucking about in Kent? He'd actually read *The House of Shade,* which is more than I have—I've never been able to struggle further than page six—so getting rid of Millicent was easy.'

'And I suppose he killed Jembe too,' said Gussie with a shudder.

'Probably. If he talks, we may know. However, Dowling appears to have landed him such a crack that there's an even chance he won't. Can't think why he couldn't have used the siphon. Sheer waste of gin.'

'Tyson, how *can* you!' said Lorraine, releasing her daughter's hands and straightening up indignantly. 'Why, it saved Dany's life!'

'She'd have been saved quite as effectively by soda water,' said Tyson. 'Or better still, a bullet! Can't think why he didn't shoot.'

'Because of Dany, of course! He was afraid he'd hit her. He told you that.'

'So he did. Well, just as well he was there. Very lucky he saw her slip away.'

'Did he know that it was Nigel all the time?' inquired Gussie.

'I don't think so. But he had a few shrewd suspicions. It seems that parts of Kent were fairly misty on the morning that Honeywood was killed, and one or two trains ran late in consequence. Dowling says that Nigel mentioned that mist twice; though as it was only localized, and there was no mention of it on the news or in the papers, how did he know a thing like that—unless he was there? But Dowling didn't know that Nigel was hoping to needle Dany into leading him to Emory's letter, and he very nearly didn't get there in time because——Oh, there you are, Dowling. How's the jaw?'

'Swell,' said Larry Dowling bitterly, '—if I may borrow an Americanism from the donor. By this time tomorrow I shan't even be able to talk.'

'Or see out of your left eye,' said Tyson. 'The boy would appear to pack a punishing left. But I still can't see why he should have thought——'

'Neither can I,' said Larry. 'Considering that I happen to be a loving husband and an indulgent father. How are you feeling, Miss Ashton?'

'Drunk,' said Dany. 'You all will keep on giving me brandy and whisky and things.'

She held out her hands to him. 'I'm sorry about your face, Larry. And—and thank you so very much. For everything.'

Her voice broke and her eyes filled with weak tears, and Larry sat down on the edge of the bed and took her hands in his.

'You haven't anything to thank me for. If I'd had the sense to look where I was going I'd have got that pro-Red so-and-so before he started any rough stuff. But because I didn't, I expect your head is a good deal worse than my jaw; so you're not really even with me yet!'

Gussie, who had been standing by the window, said: 'Here are the cars. This will be the police. Or the doctor.'

'And Holden,' said Larry Dowling, hastily releasing Dany and rising to his feet: 'Time I went. I'm not taking any chances on being found holding your hands again and getting another crack on the jaw. That boy is too impetuous by half. See you tomorrow.'

He went out, leaving the door ajar behind him, and they heard footsteps running up the stairs and then Lash's voice on the verandah outside. 'You here again?'

'And very well chaperoned,' said Larry, 'so you can keep your hands in your pockets! Have you brought the doctor?'

'Of course. I also gave him your letter.'

'Thanks. Where is he now?'

'Ministering to that murderous louse, who has apparently surfaced—worse luck!'

'Good: I'll send him up to see Miss Ashton as soon as he's finished down there.'

Larry's footsteps retreated and Dany sat up dizzily as the door opened and Lash came in.

He paid no attention at all to Lorraine, Gussie or Tyson, but came straight across to the bed and took Dany into his arms.

'Don't mind us,' remarked Tyson caustically.

'I don't,' said Lash, '—much.'

He turned his head to look over his shoulder at Lorraine, and said: 'The doc will be up here as soon as he's through with Ponting, and after that, if I know doctors, he'll throw me out on my ear. So I'd be deeply obliged if you'd all scram.'

'Of course, dear,' said Lorraine. 'Come on Gussie. Tyson——' The door closed behind them.

Dany said: 'Lash, you aren't a G-man, are you? I thought you might be—or a murderer—because you'd taken that letter, and Nigel said——And I knew I ought to hate you if you were a murderer, but I couldn't—and I'm so glad you're not a G-man! I didn't want you to be, and I'm so sorry. Lash, I'm sorry—so sorry——'

Lash said: 'All right, honey, all right. You're sorry. For Pete's sake, how much brandy did they give you?'

'Lots,' said Dany. 'Lots and lots and lots. Firs' Larry, then you, then Tyson . . . It's good for you. I shouldn't have listened to Nigel. Lash, you will forgive me, won't you? because I couldn't bear it if you didn't . . . I couldn't bear it——'

'This is just about where we came in,' said Lash. 'Only it was me last time. It's a judgment on me! Darling, you're plastered! All right, I'll forgive you—but after this if I ever catch you drinking anything stronger than a chocolate-soda, so help me, I'll take a strap to you! Darling—my darling—*my darling* . . .'

◇ ◇ ◇

The African police-constable on guard saluted smartly and ushered Mr Dowling into a small ground-floor room leading off the central courtyard, where the window shutters were further reinforced by iron grille work and the doors were stout. A room that was, oddly enough, the self-same one to which Tyson's grandfather, Rory Frost, had brought his share of Sultan Saïd's treasure for temporary safe-keeping on a wild, rainy night over ninety-five years ago. No one now alive was aware of this; yet, strangely, a superstition survived that the room was, for some obscure reason, a place of ill-omen: which perhaps accounted for the fact that until an hour or so ago it has been kept locked and unfurnished.

Now, however, having been hastily denuded of dust and innumerable spiders-webs, it contained a heavy brass bedstead, a couple of cane armchairs loosely covered in faded chintz, a bedside table, and an ornate, marble-topped Victorian wash-handstand complete with an imposing array of flower-patterned china utensils. It also contained—in addition to the doctor—Nigel Ponting and Mr Cardew: the former lying prone upon the bed with his right wrist securely handcuffed to a brass bedpost, while the latter, who had arrived at the House of Shade in response to an urgent telephone call from Larry Dowling, occupied one of the cane chairs, pad and pencil at the ready.

Mr Dowling noted with approval that the doctor had wasted no time. The wet towel that some amateur hand had hastily wound about the secretary's head, in the manner of an untidy turban, had been removed, together with his coat, and a shirt sleeve that had been rolled back disclosed the mark of a recent injection on Nigel's bare arm. An empty syringe lay on the bedside table, and Nigel's eyes were open. He was muttering to himself, and watching someone whom he could see, but the others could not, moving about the room.

'Is it going to work, Doc?' inquired Superintendent Cardew in an undertone.

'I don't know,' returned the doctor shortly. 'I've never had occasion to use it before. And, if it does, I don't guarantee that you'll get the truth. It's more likely to be a load of old rubbish or else pure fantasy. And, what's more, I'm not at all sure that this business isn't illegal and that I won't wind up finding myself struck off the Medical Register!'

'Nonsense. Besides, if anyone hears of it—and they won't—you can always say that you were only carrying out the orders of the police, and put the blame on us. We're used to that.'

'And how!' endorsed Larry feelingly. Adding a trifle anxiously that he hoped that the quality and volume of the sound was going to improve, because at present he could not make out a word that the prisoner was saying.

'Give him time,' urged the doctor, busy replacing the discarded turban with an elaborate and highly professional bandage. 'You can't expect that stuff to act with the speed of light.'

Larry sighed, and pulling up the vacant chair, seated himself gingerly in its creaking depths, produced his own notebook and pencil, and sat waiting to take down anything relevant that the prisoner might say.

Mr Ponting continued to mutter unintelligibly and the doctor, having completed the bandage to his satisfaction and felt his patient's pulse again, picked up the syringe and wrapped it in a square of surgical gauze. He was stowing it away in his bag with some ostentation—as if to forestall any request from the guardians of the law for a further injection of the drug he had been asked to administer—when Nigel Ponting began to talk: aloud and clearly . . .

'. . . There is no proof,' declared Nigel, addressing the unseen person whose movements he had been watching, and who was now apparently standing at the foot of the bed. 'I've been too clever for them. There isn't an atom of proof, and they'll never think of looking under Tyson's floorboards for that duplicate key . . . Right under his nose! And of course for any serious work I always took care to wear gloves—the pair of silk ones to match my skin that Don had specially made for me in Cairo. They've proved invaluable. There'll be no prints on the stair mechanism, or anywhere else. They teach you to cover your tracks, as you know. They're very insistent about that. Old Honeywood never noticed the gloves even though it was mid morning. Though of course it was a grey day, and I have to admit that the mist was a bonus—one might almost call it providential—if one believed in Providence, which luckily I don't . . .

'A pity it wasn't thicker . . . If it had been, that Bates woman would never have recognized me—silly bitch! *I never forget a face!* That really was bad luck. Hers not mine. Tiresome, beady-eyed old busy-body! I certainly didn't remember hers. But of course after that I had to get rid of her as quickly as possible . . . I must tell you about that. It was laughably easy and I really do pride myself on it

. . . It was a stroke of genius. All I had to do was type an urgent little note on the Ashton girl's typewriter, push it under Bates's door, set the stair trap and wait for her to fall into it. Which of course she did—*plunk!*

'. . . Yes. Terrible about Jembe—I don't know how I'm going to manage without him. I wonder who did it? We shall have to find out. I suppose the police will have searched his luggage. Let's hope he was careful: his type so often aren't . . . too conceited. It's our weakest link. Oh, well, I shall have to find a replacement. It shouldn't be difficult—three million will buy almost anything! . . . We could swing the elections for a fraction of that. It's after we've done it that the trouble will start. I know we need islands and that this one is the best one to begin on . . . but the snag is going to be the Zanzibaris. They're too damned easy-going. They'll have to be educated . . . taught to kill. And to hate. That's the important thing. Hate . . . to hate . . . to hate. And after that . . .'

The harsh, unfamiliar voice, that contained no trace of those high-pitched and carefully cultivated fluting tones that had been part of a successful disguise for so long, talked on and on, while the horrified doctor (who had been more than half inclined to take all he had been told about Ponting with a large helping of salt) frowned and fussed and muttered oaths that were certainly not Hippocratic, and Messrs Cardew and Dowling scribbled swiftly, filling page after page of their official notebooks. Jotting down names that would later be identified and their owners traced, together with dates and details that were to prove damning . . .

When at last the hoarse voice slurred to a stop, the doctor—having declared that the performance was over and that the prisoner would now sleep for several hours—departed upstairs to see what he could do for Miss Ashton, and Mr Cardew mopped his brow with a pocket handkerchief and announced that he would be jiggered.

'If you'd told me that, and I hadn't heard it with my own ears, I wouldn't have believed a word of it,' confessed Mr Cardew. 'And, whatever the Doc's reservations are about using that drug, there was nothing phoney about that performance! If ever anything came straight from the horse's mouth, that did! But I didn't follow that stuff about the three million that's going to give Jembe's dupes a walk-over in the elections, and turn Zanzibar into a Communist paradise and a base for Russian spy-rockets and atom-subs and all the rest of it. Whose three million?'

'Tyson's grandfather's,' said Larry. 'The old reprobate reportedly stashed away roughly that amount as his share of Sultan Saïd's treasure, which he and a subsequent Sultan, Majid, somehow got their hooks on. And all this murder and mayhem was apparently sparked off by a map that shows where he hid it. It seems to have turned into a nasty adult version of that popular children's party game, "Hunt-the-slipper", and to date three people—if one can count "the thin man" as one of them—have been murdered for the sake of that map.'

'Who's got it now?'

'Mr. Frost, I imagine. Unless it's still on the floor of young Holden's room in the guest annex. I forgot to ask.'

'Do you think they'll find it?—the loot, I mean.'

'I expect so. That is, if it's still there. It may not be. But if it is, at least it won't be going to swell the coffers of some local Dictator and his Commissars, and their home-picked brand of the K.G.B.'

'No, thank God! Well, Dowling, now that that's over, I'll be off to dig the Resident out of bed and see what can be done to ensure that this murderous fellow-traveller gets sent back under guard to stand trial at the Old Bailey. And a very good night to you!' The door banged behind him.

'Some hope!' sighed Larry sadly. And resigned himself to spending what remained of the night in a creaking and far from comfortable cane armchair.

◇　◇　◇

Postscript from 'Kivulimi'.

. . . it sounds to me a very dull place for a honeymoon, baby. Though I do see that you both felt you'd had enough of romantic places for a bit. It's a pity we didn't buy you a mackintosh and some sensible shoes, but anyway, I expect you can get them there, and I'm sure you're both having a heavenly time, even if you are only on parole or bail or something. And by the way, Larry said to remind you that if you don't turn up in London on the right date and the right time he'll have you both arrested and never speak to you again. So you won't go all starry-eyed and forget, will you darling? (Tyson says that if I'm referring to your husband, I mean pie-eyed. But of course I don't.)

I think we've got rid of the police at last, which is a blessing (except for darling Larry. I wish he could have stayed) and we had a bit of drama over Elf. I expect you saw the announcement in the papers. She's going to marry Sir Ambrose Yardley. She says that Tyson advised her to marry someone like that. Very naughty of him, as of course Eduardo was simply heartbroken, and we had the most exhausting scenes—and right on top of everything else: I can't tell you! Still, they've both gone, and if I know Eddie, he's already in love with someone else.

Everything else seems to have been sorted out, except for the Jembe business. I don't suppose we shall ever know about that, but it seems that Nigel didn't do it, and Tyson says he's quite sure that Seyyid Omar did. He was dining with us here the other night and mentioned that Jembe suffered from air sickness, or nerves or something, and that he'd given him something to take for it. And then he looked at Tyson with that bland smile of his and said: 'Like your revered uncle, one does what one can.' And then they both drank Barclay's health. Really— men! How could they? When one thinks of all that lovely money. Oh I forgot you wouldn't know about that—I must tell you——

It wasn't nearly as easy as they thought to find it, the treasure I mean, because of course Tyson's father had bricked up all those walls. (Tyson says he was always messing up the place with improvements.) And when we got there at last, all we found was a rather pompous letter from Barclay. It was a bit difficult to read, as it had got damp, but we read it and it seems that the silly old man had come on the gold when he was poking about in the foundations for material for that boring book of his, and believe it or not, he had carried it all out, bit by bit and night after night, and dumped it into the sea from one of those little fishing carracks, about a mile offshore. Really, darling!

He said money in a place like Zanzibar was a source of evil, because all it led to was Progress; and he was against progress, because it seldom led to happiness, and more often only meant hideous build-ings, ugly factories, dirty railway yards and noisy motor cars, and things like strikes, lockouts and exploitation. He preferred coconuts, cloves and charm.

Tyson says it's rather like a story called 'The Treasure and the Law', but I don't think I can have read it. By the way, he's sending Lash a copy of The House of Shade *as a sort of extra wedding present, and he says if the first one's a boy you'd better call him Barclay, because in his opinion there can't be too many of them.*

Tyson doesn't seem to think much of Progress either. He says it was a good idea, but that it's got out of hand.

Well, darling——

Death in Cyprus

To
MAXINE
And the Enchanted Island

AUTHOR'S NOTE

Back in 1949, while my husband's regiment was stationed in Egypt, and we were living in an army quarter at Fayid in what was then known as the 'Suez Canal Zone', a friend and I decided to spend a painting holiday in Cyprus. We went there on a ship sailing from Port Said to Limassol, and once on the Island, hired a self-drive car for the duration. (Incidentally, cars in those days were still built with running-boards, and had a luggage-grid instead of a boot!) We stayed in the enchanting house in Kyrenia that I have described in this story, and the plot was practically handed to me on a plate by a curious series of incidents that occurred during our stay. But owing to the fact that I was too busy painting and, later, because of a multiplicity of army moves, I did not get around to writing it for almost five years. Reading it now, I am interested to see that even during that halcyon holiday I must have been aware that the Cyprus I was living in and painting was much too good to last, and that one day greedy quarrelling factions were bound to destroy it. That day came sooner than I thought; and nowadays the Island is divided into two hostile sections. Kyrenia and Hilarion, lovely Aiyos Epikititos and beautiful Bellapais, and most of the places I knew best, are now held by the Turkish Cypriots, while the Greek Cypriots, who hold the remainder, have turned their sleepy little coastal towns into roaring tourist resorts, complete with vast holiday hotels and 'recreation complexes'. *'O world! O life! O time!'* . . . Shelly said it all.

1

Amanda had not been really frightened until she found the bottle. Horrified certainly: shaken by incredulity and shock, but not with fear. Not with this cold, crawling apprehension of evil . . .

One minute Julia Blaine had been alive and talking in that high, hysterical, sobbing voice. And almost the next minute she was dead —sprawled on the floor of Amanda's cabin in an ungainly satin-clad heap.

It had all happened so suddenly, and without a word of warning. Or had there been a warning? Somewhere in the happenings of the past few days or weeks had there been nothing to suggest that such an ugly and fantastic thing might possibly occur . . . ?

Amanda Derington had been staying with an aunt at Fayid in the Suez Canal Zone while her uncle and guardian, Oswin Derington of Derington and Company, looked into his business affairs in the simmering stock-pot of the Middle East.

A night raid on London during the autumn of 1940 had left Amanda an orphan, and she had been subsequently and arbitrarily annexed by her Uncle Oswin. This despite the fact that there had been several sympathetic aunts only too ready and willing to take charge of the child. But then Oswin Derington, a bachelor and a misogynist, had little or no opinion of any of them, and a great many opinions on everything else: including the upbringing of children.

The head of Deringtons—that ubiquitous firm whose name and multitudinous activities crop up like measles spots wherever the shoe of the white man has managed to gain a foothold—was a stern moralist in whom the blood of Calvinistic ancestors ran strongly. He was, in addition, successful, egotistical, selfish and frequently inclined to pompousness, and it was his firm conviction that the majority of his fellow-men led sinfully immoral lives. Anyone hearing him holding forth on his favourite subject might well gain the impression that, in the mind of the speaker at least, the entire population of the world was given over to sinful and riotous living with the solitary exception of that pillar of uprightness, Oswin Greatorex Derington.

Uncle Oswin apparently included Amanda's aunts among the ranks of the ungodly, for his action in assuming sole charge of his brother Anthony's only child was prompted as much by a desire to save a tender brand from the burning, as to put into practice various long-held theories on the correct method of bringing up the young. And Anthony having left a will in which he had lightheartedly named his brother as trustee and sole guardian of his daughter, there was nothing that anyone else could do about it.

The outlook for Amanda might well have been bleak, had it not been for the fact that she had inherited her mother's physical beauty, together with much of her father's gaiety and courage. Three useful legacies that a series of strict boarding schools, constantly changed, and her Uncle Oswin's selfish and Victorian ideas on the correct behaviour of young ladies, had done nothing to diminish.

In the years that followed on the heels of Hiroshima, and saw a startling shrinkage of those pink-tinted portions of the map that depicted territories governed by or owing allegiance to the Crown of Great Britain, the trading empire of Derington and Company saw many changes. A number of branches, mainly in the Far East, had been compelled to close down with unexpected suddenness. But other and newer branches had sprung up to replace them, and there came a time when Oswin Derington (whose harassed but resourceful medical adviser had recommended him to take a long sea voyage) decided to combine business with the pursuit of health, and personally inspect a few selected Outposts of the Derington Empire.

He had taken Amanda, now aged twenty, with him; in pursuance of a favourite and often expressed theory that women have an instinct in the matter of irregularities, and that no Branch Manager however efficient occupied—at least in Mr. Derington's opinion—the position of Caesar's wife.

He intended to visit Alexandria, Cairo, Aden, Mombasa and Nairobi, and to return via Tripoli. But finding that travel in or to various of these cities was likely to prove full of unpleasant surprises, he had, on reaching Cairo, ordered his niece to return to England forthwith, while he continued the journey alone. There being no return passage immediately available, and as he had a rooted objection to flying (except on those occasions when it happened to suit his convenience) he had packed her off to the temporary care of one of his sisters whose husband, a Brigadier, was stationed in Fayid.

Amanda enjoyed Fayid, and had ultimately administered an even more unwelcome surprise to her Uncle Oswin than his discovery of a strange tendency among certain coloured races to take an actively unappreciative view of Empire builders. She had announced her intention of remaining in Fayid for several months and, later, of visiting the Island of Cyprus.

Since she had in the meantime celebrated her twenty-first birthday and come into control of a small but adequate income, there was little that her Uncle Oswin could do about it beyond losing his temper, which he had done to exhaustion and no effect. His niece had remained sweetly adamant; aided and abetted by her aunt, who had waited a good many years for a chance to repay Oswin for a few forceful criticisms he had uttered on the subject of her choice of a husband, in the days when the Brigadier had been a high-spirited subaltern in the Horse Artillery.

Amanda had extended her stay in Fayid, and eventually carried out her intention of visiting Cyprus, where she had planned to put up in some hotel in Kyrenia. But here, after several weeks of sulky silence, Uncle Oswin had once more intervened.

Deringtons, it appeared, owned a wine business in Cyprus: a post-war venture that was not of sufficient importance to warrant a personal visit from Derington of Deringtons. The management of the business was in the hands of a Mr Glennister Barton, and— wrote Uncle Oswin—if Amanda insisted on gallivanting all over the Middle East in this unmaidenly and unladylike manner, it was only right that she should have some consideration for his good name, if not for her own, and, as an unmarried female, stay in some respectable private house rather than in a public hotel. He had therefore taken it upon himself to appraise the Bartons of his niece's arrival, and demand that they should put her up for the duration of her stay, offer her all facilities and see that she came to no harm. He had already received a favourable reply, and Mr and Mrs Barton would meet Amanda at Limassol . . .

'You are on no account to fly. I hear that there was an accident only last week. I am further informed that anti-British feeling runs high among those Cypriots who support Enosis and wish the Island to be united to Greece. If you had the slightest consideration for the name of Derington you would abandon this rash and unwomanly project and return to Hampshire,' wrote Uncle Oswin—but without much hope.

Amanda read the letter and sighed. She would have much preferred a hotel and independence, but although she could not be fond of her Uncle Oswin, she felt a certain sense of duty towards him. Despite his selfishness and pomposity, and his conviction that he had been sent into the world to reprove Vice and restore Victorianism, he was—or had been—her legal guardian. And if he had arranged for her to see Cyprus under the auspices of these Bartons, she did not feel like pouring oil on the smouldering embers of his disapproval by refusing to be their guest. She therefore wrote dutifully to say that she would be delighted to accept their kind hospitality.

To the dismay of her aunt and uncle, who pointed out that it would entail travelling to Port Said with an armed convoy and going through the Egyptian Customs, Amanda booked a passage on the S.S. *Orantares* sailing from Port Said to Limassol. They were, however, relieved to discover that others from Fayid, also bound for a holiday in Cyprus, had decided to travel the same way, and that she would be accompanied by Captain Gates, Major and Mrs Blaine and Persis Halliday.

Captain the Hon. Tobias John Allerton Gates was a pleasant young man whose more engaging qualities were at present somewhat obscured by the state of his emotions. Toby was in love—not for the first time—and his failure to make the present object of his devotion, Miss Amanda Derington, take him seriously was casting a deep gloom over a hitherto volatile nature.

Toby had not intended to go to Cyprus for his leave. He had had other plans that included Roehampton and Cowdray Park. But on hearing that Miss Derington meant to visit Cyprus, he had hurriedly cancelled these arrangements and booked a room at the same hotel in Kyrenia that his divinity had intended to patronize. And now it seemed that she was not to stay there after all. She would not even be staying in Kyrenia. She was staying instead at Nicosia with the manager of the Cyprus branch of some Derington & Co. enterprise, and Captain Gates wondered gloomily if it would be possible for him to cancel his room at the Dome Hotel and obtain one in some hotel in Nicosia instead?

Major Alastair Blaine of the 6th Hussars and his wife, Julia, were to spend three weeks with cousins who had a house in Kyrenia. They had intended to go by air, but the only passages available had been on a plane leaving on the 13th of the month, and Julia, a superstitious woman, had refused to fly on such an inauspicious date and had insisted on going by sea. The fifth member of the party from Fayid was Persis Halliday.

Mrs. Halliday, although perhaps not so well known outside her own country, would have needed no introduction to anyone living within the bounds of the United States. Persis was a writer of romances, and unlike most of that sisterhood managed to look it. Her books sold by the hundred thousand and her name on the cover of any woman's magazine could be guaranteed to boost its circulation into astronomical figures. She had been widowed by an air disaster three years previously, and her presence in Fayid was accounted for by the fact that she had been on a world tour collecting material for Love in an Eastern setting, and was a friend of Amanda's aunt.

Persis, having heard Amanda mention that Venus-Aphrodite was supposed to have arisen from the foam off the coast of Cyprus, had immediately decided to visit the Island.

'Why, honey—it's a natural for me,' declared Persis. 'The birthplace of the Goddess of Love! Say, that's wonderful. You can count me in on the tour. I just can't miss it!'

'When one thinks of the money you must have made out of the woman,' commented Julia Blaine acidly, 'I suppose the least you can do is to pay her birthplace a visit.'

That had been at a dance at the Fayid Officers' Club, and Persis had raised her brows in real or affected astonishment at the vehemence of Julia's tone, and then laughed and drifted away on a wave of expensive scent.

'Twaddle!' said Mrs Blaine angrily, watching her go.

'What is?' inquired Amanda, startled.

'Her books. Silly, sloppy, sentimental twaddle with a nasty, slimy streak of sex. I can't think why anyone ever reads the stuff.'

'Escape,' said Amanda promptly. 'Just think what life must be like for millions of girls? A deadly, boring grind. Then they read something by Persis and they think, "That might be me!" and feel a lot better.'

'Do you mean to say that *you* read them?' demanded Mrs Blaine incredulously.

'I used to. My last headmistress banned them on the strength of one about a poor but honest hatcheck girl who got mixed up with racketeers, dope peddling and white slavery. She emerged spotless

433

of course—all Halliday heroines do—but the ban was enough to make us smuggle them into the dormitories by the dozen.'

Julia Blaine produced a sound uncommonly like a snort and said sharply: 'That merely bears out what I have just been saying. Only giggling schoolgirls would read them!'

She rose abruptly and walked away, angrily jerking at a long chiffon scarf that she wore about her plump, bare shoulders, the end of which had caught on the back of her chair.

'Sour grapes, I'm afraid,' said Amanda's aunt regretfully. 'Poor Julia. She used to write herself—or at least she tried to write. She once had a short story accepted by a magazine and thought that she had really arrived. But nothing came of it and she gave it up. Nothing has ever gone quite right for Julia.'

'Whose fault is that?' grunted the Brigadier, mopping the sweat from his brow and trying to edge his chair round so as to get a more direct blast from the nearest electric fan. 'I know she's your cousin, but the woman's a fool.'

'I know,' sighed Amanda's aunt. 'She is difficult. Poor Julia! She's always angry about something—usually something that doesn't matter at all, like Persis Halliday's books. If she hadn't anything to be angry about I believe she'd invent it. It's a habit of mind. Such a pity that she's never had any children. Alastair's father was one of a family of eighteen I believe, but only two of them married. Alastair is the very last of the Blaines of Tetworth and I think Julia feels it rather. Perhaps that's why she's turned so sour. She shouldn't be sour. Stout people are usually rather placid and jolly.'

'Probably the result of all those pints of lemon juice and iced water that she drinks,' said the Brigadier. 'Enough to sour anyone. Can't think why she does it!'

'To make her thin,' said Amanda's aunt. 'Not that it seems to do much good. All the same it's really very stupid of her to be rude to Persis. Persis may seem gay and good-tempered, and her books may drip with sentiment. But underneath all that she has a good hard streak of vanity and cast iron. She wouldn't have got where she has without it. And because she makes fun of her own books, it doesn't necessarily mean that she takes kindly to other people doing so.'

'Julia,' said the Brigadier, 'is jealous.'

'I know, poor dear. But then she's always been like that ever since she was a child. She's pretty—or she was pretty—and she's got plenty of money. But she would so like to have been fascinating and famous and filthy-rich. And she's automatically jealous of anyone who has anything she hasn't got.'

'I didn't mean that,' remarked the Brigadier. 'I meant Alastair.'

'Oh *that!*' said Amanda's aunt, and sighed. 'That's just an occupational disease with her. She wouldn't speak to Amanda for days just because he started giving her those riding lessons, and she still sulks every time he asks Amanda for a dance.'

Amanda laughed. 'I can't think why,' she said. 'He's very nice and he has charming manners. But he's as dull as—well I don't believe that ditch water is dull. Isn't it supposed to be simply teeming with weird and peculiar and wriggly forms of life? I don't believe that you'd find anything weird or peculiar about Alastair Blaine if you pushed him under a microscope. He's just a nice reliable glass of water—slightly chlorinated. The sort of thing you drink at every meal without thinking about it, and pass up at once if anything better offers.'

'Such as what?' demanded the Brigadier. 'Champagne? Seen anything yet that looks like champagne to you, Mandy?'

'Yes,' said Amanda, her dimples suddenly in evidence.

They had been sitting, all three of them, in a corner of the ballroom, and Amanda's aunt had turned in her chair to watch Persis Halliday and Major Blaine, who were dancing together.

Alastair Blaine was not a particularly good-looking man, but he possessed a pleasant tanned face, the lean lines of a cavalryman, thick blond hair and a pair of frosty blue eyes. He was forty, but did not look it, and was frequently taken to be at least five years younger than his wife's stout and embittered thirty-eight. He was popular, especially with men, and his manner towards his nagging, discontented wife was generally admitted to be beyond reproach, for Julia Blaine cannot have been an easy woman to live with. She had been the spoilt only child of rich and elderly parents, and as a plumply pretty debutante with a more than adequate income she had fallen in love with young Alastair Blaine, home on leave from India, and had married him.

Julia had not liked India. Alastair, a junior officer in an Indian Cavalry Regiment, knew too many people and had too many friends there, and Julia was jealous of anyone and anything that distracted his attention from her. It was there that she first tried out a gambit that was in time to wreck her peace of mind and all prospects of a happily married life. At any party, picnic, ball or social gathering where Alastair appeared to be enjoying himself, she would develop a headache or feel suddenly unwell, and ask to be taken home.

It became her way of demanding his attention and demonstrating her possession of him, and satisfied some hungry, jealous, grasping instinct in her that could not bear to see him entertained or interested by anything or anyone but herself. She loved him with a bitter, jealous love that drove her to almost pathological extremes of behaviour in order to prove to herself that she had at least the power to wound him, and which only served to drive him further from her. The nerves and ill-health that had at first been imaginary, she pandered to and coaxed into reality. And there had been no children to direct her energies and emotions into more normal channels. The plumpness which had been pleasing in youth had turned in her thirties to fat, and the uncharitable were quick to decide that it was only his wife's money that kept Alastair Blaine from running off with some younger and more glamorous charmer. Not that gossip had ever been able to name one. Everyone liked Alastair, but despite his wife's unreasonable jealousy no one could accuse him of taking any particular interest in any other woman, and he had perhaps paid as much attention to Amanda Derington as he had ever been known to pay to anyone.

At the moment he was dancing with Persis Halliday, and Persis, slim and spectacular in flame-coloured chiffon, was flirting with him with a deliberate and malicious ostentation that was undoubtedly aimed at annoying his wife.

'I can only hope that Persis changes her mind about going to Cyprus,' murmured Amanda's aunt, watching Mrs Halliday with a troubled frown. 'Julia isn't going to like it a bit, and she really does need a holiday. The heat has been very trying and she is not at all fit.'

'You mean she's too fat,' said Amanda with the callousness of youth and a twenty-two-inch waist. 'If she took a bit more exercise, instead of sipping all that diluted lemon juice, she'd feel far better. Who are these people she and Alastair are staying with in Cyprus?'

'The Normans. He's Alastair's first cousin, and next in line to inherit Tetworth if Alastair doesn't come up with any children—which seems highly likely at this late date. I met them when I was over there last year. They have a fascinating house in Kyrenia. I rather think that Claire Norman is delicate—lungs probably—and that is why they have to live in a warm climate. They must have plenty of money, as George Norman does nothing. Julia tells me that they'll be crossing on the same boat as you are, as they've been staying with friends in Alex. You'll probably be seeing quite a lot of them.'

'I do *hope* not,' said Amanda feelingly. 'Not if it means seeing much more of Mrs Blaine. The proper place for her is flat on her back on some psychiatrist's couch being de-complexed. You can't blame Mrs Halliday for trying to take a rise out of her—she's been consistently rude all evening. That's no way to keep a husband!'

'When you have acquired one of your own, Mandy, you will be able to show us how it should be done,' said the Brigadier dryly.

Amanda laughed and made a face at him. 'If you really want to know, darling, I've decided to be a spinster.'

'What? Do you mean to say that in all this seething mob of males you see nothing that attracts your eye?'

'Only one,' said Amanda reflectively. 'Present company excepted, of course.'

'Ah!' said the Brigadier. 'That champagne you were referring to a moment or two ago. Don't tell me that young Toby has at last succeeded in making a dent in your affections?—where is he by the way?'

'He had to rush off and turn out a guard, or something equally martial,' said Amanda. 'He'll be back. No, Toby isn't my idea of champagne, poor lamb.'

'Not Andrew Carron I hope?—or is it young Haigh? or the Plumbly boy or—no it *can't* be Major Cotter! I won't believe it of you.'

'It isn't anyone you know,' said Amanda regretfully. 'In fact it isn't anyone I know either.'

She indicated by a brief gesture of the hand a lone gentleman who was lounging in a chair on the terrace just beyond the nearest door that led out of the ballroom, his long legs stretched out before him and his hands deep in the pockets of a pair of burnt-orange slacks of the type worn by Breton fishermen.

'Good God!' said the Brigadier, revolted. 'The *Artist?*'

'That's right,' agreed Amanda. 'Don't you think he looks rather intriguing?'

'No I do not. Needs a hair-cut! Where did you meet the feller?'

'I didn't. I mean I haven't. I've only seen him here and there. And as I'm off to Cyprus on Monday, I don't suppose I shall ever meet him now. A pity. He looks precisely my cup of tea.'

'You are mixing your drinks,' observed the Brigadier, hitching his chair round so as to obtain a better view. 'He probably wears sandals and manicures his toenails and thinks Picasso is terrific.'

'Well so do I, if it comes to that.'

'Tacha!' said the Brigadier. 'All you women are alike. Hand you a lot of nice clean-living normal chaps on a platter, and you won't look at 'em! But you fall over your feet at the sight of the first long-haired blighter who dabbles in art. What's he doing here anyway?'

'Painting the pyramids,' sighed Amanda's aunt. 'They will do it!' She turned an affectionate smile upon her niece: 'You are quite right, Mandy. Such a change from chlorinated drinking water or gin and lime. I must get to know him at once.'

'What on earth are you talking about?' demanded the Brigadier, bewildered.

'Champagne, of course,' said Amanda's aunt. 'So much more exciting and stimulating than—well, beer.' She rose to her feet in a swirl of grey draperies and turned towards the door.

'Muriel!' said the Brigadier, scandalized, 'even at your age you cannot go accosting strange men!'

'Watch me,' said Amanda's aunt, and left them.

It was perhaps half an hour later that her niece, leaving the ballroom for the cooler air of the terrace, was hailed by her aunt.

'Amanda dear, come over here. I want to introduce you to Steven Howard. Mr Howard—my niece, Amanda Derington.'

Mr Howard rose and Amanda held out her hand and found herself looking up into a pair of coolly observant hazel eyes that held a curious glint of speculative interest. There was no trace of admiration in that level gaze, or any recognition of the fact that Miss Derington was an exceptionally pretty girl. Only that oddly speculative interest.

Brown hair . . . light brown eyes . . . sun-browned face . . . thirtyish; he isn't really good-looking, thought Amanda confusedly: his face is out of drawing. But that's what makes it so intriguing . . .

A muscle twitched at the corner of Mr Howard's mouth and Amanda suddenly awoke to the fact that her hand was still in his and that she had been studying his face for a full minute. She snatched her hand away, blushed vividly, and was instantly furious with herself and—illogically—with Steven Howard.

'Mr Howard is an artist. He paints,' said Amanda's aunt helpfully. 'He is collecting material for an Exhibition in the autumn.'

'Oh,' said Amanda briefly.

Mr Howard said: 'I am afraid that your aunt gives me credit for more zeal than I possess. To tell the truth, I find art an admirable excuse for avoiding work and loafing around in the sun.' His voice was slow and pleasant and contained the hint of a laugh.

Amanda said: 'Really?' in the tone of one who is not amused, and the band launched into *'La Vie en Rose'*.

'I'm sorry I can't ask you to dance,' said Mr Howard, 'but as you see, I am improperly dressed. Perhaps some other time——?'

'I shan't be here,' said Amanda flatly. 'I'm leaving on Monday. Toby, isn't this our dance?'

She turned abruptly away and left him, and when the dance was over and she and Toby returned to the terrace, he was gone.

'But I thought you wanted to meet him, Mandy!' said Amanda's aunt plaintively. 'Why did you snub the poor man after I'd gone to all that trouble?'

'I don't know,' admitted Amanda ruefully. 'Because I felt I'd make an exhibition of myself, I suppose. Or else because I don't like being laughed at. And he wasn't in the least snubbed. He was amused—and I don't think I like him at all.'

'Oh well,' said Amanda's aunt, 'I don't suppose you're ever likely to see him again.'

But in this she was entirely wrong. Amanda was to see him again not five minutes after Julia died.

2

The decks of the S.S. *Orantares,* which was due to leave Port Said for Limassol, were hot and crowded, and the party from Fayid had taken refuge in the lounge where they had turned on all the fans and ordered iced drinks.

They had been joined there by Mr and Mrs Norman, who had arrived from Alexandria earlier in the day.

Claire Norman was a petite, small-boned and magnolia-skinned woman who possessed a pair of wide grey eyes fringed with silky black lashes, and a cloud of short dark curls cut like a child's. She was not particularly pretty, but her lack of inches and look of slender delicacy somehow suggested the drooping fragility of a snowdrop bending before a harsh wind, and managed to make every other woman appear, by comparison, buxom and oversized. She owned in addition a sweet, soft little voice, and her beautifully cut dress of pale green linen, small white hat and the faint scent of lily-of-the-valley that clung about her, strongly emphasized the First-Flower-of-Spring motif.

Her husband, George Norman, appeared by contrast almost aggressively solid and beefy as he fussed about his tiny wife like some large and over-anxious St Bernard dog. His square, homely face was burnt brick-red by the sun and his thick brown hair was streaked with grey, and he looked completely out of place in the hot, garish and cosmopolitan setting of the crowded lounge. One felt instinctively that he would have been more at home wearing old tweeds and a hat with salmon flies stuck into the band, drinking draught beer at some English country pub, rather than wearing thin tropical duck and accepting an iced gin sling from a coffee-coloured gentleman in a red tarboosh.

'Oh, this heat!' sighed Claire Norman, 'I'm exhausted!'

'Claire tires so easily,' explained George Norman to the assembled company. 'Darling, don't you think you should go and lie down? It's probably a lot cooler in the cabin.'

'And leave dear Julia?—and Alastair—just when we've met? Of course not! Why I've been *longing* to see them again. It's been such *years!*'

'January,' said Julia blightingly. 'Six months.'

'So it is. But it *seems* like years. It's dreadful the way one misses one's real friends . . .'

'——and before that, September,' continued Julia as though Mrs Norman had not spoken.

'And now again. It's so wonderful to see you Julia—and you too Alastair . . .' Claire Norman laid a small white hand caressingly on Alastair Blaine's lean brown one and Amanda saw him flush, and saw too that for a brief moment there was a queer, unreadable look on his face.

Julia put down her glass with a grimace of disgust and said: 'They've put sugar in it! Alastair, make that man get me another. I particularly said only lemon and water, *not* lemon squash. They don't listen!'

Major Blaine dutifully hailed a passing steward and Claire said: 'It's so good of you both to come and stay with us, Julia. I get so lonely in Cyprus—so far from home and friends.'

'Then why stay there?' demanded Julia.

Claire Norman drew a soft, quivering breath and smiled wistfully. 'The doctors,' she said gently. 'They tell me that I could never . . . But don't let's talk about me. Let's talk about something more interesting. *You!* You're looking so well Julia darling. I only wish I could put on a little weight too. George makes me drink pints of cream and eat pounds of butter, but it's no good. I cannot seem to gain an ounce. Daddy always said I was a changeling—too small for a mortal.'

Persis choked into her gin and lime, dabbed her mouth with a vast chiffon handkerchief and muttered something into its folds that sounded suspiciously like *'Teeny weeny me!'* and Amanda's dimples were suddenly visible. She turned hurriedly away, and looking out of the window said: 'We must be going to sail. They seem to be getting the gangway in.'

There was a burst of shouting and invective from over the side as two more passengers, late arrivals who had almost succeeded in missing the boat, scrambled up the gangway and stood panting and breathless on the deck.

They were an ill-matched couple. The attractive, dark-haired woman in the pink linen suit was as smartly and expensively dressed as Persis, and her white shoes and gloves, despite the heat and the coal dust, were fresh and spotless. She carried a small white leather dressing case in one hand, and what appeared to be an easel in the other. Her companion, by contrast, appeared hot, grubby and dressed with deliberate carelessness. He wore a pair of exceedingly dirty blue linen slacks topped by an orange sports shirt that could also have done with a wash, and sported a scanty ginger beard and a black beret.

Artist, thought Amanda; and was suddenly reminded of Steven Howard. No one meeting Mr Howard for the first time could have typed him, she thought. He had, it is true, worn brightly coloured slacks; but then a good many members of the Sailing Club affected them too, and there was nothing else about him to suggest his profession. He might have been anything: *Tinker, tailor, soldier, sailor,* mused Amanda; and wondered why it was that she should remember everything about him, and every line of his face, so clearly?

The blatantly artistic gentleman on the deck dropped two suit-cases and an untidy paper parcel containing canvases, and said crossly and as though continuing a previous conversation:

'Of course I declared them. What a country! Not a tube of usable paint in the place. Students' Water Colours—*Bah!* Put that down, you frightful coolie! Put it *down*—it's not dry yet! *God in heaven——!'*

George Norman, his attention attracted by the howl of fury from the desk, stood up and peered through the window over Amanda's head.

'I thought so,' he said. 'It's that chap Potter.'

Claire turned quickly. 'Lumley? Why, whatever can he have been doing over here?'

'Painting the pyramids, I suppose,' said her husband in an un-conscious echo of Amanda's aunt.

'Tell him to come in and join us,' said Claire. She turned to Major Blaine: 'You remember Lumley Potter, don't you Alastair? He has a studio-flat in Famagusta. You met him once or twice at our house when you and Julia were staying with us last year. I think I took you over to see his paintings.'

'You did,' said Julia. *'Lumley!* That wasn't what his mother chris-tened him. I met a Mrs Deadon in Cairo last winter who knew *all* about Mr Potter. I'm not surprised that he decided to settle in Cyprus. As for his paintings, I could do as well with my eyes shut—better! If that's art——'

'But Julia darling, it *is* Art—Claire pronounced it as though it had a capital A. 'You mustn't be conventional, darling. Lumley doesn't paint what ordinary, conventional people see. He paints the *soul* of a place—the spiritual aroma.'

'Spiritual garlic you mean!' snapped Julia. 'Don't be such a humbug, Claire! The man's a flop, a failure and a fake, and you know it. He can't paint well, so he dresses himself up in what is practically fancy dress, grows a beard, talks a lot of rubbish and paints as badly as he can in the hope of fooling a lot of credulous artistic snobs into thinking he's a genius. And so I told him!'

'Yes, I remember,' said Claire dryly. 'And lost him a great deal of money by doing so. That new-rich Australian couple had practically bought eight of his canvases, but when they heard you they took fright and backed out. However Alastair at least did not agree with you. He bought one—"Sea Green Cypriots"—didn't you Alastair?'

'Only because he felt he had to, to make up for the Blaggs backing out of buying those dreadful daubs,' said Julia unpleasantly.

'Oh darling! You *do* misjudge Alastair so. He has a real, deep-down feeling for truth in Art.'

'I understand Alastair perfectly, thank you Claire,' said Julia acidly.

Alastair Blaine flushed uncomfortably and Persis rose with determination: 'Well, I don't know about you, but I guess I've had all that I can take of the ship's gin,' she remarked cheerfully. 'Alastair honey, how about leaving the girls to sort out your artistic sensibilities while you escort me on deck? I'd like to take a slant at the waterfront before we pull out. Will you spare him, Julia?'

Major Blaine rose with alacrity and assisted Persis to collect her handbag and gloves, while Claire Norman watched them with a sudden frown on her white forehead. After a moment she turned abruptly to her husband and said: 'George dear, I asked you to call Lumley.'

George Norman looked embarrassed and spoke with obvious hesitation: 'Er—well—I thought perhaps I had better not. He had someone with him.'

'Oh?' Claire Norman's soft voice sharpened a little. 'Who was it? Anyone we know?'

'Anita.'

'*Who?*' said Major Blaine, turning sharply. 'But I thought——'
He glanced at Amanda, but did not finish the sentence, for Persis
took his arm and said: 'Let's go,' and they turned away together and
disappeared through the doorway.

'Anita!' said Claire Norman. There were suddenly two bright
patches of colour in her pale cheeks. Her small mouth tightened into
a hard narrow line, and for a moment it was as if the frail, pliant
snowdrop had been transformed into something made of steel.

The impression was only a fleeting one, and then the corners of
her small mouth drooped childishly and once more the sense of
wistfulness and fragility was back, and Mrs Norman was saying in
her soft, apologetic voice: 'I think after all that I will go and lie down
for a while, George dear. I feel so tired. I'll see you at dinner Julia—
if I feel strong enough.'

She bestowed a faint smile upon Amanda, directed another at
Toby Gates, tucked her small hand confidingly through her husband's arm and moved gracefully away.

Julia Blaine sat staring after her in silence and Amanda saw with
surprise that her face was colourless and her eyes wide and fixed and
filled with something that looked uncommonly like fear. It was a
disturbing expression, and Amanda tried to think of something light
and casual to say that would break the spell of that uncomfortable
silence. But before she could speak Mrs Blaine stood up, pushing
her chair back so violently that it overturned on the thick carpet, and
walked quickly out of the lounge.

The ship had sailed some ten minutes later, and Amanda and
Toby had gone out on to the deck to watch the garish waterfront of
Port Said with its blaze of flames trees slide past them, shimmering
in the heat haze.

Feluccas with their squat prows and huge triangular sails drifted
by among a clutter of shipping from almost every nation in the
world: a British destroyer bound for Colombo and the Far East; oil
tankers from England, America, Holland, France, Scandinavia; a
P & O liner, white and glittering in the hot sunshine; a troopship
returning from Singapore; a dhow from Dacca and a cargo boat
from Brazil.

They passed the long stone mole where the statue of de Lesseps
gazes out upon that narrow ribbon of water that is his memorial for
all time. Beyond and far behind the green-bronze figure, a fleet of
fishing boats lay motionless on the shallow waters that curve away
towards Damietta and the Delta of the Nile, their sails ghostly in the

haze. A cool breath of wind from the open sea blew gently across the sun-baked deck as the ship turned her bows towards Cyprus, and when the white rooftops and garish domes of Port Said had vanished into the heat haze, Amanda went down to her cabin to wash off the dust of the journey from Fayid.

The long, white-painted ship's corridor was hot and airless and smelt strongly of food, disinfectant, engine oil and that curious all-pervading and entirely individual smell of shipboard. A small but voluble group of people were standing halfway down the corridor and Mrs Blaine's voice made itself heard above the babble:

'I don't care, you'll just have to find me another cabin. I didn't notice it before, or I would never have let you move my things in. I won't sleep in there, and that's all there is to it!'

Mrs Blaine, looking flushed and angry, pushed her way through the group and caught sight of Amanda.

'Really, these people are impossible!' she announced heatedly. 'There must be dozens of other cabins!'

'What's the matter?' inquired Amanda. 'Is there something wrong with yours?'

'Only the number,' said Julia bitterly. 'It's thirteen. I won't travel in it. I'd rather sleep on deck. It isn't even as if the ship were full. Why it's half empty! And it's no good just saying that I'm superstitious. I am. Not about some things—like cats and ladders—but I am about thirteen.'

'Well I'm not,' said Amanda cheerfully. 'I'll swop with you if you like. They've given me a two-berth cabin all to myself.'

'Would you? Would you really?'

'Of course. I haven't unpacked anything yet so it won't take a minute. Mine's fourteen—right next door to you.'

The stewardess, a cabin steward, a hovering Cypriot deck-hand and a man who was evidently the purser, expressed voluble relief, and the transfer was accomplished in a matter of minutes.

'It's very good of you,' said Julia Blaine awkwardly, lingering in the doorway of her late cabin and speaking in a halting, difficult voice, 'I know it sounds silly to be so superstitious, but—well I've wanted to get away from the heat and—and Fayid so badly, and I—I do so want this leave to be a success. But when I saw that number on the door it—it seemed like a bad omen, and I . . .' Her voice trailed away and stopped.

Amanda smiled sympathetically at her, but Julia Blaine did not return the smile. She was not looking at Amanda. She was staring instead at her own reflection in the narrow strip of looking-glass behind Amanda's head, and her plump, ageing face was once again white and frightened.

Amanda had tea in the lounge with Toby Gates, and when the sun had set in a blaze of gold and rose and amethyst and the sky was brilliant with stars, they had all dined in the saloon: Amanda, Toby, Julia and Alastair Blaine, the Normans and Persis Halliday.

The saloon was far from crowded and Amanda caught sight of the ginger-bearded painter of spiritual aromas dining at a small table with his companion of the afternoon, who had changed her linen suit for a short, strapless dinner dress of scarlet lace.

Amanda had exchanged one cotton frock for another, and Julia Blaine had not bothered to change at all. But Claire Norman was looking cool and ethereal in white chiffon and pearls, while Mrs. Halliday, despite the heat, had elected to wear gold lamé and some astonishing emeralds. The glittering cloth brought out the gold lights in her copper hair and the emeralds turned her eyes to a clear, shining green. She looked stunning and knew it, and was amusing herself by flirting outrageously with George Norman.

Alastair Blaine was sitting next to Amanda, but Claire Norman, seated on his right, monopolized most of his attention, and for once Julia's acid tongue was silent. She was watching her husband and Claire Norman with a furtive and almost frightened intentness, but if Alastair was aware of this he certainly paid no attention to it. Major Blaine, for the first time since Amanda had known him, appeared to be the better—or worse—for drink. His face was un-naturally flushed and his blue eyes overbright, and he appeared to be slurring his words a little.

They were half-way through the meal when Claire leant across and spoke to Amanda:

'Alastair tells me that you've never been to Cyprus before, Amanda?—I may call you Amanda, mayn't I? Are you staying long?'

'Only ten days,' said Amanda regretfully. 'It doesn't seem nearly long enough. Ten days is such a little time.'

'Oh, but it's a very little Island. Where are you staying? In Kyrenia?'

'No, I'm afraid not. I'd much rather have stayed somewhere near the sea, but my uncle arranged for me to stay with some people in Nicosia.'

'Army people I suppose. They're nearly all stuck in Nicosia, poor things.'

Amanda shook her head. 'No. They're something to do with wine. People called Barton.'

'Barton! You can't mean *Glenn* Barton?'

'Yes, I think that must be it. Glennister Barton. Do you know them?'

'Yes, of course I know them; but you can't possibly be staying at the Villa Sosis. Why——' She stopped suddenly and bit her lip.

'But I am staying with them,' said Amanda with a laugh. 'Did you think they were away?'

'No. I mean——' Once more Claire Norman did not finish the sentence. She laughed instead; a light tinkling laugh that somehow gave Amanda the impression that she was both disturbed and angry. 'Oh well—we shall see. It will be very interesting. But personally I should have thought that Glenn would have had more respect for the convention. He is such a stickler for propriety.'

With which cryptic remark she turned her attention to Toby Gates, and Amanda had no further opportunity of reopening the subject, for it was at that point that the artistic Mr Potter and his companion rose to leave the dining saloon and paused beside their table. Amanda, looking round, saw the painter pull at the woman's arm as though he would have hurried her past, but she disengaged herself deliberately and spoke in a clear high voice:

'Hullo Claire. Hullo Mrs Blaine. Alastair!—fancy seeing you here again!'

Alastair Blaine stood up quickly. He was swaying a little. 'Hullo Anita. What are you doing here?'

'As if you didn't know!' mocked Mr Potter's companion. 'However if you don't, you soon will. Claire will see to that. Won't you, Claire?'

Claire Norman stiffened where she sat. She turned slowly and it seemed a full minute before she spoke:

'Hullo Anita. I'm not sure that I expected to see you here either. I should have thought——' She broke off with a shrug of her white shoulders and gave her tinkling little laugh: 'Oh well, it's no concern of mine, is it? Hullo Lumley. You remember Major and Mrs Blaine, don't you?'

She made no attempt to introduce the woman she had addressed as Anita, but turned instead to the three men at her own table: 'Do sit down, darlings. There's no need for you to stand around while your food gets cold. They're just going.'

Mr Potter's face, which had acquired a fiery glow that reduced his beard to luke-warm proportions, turned an even richer shade of puce and he said hurriedly: 'Yes, we—we were going on deck. Come on Anita.' He grabbed his companion's arm and almost dragged her from the dining-room.

'Say, who was that dame?' inquired Persis, interested.

'Just someone we have the misfortune to know,' said Claire in a small, cold voice, and instantly changed the subject.

Persis raised her eyebrows but did not press the question. And presently they left the table and went up to drink coffee in the lounge, and later someone turned on a gramophone and they danced on deck under a blaze of stars.

It was almost eleven o'clock by the time Amanda went down to bed, and except for a passing Cypriot deck-hand the long brightly lit corridor was silent and deserted. Her cabin was hot and stuffy after the cool night air on deck and she was pleasantly surprised to see that a thoughtful stewardess had placed a brimming frosted glass, with ice and a long strip of lemon peel floating in it, on a small stool near her berth. A moment or two later she realized that the drink must have been ordered by Julia, and placed in error in the cabin that Julia should have been occupying: she would have to take it in to her, but as she had already removed her dress it could wait until she was ready for bed. She put on a thin silk nightdress, washed in cold water and removing the pins from her hair, brushed out its long, shining length.

Amanda's hair—a deep golden brown with glints in it the colour of the first chestnuts in September—was a glorious anachronism. In the sunlight there were other colours in it too; purple and green and bronze; and it fell far below her slim waist in a rippling, glinting cloak that might well have rivalled Montezuma's fabled cloak of feathers. Yet as she brushed it she regretted—not for the first time since the advent of the hot weather—that she could not summon up the moral courage to defy her uncle and chop it off.

But Oswin Derington did not approve of short hair for women, and although Amanda was now of age and had demonstrated her independence in a drastic manner, the habit of years made her shrink from the prospect of Uncle Oswin's scandalized wrath should she cut off what he persisted in referring to as 'Woman's Crowning Glory'.

Amanda sighed and rummaged in her suitcase for a length of ribbon with which to tie it back, and she was pulling the bow tight when the door of the cabin burst open without any preliminary knock to disclose Julia Blaine, arrayed in a pink satin dressing-gown liberally trimmed with lace, a tight pink satin nightdress and feathered mules.

Mrs Blaine banged the door shut behind her and subsided heavily on the end of Amanda's berth. She was trembling violently and her teeth chattered as though she were cold.

'What's the matter?' demanded Amanda sharply; appalled by the sight of the older woman's ravaged face. 'Are you ill? Shall I call the stewardess?'

'No,' said Mrs Blaine hoarsely. 'It's—it's Alastair——'

'Alastair? You mean he's ill?'

'No. But he hasn't come to bed. He—he was dancing to that gramophone, and I told him that I wasn't feeling well and would have to go to bed, but he wouldn't come with me. He wouldn't even come as far as the cabin with me! He said I could find the way myself. I waited and waited; and then I sent the stewardess to tell him to come as I was feeling very unwell, and he—he sent back to say that I'd better take an aspirin and that he couldn't come just now. Couldn't come . . . ! It's that woman! I should have known it. I've always known that this would happen one day. Alastair . . . *Alastair . . . !*'

She broke into gulping, hysterical sobs.

'Mrs Blaine,' said Amanda gently, 'don't you think you'd better go back to your cabin and lie down? You shouldn't say these things to me—really you shouldn't. You'll feel quite differently about it in the morning. It's only because it's been a hot, tiring day that you're feeling upset. You don't really mean it. *Do* lie down.'

But Julia Blaine was beyond the reach of reason. She had to talk, and if it had not been to Amanda it would have been to someone else—anyone else—the stewardess, or a stranger.

She said violently: 'I shall say it! I do mean it! I shall tell everyone. *Everyone!* I've always known that he'd leave me one day. I've felt it; *here*——'

She struck her billowing breasts with her clenched fists, while the tears poured down her plump, faded cheeks:

'Only he couldn't leave me! I had the money and he needed that. He might have managed in an Indian cavalry regiment, but when he had to transfer into a British one he had to have money. And I had more than the others. A lot more. There might have been prettier women, and younger and—and slimmer ones, like Anita, but they couldn't give him the horses and cars and comforts that I could. But now it's different. That American woman. She's rich. You saw those emeralds! They must have cost a fortune. And Claire—it isn't George's money. It's Claire's. That's why George has to stay in Cyprus. He hates it—he's always hated it. But if he left her he wouldn't have a penny, and he's grown used to doing nothing. When she got him to give up the Army she told him that they'd buy a farm in England. But she didn't; and he hadn't even qualified for a pension. She's got him where she wants him. But I didn't realize that she wanted Alastair. He can't do this to me!—he can't!'

She wept noisily, rocking her stout body to and fro, and Amanda sat down beside her and put her arms about the fat, satin-clad shoulders, wondering desperately what she could say to comfort this hysterical, despairing woman.

'I'm—I'm sure you must be imagining it,' said Amanda help-lessly.

'I know him and you don't,' sobbed Julia, 'and I've never known him to behave like this before. But she shan't have him! I'll kill myself first! I'd be better dead than having to go through all this—this awful agony.'

Amanda began to wonder if she ought not to ring the bell for the stewardess and ask for sedatives or the ship's doctor. She said anxiously: 'Wouldn't you like a—an aspirin or something?'

Mrs Blaine turned her head slowly and looked at Amanda as though she was awakening from a deep sleep or an anaesthetic. Her blotched and tear-disfigured face coloured a slow, ugly red and she jerked herself free of Amanda's arm and stood up abruptly:

'That's what Alastair said. He said to take some aspirin. The stewardess brought me some. The one who—who brought me the message.'

She opened her hot, plump hand to show two small white tablets that were already beginning to crumble.

Amanda said: 'You take those and get into bed. They'll make you sleep, and you'll feel much better in the morning.'

'Yes,' said Julia slowly. 'Perhaps it's the heat. I always feel so dreadful in the heat. It's horrible, having to live so much in the East. I've always hated Army life . . . but Alastair likes it. Perhaps if I sleep . . .'

She put the tablets into her mouth and reached out one plump beringed hand for the glass that stood beside the berth. The diamonds on her fingers winked and sparkled in the light of the ceiling bulbs as she lifted it to her lips and drank deeply.

She made a wry grimace and drank again, swaying a little as she stood, and presently said in a harsh whisper: 'I've been a fool. I should never have let him go back to Cyprus. But I never suspected . . . Claire's too clever. We stayed with them last year, you know. And then they came and stayed with us, and we all spent Christmas and New Year together in Alex. He never seemed to pay any special attention to her. He—he always said that he didn't like little women. But tonight—tonight——'

She swayed again and put up a hand, catching at the edge of the upper berth to steady herself. Holding it, she drew herself erect and said in a voice that was no longer trembling with hysteria but cold and venomous: 'Well he can't divorce me! And I'll never divorce him. *Never!* He knows that. I'd kill myself first—I'd kill myself!'

She clung to the edge of the berth, breathing stertorously and shivering, her eyes staring blindly across the small cabin. There were great beads of sweat on her forehead that trickled down and mingled with the tears that smeared her cheeks, and the silence in the cabin, broken only by the sound of her hoarse panting breath, began to grow oppressive.

Amanda watched her anxiously and presently said: '*Do* go to bed. You're only upsetting yourself. I'm sure your husband will be along soon.'

Julia Blaine looked at her as though she did not know who she was or could not focus her, and lifting the glass that she still held, drank again, thirstily.

A minute or two later she suddenly swayed and staggered and seemed to gasp for air, and releasing her hold on the berth, doubled up, retching; her face suffused and her eyes starting from her head.

The glass dropped from her hand and rolled on its side, spilling what little remained of its contents on to the floor in a scatter of melting ice, and Julia gave a curious, choking cry and fell forward to sprawl face downwards on the narrow cabin floor.

3

She's fainted, thought Amanda frantically. What on earth does one do for a faint? Oh, *bother* the woman!

She leapt for the bell and pressed it hard. The stewardess would know what to do.

Amanda bent and attempted to lift the limp body, but the task was beyond her. She managed to turn Mrs Blaine over. But at the sight of that contorted face her heart gave an odd lurch: Julia Blaine's mouth had fallen open and her eyes were wide and fixed and staring.

'It isn't a faint. She's had a fit,' said Amanda, unaware that she had spoken aloud. She reached for the unbroken glass, and filling it with water from the cold tap, splashed it over Mrs Blaine's face and neck: the water streamed over Julia's contorted features and across her staring eyeballs. But her eyelids did not close . . .

Amanda straightened up, cold and trembling. She sprang to the bell and pressed it again, frantically, and then seized by a sudden, shuddering horror, jerked open the door and ran out into the corridor. It stretched away on either side of her, blank, brightly lit and empty, and she had no idea at which end of it the stewardess had her cabin, or where to find her. But she must fetch help, and quickly.

Julia's own cabin was empty, and there was no one in No. 12, for it was in darkness and the door stood open. She turned in desperation to the one beyond it and hammered on the door.

'Who is it?' demanded a man's voice impatiently.

Amanda tried to speak and found that she could not. The next moment the door opened and Steven Howard, pyjama clad and sleepy, was staring down at her with a mixture of amusement and unqualified surprise.

'Well, well!' said Mr Howard cordially, his interested gaze missing no detail of her unorthodox attire. His eyes went to her white

452

face and his own face changed abruptly, so that all at once it was an entirely different person who was standing there in the white, brightly lit corridor of the S.S. *Orantares*. His hand shot out and gripped Amanda's shoulder, steadying her:

'What is it?'

'It's Mrs Blaine,' said Amanda, shuddering. 'She's in my cabin. I —I think she's had a fit and I can't bring her round. And I rang and rang, but no one has answered the bell, and . . . and . . .'

Mr Howard said briskly: 'Just a minute.' He reached for a dressing-gown, put it on and said: 'Where is she?'

Amanda led the way to her cabin and stood back for him to enter, and he went quickly past her and dropped on one knee beside the sprawling figure whose pink satin attire was blotched and stained with water.

After a moment or two he lifted his head and said curtly: 'She's dead.'

He came to his feet rather slowly and looked at Amanda. It was a long, measuring look that held that same curious suggestion of speculation and intentness that she had seen in his eyes on the terrace of the Club at Fayid.

'No!' said Amanda in a whisper. 'Oh no! She can't be—she was talking to me! Why don't you get a doctor? Why don't you do something? If it's a heart attack a doctor——'

Mr Howard cut her short: 'I'm not too sure that it was a heart attack.'

'What else could it *possibly* be?'

'Well, it could be suicide.'

'No,' said Amanda loudly and definitely. 'She wouldn't have done that, because it would mean that he could——' She stopped abruptly.

'Mean that who could what?' inquired Steven Howard softly.

'Nothing,' said Amanda confusedly. 'I didn't mean . . . it was just something that she said.'

Mr Howard reached across her and shut the cabin door.

'I think you'd better tell me just exactly what happened,' he said. 'Quickly, before anyone comes. If you rang for the stewardess she may be along at any moment, so let's have it.'

He spoke quite quietly, but with an unconscious note of authority which, for some reason, it did not occur to Amanda to question, and she found herself telling him exactly what Julia Blaine had said and done: repeating the substance of that hysterical outburst almost word for word.

Mr Howard said: 'Then you saw her take the tablets herself?'

'Yes. She put them in her mouth and then drank some lemon-water, and a little while later she seemed to feel ill, and then she fell down like—like she is now, only on her face.'

'Is that the glass?'

'Yes.' Amanda's teeth chattered a little and she clenched them on her lower lip.

Mr Howard reached out and picked it up, holding it by the extreme edge of the rim. He smelt it, put it down again and said: 'Where did all that water on her clothes come from? It didn't all come out of this glass, did it?'

'I filled it again at the basin and poured it over her. I thought it might bring her round.'

'I see.' He went down on his knees again and examined the contorted, staring face and then lifted the slack hands one after another. A few coarse grains of white powder clung damply to the palm of one hand. Steven Howard sniffed it, and rubbing the tip of his finger over it, touched it to his tongue with infinite caution, and frowned.

He sat back on his heels and looked around at the floor and presently said: 'What was the last thing she said again?'

'She said she'd kill herself. But I didn't think she meant it. I thought she was only—only——'

'Quite,' said Mr Howard curtly. 'All the same it looks as though she may have meant it.'

He frowned thoughtfully down at the plump-fingered hands with their glittering rings and then stood up abruptly:

'It doesn't look as though anyone is going to answer that bell. You'd better see if you can find someone. See if you can rout out a steward or a stewardess; or grab the first ship's officer you see and tell him to send along a doctor.'

He looked Amanda over and added dryly: 'And if I were you, I'd put on a dressing-gown.'

An hour later Julia Blaine's body had been removed to the sick bay and the water had been mopped off Amanda's cabin floor. Amanda herself, having repeated her story—with several reserva-tions—at least half a dozen times, was at last left in peace.

The ship's doctor had seemed puzzled by the cause of death and he too had suggested the possibility of suicide, but the stewardess had sworn with fervour and a touch of hysteria that she had given Mrs Blaine two aspirins and nothing else. She had produced the bottle in evidence, and the doctor had taken charge of it and after careful examination pronounced the tablets to be innocuous.

Alastair Blaine, white-faced and incredulous, had agreed that his wife had been in poor spirits of late; that she was highly strung and, though her health had not been of the best, there had never been any suggestion of heart trouble, and he did not know how she could have obtained poison.

'In the East, that is easy,' commented the Captain dryly. 'A little money, and the thing is done'—he had pantomimed a sly, expressive Oriental gesture.

Amanda, prompted by Steven Howard, had agreed that Mrs Blaine had talked of taking her life. And looking at Alastair Blaine's haggard face, she had refrained from any mention of names or motives; allowing it to be inferred that a combination of nerves, ill-health and the heat had been responsible for Mrs Blaine's state of mind. She had not looked at Steven Howard, and to her relief he had failed to point out that this version differed considerably from the one that she had given him so short a time ago. He had, in fact, barely spoken. But Amanda had the odd impression that in some way that she could not define, he had directed the course of the inquiry and headed it away from dangerous ground. He had eventually, and still without appearing to do so, managed to get rid of the Captain, the First Officer, the doctor, the stewardess and sundry other spectators who had crowded in and asked questions and talked in unison. He had been the last to leave, and had stood in the doorway, his hands thrust into the pockets of his dressing-gown, frowning down at her.

'Are you sure you're all right? You wouldn't like me to knock up Mrs Halliday or get one of the stewardesses to sleep on that top berth?'

'No thank you,' said Amanda wearily. 'I'm all right. You wouldn't think that anyone could feel sleepy after all that, but I do. I feel very stupid and dopey.'

'Reaction from shock,' said Mr Howard. 'Well if anything scares you, don't wait for someone to answer that bell. Come out into the corridor and yell!'

'*Scares* me? What is there to be scared of?' asked Amanda, puzzled.

'I don't know,' said Steven Howard slowly. 'Nothing, I hope.'

He looked round the narrow cabin almost as though he were making certain that no one could be concealed there, and the frown line deepened between his brows. Then he shrugged his shoulders, smiled briefly, and was gone.

Amanda yawned. She felt unbelievably exhausted. She slipped out of her dressing-gown, leaving it in a heap on the floor, and climbing into her berth, switched off the light.

After a minute or two she became aware that there was a small hard lump either in or under her pillow, and she put up a sleepy and impatient hand to investigate.

And that was how she found the bottle.

◊   ◊   ◊

It was a small bottle, and there was something in it that rattled. Amanda lay for a time in the semi-darkness, turning it over in her hand and wondering how it could have come there. Presently she reached out to switch on the light again, and sat up to look at it.

It was an ordinary glass bottle of the type that usually contains aspirins. There were three small tablets in it and it bore a bright red label with a single warning word printed blackly across it. POISON.

All at once Amanda was frightened. She had been shocked and horrified by Julia's collapse, and frightened by the staring, sightless eyes that had not blinked when the water splashed across them. But this was a different sort of fear. A cold, creeping fear that seemed to chill her blood and slow down the beat of her heart. For the bottle had not been there earlier that evening. She was quite sure of that. And for a very good reason.

She had sat down on the centre of the berth to read some letters before changing for dinner, and, reaching for the pillow, had tucked it between her shoulders and the back of the berth. There had been no bottle under it then.

That meant that someone had placed it there some time after eight o'clock. Julia? But Julia had not come near the pillow. She had sat on the foot of the berth and had not moved from there until she had stood up and put those tablets in her mouth and reached for the glass. Amanda had been between Julia Blaine and the pillow and it was quite out of the question that Mrs Blaine could have reached across her and put anything under it without her knowledge.

Who then? And why?

Quite suddenly an answer slipped into Amanda's head as though someone had whispered it very softly into her ear.

Julia Blaine had neither died of a heart attack nor killed herself. She had been murdered. And that small bottle with the poison label proved it——!

The tablets that Julia had put into her mouth had been aspirin tablets given to her by the stewardess. The poison had been in the glass. In that innocent iced drink whose unsweetened tartness would serve to disguise any additional acidity.

Someone who knew that Julia Blaine drank lemon juice and water, but who did not realize that she had changed cabins with Amanda, had laid that deadly trap for her. Julia should have drunk from that glass in her own cabin, and she would have been found there, dead. And presently the bottle would have been found under her pillow, to ensure a verdict of suicide.

Fate had been on the murderer's side, for chance had brought Julia to her former cabin and she had, after all, drunk from the glass and died. But it was Amanda who had found the bottle. And its presence under the wrong pillow was no longer a pointer to suicide, but proof of murder.

'No!' said Amanda, speaking aloud in the hot, silent little cabin. *'No!'*

Almost without realizing what she meant to do, she slipped out of bed. The carpet was still damp and faintly sticky under her bare feet, and she groped for her dressing-gown and putting it on rang the bell. This time it was answered promptly.

Amanda could hear the stewardess rustling down the corridor, her stiff, starched uniform sounding brisk and reassuring.

'What is it, dear? Can't you sleep?' The stewardess was stout, middle-aged, motherly and, by some miracle, English.

Amanda said: 'Did you—did you put a glass of water and lemon juice in here for Mrs Blaine, by mistake?'

The stewardess looked bewildered. 'A lemon squash dear? No. Would you like one?'

'No thank you. But there was one here. It was on that stool when I came in. Did you put it there?'

'Me? Oh no, dear. We don't provide drinks for the passengers unless they ask for them. But you'd only have to ring.'

'Did Mrs Blaine ask for one? This was her cabin before, and I—I thought perhaps it was put in here by mistake.'

'She didn't ask me for one, poor lady. And no one who has to do with the cabins would have made such a mistake, I assure you. They were all aware of the exchange. So it must have been put there by one of your friends. Now what is it that you want, dear?'

'Nothing,' said Amanda, white-faced. 'I—I only wondered . . . You see when she—Mrs Blaine—swallowed those tablets she drank out of a glass that was on that stool; and I—I wondered who put it there.'

'I'll tell you what's the matter with you, dear,' said the steward-ess kindly. 'You're sufferin' from shock. That's what it is. You mustn't let it worry you. The poor lady must have been out of her mind. Now just you try and forget all about it and go to sleep. I expect she had a drink out of that tooth glass over there.'

'No she didn't,' said Amanda. 'It was another glass.'

'Then where is it now?'

Amanda turned and looked about her, but the glass had gone. It was nowhere in the cabin.

'There now!' said the stewardess cosily. 'You're lettin' your nerves run away with you, dearie. An' no wonder! I'll fetch you a nice cup of hot milk, and you'll soon be asleep.'

'No thank you,' said Amanda in a small unsteady voice. 'It's very kind of you, but I don't want anything. I'm sorry to have bothered you.'

'That's all right,' said the stewardess. 'Now you get back into bed, and I'll turn the light out, and if you should want me you only have to ring.'

She tucked Amanda into her berth and went out, switching off the light and closing the door behind her. Her starched skirts rustled crisply away down the passage, and from somewhere nearby a door latch clicked softly.

A faint light from the passage outside filtered in through a nar-row open grill above the door and thinned the darkness of the small cabin, and beyond the open porthole the sky was bright with moon-light.

Except for the soothing swish of the sea and the muffled, rhyth-mic throb of the engines, the night was still and silent and Amanda had heard no sound of footsteps. But suddenly her cabin door opened and closed again. And someone was there, standing beside her; a dark shape against the faint light from the transom.

Amanda's heart seemed to jerk and turn over sickeningly. She sat up, shrinking back against the head of the berth, and tried to scream—and could not, because her throat was dry and constricted with terror; and because there was a hand across her mouth.

A voice spoke in a whisper: 'Don't make a noise. It's I—Steve Howard.'

Amanda crumpled up in a small sobbing heap against him, and he put an arm about her, holding her hard, and sat down on the berth.

'I'm sorry. I didn't mean to frighten you'—his voice was barely a breath against her ear. 'But I had to talk to you. Come on, dear—take a pull on yourself.'

Amanda lifted her head from his shoulder and said in a sobbing furious whisper: *'Get out of my cabin!'*

'That's more like it,' approved Mr Howard. He produced a handkerchief and dried her eyes. Amanda snatched it from him, and having completed the operation for herself, reached for the electric light switch.

Steve Howard's hand shot out and caught her wrist. 'No! Don't turn on the light. I don't want the stewardess coming in here to find out why you're still awake. What were you telling her about a glass? I heard you talking to her. Your door was open. What about that glass, Amanda?'

Amanda shivered and her teeth made a small chattering sound in the silence. She said in a halting whisper: 'There was a glass of water in here—with—with lemon in it, when I came to bed. Mrs Blaine always drinks—drank—lemon and water. She did it to make her thin. And she changed cabins with me.'

'When was that?' the whisper was suddenly sharp. 'Why did you change cabins?'

'This afternoon. Just before tea. This was her cabin. But she wouldn't go into it when she saw the number. It's thirteen, and she was superstitious about thirteen. So I told her that she could have mine.'

'Who knew about it?'

'I don't know. The stewardess said that—that the ship's people would all know. But I don't suppose anyone else would. Except Alastair of course—her husband. The—the stewardess said that it must have been one of the passengers who put that glass there.'

'Yes I know. I heard her. What made you ask her about it?'

'I—I was frightened. Mrs Blaine drank out of it. And now it's gone. Someone must have taken it.'

'I did,' said Steven Howard softly.

'You! But why? I don't understand.'

'Don't you? Why were you frightened because Mrs Blaine drank out of it?'

'Because of the bottle,' breathed Amanda tremulously. 'There was a bottle hidden under my pillow, and I thought——'

'What's that!' The whispered question cracked like a whip in the silence.

Amanda turned and thrust a shaking hand under the pillow, found the bottle and held it out.

Mr Howard took the bottle from her gingerly, holding it with extreme care, and turned to face the light that filtered in through the grill above the door. The little cabin that had seemed so dark when the light had first been switched off no longer appeared dark now that Amanda's eyes had grown accustomed to the dim light, and the single word printed across the red label was clearly readable.

He turned back to her and said: 'How did you come to find it?'

'I told you. It was under my pillow. But it hadn't been there before.' She told him about that, and why she knew that it had not been there before eight o'clock.

'You don't think Mrs Blaine could have put it there while she was talking to you.' The words were less a query than an assertion.

'I know she didn't.'

'Then what *do* you think?'

Amanda did not answer him. She stared down instead at the small bottle that he held so carefully with a corner of his handker-chief.

'Why were you frightened, Amanda?'

Amanda's eyes lifted slowly to his face. His back was to the light from the passage and his face was in deep shadow, but she could see the gleam of his eyes and the line of his mouth and jaw.

She said: 'You know, don't you? That's why you took the glass.'

'Ssh! Quietly. Yes I know. You don't think that she died from a heart attack. Or that she killed herself either. That's it, isn't it?'

'What else can I think?' said Amanda shivering. 'If—if it was something in the glass and not the tablets in her hand, then it must have been—have been——'

'Murder,' finished Steven Howard softly. 'Of course. And I think you're right. Mrs Blaine took two tablets of aspirin. The stuff that killed her was in that glass.'

'How—how can you know?' demanded Amanda in a shaking whisper.

'There are only two sets of finger-prints on the glass, and both of them are quite clear.'

Amanda said: 'But of course there are only two! Only two people touched it. Myself and Mrs Blaine. Oh, and you.'

Mr Howard shook his head. 'I lifted it by the rim. Those marks are there too. But what about the person who brought it here in the first place? There should have been at least three sets of prints on it.'

Amanda put her hands to her throat. It seemed oddly constricted. 'Then she *was* murdered. No! No, it can't be true!'

Her voice rose and Steven Howard's hand was instantly over her mouth. Amanda twisted her head away and said in a shuddering whisper: 'But—but don't you see, that would mean that it was someone she knew. Someone *I* know!—Persis or Toby——No, it can't be. It couldn't possibly be!'

'It must be. Unless——'

He stopped, and Amanda said breathlessly: 'Unless what?'

Mr Howard did not answer her. His eyes had not moved from her face, but he appeared to be listening intently and his hand closed warningly about her wrist.

There was someone in the passage outside. Amanda did not know how she knew it, or how Steven Howard had known it, for her ear had caught no sound of approaching footsteps. Perhaps someone had brushed against the door in passing, or a shadow had flickered briefly across the white wall of the passage.

Steve Howard sat between her and the door so that she could only see the edge of it. The door did not quite fit and there was a thin sliver of light where age had warped the wood. But even as she looked, the slit of light vanished.

Steve saw her eyes widen, and for a brief moment his fingers tightened on her wrist. He turned his head and drew something out of the pocket of his dressing-gown, moving with infinite caution. Amanda saw the light from the transom glint on the barrel of the gun he held, and thought with a stunned illogicality, 'He's left-handed.'

Booted feet clattered noisily down a companionway at the far end of the passage and instantly the thin sliver of light reappeared at the edge of the door. Whoever had paused outside Amanda's cabin had gone as silently as they had come.

Someone, a ship's officer by the sound, passed quickly down the passage, and a distant door banged shut. Mr Howard slid the small gun into his pocket and sighed.

'I was afraid of that,' he said softly.

'Of what?' breathed Amanda.

Mr Howard turned to look at her. 'Without wishing to be an alarmist,' he said, 'I think you would be advised to walk extremely warily for the next few days. In fact I would suggest that you send yourself an urgent telegram and take the next available plane for England?'

'Why?' said Amanda. 'I don't understand——'

'Don't you? I should have thought it was obvious. It looks as though somebody planned a murder that was to pass as suicide. That someone has either realized already, or will shortly realize, that the thing has blown a fuse, in that you and not Mrs Blaine are occupying Cabin No. 13, and that you will therefore be in a position to know— or at least suspect—that Mrs Blaine was murdered. That being so, whoever planted that bottle may go to considerable lengths to get it back.'

'Then what are you going to do with it?' demanded Amanda in a dry whisper.

'Dispose of it.'

'But you can't! The Captain must see it—the police. If you don't tell them, I shall!'

Mr Howard stood up. 'I wouldn't do that if I were you,' he said quietly. 'Not unless you want to find yourself under arrest.'

Amanda shrank back against the pillow, her breath coming short. 'What do you mean?'

He stood looking down at her, his hands in his pockets, and after a moment he said softly and very deliberately: 'You see, there is always the possibility that you might have worked the whole thing yourself.'

There was a long silence in the little cabin. A silence that seemed to stretch out into interminable minutes. Outside that silence the quiet night was once again full of sounds: the rustling wash of water along the sides of the ship, the monotonous throb of the engines and the hundred and one tiny creaks and squeaks and rattles that the shudder of the screw set up in the fabric of the ship.

Amanda spoke at last. 'You can't believe that. You can't!'

'Perhaps not. But there'll have to be a post-mortem, and the police may—if this turns out to be a case of murder. You see, they would have only your own word for what happened in this cabin, and of how you came to be in possession of that bottle. If it turns out to contain the same poison that killed Mrs Blaine, they may even think that you invited her in to talk to you. And since her husband presumably inherits anything she had to leave, Major Blaine will now be an exceedingly eligible widower—and you saw quite a lot of him in Fayid, didn't you?'

Amanda caught her breath in a hard gasp. She said in a furious whisper: *'Get out!* Get out of my cabin before I call someone to put you out!'

'Don't be silly, Amanda;' Steven Howard had not raised his voice, but the words held a cutting edge that was as effective as a slap in the face. 'You are in no position to behave stupidly. You have no idea at all what it would be like to get yourself involved in a police inquiry out here. It's no joke anywhere. With this setup it would be hell. If you have any sense in that charming head you will keep your mouth shut about that bottle and the glass and let it be supposed that Mrs Blaine committed suicide. Any other course is likely to prove very sticky for you, if not downright dangerous. And you are in a sticky enough position already, without that.'

Amanda said: *'Who are you?'*

Mr Howard grinned unexpectedly. 'The name is Howard. Steve to my friends. I paint indifferent pictures and have a passion for meddling in other people's affairs. Anything else you'd like to know?'

'Yes,' said Amanda. 'Who are you really? Why do you carry a gun? What are you doing in all this? Don't tell me that you're just out here to paint pictures, because I don't believe a word of it!'

Mr Howard laughed. 'All right. Let's say that I happen, for reasons of my own, to be interested in one or two people who are on this boat.'

'Are you in the police?' demanded Amanda abruptly.

'No.'

'Then why are you taking a hand in this?'

Steve Howard grinned. 'Pure knight-errantry. Or mere meddling —take your choice. And now I think you'd better get some sleep, if you think you can manage it. There's a bolt on that door. I suggest you use it. Goodnight Amarantha.'

The door closed softly behind him.

4

Amanda shot the bolt on the inside of her cabin door with unsteady fingers, and returned to her berth to sit rigidly upright with her arms about her knees, straining to listen and starting at every unidentified sound.

The full import of Steven Howard's statement that sooner or later someone must inevitably realize that Amanda, as the present occupant of cabin number thirteen, was bound to obtain possession of evidence that pointed to murder, had only just come home to her. It was a singularly unpleasant thought; and even more unpleasant was the sudden realization that but for Julia's arrival, she would have carried that glass into Julia's cabin. Her finger-prints would have been found upon it, and there would only have been her own word for why she had handed a glass of poison to Alastair Blaine's wife.

Alastair's wife . . . Was that the key to this cruel murder? Had Alastair——? But no, that was absurd! It could not be Alastair because he at least would know of the exchange of cabins. Who then? Someone who knew Julia well enough to be aware of her lemon-and-water slimming fad, and who had made a note of the number of her cabin but had not realized that she had subsequently moved into Amanda's. Mrs. Norman——? George Norman? Persis? Toby? No, it could not be! There must be some mistake. Julia must either have had a heart attack or committed suicide after all, and there must be some other explanation for that bottle. There *must* be!

Why, oh why, thought Amanda desperately, had she ever offered to exchange cabins with Julia Blaine? But for that, no one need ever have suspected that there had been a murder. No one would ever have known. Yet because she had made that exchange, she knew—and someone else must suspect that she knew—that Julia's death was not suicide, but a carefully planned murder.

The sky was paling to the dawn, and the swish of hoses and a thump of holystones betokened the arrival of a new day before Amanda fell at last into an exhausted sleep, from which she was eventually awakened by a loud knocking on her door. Starting up with her heart in her mouth, she found the cabin full of reflected sunlight, and the stewardess demanding entrance with a lukewarm cup of tea.

In the gay morning sunlight Amanda could not remember for a moment why she should have been frightened. Her first impression was that she must have had a particularly vivid and unpleasant dream. But this was quickly dispelled by the stewardess, who on being admitted, announced with relish that the police were already on board and that the captain wished to see Miss Derington in his cabin as soon as possible.

Amanda was suddenly aware that the sea was no longer swishing past the ship and that the engines were silent.

'Have we arrived?'

'Half an hour or more ago,' said the stewardess. 'We're at Limassol. I would have woken you before, but the gentleman in number eleven said to let you sleep. *Such* a nice man! So thoughtful. It's not many that are these days. Shall I get you some breakfast, dear? You looked a bit peaked—an' no wonder.'

'No thank you,' said Amanda. 'Just coffee, if you would. What does the captain want to see me about?'

'I'm sure I don't know, dear. I expect they just want you to tell the police what happened last night—just as a matter of form as you might say—before they bury the poor lady. Very cut up her husband is. Looks like a ghost he does. As for the little lady in 31, she came over all queer when she heard the news. The dead lady and her husband were going to stay with her. Fancy! Cousins or something. Very delicate she is—Mrs Norman, that is. The sensitive kind I should say. *Dreadfully* upset she was. "Why, Mrs Norman," I said——'

A knock on the door mercifully stemmed the flow and Toby Gates' voice inquired anxiously if Amanda was all right and wasn't it ghastly?

Amanda replied in the affirmative to both, adding that she would be out in five minutes; and while the stewardess went in search of coffee she dressed hurriedly, plaiting her hair into two thick braids and pinning it swiftly about her head instead of coiling it into the heavy knot at the nape of her neck that took considerably more time and care to achieve.

The yellow cotton frock that she had worn on the previous day seemed too gay a garment in which to attend an inquiry into sudden death (she would not say the word 'murder' even to herself), and she rummaged hastily in her suitcase and found a silver-grey poplin with a narrow white belt. Gulping down the coffee that the stewardess had brought, she slipped her feet into white sandals and found Toby Gates waiting for her at the end of the passage.

'They want to see all of us,' said Toby, taking her arm and hurrying her up the stairs. 'Those of us who knew her. She must have had a brainstorm. I always thought she was a spot peculiar. Rotten for Alastair, poor devil; utter hell I should think.'

Amanda said anxiously: 'What do they want to see us for, Toby?'

'Oh, just to give them some sort of a picture of the whole thing I suppose. Matter of form an' all that. They've already had poor old Alastair answering questions for the odd half-hour or so. Jolly kick-off to a holiday for all of us, I must say!'

The ship was anchored near a town whose white-walled houses were set among green trees and the silver-grey of olives, against a backdrop of low, barren hills. The sun blazed down from a cloudless sky and glittered on the dancing water, and the blue shallow sea was streaked with bars of vivid emerald, clear cerulean and a soft, milky jade. There was an exhilaration and a sparkle in the air and once again Amanda found that it was impossible to believe that any of the events of the past night had really occurred, or that Julia Blaine was dead.

Toby said: 'Up this ladder. Left turn. Here we are.'

The captain's cabin appeared to be filled to overflowing. Besides the captain, the first officer, the doctor, purser and stewardess, there were three unidentified men in uniform, presumably police officers, one of whom, at least, was British. Alastair Blaine, the Normans and Persis Halliday were also present, and Steve Howard was standing at the far side of the room, leaning on the windowsill and looking out across the sunlit deck towards the little town of Limassol. He glanced round as Amanda and Toby Gates entered, but he did not speak and presently returned to his idle contemplation of the view.

Alastair Blaine was looking drawn and grey. He appeared to have aged ten years, and the merciless morning sunlight showed unexpected traces of silver among his thick blond hair.

Persis Halliday, looking, as ever, as if she had that moment been unpacked from an expensive bandbox, was sitting on the arm of a chintz-covered chair swinging one silken foot in a neat alligator shoe and fidgeting with an unlighted cigarette. She looked up as Amanda came in and said: ''Lo, honey. This is a pretty set up, I'll say! Did you sleep at all?'

Claire Norman said: 'Sleep? I am sure none of us did! How *could* we? Poor Julia! I shall never forgive myself. Never! Dancing, while she was dying . . . !'

Her voice was tragic and quivering and she had managed to find among her suitcases a deceptively simple and most becoming frock in black linen that made her appear smaller and whiter and more fragile than ever.

George Norman patted her shoulder with awkward tenderness and Persis, turning to face her, said: 'So you knew about it last night? Now that's very interesting. I didn't get in on it until the stewardess spilt the beans this morning. How did you hear about it?'

For a brief moment two small patches of colour appeared in Claire Norman's ivory cheeks, and she was all at once very still; her grey eyes no longer limpid with tragedy but curiously alert and guarded. She did not answer Mrs Halliday's question and it was George Norman who broke the brief silence:

'We didn't hear until this morning,' he said. 'Claire was only speaking figuratively. She's a little upset.'

The rigidity went out of Claire Norman's small body. She did not contradict her husband's statement, and there was no further chance for conversation, for the captain, clearly impatient to be done with the whole affair, was introducing the police officers and hurrying on with the business in hand. This proved to be merely a repetition of last night's questions and answers, with the sole difference that four of the late Mrs Blaine's friends and acquaintances were also present, each of whom gave their individual opinion as to her state of nerves and mind.

Amanda was asked to repeat her story, and did so; making the same reservations that she had made the night before. Mrs Blaine, said Amanda, had been overwrought and hysterical. She felt the heat badly, had complained of the East and Army life in general and had talked of taking her own life. She had been holding some tablets in her hand—no, Amanda could not say how many—and had eventually swallowed them——

Amanda's voice wavered suddenly, and looking beyond the captain's shoulder she encountered Steve Howard's deceptively lazy gaze. He shook his head very slightly. It was only a fractional gesture but in the circumstances plainly readable. Amanda turned her eyes away and looked at the ring of silent faces—the red, impatient face of the captain; the avid gaze of the stewardess; the weary resignation on the face of the ship's doctor and the alert concentrated gaze of the three police officers—and closed her lips without mentioning the glass in her cabin. She did not look at Steven Howard again but she had the impression that he had relaxed.

The police were courteous and sympathetic and the captain only too eager to wash his hands of the lot of them, and after leaving their names and addresses and completing various other formalities, the passengers were hustled out of the cabin and told that they could now go ashore.

It was perhaps twenty minutes later that they descended the gangway and were rowed away from the ship over water so crystal clear that as they neared the shore every rock and pebble and shell on the sea floor was clearly visible, and they could see the shell markings on the back of a huge turtle that flippered its way lazily through the water beneath them.

There was a man waiting on the water steps by the quay; hatless and presumably British, since he wore a thin, well-cut and very English tweed coat. He was a slim man in the late thirties, of medium height and with a face so deeply tanned by sun and wind as to make his eyes and his crisp, sunbleached and slightly greying hair seem light by contrast. But despite its brownness it gave an impression of being pale under the tan. A paleness that gave a curious greyish tint to the shadows on his face. It was a thin, pleasant face that would have been handsome except that just now it looked desperately tired and was scored with lines of weariness and anxiety.

'There's Glenn,' said George Norman. 'Do you suppose he's——' He checked suddenly and coughed in an embarrassed manner. The prow grated upon stone and a moment later the passengers were on shore and Claire Norman was holding out a small white hand to the man in the tweed coat:

'Glenn. How nice to see you! I suppose you are here to meet Miss Derington. Or did you come to meet . . . someone else?'

There was the faintest pause before the last two words, and Mr Glennister Barton's pleasant tanned face flushed deeply and the muscles about his mouth tightened. Claire Norman said: 'Amanda, this is Glenn Barton. Your host in Cyprus.'

Amanda held out her hand and found herself looking into a pair of grey eyes that were unmistakably desperate and unhappy. And she was suddenly unreasonably angry with Mrs Norman, who had said something which, though meaningless to Amanda, had undoubtedly possessed a hidden and hurtful meaning for this pleasant, rather diffident man.

Glenn Barton barely touched her hand, was introduced to her companions and exchanged a few civilities. He inquired after her Uncle Oswin and, having taken charge of her luggage and seen her through the customs, led the way to a long grey saloon car that was parked near the customs' shed. Amanda had expected to see Mrs Barton, but there was no sign of any other woman, and Glenn Barton, having piled Amanda's suitcases on to the back seat held open the front door of the car for her.

Persis called out: 'See you in Kyrenia, honey!' and Toby Gates, looking like a spaniel puppy that is being left behind from a walk, said in an urgent undertone: 'You *will* let me come over and see you, won't you?'

Amanda glanced over his shoulder, but Steve Howard, his back to her, was leaning lazily against a pillar with his hands in his pockets, talking to Claire Norman. Amanda got into the car feeling unaccountably annoyed and said: 'Why, of course, Toby,' with unnecessary cordiality and emphasis, and a moment later Glenn Barton released the clutch and the car slid out of shadow into the bright sunlight of the road to Nicosia.

The countryside, once they had left the coast and the incredible sapphire, turquoise and jade of the shallow waters that fringed it, was bleached and colourless in the hot sun. The earth was brown and stony and dotted with small shrubs, and except for an occasional olive grove there was little green and almost no shade as the road wound and twisted through barren hills and past dried-up watercourses where the heat haze shimmered on the stones and boulders.

It was all new and strange and different to Amanda, and she might well have found it fascinating but for the fact that her host was strangely silent and was driving much too fast. She wondered if he were shy or if there was something in that seemingly innocent remark of Claire Norman's that had goaded him to this silence and speed? The big car was moving with dangerous velocity, shaving corners with a screech of tortured tyres and singing down the straight stretches of road with the speed of a steel-shafted arrow, while Amanda, who was not normally of a nervous disposition, found herself unconsciously clutching at the edge of her seat with rigid fingers and watching the flickering needle of the speedometer with fixed and apprehensive eyes.

She turned her head away with an effort and covertly studied her prospective host. He was sitting hunched forward a little, as a man will sit who steadies a nervous horse at the approach of a dangerous fence, and there was a look of nervous strain and tension in every line of his brown face and slim body. His hands were gripping the wheel so tightly that the knuckles stood out white against the tanned skin and there was a deep crease between his brows. Amanda thought that she had never seen anyone look so unhappy, and she looked away quickly, embarrassed and disturbed.

The needle of the speedometer wavered on ninety and she tightened her clutch on the seat, shut her eyes briefly and swallowed hard. Making a valiant effort she attempted a few polite observations on the scenery, to which Mr Barton returned equally polite but brief replies. The car whipped between an ox cart and a bus load of Cypriot peasants on their way to market, avoiding both by a hair's breadth; flashed past a string of camels on to a narrow bridge, and missed a small boy on a donkey by a matter of millimetres.

Amanda shut her eyes again and Mr Barton inquired if she had had a pleasant trip from Fayid.

'No,' said Amanda with feeling. 'It was perfectly beastly!' She found herself telling him about Julia Blaine's death, and Mr Barton expressed concern but no surprise.

Amanda said: 'Did you know about it then?'

'Yes. You see we ship a good bit of our wine from Limassol, so there are always several of our people on those boats or at the docks and most of them had heard. There was a lot of talk about it. The Blaines were over here for a couple of weeks last year, staying with Claire and George Norman. They're related I believe. I was away on business at the time so I didn't meet them myself, but my—wife knew them slightly.' He was silent for a moment or two and then said apologetically: 'Of course I had no idea that Mrs Blaine had died in your cabin, or I should not have asked such a stupid question. It must have been a most unpleasant experience. I'm sorry that you should have had such a horrible introduction to Cyprus. I wish I could do something to make up for it.'

He turned to look at her and his tired, unhappy face broke into a smile. It was an extraordinarily pleasant smile and Amanda found herself returning it with frank friendliness.

He's nice, she thought. But he's got something on his mind. He's tired and badgered and worried sick about something—and then he has to come and meet me and put me up and look after me!

She said quickly: 'It's very kind of you and your wife to have me to stay. I do hope it hasn't been an awful nuisance. I feel rather bad about it—inflicting myself on you like this. I don't imagine that Uncle Oswin gave you much choice, did he?'

'Well—no,' said Glenn Barton with a rueful smile and a return of the anxious crease between his brows. 'But——'

He slowed the car down and said abruptly: 'Look, would you like something to eat? There's an inn just ahead. We could get some bread and cheese and olives and some goat's milk if you'd like it.'

'I'd love it!' said Amanda, suddenly remembering that she had had no breakfast. Mr Barton removed his foot from the accelerator and brought the car to a stop before a small shabby building half hidden by trees.

The little inn consisted of one large room furnished with rough wooden chairs and tables and decorated with portraits of the King and Queen of the Hellenes, torn from some illustrated paper and tacked against the walls. The charming, elfin face of Fredricka smiled out from a wreath of green leaves, reminding Amanda that this was an island where many of the inhabitants resented the British occupation and were demanding union with Greece.

The room was crowded with black-haired, dark-eyed Cypriots and redolent with garlic and the spilled lees of wine, but the proprietress, a buxom red-cheeked woman who seemed to know Mr Barton well and addressed him in rapid Greek, found them a table and fetched coarse bread, grapes, figs and lumps of cheese made from goat's milk. At Mr Barton's request she added a bottle of some colourless liquid that appeared to be gin, a carafe of water and two glasses.

Amanda ate the simple food with relish and Glenn Barton poured a small portion of the liquid into each glass and added water, whereupon the mixture turned a cloudy white.

'What is it?' demanded Amanda, intrigued.

'*Ouzo*. The national drink. Do you see that old man over there by the door?' Amanda turned and observed an ancient and decrepit greybeard who appeared to be dozing comfortably in his chair. 'He's our hostess's husband. He used to be a tough upstanding chap when I first came to Cyprus, but he took to drinking his *ouzo* straight. If you drink enough of it it's supposed to send you off your head. But it's quite harmless in small quantities. Try it.'

Amanda picked up the nearest glass, sniffed at it and wrinkled her nose expressively. Glenn Barton laughed. 'It smells pretty pungent, doesn't it? Aniseed. Don't you like it?'

'No,' said Amanda frankly, 'I've always detested the smell of aniseed ever since my kindergarten days when there was a small boy who used to sit next to me in class and suck aniseed balls. I hated him—and them.'

'It tastes better than it smells,' said Glenn Barton. He raised his glass to her. 'Here's to your first visit to Cyprus. May it be a very pleasant one.'

'Thank you,' said Amanda, and smiled at him.

Mr Barton drank and pushed away his glass. The frown was suddenly back in his forehead and Amanda saw that his hands were not quite steady and that there was a tinge of whiteness about his mouth. He offered her a cigarette, and when she refused, lit one himself and said in a jerky and difficult voice: 'I—I'm afraid that I— we—shall not be able to put you up after all. You see—my wife is not well, and I couldn't ask you to stay in the house while—while——'

He stopped and pushed his hands through his hair in a gesture that was somehow boyish and despairing.

'But of course you can't!' said Amanda, moved by a sudden warm feeling of compassion. 'Don't give it another thought—please. I'm terribly sorry to hear about your wife. Are you sure that there is nothing I can do to help?'

'No, nothing,' said Glenn Barton wretchedly. 'It's very good of you to take it like this. I feel pretty terrible about it—saying that we'd put you up, and then letting you get here and failing you like this.'

'Nonsense!' said Amanda cheerfully. 'It doesn't matter a bit. I can easily go to a hotel.'

'Oh no. I couldn't let you do that!' Glenn Barton lifted his eyes from the table and looked at her earnestly. 'I've arranged all that. A friend of mind in Kyrenia, a Miss Moon, is going to put you up instead. She's a bit eccentric, but very kind. I know you'll like her.'

'But I can't go sponging on your friends,' said Amanda dismayed. 'It was quite bad enough Uncle Oswin pushing me on to you like this, but——'

'Please!' interrupted Glenn Barton with a twisted smile. 'You're being kind and letting me down gently, but I'd be very grateful if you'd add to your kindness by agreeing to stay with Miss Moon. I'd feel much better about it. Besides, she's expecting you. She's a dear and is delighted at the idea of having you. She likes young people—specially pretty ones.'

His smile pointed the compliment and Amanda laughed and capitulated. She had been disappointed at the prospect of staying in Nicosia instead of on the coast, and Persis and Toby would be in Kyrenia. She would have preferred to be independent and stay at a hotel, but she could hardly treat Mr Barton's arrangements in a cavalier fashion.

Mr Barton said: 'Then that's fixed. We'll have to stop in at the office in Nicosia just for a minute or two I'm afraid, but we should be in Kyrenia in time for lunch. If you really won't try the *ouzo* we'd better be getting along.'

5

The buxom proprietress of the inn presented the bill and embarked on an animated conversation with Mr Barton that, judging from her laughing glance, referred to Amanda.

'What is she saying?' asked Amanda.

'She was asking where you'd come from, and she says that you are a very beautiful young lady and wishes to know if you can sit on your hair when it is unbound,' said Glenn Barton with a smile.

Amanda laughed. 'Tell her, only just!'

'You come on *Orantares,* yes? From Port Said?' said the woman in halting English. 'My man too. Is fine ship.'

She smiled broadly at Amanda, swept up the handful of small coins that Mr Barton had counted out onto the table, and hurried away to deal with an impatient patron.

'Are all the people here as friendly and cheerful as that?' asked Amanda.

'A good many of them. Why? You sound surprised.'

'I suppose I am,' admitted Amanda. 'The only things that ever get into the papers about Cyprus are articles about how discontented they are with the whole set-up.'

Glenn Barton smiled and said: 'I think you'll find them cheerful enough.'

He dropped the end of his cigarette into Amanda's glass, where it hissed out and disintegrated slowly, and sat watching it abstractedly for a moment or two with his own face anything but cheerful. Presently he gave a sharp sigh and stood up.

'Let's go, shall we?'

They walked out into the bright sunlight to the car and continued their journey towards Nicosia; but at a less dangerous speed. The interlude at the inn appeared to have lessened Glenn Barton's nervous tension, and he was more talkative and at ease; but he did not refer again to his wife's illness and it was obvious that he did not wish to discuss it.

Amanda found herself wondering what Mrs Barton was like, and if she would meet her—and passed from that to wondering whether she would meet Steven Howard again, and why it should be a matter of concern to her whether she did or not? Mr Howard had been brusque and arbitrary and rude, and had had the incredible effrontery to hint that she might have planned the murder of Julia Blaine as the result of an intrigue with Julia's husband Alastair. True, he had said nothing to suggest that he himself believed it. But that such an idea could even enter his head, infuriated and frightened her. She ought by rights to be thankful that she need have no more to do with him and could put him out of her mind and forget him.

But she found that she could not stop thinking about him. Who was he? Why had he been on the *Orantares?* What had he been doing in Fayid and who was it that he had followed to Cyprus?

The road twisted downwards through the sunbleached hills and ran out upon the wide, flat, dusty central plain of Cyprus, and it was midday by the time they came in sight of the green trees, jostling rooftops, Byzantine churches and Gothic mosques of Nicosia.

The heat danced in the narrow, crowded streets; on minarets and domes and fretted balconies, the concrete walls and roofs of innumerable newly built suburban-style houses, petrol pumps, jeeps, Army lorries and creaking carts drawn by oxen.

Presently the car turned in between whitewashed gateposts shaded by flamboyants and oleanders, and drew up before a small bungalow.

'This is our Nicosia office,' explained Glenn Barton. 'Would you like to come in? I won't be more than a few minutes.'

The office walls were bare and white-washed. There was coarse matting on the floor, and green wooden jalousies over the windows kept out the midday heat and made the rooms cool and dim. A woman who had been seated at a littered desk rose quickly as they entered and Glenn Barton said: 'This is Miss Ford—my secretary. Monica, this is Miss Derington.'

Miss Ford was plain, solidly built and verging on middle age. She had slightly protruding teeth and her hair—of that indeterminate shade that is usually described as 'mouse'—was drawn loosely back from her forehead and confined in a small hard bun at the nape of her neck.

Glenn Barton said: 'I didn't think you'd be here today, Monica.

Sure you're all right? You needn't have come you know.' There was concern in his voice and he put a hand on the thick shoulder and pressed it affectionately, and turning to Amanda said: 'Monica's not only my secretary. She's my right hand—and my left one! I don't know what I'd do without her. She practically runs the business.'

Miss Ford's sallow face flushed with pleasure and for a moment she looked almost girlish. 'That's nonsense, of course,' she said to Amanda. 'Glenn works far too hard. I'm always telling him that he'll have a breakdown if he doesn't let up a bit. How is your uncle, Miss Derington? I haven't seen him for over a year. He got me this post you know. I used to work in his London office.'

'Uncle Oswin is fine,' said Amanda. 'He's ramping round the Middle East putting the fear of Derington into Deringtons, which is his idea of bliss.'

Glenn Barton laughed. 'Then we can consider ourselves very lucky that he has sent us such a charming representative instead of paying us a personal visit.'

'Oh, I'm not a representative,' said Amanda, smiling back at him. 'I'm merely having a holiday on my own. Uncle Oswin would have come himself if he could have fitted it in, but he couldn't, and once he's worked out a programme nothing will induce him to alter it by an hour—let alone a day. So he decided that you would have to get along without a personal pep-talk for another year or so.'

'It's a pity he couldn't come,' said Glenn Barton with a sigh. 'We have a lot of problems to contend with that I don't think your uncle fully understands. They lose a lot of force when they are reduced to official reports, but a few days on the ground would have brought them home to him. Perhaps you could persuade him to come over on his way back?'

'I'm afraid not,' said Amanda lightly. 'He'll be in Kenya now, and he flies to Tripoli for a few days this week-end, and goes back to London from there for a conference. I don't believe he'd alter a schedule for the H Bomb. That is, not unless you could think up something that would really lure him; like flagrant immorality among the staff! Uncle Oswin is very hot on the Purity of Deringtons. It's his hobby.'

Amanda laughed, but there was no answering smile on the faces of her two companions. It was, on the contrary, instantly and painfully obvious that she had made an exceedingly tactless remark, for once again there was a white line about Glenn Barton's mouth while

Miss Ford's sallow face had flushed a dull and unbecoming shade of red.

There was a brief uncomfortable silence and then Miss Ford turned hurriedly to Mr Barton:

'Kostos is here, Glenn. He arrived just before you did. I don't know why he didn't see you in Limassol and save himself the journey. These people never think.'

'He couldn't,' said Mr Barton. 'They had a bit of trouble on the ship. One of the passengers died, and things got a bit held up. I'll see him now. Will you look after Miss Derington?'

'Yes, of course. Wouldn't you like a wash, Miss Derington? I—I know how dusty that road is. And what about some orange juice or sherry or something? Or there's some iced coffee if you'd prefer that? Glenn will be here about ten or fifteen minutes; there are some invoices he'll have to look at.'

'Iced coffee sounds wonderful,' said Amanda gratefully. 'And so does a wash. I'm stiff with dust and parched with thirst.'

Glenn Barton said: 'I'll be as quick as I can,' and Monica Ford led Amanda away. 'Come on to the verandah when you're ready,' she said. 'It's through that door over there. I'll have the coffee ready for you.'

The verandah was wide and shady but it seemed intolerably bright after the cool dimness of the shuttered rooms. Monica Ford had set out two chairs and was pouring out iced coffee from a frosted jug.

'Lovely!' said Amanda, drinking thirstily. 'I needed that!'

She smiled gratefully at Miss Ford and noticed that in the full light of the verandah the sallow, sensible face looked older, and somewhat ill. There were dark shadows under Miss Ford's eyes that the wide pink plastic rims of her glasses failed to hide, and Amanda suspected that she had been crying. The square, plain face with its pale blue eyes, sandy lashes and entire absence of make-up, looked sensible and efficient. An impression that was somewhat belied by Miss Ford's choice of costume, for she wore a gaily coloured and full-skirted cotton frock which did nothing to improve either her thick waist or her unadorned complexion. To this she had added as a final incongruous touch a necklace and ear-rings of large plastic flowers and a liberal application of some cheap scent that smelt like violet hair oil

Amanda suspected that the ear-rings at least were a recent and unusual adornment, for Monica Ford could not keep her hands from them. She kept touching them while she talked, as though they worried her; loosening the screws and tightening them again; her strong, square-fingered, sensible hands with their short unvarnished nails providing a sharp contrast to the glittering transparent petals of the plastic flowers.

She had arrived in Cyprus less than a year ago, she told Amanda, at the instigation of Mr Oswin Derington in whose office she had previously worked for over five years: 'He thought that Mr Barton needed someone to help him,' explained Miss Ford. 'Things were not going so well at first, and these little local typists are often worse than useless. There was a great deal of work. You've no idea what Glenn has had to contend with. Labour troubles and customs troubles and local prejudice, and no one to give him any help or encouragement. It's been an uphill fight. He ought to go on leave, but he won't. He works himself until he drops. He doesn't know how to spare himself. Some men are like that—Bobby was like that too . . .'

Her voice suddenly broke and stopped and Amanda saw to her horror that the pale eyes had filled with tears.

Miss Ford fumbled in one of the large pockets that ornamented her skirt and producing a damp handkerchief blew her nose fiercely. 'Do forgive me. I—I'm not quite myself today. I—Hay fever you know——'

'How horrid for you,' said Amanda politely. 'But I'm not surprised, with all these gorgeous flowers around.'

'They are lovely, aren't they?' said Miss Ford recovering herself. 'It's odd to think that I didn't want to come out to Cyprus at all.'

'Then you like it here?'

'Oh *yes!*' said Monica Ford clasping her hands together in a sudden convulsive gesture. 'It's—it's a beautiful island. I couldn't bear to leave! I won't leave!—I *won't*—I——'

She stopped abruptly and the colour flamed up into her sallow cheeks. There was a brief embarrassed pause and Amanda said sympathetically: 'I suppose Uncle Oswin is trying to drag you back to London or Liverpool or somewhere? He is an old bully, isn't he? Pay no attention to him! I was scared stiff of him for years and then one day I suddenly realized that I wasn't a schoolgirl any longer, and I staged a token strike and got away with it. All you've got to do is to stand up to him.'

Monica Ford smiled uncertainly and said: 'Have some more coffee?'

'I'd love some.' Amanda held out her glass and said: 'I'm sorry to hear that Mrs Barton is ill. What's the matter with her? I didn't like to ask her husband; he seemed rather upset about it. Is she really bad?'

Inexplicably the hot colour deepened in Monica Ford's plain face and she fumbled with the jug so that the coffee spilt in a pale brown stream down the skirt of her gaily patterned cotton frock. She sprang up hurriedly, her face crimson, and said in a muffled voice: 'Oh dear!—and it stains so! Excuse me just a minute——' and fled.

Amanda looked after her in considerable surprise. What *was* the matter with Mrs Barton? Had she perhaps gone off her head? Or contracted some illness like poliomyelitis that the authorities wished to hush up for fear of creating a panic? It was all rather mysterious and Amanda was suddenly intensely sorry for Glenn Barton. What with work and worry, a wife who was ill—or worse—and a secretary who was quite obviously suffering from nerves (Amanda did not believe the hay fever story) her own arrival at this juncture must have seemed to him like the proverbial last straw.

A door at the far end of the verandah opened and Mr Barton himself walked quickly towards her.

'I'm sorry to have kept you waiting. I hope that Monica kept you entertained. Where is she?'

'She spilt some coffee down her frock and she's gone to mop it off,' said Amanda, rising. 'I don't think she's feeling very well.'

A shadow crossed Glenn Barton's pleasant face and he glanced towards the door and lowered his voice:

'I know. Poor Monica. She's had a ghastly shock, but she's taking it splendidly. She's got lots of guts. She only heard yesterday that her brother was shot by Mau Mau terrorists in Kenya. He had a farm out there, and they attacked the place and wiped it out. He was all the family she had. There don't seem to be any other relations, and she was devoted to him.'

'I *am* sorry! said Amanda, smitten. 'How dreadful for her. No wonder she seemed so upset.'

She turned to look out across the sun-drenched garden with its blaze of flowers, and all at once, in that hot, quiet verandah, she shivered as though she were cold.

'What is it?' asked Glenn Barton, his voice suddenly gentle.

'Nothing. I—I was only thinking that—that it's such a lovely day, and it doesn't seem possible that awful, tragic things can happen to people. And yet they do. To ordinary, nice people like Alastair Blaine—and Miss Ford——'

'I shouldn't have told you about it,' said Glenn Barton contritely. 'I'm sorry. You've had quite enough to upset you already. Tragedy is not for the young. Forget it and enjoy yourself. It *is* a lovely day!'

He held out a hand to her: 'Come on, or you will be late for luncheon and Miss Moon will never forgive me.'

6

The road from Nicosia to Kyrenia runs for a few miles across the plain and then begins to climb the long narrow barrier of the Kyrenia range that forms a rampart between the plain and the north coast of the Island.

The car topped the pass and began to descend, swinging and turning to the curves of the winding road, and there below them lay the sea—an impossible cerulean blue streaked with sapphire and viridian, with the white, beautiful coastline fading away into the heat haze until the sky and sea and coast seemed to merge and melt into one.

Olive groves, the tree trunks so gnarled and twisted with age that some of them must surely have seen the Crusaders come and go, stood dark against the glittering expanse of blue, and below them the little white town of Kyrenia lay basking in the noonday sun like a handful of pearls and white pebbles washed up by the sea.

They drove down a long road that wound and curved between olive, carob, cypress, mulberry and mountain fir, and which finally ran straight from the foot of the hills to the sea.

A quarter of a mile short of the harbour the car turned off into a side road and drew up before a large square, two-storeyed house that was separated from the road by a white wall, a line of cypress trees and a tangle of oleanders.

'Here we are,' said Glenn Barton. 'This is the Villa Oleander. Andreas will bring in your suitcases.'

The house was high and old, weather-worn and beautiful. Its walls had been colour-washed a flaking and discoloured pink that had bleached to a warm, uneven shade of apricot, and the wrought-iron balconies and wooden shutters at the windows were a soft, faded, dusty emerald green. The roof tiles had probably come from the South of France, for they were not red, but a deep beautiful pink, each one curved and marked with the outline of a heart.

A short, flagged walk and six shallow stone steps led up to a massive front door whose heavy bronze knocker was green with age, and the garden was a neglected tangle of orange and lemon trees, figs, plum trees, oleanders, roses, and cascades of yellow and white jasmine. A vine grew along the wrought-iron of a balcony to the right of the front door, and water trickled from the mouth of a bronze dolphin into a deep pool full of lily pads and reeds; the sound of its fall providing a tinkling counterpoint to the cooing of pigeons from among the warm shadows of a gnarled olive tree.

Amanda stood with her hands on the gate and looked about her with a feeling of awe. It was all so right. So exactly right—the quintessence of serenity and enchantment.

Glenn Barton, watching her, said a little anxiously: 'I'm afraid it's a bit neglected. But Miss Moon says that she can't be bothered with keeping up the garden and that she likes it like this.'

'So do I,' said Amanda on a breath of rapture. 'It's beautiful! It's just exactly like a picture I've always had in my mind of what a house on a Mediterranean island should look like, but I've always been afraid that it wouldn't. It's like a dream!'

Glenn Barton looked relieved but uncomprehending, and it was obvious that he himself saw little to admire in the shabby house and neglected overgrown garden. He led the way up the short flight of stone steps to the front door and banged on the knocker. There was a sound of quick footsteps and the door swung open on well-oiled hinges to show a stout black-eyed woman who wore a voluminous and rather dirty apron and a brightly coloured cotton handkerchief tied over her abundant greying hair.

'Ah! Kyrie Barton! Kalossorisis. Ti habaria. Kopiase messa!'

'This is Euridice,' said Glenn Barton turning to Amanda. 'She's the cook and housekeeper and housemaid and everything rolled into one.'

Amanda smiled at her, and the woman beamed back and breaking into a flood of unintelligible speech, led the way across a wide hall into a large dim drawing-room full of old, beautiful furniture and dusty curio cabinets, where the shutters had been closed against the hot sunlight.

'Can't she speak English?' whispered Amanda apprehensively.

'Quite a lot. You'll find that she speaks enough to manage on. But Miss Moon has always refused flatly to speak to her in Greek so

Euridice, who has been with her for over thirty years, refuses to admit to any English. It's a point of honour with both of them.'

'How do they manage?'

'They both speak to each other very slowly and at the tops of their voices in their own languages. Here, I think, is your hostess——'

High heels clicked rapidly on the hall staircase: there was a jingle of jewellery and a strong scent of heliotrope, and Miss Moon was with them.

Miss Moon was small and bony and birdlike, and somehow managed to suggest a homely British sparrow that has gone to a fancy dress ball dressed as a peacock. Her thin hair, which she had thought fit to dye an improbable shade of scarlet, was dressed in innumerable frizzy curls and decorated with a bow of violet gauze. Her dress, also in shades of violet and mauve, was of the type known to an earlier generation as a 'tea gown', and she had confined it at the waist by a wide belt of silver filigree adorned by an enamel buckle in a design of irises. She wore a number of necklaces and bracelets of silver filigree, amethysts and opals, and a pair of amethyst ear-rings of rococo splendour.

'Glenn! Dear boy. How it warms me to see you! And this is Amanda? Let me look at you, child. Beautiful! You refresh my eyes. How *good* of you to come and stay with me. So few young people care to do a kindness to the old these days, alas! It will be delightful to have you in the house. Quite delightful—it needs cheering up, and so do I. You are looking at my dress. Not *quite* the thing to welcome a guest in. It should have been pink for that. Pink for joy! But it's Tuesday you know, and so it had to be mauve. I always wear mauve on Tuesdays. Monday is my pink day. I do so resent it when people speak of *black* Monday. Why, Monday is a new start! A fresh week—anything might happen! And so, of course, I always wear pink. In welcome. I think that colours are *so* important, do not you? But here I am keeping you talking when you must be quite famished! Glenn, dear boy, will you not change your mind and stay to luncheon?'

'I'm afraid I can't. Nothing I would have liked better, but I have to meet Gavriledes at the Dome. He's giving me lunch and we can get through our business at the same time.'

'Oh dear. How disappointing. You know, of course, that Lumley Potter has taken the top floor of one of the houses on the harbour, don't you? He arrives today.'

'Potter—who told you?' Glenn Barton's face was suddenly white.

'So you did *not* know! I think Anita should have told you. So awkward if you met. Lady Cooper-Foot told me. The flat—if you can call it that—belongs to her cook's second cousin. Mr Potter intends to set up a studio.'

'But—but I thought he was staying on in Famagusta.'

'He wishes to paint in Kyrenia. Famagusta has not enough spiritual essence. I could have told him that.'

Glenn Barton's eyes were wide and blank. He turned to Amanda as though he were about to say something, and checked. After a moment he said instead, in an uncertain, rather formal voice: 'I must go now, I hope to see you again soon. If you are by any chance writing to your uncle, let me have the letter and I will see that it is sent with the office mail. It will go quicker that way. I will see that someone calls every day in case you should want to send anything. I am sure Miss Moon will look after you well. I won't say good-bye. Only *au revoir.*'

He took Miss Moon's withered, be-ringed hand and kissed it in an affectionate gesture that was entirely without affectation, and went quickly away.

Miss Moon drew a gusty sigh. 'Poor boy! How that woman *can*— —But I must not stay gossiping here all day, must I? I will show you your room. Andreas will have taken up your luggage. And then we will have luncheon and hear all about each other. So stimulating!'

She led the way back through the high, dark hall and up a wide, shallow stepped staircase. 'This is the bathroom, dear, and there is a lavatory. That is my room, and here is yours——'

She opened a door and Amanda found herself in a large, high-ceilinged room that was painted a soft green and carpeted with coarse matting. There were flowers in tall jars and the furniture, like that in the drawing-room, was old and beautiful and dusty from neglect. A portrait of a girl in a green satin dress of the Restoration period hung on one wall, while on another a vast silvery looking glass, spotted with age and wreathed with garlands, ribbons and cupids of tarnished gilt, hung above a small painted French bureau that served as a dressing-table. A graceful Venetian glass chandelier, not entirely innocent of cobwebs, hung from the ceiling, and only the bed struck an incongruous note. It was a narrow cheap iron bedstead that supported, on four poles of varying size that had been lashed to it with string, a somewhat darned mosquito net. The shutters were closed against the heat of the day and the room was dim and green and smelt of lilies and syringa, dry rot and dust.

Amanda turned to her hostess with shining eyes:

'It's is so good of you to have me. This is the most *beautiful* house!'

'Oh, I *am* so glad that you should feel like that!' said Miss Moon, suddenly embracing her. 'I knew the moment I saw you that you were *right,* and that the house would like you. So many people are wrong. Such a pity! It is indeed beautiful—the whole island. I came here with dear Papa forty-three years ago. That is a very long time, is it not? I cannot have been much older than you are now. He died here, and I meant to go back to Norfolk. But somehow I never did. I had walked through the looking-glass like Alice, and I could not get back. The enchantment had got me. I bought this house and I have been here ever since. And when I die I shall be buried among the lemon trees and the oleanders in the garden. I have it all arranged. Ah, Kyrenia——! The very name sings, does it not? Like a warm wind through the olive trees. How delightful that you should feel it too. Are you ready, dear? Euridice will be waiting to serve luncheon.'

The dining-room looked out across a froth of lemon trees to an old stone wall with deep, arched embrasures, crumbling into ruin, in which fantailed pigeons strutted and cooed, and the meal began with fruit. Purple and green figs, melons, oranges, grapes, and tiny plums like balls of blue velvet: ice-cold and piled in careless, colourful profusion on shallow dishes of Venetian glass. There were tall glasses flecked with gold, also Venetian, into one of which Miss Moon poured a white wine of local manufacture:

'It is quite harmless, dear. A child could drink it. Glenn lets me have it. The firm exports it in bottles, but bottling seems to spoil the flavour, and it is never so good afterwards. This is straight from the cask, and really very pleasant. Or so I am told. I myself never take anything but barley water. Euridice makes it for me after breakfast, fresh every day.'

Amanda said: 'You know, I think I am going to be very grateful to Mrs Barton for being ill.'

'Ill?' said Miss Moon sharply. 'Who told you that she was ill?'

'Mr Barton. That's why I'm here. I was to have stayed with the Bartons in Nicosia. My uncle arranged it. But they couldn't have me after all because Mrs Barton was ill. Didn't he tell you?'

'Yes he did, now that you mention it, dear. But I never thought that he would really do it. Pretend that she was ill, I mean. So *much* better to stick to the truth, however unpleasant. I cannot see why Glenn should try and shield his wife at his own expense. He did ask me not to tell you, but now that they will actually be here in Kyrenia of course you are bound to find out.'

'Find out what?' inquired Amanda, puzzled. 'Isn't Mrs Barton ill?'

'She most certainly is not!' said Miss Moon with an indignant clash of bracelets. 'On the contrary, it is her poor husband who appears to be heading for a nervous breakdown. I cannot understand it—she seemed such a nice girl. But in my young days there was a good old-fashioned word for people who behaved as Anita Barton is behaving. We called them trollops.'

'Anita?'—the name struck a sudden chord of memory.

'That is her name,' said Miss Moon, and sighed. 'I should never have thought it of her. But I suppose that she found Glenn dull. He has been sadly overworked. And she is so good looking. Perhaps she felt the need for more excitement and attention and admiration than he could offer. No, she is not ill. She has merely left Glenn and run away with a painting person who calls himself Lumley Potter. She has not even left the Island. They are living together quite brazenly, and she has attempted to justify her flagrantly immoral behaviour by spreading scandal about her husband and his secretary, Miss Ford.

'*Oh!*' gasped Amanda, her eyes wide with horrified dismay. 'So *that* was why——' She was remembering her light-hearted remark of that morning on the subject of Uncle Oswin and flagrant immorality. Could they possibly have imagined that she had said anything so cruel and unkind on purpose? A hot wave of colour mounted to her cheeks at the very thought.

'What is it, dear?'

'Nothing,' said Amanda hastily. 'I was just thinking of—of something I said to Miss Ford.'

'You have met her then?'

'Yes. We stopped at the office on our way through Nicosia.'

'Then you will know what I mean when I say that Anita must have taken leave of her senses. If she felt that it was necessary to slander Glenn in order to justify her own quite unjustifiable behaviour, she should have picked on a more plausible story. Monica Ford is a nice, sensible woman and a most efficient secretary—and she worships Glenn. But speaking entirely without malice, she possesses no feminine charm whatsoever. There are plenty of pretty girls in

Cyprus, and if that was what Glenn Barton was after he could have taken his pick. But Monica Ford——!'

Amanda was suddenly reminded of Julia Blaine and her equally senseless suspicions, but she pushed the thought quickly from her, and said lightly: 'She isn't exactly glamorous.'

'Glamorous! The poor girl is *Plain!* If she had even been ugly she might have stood more chance. Ugliness is at least arresting. The trouble with Glenn Barton is that he is too *soft*. You need to be hard if you marry a girl like Anita—as hard or harder than she is. She has accused him of carrying on with all sorts of people. Claire Norman for one. I would put nothing past Claire, and I am well aware that she cast a handkerchief in Glenn's direction—oh very discreetly of course; Claire is always discreet—and that she is not likely to forgive him for not picking it up. Dear me! What a lot of scandal I have been talking. *So* stimulating! You know, dear, there are a great many people—women of course—who will assure you that they *never* gossip, and that in fact they detest and abominate gossip. It is hardly ever true (the ones who say that are *always* the worst I find!) but if it *were* true, what a lot they must miss! Just think how much we should *all* have missed if people like Somerset Maugham had refused to listen to gossip? What would you like to do this afternoon, dear?'

'Sleep,' said Amanda promptly. 'I know that sounds very dull of me, but I feel as if I could sleep for hours. So much has happened, and—and I didn't get much sleep last night.'

'Not a rough crossing, I hope?'

'No,' said Amanda slowly; and for the third time that day told, with reservations, the story of Julia.

'You poor, *poor* child!' exclaimed Miss Moon in horrified sympathy. 'But how terrible! How too shocking. How fortunate that it should be a Tuesday. I should never have forgiven myself if I had been wearing orange or yellow when you arrived. So upsetting for you. Blue perhaps—blue is so soothing. But *not* orange. Certainly you must sleep. So sensible.'

She accompanied Amanda to her room at the conclusion of the meal. 'Just come down whenever you wake up,' urged Miss Moon. 'We pay no attention to the clock in this house. Time is our servant here, Amanda. We are not the servants of Time. *Amanda!* such a pretty name. So unusual. Amanda—"worthy to be loved".'

Amanda said abruptly, following a sudden train of thought: 'Did you ever hear of anyone called Amarantha?'

'Now I wonder who has been calling you that!' said Miss Moon, beaming. 'A man, of course. And one with a very pretty taste in compliments. Not Glennister Barton; he is *lamentably* unread. Amarantha was the subject of a charming poem by a cavalier named Richard Lovelace. He addressed some verses *To Amarantha, that she would dishevel her hair.* I am not sure that I remember them aright. My memory is *not* what it was, alas. Let me see—*"Amarantha sweet and fair, braid no more that shining hair. As my curious hand or eye hovering round thee, let it fly——"* something like that. Ah, I see that you are blushing! *Such* a charming accomplishment. You must tell me all about him when you wake up.'

Miss Moon withdrew, leaving behind her a scent of heliotrope to mingle with that of the lilies, the syringa, the dry rot and the dust. And Amanda, barely pausing to remove her dress and kick off her shoes, wriggled in under the mosquito net and was instantly and deeply asleep.

7

Amanda had awakened too late to be able to see anything of Kyrenia that day, but shortly after breakfast on the following morning Toby Gates called at the Villa Oleander.

'I heard you were here,' he told Amanda. 'Mrs Norman told us. They asked us all to dinner at their house last night; those of us who were on the boat; and she'd heard that you were staying here. We came here from Limassol in their car. The hotel had a car laid on for us, but a jeep ran into it just outside Nicosia, so we all piled into the Norman's car.'

'Who's "we"?' asked Amanda, sniffing ecstatically at a foaming torrent of jasmine that tumbled over the edge of the verandah rail outside the french windows of the drawing-room.

'Claire and Persis and Howard and myself. Claire—Mrs Norman —said that she was sure you wouldn't be staying at the Barton's house, because Mrs Barton has run off with that painter chap and you couldn't very well stay in the house with just Barton there. Funny that we should have seen them on the boat.'

So Steve Howard was staying in Kyrenia! Amanda said quickly: 'What happened to Mr Norman? Or did he have to come by bus?'

'Oh he stayed behind to help out Alastair Blaine. They didn't get in until late last night. I gather the body was taken to a hospital in Nicosia for a post-mortem, and he'll have to go over there this afternoon for some sort of an inquest. But they had the funeral yesterday evening.'

'So soon?' said Amanda, startled and distressed. Somehow, although she could have not explained why, Julia had not seemed really dead until this moment. Now that she was buried—hidden under six feet of foreign soil in an alien country—the fact and the finality of her death came home to Amanda with a renewed sense of shock.

'It's a hot country,' said Toby uncomfortably. 'You have to bury people pretty quickly in this sort of climate.'

'What is he going to do? Alastair, I mean.'

'He's staying on with the Normans. No point in his doing anything else, really. He and Norman got in about ten o'clock and he went straight off to bed. Claire met Barton in the town yesterday afternoon and he told her you were here, so we rang up to ask you to join us, but the Moon woman said that you were asleep, and she wouldn't wake you. I say——' Toby sank his voice to a conspiratorial whisper—— 'she's a bit peculiar, isn't she? She told me that I shouldn't be wearing a blue shirt because it was Wednesday. Do you suppose she's all there?'

'She's not dangerous, if that's what you mean,' said Amanda laughing. 'She just has a theory about wearing different colours on different days. If you'd turned up in cerise you'd have been dead right.'

Toby looked relieved. 'Oh I see. I thought the old girl was bats. She asked me if I had called to see Amarantha—sounded rather Biblical to me—must be one of her servant girls I suppose. I said no, as a matter of fact I'd called to see Miss Derington, and she said "Ah, I thought not. You do not look at all the sort of man who could quote Loveless to the point." I began to think I'd got into the local looney bin. What on *earth* do you suppose she meant?'

'I haven't an idea,' said Amanda shamelessly.

'By the way,' said Toby diffidently, 'I—er—asked her if she'd mind if I took you out to luncheon and she said not at all. So would you come? It's not really just me—I wish it were—I mean, we arranged last night to have luncheon together at the Dome. Claire—Mrs Norman—thought it would cheer Alastair up, and it's their cook's day off. I said I'd like to ask you along too, and——You will come, won't you?'

'I'd love to.'

'That's marvellous,' said Toby enthusiastically. 'Let's go now!'

'It isn't ten yet,' pointed out Amanda, 'and there are lots of things I want to do this morning. I want to prowl around and explore.'

'I'll come with you. I must get hold of a car. Howard's hired one. A pound a day and you drive yourself; something like that. You know he's really an astonishingly good type, for an artist.'

'What do you mean—for an artist?' demanded Amanda, unaccountably annoyed.

'Oh I don't know. So many of them look like that bearded blighter in sandals; the one Barton's wife ran away with. Well I mean to say—if you're any good, surely you don't have to go about practically in fancy dress just to show what you are?'

'Nonsense!' said Amanda briskly. 'Look at you when you're on duty. You wear a weird khaki outfit with pips here and badges there and a peculiar hat with feathers that would make a man laugh his head off if he saw his wife wearing it. If you can go around in fancy dress just to show what you are, why can't he? It's the same idea. Which reminds me—wait while I get a sun-hat and I'll be with you!'

They spent the morning exploring Kyrenia, and towards twelve o'clock came down to the little harbour where the pastel-coloured houses, the ancient, glowing walls of Kyrenia castle, the minaret of a mosque and the white walls of the Greek Orthodox Church reflect themselves in the clear, luminous greens and blues of the harbour water and look as though they had been designed by an inspired artist as a Mediterranean mural.

A voice hailed Amanda from one of the small tables outside a café on the quay, and there was Persis, as decorative as the morning.

'Hi there, honey! I hear you're parked right here in Kyrenia after all? Nice work. I thought nothing of Nicosia from what little we saw of it. Nothing *at* all. Now this!—this is quite a town, and I shall write a romance that will go into half a dozen editions in as many months. Why, it's just made for love! I must get me a beau.'

'Won't your imagination do?' inquired Toby solicitously.

'No, honey. My imagination is Grade A plus, but when it comes to Love, I like 'em over six foot and solid.'

'What about me?' offered Toby.

'That's just sweet of you, honey, but I prefer my beaus to keep both eyes on their work; and if you watch Amanda over my shoulder I can't see myself getting really in the mood. Still, there's a lot of talent lying around; as well as some pretty stiff competition.'

'Meaning me?' inquired Amanda showing her dimples.

'Of course, honey. Who else? Though to tell you the truth I was casting a mental eye over Mrs Norman. That gal is a smooth worker. I am no amateur myself, and Lord knows I count my calories. But when she's around I feel just a shade like Sophie Tucker's twin sister; and say what you like, that is lowering to the morale. Besides, she has the edge on outside operators. It's her own ground and it kinda looks as though she's worked it well. Remember that guy with the beard and an outfit like sunset in technicolor?'

491

'Lumley Potter,' said Amanda, recognizing the description.

'That's the boy. The one who beat it with your pal Barton's ball and chain. Well, who do you suppose was whispering to him on the boat deck at two o'clock in the morning the other night? Lil' Claire, no less.'

Toby said sharply: 'That's impossible! I mean—how can you know?'

'How? By using my great big eyes, Grandma. That two-by-four cabin of mine was as hot as Broadway in a heatwave, and I slid out for a breath of air. I passed No. 31—that was the Normans' cabin—on my way. George was snoring fit to shift the deck plates and I spared a sympathetic sigh for his life partner. I need not have wasted my sympathy. The little woman was on the boat deck—taking, we must suppose, an intelligent interest in Art. She's quite a gal!'

'But he's run off with Barton's wife!' said Toby indignantly.

'Maybe the guy's a Mormon.'

Amanda said slowly: 'So *that's* how she knew——'

'About Julia? I guess so. Potter had probably gotten the dirt from the first officer or the doctor or someone by that time. I imagine that there must have been quite a ruckus going on about it, and most of those who were out and about probably got an ear full. Yes, little Claire is certainly stiff competition. I shall have to brush up on my technique.'

'Who are you thinking of starting on?' inquired Toby, interested.

'Well there's always Major Blaine; and though it may be bad taste to pursue a bereaved widower, we heard plenty last night from his hostess about not letting the poor boy mope, so I guess I may as well try my hand at a little light consolation. And then there's Steve Howard. He's quite a guy. Plenty of looks and charm—and has he got that certain something! Claire seems to have noticed it too.'

'He's *not* good looking!' said Amanda with something of a snap. 'His face is out of drawing.'

'Well as far as I'm concerned, honey, it can stay that way. I never could draw anyway.'

Toby said: 'Persis darling, I never remember you sounding so aggressively American when I knew you in the States. Or did you always talk that way?'

'Not when I'm back home,' said Persis placidly. 'I keep it for foreign travel. It amuses the natives.'

Toby laughed. 'You're just a highly coloured fake and I adore you!'

Persis gave him an odd, slanting look and said: 'Do you, honey? Well maybe you did once. Or maybe you're like this guy Potter—or any other guy for that matter!—just a Mormon at heart.'

For a moment there was an unexpected tinge of bitterness in Persis Halliday's clear incisive tones and Toby said quickly: 'What's that stuff you're drinking? It looks like ammonia.'

'Maybe it is, at that. The boy with the dinky white apron calls it *oozoo* or *ouzo*—and is it filthy! Still, I'm all for trying anything once. Drag up a chair and join me.'

'Do you mean to tell me that you're knocking back drinks alone and unprotected?' demanded Toby, astounded.

'Not quite. I am not entirely lost to all sense of what is due to me. My escort is in back—trying to get something under the counter if you ask me. Ah, here he is. Okay, George?'

George Norman appeared from the interior of the café bearing a bottle of beer. 'Got it!' he announced triumphantly. 'I knew they had some stored away. Good morning, Miss Derington. 'Morning, Gates. I'm showing Mrs Halliday the sights.'

Toby said: 'Is your wife here?'

'She'll be along in a minute. Alastair had to send off some cables and she went along to the Post Office with him. Here they are now.'

Claire Norman, still in black and wearing a wide-brimmed black hat that shaded her small face in a most becoming manner, appeared round the corner of the quay, her hand through Alastair Blaine's arm. Major Blaine looked tired and grim and as though he had had remarkably little sleep, if any, during the last forty-eight hours.

'Why—Amanda,' said Claire in her soft, light voice. 'How nice to see you. And Toby. Have you two been exploring the harbour?'

'No,' said Amanda. 'We've been exploring the town. I'm going to look at the harbour now, from the sea wall.'

'I'll come with you,' said Toby.

'I don't want you, Toby,' said Amanda perversely. 'I just want to sit and look at it and not talk. I'll be back.' She turned on her heel and walked quickly away.

Toby made a move as though to follow her, but Claire Norman laid a small hand on his arm and asked him prettily to fetch a chair for her, and by the time he had done so Amanda had gone.

A long stone wall with a small lighthouse on the end of it protected the tiny horseshoe-shaped harbour of Kyrenia from the seaward side, and walking along it Amanda looked across the translucent harbour water to the towering walls of the old Crusader castle, golden in the sunlight, and the beautiful curving coastline that faded into the shimmering heat haze beyond the age-old buttresses.

There were several other people on the sea wall, one of whom, a man who was sitting on the edge of the wall at the harbour side with his legs dangling above the water, was surrounded by an interested crowd of children. He was sketching swiftly with quick, bold strokes of a conté pencil on a large loose-leaf drawing block, and Amanda paused involuntarily, attracted by a burst of childish laughter.

The man spoke without turning his head: 'Good morning, Amarantha.'

'How did you know I was here?' demanded Amanda, startled.

Steve turned about and grinned up at her. 'I have eyes in the back of my head. Or perhaps I'm like that chap in *Maud* whose *"heart would hear her and beat, were it never so airy a tread".*'

Amanda flushed and turned away. Mr Howard spoke one quick sentence in Greek and instantly Amanda found her way barred by half a dozen laughing children, while three more laid hold of her arms and the belt of her grey linen frock. Amanda's sense of humour got the better of her and she laughed.

'Is this a hold-up?'

'It is. Now come off your high horse, Amarantha, and sit down and relax. I want to talk to you. You can sit on this——'

He ripped off a sheet of cartridge paper from the drawing block and laid it on the edge of the harbour wall. Amanda, surrendering to curiosity and *force majeur,* sat down beside him, and looking downwards at the clear harbour water beneath her dangling feet, saw her own reflection and that of the group of children behind her.

'So much for the eyes in the back of your head. You saw my reflection.'

'I did,' admitted Steve.

Amanda turned to look at him and her gaze fell on the drawing block in his hands. The page was covered, surprisingly enough, with quick, vivid sketches of elephants, tigers, a sailor in bell-bottomed trousers, a witch on a broomstick, a horrific dragon, a sea serpent and a pirate brandishing a cutlass.

Mr Howard had the grace to look abashed. 'Not what you would call a hard morning's work,' he remarked, 'but popular with my public.'

Amanda said in a voice of blank amazement: 'So you *can* draw!'

'Why this unflattering incredulity? Or do I look like a painter of

Spiritual Aromas, like my brother-of-the-brush, that dashing home-breaker, Mr Potter?'

Amanda flushed and bit her lip. 'I thought——' she began, and stopped.

'You thought it was merely an act,' concluded Steve. 'But no one should put on an act unless they can also put it across.'

He turned over to a fresh page and idly sketched in the outline of a girl's face and figure that turned suddenly into Amanda as she had looked in the cabin of the *Orantares*. Amanda in a nightdress with her long hair falling below her waist and her eyes wide and frightened.

There was a murmur of admiring recognition from the audience of children, and Amanda reached out, and snatching the pencil from his hand, said abruptly: 'What did you want to talk to me about?'

Steve turned his head and spoke briefly to his youthful audience, and received what appeared to be a chorus of assent.

Amanda said: 'What did you say to them? And how is it that you speak this language so well?'

'There is no end to my accomplishments,' said Mr Howard airily. 'And if you really want to know, I told them that I wished to declare my love to this so beautiful lady, and should any of the English approach I relied on them to give me due warning. The gang are with me to a man, so we can now relax and talk without fear of being overheard.'

'Oh,' said Amanda in a small voice.

Steve laughed. 'Don't worry. I only make love by moonlight. At the moment I merely propose to discuss crime.'

He retrieved the pencil and turning over another page began to sketch the houses on the far side of the harbour, but he was no longer smiling and his voice when he spoke again was terse and low pitched.

'The results of the post-mortem show that Mrs Blaine took poison. And I was right about that glass in your cabin. There are only two sets of finger-prints on it: yours and Mrs Blaine's. The bottle has only one set—yours. Which means that it was polished very carefully before it was put there, and probably handled with gloves. And the tablets in it were the same stuff that was in the glass: pilocarpine nitrate.'

'But—but you can't be sure that there was anything more than just lemon juice and water in that glass,' said Amanda, forcing the words past an uncomfortable constriction in her throat. 'I filled it again with water from the tap—to throw over her.'

'I know. But the remains of the original stuff had spilt and soaked into the carpet. I mopped it up with a handkerchief. There wasn't much of it, but with that bit of peel it was enough. The analysis shows that it contained a solution of pilocarpine nitrate which was probably sufficient to kill a dozen people. A single mouthful would have been enough to kill Mrs Blaine, though it would have taken a good bit longer.'

Amanda said: 'But the bottle! No, it can't be true, because don't you see, if Julia hadn't changed cabins with me, there wouldn't have been *any* finger-prints on the bottle and someone would have noticed it.'

'I wonder. How did you find it?'

'I felt it when I lay down. It made a hard lump.'

'So that you found it almost as soon as your head touched the pillow. The chances are that Mrs Blaine would have done the same, and would have touched it, as you did, and probably thought that some previous occupant of the cabin had left it behind by mistake. It only meant something to you because you had seen Mrs Blaine die of poison. Even if she had not found it, it is an even bet that several people would have handled it before it occurred to anyone to see if it had her finger-prints on it. Now let's have your story again. Right from the beginning this time. Anything that you knew or noticed about these people when you were in Fayid, and why they—and you —are in Cyprus, and as much as you can remember of what they did and said in Fayid and on the way to Port Said and on the boat. In fact the whole works.'

Amanda turned her head and looked at him, but his entire attention appeared to be concentrated on the drawing that was taking shape under the leisurely, unerring strokes of the conté pencil.

She said uncertainly: 'Then you *are——*'

Steve Howard threw a brief glance in the direction of the café on the quay where Persis Halliday, the Normans, Major Blaine and Toby Gates were seated about a small table in the shade, and said curtly: 'Quickly, Amanda!'

There was not much to tell, and what there was seemed to date back to the evening at the Club in Fayid when her aunt had introduced her to Steven Howard. And yet Amanda had a queer feeling that it went farther back than that, and that Steve himself had been in Fayid for some specific purpose that was entirely unconnected with art, and that his presence at the Officer's Club that night had not been accidental.

She told him what she knew, thinking as she did so that it all sounded very trivial and unimportant. But he questioned her exhaustively on a number of points, and seemed interested to hear that Toby had met Persis in the States while visiting a married sister whose husband was attached to the Embassy Staff in Washington. She re-told yet again how she had come to occupy the cabin that had been allotted to Julia, and everything that she could remember of that last hysterical scene.

Steve said: 'What time did she go down to her cabin? Was she still on deck when you left?'

'No. She went quite early. About ten I think. Someone put on a gramophone record and people started dancing. Alastair danced with Mrs Norman, and I think Julia must have left about then. She started making rather a fuss about having a headache, and went off to her cabin.'

'When did you go down to yours?'

'Just about eleven. I remember the time, because I wound up my watch when I took it off to wash.'

'And Mrs Blaine came into your cabin around five or ten minutes later. Is that right?'

'Yes.'

Steve was silent for a moment or two, and then he said: 'Did all of you know that she made a habit of drinking unsweetened lemon juice?'

'Yes. She used to make rather a virtue of it. She took it to take down her weight. People always seem to advertise their dieting fads. She'd never touch a sweet drink, yet she'd eat ice creams and sticky puddings and chocolates by the ton.'

Steve said: 'Are you quite sure that you've told me everything you know?'

'Quite. Oh there is one other thing, but it can't possibly have anything to do with all this.'

'Never mind; let's have it.'

'Persis says that she went on deck much later that night, because her cabin was hot, and that she saw Mrs Norman and Lumley Potter together on the boat deck.'

Steve made no comment, but his pencil checked and he sat quite still, staring across the lovely harbour with eyes that did not appear to see the charm of the scene that lay before him.

After a moment or two he shrugged his shoulders and returned to his work, and presently one of the children called out something in a shrill piping tone, and he looked round.

'I rather think that a search party is about to be sent after you,' he observed, 'so let us talk of other things in a bright and audible manner. What are you doing in Kyrenia, for instance?'

'You know quite well why I'm here,' said Amanda accusingly. 'You were dining at Mrs Norman's house last night, and she seems to have broadcast the whole story.'

'Oh yes—of course. You couldn't stay unchaperoned with the manager of your uncle's Cyprus venture, so this man Barton has parked you instead *chez* Moon. His loss is our gain. Did you have an entertaining journey from Limassol?'

Amanda embarked on an account of her drive, her stop at Nicosia and her arrival at Miss Moon's, and was still talking when a shadow fell across them and Claire Norman's soft fluting voice said: 'Why, *Steve!* I'd no idea it was you who were monopolizing Amanda. We wondered what was keeping her. Have you been here all morning? You're supposed to be meeting us at the hotel at one o'clock, you know, and it's five past now.'

Steve closed his sketch book, pocketed the pencil and stood up:

'Hullo, Mrs Norman. 'Morning, Gates. Yes, I have been pursuing my vocation in an industrious manner. Miss Derington has been offering advice.'

He leant down and pulled Amanda to her feet.

'Do let me see,' begged Claire Norman. 'If you only knew how I envy people who are *really* creative! Do show us what you have been doing.'

Steve held up the sketch book to display the drawing of the harbour and Toby Gates said involuntarily: 'Why that's damned good! I suppose you make a packet out of this sort of thing?'

'Alas, no,' sighed Mr Howard regretfully. 'I shall never make a fortune from my art. It contains a fatal flaw: anyone can instantly recognize what it is intended to represent. One can only make a packet nowadays if one's creative efforts are of the type that the purchasing committee can hang upside down without anyone—including the artist—spotting the error.'

A sudden and unexpected breath of wind ruffled the quiet water of the harbour and lifted the sheet of paper, disclosing the page that lay beneath it. It was only for a brief moment, but quite long enough for both Claire Norman and Toby Gates to see and recognize that quick, brilliant sketch of a girl with unbound hair.

Tony Gates said in a thunderstruck voice: 'But that's Amanda! How on earth——' He stopped, red-faced and scowling, and Claire Norman laughed her light, tinkling laugh and said: 'Why, Steve! How secretive you are! I had no idea that you and Amanda knew each other so well.'

Steve closed the sketch book and tucked it under his arm. He smiled down at Claire with lazy pleasantness, but Amanda was suddenly and vividly aware, without knowing why she should know it, that he was angry.

'I am afraid,' said Steve gently, 'that that was merely an example of what is known as artist's licence. I do not know Miss Derington well. But that, fortunately, is an error that can be remedied. And now what about some food?'

Claire Norman's glance went swiftly from Mr Howard's smiling face to Amanda's entirely blank one and Captain Gates' scowling countenance, and she laughed again: a laugh that this time was not quite so sweet and tinkling:

'Yes, let's!' she said. 'I'm famished.'

She slipped one small hand through Steve Howard's arm and laid the other on Toby's sleeve, and they walked away towards the Dome Hotel, four abreast in the bright glittering sunlight, their shadows foreshortened on the hot stones at their feet.

8

The dining-room of the Dome Hotel was long, spacious and cool, and a little breeze blew in from the line of windows that opened on to the burning blue of sea and sky.

Amanda looked about her with interest and decided that most of the guests were tourists, with a sprinkling of permanent residents. The Normans and Alastair Blaine were seated at a small table just beyond the one occupied by Persis, Steve Howard, Toby and herself: Claire Norman having suddenly decided that owing to Alastair's recent and dramatic bereavement, it might cause comment if he were to appear as one of a large and cheerful luncheon party at the hotel.

Amanda wondered why, in the circumstances, Claire could not have managed to give him a meal in the privacy of her own home? But Claire was a law unto herself, and Alastair, silent and stunned, was in the mood to do anything he was told without question.

Amanda's gaze, wandering farther, stopped at a strapless and backless white sunsuit printed with several huge scarlet roses and apparently remaining in position upon its wearer by faith alone. She was puzzling over the mechanics of this arresting garment when she became suddenly aware of the identity of the owner. The lady in the sunsuit was none other than Mr Glennister Barton's errant wife, while her companion, temporarily hidden from Amanda's view by an attentive waiter, was presumably her partner in guilt, the improbable Mr Potter.

Amanda was both interested and surprised. Somehow she had not expected Anita Barton to flaunt her liaison in such a public spot as the dining-room of the Dome Hotel. The attentive waiter removed himself, giving Amanda an uninterrupted view, and she studied the couple with considerable interest.

Lumley Potter, she decided, was not enjoying himself. He was

500

looking morose, sulky and more than a little apprehensive, and kept darting anxious glances in the direction of the Normans' table. Anita Barton, however, appeared to be entirely at ease. She was laughing and talking—perhaps a shade too loudly.

Mrs Barton was a dark-haired woman of about twenty-five, with an excellent figure and striking good looks that owed much of their impact to a lavish and theatrical use of make-up. Altogether an unexpected wife, thought Amanda, for someone as quiet and fine-drawn as Glenn Barton.

As though she had felt Amanda's interested gaze, Anita Barton turned full face towards her. Her dark, over-bright eyes looked Amanda over with cool and deliberate insolence and her wide scarlet mouth curved in a mocking smile. She made some remark to her companion and shrugged one bare, sunburnt shoulder. And then all at once her eyes became fixed and hard and her red mouth tightened into a thin line. But she was no longer looking at Amanda. She was looking at someone immediately behind her, and, involuntarily, Amanda turned.

Glenn Barton was standing in the doorway, searching the room with anxious eyes. He did not see his wife, but he saw Amanda and came quickly towards her, threading his way between the tables.

'Glenn!' Claire Norman's voice arrested him as he was about to pass their table, and he paused beside her. She looked up at him with large, luminous eyes and said reproachfully: 'Glenn, you've been overworking again. You look as if you've had no sleep for weeks. You don't know Major Blaine, do you? I think you were over in the Lebanon on business when they were here last year, weren't you?'

'No, we haven't met. But of course I heard about you from——' Glenn checked suddenly and Claire said: 'Stay and have something to eat. We've only just started.'

'I'm afraid I can't. I've a lot to do.'

'Then what about tea? Drop in at the house on your way back.'

'I will if I can,' said Mr Barton hesitantly.

'We shall expect you,' said Claire, smiling up at him.

He nodded absently and made his way across to Amanda. Claire's smile faded and her wide childlike eyes were suddenly narrowed and speculative.

Amanda turned in her chair: 'Hullo, Mr Barton. Were you looking for me? Persis, this is Mr Barton. He very kindly collected me at Limassol.'

'Yes. We met,' said Persis, producing her most dazzling smile. 'But I'm just delighted to meet you again, Mr Barton. Any friend of Amanda's is a friend of ours. Say, why not get a chair and join us?'

Mr Barton blinked and his drawn face relaxed in a smile:

'I—I'd like to very much. But I'm afraid I can't just now.'

'Some other time then,' said Persis warmly.

As one angle of the local triangular scandal, Glenn Barton represented copy; and Persis, whose interest had been aroused by the story, had been determined to make his closer acquaintance; though it is doubtful if her interest would have been so great had he proved to be a less personable man.

'Thank you,' said Glenn Barton. He turned rather abruptly to Amanda and said: 'I really came to ask you if you'd be in this afternoon. At the Villa Oleander I mean. Could you spare me half an hour of your time if I came in about three? I——' he hesitated a moment and glanced at her three openly listening companions. 'I have had a letter from your uncle. He has some messages that he wishes me to give you.'

'Of course,' said Amanda. 'I'll expect you about three o'clock.'

'I'll try not to keep you waiting.'

Persis said: 'Say, Mr Barton, I hear you run a wine business. Vineyards and vats and pretty girls treading out the grapes and all the rest of it.'

'He does,' said Amanda. 'Miss Moon gave me some of his wine yesterday. It was delicious.'

Glenn Barton laughed. 'I'm glad you liked it. You were lucky not to get barley water. I thought that was the only thing that she drank.'

'It is. But thank goodness, she doesn't expect her guests to drink the stuff. It always tastes to me like water in which someone has stewed up half a lemon and three yards of flannel.'

Persis said: 'To get back to your vineyards, Mr Barton. I'm just crazy to see the whole works. Would you take pity on a poor foreigner and show me round one day?'

'I'd be delighted to.'

'Then how about tomorrow?'

'You can't go looking at vines and vats tomorrow, Persis,' said Toby Gates firmly. 'We're all going for a picnic to St Hilarion. Amanda's coming too. You know you arranged the whole thing with George Norman only this morning.'

'So we did. I'll tell you what, Mr Barton—suppose you join the picnic? Then we can get together and fix a day for the vines. Tomorrow at two-thirty. You can give me a lift to Hilarion. Is that a date?'

'I ought not to,' said Glenn Barton with a rueful smile, 'I'm rather busy just now, but—all right. I'd like to come. But I shan't be able to give you a lift I'm afraid. I can't get off as early as that. I could be at Hilarion about four o'clock if that's all right?'

'Sure. That's okay by me. Be seeing you then.'

Glenn Barton smiled at her, turned away and then stopped suddenly, his face rigid, and Amanda, following the direction of his fixed gaze, saw that he was staring at his wife. It was obvious that he had not noticed her until then, and highly unlikely that he would in any case have expected to see her lunching openly at the Dome with Lumley Potter.

Anita Barton had turned in her chair so that she faced him directly. Her eyes were bright and defiant and her painted mouth was hard and ugly. The room was noisy with chatter and the chink of glasses and cutlery, but the four at Amanda's table and the three at Claire's were suddenly silent with the silence of embarrassment and curiosity.

There was a queer grey look about Glenn Barton's thin, tanned face, and his mouth had shut hard. A muscle twitched at the corner of his jaw and his hands had clenched so tightly that the knuckles stood out bone white.

He stood there for perhaps a full minute, and then suddenly swung about and walked quickly and unsteadily from the room.

'Well, what do you know!' remarked Persis into the silence. 'Did you see that guy's face? If I had a dollar for every time I've written *"he turned white under his tan"* I'd buy the Koh-i-noor. But, so help me, I've never seen it happen until now. Fiction is certainly no improvement on nature.'

Steve said: 'Tell me, Mrs Halliday, are all American women as ruthless as you are?'

'Persis to you, Steve honey. And why ruthless? Why, I was *charming* to the poor guy.'

'That's what I meant,' said Steve with a grin. 'But what are you going to do with him when you've got him? Gaff him, or throw him back into the pool?'

'Steve *daaarling!* All I want is to get to know him. Can't you see what divine copy he is?'

'I see all right. You're a ruthless vamp and should be kept under lock and key. And don't bat your eyelashes at me—I suffer from extreme susceptibility.'

'But that's just *wonderful,*' said Persis warmly. 'I can see that you and I have a lot in common. You can drive me to Hilarion.'

'It's a date,' said Mr Howard.

Toby escorted Amanda back to Miss Moon's after luncheon and she dismissed him at the gate. She was feeling unsettled and restless and on edge, and the feeling of enchantment that she had experienced on her arrival at the Villa Oleander had vanished. Miss Moon peered over the landing rail as she closed the front door behind her.

'Ah, you're back, dear. Glenn Barton was asking for you. I told him that I thought you were taking luncheon at the Dome.'

'Yes I saw him, thank you, Miss Moon. He's coming to see me this afternoon. I hope that's all right? My uncle has been writing to fuss him about me.'

'Quite all right, dear. I usually rest in the afternoon, so you will have the drawing-room to yourselves. I shall be down to tea about four o'clock. Ask Glenn to stay. He'll let himself in. Euridice is out for an hour.'

She disappeared and Amanda heard her bedroom door shut. A clock in the hall struck three mellow notes, and almost before the echo had died away in the quiet house there was a sound of quick footsteps on the stone-flagged path and Glenn Barton was there, breathing a little quickly as though he had been hurrying.

'I haven't kept you waiting, have I?' he asked anxiously.

'About two seconds,' said Amanda with a laugh. She led the way into the drawing-room and sat down in a straight-backed chair, carved and gilded and upholstered in faded green velvet. Glenn Barton stood looking down at her with a deep crease between his brows and did not speak.

Amanda said: 'Do sit down. What is it? Has Uncle Oswin been devilling you about me?'

Glenn Barton sat down on the sofa and pushed his hands through his hair in the same boyish and despairing gesture that Amanda had seen him use on the previous day.

He said jerkily: 'I haven't heard from your uncle. That was just an excuse; I had to say something.'

He raised his eyes and looked at her wretchedly.

Glennister Barton must have been at least fifteen years Amanda's senior, and his hair was already flecked with grey at the temples. But all at once Amanda felt as maternal as though she were twice his age and he was a small boy in trouble.

She said quickly and warmly: 'What is it? What's the matter?'

'I had to tell you——' his voice had a ragged edge to it—'I had to. About Anita—my wife. You see I didn't know that she would be here. I hoped that you wouldn't find out. So I—well I said she was ill. It was a lie of course.'

'Look, Glenn,' said Amanda, unconsciously using his name, 'it doesn't matter. You were only covering up for her. You couldn't have done anything else. I do understand, so don't worry about it— please!'

Glenn dropped his head into his hands and said in a low, uneven voice: 'It's all such a mess. Such a ghastly mess! I didn't believe that it could happen. But it did. I didn't mind what other people said or thought, but this involves the good name of the firm, and you are a Derington. I wanted to hush it up, but I see now that it isn't possible. I—I did what I could.'

'Of course you did,' comforted Amanda, distressed. 'But it's no good trying to cover up for your wife if she doesn't care what people say.'

'I don't understand it,' said Glenn tiredly. 'I don't know why she should behave like this. Perhaps it's some sort of defence mechanism. She's such a child really. A spoilt child who is trying to cover up its own naughtiness by accusing other people of worse things.'

'You mean those stories about Miss Ford?' said Amanda.

Glenn looked up, his face haggard. 'So you've heard about that already!'

'Miss Moon told me. But you don't have to worry, Glenn. She says that no one believes it.'

'How can she know?' said Glenn bitterly. 'There are people who will believe anything.'

He dropped his head on his hands again and after a moment spoke in an almost inaudible voice, as though he had forgotten about Amanda and was finding some relief in speaking his troubled thoughts aloud:

'Anita doesn't like Monica—she never has. Monica is efficient and she has brains, but she's not very tactful. Anita is so gay, and so careless about money and housekeeping and things like that. She likes expensive clothes and parties and late nights, and admiration. She's young; it's only natural. And I suppose I was a bit dull—there was always so much work. Monica used to drop hints; very heavy ones I imagine—and it annoyed Anita. Then one day she lost her temper and they had a quarrel. A silly, rather childish quarrel——'

Glenn sighed and pushed his hands through his hair again: 'Anita told me that either Monica went or she would. She wouldn't see that I *could* not sack Monica—she was Mr Derington's personal nominee for the post, and until she arrived things were in a bit of a mess in the office. Monica got the whole thing into shape and worked like a demon. I couldn't replace her without damaging the firm's interests. I told Anita that she need never see her or speak to her—I would have seen to that—but that I had to keep her. I *had* to. I can't deal with all the stuff she copes with, as well as my own work; it isn't possible. But Anita wouldn't see it. She just went on saying that if I didn't sack Monica immediately she'd go. I—I didn't think she could mean it. But she did. And now that she's gone she's too proud—and too young—to admit the truth, so she has spread it about that she was forced to leave me because I was having an affair with the woman. An *affair!* With Monica Ford of all people! *Monica!* Oh God, if it wasn't so tragic it would be damnably funny!'

Amanda, looking at him with an aching pity beyond her years, was once again reminded of Julia. Julia whose jealous love of her husband had prompted her to accuse him of entirely imaginary affairs with any and every woman he paid the smallest attention to. Was Mrs Barton only another Julia? Did she really love her husband with the selfish, jealous love that Julia had had for Alastair? And had he, because of his work, neglected her and so driven her to much the same hysterical extremes of behaviour that Julia had indulged in? Could love really do such dreadful things to people? Drive them so mercilessly?

She said quickly: *'Don't,* Glenn! I don't want to sound catty, but anyone who has ever met Miss Ford will know that it's all nonsense. No one would believe it.'

Glenn lifted his head from his hands and looked at her.

'No,' he said with a wry smile. 'I don't suppose they would. But there are a good many people who have not met her, and it makes an unsavoury story. God knows I can't spare her from the office just now, but for her own sake I've tried to make her go. I can't let her name be spattered with mud by every gossip in the Island. It isn't fair on her. I have got some sort of duty towards the woman—and to your uncle for that matter. But she won't go. She says that if she went now it might look like an admission of guilt, and that anyway she will not be forced to leave by an entirely baseless scandal. I've done my best to persuade her, but it's no use.'

'She's quite right,' said Amanda warmly. 'If you wouldn't sack her because she had a row with your wife, I don't see why she should lose her job now, just because your wife is telling everyone that she was your——' She stopped abruptly and flushed.

'Mistress,' finished Glenn Barton wryly. 'I suppose not. But she is the only one I worry about. The others can not only take care of themselves, but give as good as they get.'

'What others?' asked Amanda, puzzled.

'Didn't Miss Moon tell you that too?' inquired Glenn Barton bitterly. 'Monica is not the only one I am supposed to have carried on with. Anita has been very generous with her accusations. I am supposed to have made love to half a dozen women—Mrs Norman for one. In fact it seems that no woman is safe from me. You wouldn't think it to look at me, would you?'

He laughed again. A short, harsh laugh that was entirely devoid of amusement.

'Why don't you strangle her!' demanded Amanda indignantly.

'Anita?'

'Yes. It sounds to me as if it would be justifiable homicide!'

Glenn smiled a curious, twisted smile. 'You don't understand. You see she doesn't really mean it. She's just a spoilt kid who has found that the party isn't as much fun as she thought it would be. She drinks a little too much, and that doesn't help. She's only hitting about her because she's bored and disappointed—with me and marriage and Cyprus.'

'She sounds to me,' said Amanda candidly, 'as if she needed a dozen with a good solid slipper. It's a pity you didn't try it.'

'Perhaps,' said Glenn wryly. 'But it's too late for that now. She wants me to divorce her.'

Amanda said: 'Of course you're going to?'

Glenn Barton got up suddenly and walked over to the open french windows that gave out onto a small covered verandah shadowed with jasmine and climbing roses. He stood with his back to Amanda and his hands in his pockets and spoke without turning his head.

'I *can't!*'

'Why, Glenn? Do you mean because of your job? I know that Uncle Oswin is pretty rabid on the subject of divorce, but it's not your fault.'

'It isn't the job,' said Glenn Barton, still without turning. 'I don't care a *damn* about the job. It's Anita. You see I—I love her so much.'

He swung round suddenly to face Amanda and said harshly, 'I suppose you find that difficult to believe? It's absurd, isn't it, to go on loving someone who can do that to you, and to be unable to stop? I know it doesn't make sense, but it's true all the same. I want her back—on any terms. I don't believe that she loves Lumley Potter. It's only a silly escapade, and if I don't divorce her she'll get over it one day and—and come back to me.'

He looked appealingly at Amanda; his tired, desperate eyes pleading with her to agree with him; to reassure him. Amanda got up swiftly and went to him, gripping his arm:

'Don't look like that, Glenn! Please don't. I'm sure it will all come right in the end. Oh, Glenn, I am so sorry! Isn't there anything I could do? Perhaps if I saw her?—talked to her?'

A sudden light leapt into Glenn's grey eyes and for a moment his whole face seemed to change and the lines in it to alter; the avid, incredulous look of a cornered animal who is suddenly presented with an avenue of escape. It faded as quickly as it had come and his eyes fell.

'No. No, I couldn't possibly ask you to. I shouldn't have talked to you like this. I didn't mean to—honestly I didn't. I only thought that you should know something about it because—well because you're a Derington, and because I'd lied to you. I apologize. It was unforgivable of me to go to pieces and bore you with my sordid private affairs. Will you forgive me and—and try and forget about it?'

He covered her hands with one of his own, and despite the warmth of the hot Mediterranean day she could feel that it was cold and quivering.

'Now you're being silly,' said Amanda with a light laugh. 'You know very well that you don't have to apologize for anything. I'm the one who should do that. Here you are, in the thick of a perfectly beastly crisis in your life, and on top of everything else Uncle Oswin orders you, practically at pistol point, to put me up and show me round. You must have wanted to murder me!'

Glenn's cold fingers tightened convulsively on hers and he said quickly: 'Don't talk like that. You weren't to know. If I'd had any guts I'd have written and explained the whole thing, but—but I couldn't believe that she wouldn't come back. I couldn't think about anything else. My brain seemed to have stopped working, and if it hadn't been for Monica Ford I'd probably be without a job by now as well as without a wife. You've helped me quite enough by letting me talk to you, and I can't let you get involved any further in an affair like this. There's a proverb about touching pitch, and I won't have you touching it.'

'What nonsense!' said Amanda warmly. 'You told me yourself that this involved the good name of the firm. Well, I am a Derington, so you can't keep me out of it. If you'd like me to see your wife, I will.'

Glenn dropped his hand and turned away to stare once more at the sunlit garden beyond the shadowy verandah.

He said slowly: 'I don't know. I simply do not know. You see she refuses to see me, and I don't think she even reads my letters. She says that until I agree to a divorce she has nothing to say to me. If I could only talk to her!—but perhaps she might talk to you.'

'It's worth trying anyway,' said Amanda. 'At the worst she can only show me the door, and after being brought up by Uncle Oswin I am practically immune to snubs!'

Glenn Barton turned quickly and took her hands in a brief hard grasp:

'You're a brick, Amanda. I can't thank you enough. I know I shouldn't let you do this, and probably no good will come of it, but I've reached the stage where I feel I'd try almost anything!'

'Then that's settled,' said Amanda. 'When would be the best time to see her? Now?'

'A good bit later I should think. She's sure to be out bathing or watching Lumley paint during most of the afternoon and evening. Lumley's the snag, of course. He'll be there.'

'I'll go down after supper tonight,' decided Amanda, 'and just walk in. And you're right about Mr Potter. He's going to be terribly in the way. Couldn't we think up some method of getting rid of him, just for an hour?'

Glenn Barton frowned thoughtfully. 'Yes,' he said hesitantly. 'I think it might be done. I could send him a message or something.'

'That's it!' said Amanda with enthusiasm. 'We'll pretend that someone at the hotel wants to see his pictures with the idea of buying one. That's sure to fetch him. I'll get Toby to do it.'

Glenn Barton said uncertainly: 'I think I'd better do it myself. I don't quite feel like explaining this whole sordid set-up to anyone else.'

'We don't need to. But Mr Potter probably wouldn't come for

you, and I shall merely tell Toby Gates that I have a date with your wife and as I do not want Lumley Potter around, will he be an angel and decoy him away for an hour? I know he'll do it if I ask him. How do I find the house?'

'It's on the harbour,' said Glenn Barton; and gave directions in detail.

'I'll go down about half past nine,' said Amanda, 'and wait until I see Mr Potter leave, and then go straight up. And as Toby is far too rich for his own good, it won't hurt him at all if he finds that he has to end up by buying a genuine Potter Masterpiece.'

The tense lines around Glenn Barton's mouth relaxed and he laughed.

'How nice to hear you laugh again,' said an approving voice from the doorway. They had not heard Miss Moon's approach and they turned, startled and looking a little guilty.

'I see that dear Amanda has been cheering you up,' said Miss Moon cosily. She was wearing today a linen skirt patterned in shades of cerise, with a blouse of cerise organdie copiously ornamented with narrow frills of lace. Her improbable hair was adorned with a gay bow of tulle in the same shade, while a scarf composed of several yards of the same material encircled her thin neck and floated behind her. The amethysts and opals of yesterday had been replaced by a set of garnets that did not tone well with the prevailing colour scheme, but the chains of silver filigree were the same and the scent of heliotrope accompanied her in an almost visible wave.

She reached up and patted Glenn Barton's thin, tanned cheek with a be-ringed hand: 'Dear boy! It does me good to see you in spirits. Amanda dear, I trust that you will insist on Glenn showing you some of our beauty spots. He should get about more.'

'He's going to,' said Amanda. 'He's coming on a picnic to St Hilarion tomorrow. But I can't take the credit for that, I'm afraid. He was shanghaied into it by a glamorous American authoress. We're all going. Come with us Miss Moon—do!'

'You're a dear child,' said Miss Moon approvingly. 'I wish I could. Although I must admit that I have never enjoyed picnicking. Ants, you know. Not to mention wasps. But I shall be out tomorrow. Lady Cooper-Foot is giving a small afternoon bridge party and tea. Three o'clock to six-thirty. Rather a nuisance, as Andreas and Euridice will both be out for most of the day, though they have promised to be back by seven-thirty at the latest. There is some festival or fête at Aiyos Epiktitos that they wish to attend. There is always some fête somewhere that they cannot miss. Very trying. Though why should they not be gay? So it is probably just as well, now I come to think of it, that we shall both be out for the afternoon. Here is Euridice with the tea. Glenn dear, you will stay and have tea with us, will you not?'

'I'm afraid I can't. I have to get back to the office. Monica has one or two things on the files that have to be dealt with before the post goes tomorrow. Any letters I can post for you, Amanda?'

'I haven't had time to write any yet,' confessed Amanda with a laugh.

Mr Barton bent to kiss Miss Moon's hand—evidently an established ritual that pleased the old lady enormously—and Amanda accompanied him to the front door.

'I'll hunt up Toby after tea and explain about Lumley Potter,' she said in a conspiratorial whisper.

'Bless you!' said Glenn Barton with a catch in his voice.

He turned and ran quickly down the steps and a moment later the front gate clanged behind him and Amanda heard his car start up and purr away up the long rising road that led to Nicosia.

9

It was close on half-past nine when Amanda walked quietly down one of the narrow lanes that led to the harbour, and paused in a patch of deep shadow near the quay.

The warm night was milky with moonlight and the air smelt richly of dust and garlic and fishing nets, and fragrantly of flowers. The streets and the quay were full of idlers and no one turned a head to see Amanda pass. Her short, full-skirted frock of coffee-coloured poplin blended equally well with the white moonlight and the dark patches of shadow, and she had tied a scarf of matching chiffon loosely about her head, peasant-wise, that helped to conceal her face.

She did not expect to meet anyone she knew in the narrow lanes at that hour, but she preferred to be on the safe side as she did not in the least wish to explain her mission to any of her friends or acquaintances.

Alastair Blaine had passed her as she crossed the main road. He was hatless and walking very slowly, his hands in his pockets, and the light from a street lamp had glittered for a moment on his blond hair. But Amanda did not think that he had seen her, for his eyes had been blank and unobservant and he had passed her without pausing.

Thanks to Glenn Barton's directions she had no difficulty in locating the house on the harbour where Lumley Potter had rented a studio flat, and she waited in the shadows of an alleyway, sniffing the spicy air and revelling in the warm beauty of the moonlit night.

Presently she was aware of muffled footsteps clattering on a wooden stair near-by. A door creaked and a moment later Lumley Potter hurried past clutching a large portfolio under one arm, his ginger-coloured beard looking grey in the moonlight.

Dear Toby! thought Amanda gratefully. She waited until Mr

Potter turned the corner of the quay, and then left the shadowed alleyway and walked quickly up to the door that Lumley had left open behind him.

A single oil lamp dimly illuminated a narrow hall with flaking plaster walls and a long flight of rickety wooden stairs that led up into darkness. Amanda squared her slim shoulders and started upward.

She passed several landings giving on to rooms that appeared to be unoccupied, for no chink of light showed from under any door and their sole illumination came from the moonlight beyond the grimy landing windows. Glenn had said the top floor. Then this must be the Potter Love-Nest . . .

A strip of light showed from under an ill-fitting door, and a single guttering candle, in a ship's lantern hanging from an iron bracket on the wall, provided a faint, flickering illumination. On the other side of the door a gramophone or a wireless was playing dance music, and Amanda took a deep breath and knocked on the door. She did not wait for an answer but turned the handle and walked in.

The big oblong room was ablaze with light, and Amanda blinked, momentarily dazzled by the contrast from the dimness of the landing and the dark flights of stairs outside.

The room had been colour-washed a vivid shade of salmon pink and there were thick white hand-woven curtains by the open windows. The floor was covered with rust-red matting, and enormous canvases, presumably the work of Mr Potter, hung against the salmon-pink distemper or were stacked in rows against the walls. Mr Potter evidently believed in Paint, and applied it by the pound with the aid of a palette knife or possibly a small trowel. He also, apparently, believed in Gloom and Prussian blue.

A voice said *'Pios ine?'* and Amanda turned quickly and saw Anita Barton.

Mrs Barton presented an incongruous picture in that setting. She was lying face downwards and at full length on a large divan, putting records on a gramophone that stood on the floor beside her. She turned over lazily, and seeing Amanda, came suddenly to her feet.

She was wearing a subtle, clinging dress of black chiffon that breathed Paris in every line, and there were pearls in her ears and at her throat. Her dark hair was cut short and brushed back in smooth shining waves and she looked like a professional fashion model waiting for the photographer.

She stood quite still and stared at Amanda while the record on the gramophone ground to a stop.

'Well I'm damned!' said Anita Barton loudly. 'What are you doing here? Who let you in?'

'I let myself in,' said Amanda apologetically. 'I do hope you don't mind. The downstairs door was open; and I wanted to meet you.'

'I suppose Glenn sent you,' said Mrs Barton, her voice suddenly strident. 'Well in that you can just turn round and walk right out again!'

'No one sent me,' said Amanda composedly. 'It was my own idea. May I sit down?'

'It's a free country,' said Mrs Barton. She sat down herself with some suddenness on the divan, and Amanda realized with a sharp stab of dismay that she had been drinking and was not entirely sober.

'Well, what is it?' demanded Anita Barton. 'Sob stuff? or Good-Name-of-the-Firm? And where do you come in on this—that's what I'd like to know.'

Amanda said abruptly: 'Are you in love with Mr Potter?'

It was not at all what she had intended to say and the moment the words were out she would have given much to recall them, for Anita Barton flung her head back and went off into a peal of laughter.

'With *Lumley!*' Mrs Barton controlled herself and looked at Amanda with frowning brows:

'Listen—you look a good kid. I don't know what you're after, but whatever it is I bet Glenn's behind it. Have a drink—come on, have one.'

She filled a glass and handed it to Amanda. 'Ouzo. Local poison. Go on, drink it. It won't kill you. They say it's an acquired taste. Well now's your time to acquire it.'

Amanda sipped it with repugnance and suppressed a shudder of distaste.

'What were we talking about?' demanded her hostess, refilling her own glass. 'Lumley! So we were. Dear Lumley. No one could love Lumley unlesh—unless—it were his mother. And do you know what *she* christened him? Well I'll tell you: Alfred! Alf Potts. He didn't think that was dish—distinguished enough, so he changed it to "Lumley Potter". Shall I tell you why he let me run away with him? Two re-reasons. To annoy Claire, and because he wanted to show off. The "Free Life"—t'hell with the conventions! The Creative Artist is above the laws that g-govern the uncreative herd. Long live the Revolution!'

Mrs Barton described an airy circle with her glass, splashed a generous proportion of its contents on the floor and drank the remainder.

'No,' she said, scowling. 'I don't love Lumley. Lumley loves Claire. Claire de la lune! They all love Claire—or that's what *she* thinks. And what a surprise she's going to get one day!'

She dropped her empty glass on to the floor where it rolled in a circle on the matting, and for an appreciable interval she sat staring at it with fixed unseeing eyes, and at last she said in a half whisper: 'But I had to run away with someone. I had to get away from Glenn. You don't know what it was like. You don't know! I want to *live*. I must get away. Right away from this narrow deadly little island—escape. I'd have divorced him if I could, but there wasn't any evidence. What's the good of telling people things? It hurts him and he hates it like hell, but it isn't evidence in court. So I have to make him divorce me. He'll do it. He *must*. I sh-shall make such an exhibition of myself that in the end he'll have to do it f' his own sake'—she appeared to have forgotten Amanda—'I've got to get away. Right away——'

Amanda said tentatively: 'If you hate the life here so much couldn't you persuade him to get a job somewhere else? Wherever you *would* like to live? I'm sure he could get a transfer. If you went back to him I'm sure he'd try. He said that he only wanted you back —on any terms.'

Anita Barton lifted her head and stared at Amanda. She said loudly and harshly: 'You don't understand. I don't want to be dead and buried. I want to live! I want to have fun. I want to laugh and enjoy myself; and I will-I will! If I had to go back to Glenn I should die. Thash what—die! Nice, quiet, hard-working, dull, *deadly* little Glenn——!'

With a sudden violent gesture she picked up the fallen glass and hurled it at the wall, where it smashed against one of Mr Potter's eccentric canvases and fell in a shower of broken fragments on to the rust-red matting.

'And now,' said Mrs Barton, rising unsteadily, 'I think you'd better go. So nice of you to call. Good-bye.'

Amanda rose. There seemed to be no point in prolonging the interview, as Mrs Barton was obviously in no condition to listen to reasoned arguments that night. But the interview had at least produced some interesting information, even if it had done little towards helping Glenn Barton. She said good-bye and left.

The candle in the ship's lantern had evidently burned out, for the landing was in darkness and she wavered, wondering if she should turn back and ask Anita Barton to lend her a torch or a box of matches. But Mrs Barton had put another record on the gramophone and Amanda could not face a return to that room. She lingered on the landing for a moment or two, waiting until her eyes should accustom themselves to the gloom, and aware of an inexplicable reluctance to return down that narrow dark staircase.

Presently she walked cautiously forward, and groping for the stair-rail began to move downwards, feeling for each step.

The moonlight beyond the small window on the landing below provided a faint light, but Amanda, peering down the well of the staircase in expectation of seeing the glow of the oil lamp in the hall, could see nothing but blackness below her. Had the hall light too burned out, or had someone blown it out? Or were there three more landings between her and the hall? She could not remember.

Amanda hesitated at the top of the next flight of stairs. Above her she could hear a voice from Mrs Barton's gramophone singing a familiar, lilting French song. *La Mer: 'Voyez—ces oiseaux blancs—et ces maisons rouillées . . .'*

It should have been a friendly and encouraging sound, but somehow it was not, and quite suddenly and for no reason Amanda found that she was shivering, and that her heart was beating in queer uneven jerks as though she had been running. She looked quickly over her shoulder, but beyond the faint square of moonlight the landing stretched away into dusty blackness, and if there had been anyone there she could not have seen them. But of course there was no one there! It was absurd to imagine such a thing. She was being ridiculous and childish—afraid of walking down a staircase in the dark!

There was nothing to be frightened of, for she had only to keep one hand on the stair-rail and walk straight down, and in less than a minute she would be out on the open quayside in the bright moonlight. Amanda straightened her shoulders and gripping the flimsy rail, felt for the top step and moved downwards once more into blackness.

She began to count the steps—*four—five—six—seven*. Then all at once she stopped, and stood frozen and still.

There was someone on the stairs behind her. She was quite sure of it. She listened intently, every nerve strained and alert, but she could only hear the muffled music of the gramophone two floors above her. There *could* not be anyone on the stairs behind her! It had only been an echo—or imagination. She must go on—*eight—nine—ten——*

'. . . *La Mer—a bercé mon coeur—pour la vi-e* . . .' The music stopped on a last, long note, and in the silence she heard the stairs above her creak to the soft footsteps of someone who was following her down.

Amanda fought down a rush of blind panic. How many steps to the next landing? *Was* there a next landing? Surely there should be a window? The footsteps behind her had stopped when she stopped, and the house was deathly quiet. But in that stillness she could hear someone breathing in the blackness above her. Or was it only her own frightened breathing?

From somewhere outside the house someone approaching along the quay was singing the tenor part of the love duet from *Butterfly* in a loud and tuneful voice that somehow conveyed the impression that the singer, if not exactly intoxicated, was somewhat elevated by liquor. Amanda took courage from the sound. There were people out there on the quay. Nothing could harm her. She had only to reach the quay——

She went on again, quickly; stumbling in the dark. And instantly those other soft, furtive footsteps followed her. They were quicker now, and closer; and it was not her own frightened breathing that she could hear, but the short hard breathing of someone who followed her. Someone who breathed as an animal breathes, avid and panting, and who, in another moment, would reach out and clutch her——

Amanda stumbled and came hard against the turn of the stair, and turning, pressed frantically back into the angle of the wall, trying not to breathe. She heard a groping hand brush against the rough plaster within a foot of her head . . . and then suddenly, in the hall below her, the heavy door was flung wide and the bright glow of a torch showed in the well of the stairs.

Amanda heard a short hard gasp above her, and then the quick pad of running footsteps that retreated into the darkness.

She turned swiftly, but the stairs above her were empty, and whoever had entered the hall below was coming up the staircase towards her, humming softly. It was, oddly enough, the same song that Anita Barton's gramophone had played so short a time ago:

'. . . *Et d'une chanson d'amour—La Mer—a bercé mon coeur——*'

The beam of a torch fell full on her face, blinding her, and the song stopped short.

'Amarantha!—well, well! And who has been dishevelling your hair this time?'

Amanda spoke in a breathless, sobbing whisper: 'There-there was someone on the stairs! Behind me. I——'

Steve caught her wrists in a painful grip that spoke as clearly as any words.

He raised his voice a little and said: 'I suppose you've been visiting the Potter studio? Then you can introduce me. Met a fellow at one of these cafés who says that Potter is a newer and bigger and better Picasso—and how! I told him that Potter was probably a mere painter of pot-boilers, but as a brother of the brush'—Mr Howard was slurring his words a little—'it behoved me to prove his worth before presuming to criticize. I say, that's pretty good, isn't it? Let's go up and see him. There is no time like the present—Napoleon said that. Or was it Josephine?'

'He's out,' said Amanda, still breathless.

'Out? Then don't let's waste our time on the chap. Probably can't paint for pineapples. Let's go out and paint the town instead!'

'But——'

'*Shut up!*' said Steve softly and savagely.

He pulled her arm through his own, and holding it hard against him, turned and went back down the stairs, singing '*Dolce notte! Quante stella*' in a loud and cheerful voice.

The door banged behind them and Mr Howard, still retaining his hold on Amanda's arm, walked rapidly away along the quay and continued to sing.

He did not turn towards the town, however, but swung instead down the sea wall of the harbour, dragging Amanda with him. The loiterers whom she had observed earlier that evening were gone and the wall was deserted. Half-way along it he stopped and jerked her round to face him. She saw his gaze search the length of the wall, the open sea on one side and the dark harbour water on the other. But there was no boat anchored near them and the wall itself lay white and empty in the brilliant moonlight.

Steve drew a quick breath of relief and his voice when he spoke was no longer either loud or slurred, but low pitched and incisive:

'At least we can't be overheard here; which is more than I can say of any other spot in this damned town! However just in case anyone has a pair of night glasses and is curious, I propose to convey the impression that conversation is not what is on my mind. Stand still!'

The next minute his arms were about Amanda and his cheek was against her hair: 'And now,' said Steve tersely, his voice hard and curt and entirely devoid of any emotional content, 'perhaps you'll tell me what the hell you were doing in that house! Toby Gates told me that you'd gone to see Mrs Barton, and I got down there as quick as I could. What were you doing there?'

His shoulder was warm and firm and smelt comfortingly of shaving soap, clean linen and Turkish cigarettes, and Amanda struggled with a childish desire to turn her head against it and burst into tears. It is possible that Mr Howard was aware of this, for he said sharply: 'Take a pull on yourself, Amanda!'

Amanda steadied herself with an effort and said: 'It was Glenn——'

'*Glenn?* You mean Barton? Was he there?'

'No. He came to tell me about her—Anita. Because he'd pretended that she was ill, and when he heard that she was in Kyrenia he knew that I'd find out . . .'

She told him the story as Glenn had told it to her that afternoon, and how she had offered to see Anita Barton and had arranged with Toby Gates to get Lumley Potter safely off the premises.

'And what happened when you got there?' demanded Steve brusquely.

He listened without interruption to her account of that unsatisfactory and abortive interview with Anita Barton, and when she had finished he said:

'What was that about someone on the stairs?'

'There *was* someone,' whispered Amanda, and shivered.

'Steve's arms tightened about her momentarily and he said: 'Go on. Tell me.'

She told him of that brief, ugly, terrifying interlude on the dark rickety staircase, and when she had done he said curtly: 'Quite sure you didn't imagine it?'

'Quite sure,' said Amanda, and shivered again.

'Any idea who it was?'

'No.'

'Could it have been Mrs Barton?'

'No,' said Amanda again, entirely positive.

'What makes you so sure?'

'She had the gramophone on. If she had opened the door it would have sounded louder at once.'

'H'mm. Maybe. On the other hand there is probably another door.'

He brooded for a moment or two, absently rubbing his cheek against her hair, and then said abruptly: 'Who knew that you were going there?'

'No one. Only Glenn—Mr Barton. And Toby of course. No one else.'

'And Toby told me—choosing a nice public spot to do it in—and probably half a dozen other people as well. So that's not much help to us.'

Amanda said with a quaver in her voice: 'What's wrong with that house?'

She was aware of a brief, fractional tension of Steve's body, but he only said: 'Nothing that I know of.'

'Then why did you come there as soon as Toby told you where I was?'

'Because,' said Mr Howard with commendable restraint, 'I do not consider it healthy for you to wander around alone after dark. I warned you once that you'd have to watch your step. Well I meant it. In case you're not aware of it, this afternoon, in the absence of any other evidence, a verdict that amounted to "suicide while of an unsound mind" was returned on Mrs Blaine.'

'But—that means it's all over!' said Amanda. 'If the police think it was suicide, then no one would want to——'

'Can't you understand?' interrupted Steve roughly. 'Mrs Blaine was murdered; and as far as the murderer knows, you are the only person who may be aware of it. If you had talked—if you talk now— that verdict would not stand. Use your head, Amanda!'

'Then you think that-that someone in that house meant to stop me talking by——' Amanda's voice died in her throat.

'I don't know about that. You can't say that because you heard someone coming down a staircase behind you it was necessarily someone who meant to harm you. Or, for that matter, that he or she even knew who you were. It is just on the cards that another visitor may have been expected to pay a call on Mrs Barton tonight, and that in the dark you were mistaken for someone else.'

'For-for someone who . . . somebody meant to kill? You mean another murder? Oh no!'

'It's possible. An attempt at one, shall we say?'

'I don't believe it. Why? Why should there be?'

'I'm not sure yet. It's just a theory. But it might account for that incident on the staircase. There are, of course, various other possibilities——' There was an odd inflection in Steve Howard's voice.

'I know,' interrupted Amanda bitterly. 'One of which is that I might really have murdered Julia Blaine, and then invented a story of someone on the stairs just to make it look as though it couldn't possibly have been me!'

'Yes,' agreed Steve thoughtfully. 'There is always that of course. I hadn't lost sight of it.'

He heard Amanda's quick gasp of rage and continued reflectively: 'Poison, you see, is a woman's weapon. Women do not as a rule use a gun, and hardly ever a knife. They don't like noise or blood. They prefer poison or pushing someone off a cliff—something which produces death, but death at arm's length so to speak. Men don't mind the bang, or the blood getting on their hands.'

'You-you——' words appeared to fail Amanda. 'You dare to think that I——' She attempted to wrench herself free and Steve tightened his hold.

'There's no need to fly off the handle, Amarantha. One has to look at every angle. It's a possibility. There are, as I said, others.'

Amanda pulled back against his arms and stared up at him; but the moon was behind him and his face was only a dark shadow against the pale sky and the silver sea. She said in a breathless, furious whisper:

'There's something I haven't lost sight of either! *You* told me not to tell about that bottle. And *you* took it away—*and* the glass! How do I know that you didn't do that because your own fingerprints were on both? I don't believe that you were in Fayid, or on the ship, just because you paint. You were there for a reason. Something to do with Julia—or Toby, or Persis, or someone who was on that ship. There's something horrible going on, and you're mixed up in it!'

She stopped, breathless and trembling, and Steve said reflectively: 'You look charming when you're angry. Like an infuriated kitten.'

Amanda made another ineffectual attempt to free herself, but the arms about her were suddenly like a vice, hard and painful, and there was no longer any trace of levity in Steven Howard's voice. He said harshly: 'Keep out of this, Amanda! I mean that. Murder is a diabolical thing. You can't risk taking an interest in the private affairs of anyone who was on that boat. It isn't safe.'

'Why?' asked Amanda uncertainly.

'Because it's essential that you avoid any appearance of suspicion or meddling. It's no secret that you were with Julia Blaine when she died, and someone knows that there was a small bottle containing the poison she died of under the pillow in that cabin. That someone is bound to wonder what you thought when you found it, and why you never mentioned it, and what you have done with it. Remember that a murderer always has a guilty conscience, and that a killer knows quite well that even if he kills a dozen people—or twenty—he himself can only hang once.'

Amanda said in a choking whisper: 'But I don't know anything— I don't want to!'

'You know about the bottle,' said Steve grimly. 'You also questioned the stewardess about that glass. I heard you, so the chances are that several other people did as well. And because of that, someone may be interested enough—or scared enough—to keep a pretty wary eye on you and to get unpleasantly upset when you behave as you did tonight.'

'But I only called on Mrs Barton. There's nothing suspicious in that!'

'No? Not when you tell Toby Gates to lure Mr Potter out of the house? Not when you slip out after dark and—I am willing to bet— sneak along in the shadows with a veil half over your face and lurk in some alleyway until Potter has left, and then steal into the house like a stage conspirator in Act II about to plant the time bomb in the Prime Minister's portfolio? You did, didn't you?'

'Well——' began Amanda defensively, and stopped.

'I thought as much,' said Mr Howard, resigned. 'Listen to me, Amanda—and I'm not going to tell you this again. You are in the unfortunate position of being able to produce evidence that what has scraped past as suicide was, in reality, murder. If, on top of that, you start paying elaborately furtive visits to a woman whom you have never met before, but who was a fellow passenger on board the *Orantares,* someone with a guilty conscience and a single-track mind may begin to ask themselves why all this First Conspirator stuff, if your visit to Mrs Barton is just a social call?—or could it be that you are beginning to make discreet inquiries among the passengers, and if so, what are you after? On the other hand, provided you behave in a perfectly normal manner, whoever was responsible for the murder of Mrs Blaine may be led to believe that you made nothing of that bottle after all, but merely threw it out of the porthole and dismissed the incident—maybe! Now do you get the idea?'

'Yes,' said Amanda with a shudder.

'Good. Keep thinking of it. And keep out of it!'

Amanda said haltingly: 'But—but Julia—If somebody killed her it isn't right that they should get away with it just because I—I hadn't the courage to tell.'

'Don't worry; they won't,' said Steve grimly. 'I promise you that. And it wasn't a question of your not having the courage to tell. You'd have told all right, if I hadn't stopped you.'

'Why did you?'

'Because it was too late to do anything for Mrs Blaine by then, and I had an idea or two of my own that I preferred to follow up without the issue being confused by a cat among the pigeons.'

'Ideas about what?'

'Limes, Times and Temperature,' said Steve lightly. 'And now, as I am beginning to get a cramp, I think that the sooner we terminate this tender interlude, the better. Look at me!'

Amanda looked up, startled, and Steve bent his head and kissed her.

It was, as Persis would have said, quite a kiss, and indicated if nothing else that Mr Howard must have had plenty of experience in such matters. Amanda, who owing to a strict policy of chaperonage enforced until recently by Uncle Oswin, had not, had the oddest conviction that the ground under her feet was no longer solid and that for a long moment the moon and stars were describing circles about her head.

'That,' said Mr Howard, releasing her, 'was just for the record.'

'Was it?' said Amanda breathlessly. 'Then this is just for——'

Steve caught her hand a fraction of a second before it reached its mark.

'That would have hurt you much more than it hurt me,' he remarked reprovingly. 'Another time use your fist instead of your palm, and go for the point of the jaw. Like to have another shot?'

'Yes!' said Amanda, breathing stormily. 'With a flatiron!'

'Very wifely,' commented Mr Howard. He looked down at her and laughed.

'I apologize—there! But it was quite irresistible. Don't quarrel with me, Amarantha.' He kissed her hand lightly and tucked it under his arm. 'Come on; it's quite time you got back, or Miss Moon will begin to wonder if you really are a nice girl after all.'

He turned her about and walked her back along the sea wall and up through the moonlit town to the gates of the Villa Oleander.

10

Amanda avoided the harbour on the following morning. In the hot, brilliant sunlight that streamed through the open windows of the Villa Oleander and filled the dusty, gracious rooms with sunbeams, the events of the past night seemed unbelievable and unreal, and even faintly ridiculous. Amanda was almost tempted to wonder if she had not, after all, imagined the sound of those furtive feet on the stairs. Had they perhaps been only an echo of her own footsteps, or a trick played upon her nerves by darkness and an unfamiliar and empty house?

There was only one thing about the happenings of the past night that was entirely real. The fact that Steve Howard had kissed her.

Amanda, standing in the hot sunlight of the garden and remembering that kiss with a return of the curious sensation of dizziness that had accompanied it, was inclined to discount all that Steve Howard had told her, and to suspect that it had merely amused him to see how long he could keep her standing in a close embrace in the moonlight. Hadn't he made some flippant remark on the previous morning about only making love by moonlight?

'I wouldn't put it past him to have done it for a bet!' thought Amanda with sudden bitterness. 'He probably makes a habit of it, and I expect he has kissed Persis already!'

The reflection annoyed her unreasonably, and she did not realize that in the process of brooding over Steve Howard's outrageous behaviour she had very nearly lost sight of the terrifying and infinitely more important fact that she had been indirectly involved in what was almost certainly murder, and that she had entirely forgotten to be frightened. An end that Mr Howard may possibly have had in view when he had terminated their macabre conversation on the harbour wall in that particular manner.

Amanda stood among the freckled shadows of the lemon trees,

with the pigeons cooing and fluttering in the deep stone arches of the ruined wall behind her and the scent of roses and syringa and sunbaked dust sweet on the windless air, and thought exclusively of Steven Howard and not at all of Julia Blaine . . .

Miss Moon, a blaze of emerald green, appeared upon the creeper-covered verandah outside the drawing-room windows and called down to say that Captain Gates was on the telephone asking if Amanda would go bathing with him.

'Tell him I've gone out!' begged Amanda.

'Certainly, dear. Where to?'

'Just out,' said Amanda, seized with an urgent desire for solitude and a feeling of inability to cope with the conversation of Toby Gates or anyone else—with one possible exception.

She ran across the garden and out into the road, and taking the first turning that offered, presently found herself leaving the town behind her.

The houses became fewer and the road wandered between olive groves, dark pointed cypress trees and stony sun-baked fields where goats grazed among the coarse grasses, weeds and asphodel. An ox cart creaked towards her and a black-haired, black-eyed, bare-footed urchin riding a donkey flourished a branch of oleander and grinned at Amanda as he ambled past. The road was hot and white under her feet and she began to wish that she had thought to bring a hat.

A car swept past, covering her with dust. It drew up abruptly some distance ahead, and reversed until it drew level with her.

'Amanda!' said Alastair Blaine, leaning out over the door. 'What do you think you're doing?'

'Walking,' said Amanda. 'Hullo, Persis. Where are you two off to?'

'We are doing our duty as self-respecting tourists,' said Persis. 'According to the Guide Book, we should not fail to see the Abbey of Bellapais. We are not failing.'

'Come on Amanda,' said Alastair Blaine, leaning out to open the back door. 'Get in. You'll get heat-stroke or a peeling nose or both if you wander around the countryside in this sun, and as you'll have to do the sights some time you may as well do this one now.'

Amanda looked back down the hot dusty road and capitulated. She said: 'You will get me back by one o'clock, won't you?'

'Of course. Half an hour is about my limit for looking at ruins. Hop in.' He slammed the door behind her and changed gear.

Persis had not seconded the invitation and Amanda had the sudden and uncomfortable impression that she was not too pleased at the addition of a third person to the party. But it was too late now, for the car was already moving again.

The white road ran parallel to the sea and the long, narrow barrier of the Kyrenia range that lay between the coast and the central plain. The mountains were blue in the hot sunlight; a clear transparent blue that made them look as though they had been fashioned out of Lalique glass, and their pale serrated peaks, shimmering in the heat haze, had the strange beauty of those distant ranges that Leonardo da Vinci has painted as a background to the Mona Lisa and the Madonna of the Rocks.

A light breeze blew in from the sea, turning the olive trees to silver, and Amanda relaxed into a day dream and made no attempt to talk. Even Persis Halliday's clear and incisive voice had softened and slowed as though the warm peace of the morning was also having its effect on her, and she conducted a low-toned conversation with Alastair Blaine to which Amanda, occupied with her own thoughts, paid no heed.

The car changed gear as the road wound up through a village perched on a low hill. A village of white-walled, pink-roofed houses, bell towers and minarets, encircled with olive groves, silver in the wind, and spiked with the sharp dark green of cypress trees.

Persis said: 'Say, isn't this the cutest place you ever saw! Where's that map? . . . Aiyos Epiktitos. That'll be it. Do stop, Alastair, I want to take a photograph.'

Major Blaine looked at his watch and said, resigned: 'I'll give you five minutes. And no wandering round the place if you want to see the Abbey and get back by one.'

The streets were full of people in holiday attire and gay with a flutter of paper flags and green branches, and Amanda suddenly caught sight of a familiar face. It was Euridice, the prop and stay of the Villa Oleander, and Amanda remembered that Miss Moon had mentioned a fête at Aiyos Epiktitos that both Euridice and her nephew Andreas, the odd-job man, were to attend that day.

Euridice, however, appeared to be in anything but a festive mood. She was talking to a small group of black-clad women, one of whom was wailing aloud, and her normally cheerful face was full of woe. She looked up and, seeing Amanda, hurried over to the car.

This meeting, it was providential! declared Euridice. Her English was strangely scrambled and interlarded with whole sentences in her native tongue, but Amanda gathered from her flood of agitated speech that neither she nor Andreas would be able to return to the Villa Oleander that day, and that she wished Amanda to convey this information and her apologies to Miss Moon.

'Tomorrow morning, for the breakfast I come,' said Euridice. 'Today, no.' A relative had died, she explained; the husband of a cousin who kept a Taverna on the road beyond Nicosia. Apparently the cousin's husband had got into some bar-room brawl in Nicosia and had ended up in a culvert with a knife in his back.

Ah, these seafaring men! said Euridice, throwing up her hands. On the ships they would work like oxen at the plough, but on shore they pursued pleasure and conducted themselves in a truculent manner. The poor Almana!—Euridice mopped her eyes—what sadness to lose a husband thus! This had been her home village before her marriage, and her family, together with Euridice and Andreas, were to leave shortly by bus for Nicosia to attend the funeral, and would not be back that night.

Amanda offered her condolences and promised to inform Miss Moon. Euridice thanked her tearfully and departed.

'Who was your lady friend?' demanded Persis, returning. Amanda explained the circumstances as Alastair Blaine restarted the car and they continued on their way.

The ruined Abbey of Bellapais lay on the knees of the hills, its pale stone walls, arches and tall campanile rising up out of a silvery sea of olives so graciously, so softly opalescent, that it seemed more like a mirage than something built by men, and as though a breath could blow it away.

Beyond and above and below the pale gold walls and empty archways lay a wash of blue; the intense cobalt blue of the distant sea, the cloudless blue of the sky and the soft blue barrier of the Kyrenia range.

Major Blaine braked the car in a patch of shade and Amanda said suddenly: 'I don't think I'm coming in. I'd rather look at it from the hillside. If I go inside there's sure to be a guide and instructive notices, and I couldn't bear to turn it from a dream into a string of dates. I shall sit under one of those olive trees and just stare at it.'

Persis laughed. 'You know what, honey? You are too romantic for your own good—or else you must be in love. Well I guess I won't dissuade you. We're only young once. But speaking for myself I do not intend to miss a trick. I've come to Cyprus to see the sights, and I'll see 'em if it kills me. Where's that dam' guide book? Alastair honey, if you think you're going to lie on your back under any olive tree and go to sleep, you have assessed the situation incorrectly. You were taking me on a conducted tour—remember? You start conducting right here. Lead on!'

They passed under the shadow of a stone archway and Amanda, left alone, turned away and climbed the slope above the road, and presently settled herself in the shade of an ilex with her back against the rough bark and gave herself up to a fascinated contemplation of the view.

I should like to live here, thought Amanda dreamily; and remembered what Miss Moon had said about Time . . . that in the Villa Oleander, Time was their servant, and not they the servants of Time. Perhaps that was true of all Cyprus. Certainly this shimmering blue day held a timeless and dream-like quality. But it was a deceptive quality, for Time must move on here as relentlessly as it did in colder and harsher countries, and it was only a pleasant illusion that here it drifted slowly and lazily. One day the world would catch up with Cyprus. One day politicians and greedy, frightened, quarrelling factions would engulf the sleepy, enchanted island—as they had engulfed so many other lazy, beautiful places—in a wave of Progress, reinforced concrete and Town Planning.

The sun moved slowly across the sky and the shadow of the ilex moved with it. The bark of the tree trunk began to feel unpleasantly hard through the thin green cotton of Amanda's frock and there was an ant crawling down her back and several more investigating her ankles.

She rose reluctantly and made her way back to the car. There was still no sign of Persis and Alastair, and abandoning her decision not to enter the Abbey, she paid over the small entrance fee to the drowsy custodian at the entrance and walked into the Abbey grounds.

Only the shell of the gracious building remained. But the old stone cloisters were cool and quiet and the ruined arches gave on to soft blue distances and the grey-green of olives on the hillside below. Bellapais—The Abbey of Peace. It had been well named.

Amanda wandered across a square of emerald green turf surrounded by shadowed cloisters. There was a rose bush growing at one side of it and a single tall cypress tree. The close-cut turf looked more comfortable than the stony hillside, and she lay face down on it, stretched out at full length on the warm grass in the small patch of shade thrown by the scented sprays of the roses that curved above her. Amanda pulled a grass stem and chewed it reflectively, and presently, feeling pleasantly drowsy, closed her eyes . . .

She was aroused by a sound of voices from under the arch of the cloisters on the far side of the rose bush. It was Alastair Blaine who was speaking, though it did not seem like his voice, for its slow, pleasant drawl was entirely missing and the words had a sharp, ragged sound:

'My dear, don't! Not now. You don't understand——'

Persis Halliday answered him, and her voice too was almost the voice of a stranger: hurt and uneven and somehow vulnerable.

'I think I do. Cyprus isn't London, this isn't last year, and Time Marches On. That's it, isn't it? You've changed—and I haven't. Once I thought that you might almost walk out on everything— Julia, your career, everything, anything—for me. Almost—not quite.'

'Persis, you knew it wasn't possible.'

'Because you hadn't a penny beyond your pay and the money was all Julia's? But it's different now, Alastair. She's dead, and it's all yours.'

'You don't understand,' said Alastair tiredly.

'What don't I understand? I came out to Egypt because I had to see you. And her. To see what she was like. I knew the minute I saw you together that you didn't even care for her. But you didn't care any more for me either. Who is she, Alastair?'

'She? I don't know who you are talking about.'

'Neither do I. But I feel that there is someone. Is it Claire? You stopped off here, after that fortnight in London, to stay with the Normans. Oh yes, I know that Julia was here too, and that when you were flown home to London for that conference I had a fair field because she couldn't come with you. But a little thing like having your wife around wouldn't stop Claire!'

'Oh God,' said Alastair Blaine. 'You too!'

Persis said: 'Don't fool yourself, darling—it isn't you she wants. She likes men around, but it's George she really relies on. George, who puts up with all her whims and whimsies and provides her with a nice safe respectable background and fetches and carries for her. Things no one else would do. Is it Claire?'

'I don't know what you're talking about,' said Alastair wearily. 'I have no interest in Claire Norman, and George is my first cousin. In fact now that Julia's dead he's my next of kin, so is it likely that I'd even think of—Oh, leave it!'

'Now you're angry. But if it isn't Claire, who is it? Is it Amanda? Have you fallen for those big grey eyes and that wonderful hair, like Toby Gates? You and Toby! And just over a year ago he was tagging round after me like Mary's little lamb. Oh well, who can blame him. She's a sweet kid, and worth anyone's while for half an hour in the moonlight.'

'Don't be ridiculous!' Alastair's voice was both angry and exasperated.

'Then who?'

'There isn't anyone, I tell you. Can't you see that after Julia——'

Persis cut across the sentence sharply and cruelly: 'You didn't give a dam' for Julia! I know. I've seen you look at her. The best turn she ever did you was to kill herself! That's true, isn't it?'

'Yes,' said Alastair Blaine heavily. 'It's true. But—but you can't shrug off death, Persis. She was my wife, and—oh I don't want to talk about it. I don't want to *think* about it. Can't you see that all I want is a little peace and quiet? I've had nothing but scenes for years. Scenes and tears and hysteria, and nagging, senseless, silly accusations. God! I'm sick of it!'

'Alastair, darling——'

'Don't darling me!' Alastair's voice was suddenly ragged with exhaustion and rage. 'All right, you asked for it and you shall have it! I did make love to you in London last year. Would you like to know why? Because you wanted me to. You shouted for it like a spoilt kid banging the table with a spoon. And you were attractive and amusing and you treated the whole thing as a joke. And because I knew—I knew so damnably well!—that when I got back to Julia she would accuse me of having had an affair with some woman, even if I'd spent the entire bloody fortnight locked in the cell of a monastery!'

'But Alastair——'

'Shut up! I'm talking now. I've never had affairs with women. Do you realize that? Julia was the first woman I ever fell in love with, and I married her. In all the years of our marriage I had never been unfaithful to her—never once! Do you know why? Because I'm not built that way. I cannot be rude or curt to women who put themselves out to be pleasant to me, but I don't want to make love to them. And believe me, they don't want it either! But Julia would never believe that. She preferred to imagine that I was some frightful Lothario, instead of a perfectly ordinary, dull sort of chap without an ounce of sex appeal. And now you!—it's too much! I'd put up with Julia's senseless, endless, *futile* suspicions for years, and I suppose there was bound to be a breaking point one day, and——'

'And I was it,' finished Persis quietly.

'Yes! Oh it wasn't you——No, I don't mean it like that. But it was knowing so well that as soon as I saw her again I should have to listen to the same old sordid accusations. I suddenly felt that I couldn't take it any more.'

'So you said to yourself "What the hell? If I'm going to be accused of playing around anyway, okay, I'll play around!" '

'Yes!'

'And that's really all there was to it? Just—just a ten-day flirtation with someone who was attractive and amusing and who treated it all as a joke?'

'I'm sorry. I didn't imagine for a moment that you——'

Persis' voice interrupted him before he could finish the sentence:

'Don't, dear! You don't have to say any more. And so there isn't even anyone else!'

She laughed; a little bitter laugh. Alastair did not answer and there was silence for a moment or two. Presently their footsteps moved slowly away together, echoing hollowly under the curved stone arches of the age-old cloisters.

A shadow moved on the grass beside Amanda and a quiet voice quoted Puck's words: ' *"Lord, what fools these mortals be!"* '

Amanda started up. *'You!'* she said on a gasp. 'What are you doing here?'

'The same as you,' said Steve Howard amiably. 'Eavesdropping.'

Amanda's face flamed. 'I was not eavesdropping!'

'Perhaps not intentionally, but the result was the same. Very instructive, wasn't it?'

'Why are you spying on us all?' demanded Amanda hotly.

'You sound very cross, my sweet. Why shouldn't I come here if I wish? A good many people do. In fact all self-respecting tourists are urged not to miss it. I have been pursuing my Art.'

'I don't believe a word of it!' said Amanda. 'And I'm not cross and I'm not your sweet!'

'I withdraw the adjective. There is, alas, a distinct trace of acidity in your manner this morning; and you are not only cross but getting crosser every minute.'

Amanda opened her mouth and shut it again without speaking. She had remembered an admirable piece of advice frequently given to her by Miss Binns, her Uncle Oswin's elderly and placid house-keeper. She drew a deep breath and counted twenty.

'Why are you here?' she inquired in a more reasonable voice.

'To keep an eye on you.'

'On *me?*' said Amanda, startled. 'Why?'

'I find you so attractive that I cannot keep away.'

There was a mocking gleam in Mr Howard's eye and once again Amanda felt her cheeks burn, counted fifteen and said coldly: 'Don't talk nonsense.'

'Don't you believe me?'

'No I don't!' snapped Amanda.

'All right then. I have a brilliant theory that sooner or later someone is going to murder you, and I wish to see who does it. Will that do?'

'Don't you ever speak the truth?' demanded Amanda frostily.

'Not if I can help it,' admitted Steve with disarming candour. 'Truth, Amarantha, as your classical studies will no doubt have informed you, is a naked lady who lives at the bottom of a well. It therefore behoves any gentleman who inadvertently dredges her up in his bucket to look the other way or hurriedly shroud her in a mackintosh.'

Amanda looked at him doubtfully. His brown hair was ruffled into disorder and there was a smudge of blue paint on one side of his chin. He was wearing a blue sports shirt and a pair of grey flannels that had seen better days, and there were paint marks on both.

She said abruptly: 'What have you been painting?'

Mr Howard made an airy gesture of the hand towards the surrounding walls. 'This. From a couple of hundred yards down the road.'

Amanda said: 'I'd like to see it.'

'Suspicious little thing, aren't you? All right—come on.'

They walked back through the Abbey and down the road, and he led the way up a goat track to a point on the opposite hillside some fifty yards to the left of the ilex tree under which Amanda had been sitting.

'Where's your car?' asked Amanda.

'On the upper road; it's not much more than a track.'

There was a clutter of painting gear in the shade of some trees, and Steve picked up a canvas that he had left propped against a tree trunk, and held it up for her inspection.

It was a rough sketch in oils, showing the Abbey of Bellapais lifting above a haze of wind-ruffled olives. The thing had apparently been done entirely with a palette knife, for the paint was laid on with a lavish hand; but it in no way resembled the efforts of Mr Lumley Potter. Despite the strength of the technique the unfinished sketch had captured all the dreamlike, ethereal quality of the ruined Abbey that had so forcibly struck Amanda at her first sight of it, and she said again, and unconsciously, almost the same words that she had used on the harbour wall on the previous morning.

'But you *can* paint!'

She lifted her eyes from the picture and looked at Steve Howard, puzzled and uncertain.

'Poor Amarantha,' said Steve softly. 'You don't know whether you're coming or going, do you? Well if it's any consolation to you, I'm not so sure myself. Why did you come to Cyprus?'

The question was abrupt and unexpected, and Amanda looked startled. 'I wanted to come.'

'Why? Any special reason?'

'Yes,' said Amanda slowly, her mouth curving in a reminiscent smile: 'A poem I read at school. Have you ever read something that made you want to see a special place? That—that sort of haunted you?'

Steve's eyes were no longer mocking. 'Flecker,' he said, smiling, and quoted the lines that had captured the schoolgirl Amanda's childish imagination: ' *"I have seen old ships sail like swans asleep beyond the village which men still call Tyre, with leaden age o'ercargoed, dipping deep for Famagusta and the hidden sun that rings black Cyprus with a lake of fire."* '

'Yes,' said Amanda. She turned to look out across the grey-green mist of olives to the far blue sea beyond them, and spoke in the soft abstracted voice of one who speaks a thought aloud:

' *"Famagusta and the hidden sun . . ."* The names are so beautiful. Famagusta—Kyrenia—Hilarion—Paphos.' Her voice changed to every name, lingering on the syllables. 'Do you know what the castle on that peak over there is called? Miss Moon told me. It's called Buffavento. That means "the wind blows". *The wind blows . . .* ' Her voice sank to a whisper.

Steve forbore to correct her translation, and just then a car horn sounded from the road below.

'That'll be Blaine,' said Steve. 'You'd better get back. See you at the picnic this afternoon.'

Amanda turned to look at the square of canvas again. She said a little hesitantly: 'Could I buy it? I'd like to have it for my own. You do sell them, don't you?'

'I do,' said Steve. 'But not, generally speaking, off the peg. However, I'd like to give you this one. You can consider it as an unbirthday present. It's only a rough sketch.'

Amanda smiled at him with a sudden glow in her eyes and reached out a hand for it. 'It's wonderful!' she said.

'It's wet,' said Steve, removing it. 'I'll keep it for the moment. You shall have it later.'

Amanda nodded absently, and went slowly back down the hillside between the olive trees. And all the way back to Kyrenia, while Persis laughed and chattered as though that brief, emotional scene in the Abbey cloisters had never taken place, Amanda was silent and thoughtful.

She was remembering something that Steve Howard had said in the cabin of the *Orantares:* 'I paint indifferent pictures and have a passion for meddling in other people's affairs.' She had put her own interpretation on that and had come to the conclusion that he was some sort of private inquiry agent, and that it was even possible that Julia had employed him to watch her husband so that she might have something besides hysterical suspicions with which to confront Alastair, and acquire thereby an additional hold over him.

But Steve did not seem to fit into that role. And he could paint: there was no doubt at all about that. The conté drawings she had seen on the previous morning had betrayed a considerable talent, but the rough sketch in oils of the Abbey of Bellapais was in an entirely different category and Amanda began to wonder if her imagination had not run away with her.

Had Steve Howard after all come to Fayid and to Cyprus by chance, and with the sole object of painting, and had his subsequent proceedings stemmed, as he himself had suggested, from an amused and analytical interest in the behaviour of his fellow men?

Then there was Persis: Persis and Alastair Blaine, who had apparently met and had a brief affair in London during two short weeks the previous summer, when Alastair had been flown to London on the General's staff to attend some conference. Amanda remembered having heard Julia refer to it once. The conference had been delayed and instead of staying in London for a few days, Alastair had stayed two weeks and—probably as a result of some foolish letter from Julia—reached at last that breaking point to which he had referred. And Persis had fallen in love with him.

Amanda was conscious of a sudden intense pang of pity for Persis Halliday, who had proved to be so vulnerable under that surface shell of glittering, cynical sophistication. It was followed by a surge of admiration. If Persis had indeed received a shattering blow to her heart and her hopes and her pride, there was nothing in her manner to indicate it.

What did she see in Alastair Blaine? wondered Amanda. What had Julia seen? He was tall, blond, sun-tanned and blue-eyed, but not particularly good looking. It was an unremarkable, pleasant and entirely Anglo-Saxon face, and he was in fact, as he himself had said, a 'perfectly ordinary dull sort of chap without an ounce of sex appeal'. Women liked Alastair Blaine, but in much the same way as they liked their brothers. They made use of him and discussed their problems with him in a way that they would never have done had their emotions been involved. It was only Julia's jealousy, Amanda realized, that had built up a picture of Alastair as an irresistible charmer.

Julia was probably the only woman who had ever fallen deeply in love with Alastair Blaine—Julia and Persis. What *did* Persis see in him?

It's because she's an American and she writes, thought Amanda with a sudden flash of understanding.

Persis did not see Alastair as other people saw him. He had looked like her idea of a strong, silent Englishman, and his very indifference to women, as women, had probably lent colour to that view. She had fitted him with a ready-made character and attributes of her own devising, and fallen in love with the result. In love with something that was no more the real Alastair Blaine than a tailor's dummy is flesh and blood.

I wonder what he is really like? thought Amanda. But then what was the real Persis like?—or the real Toby?—or jovial, stupid, easygoing, devoted George Norman? Or, for that matter, Steve Howard?

Amanda frowned unseeingly at the olive groves and the sea; puzzled and disturbed for the first time in her twenty-one years by the realization that despite the dictates of John Donne, each man and woman is, in some way, 'an island unto themselves'.

11

Amanda delivered Euridice's message to Miss Moon, and Miss Moon tut-tutted absently and said: 'I only trust that she will return early enough to cook us some breakfast. At what time are you leaving for this picnic, my dear?'

'Half past two,' said Amanda. 'I'm being collected.'

'I,' said Miss Moon with a regretful sigh, 'shall be leaving a quarter of an hour later. Such a pity that I cannot come with you. St Hilarion always gives me such a feeling of spiritual refreshment and affinity with Time. So much more soothing than Lady Cooper-Foot's bridge afternoons. I shall not enjoy myself at all I fear, and I have a headache coming on—I only trust it does not develop into migraine. But one must not neglect one's duties towards society.'

Amanda said: 'How do I get in if I get back before you, now that Euridice isn't in?'

'Oh, I never lock the house, dear. I have always maintained that any dishonest person who wishes to enter a house will do so despite all the locks and bolts in the world. Locks only serve to incommode the innocent and innocuous. You will find the house open.'

Toby Gates arrived with commendable punctuality on the tick of two-thirty, and Amanda fetched a wide-brimmed hat and a pair of sunglasses and called good-bye to Miss Moon. She received no answer and thought it probable that Miss Moon had already left.

'How are we going, Toby?'

'I've hired a car for the afternoon. Not a bad little bus. The Normans offered to give us both a lift, but as they're already taking Alastair Blaine and all the tea things, I thought it sounded a bit of a squash.'

He ushered her into the front seat of a small grey saloon car and Amanda said: 'What about Persis?'

'Howard is taking her.'

The car drew away from the kerb and gathered speed on the long rising road that leads up from Kyrenia to the pass in the hills, from where it drops again to Nicosia and the plain.

'I can't think why I'm doing this,' said Toby. 'If I were in my right mind I should not be on speaking terms with you.'

Amanda turned to look at him in frank surprise. 'Why, Toby? What have I done now?'

'I like that!' said Toby forcefully. 'Do you realize, you long-haired hussy, that entirely owing to you I am down a matter of fifty quid and in possession of two of the most god-awful eyesores that ever defaced a wall?'

'Oh Toby!' Amanda was suddenly stricken with guilt. 'I'd quite forgotten. You *didn't* buy a genuine Potter?'

'My dear girl, I couldn't possibly avoid it! I sent along a note as per order, and then I quite forgot about the chap and went for a stroll in the town. It was meeting Howard that reminded me of him. And when I got back, there he was, planted in the lounge with a portfolio the size of Cyprus, still waiting. So of course after that I had to do something about it. He stayed for hours! Fortunately it didn't seem to matter if I said anything or not. I let him do the talking, and he thinks I am a connoisseur of the Arts. Well I'm sending you those pictures as a small present, and you can jolly well hang them on your walls. And what is more, you can dine with me tonight. You owe me that at least.'

'Toby darling, I *am* sorry. Yes of course I will. The staff is out for the day, so Miss Moon will probably be only too pleased to have one less to cook supper for.'

'Good show. How did your party with the erring wife go? Did she give you the inside low-down on the whole affair?'

'No,' said Amanda repressively. 'We—just talked. Are you sure you know the way, Toby?'

'No,' said Toby. 'But the chap who hired me the car said we can't miss it.'

The road wound up and up through olive groves, firs, cypress, carob, and sunbaked grassy slopes, and just short of the pass Toby turned the car right-handed into a side road signposted to Hilarion. As they turned, a car coming from the direction of Nicosia passed them on its way down to Kyrenia. It was a small green two-seater with a sports hood, driven by a woman, and Amanda thought that she recognized Glenn Barton's secretary, Monica Ford.

Their road skirted the mountain side and presently ran between an outcrop of the hills and past a wide saucer-like depression that Toby said had been a tilting ground—adding that his informant was Persis Halliday, who had been reading up on the subject of Hilarion and had evidently held forth during luncheon.

Rising sheer above it on a pinnacle of rock, over two thousand feet above the sea and silhouetted against the cloudless blue of the sky, stood the ruins of the Crusader castle of St Hilarion—the castle to which, legend says, Richard of the Lion Heart brought his newly-wed bride, Berengaria of Navarre. From this castle he went forth to the Crusades. And from its arched windows Berengaria the Queen must often have looked out on to that same sea to watch for the sails of his ships.

There was another car parked in the shade of some trees below the slope that led up the outer walls of the castle. But it did not belong either to the Normans or to Steven Howard.

'Tourists,' said Toby with contempt.

'Tourist yourself!' retorted Amanda, scrambling out of the car. 'Don't let's wait for the others. Let's go and explore.'

They climbed the stony slope in the hot sunlight and passed into the cool shadow of the Keep. A long flight of worn stone steps led upward to the main bulk of the story-book castle that soared above them, clinging to the naked rock whose sheer sides formed many of its walls. At the foot and to one side of the stairway a man in a vividly patterned sports shirt was seated on a small canvas stool before a large easel. It was Lumley Potter. He turned his head as they approached and his scowl turned to a delighted smile:

'Hullo Gates. Just the man I wanted to see. How does this strike you? Early stages yet, of course, but I feel I have captured something of the tempo and perhaps a *hint* of the aura. At the moment the inner essence eludes me—yes, frankly it eludes me—but I feel that I shall ultimately grasp it.'

'Er—yes—I'm sure you will,' said Toby, staring in horrified disbelief at what appeared to be the portrait of a suet pudding in the making, into which someone had inadvertently stirred a generous dollop of schoolroom ink.

'Well?' said Mr Potter.

'Oh—er—terrific!' said Toby Gates hurriedly. 'I don't think you've met Miss Derington. Amanda, this is Mr Potter.'

Mr Potter expressed himself as pleased to meet Miss Derington and plunged into a discussion of his work that was only terminated by the arrival of the Normans, Major Blaine, Mrs Halliday and Steve Howard.

They left Claire and Major Blaine talking to Lumley—Claire it seemed was entirely familiar with the tempo and aura of art—and continued their exploration of the castle, Persis instructing their ignorance with the aid of a guide book.

Some minutes later, turning a corner, they came unexpectedly upon Anita Barton.

Mrs Barton had spread a travelling rug in a shady corner and lain down at full length with a book and a box of chocolates. The pages of the book were fluttering in a light breeze and a colony of ants were investigating the chocolates. Mrs Barton was asleep. She was wearing an exceedingly becoming dress of corn-coloured linen decorated at the hem and the deep neckline with innumerable small flat flowers cut from white linen and loosely attached by their centres. The effect was charming, but conveyed the impression that Mrs Barton must be exceedingly expensive to dress.

Amanda, gazing down at her, thought that she looked much younger than she had seemed last night—younger, and somehow defenceless—and remembered that Glenn Barton had spoken of his wife as being 'such a child'. Amanda could see now what he had meant. Despite the blue-tinted eyelids, the lavish use of mascara and lipstick and the scarlet lacquer on fingers and toes, there was something oddly childlike about the slumbering figure in the absurd and charming frock.

They turned away noiselessly and left her sleeping.

'This,' said Persis when they were out of earshot, 'is quite a situation. Do we warn her husband that his erring wife is among those present? The guy is due at any moment now. It's almost four. Or do we just ignore the whole thing and let him fall over her and the hell with it?'

'The latter,' advised Mr Howard lazily.

Amanda said anxiously: 'I'd forgotten that Glenn was coming. What time did he say he'd be here?'

'Four, if he could make it.'

Amanda peered over the battlements but could see no car on the white ribbon of road far below. Which was not surprising, for Mr Barton had been delayed . . .

Glenn had intended to drive directly from Nicosia to Hilarion, but had found it necessary to go into Kyrenia to deliver some documents to a client who was staying at the Dome. He had been additionally delayed by a puncture just short of the town, and had left his car at a garage on the road and walked down to the hotel, discharged his errand and returned.

He was on his way back to collect his car when he saw Monica Ford's small, shabby two-seater cross an intersection ahead of him and turn down the side road that led past the Villa Oleander.

He was conscious of a slight feeling of surprise. What could Monica be doing in Kyrenia? He had seen her briefly in the Nicosia office that morning, but his work had taken him out to the vineyards and he had not been back to the office. Monica had made no mention of driving over to Kyrenia, and he had never before known her to leave the office unattended in his absence. Had something cropped up that required his immediate attention and had Monica come over in search of him?

Glenn glanced at his watch and saw that it was already a quarter to four. He hesitated on the pavement, puzzled and undecided, and then crossed the road and turned down to the Villa Oleander.

Monica's car was not outside the house, but he caught a glimpse of green paint and realized that she had parked it at the mouth of a narrow lane shadowed by mulberry trees on the opposite side of the road. Monica herself had just crossed the road and he saw her push open the gate of the Villa Oleander and disappear from view.

Perhaps there had been some message from Oswin Derington for his niece? But Amanda would be at Hilarion and Miss Moon at Lady Cooper-Foot's, while Euridice and Andreas were attending a fête at Aiyos Epiktitos. Monica would find the house empty.

Glenn turned in at the gate which Miss Ford had neglected to close behind her, and walked up the short flagged path. The front door swung open on oiled hinges and he was in the welcome coolness of the high, dim hall. He heard a movement from the direction of the drawing-room and walked across the hall and through the open doorway.

Monica Ford was standing near the french window and he checked abruptly at the sight of her face.

'Monica! My dear—what's the matter?'

Miss Ford did not answer him. Her face was ashy white and blotched with weeping; so drawn and haggard and aged with grief and emotion that it was almost unrecognizable.

'Monica!'

He went quickly towards her, but she shrank back and he stopped. He saw her lick her dry, trembling lips and she said in a

541

harsh, high whisper: 'What are you doing here? I—I thought you were in Limassol.'

'Monica, what is it? Has anything happened?'

She stared at him for a long moment, her red-rimmed eyes wide and fixed, then turning away she walked stumblingly to the sofa and sank down upon it with her back to him and her head in her hands, and burst into tears.

Oh God! thought Glenn despairingly. Another emotional woman! Anita—and now Monica. For Monica had begun to talk; a flood of hysterical words that fought with her sobs; jumbled, desperate, incoherent, from which a few words stood out, constantly repeated. Her dead brother's name; Anita's; his own—Glenn—Glenn —Glenn.

'. . . I didn't realize . . . I—I loved you, Glenn, I loved you . . .'

Glenn shut his eyes and tried to shut out the sound of her gasping voice; aware of a feeling of sick disgust and cold anger. But Monica's voice went on and on. Thick, ugly, choked with tears: '. . . I didn't realize it until today. I didn't know . . . I wouldn't face it. I've always felt that there was something—something I shouldn't . . . But I wouldn't admit it. And today you were away and Pavlos came to the office about a damaged case. He said you had gone to Hilarion with—with Claire Norman . . . and—and then—then I knew. I loved you . . .'

Glenn opened his eyes and looked at the huddled jerking shoulders with rage and despair. A faint scent of jasmine drifted in through the open windows and mingled with the cheap violet scent that Miss Ford affected, borne on a little breeze that billowed the curtains and fluttered the ends of a vivid green *crêpe de Chine* scarf that Miss Moon had left hanging over the back of the sofa. 'Thursday' thought Glenn automatically, noting the colour.

He tried to speak, but could find no words. There was nothing he could say. Nothing that could do any good now. He ought to have sent her away. He ought to have made her go. The ragged, sobbing voice went on and on and he winced at the sound of his wife's name.

'Anita . . . Anita must have known. That's why she left you. I should have known too. But I wouldn't let myself know! I wouldn't face it. It's all my fault . . . I pretended that everything was all right. But Anita must have known——'

Anita, thought Glenn with a sudden twinge of almost physical pain. Was it true? Had she known? He had always suspected that she did not really believe the things she had said about himself and Monica Ford—that there was something else behind her sudden defection, and that Monica Ford had been only an excuse. Now Monica herself said that she must have known. And so she had run away. Anita——

The gasping, weeping voice filled the quiet room with ugly sound: 'I don't know what to do! If only it hadn't been for Bobby I could have borne it. But I had to talk to someone—I had to! Glenn! . . . Glenn . . .'

Monica Ford's voice choked and stopped at long last, like a gramophone record that has run down, and silence flowed back into the dusty, gracious room.

The sun had moved down the sky and now it shone in through the french windows and lay in a bright square of gold on the faded carpet, illuminating Monica Ford's ungainly body and filling the room with a mellow glowing warmth.

Glenn looked down at the slumped, twitching figure with sick distaste. And presently, realizing that there was nothing else he could do, he turned abruptly away from her and walked quickly out of the room.

A clock struck the quarter hour as he crossed the hall, and his hand was on the latch of the front door when he thought he heard a soft sound from somewhere on the bedroom floor.

He turned quickly and looked up. But there was no one on the stairs and nothing moved on the shadowed landing above. Miss Moon was out, and so were Andreas and Euridice, and the upstairs rooms should have been empty. There could be no one there. Perhaps the sound he had heard had been caused by a pigeon or Euridice's grey cat. He hesitated, frowning and uncertain, his nerves on edge and a cold tremor running down his spine. But there was no repetition of the sound and he did not wish to remain any longer under the same roof as Monica Ford. He turned away and left the house, shutting the door quietly behind him. And it was almost a quarter to five by the time he reached Hilarion . . .

He found the picnic party seated about the remains of tea on a grassy space by a ruined buttress, and because he was disturbed and preoccupied he did not notice—or at least did not recognize—Lumley Potter's ramshackle car among the cars parked beside the road.

'So you finally made it,' remarked Persis, making room for him beside her. 'We'd given you up.'

Glenn subsided wearily on to the grass and accepted a lukewarm cup of tea which he drank thirstily.

'I'm sorry I'm late,' he apologized. 'I had to go into Kyrenia first, and I had a puncture just short of the town. And then I met Monica, and that held me up a bit.'

He frowned at the recollection of that interview, and for a moment his mouth twisted in a wry grimace of distaste.

Claire said: 'Monica? What was she doing in Kyrenia?'

'Nothing much. She thought she'd pay a call on Miss Derington, but of course there was no one in the house.'

'On me?' said Amanda, surprised. 'I hope you explained that I was out on a picnic and that the house would be empty until after seven, what with Miss Moon and the servants both out. She won't even get any tea! You ought to have brought her along with you.'

The frown in Glenn Barton's eyes deepened. He said uncomfortably: 'She wasn't really in a picnicking mood. She's feeling pretty upset, what with her brother's death and——' He broke off and after a short pause said heavily: 'You'll probably be seeing her later anyway. She may wait if she's nothing else to do,' and changed the subject.

They cleared away the tea things and repacked the picnic baskets, and Amanda seized the opportunity of drawing Mr Barton apart and telling him something of her abortive mission on the previous night.

'I'm sorry it was so useless, Glenn,' she finished, 'but I'll try and see her again when—when she's feeling a bit better. At least you know that you were right and that she's not a bit in love with Lumley Potter.'

'Yes,' said Glenn slowly. 'I suppose that's something; though I was always sure she couldn't be. She's too—too fastidious for such an untidy, messy sloppy sort of chap as Potter.' He smiled at Amanda and added a little awkwardly: 'Anyway it was more than kind of you to go, and I'm very grateful. I am really.'

He took her hand and held it for a brief moment in a hard grip, and Amanda's fingers returned the pressure sympathetically. She smiled warmly at him, and in the next instant became suddenly aware that Steve Howard was watching them with an odd look in his eyes. A hard, bright, speculative look that held more than a hint of anger, and that for no reason at all caused Amanda's heart to give a queer little lurch and brought the bright colour up into her cheeks.

Claire called out: 'Glenn, come and give a hand with these

baskets and things,' and Mr Barton dropped Amanda's hand and turned away. Presently he and George Norman carried the baskets and rugs down to the cars, Persis accompanying them.

The sun was low in the sky and the ruined walls threw long purple shadows on the grass and the wild thyme and the sheer rock faces that fell away almost vertically to the olive groves and the quiet blue sea far below.

The sea was as smooth and unwrinkled as polished steel, but high above it the breeze had strengthened with the approach of sundown and blew strongly about the castle, whistling shrilly through the stone arches and along the deserted battlements.

Claire and Toby had walked away together deep in conversation, and Amanda, leaning against a parapet of stone and looking downwards, saw Alastair Blaine standing in an embrasure of the battlements below, talking to Anita Barton. She wondered idly if Alastair too would shortly be the possessor of another Potter masterpiece in Prussian blue, and hoped that Glenn would not meet his wife on his return from the cars. He had looked tired and ill and quite incapable of coping with a situation that involved being faced with a runaway wife and her lover.

Amanda turned her attention to the tilting ground that lay far below, and tried to imagine what it must have looked like when banners and pennants had flown there, and knights in armour had jousted before Richard of England and Queen Berengaria on their wedding day in Cyprus almost eight hundred years ago . . .

'What are you thinking of, Amarantha?' inquired Steve Howard coming to lean against the wall beside her. She had not heard him approach because of the croon of the wind, and she turned quickly, considerably startled.

'Penny for them,' offered Steve. 'Or are they worth more?'

'If you really want to know, I was thinking that you and Toby and Glenn and the rest of them ought to be in armour, and Persis and Claire and I should be wearing wimples and "camises of fine white linen" and—and ermine lined pelicons—or do I mean surcotes?'

'Anyone mad enough to wear armour in this climate would be toasted to a crisp inside ten minutes,' observed Mr Howard prosaically. 'And you are wrong about the wimple. You should by rights be leaning out of the nearest window letting your hair down—like Rapunzel. How long have you known this man Barton?'

The question took Amanda by surprise. 'Glenn? I met him at Limassol. You know all about that. Why do you ask?'

' "*Glenn*",' murmured Steve, and went on to observe with some asperity that considering the shortness of their acquaintance they appeared to be on remarkably intimate terms with each other.

'Hardly that,' said Amanda sweetly, 'though he, like me, is probably worth anyone's while for half an hour in the moonlight.' She saw with satisfaction that she had made him angry, and added with deliberate provocation: 'I must find out.'

'Try it!' said Steve, smiling unpleasantly.

Something clattered on the stone behind them and a mangled tube of Hooker's Green fell at Amanda's feet. Lumley Potter had joined them.

'Damn!' said Mr Potter fretfully.

He deposited a folding easel and a virgin canvas on the ground and stooped to retrieve half a dozen tubes of paint that had fallen from an insecurely fastened box under his arm.

'Thought I'd make a quick study from here,' said Mr Potter. 'Hullo, Howard; you working on anything here?'

Amanda turned to look at Steve in some surprise. She had not realized that he had made Lumley Potter's acquaintance.

'No, alas. I find that it has nothing to say to me,' said Steve with perfect gravity. 'To the eye perhaps; but spiritually, no.'

'Now that's very interesting,' said Mr Potter earnestly. 'I, on the other hand——'

He plunged with enthusiasm into a pond of theory, and Amanda, who considered that Steve had asked for it, wandered away and left them to it.

She had already been up to the topmost part of the castle, but she thought that she would go again, and alone, to sit by the Queen's window where Berengaria must so often have sat, and watch the sun go down. She climbed a long flight of ruined stone steps with a high curtain wall above her and a steep grassy slope falling away below, and passed under an arch of lichened stone and through small, walled enclosures, partially roofless, that had once been guardrooms, granaries, galleries and *garderobes*.

The Queen's chamber was open to the wind and the evening sky, and a large part of the outer walls had fallen away, so that from the edge of the stone-paved floor one looked down on to tree tops and a yawning gulf where the rocky peak on which the castle of St Hilarion was built fell sheer away in a drop of well over two thousand feet.

Only one portion of the outer walls still remained, and from this the Queen's window, a graceful double arch in stone, looked out across the dreamlike landscape spread far below.

The sky and the sea had lost the deep, intense blue of the earlier afternoon and were pale in the evening light, and along the far horizon lay a faint lilac shadow that was the mountains of Turkey.

Amanda turned from the window and wandered away to where the weather-worn stone gave on to nothingness.

The evening wind whistled shrilly past her, whipping back her thin frock and tugging at her hair so that the heavy coils were loosened and fell upon her shoulders, tumbling down her back. Amanda put up a hand to arrest them, and yet another hairpin slid out, bounced upon the stone and fell into the void.

The song of the wind drowned the sound of footsteps behind her. A hand thrust hard against her and she fell forward and plunged downward into that horrible gulf, her scream of terror whipped away on the wind.

◇   ◇   ◇

It was her hair that saved Amanda. Those long, thick, golden-brown tresses. Her hair and an aged and twisted fir tree that grew outwards from a fissure in the rock-face below the castle wall.

The branches whipped her face and broke under her, but they caught her hair; tangled it and wrenched at it, but held it as Absalom's had once been held. It checked her fall and gave her just time to clutch at a stronger bough.

Amanda hung there, blind and breathless with terror, her hands clinging frantically to the creaking bough, her long hair dragged taut above her and her feet swinging over emptiness.

She heard a shout above her, but she could not turn her head and she dared not move. The muscles in her arms hurt agonizingly, her clutching fingers were numb from her weight, and the wind sang through the pine needles and drowned out all other sounds.

She heard the bough crack, but it did not break, and she knew that she should move her hold and try to swing herself backwards on to the tree trunk; but she could not do so. If she attempted to relax her hold, she would fall.

The tree shuddered as though something heavy had struck it and a voice that she did not recognize shouted to her to hold on. It seemed to come from somewhere close behind her. But no one could climb down that rock-face below the wall—it would be suicide.

547

Someone else was shouting now and a woman was screaming. Amanda felt the tree shake again and the bough to which she clung cracked ominously. And then hard fingers closed about one wrist and a voice said breathlessly:

'Try and get your foot on to the branch behind you. Your left foot. Swing it straight back.'

She obeyed automatically, and could not afterwards remember how she had got from the tree trunk to a narrow ledge of rock that had been concealed from above. Once there, with an arm steadying her, it had not been too difficult to reach the level of the ruined battlements.

Someone above her leaned down and caught her hands, and a moment later her feet were on level ground and she had fainted for the first time in her life.

12

Amanda swam slowly up out of blackness into the warm golden glow of the evening sunlight.

Someone was pouring an unpleasant and fiery liquid down her throat and she choked and coughed; swallowed a considerable quantity of the stuff in the process, and choked again.

Steve Howard, very white about the mouth, was looking down at her with a grim anger that startled her. Amanda stared up at him, puzzled and shaken, and momentarily at a loss to know where she was or what she was doing, and why Steve should be in a rage.

She shut her eyes for a brief moment and opened them again. They were all still there, staring at her with pale excited faces. Claire and George Norman, Persis, Toby, Alastair and Glenn.

'What happened?' asked Amanda. 'Did I——'

And then suddenly she remembered, and stopped on a harsh gasp.

'You fell,' said Steve grimly. 'And I'd like to know what the hell you mean by wandering along parapets that a child of two would realize were unsafe! It's not your fault that you are not unpleasantly dead at this moment.'

It is possible that Mr Howard had a sound knowledge of psychology, for sympathy at this juncture would undoubtedly have reduced Amanda to tears and a return of terror. His curtly callous observation had an entirely opposite effect.

Amanda sat up, her breath coming short, and opened her mouth with the intention of informing him furiously that she had not fallen, but had been pushed.

But she did not say it.

She sat quite still, realizing, with a sudden, appalled clarity, that except for the Cypriot caretaker, Lumley Potter, Anita Barton and herself, there had been no one else at Hilarion that evening but the seven people who faced her.

Then one of nine people—seven of whom stood looking down at her, so close to her that by merely reaching out her hand she could touch any one of them—had meant to murder her. *Her*—Amanda Derington! What was it that Steve had just said? 'It's not your fault that you are not unpleasantly dead at this moment.' It was not someone else's fault either, for one of these people had meant her to be dead. Had tried to kill her——

Amanda shrank back against the sun-warmed stones of the wall, her wide, terrified eyes going from face to face in that circle.

Claire—Alastair—Toby—Glenn—Persis—George—Steve——

No. Not Steve! He was the only one she could be sure of. The only one. Her frightened eyes turned to him and she reached up and clutched at his sleeve.

Steve leant down and jerked her ungently to her feet, and Amanda said breathlessly: 'Please will you all go away. Please! I'm all right. I am really. I'm sorry I gave you all such a fright. I—I think I'd just like to sit here alone for a bit until I feel less peculiar. Please go!'

Her frantic fingers on Steve Howard's arm said *not you! not you!*

Persis said: 'Nonsense! Now see here honey——'

'Persis honey,' remarked Steve pleasantly, 'Scram! I'll see that she doesn't trip over any more walls.'

He glanced at his wrist watch and turned to Toby Gates:

'Would you mind giving Mrs Halliday a lift home, Gates? I'll drive Miss Derington back when she's feeling less scrambled.'

'Of course,' said Toby, looking uncertainly from Persis to Amanda and back again.

'Good idea,' said George Norman, his ruddy features resuming their normal hue. 'Beastly shock for her. Might have been a nasty accident. They really should rail off these dangerous spots. It's a scandal!'

They departed and Amanda was alone with the wind and Mr Howard.

She relaxed her grip on his arm, turned her back on him and said in a muffled voice: 'Would you mind going to the other side of that wall.'

'Why?' inquired Steve. 'Are you going to cry?'

'No,' said Amanda indistinctly. 'I'm going to be sick.' And was.

Mr Howard bore this unalluring spectacle with commendable

fortitude, and having provided assistance in the form of a clean handkerchief, remarked that it was a waste of a good brandy and that he hoped for the sake of subsequent visitors that it would rain during the night.

'Feeling better?' he inquired presently.

'Yes thank you. Could we go somewhere where there are four walls and no edge, do you think?'

'Nothing easier.' He drew her hand through his arm and walked her away, keeping her between him and the solid inner wall. They had gone less than half a dozen yards when he checked suddenly and bent down to pick up something that lay wedged between two slabs of stone. It was a small, twisted tube of oil paint from which the top was missing. He turned it over in his hand, looking at it thoughtfully, and then slipped it into his pocket without comment.

They walked back through the roofless rooms, and once again the steep flight of stone steps lay below them.

Amanda stopped and shut her eyes. She had never been in the least affected by heights, but now she knew that she would never be able to look down from any height again without being afraid. She knew that it was ridiculous and absurd; the ruined stairway was wide and safe and the slope that fell away along one side of it was covered with grass and shrubs, trees and fallen boulders. But the fear of falling was on her and she could not move.

Steve Howard picked her up without ceremony and carried her down the long, uneven flight to the quiet and shelter of a grass-grown level, where the solid walls of the Outer Bailey towered comfortingly above them and the last of the sun turned the dry grasses to bright gold.

'All right here?'

'Yes,' said Amanda gratefully. 'I'm sorry about that.'

'You'll get over it,' said Steve, striking a match against the stones and lighting himself a cigarette.

Amanda sank down cross-legged on the warm grass and said in a voice that she tried to keep steady: 'I haven't thanked you yet for—for saving my life. That branch wouldn't have held much longer.'

'You don't have to thank me,' said Steve shortly. 'Barton got you out of that.'

'Glenn?'

'Yes—Glenn.'

Steve's mouth twisted a little wryly on the name. 'He's the one you have to thank. He thought he heard someone scream, and ran out and saw you. I was on my way up, and he yelled out to me, and the next thing I knew he had lowered himself down over the edge and found some sort of a foothold and dropped down onto the trunk of that tree. He must have plenty of nerve. I wouldn't have cared to do it myself.'

'And I let him go without saying anything!' said Amanda, distressed. 'I thought it was you——'

'Alas, no,' said Steve satirically. 'I was merely among those present. How did you happen to do it?'

'I was pushed,' said Amanda in a whisper.

'Say that again!'

'S—someone pushed me.'

Steve stood very still, looking down at her, his mouth a tight line and his eyes blazing.

Presently he said quite softly: 'Who?'

'I—I don't know,' said Amanda, a terrified break in her voice. 'The wind was so loud—I didn't hear any other sound. And then suddenly someone pushed me hard and—and I fell . . .' Her voice died out in a whisper and she shuddered uncontrollably.

'You are quite sure it wasn't a sudden gust of wind?'

'Don't be ridiculous!' said Amanda, retreating from the verge of tears. 'It was a *hand.'*

'Man or woman?'

'I tell you I don't *know!* I didn't hear or see anyone.'

'Come on, Amanda—think! Try and remember what it felt like. Was it a small hand or a large one? Hard? Thin? Warm? That dress you're wearing is pretty flimsy, you must have some idea.'

'But I haven't! You see my hair had come down and it was all over my back.'

'Hell!' said Steve softly.

He dropped his cigarette on the grass, put his foot on it and sat down beside her with his hands clasped about his knees, and stared fixedly ahead of him at the massive walls of the Outer Bailey. Amanda, watching him, saw that there were harsh lines on his forehead and about his mouth that she did not remember having noticed before, and that his eyes were blank and unseeing.

After a time he said curtly and without turning his head: 'What made you keep quiet up there?—about being pushed?'

'I was just going to say it, and then——' Amanda's voice seemed to dry in her throat and she swallowed convulsively.

'And then——?' prompted Steve.

'Then I suddenly realized that it might have been one of them. People I know——' Amanda's voice wavered and she said desperately: 'Why? I haven't said anything to anyone. Why should someone want to kill me now that it's all over?'

'It isn't all over,' said Steve curtly. 'Not by a long chalk.'

He dropped his chin on his knees and relapsed into silence, brooding with the concentration of a Buddhist considering infinity.

The shadows lengthened and soon the ruined walls of Hilarion would no longer be warmly gold but a cold forbidding grey. The sky above the battlements had already turned to a pale clear green, and the level floor of the tilting ground below the castle began to fill with soft purple shadow.

Steve sighed and moved at last. He stood up, stretching himself, and leaned down to pull Amanda to her feet:

'Come on; it's time we got going. If we don't watch it we shall find ourselves being locked in for the night.'

He put out a hand and lifted a long shining strand of the hair that tumbled in tangled disorder to well below Amanda's waist.

'Beautiful stuff,' observed Steve reflectively. 'I wonder why women will cut it off? Well you can thank your lucky stars you didn't. A crew-cut wouldn't have saved you today, Amarantha. Go on— plait it up or get it out of the way. It gives me ideas—and this is no time for ideas; at least not of that category.'

Amanda's white face flushed with colour and she jerked her head away and plaited her dishevelled hair with quick, unsteady fingers into two heavy schoolgirl plaits.

'You look about six,' commented Steve. 'Can you manage the rest of the way on your own feet?'

'Of course I can,' said Amanda with dignity. 'It was only those stairs.'

He turned on his heel without further comment and walked down ahead of her, whistling abstractedly, his hands deep in his pockets.

There was only one car left beside the roadside at the foot of the slope below Hilarion. The others must have left at least half an hour before.

'Twenty past six,' observed Steve, releasing the clutch and glancing at the dashboard clock. 'You'll just make it.'

'Make what?'

'I gather that you are dining out with young Gates; drinks at seven. He mentioned it during tea.'

'Oh!' said Amanda blankly. 'I'd forgotten. Perhaps he could dine with Persis instead.'

'Going to cut your date?'

'Yes. I—I don't think I feel like facing any of them just now. I feel like getting back to my bedroom and looking under the bed and inside and behind all the furniture, and locking every door and window and then getting into bed and pulling all the bedclothes over my head. And that's just what I'm going to do!'

'A very sound programme,' approved Steve. 'You'll feel braver in the morning. Want me to make your excuses to Toby Gates?'

'Would you? Tell him that I—No; don't tell him anything. I'll write a note if you don't mind waiting while I write it. Then you could give it to him. Would you do that?'

'A pleasure, Amarantha.'

Kyrenia and the coast were still bathed in the last warm glow of the sunset when they turned into the quiet side road and stopped before the Villa Oleander. But the shadows were moving swiftly across the garden and up the face of the house, and only the tops of the tallest cypress trees were still touched with gold.

The water trickling from the mouth of the bronze dolphin made a cool, pleasant sound in the silence, and now that the sun had left the garden the scent of roses and jasmine and dust filled the windless air with fragrance. In the embrasures of the old wall behind the house the pigeons cooed and fluttered as they settled down for the night, and the drowsy hum of the town rose murmurously from beyond the trees and the garden wall. But the house itself seemed strangely silent.

Amanda pushed open the heavy front door and stood in the cool, shadowed hall, listening to that silence.

Miss Moon could not be back yet. She was not given to silence except when resting, and the sound of her voice and her jingling jewellery was almost an integral part of the Villa Oleander.

'What is it Amanda?' inquired Steve Howard, watching her face.

'Nothing. It—it's very quiet. I thought perhaps that Miss Moon would be back.'

'Scared?'

'Yes!' said Amanda with a shiver. 'Steve——' she turned to him quickly, unaware that she had for the first time used that familiar abbreviation of his name that Persis and Claire used so lightly—'would you—would you stay until she comes back? I know it's ridiculous of me, but the house feels so empty.'

'Yes of course,' said Steve, in the manner of one who has been asked to pass the salt. His tone was entirely matter-of-fact and oddly steadying. 'Like me to go upstairs and look under the bed for you?' he suggested with a satirical gleam in his eye.

'Do you think I'm being very silly?' demanded Amanda abruptly.

Steve smiled at her. 'No dear. In fact for a girl who has just escaped a particularly messy end by inches, you are behaving like the entire George Cross Island rolled into one, and I'm proud of you, Amarantha. Do you realize that nine hundred and ninety-nine women out of a thousand would have had shrieking hysterics, burst into tears, died of heart-failure and then rushed screaming to the telephone to book an immediate passage to Baffin Bay or North Borneo?'

Amanda laughed a little shakily. 'I've wanted desperately to do all those things,' she confessed. 'In fact with any encouragement at all, I'd have done them!'

'I know,' said Steve with a grin. 'That's why you didn't get any!'

'You've been quite beastly!' said Amanda accusingly.

'The situation,' observed Steve caustically, 'is sufficiently unpleasant as it is, without being further gummed up with tears and hysteria. Is there by any chance a lavatory in this building?'

'Yes of course. Down that passage and first door on your left.'

'Thanks.'

He departed and Amanda, remembering her decision to write a note to Toby Gates, crossed the hall and went into the drawing-room.

The last of the sunlight had only recently faded from the room, but except before the french windows that gave on to the verandah the green wooden shutters were still closed, and the room was hot and airless and very dark. Amanda threw open the shutters to let in the fast vanishing daylight, and sitting down at Miss Moon's cluttered ormolu desk, reached for writing paper and a pen.

She began to write, aware as she did so that the scratching of the pen sounded astonishingly loud in the quiet room. But after completing no more than two lines she paused: listening, as she had listened in the hall, to the silence.

The windless evening was quiet and very still, and there was no sound in the darkening house. But she was not alone in the room. It was not a suspicion but a certainty. There was someone else in the room besides herself. Someone was hidden there . . .

Amanda sat rigid while her blood seemed to turn cold and run slowly. She dared not move, and it seemed that she had lost the power to breathe. She knew that she should turn—she would be safer, surely, with her back to the wall? But she could not move. She must call out; scream for Steve Howard——

Steve! Why of course! it was Steve who had returned across the hall without her hearing him.

She whirled round on a gasp of relief. But there was no one there. The dusty beautiful furniture looked back at her, composed and calm and watchful with that curious sense of watchfulness that many old and inanimate objects possess. The open doorway gaped emptily on the dark and silent hall, and there was no sign of Steven Howard.

It was imagination, Amanda told herself—imagination and the silence of an empty house. There was no third person in the Villa Oleander; no one in the room but herself. She forced herself to turn and face the desk; to pick up the pen. But she could not force her hand to write. She could only sit still; and listen——

The scent of roses and jasmine and violets filled the airless room with a cloying sweetness: odd that she should not have noticed that there were violets growing in the garden. Amanda laid down her pen very carefully. She seemed to be under some curious compulsion not to make any sound that might break that alert and listening silence. There was—someone else in the room—there was.

She stood up quickly and turned, gripping the carved chairback with cold hands and fighting to control a rising panic. Her wide, frightened eyes searched the darkening room, but except for the solid back of the sofa that stood between her and the french windows the furniture was either too frail or so placed as to afford no opportunities for concealment. The glass-fronted cabinets of buhl and marqueterie stood backed against the corners of the room, their cluttered contents making splashes of pure, gleaming colour in the shadowy room. The fading light glinted on carved jade and ivory, enamelled snuff boxes, bottles cut from rose quartz, chrysoprase and lapis lazuli, and on the tiny, twinkling diamonds that formed the cypher of a murdered Empress on a fabulous Fabergé egg of crystal.

The faded brocade curtains hung straight and motionless and it was not possible that anyone could be standing concealed behind them. An ornately framed looking-glass that hung above the writing table reflected another and similar mirror on the opposite wall, and Amanda could see herself in it; endlessly repeated. A long line of slender, frightened girls standing in a dim, silvery corridor in the disk.

But it reflected something else as well. Something that lay beyond the range of her vision, though not beyond the compass of that glimmering oval. A hand——

There was someone crouching on the floor in front of the french windows, concealed by the sofa.

Amanda froze into stillness; her wide eyes fixed upon the reflection of that hand whose fingers were crooked, claw-like, on the faded carpet; waiting for it to be withdrawn—to slide quietly back into hiding. But it did not move.

A sudden stabbing thought broke the web of terror that held her. It's Miss Moon! She turned and leapt across the narrow space that lay between the writing table and the sofa, reached it and was round it.

But it was not Miss Moon. It was someone who lay sprawled face downwards on the floor. A woman in a tight blue cotton frock patterned with rosebuds, who wore a vivid scarf of emerald green *crêpe de Chine* tied about her neck.

Amanda dropped on her knees and touched that outstretched hand. It was slack and warm, and a wave of incredible relief engulfed her. What a fool she was! This must be some visitor who had waited for Miss Moon, and had fainted. She tugged at the limp, warm bulk and turned it over . . .

There was nothing she could recognize in that swollen, horribly discoloured face with its glazed, protruding eyes and lolling tongue. Nothing except a necklace and ear-rings of garish plastic flowers and the odour of a cheap violet scent that suggested hair oil.

Amanda let the heavy, lifeless body drop back on to the floor and sprang to her feet, backing away from it, her hands at her throat.

There was a sound of leisurely footsteps crossing the hall and then Steve was standing in the doorway——

The next second he had crossed the floor in three strides and his hands were gripping her shoulders so tightly that they hurt.

'What is it!'

Amanda did not speak but her head turned and Steve's eyes followed the direction of her frozen gaze.

His fingers tightened convulsively on her shoulders so that she winced with pain, and then he had thrust her roughly to one side and was on his knees beside that appalling figure.

He touched it once only, noting, as Amanda had done, the warm slackness of that outstretched hand, and after that only his eyes moved, quickly and intently.

He looked up at Amanda and said harshly: 'Did you touch her?'

Amanda wet her dry lips with her tongue. 'I—I turned her over. I thought she had fainted.'

'You know her?' It was less a query than a statement of fact.

'Yes. It's—she's Glenn Barton's secretary. Monica Ford. He—he said that she had called to see me.'

'I remember. That must have been somewhere between four and half-past. Three hours ago,' said Steve thoughtfully.

Amanda said shuddering: 'Then—then she did wait for me. She's warm. She can't have been dead for three hours!'

'Probably less than half an hour, at a guess.' He looked down at the distorted face and said slowly: 'Both you and Barton mentioned at the picnic that this house would be empty. Someone who did not really believe that Miss Ford would wait for you may have seized the opportunity to slip in here and look for something—perhaps that bottle, or the glass—and been surprised by her on their way out.'

Amanda said in a high, breaking voice: 'But I haven't got them! I haven't got them!—I——'

Steve stood up swiftly and caught her clutching hands in a hard and exceedingly painful grasp.

'Stop that, Amanda. I'm not standing any nonsense from you! Come on, George Cross Island—pull yourself together!'

Amanda gasped, gulped, and clenched her teeth on her trembling lip, and her breathing steadied.

'That's better,' approved Steve. 'Is there a telephone here?'

'Y—yes. At the end of the passage off the hall.'

'Afraid to go there by yourself?'

'No!' Amanda wrenched her hands from his hold and her chin came up with a jerk.

'That's the girl. All right; go and ring a number for me——' He gave her a number and made her repeat it. 'Tell whoever answers it that Steven Howard would like to see Mr Jurgan Calder at the Villa Oleander in Kyrenia and that it will be a late party. Got that?'

'Yes.'

'Repeat it . . . That's right. Don't say anything else. Only that, and ring off. And when you've done that you'd better get through to the Dome and leave a message for Toby Gates to say that you will not be able to dine with him tonight. Otherwise we shall have him turning up here to fetch you before we know where we are. Cut along.'

He did not watch Amanda go, but turned back immediately to the huddled, hideous figure on the floor. He was on his knees beside it when she returned, but he had switched on two of the lights, and he did not look up or trouble to inquire if she had done as he asked. It was after seven, but Miss Moon had still not returned. They had been back for just over twenty minutes, thought Amanda numbly—how was it possible to live through so much in so short a space of time?

The sun had set and the sky was green with gathering dusk and pricked with the first stars. The house was very still again. And in that stillness Amanda heard the soft, unmistakable pad of shoeless feet in the room above them.

Steve had heard it too, for his head came up with a jerk and his eyes were wide and bright and intensely alert. Presently the sound was repeated and all at once he was on his feet and at the door. He seemed to move with a swiftness and lack of noise that was, in its way, remarkable.

He swung round suddenly and looked at Amanda. His eyes went from her to the open windows and the garden beyond the verandah, and she saw that he was holding something in his left hand. That same small gun that she had seen once before in the cabin of the *Orantares*.

He said curtly: 'You'd better come with me,' and turned away again without looking to see if she followed him or not.

They went up the stairs swiftly and—on Steve's part—silently. But Amanda's white, flat-heeled sandals clicked on the polished treads and she stumbled and clung to the stair-rail.

It was Miss Moon's bedroom that lay directly above the drawing-room, and Steve glanced over his shoulder at Amanda, and pushing her back against the landing wall with one hand, turned the handle and kicked the door open with his foot.

There was a shrill, feminine shriek and a familiar clash of silver filigree bracelets, and Amanda said on a sob: 'It's Miss Moon!' and brushing past him she ran into the room.

Miss Moon was standing at the foot of her tumbled bed, wrapped in an elderly cotton kimono patterned with a design of storks and chrysanthemums that suggested that its origin was Manchester rather than Matsumoto. She was wearing what at first sight appeared to be a hat, but which, on inspection, turned out to be an ice-bag of antediluvian design tied on to her head bonnet-wise with a black silk stocking. Bedroom slippers of scuffed kid and an assortment of bracelets completed the ensemble.

'Who is this man?' demanded Miss Moon in outraged tones. 'Amanda, send him away at once! I will not have strange men in my bedroom!'

Amanda flung her arms about Miss Moon and burst into overwrought tears. Miss Moon enfolded her in a protective clutch that smelt of mothballs, menthol and heliotrope, and glared at Mr Howard. Mr Howard looked thoughtfully back at her. The gun was no longer in evidence and he looked entirely relaxed and innocent of guile.

'There, there, dear!' said Miss Moon, patting Amanda's shuddering shoulders. 'Has he been annoying you? Well I shall know how to deal with him. Sir—you should be ashamed of yourself!'

'I must apologize,' said Mr Howard. 'I didn't know that you were in.'

'That,' observed Miss Moon haughtily, 'is quite evident!'

'How long have you been back, Miss Moon?'

'I cannot see that it is any concern of yours, young man. But if it is of any interest to you, I have not been out.'

'What?' Amanda lifted a tear-wet face from Miss Moon's bony shoulder. 'But the bridge party . . .'

'I was compelled to send my excuses,' said Miss Moon. 'I am subject to sudden and severe attacks of migraine, and it proved quite impossible for me to go.'

Amanda said: 'Then—then you have been here all the time?'

'I have.'

'That's very interesting,' said Steve.

Miss Moon bristled. 'Interesting? Why should it be interesting?'

'Because,' said Steve gently, 'it means that someone is due for the shock of their life, and I would most earnestly advise you, Miss Moon, not to mention to anyone that you did not go out this afternoon.'

'Young man,' said Miss Moon, drawing herself to her full height, 'I do not understand you. Naturally Lady Cooper-Foot and all those who attended her bridge party are fully aware that I remained at home.'

'Then that's torn it!' said Steve.

Miss Moon looked from Amanda to Steve, and her eyes, despite the heaviness that pain and drugs had lent them, were suddenly sharp and shrewd:

'Tell me what has happened,' she demanded crisply. 'Why would it have been advisable to conceal the fact that I have not left the house?'

'Because,' said Steve softly, 'less than an hour ago a woman was murdered in the room directly below this one—by someone who had every reason to believe that there was no one else in the house.'

13

Awakening late on the following morning, Amanda lay for several minutes staring idly at the misty folds of the mosquito net and wondering why the room seemed so airless. She felt drowsy and relaxed and curiously stupid. It can't be more than six, she thought; the room is still dark.

But the air was always cool and fresh in the early morning, not hot like this. Turning her head she saw that the dimness of the room was due to the fact that the shutters, which were always thrown back at night and only used during the heat of the day, were closed and bolted, and she frowned at them; realizing, from the bright chinks of sunlight that showed between the slats, that it was far later than she had supposed, and puzzled by a vague recollection that it was she herself who had insisted on closing those shutters.

A moment later she was sitting bolt upright with all trace of drowsiness gone, for she had remembered why it had seemed so necessary to lock herself into her room last night.

Amanda pushed back the mosquito net and went over to open the shutters, aware as she did so that it was at least midday. And also that someone must have given her a strong sleeping draught, for her head felt unaccountably heavy.

Steve Howard, of course! He had made her drink a cup of coffee. It had been black and sweet and had left a faintly unpleasant taste on her tongue. That must have been late last night, after the police and the doctor had left and an ambulance had taken Monica Ford's body away to the Nicosia General Hospital, and the endless questions were over at last.

There had been so many questions.

The man she had telephoned for, the man with an odd name, had arrived while they were still explaining the ugly situation to Miss Moon. Steve had gone down to meet him, and Amanda, who had

562

remained with Miss Moon, had not been present at that interview. She had come out onto the upper landing just as he was leaving and had heard him say: 'All right; we'll play it on those lines. It's your deal. I can stack the deck at my end, and——' He had heard Amanda's sandals click on the stairs and had stopped.

'This is Miss Derington,' said Steve. He did not complete the introduction and Amanda found herself shaking hands with a slim, quiet man who seemed a little shy and very ordinary. The sort of man, thought Amanda, whom one might meet a dozen times and still not remember. There was nothing in any way remarkable about him except perhaps his eyes, which were as cool and quiet and yet as disconcertingly observant as Steve Howard's own.

A moment later he had gone. It was after that that Steve had telephoned for the police and the doctor, and when they arrived he had gone into the drawing-room with them and shut the door. After what seemed a very long time they had sent for Amanda and Miss Moon and had questioned them. Two of the police officers had been British. C.I.D. men from Nicosia. The third had been a Cypriot who spoke excellent English.

Miss Moon had little to tell them. A migraine had descended upon her with sudden and all too familiar severity, and she had telephoned her excuses to Lady Cooper-Foot and retired to bed in a darkened room with an ice-pack and sedatives. Yes, she had been aware of voices in the drawing-room some time during the afternoon. She could not say when. Three-thirty perhaps? Four? She had been in considerable pain and had paid little attention beyond wishing that whoever was speaking would use a less hysterical tone. Oh yes, it had been a woman, and she had sounded upset. No: Miss Moon had not gone down. She had imagined that it must have been Euridice returned unexpectedly, but soon afterwards the drugs had taken effect and she had slept until past seven o'clock and had barely arisen when Amanda and Mr Howard had burst into her room.

But surely, said a police officer, she must have been aware of some sounds, however slight? The woman had been murdered——

' *"Strangling is a very quiet death,"* ' murmured Steve Howard meditatively.

Apparently Miss Moon was familiar with *The Duchess of Malfi*, for she had looked at Mr Howard with a distinct gleam of appreciation in her eyes and said: 'Exactly! No, I not only heard no other sounds, but I have no idea—if the woman whose voice I heard was indeed Monica Ford—whom she can have been addressing.'

'Glenn,' said Amanda. And explained that Mr Barton had mentioned meeting his secretary and had added that Miss Ford had wished to see her—Amanda—and that she had seemed upset.

They had questioned her as to her previous meeting with Miss Ford on the day of her arrival in Cyprus, and made her repeat as much of their conversation as she could remember. And then they had asked her to tell them again exactly what Glenn Barton had said on the subject of his secretary at the picnic that afternoon, and having received corroboration from Mr Howard, they had sent for Mr Barton.

Glenn had arrived shortly after half past nine, having driven from Nicosia at a speed considerably in excess of the recognized limits. He had looked grey and drawn and somehow apathetic. Steve had poured him out a stiff portion of Miss Moon's liqueur brandy and he had swallowed it gratefully.

Yes, he had been to the Villa Oleander that afternoon and had spoken with Miss Ford in this room. He explained the circumstances and agreed that his secretary had been upset. She had recently lost her only brother and sole close relative. And there had been other things on her mind——He checked abruptly and frowned.

What other things?

Glenn's tired face seemed to grow greyer and he had explained in a halting, difficult voice something of what he had told Amanda in that same room on the previous afternoon: of Anita's suggestions concerning the relations between Miss Ford and himself.

'Of course there was nothing in it,' he explained wearily. 'My wife could never believe such a thing. She only spread that story in order to—well, to make trouble I suppose. They had quarrelled and Miss Ford had probably been rude to her.'

'Anita,' put in Miss Moon crisply, 'was well aware that people would be only too willing to believe that Monica had fallen in love with her employer, but that no one in their senses would believe that he was in love with her. So that from Monica's point of view the story would be doubly wounding.'

'Was she in love with you?' asked a police officer.

The colour came up into Glenn's haggard face and his mouth tightened and set hard. He looked at the man who had asked the question and his eyes did not waver.

'No.' The single word was curt and entirely final.

But they had not finished with him. They went back again to the quarrel between his secretary and his wife, and again and again to his conversation with Miss Ford in the Villa Oleander that afternoon. Was he quite sure of the time? Why was he sure? So he had seen the green scarf? Why, having heard a sound from one of the upper rooms, had he still said at Hilarion that the house was empty?

'I didn't know that Miss Moon was in,' said Glenn wearily. 'I thought it must be a pigeon or the cat.'

He turned to look at Miss Moon. 'I'm sorry, Mooney. If I'd known you were ill I'd have come up.'

'I wouldn't have let you in,' said Miss Moon tartly, and departed to cut sandwiches and brew hot coffee.

They turned back to the picnic at Hilarion:

How many people had been present when Mr Barton had spoken of his secretary and mentioned that there was no one at home in the Villa Oleander? At what time had Mr Barton left Hilarion, and where had he gone?

'To Nicosia,' said Glenn tiredly. 'Prove it? Well as a matter of fact I can. The Normans saw me go. We all left at the same time—except Howard and Miss Derington. There were only four cars there. Gates and Mrs Halliday went ahead of my car and turned left for Kyrenia. I turned up right, and the Normans and Major Blaine were behind me and must have seen me turn. They went down to Kyrenia too, of course. I drove straight to the Nicosia office, and as it happens I can prove that too, because I gave a lift to a couple of troops. You can probably check with them. I dropped them off in the centre of the town just after six. Anything more you want to know?'

There appeared to be a great deal more. But they left at last, and it was just as they were leaving that one of the police officers found the little linen flower.

There was a massive carved chest in the hall, black with age and decorated with medallions of beaten silver, and the small white flower had caught on a rough edge of metal at a level where the hem of a woman's skirt might have brushed past it.

The officer reached down and removed it and turned it over between his fingers. There was a thread hanging from the centre of it as though it had been torn from something.

Amanda said incredulously: 'But that's——' and saw Glenn Barton's face, and stopped.

Glenn was staring at her with a tense and desperate appeal in his eyes. Amanda looked away quickly and became aware that Steve had been watching them.

The police officer said: 'This is yours, then?'

'Yes,' said Amanda without hesitation. She saw Glenn shut his eyes for a brief moment and catch at the edge of the chest as though to steady himself, and she held out her hand for the flower.

The police officer looked at her long and thoughtfully, and then put it into his pocket. 'If you do not mind, I will keep it. It will be returned of course.'

And then they had gone. Glenn first, and the three police officers perhaps five minutes later. The doctor had already left in the ambulance that had taken Monica Ford's body to Nicosia an hour earlier.

Miss Moon departed to the kitchen to make more coffee and Amanda would have followed her except that Steve Howard stood between her and the door that led through to the kitchen, and he did not look as though he intended to move aside for her as he had moved for Miss Moon.

'Amanda,' said Steve softly, 'you are a damned bad liar and several kinds of a fool into the bargain. What possessed you to do such an idiotic thing?'

Amanda did not pretend to misunderstand him. 'I couldn't do anything else,' she said unhappily. 'You didn't see his face——'

'Oh yes I did,' interrupted Steve brusquely. 'But that is no reason why you should have laid claim to the thing.'

'What else could I have done? If I'd said it wasn't mine, they'd have asked Miss Moon; and as it wasn't hers, they would have traced it.'

'They'll trace it all right,' said Steve grimly. 'And when they do you are going to find yourself in an exceedingly unpleasant position.'

'Why?' said Amanda defensively.

'There is such a thing as being an accessory after the fact,' pointed out Steve dryly.

'I can't help it,' said Amanda. 'I—I owed him something.'

'For saving your life?' said Steve with an edge to his voice. 'Perhaps. But he had no right to let you do it.'

'You don't understand,' said Amanda. 'He's in love with her.'

'And are you by any chance in love with him?' inquired Steve unpleasantly. 'Is that the real reason for this quixotic gesture?'

Amanda hit him.

She had not meant to do it or known that she would do so. The gesture had been an entirely unexpected and instinctive reaction born of the accumulative terror and shock and emotional strain of the past hours and the last few days. This time he either did not anticipate the action or did not trouble to avoid it.

Amanda stared in stunned dismay at the red mark that her palm had left on Steven Howard's hard cheek; her grey eyes very wide and young.

'I—I'm sorry,' she said in a small, unsteady voice. 'I didn't mean to do that. I——'

'Don't apologize,' interrupted Steve sardonically. 'After all I did offer you a second try, didn't I?—and they say that practice makes perfect.'

'You're very angry, aren't you?' said Amanda in a subdued voice.

'If I am, it's probably with myself,' said Steve curtly.

And then Miss Moon had reappeared with a fresh pot of coffee and they had drunk it sitting round the dining-room table because none of them wanted to go into the drawing-room again, and because Amanda flatly refused to go to bed.

Amanda had not wanted the hot coffee either, and had asked for a cold drink instead. Steve had ignored the request and had poured out a cup of black coffee to which he had added sugar and, undoubtedly, some drug that he had presumably obtained off Miss Moon or the doctor, and had handed it to her without further words. Amanda had looked at his coolly unemotional eyes and uncompromising mouth and had been too tired to argue. She had drunk it, and it had left an unpleasant taste on her tongue.

Steve had embarked on a long conversation with Miss Moon who, it was soon obvious, had entirely revised her first opinion of him and was already addressing him as 'dear boy'. He had not spoken directly to Amanda again, and presently his voice and his face had begun to fade into a misty background in which only a flight of pseudo-Japanese storks and the jingle of Miss Moon's bracelets stood out at all clearly.

Amanda's eyelids had begun to feel strangely heavy and she found that she could no longer prevent them from closing. She slid down a little lower in her chair and a voice that seemed to come from the other end of a long tunnel had said faintly but distinctly: 'I think, dear boy, that she is almost asleep now,' and another voice, equally far away said: 'And about time too!'

Amanda had forced open her eyes in order to see who was asleep, and had looked up into Steven Howard's face and remembered that he had been angry about something; something to do with Glenn Barton. She must explain about that. Steve had not understood. She found that it was an effort to speak, and said drowsily and with difficulty: 'Glenn——' and the face above her was suddenly blank and hard and completely expressionless.

Then her eyes closed again and Steve had lifted her and carried her up a long dark flight of stairs, and she had turned her face against his shoulder and clung to him with terrified desperation, because these were the ruined stone steps of Hilarion once more, and she was afraid of falling.

◊ ◊ ◊

The door opened with a faint creak of hinges and Amanda turned quickly to see Miss Moon peering cautiously around it.

Miss Moon, a vision in lemon yellow, brightened at the sight of her and said approvingly: 'So you are awake at last! I have looked in several times, but did not wish to wake you. How are you feeling, my dear?'

'A bit stupid,' said Amanda with an attempt at a smile. 'Is it very late?'

'Ten minutes to one, dear. Luncheon will be ready in a moment. I expect you are hungry. I do trust that you feel no ill-effects from those sleeping powders? I have always found them remarkably effective, although I confess I have never taken more than one. But Mr Howard thought that in the circumstances two would be advisable. *Such* a dear boy! So thoughtful—and so well read. How *few* people one meets who have read *Il Conte de Carmagnola* in the original and can discuss it intelligently! Dear Papa would have enjoyed conversing with him. I will tell Euridice to run you a bath.'

'Miss Moon,' said Amanda in a halting voice, 'I—didn't dream it by any chance, did I?'

Miss Moon's face changed and her mouth closed for a moment into a tight line.

'No my dear. I am afraid not. We have had the police here the whole morning. I would not permit them to wake you, since you could have told them nothing more than you told them last night. Several people called to inquire after you. That young Captain Gates, and a Mrs Halliday—American I think, and very striking. And Glenn has been here too. There will have to be an inquest, of course, but the police have satisfied themselves as to the reason for poor Monica Ford's dreadful end.'

Amanda sat down rather suddenly on the edge of her bed. 'Who —who do they think did it?'

'A thief of course,' said Miss Moon, and wrung her hands so that the bracelets jingled. 'Oh, Amanda dear, I fear it was *all* my fault!

'Darling!' said Amanda, jumping up and giving her hostess a sudden impulsive hug. 'Don't be silly! How could it possibly be your fault?'

'Well you see, dear, there are a great many valuable things in this house. My dear Papa was a great collector. And of course I have never kept anything under lock and key, and everyone knows that I never lock the house up—except of course at night. Euridice insists on that. It must have been a temptation. I see that now. Some dishonest person must have come to hear that the house would be empty yesterday afternoon, and have crept in intending to steal what they could. They would not have expected to find anyone in the drawing-room, and may not have noticed Monica until she had time to see and perhaps even recognize the thief. They think that he lost his head and picked up the scarf only intending to stop her from calling out, and did not mean to kill her—I do *hope* he did not!'

Amanda said: 'But nothing was missing.'

'Oh yes there was, dear. Several of the smaller and more valuable items from dear Papa's collection had been removed from the cabinets in the drawing-room. There are so many things there that I did not immediately realize it.'

Amanda was aware of a sudden and overwhelming wave of relief.

She could not have told why she should be so inexpressibly relieved. Surely she could not have believed that one of a small group of people who were personally known to her could have deliberately strangled poor, harmless, unhappy Monica Ford? No of course she had not. All the same she felt as if a black, crushing weight had been lifted off her shoulders.

'It will be a lesson to me,' sighed Miss Moon. 'I shall have to send dear Papa's collection to the bank. So foolish. Beautiful things should be looked at and appreciated; not locked away in vaults. I think I hear Euridice in the hall. Luncheon will be ready and here I am keeping you talking.'

She hurried away and Amanda bathed and dressed quickly, and having brushed out her tangled hair, rolled it up and bundled the shining mass into a coarse white net in the style that had been fashionable in the days when the young Empress Eugenie had netted her beautiful tresses in a similar manner. Amanda would not let herself think of those desperate moments at Hilarion when her hair alone had saved her from a horrible and disfiguring death, but some frightened instinct would not allow her to pin it securely. She had to feel that it was free and unbound.

She turned to look at herself in the long silvery expanse of looking-glass on the wall. The heavy chignon tilted her head back with its weight and made her face appear smaller and more pointed and her slender neck as long as the stem of a flower. White linen dress. White linen sandals. *White linen*—a small flat, white linen flower clinging to a rough edge of metal on the chest in the hall . . .

Amanda caught her lip between her teeth. She had forgotten that sinister little flower. But it couldn't mean anything! Supposing Anita Barton *had* been to the Villa Oleander on her return from St Hilarion? Supposing, even, that she was (as her clothes suggested) extravagant and possibly in debt? That still did not make her a thief, any more than her dislike of Monica Ford made her a murderess. Recalling Anita Barton's relaxed and sleeping face, Amanda was suddenly and comfortingly sure of that.

The police and Miss Moon were right. Some petty thief, snatching the jade and crystal trinkets from the drawing-room cabinets, had been surprised by Monica Ford, and had panicked and killed her.

Amanda applied rose-pink lipstick with a steady hand, made a face at herself in the glass and ran downstairs to join Miss Moon.

The dining-room smelt pleasantly of flowers and fruit and Euridice's special brand of ravioli, and beyond the open windows the garden was brilliant with sunlight and noisy with the coo and flutter of pigeons and the sound of Andreas chopping wood. Euridice was conducting an excitable conversation with a friend in the kitchen and Miss Moon was as talkative as ever.

'No,' said Miss Moon, waving away the barley water: 'I never drink with meals, dear. So bad for the digestion; it dilutes the gastric juices. Only between meals. Though of course one so often forgets to do that, and then so much of it is wasted. It does not really keep in this weather. Try some of this melon, dear——'

Everything was suddenly safe and sane and ordinary again, and the house no longer held its breath to listen but basked comfortably in the hot sunshine. Colour came back to Amanda's cheeks and some of the sparkle to her eyes, and with the resilience and optimism of youth she pushed the recollection of the past few days behind her and felt her spirits rise to meet the challenge of the gay, glittering day. She would forget about all the horrible things that had happened. She would not think of them. She was in Cyprus—in Kyrenia—and the sun was shining. She would go out and bathe with Toby and laugh with Persis, and buy embroidered linen in the shops in the town and photograph the harbour as a hundred thousand carefree tourists had done before her.

Her mood lasted until the end of the meal, and it was Miss Moon who shattered it.

Amanda, admiring a Venetian glass fruit dish, had been suddenly reminded of Miss Moon's stolen treasures. 'And I never even asked you about them,' she said remorsefully. 'How horrid of me. Were they things that you were specially fond of?'

'Oh, but I have not lost them,' said Miss Moon placidly. 'They were all found, you know.'

'*Found?* But where? Then they *have* caught the man!'

'No dear. It was Euridice who found them this morning. Or rather Katina, Euridice's cat. *Not* a very engaging animal. She was playing with something on the path—rolling it about—and Euridice saw it glitter and went to pick it up. It was that crystal egg. The Fabergé egg, you know. And there they all were, in the grass by the path. The thief must suddenly have realized that if he were caught with them it would mean a sentence of death for murder, and dropped them.'

'The—the Fabergé egg?' repeated Amanda in a whisper.

'Yes dear. Such a pretty thing. He made a great many of them. For the poor Czarina, you know. This was a specially beautiful one, and of course the diamonds probably add to its value. There is a jewelled bird in it, that sings. I am not very fond of it. Such a tragic story. It makes one wonder, does it not, if Russians are ever to be trusted?'

But Amanda was not listening. She was seeing again the shadowed drawing-room as she had seen it on the previous evening when, rigid with the terrified conviction that the silent room contained someone besides herself, she had looked about it with panic-stricken eyes. The diamonds on the Fabergé egg had sparkled in the last of the daylight.

The egg had been in the buhl cabinet less than a minute before she had discovered the dead body of Monica Ford. It had not been stolen. Someone had removed it later in the evening, together with a handful of similar small objects, in order to convey the impression that Monica Ford had been murdered by a thief. And quite suddenly Amanda knew who had done it and when.

Steve Howard had sent her out of the room to make a telephone call that he could have made with more speed himself. But it had served a double purpose. He had got her out of the way for at least ten minutes, and it must have been then that he had opened the corner cabinet.

Amanda could see him doing it—moving with that noiseless swiftness that had surprised her. Lifting each small, gleaming object in his handkerchief so as to leave no finger-prints, as he had lifted the small bottle with the red poison label in the cabin of the *Orantares*.

'All right—we'll play it on those lines; it's your deal,' the slim, ordinary-looking man with the odd name had said; and the half a dozen or so trinkets from Miss Moon's cabinet had almost certainly been in his possession as he said it. He had shaken hands with Amanda and gone out into the darkness and had dropped that misleading evidence in the overgrown grass by the edge of the flagged path, to lend colour to the theory that Monica Ford's murder had been a chance occurrence instead of part of a hidden, ugly pattern that had begun to form in Fayid, and that involved that small group of people who had sailed for Cyprus on the S.S. *Orantares*— one of whom must have planned the death of Julia Blaine.

14

Amanda did not do any of the things that she had meant to do that afternoon. She ran up to her room instead, and having looked under the bed and inside the cupboards and behind every piece of furniture, she locked the door and wrote three letters. One to her Uncle Oswin, one to her aunt in Fayid, and the third to the shipping company. After which she threw herself on her bed and wept stormily, and had not the least idea why she should do so.

Whatever the reason, she felt considerably better for it; and more than a little ashamed of herself. Presently she heard the clock in the hall strike four and realized that the afternoon had almost gone, and Euridice would be laying tea in the verandah outside the drawing-room.

Amanda sat up and pushed her tumbled hair out of her eyes. She went over to the dressing-table and stopped with a sudden shock of dismay at the sight of her own reflection in the oval looking-glass.

She stood there for a long time, staring at herself. Her hair had escaped from its confining net and had tumbled about her shoulders and half-way down her back in tangled disorder. Her white face was blotched with tears and her dress crumpled and creased.

Looking at herself, she had a sudden and disturbing vision of Julia Blaine, tear blotched and unsightly, giving way to hysteria in the cabin of the *Orantares*. If she wasn't careful, she, Amanda Derington, would soon be behaving as Julia Blaine had behaved. There was already something about her tear-stained face that was unpleasantly reminiscent of Julia's.

A familiar, mocking voice seemed for a moment to speak in Amanda's ear: *'Come on, George Cross Island—pull yourself together!'*

Amanda straightened her bowed shoulders with a jerk and set her small jaw, and there was a sudden defiant sparkle in her eyes.

The three letters that she had written lay on the writing table by the window. She picked them up, tore them into small pieces and dropped them into the waste-paper basket, and ten minutes later went down to tea with her head high and her red mouth set in lines of determination.

There were voices on the drawing-room verandah and Amanda suffered a momentary qualm. Could it be the police again?

But it was only George Norman.

Mr Norman, who was holding a tea-cup in one hand and a small plate in the other, stood up hurriedly at the sight of Amanda and instantly dropped a piece of toast butter side down on the matting.

'Mooney's been telling me about this terrible business of Glenn's secretary,' explained George Norman, stooping to retrieve the toast and spilling his tea in the process. 'Ghastly show! I can't tell you how shocked we all were. Told Mooney a thousand times if I've told her once that having all that stuff lying round loose was simply asking for it! Ought to be in a bank. Terrible business! Claire's very upset about it. Couldn't sleep a wink last night.'

'Last *night?*' Amanda's voice was startled and incredulous. Did Claire always get bad news ahead of other people? How could she possibly have known last night about Monica Ford?

'Glenn told her,' said George Norman, spreading bloater paste on his toast. 'He telephoned at about half past ten last night. Extraordinary chap. Actually wanted us to go at once and see Anita about something. Seems he didn't dare go himself. Some silly idea that the police might see where he went. He said he couldn't ask you because the police were in your house, and that only left us. Well of course we've been friends of Glenn's for years, but there are limits! He knows perfectly well that Claire and Anita never hit it off. And since then Anita has been spreading all that scandal about him and Claire. However urgent the matter was I do not feel that he should have traded on our personal friendship for him to that extent. Anita Barton is a thoroughly bad lot and he is lucky to be rid of her.'

Miss Moon said: 'I confess I do not understand Anita. I would never have thought her capable of such crudely vulgar behaviour. It does not seem to be at all in keeping with her character. She has changed sadly of late.'

'Drink,' said George Norman succinctly.

'My *dear* boy!' said Miss Moon in horrified protest, 'I am quite sure you are mistaken. Although of course I have heard rumors——'

'I bet you have! It's true, I'm afraid. Drinks like a fish. And that's the girl who never used to touch anything stronger than tomato juice.'

'Perhaps there is a reason for it,' said Miss Moon with a small sigh. 'I cannot help feeling that despite her brazen behaviour Anita is very unhappy. Perhaps she hoped that drink would give her forgetfulness—or courage. "Dutch courage", my dear papa used to call it.'

'She deserves to be unhappy,' said George Norman. 'Impossible woman!' He drained his tea-cup and helped himself to a slice of cake.

Amanda said abruptly: 'What did you all do yesterday? After you left Hilarion?'

'Eh? Oh yesterday. Nothing much. Came down to the Club, you know. I wanted to see a chap who I thought would be there, but he wasn't. Hardly anyone there. Lumley dropped in for a minute or two. He's not a member as a matter of fact. Came up to show a chap some pictures. Claire went off to do a bit of shoppin' and Alastair went for a stroll, and we all forgathered at the Dome for a drink about eight. Alastair was dining there with Mrs Halliday, and she suggested we all stay, so we did. Didn't get home until half past ten, and then the telephone went and there was Glenn going on about this appalling business. Couldn't believe it when Claire told me. Thought the poor chap had finally gone off his rocker.'

Amanda said carefully: 'What happened to Toby—Captain Gates?'

'Oh, he fetched up too. I think he dropped Mrs Halliday at the hotel and drove the car back to the chap he hired it off. He joined us for dinner.'

Amanda relapsed into silence. So they had all separated. All or any of them could have come to the Villa Oleander and gone away again without anyone else knowing about it. They had all been within five minutes' walk of it, and there were three seperate entrances to the garden: the front gate, the gate at the far end of the garden that led to the garage, and the small, sun-blistered door in the old Turkish wall that ran the length of the back garden, and which gave onto a narrow secluded lane.

I won't think about it, thought Amanda. I won't . . . It was somebody who broke in to steal . . . It must have been . . . Ordinary, nice people—people that you know—don't do these things. And yet—there was Hilarion. I won't think of it, Amanda told herself again and with desperation.

Miss Moon was saying: 'Yes, a great many people have called. To

575

offer sympathy of course. And two of Amanda's friends came to inquire after her. Lady Cooper-Foot and Mrs Teenley telephoned. Everyone realizes what a shock it must have been to me. But I could not see them all this morning. The police were here you know. And after luncheon dear Amanda went up to her room to rest, so I told Euridice to say that we were "not at home" and to take the receiver off the telephone. So kind of people; but in the circumstances——'

'Nosey Parkers!' snorted George Norman indignantly. 'All the old gossips dying to get the details.'

'Oh surely not, dear boy,' protested Miss Moon, shocked. 'After all, *you* are here, and although of course we did discuss the whole affair, I am sure that you did not come only for that.'

George Norman's already ruddy countenance turned a rich shade of puce and he said hurriedly: 'No, of course not. I mean Claire told me to—I mean——'

He floundered into incoherence and Miss Moon, taking pity on him, offered him another cup of tea and urged him to move his chair a little farther into the shade afforded by the climbing roses.

'I always like to take tea out here,' said Miss Moon. 'The view is so beautiful. Quite uninterrupted. I often sit here to watch the sunset, though facing west, it has its drawbacks. Almost too much sun; it has sadly faded my drawing-room carpet. But then I myself am a sun-worshipper. I do not think—except during the real heat of the day of course—that one *can* have too much of it. Do you not agree?'

George Norman sighed, and for a moment his face had a wistful look. 'Yes. I suppose so.'

'You sound rather doubtful,' said Amanda, only too anxious to keep the conversation firmly on the weather. 'Don't tell me that you prefer grey skies and drizzle to this heavenly climate?'

'But of course I do,' said George Norman, surprised. 'England is my own country. This foreign stuff is all very well for a time, but one gets tired of it. The heat and the smell and jabbering foreign voices, and this damnable sun, sun, sun. No; give me Suffolk on a grey day with the wind blowing over ploughed fields, and chaffinches and yellow-hammers in the hedges, and——' He broke off with a sharp sigh. 'Oh well; no good talking about it. It doesn't suit Claire. If it wasn't for Claire——' His voice trailed off into silence and he sat staring at the slowly cooling tea in his cup as though he had temporarily forgotten Amanda and Miss Moon, his square, ruddy face suddenly bleak and bitter.

Miss Moon, said: 'Try a piece of the gingerbread, dear boy. I made it myself. A recipe of my dear grandmother's.

George Norman awoke from his meditations with a visible start and said hurriedly: 'No thank you. I must be getting back.' He gulped down the contents of his cup and added that he had not meant to inflict himself on her for tea: 'I really only came to——'

'I know. To collect the details,' finished Miss Moon wickedly. 'Well I hope you have them all. Tell Claire that I am sorry to hear that she is feeling so upset, and that I advise a strong dose of Gregory's powder. My dear Papa used to say that it was a sure cure for all imaginary ills. Good-bye, dear boy. So kind of you to call.'

Miss Moon watched him depart and clicked her tongue impatiently.

'It is frequently a matter of surprise to me,' she remarked tartly, 'what some men will put up with. And the nicest men put up with the most. Look at Glenn! As for George, he puts me out of all patience.'

'Why, Miss Moon?' Amanda was interested in the Normans. She was interested, with a shrinking, frightened, fascinated curiosity, in every one of that small group of people who had known Julia Blaine and who had picnicked at Hilarion.

'Because,' said Miss Moon, 'he has got into the habit—Claire has seen to that!—of putting his own wishes and desires and convenience second to those of his wife. There is nothing wrong with Claire's health and George knows it! But he has to keep up the fiction of believing in it for the sake of his own self-respect. It is, of course, a case of "he who pays the piper calls the tune." The money is Claire's, and that has put her in a position to dictate. All the same, George is able bodied and reasonably intelligent. There is no reason why he should not be able to obtain some remunerative employment in his own country if he insisted returning there. With or without his wife!'

Amanda said: 'But he's so devoted to her.'

'Is he? I suppose so. But I have frequently wondered of late if perhaps he might not be almost relieved were she to emulate Anita Barton. Poor Anita: I fear she made a bad enemy when she came up against George's wife. So foolish of her! But she was always high-spirited and reckless. Anita will always "rush her fences", as my dear Papa would have said. And that so frequently leads to disaster. Claire is far more subtle. Yes, I am afraid that Claire is a bad enemy.'

Miss Moon sighed and Amanda said: 'You like Mrs Barton, don't you?'

'Well . . . yes, dear. One could not help being fond of her. She was such a child.'

'Glenn said that too,' said Amanda slowly.

'He was right. Some adults seem to retain the more endearing qualities of childhood longer than others. Though many, of course, retain the worst ones for ever. Anita Barton was one of the former. A little spoilt perhaps, but very trusting and honest, and not very clever. A woman like Claire Norman, for instance, could make rings round her. It seemed that Anita and Glenn would be perfectly happy. Of course she was gay; she always liked parties and people and pretty clothes. And Glenn, poor boy, was very overworked and perhaps did not take her about as much as he should, so that——'

Miss Moon stopped suddenly and was silent for a moment or two, frowning.

'What is it?' asked Amanda curiously.

'Well dear, it suddenly struck me that if one hears a thing repeated sufficiently often, one begins to believe that it is true, even if it is not. We have all heard so often of late that Glenn neglected Anita. But now I come to think of it, they appeared to go about together a great deal. One certainly never heard that he was remiss where the social side of life was concerned. Of course she may just have found him dull. One does not know.'

'I don't see that she can have it both ways,' pointed out Amanda. 'If—as she says—he was behaving like a Don Juan and making love to about six different women at once, he can't have been exactly dull. He must have had *something*—plenty of spare time, for a start!'

Miss Moon sighed again. 'One would think so. Although of course women do like Glenn. I am very fond of him myself. And so was Claire. She was not at all pleased when he married Anita. All the same, it was exceedingly foolish of Anita to be rude to her, and I have always had a suspicion—uncharitable of me, I fear—that Claire was in some way responsible for the break-up of that marriage. What is it, Euridice?'

Euridice was standing in the french windows behind them, wearing the patient expression of one who has been waiting for at least five minutes. She made a brief and unintelligible remark and went to collect the tea-cups, and Miss Moon turned to Amanda and said: 'Someone asking to see you, dear. If it is that nice Mr Howard, ask him to stay and dine with us.'

Amanda stood up quickly and put her hand to her hair in a gesture that was purely instinctive and feminine.

Miss Moon smiled at her with warm understanding and said: 'You look exceedingly nice, dear. In fact, if I may say so, quite charming.'

Amanda blushed, laughed and went quickly through the french windows and across the drawing-room into the hall: to check abruptly at the sight of her visitor, aware of a sudden and ridiculous sense of disappointment.

It was not Steven Howard who stood waiting for her in the hall of the Villa Oleander. It was, surprisingly enough, Anita Barton. And Anita Barton was frightened. That fact was immediately and startlingly apparent, and it sent an odd cold shiver of apprehension through Amanda.

In the dimness of the high, dark hall Mrs Barton's face had the appearance of a white paper mask on which a child has scrawled features in crudely coloured chalks. The patches of rouge on her cheeks, the vividly lipsticked mouth, the blue-tinted eyelids and heavily mascara'd lashes, stood out in harsh and painful artificiality in a face that was drawn and drained of all natural colour, and eyes that were as wide and glittering as a terrified cat's.

There was no longer any trace of prettiness in that face, but strangely enough its look of haggard fear was not ageing, and with the loss of her hard defiant assurance, Anita Barton seemed to have become all at once younger, and as though she were indeed only the foolish, frightened child to which both her husband and Miss Moon had likened her.

Amanda was aware of a sudden pang of pity and an instinct of protectiveness, and she went forward quickly with her hand outstretched. 'What is it? Did you want to see me?'

'Yes——' Anita Barton's frightened-cat eyes darted quick glances about the hall and the long staircase that stretched up into the shadows of the upper landing, and her fingers tugged nervously at a small lace-edged handkerchief so that the delicate fabric tore with a small ripping sound. She dropped it, startled, and said breathlessly: 'But not here. Can't we go somewhere else. Will you walk down the road with me?'

Amanda looked at her, puzzled and disturbed. 'All right. Just wait a moment while I tell Miss Moon.'

She returned to the verandah and informed Miss Moon that she

579

would be going out for a short walk. Miss Moon looked interested. 'Anita, you say? I was not aware that you knew her. *Hardly* a suitable companion for you just now dear. People talk so. Do you not think that perhaps it would be wiser to decline the invitation—tactfully, of course?'

'I can't,' said Amanda, distressed. 'I think she's in trouble. I don't suppose I shall be long.'

Once outside the gates of the Villa Oleander Anita Barton turned to the right and away from the main road, and as soon as they were out of sight of the house she clutched Amanda's arm and spoke in a harsh, breathless voice:

'Is it true that something of mine was found in Miss Moon's house last night?—a flower off that dress I was wearing?'

'Yes,' said Amanda briefly.

She heard Anita Barton catch her breath in a hard gasp and the fingers that held her arm tightened convulsively so that the pointed scarlet nails dug painfully into her flesh.

Mrs Barton stumbled and recovered herself and stopped near a group of dusty tamarisk trees by a high, white-washed wall in what appeared to be a deserted cul-de-sac:

'Then it is true! I didn't believe it. I thought that it was only— only a spiteful story. But Lumley said——' she stopped, and her wide, hunted eyes searched Amanda's face with a desperate intensity. 'Tell me about it, please. I must know.'

Amanda told her. There was not much to tell, but the bare facts were ugly enough and Anita Barton's white face seemed to grow whiter and more pinched as she listened.

She said at last in a harsh whisper: 'Didn't they ask whose it was?'

Amanda hesitated and once more the lacquered fingernails dug into her arm. 'Didn't they?'

'Yes,' said Amanda unhappily. 'I—said it was mine.'

'You *what?*' Mrs Barton's voice was suddenly strident. 'Why did you do that? Why should you do a thing like that for me?'

'I didn't, confessed Amanda. 'I did it because of your husband. You see——'

'*Glenn?*' Anita Barton relaxed her grip and took a quick step backwards, staring. A stare that changed suddenly to a look of scornful comprehension:

'Glenn,' repeated Mrs Barton, her mouth no longer slack-lipped with fear but twisted and derisive. 'So you've fallen for him too, you silly little fool!'

Amanda's chin came up with a jerk. Her grey eyes were suddenly cold and angry and her voice as scornful as Mrs Barton's own:

'I think it is you who are the fool, if you really imagine that I have any interest at all in your husband. Perhaps no one else has ever had any interest in him either, and you are just another Julia Blaine. Someone who imagines that no other woman can speak to her husband without falling in love with him. You do love him, don't you? You're only behaving like this because someone has made you jealous. Julia was like that.'

For a long minute Anita Barton did not speak, but the scorn and bitterness left her face and it was once more frightened and quivering. She put her hand up to her throat and said in a voice that was barely above a whisper: 'Yes, Julia was like that. And Julia died. But I don't want to die!'

She swallowed convulsively and her eyes came back to Amanda:

'If Glenn doesn't mean anything to you, and I don't, why did you tell the police that the flower was yours?'

'Because I owed your husband something. My life,' said Amanda bluntly.

'Your *life?* What do you mean?'

Amanda told her, omitting only the fact that her fall had not been accidental. 'So you see,' she concluded, 'I thought that I owed him something in return.'

'So that's why you said that flower was yours!' Suddenly and without warning Anita Barton threw back her head and laughed. A loud peal of hysterical mirth that was somehow incredibly shocking. It stopped as abruptly as it had begun and she reached out and clutched at Amanda's arm once more:

'Listen, I never went near Miss Moon's house yesterday. Do you hear? I never went near it?'

Her teeth chattered suddenly as though she were cold, and Amanda said quickly: 'If you didn't, you'll be able to prove it, and then——'

'But I can't prove it!' interrupted Anita Barton desperately. 'Someone telephoned the cafe on the quay and asked them to give a message to Lumley. Some visitor who wanted to know if he would take a few of his pictures up to the Club. But the man never turned up, and Lumley waited and didn't get back until late. I was alone in the flat; but I can't prove it. I might have gone out. The floors below are empty. They're used for storage. And there are two ways out of that house.'

'Perhaps you wore that dress to Miss Moon's house some other time?' suggested Amanda. 'That flower thing could have been there for ages, you know. Euridice doesn't seem to be very good at dusting and I don't suppose that anyone would have noticed it.'

'I haven't been at the Villa Oleander since the winter,' said Anita Barton, 'and that flower couldn't have come off my dress there because I've never worn it to the house. Someone put it there; and I know who it was. I know how they could have got it and why they did it. And then you said it was yours, which might have spoilt it all. But it won't—you'll see! The police and everyone will know soon enough.'

Her voice died out in a frightened, hopeless whisper and Amanda's fingers closed over the hand on her arm in a comforting grasp.

'No they won't. Don't look like that, Mrs Barton. The police think that it's mine; and they won't worry about it any more because Miss Moon says that they think it was a thief who killed Miss Ford.'

Anita Barton drew a long shuddering breath and her eyes seemed to look through and beyond Amanda as though they did not see her. She said in a barely audible whisper: 'I shall have to be careful. I shall have to be very careful . . .'

The sky beyond the dusty tamarisk trees was tinged with gold and the deserted lane was in shadow, and high above the tree tops Amanda could see the distant, rocky outline of St Hilarion, bright with the sunset. It would not be long now before the swift tropical twilight would be upon them, to merge once more into another night of moonlight and stars. She heard a cart creak past the end of the lane, and from somewhere behind the high, white-washed wall a woman began to sing a plaintive Turkish ballad that was old when the Empire of Byzantium was young.

Anita Barton's eyes seemed to focus Amanda again and she drew a short, hard breath and said: 'Thank you for trying to help. It was kind of you. I don't think you'd better be seen with me, so I'll go back a different way.'

Amanda said, impulsively: 'If there is anything I can do—to help I mean—I'd like to do it. I really would.'

Mrs Barton smiled crookedly. 'That's nice of you. I'll remember.'

She turned on her heel and walked quickly away, and Amanda,

following more slowly, saw her take the turning that led into the narrow lane behind the wall where the pigeons of the Villa Oleander cooed and paraded in the ruined embrasures of the time-worn stone.

15

Amanda walked slowly back to the house, but at the gate she suddenly changed her mind, and instead of going in, went on and turned down towards the centre of the town.

She would go and see Steve Howard and tell him about that odd, disturbing interview with Anita Barton. Steve would know what to do.

There was a man loitering at the corner of the road, and as she passed him Amanda had the odd impression that he had taken note of her; not as a pretty girl, but as one who observes and files away a piece of information.

She looked quickly back over her shoulder, but the man was leaning against the wall, apparently intent upon removing a stone from the sole of his shoe, and she wondered if her imagination had tricked her, or if the police were not so satisfied as Miss Moon supposed with the theory that Monica Ford had been killed by a thief, and were watching the Villa Oleander?

It was an uncomfortable thought, and yet she had to admit that she would sleep easier that night if she could be assured that the police were keeping an eye on the house.

She saw Claire Norman and Toby Gates in the town, but they did not see her. They were talking earnestly outside Karafillides' shop, and as she approached they turned and walked away together.

Amanda saw no one else that she knew, with the exception of several children who grinned cheerfully at her and were presumably among those admirers of Steve Howard's whose acquaintance she had made on her first morning in Kyrenia. And struck by a sudden thought, she did not go directly to the Dome, but turned instead towards the harbour, where the low rays of the setting sun had turned the massive walls of Kyrenia Castle to molten gold, and dyed the long range of the hills with rose and cyclamen and lavender streaked with soft blue shadows.

The quiet water of the sleepy little harbour lay like a vast opal in the shelter of the sea wall, mirroring all the clear colours of the evening and the orange-brown mainsail of a small blue sailing boat whose owner was manoeuvring her to her moorings at the far side of the harbour. It was a picture to delight the eye of the least appreciative: a back-drop for a ballet or the setting for an opera by Puccini. But there was no one painting on the wall that evening and Amanda could see no sign of Steve Howard.

She turned to look at the row of tall, flat-roofed houses that ringed the far side of the harbour, one of which contained Lumley Potter's studio flat. The french windows of the Potter studio gave on to a small iron-railed balcony, and Amanda saw a man step out on to the balcony and peer down on to the quay beneath. The distance was too great for her to be able to make out his features, but against the dark square of the open window behind him the man's blond head stood out in sharp relief, and Amanda wondered if Alastair Blaine— if it was Alastair—was being inveigled into purchasing a companion piece to 'Sea Green Cypriots'?

The man turned and went in again and Amanda's gaze wandered along the quays and over the crowded tables of the little café, but Steve Howard was definitely not among those present, and after a time she turned away and walked slowly back towards the Dome Hotel.

The girl at the desk glanced at an array of keys and said that she was afraid Mr Howard must be out. He had left his key at the desk and had not reclaimed it. Perhaps Amanda would care to wait?

Amanda lingered, uncertain whether to stay or to leave a message asking Steve to call at the Villa Oleander. But as she hesitated, there was a click of high heels on the floor behind her, a waft of 'Bois des Iles' and Persis Halliday said: 'Hullo there! Just the girl I wanted to see! Amanda honey, I was round at the old Palazzo of yours this morning trying to see you, and I rang up twice this afternoon. But your phone must be out of order. I hear you've been right spang in the middle of a front page story? Come and have a shot of something and tell me all about it at once. Am I thrilled!'

She took Amanda's arm in an affectionate and possessive clasp and swept her off to a corner of a wide lounge where the lights had already been lit and the windows that looked out onto the placid ocean were filled with the last daffodil glow of the sunset.

Persis, thought Amanda, was showing signs of strain. There were lines about her eyes and mouth that Amanda did not remember having seen before, and she looked less glossy and well dressed than usual. There was a large flake of crimson lacquer missing from one fingernail, and for the first time since Amanda had known her, her gleaming hair was less than immaculately sleek.

She questioned Amanda about the events of the previous evening in a low, eager voice that was entirely unlike her usual gay, high-pitched and incisive tones.

Amanda gave her an outline of the story, but avoided details, and eventually Persis abandoned the catechism and relaxed in her chair.

She had apparently called at the Villa Oleander that morning, after hearing the news of the murder from a hotel acquaintance, and had met Miss Moon.

'She wouldn't let me see you,' explained Persis. 'Seems you were asleep. The place appeared to be crawling with cops and your hostess was dealing with them with considerable firmness. She's quite a character. Glenn was there too. And Toby dropped around to ask after you. We all went upstairs and sat in the boudoir and had a quiet smoke, while the cops milled around in the drawing-room. It was quite a party.'

'Why was Glenn there? Were they——?'

'They'd been doing a bit of reconstructing the crime I gather,' said Persis, hailing a passing waiter and throwing him into temporary confusion by demanding rye-on-the-rocks:

'It seems that Glenn was their Public Enemy Number One, until someone tripped over a handful of valuables on the garden path. Will you have sherry or gin? Okay waiter, make it tomato juice.'

Amanda said: 'You mean they thought that *Glenn* had killed her?'

'Sure. Why not? After all, on his own say-so he was the last person to see her alive, and it seems that his wife's been tooting it all over town that he had an affair with the dame. They had it all doped out. Even the local cops have read that one about the secretary who is seduced by the boss!'

'Did you ever see Monica Ford?' demanded Amanda heatedly.

'Nope. But I've heard plenty from those who had that privilege. I gather that she would not exactly have reached the finals of the Beauty Contest at Mud Flats, Pennsylvania. Am I right?'

'You are. She was plain and efficient and thick and thirty-five-ish, and——'

'I get you, honey. But I guess the cops must have been reading *Candid Confessions,* for they were quite a little taken with their theory. Seems they thought the guy had gotten tired of amorous games around the office and had tried to toss the gal aside like a soiled glove, and she wouldn't toss. So he upped and strangled her, left the corpse in Miss Moon's drawing-room, came on up to Hilarion and callously ate a hearty tea to celebrate. That was their theory and they were crazy about it.'

'They must be mad!' said Amanda. 'She hadn't been dead for any time at all. She was *warm!*'

'Yeah, I know. But they probably thought he just pretended to turn off to Nicosia and really turned back and followed the Normans to Kyrenia, whipped into Miss Moon's, strangled his secretary, sprang for his steed—I mean his Studebaker—and hey, for that mad ride for the border! Could be.'

Amanda said scornfully: 'How was he supposed to know that she would still be there? It sounds a lot of poppycock to me.'

'Well it blew a fuse early on. Seems the guy gave a lift to a couple of enlisted men just back of that turn, and they've turned 'em up and checked the times, and he couldn't have made it. Not unless he's mastered the art of being in two places at once. And then there was all that jade and junk lying around the garden path, and they figured that though he might indulge in a little murder, he'd probably draw the line at theft.'

'How did you hear all this?' demanded Amanda. 'Did Miss Moon tell you?'

'Good grief no! She was too busy telling the police what she thought of them. Glenn told me. I brought him back here with me and we had a few drinks and discussed this and that. I like that guy. It's a pity he's still carrying a torch for that wife of his. She sounds a bit screwy to me. Anyone who could leave a nice guy like Glenn, to elope with a set of ginger whiskers and a smell of turpentine, must be rocking on the rails with their signals mixed.'

Persis sipped her drink in silence for a moment or two and presently said thoughtfully: 'Steve was there too.'

'Where?' asked Amanda sharply.

'At your Miss Moon's this morning. That guy's a smooth operator. He's wasted on art. He ought to be giving Dulles and Eden a few lessons in diplomacy.'

'What do you mean?'

'When I gate-crashed your villa this morning,' said Persis with a reminiscent grin, 'the situation was a little complicated. Glenn was not taking too kindly to the suggestion that this Monica had been his mistress, and your Miss Moon was addressing the senior cop in a manner which many a high-school teacher would have envied. Then that housemaid of hers—or cook or what-have-you—was having hysterics in the kitchen, and the boot-boy was offering to fight a cop who seems to have suggested that he might have tipped off a pal that the villa would be empty yesterday afternoon, so why not slide in and swipe a few trinkets? It was quite a situation and I doubt if U N O could have done much better. Then in strolls Steve like a flock of doves bearing olive branches, and in no time at all everyone is sitting around drinking vino and relaxing, and Miss Moon is calling the Head Cop her dear boy. Yes, it was certainly quite a performance.'

Persis lit a cigarette from a small diamond and platinum lighter and looked thoughtfully at Amanda through the smoke:

'You're in love with him, aren't you?'

'Who? Steve Howard? Don't be absurd! I hardly know him.'

'You sound almost convincing, honey—but not quite. And it isn't necessary to know someone to fall in love with them. In fact the less you know about 'em the easier it is.' There was a trace of bitterness in Persis' voice. 'Has he kissed you?'

She saw the vivid colour flood up into Amanda's face and said dryly: 'I see he has. Ah well, some girls have all the luck.'

'Persis,' said Amanda severely, 'don't you ever think of anything but love?'

'Not if I can help it,' said Persis candidly. 'I'm nuts about love! Romance is my business—and a very paying proposition I have found it.'

'Are you going to use everything that has happened here for one of your books?'

A shadow seemed to pass over Persis Halliday's face, and then she laughed. It was a short and rather bitter laugh.

'No. Not quite everything.'

Amanda looked at her curiously and said suddenly: 'Persis—are we real to you? Or are we—are we all just people acting out parts that give you ideas for stories?'

Persis leant back in her chair and blew a smoke ring at the ceiling. She said in a soft, abstracted voice: 'You know, it's queer that you should ask that. Sometimes I do feel that way. As if I was on the other side of a sheet of plate glass, watching a puppet show and thinking "that's interesting". Sometimes the people I write about seem more real to me than a lot of people I meet, because I know them and I own them. It's—I suppose it's a little like being God. I can make my characters do just what I want. Fall in love, get married, hate each other, jump through hoops. I can kill 'em off or make 'em achieve fame and fortune in a coupla' lines of print. But—but real people won't always do what one wants . . .'

Her voice sank to a half-whisper on the last words and she relapsed into silence, leaning back in her chair with her abstracted gaze on the darkening sky and the first stars that lay beyond the open windows, while the cigarette burned out between her fingers.

A soft, fluting voice made itself heard from the direction of the door and Persis dropped the stub of her cigarette into her glass and looked over Amanda's shoulder.

'Here comes Teeny-weeny-me,' she observed. 'Why, hullo Claire. Brought the baseball team with you I see.'

Claire Norman, accompanied by her husband, Alastair Blaine, Toby Gates and Lumley Potter, crossed the room and sinking into a chair, announced that she was exhausted. She appeared surprised at seeing Amanda and murmured a few soft words of sympathy on the subject of the *terrible* ordeal that Amanda must have been subjected to.

'We've just been to see Miss Moon,' she said. 'We thought you'd be there too of course, but Mooney said you'd gone out. She was rather secretive about it. She wouldn't say who with. I thought it must be Steve. I didn't think of Persis. Lumley, you're not going, are you?'

'Afraid I must,' said Mr Potter reluctantly. 'I said I'd be back around six, and it's well after seven, and——'

'*Poor* Lumley!' interrupted Claire in her soft, clear voice. She reached up a small hand and laid it on his arm in a brief gesture indicative of sympathy and understanding, and Mr Potter flushed pinkly.

Persis, who had watched this bit of byplay with considerable interest, caught Amanda's eye and winked, and Amanda bit back a laugh and turned hurriedly to Toby Gates who had seated himself on the arm of her chair and was inquiring solicitously as to her health.

Mr Potter removed himself, Alastair Blaine ordered a round of drinks, and George Norman asked Amanda to supper at their house:

'Would have asked you before,' he said, 'but didn't think you'd feel up to it. Be delighted if you'd come. Only pot luck of course. Claire, I've just asked Miss Derington to join the party for supper tonight.'

Claire Norman raised her delicate brows and smiled charmingly at Amanda, but Amanda received the sudden and distinct impression that she was not pleased, and said quickly: 'I'm so sorry, I'm afraid I can't come. I couldn't walk out on Miss Moon at such short notice. She had a horrid time yesterday, and today hasn't been exactly peaceful for her.'

'Of course,' sympathized Claire. 'We quite understand. Some other time perhaps.'

Toby said in a low voice: 'Why didn't you give me a ring last night and tell me what had happened? It must have been hellish for you. You know I'd have come up.'

'Thank you Toby,' said Amanda with real gratitude. 'But there wasn't anything you could do.'

'I gather Howard was there,' said Toby with a trace of resentment in his voice.

'He brought me back from Hilarion, that was why. Toby, did you really all call in on Miss Moon again this evening?' She indicated Claire and her entourage with a brief gesture of the hand.

'We just thought we'd look in and see how you were. We all happened to meet rather by accident up at the top of the town, and as it was only about two minutes' walk we went along. It's an astonishing house, isn't it? The old girl took us all over it. Simply crammed with stuff that would make an antique dealer drip at the mouth. Do you know that there's a Constable sketch in one of those bedrooms? Must be worth a packet. No wonder some enterprising burglar had a crack at it. The only thing I can't understand is why the whole shooting match wasn't pinched years ago. I don't believe the old girl would have noticed it if it had been!'

Claire was saying, '——Toby will tell us. Toby dear, is it true that your Regiment is coming here in the autumn? Alastair is being very cagey and Security-Minded about it. As if it mattered!'

Major Blaine laughed. 'I'm not being in the least cagey. I don't know. And I bet Toby doesn't know either. It is commonly supposed that the policy of the Broadmoor graduate responsible for the placing of units is to decide all changes at the last possible moment with the aid of a pin, in the hope—only too frequently realized—of causing the maximum confusion not so much to the enemy but to the units involved. Amanda, now that you've dealt with that tomato mush, how about trying the effects of a gin and lime?'

Amanda smiled and shook her head. 'No thank you, Alastair. I'm afraid it's time I was going. I don't like to keep Miss Moon waiting.'

'Nonsense. You've masses of time for another drink.'

'This is my round,' said Toby quickly. He rose and went to the bell and Alastair Blaine crossed over, and having removed Amanda's empty glass took Toby's place on the arm of her chair and began to make desultory conversation to which Amanda paid little attention.

She was watching the clock and wondering if Steven Howard had returned, and if he too was dining with the Normans? If so it would be too late to tell him about Anita Barton tonight, and she would have to let it keep until tomorrow.

She became aware that Alastair Blaine had lowered his voice to an undertone and had asked her some question. Amanda jerked her gaze from the clock and looked at him.

'I—I'm sorry, Alastair. What did you say?'

Alastair glanced quickly at the four other members of the party, but George was explaining the intricacies of cricket to Persis, and Claire and Toby were discussing a mutual friend in Alexandria. His gaze came back to Amanda and he asked a low-voiced question that was an echo of one that Amanda had already heard once that evening:

'Is it true,' asked Alastair Blaine, 'that something off Anita Barton's dress was found by the police last night?'

'Who told you that?' asked Amanda, startled. 'Did Miss Moon?'

Alastair shook his head. 'No. Claire told me.'

'*Claire?* How did she know?'

'Seems that Barton told her. He rang up in a bit of a stew last night and wanted her to go down and see his wife or Lumley and warn 'em to burn the dress or bury it or get rid of it somehow. Didn't dare go himself for fear the police were tailing him. But I think he must have been a bit worked up to suggest it, as Claire isn't exactly sympathetic to Mrs Barton. However, she and George have always been pretty good friends of his so I suppose he felt that in the special circumstances she might rally round for his sake, if not for Anita's.'

'And did she?'

'No,' said Alastair Blaine slowly, and frowned.

'She seems to have made it her business to tell a good many

other people,' said Amanda tartly. 'Is that why you were down at Lumley Potter's?'

Alastair Blaine looked startled.

'I thought I saw you on the balcony,' explained Amanda.

'I did drop in for a minute,' admitted Major Blaine uncomfortably, 'I thought someone should tip her off. But she wasn't in, and Lumley said he'd already told her. Don't know how he got hold of it. Then we met the Normans and Toby in the town and went up to see you. I thing Claire wanted to find out from Miss Moon if it were true. But your peculiar old hostess wasn't giving anything away. *Is* it true?'

Amanda hesitated, but before she could reply Claire looked up and called out in her sweet, flutting voice:

'Steve! What have you been doing with yourself? You're looking very well dressed. Is this in honour of dining with us?'

Amanda turned quickly, aware of an odd breathlessness.

Mr Howard had not, apparently, been occupying himself with art. His hair was unusually smooth, and in place of his normally somewhat casual attire he wore a thin checked suit. He had, it is true, removed the coat, which he carried slung over one shoulder, but his silk shirt was impeccable and he wore the tie of a famous public school.

'No,' said Steve smiling lazily down at Claire. 'Nothing short of a white tie and tails could do justice to that, but as I omitted to pack 'em, this is the best I can do. And damned hot it is too.'

Persis said: 'Where have you been, Steve?'

'Troodos,' said Steve, and offered no further comment.

'*Troodos?*' exclaimed Claire surprised. 'Do you mean you've been the whole way there and back this afternoon? Whatever for?'

'Oh, just to see a man about a dog,' said Steve amicably.

He pulled up a chair and sat down, stretching his long legs before him and driving his hands deep into his pockets.

Claire smiled archly at him and said: 'I don't believe a word of it! Who is she, Steve? I am quite sure that you would never have dressed up in a suit for any mere male—unless you've been to see the Governor, of course!'

She laughed, as though such an idea was preposterous, and Steve grinned at her and turned to George Norman with some query as to whether there was any fishing obtainable in the Island? George rose to the bait with the alacrity of a trout in May and Claire's question remained unanswered.

Persis stood up and said: 'Well I'm for a bath. Toby, collect me in about half an hour and we'll walk up to Claire's.'

Amanda looked at the clock again and rose hurriedly to her feet. 'I'm afraid I must be going too,' she said, addressing the company in general. 'I hadn't realized it was so late.'

George said: 'Change your mind and come on to supper.'

Amanda smiled and shook her head, and Steve, who had risen, said: 'I'll see you home,' thus checkmating Toby Gates who had been about to make a similar suggestion.

Amanda, catching Persis Halliday's amused and mocking eye, said a little stiffly: 'Please don't bother. It's no distance, I can easily go by myself.'

'I'm quite sure you can,' said Steve equably, 'but as I have sundry messages to deliver to Miss Moon, I might as well go up now as later.'

'What messages?' asked Amanda. 'Can't I take them?'

'One or two things about the inquest. It's for eleven tomorrow in Nicosia, and we shall all have to put in an appearance.' He grinned at Amanda with a good deal of comprehension in his gaze and said: 'Of course if you are averse to my company, I can always give you three minutes' start.'

'Don't be ridiculous,' said Amanda with dignity, and walked towards the door.

'Dinner at 8.15, Steve,' Claire called after him. 'Don't be late.'

'I won't.'

Persis said: 'Goodnight honey. Enjoy yourself!' And then they were crossing the hall and a moment later were out in the warm moonlight under a sky that was thick with stars.

Amanda started off at a brisk pace, but as Steve refused to be hurried she was compelled to slow down as the only alternative to having him wandering up the road a yard or so behind her—a proceeding that must appear more than a little ridiculous.

'That's better.' approved Steve, linking his arm casually through hers. 'I have had a tiring day, and just at the moment a marathon race is not in my line. What did you want to see me about?'

Amanda checked and stumbled. 'How did you know I——?'

'No, I am not omniscient, worse luck,' said Steve regretfully. 'The girl at the desk told me that a young lady had been inquiring for me. She added a description that was flattering but reasonably accurate, and a natural modesty forbade me to suppose that all you required was the pleasure of my company. What is it?'

Amanda hesitated, frowning and uncertain.

'Changed your mind?' inquired Steve.

'No,' said Amanda doubtfully. 'Perhaps there isn't anything in it, but Mrs Barton came to see me this evening——'

Steve Howard's leisurely pace did not alter but Amanda had a fleeting impression that the muscles of the arm that was linked through hers had tightened for an infinitesimal moment.

'Did she indeed? What about?'

Amanda told him, repeating that short conversation word for word as accurately as she could remember it. Steve made no comment, except to ask her if she had mentioned the finding of the small linen flower to anyone.

'No,' said Amanda. 'It was Glenn.'

This time there was no mistaking the sudden rigidity of that arm, and perhaps Steve was aware of it, for he released Amanda's arm and thrust his hands into his pockets.

'Ah, the hero boy,' he remarked satirically. 'So he blew the gaff, did he? Now I wonder why?'

Amanda explained the circumstances, her voice quick and indignant, and Steve said caustically: 'Dear Glenn would appear to make quite a habit of getting his girlfriends to pull his chestnuts out of the fire for him.'

'Why must you always sneer at him?' demanded Amanda with some heat. 'I know you all think he's a fool not to say "good-riddance" to Anita, but he can't help it if he's still fond of her. You can't stop loving people just because you want to. It's nothing to do with sense or logic or——'

She stopped suddenly and Steve gave her an odd sideways look and said: 'You do rush to his defence, don't you? No; love has nothing to do with sense and even less with logic. In fact, taking it all round, it is an infernal nuisance and a booby trap laid by Mother Nature with a view to spreading alarm and confusion, defeating the ends of justice and leading inevitably to over-population and the atom-bomb.'

Amanda laughed and Steve said sadly: 'It is no laughing matter I assure you. Just as it becomes vitally necessary to keep one's eye on the ball, along comes a naked and nauseous infant with a brain suitable to its tender years, whom someone has inadvisedly armed with a lethal weapon in the form of a bow and arrow. And *whang!*— there is a spanner in the works.'

'Are you speaking from personal experience?' inquired Amanda with interest.

Mr Howard sighed. 'Yes, alas!' he looked down at her and grinned. 'In fact you can take it that my recent crispness on the subject of dear Glenn is caused by the demon of jealous gnawing at my vitals. No one ever rushes to my defence or sobs sympathetically over my woes. And neither do I win rounds of applause by risking my neck rescuing damsels from certain death. I find it very discouraging.'

Amanda looked at him doubtfully. There was a derisive gleam in his eye and she was quite sure that he did not mean a word of what he had said. Or was there, perhaps, a grain of truth in it?

They had reached the turn down to the Villa Oleander and Amanda noted that once again there was a man standing in the shadow of the wall, lighting a cigarette. It was not the same one who had been there when she had passed earlier that evening, but there was about him the same indefinable suggestion of deliberate and observant loitering that the other man had had.

The quiet, tree-lined road was white with moonlight, but the pavement was a dark patchwork of shadows and Amanda was suddenly intensely grateful to Steven Howard for insisting on accompanying her. It would not have been pleasant to walk through those black shadows alone.

Steve stopped at the gate, glanced at the luminous dial of his watch and said: 'See you tomorrow at the inquest. Don't let them faze you and don't get led off into side issues. Just answer the questions in as few words as possible and lay off unnecessary detail. Keep it short and you'll be okay. Goodnight.'

Amanda said: 'But I thought you wanted to see Miss Moon.'

'She'll have been told all about it by now. You were being a bit haughty about accepting my offer to escort you, so I had to bring pressure to bear. Be seeing you.'

He turned away and Amanda said: 'Steve——

Steve Howard stopped and turned rather slowly. 'Yes?'

Amanda said: 'It *was* you who took those things from the cabinet, wasn't it? The——'

Steve took a swift stride towards her and the palm of his hand was hard and warm over her mouth. She saw him throw a quick look left and right into the shadows and draw a short breath of relief. He dropped his hand and said low and tersely: 'What makes you think that?'

'The Fabergé egg,' said Amanda in a whisper. 'I noticed it in the cabinet just before I—before I found Monica Ford. The diamonds glittered——'

'*Damn!*' said Mr Howard softly.

He looked down at Amanda and the moonlight showed a deep crease between his brows.

'Have you mentioned that to anyone?' he demanded curtly.

Amanda shook her head.

'Then don't! Not to anyone at all—do you understand?' His voice held a large edge of command.

'Yes,' said Amanda in a whisper.

Once again he turned his head to look into the shadows and then he shrugged his shoulders in a faintly fatalistic gesture and turned and walked quickly away, his footsteps audible in the silence long after his tall figure had been swallowed up by the shadows.

16

'Is that you dear?' called Miss Moon, peering over the banisters of the upper hall. 'I shall be down in a moment. Tell Euridice we will dine at once.'

Amanda delivered the message to the kitchen and went upstairs to brush her hair. She came down to find Miss Moon awaiting her in the dining-room, arrayed in a regal robe of yellow velvet and wearing a magnificent parure of topazes that would have been greatly improved by cleaning.

Amanda looked down a little guiltily at her own short cotton frock and apologized for not changing.

'Nonsense dear. You look exceedingly nice as you are, and had you delayed to change, the soup would have been cold. I only change from habit. Dear papa would have considered it most odd had I not, but I often think how foolish I am to continue doing so. What did Anita wish to see you about? Such a pity she should have called just then, for Claire and several of your friends dropped in not so very long afterwards. I had a most social evening. They inquired so kindly after you: although I fear that on Claire's part it was less a visit of condolence than of curiosity. But perhaps I am being unkind. That Major Blaine is a very quiet, pleasant-mannered man. His wife committed suicide I hear—so tragic for him. It seems that she——But of course dear, you know all about it. You were on the same boat. Quite dreadful.'

'Yes,' said Amanda in a colourless voice. She did not in the least wish to discuss the death of Julia Blaine, and hoped that Miss Moon would not pursue the subject. Miss Moon did not. She was far more interested in the fact that Lumley Potter had had the effrontery to accompany Claire and her friends to the Villa Oleander.

'*Such* impertinence, dear! I have always considered him a most tiresome man. Spiritual aromas indeed! Anyone who can depict our enchanting harbour in a *welter* of dirty browns and blacks—and that particularly unpleasant shade of Prussian blue—I cannot but feel to be lacking in *honesty*. And when he knows quite well how fond I have always been of Glenn—not to mention Anita—his action in calling at this house becomes quite inexplicable. Naturally I could not turn him from the door; particularly as Claire had brought him. But I let him see *quite* plainly that I considered his visit an unwarrantable intrusion. He did not look at *all* comfortable,' added Miss Moon with satisfaction.

Amanda was suddenly reminded of something that Anita Barton had said about Lumley Potter and Claire, and she turned to Miss Moon and said abruptly: 'Do you think he wants to marry Mrs Barton?'

'Marry Anita?' said Miss Moon as though such a thing had never occurred to her. 'I am quite sure he does not.'

'Then why do you suppose he ran off with her?'

'I do not think he did—though of course I may be wrong. I think Anita ran off with him. Just to make a scandal. So that Glenn would divorce her. She is obviously quite determined, for reasons of her own, to obtain her freedom; though I am convinced that her object cannot be marriage with Lumley Potter. But Anita—as I think I told you—has a strangely childish streak. When she wants something, she wants it badly and at once and without counting the cost. And you would be surprised, dear, what silly and quite childish things many people will do when their tempers and emotions get the upper hand of them. Things that they would never *dream* of doing if only they would give themselves time for reflection.'

'No I wouldn't,' said Amanda sadly. 'I'm just as bad. I lost my temper and slapped someone across the face the other day. I didn't think that anyone ever really did things like that.'

'Mr Howard,' said Miss Moon placidly. 'It left quite a mark did it not? I own I was interested. Such a dear boy! What had he done to provoke you?'

Amanda laughed, and followed the laugh with a frown. 'He asked me if I'd fallen in love with Glenn Barton.'

'What a foolish question!' said Miss Moon. 'But then gentlemen are often *so* unobservant, dear. Even the most intelligent of them. And when they are jealous they can behave with quite surprising stupidity. Look at Lumley Potter, who has always been devoted to Claire. Not that I consider *him* intelligent: quite the reverse! I imagine that Mr Howard thought that you had laid claim to that flower of Anita's to please Glenn.'

Amanda said: 'Do you notice everything, Miss Moon?'

'Oh I wouldn't say that, dear—but I hope that I am not *too* unobservant.'

'How did you know that it belonged to Mrs Barton?' inquired Amanda curiously. 'Had you seen her in that dress?'

'No,' said Miss Moon. 'Not to my knowledge. But I was aware that both you and Glenn had recognized it, and when I saw him look at you like that of course I knew at once that it must be something of Anita's. I supposed that you had seen her wear it.'

Miss Moon selected a peach and peeled it while Amanda wondered how many other things Miss Moon had noticed and had kept to herself?

'Claire had heard about it too,' said Miss Moon presently. 'She was trying to pump me. I soon put a stop to that! I imagine Glenn, poor boy, must have asked her to warn Anita. He should have known Claire better. But then, as I have said, gentlemen are lamentably unobservant in such matters, and I do not think that Glenn is a particularly good judge of character, or he would have seen through Claire years ago. Let us take coffee in the drawing-room.'

She rose with a clash of bracelets and jewellery, and over the coffee informed Amanda that a police officer had called earlier to notify her that both of them would be expected to attend the inquest on Monica Ford the following morning.

'Only a formality, my dear,' said Miss Moon. 'Nothing to worry about. I understand that all those who were at Hilarion that afternoon have also been asked to attend. I cannot think why. Corroborative evidence on the times of arrival and departure I suppose. Even Lumley and Anita have been requested to be present. Quite unnecessary I should have thought. So hard on poor Glenn.'

Miss Moon turned the conversation on to general topics and shortly after nine o'clock expressed her intention of retiring to bed:

'I feel that we could both do with an early night, dear.'

Amanda was feeling far from sleepy, but she had no intention of remaining alone in the shadowy drawing-room with those shimmering circles of looking-glass that had reflected Monica Ford's lifeless hand.

Euridice had already retired to bed—Andreas slept out—and Miss Moon turned out the lights, closed and bolted the french windows and went into the dining-room to fetch a jug of barley water off the sideboard, the train of her yellow velvet dress trailing regally behind her and collecting a small wash of dust.

'I usually take a jug of this up with me to my bedroom during the hot weather,' said Miss Moon. 'Can I offer you a glass of anything, dear? No? Then let us turn out the lights.'

Amanda relieved her of the jug and carried it upstairs to her room, and Miss Moon said: 'Thank you, dear. Just put it on the bedside table.'

Amanda did so and turned to look about her. She had not been inside Miss Moon's bedroom before, except for those few frantic minutes on the previous evening, when she had had no attention to spare for her surroundings. Miss Moon's bedroom was worth a second look, comprising as it did a magnificent mixture of French baroque and Victorian mahogany. The massive dressing table and wardrobes belonged to the later period, while the carved and gilded vastness of the canopied bed would have done credit to the Pompadour in her hey-day.

On either side of the bed two marble-topped console tables supported a clutter of books, bottles and other oddments, and on one of them stood a massive silver candelabrum that had been converted into a bedside lamp. Amanda switched it on, and the warm glow illuminated the jumbled contents of the table and glinted on gilded garlands and the worn brocaded hangings of the bed.

Something moved on the pillow and she gasped and took a quick step backwards. But it was only Euridice's grey cat, who had been lying curled up in a warm nest formed by an elderly lace-edged bed jacket.

'What is it, dear?' inquired Miss Moon, looking round. 'Oh it is that dreadful cat! Chase it off, dear. I do wish that Euridice would get rid of it. I suppose that there will now be hairs all over the pillow. How very vexing.'

Amanda scooped up the cat, deposited it in the passage, and returning, shook out the bed jacket and picking up the pillow beat off the few short grey hairs that clung to it.

She bent to replace it and stood suddenly very still, her eyes wide with shock and an icy prickle of panic running down her spine.

Something had been lying under that pillow. An insignificant object that was yet horribly familiar.

A small bottle containing a few white tablets and bearing a red poison label.

But it could not be the same one! It could not possibly be! She had not brought it away with her. Steven Howard had taken it. He had wrapped it carefully in his handkerchief and had put it into the pocket of his dressing-gown. Yet it was the same bottle—or its twin.

Amanda found that she was shivering, and she caught her lip hard between her teeth to stop it trembling.

Miss Moon had seated herself before her dressing table and was engaged in removing various necklaces, bracelets and rings and re-placing them in an old-fashioned and much worn morocco jewel case the size of a small hatbox. She was still talking, but the flow of her words slid over Amanda without making any impression on her. She could only stare and shiver.

Discovering that she was still holding the pillow, she laid it down carefully on the bed and reached out a shrinking hand for the bottle. But just before she touched it she remembered what Steve had said about finger-prints, and stopped.

There was a small, crumpled lace-edged handkerchief on the table beside Miss Moon's bed, and Amanda picked it up and lifted the bottle with it, holding it with extreme care.

She looked at Miss Moon's unconscious back and suddenly her brain seemed to clear, and she knew——

She knew that there would be no finger-prints on that bottle and just exactly why it had been placed there.

There was to have been a repetition of a scene that had been planned to take place in a cabin of the S.S. *Orantares*. But this time it would be Miss Moon and not Julia Blaine who would die. Miss Moon who should have been at Lady Cooper-Foot's bridge party, but had stayed at home instead, and who might therefore have heard or seen something or someone at the hour that Monica Ford had died. Miss Moon who knew and noticed so much and who might be waiting her chance to say a word that might lead to the hanging of Monica Ford's murderer . . .

She would have laid her head on that single down pillow and have felt the small hard lump of the bottle, and would have removed it, looked at it in some surprise and put it aside until the morning—as Julia would have done.

Amanda could almost hear the coroner's verdict. Elderly and eccentric lady, shocked by Miss Ford's murder and distressed by the consideration that her own refusal to keep her house locked was responsible for it, felt herself unable to face a public inquiry and allowed the tragedy to prey on her mind, and the recent suicide of Mrs Blaine to suggest a way out. Yes, it would have been something like that. And but for Euridice's cat and the fact that Amanda had carried up the jug of barley water for her, Miss Moon would have been found dead in the morning.

The barley water!

Amanda whirled round and stared at it. Someone who knew that Julia drank lemon juice and water had made use of that knowledge to disguise the acidity of a poison. Because Miss Moon drank barley water, had that someone laid the same trap for her? There was no innocent iced drink on Miss Moon's bedside table, but there was an empty glass—and the jug that Amanda herself had placed there.

Amanda forced herself to speak, waiting until Miss Moon ceased talking, and not having heard one word that she had said.

'May I have some of your barley water please?' Her voice sounded high-pitched and like a gramophone record, as though it did not belong to her.

Miss Moon turned. 'Why, of course dear. Help yourself.'

Amanda said: 'There's a glass in my room. I'll take some if I may and bring the jug back.'

'Do, dear.'

Amanda thrust the small bottle in its crumpled handkerchief into her pocket and picked up the jug. Once in her own room she filled her own glass from it, her hands shaking so badly that the liquid splashed on to the table. She poured the remainder out of the window, and ran down the passage to the bathroom where she turned on both taps and rinsed the jug again and again. Having dried it on a towel she half-filled it with cold water, and returned to Miss Moon; her face chalk white and her hands still shaking uncontrollably.

'I'm most awfully sorry,' explained Amanda breathlessly, 'but I'm afraid I've spilt your barley water. I've brought you some water instead.'

Miss Moon tutted indulgently and said that Amanda was not to bother about it.

'I—I have to telephone someone,' said Amanda, finding it difficult to keep her voice under control. 'Something I have to ask about. Do you mind?'

'No dear, of course not. You know where the telephone is, do you not? Now don't stay up too late. You are not looking at all well.'

Amanda said goodnight and left the room hurriedly, shutting the door behind her and standing for a moment with her back to it, fighting off an absurd feeling of faintness and aware that her heart was beating unpleasantly fast.

The stairs stretched down into the blackness below, and she was suddenly afraid to go down into the darkness of the deserted hall and past the open doorway of the drawing-room where Monica Ford had died. Supposing that there was someone hiding there, waiting to make sure that Miss Moon died too? Waiting to make sure that they were safe for ever from Miss Moon's observant eyes and chattering tongue?

But of course that was absurd! Whoever had laid that deadly trap for Miss Moon would make certain of being as far away as possible from the Villa Oleander that night. There was nothing to be afraid of. Nothing except the darkness and the silence . . .

Amanda set her teeth and forced herself to walk down that long dark stairway, remembering as she did so that other stairway and the footsteps that had crept down behind her. She groped her way to the electric light switch, and a moment later the hall was flooded with soft light from the few candle bulbs in the dusty crystal chandelier that hung from the high ceiling.

The passage off the hall yawned shadowy and silent, and facing it the door stood open on to the dark drawing-room. Amanda shivered and walked resolutely down to the end of the passage, and after a few moments of ineffectual groping, found the switch of the small lamp that hung above the telephone.

It took an absurdly long time to find the number she required. The pages of the telephone book fluttered in her unsteady hands and her fingers refused to obey her, but she found it at last.

It was George who answered the phone:

'Who? . . . Oh, Howard. Yes, he's here. Do you want to speak to him?'

'Yes please,' said Amanda, trying to keep the fear and urgency from her voice; trying to speak quite calmly.

'Who is it?' George's voice was maddeningly loud and slow. 'Who? I can't hear you. Amanda?—Oh, Miss Derington! Sorry; didn't recognize your voice. Like me to give him a message? Or would you rather——'

The receiver was abruptly removed from his grasp and Steve's voice said crisply: 'What is it, Amanda?'

'*Steve!*' Amanda's voice wavered suddenly and she clutched at the edge of the table to steady herself. 'Steve, I must see you! Could you—could you come here? At once. I know it's late but—Steve *please!'*

Mr Howard's voice said cheerfully and surprisingly: 'Oh she does, does she? I can't have made myself clear. Perhaps I'd better come around and have a word with her. No, tell her it's no trouble at all. I'll be right along.'

There was a click and he had rung off.

Amanda stared stupidly at the receiver in her hand and was just about to ring the number again and tell him that he had not understood her, when it dawned on her that Steve was once again manufacturing an alibi for the benefit of those who might be unduly interested.

She replaced the receiver slowly, but she could not return to the hall. There were too many doors leading off the hall into too many dark and silent rooms. Too many old, beautiful, silvery mirrors that reflected her and watched her . . . as they had watched Monica Ford.

The passage was narrow and bare and smelt strongly of dust and boot-polish and faintly of garlic, and the house was uncannily silent: it did not creak or stir as many houses do after dark. And outside it the windless moonlight night was as silent and as still as the house.

Amanda was seized with a sudden fear of that silence. Surely she should be able to hear Miss Moon moving about in her room? Or had there been another glass somewhere in that room? A glass that she had overlooked? Was Miss Moon even now lying sprawled face downwards on the floor like Julia Blaine? Like Monica Ford——?

Amanda ran down the short passage and raced up the stairs, taking them three at a time, and burst into Miss Moon's room, white with panic.

Miss Moon, clad in a nightgown reminiscent of the one in which the Princess Victoria was popularly supposed to have received the news of her accession, was seated before her dressing-table rolling her hair up in curl-papers. She said: 'What is it, dear?' without looking round.

Amanda clung to the door handle and strove to regain her breath.

'N-nothing. I—thought I heard you call.'

'Probably someone in the road, dear. Did you put your call through?'

'Yes,' said Amanda, her eyes searching the room and seeing no sign of any other glass. 'Steve—Mr Howard—asked if he could come round for a minute or two. About—about the inquest I think. I hope you don't mind.'

'Of course not, dear. I did not realize that it was Mr Howard you were telephoning. Such a delightful man. You will find biscuits and brandy in the sideboard. Gentlemen usually like brandy; although I have often wondered why. *So* unpleasant—except in hard sauce. Do not let him keep you up too late.'

'I won't,' promised Amanda.

She went slowly downstairs again, feeling a little foolish and wondering if she had not, after all, dragged Steve Howard out on a fool's errand? Supposing there was nothing in the barley water, and that the bottle contained some drug that Miss Moon took for her migraines? She should have questioned Miss Moon about it instead of leaping to wildly melodramatic conclusions. Her nerves must be badly on edge and Steve would undoubtedly laugh at her. She had better go up at once and ask Miss Moon.

She turned back, but as she did so someone came rapidly up the flagged path and took the six stone steps in two. The fall of the knocker echoed through the quiet hall and Amanda went slowly to the door, thinking that if it was Steve Howard he must have run most of the way.

If he had, he gave no sign of it. He looked very tall and slender silhouetted against the bright moonlight, and he did not appear to be in the least out of breath. He studied Amanda's face for a long moment and the tension went out of his own.

He said amicably: 'Are you coming out or am I coming in?'

Amanda flushed and drew back, and he strolled into the hall and closed the door behind him. He looked about him, glanced up at the landing above the staircase, and evidently deciding that the hall was an unsuitable spot for conversation, moved towards the drawing-room.

'No!' said Amanda sharply. 'Not in there.' She went past him into the dining-room and switched on the lights.

The dining-room was friendly and lacked the shadowy corners and the ugly memories of the drawing-room. Steve followed her in and shut the door.

'Well, Amarantha? What is it now? Judging from your voice on the telephone I rather expected to find another body on the door-step.'

'I'm sorry,' said Amanda uncertainly. 'I found something and I got into a panic. And now I think that perhaps it doesn't mean anything after all, and that I've made a fool of myself.'

'Let's see it,' suggested Steve, and held out his hand.

Amanda drew the small bundle of lace and cambric from her pocket and handed it over. He accepted it without much apparent interest, unfolded it, and then stood very still.

A minute ticked away into the silence and there was no longer any trace of casualness in Steve Howard's face or his tall figure, and his eyes were wide and bright and intent. Presently Amanda heard him let his breath out between his teeth and he lifted his head and looked at her.

'Where did you find this?'

Amanda told him, and he listened without interruption, his eyes on her face, and when she had finished told her curtly to fetch the glass of barley water. Amanda left the room and came back a few moments later, breathing a little unevenly, with the glass in her hand.

Steve was standing where she had left him. He had unscrewed the top of the bottle, and two small white tablets were lying in the full glare of the lamplight on the polished surface of the dining-room table. He took the glass from her hand, smelt it, and then wetted the tip of one finger in the contents and touched it to his tongue.

He made a quick grimace and jerking a handkerchief out of his breast pocket, rubbed it over his tongue. Amanda said breathlessly: 'Then it is poison?'

'H'mm?' said Steve in a preoccupied voice.

Amanda repeated the question and he looked at her as though he had momentarily forgotten her existence, and said impatiently: 'Of course it is.'

He pushed the glass away and sat down on the nearest chair with his elbows on the table and frowned at the two white tablets. Something about the handkerchief caught his attention and he reached out a hand for it and spread it flat. It was, or it had been, an expensive trifle. A monogram consisting of three entwined initials was embroidered in one corner, and the lace had been badly torn along one edge.

'A.B.H.,' said Steve pensively. 'Where did you get this, Amanda? It isn't yours.'

'It was on Miss Moon's table, by her bed,' said Amanda, leaning over to look at it. 'And it isn't A.B.H. The centre initial overlaps the other two. Its A.F.B.'

'Anita F. Barton in fact,' said Steve thoughtfully.

'Why, of course!' said Amanda suddenly. 'I remember seeing her drop it. She had it here, in the hall. I suppose Miss Moon picked it up and took it upstairs, meaning to ask whose it was.'

'Mrs Barton seems to be a bit careless with her possessions,' observed Steve grimly. 'Her husband's secretary is found murdered, and a bit of nonsense off Mrs Barton's skirt is discovered in this hall. And if Miss Moon had been found dead tomorrow morning, that handkerchief wouldn't have looked so good; however innocently it came to be there. 'Unless . . . I wonder——'

He twisted it absently about his hand, frowning the while, and after a moment inquired abruptly if Miss Moon always took a jug of barley water up to her bedroom at night.

'She told me that she usually did in the hot weather,' said Amanda. 'She doesn't seem to drink anything else. Euridice makes it fresh every day.'

'Have you ever drunk it?'

'No. Only Miss Moon. But no one else would know that.'

'Oh yes they would. I have a tolerably retentive memory, and someone, either you or Glenn Barton—I think both—mentioned the fact at that lunch party at the Dome. Which means that quite a few people knew of Miss Moon's addiction to barley water, and someone put the knowledge to good use.'

'Like—like Julia,' said Amanda, shivering.

'Julia?'

'The lemon juice.'

Steve's face was suddenly blank and unreadable. He looked at Amanda for a moment or two and seemed about to say something, but changed his mind.

Amanda said in a voice that was little more than a whisper: 'You thought that something like this might happen, didn't you?'

'Yes. It had occurred rather forcibly to me that whoever put paid to Monica Ford was going to be scared into next week by the news that Miss Moon had been in the house the entire time. We took certain precautions.'

'Then the house *is* being watched! I thought it was.'

'You could hardly miss it,' said Steve dryly. 'In fact, you were not meant to. The knowledge that the place was bristling with cops would, it was hoped, tend to discourage any rough stuff. And then,' he added bitterly, 'someone walks in right under our noses and plants this neat little booby trap. Mind if I touch you?'

He reached out and laid the tips of his fingers briefly against Amanda's arm.

'What's that for?' inquired Amanda, puzzled.

'For Luck. If it hadn't been for you and that cat of the cook's, Miss Moon would have gone the same way as Julia Blaine. In addition to which you appear to bear a charmed life. You ought by rights to be sliced into small sections and distributed in the form of amulets.'

Amanda said in a small, frightened voice: 'But if there are police watching the house they must know who came in——'

'My dear child,' said Steve impatiently, 'of course they know who came in! And that's the hell of it. I can give you a list myself. Barton was here for most of the morning, and during that time Mrs Halliday and young Gates called round to ask after you and stayed a considerable time. George Norman dropped in to tea and then Anita Barton came in to see you, casually shed her handkerchief on the premises and took you out for a walk. While you were out, a squad of sympathizers that included Claire Norman, Major Blaine and Lumley Potter called round and were actually taken on a conducted tour of the house. That makes quite a nice little list of people, all or any of whom could have easily dropped a slug of poison into the barley water and slipped that bottle under Miss Moon's pillow. The thing was a gift, and I ought to be shot for not thinking of it. I considered a good many other possibilities, but not a repeat performance of a previous flop.'

Amanda said: 'Mrs Barton couldn't have done it. There wasn't time. And she didn't go upstairs.'

Steve lifted his eyes from a contemplation of the exhibits before him and looked thoughtfully at Amanda.

He said: 'Let's hear about that visit of hers again. Details please. Exactly when did she arrive and how long was she alone in the hall and where was she standing when you first saw her? Everything.'

Amanda told him all that she could remember; hesitantly but in detail.

Steve leant back in his chair, drove his hands into his pockets and frowned at the ceiling: 'H'mm. I wonder. She would probably have had plenty of time to doctor the barley water, and as she knew Miss Moon fairly well the odds are that she not only knew about the stuff, but where it was kept. Thirty seconds would have been enough for that job. But from what you say, it sounds impossible for her to have made a quick trip to Miss Moon's bedroom and back in the time. Anyway, the risk would have been too great, for if you'd seen her coming down the stairs you would have been curious, to say the least of it.'

He brooded for a while, rocking his chair gently to and fro until it creaked protestingly, and presently he said in a softly meditative voice: 'I think a few words with the cook-general would be in order. I'll get on to that in the morning. However it begins to look as though Mrs Barton is in the clear, and that means . . .'

He did not finish the sentence, and presently began to whistle 'Sur le pont d'Avignon' very softly through his teeth.

Amanda waited for a minute or two and then, as he did not speak, asked anxiously: 'What does it mean?'

Mr Howard transferred his gaze from the ceiling to Amanda's white face and said thoughtfully: 'It means that one should not go to Birmingham by way of Beachy Head. In other words, if one wished to get from A to B with the minimum loss of time and temper, one should stick to the main road and not allow oneself to be lured down intriguing but unprofitable bypaths. An error to which I must regretfully plead guilty.'

'I don't understand,' said Amanda with a catch in her voice.

Steve returned the front legs of his chair to the floor with a crash and stood up:

'God forbid that you should! But I should have known better. I had the whole thing cold, but owing to the entirely fortuitous fact that a varied assortment of emotional crises got mixed into the works, I began to look at this thing from another angle. In fact from several other angles. A mistake, Amarantha. There was only one angle. Just as there was only one person who could possibly have been able to push you over the battlements at Hilarion.'

Amanda said in a small, frightened voice: 'Does that mean that you—you know who it is?'

'I think so,' said Steve soberly. 'But the difficulty is going to be to prove it. The obvious procedure of course is to tie up a kid with the object of luring the tiger. That would probably work all right. But I'm not sure that I'm a good enough shot.'

'You mean—you mean deliberately let a murderer have another try at killing her just so that you could see who it is? Steve, you can't! You can't risk it!'

Steve Howard looked down at her and his face and voice were suddenly and inexplicably raw with anger and bitterness:

'No!' he said savagely. 'I can't risk it. That's the damnable part of it. I should, but I daren't—because I've lost my nerve!'

He stared down at Amanda for a long moment as though he hated her, and then swung round violently and jerking open the door walked out of the room.

A minute or two later Amanda heard him strike a match, and followed him into the hall, bewildered and shaken by his sudden rage.

He was standing with his back to her under the dusty chandelier, the light turning his brown hair to bronze, and he must have heard her but he did not turn.

Amanda waited in silence, studying the back of his head and thinking that she could draw it with her eyes shut, and wondering why this should be so when she had only known him for so short a time? The smoke from his cigarette spiralled up into the still air and the scent of it mingled pleasantly with the smell of beeswax and dust and the tall orange lilies that filled a vast copper jar by the carved chest.

Presently he reached out a hand behind him and drew Amanda absently into the curve of his arm, still without turning his head.

He continued to stand quite still, holding her against him; staring ahead of him and drawing thoughtfully at his cigarette as though his mind were several hundred miles away—as indeed it was.

After a time he looked down, blew a smoke ring at the top of Amanda's head, released her and dropped his cigarette end into the jar of lilies:

'Time you were in bed, Amarantha. And quite time I got back to the Normans'. I am supposedly instructing Miss Moon in the procedure at an inquest, and there is no point in overdoing it. Do you think you can find me an empty bottle that'll take the remains of that barley water?'

'I can try,' said Amanda. She disappeared in the direction of the kitchen and presently returned with a bottle that had once contained cooking sherry.

Steve had gone back into the dining-room and was engaged in replacing the tablets and wrapping the small bottle in a sheet of paper.

'Is it the same stuff that killed Julia?' asked Amanda in a half-whisper.

'No. That would have been inviting odious comparisons.'

'But there would have been anyway. Because of that bottle——'

'You've forgotten something. You kept quiet about that first bottle. Which is why it was tried again—for the simple reason that having once kept your mouth shut you would have to continue to do so, or else land yourself in an exceedingly nasty spot indeed. An angle which I admit should have occurred to me, but didn't.'

Steve decanted the barley water into the sherry bottle with infinite care and pushed the empty glass over to Amanda.

'Run that under the tap half a dozen times, will you? Oh, and you'd better take this——' He tossed over Anita Barton's torn handkerchief. 'Ask Miss Moon about it in the morning and let me know what she says.'

Amanda nodded and put it in her pocket. She removed the glass and carrying it out into the pantry, rinsed it and left it on the draining board and returned to find Steve waiting for her in the hall.

He glanced at the clock and said: 'See you in court,' and pulled open the front door.

Amanda said with a catch in her voice: 'But aren't you going to call in the police?'

'What for?'

'To tell them about the poison, of course!'

Steve shook his head. 'No. I don't think we'll tell anyone for the moment. Not even Miss Moon.'

'But—but surely whoever did it will try again?'

'Oh, sure to. But not that way. It was a good idea, but it's backfired twice. Someone is due for an unpleasant headache tomorrow trying to work out what went wrong this time; and because they won't know they will lay off that tack and try another. And I think we can block anything else.'

He saw Amanda throw a quick look over her shoulder at the empty hall behind her and said: 'There's nothing to be frightened of tonight, dear, I promise you. The person who planted that stuff is going to make quite sure of being well in the public eye and surrounded by alibis up to a late hour tonight. Nor are they going to come near the place or ask any questions tomorrow. And in any case, the chaps who are watching this house won't let so much as a bluebottle past them between now and tomorrow morning.'

'They let you in,' said Amanda unsteadily.

'That,' said Mr Howard, 'is different. Word has gone round that

I am really Marilyn Monroe in disguise, and they are all hoping to get my autograph.'

He removed himself into the night and Amanda bolted the door behind him and went upstairs to bed; but not to sleep.

17

The inquest on Monica Ford was unexpectedly brief. The jury system did not prevail in Cyprus, and an apparently bored judge listened without much interest to the pathologist's report and an account of the police findings. But Amanda received the unpleasant impression that the perfunctory questions did not add up to lack of interest or any conviction that the comfortable theory that a casual thief had been responsible for the murder was necessarily correct. It seemed more as though the officials involved were acting under orders, and she wondered uneasily if someone was being lulled into a false sense of security.

The proceedings had been too smooth—too suave. The voices too silkily polite and the eyes too hard and watchful.

They were all there. Claire and George, Persis and Toby, Alastair and Glenn, Lumley and Anita, Steve, Miss Moon and herself.

Amanda had found that she too was watching them with furtive, frightened eyes, afraid that one face might betray surprise or fear at the sight of Miss Moon. But she had surprised no such expression and did not know whether to be relieved or sorry.

She and Steve Howard had described the finding of Miss Ford's body, and Glenn had told of his meeting with his secretary earlier that afternoon and explained about her brother's death and her recent agitation of mind. He had not looked at his wife, and no further questions had been put to him beyond asking him for the time of his departure from Hilarion and his arrival at Nicosia. The latter had been corroborated, according to the police, by the two young National Service Men to whom he had given a lift, and the various members of the picnic party had confirmed the times of his arrival and departure from Hilarion.

Miss Moon had stated that owing to an attack of migraine she had, in fact, been in the bedroom in the Villa Oleander throughout the afternoon, but had heard nothing beyond the sound of a woman's voice raised in apparent agitation some time during the earlier part of the afternoon.

They had accepted the statement without comment and had returned unexpectedly to Amanda. They had asked her four questions, and this time the suave voices had been considerably less suave.

Was it true that she had seen a great deal of Major Blaine in Fayid?

Was it true that Mrs Blaine had died in her cabin on the way to Cyprus?

Was it true that she had been alone in the drawing-room of the Villa Oleander for several minutes—perhaps five or even ten?— before Mr Howard had found her standing beside the body of Miss Ford?

What dress had she worn that day, and would she describe it?

The room had been stiflingly hot and airless and it was pleasant to get into the open again and feel a faint breath of breeze and smell the scent of sun-baked dust and flowering trees.

Miss Moon declined an invitation from the Normans to return to their house for a glass of sherry, and announced her intention of returning home immediately. Andreas was driving her in her own elderly car, and Toby had offered Amanda a lift. Miss Moon went over to talk to Persis Halliday, and someone touched Amanda's arm and she turned to see Glenn Barton.

'I haven't had a chance to talk to you before,' said Glenn in a low voice. 'I wanted to thank you. For saying what you did. I—can't tell you how grateful I am. I know I shouldn't have let you do it, but— well I think you're a brick!'

Amanda said quickly: 'Don't Glenn. Anyone would have done the same; but not many people would have risked their necks for me at Hilarion. And I never even thanked you for that.'

Glenn Barton smiled at her and held out his hand. 'Shall we call it quits?'

Amanda put her hand into his, and an exceedingly dry voice behind them said: 'I'm sorry to interrupt you, but I'd like a word with Miss Derington.'

Amanda snatched her hand away and turning quickly looked up into Steven Howard's face and experienced a sudden shock of dismay.

Steve was looking at her as though she were some complete and not particularly attractive stranger whom necessity compelled him to address, and his voice was cold and remote and entirely devoid of expression.

He said: 'I understand that you have a guardian who is at present somewhere in the Middle East. I suggest that you write to him as soon as possible and ask him to come over.'

Amanda stared at him, bewildered. 'But—but why?'

'Because it looks as though you are going to need some responsible person to advise you. You made a statement to the police two nights ago that was entirely untrue and which looks like leading a to a lot of trouble.'

He threw a glance of cold dislike at Glenn Barton, and continued curtly:

'In these circumstances I think that you would be well advised to let your uncle know what is going on, and let him decide if he thinks it is worth coming over or not. You won't find that it is in the least amusing being mixed up in a murder case in this part of the world.'

'But he's in Tripoli!' said Amanda.

'I know. Miss Moon told me. That's why I wanted to speak to you. I have a friend in the R.A.F. here who happens to be flying to Tripoli tomorrow, so if you can let me have a letter before midday tomorrow I'll see that your uncle gets it the same evening. He can probably pull enough strings to get here by Monday or Tuesday at the latest. Think it over.'

Steve turned on his heel and walked away and Amanda stared after him; helplessly aware that there were tears in her eyes, and restraining herself with a strong effort from running after him to catch at his arm and demand to know why he had looked at her and spoken to her like that? He could not be jealous of Glenn Barton!— he could not be. Couldn't he *see*——?

Glenn said soberly: 'He's right you know. You ought to let Mr Derington know about this. Would you like me to cable him instead?'

Amanda winked the tears from her eyes and said: 'I—I'll think about it.'

She did not believe for one moment that she was in any danger of arrest. The idea was too ludicrous to be entertained even for a second. She had not, as Glenn Barton and several others had, taken in the significance of those three final questions, and she did not think of them now. She could only think of Steve's face and voice and feel hurt and bewildered and angry.

A police officer came up and spoke to Glenn Barton and Glenn excused himself and they walked away together and re-entered the building.

There was a jingle of bracelets and Miss Moon patted Amanda's arm with a be-ringed hand and said affectionately: 'There, there dear. You must not mind. He is not in the least annoyed with you. Only with himself. And with Glenn of course. Gentlemen are *so* foolish!'

Amanda laughed a little shakily and said: 'You don't miss much, do you Miss Moon?'

'No dear. It is only the young who seem unable to see what is under their noses. Of course he knows quite well that you cannot really have the slightest interest in poor Glenn, but I think that he has a great deal on his mind that it annoys him to realize that he cannot prevent his attention being distracted by—by extraneous emotions, shall we say?'

'Not extraneous emotions,' corrected Amanda with a somewhat watery chuckle. ' "Unprofitable by-paths".'

'Is that what he said, dear? Well there you are! What did I tell you. And now, as I understand that Captain Gates wishes to drive you back to Kyrenia, I think I will return home. I shall be seeing you for luncheon.'

She turned away as Persis and Toby, who had been buttonholed by Lumley Potter, detached themselves at last and came towards Amanda. A few yards away George Norman, Alastair Blaine and Claire were standing on the kerb in a patch of shadow talking to Steve Howard who was sitting at the wheel of his car. Amanda noted resentfully that he appeared to be in excellent spirits and that the group beside his car, despite the fact—or possibly in reaction to it— that they had just been attending an inquiry into murder, were laughing at something that he had just said.

Anita Barton was standing by herself, a little apart. She was looking forlorn and unhappy and there were dark shadows under her eyes. Her usual air of defiant disregard for public opinion was entirely lacking and she looked noticeably ill at ease.

Amanda, studying her, saw that she was not quite steady on her feet and suspected that she had been drinking—perhaps to give herself courage to face the curious gaze of those who knew how much she had disliked her husband's secretary.

Persis, looking as usual like an advertisement for Saks, Fifth Avenue, caught Amanda's arm in an affectionate clasp and said in plangent tones: 'Well honey, how does it feel to be Suspect Number One?'

'Shut up, Persis!' said Toby crossly. 'Your humour is misplaced. Come on Amanda darling, we're all going along to the Normans' to get drunk. Only possible course, after a session like that.'

'Who's "all"?' inquired Amanda.

'The gang, honey,' supplied Persis. 'The Associated Society of Suspects. Little did I think when I decided on visiting the birthplace of Venus that all I should get handed in lieu of Love would be a coupla' corpses. It's time the boys at the Tourist Bureau rewrote that "Come to Sunny Cyprus!" stuff, and urged the prospective visitor to pack a gat and bring a lawyer with them.'

'The trouble with you, Persis,' said Toby sourly, 'is that you can't really believe anything you don't see with your own eyes. None of this is any more real to you than one of your own stories, merely because you never saw the bodies of either Julia Blaine or this secretary woman.'

'And did you, Toby dear?' inquired Persis softly.

'No. But Amanda did.'

Persis turned swiftly to Amanda and said contritely: 'He's right. I keep forgetting what heck and hades it must have been for you honey. What would like me to do? Prostrate myself on the pavement as a penance, or dedicate my next book "To Amanda, who stole all my beaux"?'

'Meaning Toby?' inquired Amanda with a smile. 'Was he your beau?'

'He certainly was. But humiliating as it is to own it, I am compelled to classify him as one of the ones that got away.'

'What you really mean is one of the ones you couldn't even bother to gaff,' said Toby, lifting one of her hands and kissing it.

'Toby! What a Continental gesture!' exclaimed Persis in mock admiration. 'I had no idea that——' She broke off and said rather sharply: 'Say, what's bitten Glenn?'

Amanda, turning to follow the direction of her gaze, saw Glenn Barton come quickly out into the sunlight, and realized what had prompted that startled exclamation.

Glenn's mouth was compressed into a tight line and he looked frightened and desperate. He stood for a moment looking about him with his eyes narrowed against the glare, and then seeing his wife walked swiftly over to her and put a hand on her arm.

'Anita——'

Anita Barton whirled about, her face white under its heavy make-up, and almost in the same movement she wrenched his hand from her arm and turned as though to walk away.

Glenn's hand shot out and he caught her arm again and swung her round to face him. 'Anita, please! I've got to talk to you. Just for a few minutes. It's for your own sake. Darling *please.*'

His voice was hoarse and desperate and he appeared to be entirely oblivious of the fact that his words were perfectly audible to everyone within a dozen yards and that at least as many inquisitive, interested or appalled pairs of eyes were openly watching him.

An ugly wave of colour flooded up into Anita Barton's livid face and she wrenched herself from his grasp and struck him across the face with the full force of her arm. She stood there for a moment staring at him, her breath coming fast, and then turned on her heel and walked rapidly away, leaving her husband standing in the bright sunlight with the red marks of her fingers showing clearly against his haggard face.

Persis was the first to recover herself and to rush in where angels might justifiably have feared to tread. She went swiftly across to him and said: 'Why, Glenn Barton—I thought you'd gone!' and slipping her hand through his arm almost forcibly turned him round: 'Have you got a car here? Because if you have, you've gotten yourself a passenger. Will you take me some place to get a drink before I drop dead from sunstroke?'

Glenn looked at her with dazed expression, and then seemed suddenly to focus her, for he smiled a stiff-lipped puzzled smile and said: 'Why—why of course, Mrs——?'

'Persis,' supplied Persis briskly. 'Is that your car over there? Good. Let's go.'

She led him firmly away, talking animatedly and at random, and the entertainment was over.

Steve Howard's car, followed by the Normans', slid away down the road. Lumley Potter hurried off in the wake of Anita Barton, and Amanda, suddenly deciding that she could not bear the prospect of a social gathering at the Normans', asked Toby to drive her instead to the Villa Oleander.

She was feeling mentally and physically exhausted, and by two-thirty was much inclined to follow Miss Moon's example and retire to her bedroom for a siesta. She was still considering the advisability of this course when she heard someone run quickly up the front steps and walk into the hall without knocking. It was Glenn.

'Amanda——!' He gave a quick gasp of relief at the sight of her. 'Amanda, can I talk to you please? Somewhere where we can't be overheard?'

His voice was jerky and uncontrolled and he appeared driven to the verge of collapse. Amanda looked at him for a long moment and then turned without a word and led the way into the drawing-room.

He came in after her, and shutting the door, leant against it.

'What is it, Glenn?'

'Anita,' said Glenn desperately. 'She won't see me. She doesn't understand! Amanda, I know she didn't kill Monica. I *know* she didn't. She may do rash, silly things, but she *could* not kill. I tell you I *know*. Good God!—who should know, if I don't? I don't pretend to know what she was doing in this house that day; she must have been here I suppose, because of that hellish flower. But whatever the reason, it can have had nothing to do with Monica Ford's death. She probably came in to see you, or Miss Moon, and found Monica dead, and panicked. No one could blame her for that!'

Amanda said urgently: 'Glenn, don't stand there. Come and sit down here and tell me what has happened. There's no sense in tearing yourself to pieces like this.'

Glenn laughed. It was a short, curiously wavering laugh that had no amusement in it. He walked unsteadily to the sofa and sank down on it as though his knees had suddenly given way under him.

Amanda looked at him with an anxious frown and left the room abruptly; returning a moment later with a glass containing a stiff proportion of Miss Moon's brandy. Glenn took it from her hand and gulped it down gratefully.

'You're a brick, Amanda. I seem to have said that a good many times of late, don't I?'

He looked up at her with a crooked attempt at a smile and Amanda said: 'What is it, Glenn? What has happened?'

'The police,' said Glenn wretchedly. 'It's that damnable flower. I think they've found out who it belongs to. They asked me if I'd recognized it. And—they asked a hell of a lot of other questions too. About her quarrel with Monica, and wasn't it true that she had told me that either I sacked Monica or she'd leave me, and—and that when I wouldn't, she had left me. They went over and over it. And then they—they wanted to know if I knew that she was friendly with Major Blaine——

'With *Alastair!*'

'Yes. Oh, I know they asked you the same thing, but that was just routine. This was far more serious.'

Glenn stood up abruptly, and walking over to the french windows stood staring blindly out across the garden, his back to Amanda.

He said in a harsh, jerky voice: 'They suggested that she knew him rather well and that—that his wife's death had made him a rich man. They pointed out that she—Anita——' His voice failed suddenly and Amanda saw his shoulders jerk in a small shudder. Presently he said in a more normal voice:

'They wanted to know if she could have got her hands on any poisons, and asked if it were true that her father had been a doctor. They—they seemed to know so many things. I got scared then, and I tried to talk to her, but she wouldn't speak to me——'

His voice held a sudden hurt, bewildered note. He turned and walked back to Amanda and stood looking down at her, his hands clenching and unclenching at his sides, and said in a flat, exhausted voice: 'I know I shouldn't ask you—I know it's an unforgivable thing to do, but I can't think of any other way out. Will you help me?'

'Yes,' said Amanda, lightly and quite steadily.

Glenn stooped quickly and lifting her hand, kissed it. 'Bless you!' There was a sudden break in his voice.

'What do you want me to do?'

'Persuade her to go away. Lumley's a useless fool. He'll be no help to her. She must get away for a while; to give them time to find out who really did kill Monica.'

'But Glenn, how can I! Persuade her to go where?'

'Lebanon. We have friends there who I know would take her in. And I've got a good many friends among the local fishermen here. I could arrange all that; if only she could be persuaded to go.'

Amanda looked at him with a crease between her brows. She said slowly: 'Glenn you know that won't work. You must know that if they are suspicious of her, and she disappears, it would only confirm their suspicions, because then they'd be sure that she had done it.'

'Yes,' said Glenn heavily. 'I know.'

'Then—then there must be some other reason why you want to get her away. What is it?'

Even as she spoke she was aware of a sudden suspicion that Glenn, whatever he might say to the contrary, was secretly and terribly afraid that his wife might just possibly be more deeply involved than he would admit.

Glenn lifted his tired, red-rimmed eyes to hers and looked at her for a long moment. And when he spoke it was in a voice that was so low that it was barely audible:

'Yes. There is another reason. There is something about all this that I don't understand, and it frightens me. You see I think—I think there is going to be another murder. An attempt at one anyway. If I'm right, there's got to be.'

He heard Amanda catch her breath and did not know that she was remembering that Steve had said almost those same words that night on the harbour wall.

Glenn said: 'Perhaps I'm wrong. I hope I am. But I'm beginning to think that there's—oh, I don't know—something behind all this. A plan. Something that may even have been worked out a long time ago. But now it hasn't gone right, and someone who still means to go through with it is getting frightened and needs a scapegoat. That's why I wanted to get Anita away. Because I think that she is playing straight into—someone's hands. Once she is safe with friends in the Lebanon, whoever is trying to hide behind her will have to think of something else. And then, if there is another attempt, we can tell the police at once where she is and why she went there. She'll be safe then. But I can't guard against something that I can only sense and guess at, but not see . . .'

His voice died out in a whisper and Amanda said quickly: 'You think you know who it is, don't you?'

He did not answer, and she repeated the question. Glenn's eyes came back to her again.

'Yes.'

'Who?' There was an odd tremor in Amanda's voice.

Glenn shook his head. 'I wouldn't tell you, and even if I were sure—and I'm not. It might be dangerous. And I can't be sure; not yet. I think that there is a way to find out, but I daren't use it as long as Anita is here to—to pin things on. Once it cannot possibly be her, then it must be someone else. You do see that, don't you? That would prove it.'

Amanda was conscious of a sudden stab of fear and a vivid recollection of Steve Howard's words about tying up a kid to lure the tiger. So Glenn intended to use himself to lure a tiger into another killing. And provided Anita was safely out of the Island, even if he failed to avoid death himself, it would at least be proof that she was in no way responsible. But he must not do that!—it was too fool-hardy a risk. Steve had said 'a killer knows quite well that even if he

kills a dozen people, or twenty, he himself can only hang once.'
Someone who had killed twice would not hesitate to kill again.

She said breathlessly: 'You can't do it, Glenn. If it's dangerous
for Anita it's just as dangerous for you.'

'Me? Oh I can look after myself. But Anita's got no one but that
ass Lumley. I've *got* to get her out of it. If I can only do that, without
anyone knowing or even guessing that she's gone, there is a chance.'

'But Glenn! even if you do, don't you see that if someone is
really trying to pin this on Anita, and—and nothing else happens,
and she has disappeared, their object is achieved?'

'Anita's suicide would achieve it in a far more final and satisfactory manner,' said Glenn grimly.

'*Suicide!*'

'Yes. An artistically staged suicide. It wouldn't be so very difficult to arrange. Anita found dead: verdict, suicide rather than face
trial and conviction for murder.'

'*No!*' said Amanda in a whisper. 'Oh no, it couldn't be——'

But she knew that it could. Once again she saw, in an ugly flash
of memory, Julia Blaine lifting an innocuous, frosted glass, drinking
from it, and dying. Felt again the little hard lump of a bottle under
her pillow, and stared down with wide, frozen eyes at a similar bottle
that had lain under Miss Moon's pillow only last night.

Glenn was quite right. Someone needed a scapegoat, and Anita
Barton's death—supposedly by her own hand—would tie up a good
many loose ends in a very neat and final manner.

Glenn said: 'She may refuse to go. If she does—well I shall just
have to think of something else. But if you can persuade her——'

'I'll try,' said Amanda unsteadily.

Glenn turned quickly away and began to pace up and down the
room, his hands in his pockets and frowning concentration on his
face. Presently he came to a stop in front of her again and said
abruptly: 'It must be tonight. Tomorrow may be too late. If she
agrees, would you help her to go? To see that she is safe.'

'Yes.'

'Can you drive a car?'

Amanda nodded.

'Then this is what we'll do. I'll leave a car on the road tonight—
against the kerb by that open bit of ground on the main road about
fifty yards below the turn out of this road, opposite that house with
the blue shutters. If you can get Anita to agree, tell her to take only
what she can carry, and to give out that she's got a bit of a headache

and intends to go to bed early. There's a little cove just beyond the five-mile beach on the road to Larnaca. Anita will know it. I'll get Yiannopoulos to be there with a boat not later than ten. It will mean leaving here around nine-thirty, which will give her an alibi from then on, as you would be with her. And as it's in the opposite direction from Nicosia, if anything should happen tonight they can't think——' He checked abruptly and then said: 'As soon as she's away, drive back here and leave the car in the same place. I'll pick it up later. There's only one other thing . . .'

Glenn pushed his hand wearily through his hair and his mouth twisted bitterly:

'You'll have to pretend that it's your own idea, or Miss Moon's. If she thinks that I've had anything to do with it, she won't touch it. Just at the moment I really believe that she'd rather be arrested for murder than be beholden to me. You see she doesn't understand. She thinks that she can do what she likes and get away with it. She doesn't realize that murder is a deadly thing.'

Once again the words brought an echo of Steven Howard. Steve standing in the bright moonlight on the harbour wall with his arms about Amanda and saying: 'Murder is a diabolical thing.'

Amanda said: 'I'll do my best.'

'I know you will. Make her see that it's serious. Don't let her brush it aside and take the line that nothing can really happen to her.'

Amanda nodded wordlessly.

Glenn said: 'I can't thank you enough, dear. I shouldn't risk getting you involved in anything; I know that. But I'm in a corner. If I could think of any other way out I'd take it; but I can't.'

He was silent for a moment or two, and then his mouth twisted in a wry smile and he said: 'I did try one other way. But it didn't work and I only made rather an ass of myself.' The smile faded and he said: 'The car will be there at nine o'clock. If Anita won't go well——'

He shrugged his shoulders and turned away, and a moment later Amanda heard the hall door close behind him.

18

Amanda came out on to the quay and walked slowly in the direction of the café at the corner of the harbour.

She felt curiously exhausted, but her exhaustion was mixed with a feeling of elation. Anita Barton had been difficult and suspicious and more than a little tipsy. But she had been frightened too, and it was her fear that had tipped the scales. She had agreed to go.

Amanda had succeeded in convincing her that she and Miss Moon were responsible for the scheme, and perhaps it was Miss Moon's name that had brought about Anita Barton's sudden capitulation. That, and the fact that Amanda had reported the gist of the questions the police had asked Glenn Barton about his wife, hinting mendaciously that they had been put to Miss Moon. She had also allowed it to be supposed that Miss Moon had arranged with the owner of a fishing boat to convey Anita away from the Island; it being unlikely that she herself would have been able to arrange such a thing.

She was to pick up Mrs Barton at a turn of the road near the Post Office at half past nine. Less than half an hour's driving would bring them to the beach where the boat was to wait, and that would give them an ample margin in which to get from the road to the shore—a matter of less than a hundred yards of rough ground and rocks.

The sun was setting in a blaze of gold and rose and apricot and the tall, picturesque houses that ringed the harbour threw long lilac shadows across the quays and the quiet water. A church bell was ringing and from the minaret of a mosque a muezzin intoned the call to prayer.

Amanda turned down the sea wall of the harbour and sat down tiredly on the warm stone. She wished desperately that she could discuss the coming night's work with someone. Glenn had not bound her to secrecy in the matter; but then he would not have considered such a course necessary. It was so obvious that if danger threatened Anita Barton, her departure must not be known or talked about.

Amanda thought longingly and resentfully of Steven Howard. Steve at least would be safe. She could have gone to him and asked for his advice and help. But she could not forget the caustic words that he had spoken only last night on the subject of Glenn Barton: 'Dear Glenn would appear to make a habit of getting his girlfriends to pull his chestnuts out of the fire for him.'

Mr Howard, apprised of the present situation, would undoubtedly consider that dear Glenn had no right to ask Amanda to involve herself in anything that might conceivably be dangerous, and be correspondingly scathing on the subject. He would, in addition, refuse to allow her to have anything whatever to do with the scheme, and might even take steps to prevent Anita Barton leaving the Island. However, even if she had wished to tell him, she could not, for she had passed him on her way to the harbour. He had been driving up the main road that led out of Kyrenia towards Nicosia, and though he had undoubtedly seen her, he had given no sign of having done so.

Amanda sighed and rested her chin on her hand.

A shadow fell across her and a cheerful voice said: 'What's eating you honey? Is it love—or indigestion?'

Amanda turned quickly. 'Persis you beast! You've nearly made me bite my tongue in half? No it isn't love—*or* indigestion. And nothing's eating me.'

'No? Then you're lucky!'

Persis subsided gracefully on the sea wall beside Amanda and said abruptly: 'Honey, I'm worried.'

Amanda turned sideways to look at her and saw that Persis was staring out to sea, her white forehead wrinkled in a frown.

'What's worrying you?'

'It's Glenn,' confessed Persis. 'You know, I like that guy. I like him quite a lot. He makes me feel all maternal; and that's something I've certainly never felt about anyone before. Maybe it's a sign of old age!'

Amanda said cautiously: 'What has he been doing now?'

'Acting like a fool!' said Persis with unexpected violence. 'Do you know what that crazy guy did this morning? He walked right back to see the police and confessed to murdering his secretary!'

'He *what?* He must be mad!'

'That's right. Plain cuckoo! I tried to drag him out. Told the boys he'd had a brain storm. But he had it all doped out and he was perfectly sober about it. Talked away as cool as a mint julep in July. Said he had not gone straight back to Nicosia from Hilarion after all. He'd lied about it. He'd waited out of sight until George's car had turned down to Kyrenia, and then followed it, gone into Miss Moon's, strangled this dame and streaked for home. So they asked him what about the two hitchhikers he'd given a lift to? And he had that taped too. Said he'd put back the hands of the dashboard clock to fake an alibi, and the boys had taken their time from that. He said it had been preying on his mind, and asked to be arrested.'

'What happened then?' demanded Amanda breathlessly. 'Why didn't they arrest him?'

'Because they aren't that dumb,' said Persis with a sigh. 'They'd thought of that one too. They turned up the statements of the two guys, and the thing came unstuck at once. Seemed the boys hadn't taken their time from any dashboard clock—it's busted anyway. They both had wristwatches and they swear to the time they got back. Glenn tried to argue it, but the cops threw him out with the greatest charm. I thought he was going to cry, and I don't mind telling you honey that it was all I could do not to put my arms round him and kiss him right there in the roadway and say: "There, there, son! Tell Momma all about it and she'll see that you're arrested for murder if that's the way you want it!" And what I want to know,' said Persis with feeling, 'is am I nuts, or is he?'

'So *that's* what he meant!' said Amanda, enlightened.

'How's that?'

'Nothing much. Just something he said about trying something, but that it hadn't been any use and he'd only made rather a fool of himself.'

'When did he say that?' demanded Persis quickly. 'Have you seen him this afternoon?'

'Yes,' said Amanda hesitantly.

She looked at Persis Halliday, frowning and uncertain. Persis could never have seen or heard of Anita Barton until that afternoon on the S.S. *Orantares* at Port Said, and could not previously have been aware of her existence, or that of Monica Ford. She had never been to Cyprus before, and she could have no possible reason for wanting to pin a murder—two murders!—on Glenn Barton's wife.

Quite suddenly Amanda made up her mind. The terror and strain and emotional tension of the last few days had been too much for her, and she had to confide in someone. It should have been Steve, but Steve had been curt and unkind, and he had apparently gone to Nicosia.

Amanda said: 'Persis, if I tell you something, will you promise me that you won't tell anyone else?—anyone at all?'

Persis looked at her for a long moment with narrowed speculative eyes, and then held out her hand. It was a strong hand, with long, intelligent, square-tipped fingers, and its clasp was comfortably firm and reassuring.

'Shoot!' said Persis laconically.

She listened to Amanda's account of the afternoon's interview with enthralled interest, and when it was finished said: 'Well if this doesn't beat Erle Stanley Gardner! When do we start?'

'We?' echoed Amanda.

'Sure. I'm going with you. You don't really think I'm going to let you stick your neck out like this without standing by with a blackjack just in case anyone tries any rough stuff? Why I wouldn't miss it for a million dollars! I'm in on this, honey, and you can't get me out.'

Amanda laughed, conscious of a sudden and overwhelming flood of relief. She would not have admitted to anyone how little the thought of that coming night's adventure had appealed to her, or how frightening she had found the prospect of that long, lonely drive back to Kyrenia. But now that Persis would be with her the affair lost its terrors, and became instead merely an exciting escapade.

Amanda threw an arm about Persis and gave her a sudden and impulsive hug.

'Persis, you're an angel!'

'So I have frequently been informed,' said Persis dryly. 'And now let's take a stroll up to that villa of yours and break it to Miss Moon that you will be dining with me at the Dome. Then there will no hitch over getting to that car on time. What do you say?'

They scrambled to their feet and carried out this programme, and Amanda, not without some qualms, left Miss Moon to dine alone. She reassured herself, however, with the reflection that Steve Howard would have taken every possible precaution to safeguard Miss Moon from further danger, and was relieved to see that the usual loiterer was industriously engaged in doing nothing at the corner of the road.

They met Alastair Blaine coming out of the Dome. He appeared to be in a hurry and said that he had a date to dine at Antonakis' Restaurant in Nicosia.

'I'm told that the speciality is octopus,' said Alastair. 'I've always wanted not to eat octopus, but life catches up on one. I'll probably be seeing you sometime tomorrow—if I survive!'

Persis said: 'Who's your date with, Alastair?' But Alastair was already striding rapidly away into the dusk, and it is doubtful whether he heard the question.

Claire came out of Zari's lace shop opposite the hotel, and seeing them, waved, but did not come over to speak to them and also appeared to be in a hurry.

They saw no one else they knew, beyond a few hotel acquaintances of Persis Halliday's, and Lumley Potter, who was eating a lonely meal in a far corner of the dining-room, and who left early. Anita had evidently thought it best to send him out for the evening. There was no sign of either Toby Gates or Steven Howard, both of whom were obviously dining elsewhere that night.

They lingered over their meal as long as they could, but the hands of the clock seemed to crawl and stop and crawl again. Even Persis began to be affected by tension, for she lit one cigarette from the next in endless succession, jerking the ash on to the floor with nervous fingers and fidgeting restlessly in her chair.

At last it was nine o'clock and Persis glanced at the tiny diamond-ringed dial of her wrist-watch, checked it with a hotel clock, and rose:

'Let's go.'

They went first to her room where Persis fetched a thin tussore silk coat from the cupboard and peered intently at her face in the looking-glass. She tied a chiffon scarf over her smoothly waved hair, applied some lipstick with careful concentration, and declared herself ready.

They walked up through the town, and were pausing at the junction of two roads when George Norman passed them, driving his car. As he slowed down for the cross traffic, the headlights of an approaching car fell full on him, and they saw that his pleasant, rubicund face was looking as sulky as that of a small boy whose play has been interrupted by a request to help with the washing up. He did not see Persis and Amanda, but drove on up the main road out of Kyrenia.

'A dime'll get you a dollar that Teeny Weeny Claire has sent him out to run errands,' commented Persis with a grin. 'What that guy needs is a nice bellhop's outfit with a dandy set of buttons down the front. Then he'd be right in character.'

They found a car parked in a patch of shadow near the edge of the vacant lot. But it was not Glenn's car.

'Sure this is it?' inquired Persis, speaking entirely unintentionally in a whisper.

'It must be. It's empty and the key's in it. He wouldn't have left his own, because his wife would have recognized it.'

'You're dead right. Okay, get in. I'd better sit in the back and put up a silent prayer that this contraption does not belong to some honest but absent-minded citizen who has chosen an unfortunate spot to park his jalopy. I do not fancy the prospect of spending the rest of my stay in Aphrodite's Island in the can!'

Amanda settled herself behind the wheel and turned on the dashboard lights. The ignition key was already in place, and she switched on the engine and pressed the self-starter. A moment later the car moved softly off down the road.

Anita Barton was waiting in the shadow of a jacaranda tree. She wore a dark linen coat and a scarf over her head, and was carrying a small suitcase.

Amanda threw open the car door and the next moment Mrs Barton was beside her, breathing quickly and shivering with fear or tension. She slammed the door behind her, and as the car drew away from the kerb, caught sight of Persis Halliday's reflection in the windscreen and whipped round with a choking cry that was almost a scream.

'Who's that!'

'It's all right,' said Amanda quickly. 'It's only Mrs Halliday. She's a friend of mine. She came along to—keep me company on the way back.'

'I don't think we've met,' said Persis sociably. 'I'm pleased to know you. I hope you won't think I'm butting in, but I thought maybe Amanda could do with a bit of support. It's going to be a long ride home.'

'You're an American, aren't you?' said Anita Barton in a hard voice.

'Dyed in the wool,' said Persis.

Mrs Barton fell silent, but it was not a relaxed silence. She sat tense and quivering, and every now and again she threw a quick, hunted look over her shoulder as if she feared to see the headlights of a pursuing car. Twice a car overtook them and passed in a cloud of dust, and she cowered down in her seat; bending her head so that her features were hidden by the dashboard.

The winding road and the olive groves, and the steep stony sides of the Kyrenia range, were milky with moonlight. The sea was a placid sheet of polished silver, and the night was warm and white and wonderful. The road dipped and turned and climbed through the streets of little white-walled villages and fell away into miniature valleys where small stone culverts spanned the stony beds of streams; and the miles unwound behind them . . .

'We're nearly there,' said Anita Barton, speaking for the first time in almost twenty minutes. 'Stop here. By those trees. We can see from here if the road is clear and if it's safe to go on.'

Amanda pulled the car to a stop where a ragged clump of scrub and casurina trees made a pool of freckled shadow.

'Turn off the lights,' commanded Anita Barton in a harsh whisper.

Amanda switched them off obediently, but left the engine running softly as Mrs Barton opened the car door and stepped out into the moonlit road and Persis and Amanda followed her.

The shore lay some fifty yards or so to the left of the road and was separated from them by a stretch of rock-strewn ground covered with coarse grasses, stunted shrubs and mulberry trees.

Anita Barton spoke in a whisper: 'I'm going to walk to the turn of the road to see if all's clear. Sometimes there are picnic parties here on moonlight nights. Miss Derington had better stay by the car. You'—she turned to Persis—'will you go to the cliff edge and see if you can see a boat out there? It should be off the rocks about half a mile ahead. You can see straight across from this point. We won't go on if it isn't there.'

'Okay,' said Persis with a sigh. 'I guess it will ruin my nylons to say nothing of my nerves, but it's all in a good cause.'

She turned away and vanished into the shadows of the casurina scrub, her high-heeled slippers making no sound in the soft, sandy soil beyond the road's edge.

Anita Barton waited for a moment or two and then walked round to the front of the car. She stopped suddenly and bent down, and Amanda heard her catch her breath.

'What is it?' asked Amanda sharply.

'Look!' said Anita Barton in a frightened whisper.

Amanda ran round to her and bent down, staring at the white, dusty road where Anita Barton's trembling finger pointed.

'What is it? she said. 'I don't see——'

And then she saw the shadow on the moonlit road.

Anita Barton's shadow. A shadow that held something in its hand and swung its arm silently upward and swiftly down again.

Amanda tried to turn, but it was too late. Something crashed with a cruel force on to the back of her bent head and she fell forward into blackness and lay sprawling on the moonlit road.

Anita Barton laughed. A soft, unsteady, hysterical sound in that silver silence.

She looked behind her with wide, panic-stricken eyes, but there was no sound or sign of Persis Halliday, and she turned back to Amanda and stooping down, gripped her by the shoulders and half dragged, half lifted her into the car. She closed the door on her, ran round and climbed into the driver's seat and released the brake.

The car slid away with barely a sound down the moonlit road, its lights still switched off—a grey shadow in the black and white and silver of the night. At the bottom of a long slope the road swung round a curve and began to climb again, and the car, having gathered speed, took the gradient at fifty and roared on down the coast road with the needle of the speedometer touching seventy-five.

The rush of the night air revived Amanda and she stirred and moaned with pain and opened her eyes.

For a minute or two she could not remember where she was, or think of anything but the agonizing pain of her head. It seemed to her that she was looking into a red haze shot with stabbing scarlet lights. Then the haze lifted slowly and the night air was cool and pleasant against her throbbing forehead, and she remembered Anita Barton's shadow on the moonlit road . . .

Anita had hit her with something; something hard and heavy and made of metal. But the thick coils of her hair had cushioned her from the full force of the savage blow.

Anita——

Amanda lifted her head slowly and painfully and saw Anita Barton's face in the faint glow of the dashboard light. A white mask of a face, the red lips drawn back over the teeth in a purely animal grimace. There was a touch of froth at the corners of that mouth and the wide eyes were fixed and glaring and bright with fear.

She felt Amanda stir, and turned her head. The next moment she had taken her foot from the accelerator and jammed on the brakes.

The car screeched to a standstill and the shock of its sudden stop flung Amanda's numbed body forward against the dashboard.

Anita Barton drew something out of her pocket, and the moonlight glinted along the barrel of a heavy service revolver.

'Don't do anything silly,' she warned, her voice harsh and high and uncontrolled.

She put up her left hand and tore at the silk scarf that was tied about her head, jerked it free and said: 'Turn round with your back to me and put your hands behind you. Quickly!'

Amanda, with that cold ring of metal thrust against her, obeyed numbly. She felt Anita Barton's hot unsteady fingers winding the silk about her wrists and wrenching the knots painfully tight, and realized that she must temporarily have laid aside the gun.

'That's right,' Mrs Barton's voice was panting and breathless. 'Now your ankles.' She dragged Amanda over roughly and tied her ankles with a length of cord that she must have brought with her and then savagely and unexpectedly thrust a handkerchief into Amanda's gasping mouth and wound another length of material across it, pulling down her hair with a ruthless hand so that it would not impede the tightness of the gag. It was quite obvious that she had made her preparations with some care.

'There!' said Anita Barton with breathless satisfaction.

She stared down into Amanda's wide, terror-filled eyes and laughed long and loudly; a high, hysterical laugh.

'So you're another of Glenn's girls, are you. You planned this with him, didn't you? Darling Glenn! What a fool you must have thought me! So he's going to wait for me with a boat, is he? He's going to get a surprise. The very last surprise of his life. He arranged it all so beautifully, didn't he? But he's the one who is going to disappear. Not me. I've kept this gun for him. I thought of using it on myself once, but I shall use it on him instead. It *was* Glenn who put you up to this, wasn't it?—*wasn't it!* Of course it was. Well it's the last thing he'll do. You thought you'd fooled me, didn't you? All that stuff about doing this for my sake; for my safety; when all the time you were doing it for the sake of dear Glenn. Why you little——!'

She used an unprintable word. Her eyes were not sane and her face was ash-white in the moonlight and contorted with rage and fear—the rage and fear of a hunted animal turning at bay. She glared at Amanda, her breast heaving with her panting breath, and suddenly and unexpectedly she laughed again and turned to release the brake.

She drove more slowly now; and presently, at the top of a rise, switched off the engine and let the car coast down a long, gentle sloping stretch of road, and braked it softly near the edge of a patch of shadow thrown by some tall, windworn rocks.

She sat quite still, listening intently, and after a moment or two opened the car door and slipped out.

She turned and looked back at Amanda and said in a whisper that was barely a breath of sound: 'When you hear a shot you'll know that you've helped dear Glenn to a death that will probably be painful. I've never used a gun before, so I shall make quite sure I don't miss him. You can stay here and listen for it. I'll deal with you later.'

She turned away and moved silently out into the moonlight to vanish down a narrow, sandy track between tumbled rocks that led to a low headland, some fifty yards distant, below which the unseen sea purred softly against a shelving beach.

Amanda turned and twisted frantically, wrenching helplessly at her bound wrists. Glenn would not be there, but since his wife did not believe that, it would be some harmless, friendly fisherman who would die. He would be waiting for her, and she would shoot him down without mercy and without warning—killing him as she must have killed poor, helpless Monica Ford. And because she had never used a gun before she would play for safety and fire at the man's chest or stomach, and he would die horribly, coughing blood.

Anita Barton was not sane. Fear for her own safety had driven her over the narrow line that lies between sanity and madness. Had Glenn really suspected all the time that she might be a murderess? Was that why he had tried to get her away—and used any and every excuse to that end?

Amanda writhed and wrenched and tugged at her bonds in helpless, frantic fear. She must not let Anita kill again. She could not lie there and wait for the sound of a shot, and know that she herself would be the next to die. She tried to get her chin on to the car horn, thinking that if she could sound it, it might cause Anita Barton to take fright; but she slipped and fell to the floor, and hit her head on the steering wheel trying to get upright again.

Then all at once hands were gripping her and dragging her up, and there was an urgent, hissing whisper in her ear:

'For Pete's sake stay still! How in heck can I get you outa this while you're hopping like a jumping bean?'

Persis! Amanda's slim body was suddenly limp with relief. Fingers fumbled at the knot behind her head and Persis' voice whispered: 'Damn and blast this hair of yours! Why the heck you want to——'

And then the bandage was whipped away and Amanda spat out the sodden handkerchief and was breathing in deep gulps of air.

'Persis!—how did you get here?'

'*Ssh!* Keep quiet! Do you want that dame back on us?' Persis started on the knotted scarf that bound Amanda's wrists and explained in a whisper:

'I didn't like the look of the set-up. There was a gleam in that gal's eye that I've seen in the eye of a horse in my day. And I don't buy nor ride those horses! I walked round the back of those trees and counted ten and came right back again, and found you out like a light and the girlfriend making a getaway. So I jumped a ride on the luggage grid, and here I am. A very dusty and unpleasant journey, and I nearly broke my neck when she slammed on the brakes a mile or so back. There you are——'

Amanda's wrists were free. She bent and tugged at the knots about her ankles, and a minute later she was out of the car and standing in the bright moonlight.

'Hey, come back!' hissed Persis. 'This is where we beat it!'

'I can't,' said Amanda desperately. 'She thinks it's Glenn down there on the beach, and she'll take a shot at him. Can't you see, I've got to stop her!'

'Okay,' said Persis, resigned. 'I guess I'll come with you. Let's go.'

She jumped out into the road and gave a brief and muffled yelp of pain.

'Holy cat!' gasped Persis, hopping on one foot.

'What is it?'

'Lost a shoe back there, and I've trodden on a rock.'

'Well you can't come on one foot,' said Amanda in a feverish whisper. 'Stay here and find a spanner or something, and if she comes back, see if you can lay her out!'

She turned and ran in the direction that Anita Barton had taken a few minutes before.

The path came out on the top of a low cliff below which lay a tangle of sea grass and huge tumbled rocks. Amanda could see no sign of Anita Barton and imagined that she must be lying in wait in the shadows of one of the big boulders. She crept forward, grateful that the wash of the sea on the shelving beach blurred the sound of her movements, and reached the level of the shore.

The sand was warm and dry and deep and she edged her way between the high, wind-worn rocks and found herself looking out on a small curving beach bounded on one side by the low headland that she had just descended, and on the other by a long natural breakwater of tumbled rocks.

A boat was drifting in from the shining sea; a boat that had evidently been waiting off the point of the rocks. She could hear the soft splash of oars above the hush of a slow tide that broke gently on the beach with a sound like the rustle of dry leaves in a light autumn breeze. Then a keel grated on wet sand.

There was only one man in the small boat, and Amanda saw him ship the oars and jump out into the creaming surf to draw the prow a little farther up the beach.

He turned and walked towards her, and the moonlight fell full on his face.

It was Glenn Barton.

For a moment the shock of that knowledge deprived Amanda of the power to call out. Then she opened her mouth to scream a warning and stopped—checked by the terrified knowledge that Anita must be somewhere ahead of her, and that if she cried out Glenn would stop and Anita, realizing that she was discovered, would fire.

She edged her way forward, keeping to the shadow of the rocks and nearing the point where Anita must be standing.

Someone moved out of the shadows barely half a dozen yards ahead of her and Glenn stopped and said quietly: 'Anita.'

The single, softly spoken word sounded astonishingly loud in that white silence where the only other sound was the lazy, murmurous whisper of the tide.

Anita Barton moved out into the moonlight, one hand in the pocket of her loose linen coat. She drew the hand out slowly, and Amanda raced forward and flung herself on Mrs Barton's arm, dragging it down so that the shot went harmlessly into the sand.

The small bay seemed full of the echoes of that sound, and Amanda's hands were on cold metal, wrenching it, twisting it free and flinging it away.

Glenn stooped slowly and picked it up, and Anita Barton turned on Amanda screaming; clawing at her like a frenzied cat:

'*You fool!* Oh you fool! Can't you see he'll kill us. *No* Glenn!—no —no! I don't want to die!'

She crumpled at Amanda's feet in a sobbing, shuddering heap.

Glenn Barton looked down at the weapon in his hand and then at his frantic wife. He raised the revolver quite steadily and said in a pleasant, soft voice:

'Yes. I shall kill you. You were really becoming too dangerous altogether. Both of you. No, don't move, Amanda! I am an excellent shot and I happen to have my own gun as well as the one my dear wife—my very dear wife—has so thoughtfully provided me with. I am sorry that you will have to disappear too. You will, of course, have accompanied Anita to the Lebanon and a telegram to that effect will be handed in there in a day or two. Anita, naturally, has left a letter which will explain everything to Miss Moon and to anyone who may be interested: I can really copy her handwriting very well. When, eventually, you fail to reappear, it will of course be obvious that my wife has committed another murder.'

Amanda said breathlessly: 'Glenn!—Glenn, what are you talking about? I don't understand——' Her voice did not seem to belong to her, but to some stranger.

'I think you do,' said Glenn softly. 'You came here to spy on me, didn't you Amanda? To report on me to your uncle. I'm sorry that I shall have to shoot you. It's noisy and bloody, and I dislike noise and blood. But there appears to be no alternative. You seem to be immune to poison. Some friend of yours drank the stuff that was meant for you on the ship, and you wouldn't even touch the drink I offered you at the Inn. I'd got either contingency worked out to look like suicide, and it would have saved a great deal of trouble. Then I had what looked like the chance of a lifetime at Hilarion, but a fluke saved you, and when I tried to get back I found Howard was on his way up behind me. As there was no other way down and no one else up there, the only possible way out of a very sticky situation was to risk my neck and save you. The irony of that should appeal to you.'

'No!' said Amanda in a sobbing whisper. 'No Glenn. You're mad. You don't know what you're saying!'

'Oh yes I do. I thought I could get you both once before. You practically handed it to me on a plate. I meant to throw you down Anita's stairs, and then go up and send her after you. They'd have said she must have been drunk and pushed you, and then fallen herself. Those banisters are like matchwood. But that interfering idiot Howard wrecked that too.'

Amanda said chokingly: 'I don't believe it! It isn't true.'

'Anita believes it. Don't you Anita dear? Stand up Anita—stand up my darling. You won't like it if I put a bullet through you while you're on the ground. It might hit you where it would hurt. You won't know anything about it if you stand up. The fish will leave nothing that can be identified if you should ever come up on a trawl. But I don't think you will. I'll weight you well. Stand up Anita——'

Anita Barton grovelled in the sand, sobbing and choking and pleading. She crawled forward on her knees, her face a mask of tears and sand, crazy with terror.

Glenn Barton looked down at her with cold disgust and fired with complete indifference.

Anita screamed at the sound of the shot and leapt to her feet, but Glenn did not fire again.

He stood staring, wide-eyed, at the gun in his hand; then he dropped it on to the sand and whipped a second one from the pocket of his coat.

A shadow moved out of the shadows of the piled rocks: and another, and another, until the moonlight curve of the narrow beach was ringed with silent men, and a familiar voice remarked pleasantly:

'You won't find that one any good either, I'm afraid.'

19

Glenn Barton whipped round on the speaker, gun in hand, and Amanda flung herself frantically between them.

'Steve——!'

There was an orange flash of flame and for the third time that night the quiet cove echoed to the sound of a shot.

Steve Howard removed Amanda's clinging fingers and said: 'It's only blank,' and Glenn Barton flung the useless weapon savagely at his head.

Steve ducked, thrust Amanda to one side, and leapt at him.

Amanda heard the blow go home on Glenn Barton's body and saw him bend double and throw his head up, gasping for air. There was the crack of a second blow to the jaw; a crisp, sharp sound that seemed almost as loud as the report of the useless revolver. Glenn Barton's body appeared to leave the ground, and came to rest a yard or so away, spreadeagled and unconscious on the sand.

'I have been aching to do that for days!' observed Steve, breathing a little unevenly.

He turned to a man who was standing beside him, and Amanda saw with a numbled lack of surprise that it was the man with the odd name whom she had seen once before in the hall of the Villa Oleander on the evening that Monica Ford had died.

'Well there he is,' said Steve. 'He's all yours.'

He turned to Anita Barton: 'If you're feeling all right, Mrs Barton, we'll get back to the car. Amanda, you can't cry here! Save it for the journey back and I'll lend you my shoulder.'

He took hold of Anita Barton's arm with one hand and Amanda's with the other and urged them up the narrow path towards the car. Someone was limping towards them down the path and Steve checked suddenly.

'It's Persis,' said Amanda.

'Good grief!' said Mr Howard, exasperated. 'What the hell is she doing mixed up in this?'

'She came with me,' explained Amanda.

Persis materialized out of the moonlight.

''Lo Steve. Sugar Ray Robinson in person, I presume? I'm sorry I missed the first two acts and the intermission, but I had a grandstand seat for the finale. It certainly packed a punch.'

She turned and accompanied them back to the car, limping a trifle, and subsided abruptly on to the running board.

Steve produced a flask from his coat pocket, removed the cap, filled it and handed it over.

'Thanks a lot,' said Persis, gulping the contents. 'Boy! did I need that. Sling some into Anita; her need is greater than mine.'

Anita Barton drank with chattering teeth and looked at Steve Howard. Her face was still white and tear-streaked, but her voice was no longer hysterical.

'I can't thank you enough. When did you—how did you know about Glenn?'

'You knew, didn't you?' said Steve gently.

'Of course. That was why I left him. I tried to warn that fool Monica, but she wouldn't listen. She was crazy about him.'

'How did you find out?'

'Oh—little things. A lot of little things that all added up. Then I began to watch him, and—and in the end I found out. I was frightened then. I knew that if he once realized that I knew, he—he'd kill me. He was always a killer. Quiet and decent and—and *deadly*. He'd been making love to Monica, and I used that as an excuse. I had to get away from him. I *had* to!'

Persis said sharply: 'I'll believe almost anything after what I've seen tonight, but I will not believe that guy ever made a pass at a middle-aged dame with buck teeth and a forty-two inch waist!'

'But he did,' said Anita Barton drearily. 'You see she'd been sent out to see what was going on. Mr Derington sent her. He always believed that women had an instinct over shady business. I think he must have heard a few rumours, so he sent out a competent secretary who was to find out what went on, and report.'

Anita Barton subsided wearily onto the running board beside Persis, and leaned her head back against the car door. She said: 'Glenn made love to her. He could always make women fall for him. He has that "little-boy-lost" look about him that makes fools of the best of them—it made a fool of me too! Monica went overboard about him. He was probably the only man who had ever looked twice at her, and he reduced her to a pulp. After that he could do anything with her and make her swallow any lie. I'd stood for his affairs with half a dozen other women including Claire—Claire used to send and carry messages for him that he couldn't risk sending himself. I don't think she realized what he was doing. He probably told her some convincing lie; and anyway she can look after herself. But the Monica business sickened me. When I tried to warn her she was rude and hysterical, and I got Lumley to let me move in on him. He only did it to score off Glenn and Claire, and because he has an inferiority complex as a result of being a Conscientious Objector during the War, so he feels he must pose as a flouter of public opinion.'

Amanda said helplessly: 'I don't understand! What was Glenn doing?'

'Gun running,' said Steve Howard briefly.

'*What?*' Persis straightened up abruptly and nearly fell on her face on the roadside. 'Why—say Steve, where do you come in on all this?'

'Oh, I'd been told off to find out who was back of the racket,' said Steve. He looked over his shoulder and said impatiently: 'How much longer do you suppose those sleuths are going to be?'

'Never mind them,' said Persis firmly. 'Spill it, honey—you have our undivided attention. I for one am not shifting from this spot until I've got all the dirt, and you can't drive off with a gal on the running board!'

Steve laughed a little grimly. He accepted one of Persis' cigarettes, lit it from her lighter, and said:

'We knew that someone was shipping guns into Africa and we knew that they were coming from a satellite country, via Cyprus. We did not know how it was done, but we narrowed it down a bit and became interested in, among others, Glennister Barton. It seemed just possible that he was using the wine business as a cover for something more profitable. He was. And things were going tolerably smoothly for him until Amanda suddenly put a cat among his pigeons.'

'*I* did?' said Amanda incredulously. 'How?'

'You decided to go to Cyprus, and your Uncle Oswin sent an exceedingly official letter demanding that you be put up and taken round and offered all facilities, and all the rest of it. It was a misleading document, and bearing in mind your uncle's preference for females in the role of snoopers, Glenn Barton imagined that you were being sent here expressly to spy on him—as Monica had been. He might have tried to carry it off, if it hadn't been for his matrimonial mess-up.'

Amanda said: 'But why should that matter?'

'Your uncle,' said Steve Howard, 'is a notorious prude in such matters. A hint from you that his nominee for the post of Barton's secretary was rumoured in love with the Boss—not to mention the rest of the set-up!—and Barton would probably have had the sack by wire. Or—more likely—your Uncle Oswin would have arrived on the next plane in order to clean the matter up.'

'Yes,' said Amanda slowly. 'He might have done. He's a bit rabid about that sort of thing.'

'Exactly. Barton couldn't risk it either way. He had a hell of a big deal coming off, and all he needed was just three more weeks and he'd have been in a position to clear off to some salubrious spot like South America, and keep himself in champagne and caviare until he died. It was as close as that. He daren't say that he couldn't have you, so he tried to stop you getting here. The stuff that Julia Blaine drank was meant for you.'

Persis said sharply: 'Julia! You mean that was *murder?*'

'But—but it was in her lemon juice,' said Amanda helplessly.

'It wasn't lemon. It was sweetlime. And there was plenty of sugar in it as well. The carpet was sticky with it. You merely jumped to the conclusion that it was lemon juice and meant for Julia because you hadn't ordered it, and, by a fluke, had happened to change cabins with Mrs Blaine much earlier in the day. Julia would never have ordered or touched such a thing. But a nice icy lime squash left in a cabin on a hot night was a pretty tempting bait. And when you told me that Mrs Blaine had gone to bed around ten o'clock, it began to look even more as though that glass had not been in the wrong cabin after all.'

'But why, Steve?'

'Ice. You didn't go down until nearly eleven, but there was still ice in that glass. There were chips of it on the carpet when I got there. If that drink had been in your cabin before ten the ice in it would have melted. Yet if it had been meant as a trap for Mrs Blaine it would never have been put there almost three-quarters of an hour after she had left the deck and gone to her cabin with a certain amount of attendant publicity. You, however, were dancing.'

Amanda said on a gasp: 'But—but Glenn! . . . Glenn couldn't have done it. He wasn't even there!'

'No. But one of his thugs was. You don't really suppose that anyone could run a racket of that description single-handed, do you? There were a gang of 'em up to their necks in it! This was a man called Kostos who was masquerading as a deck-hand. The husband, incidentally, of a woman who keeps an inn on the road to Limassol where you appear to have almost lost one of your nine lives.'

'It can't have been! Glenn told me that her husband was an old wreck of a man who——' She stopped suddenly and said in a shaken voice: 'I see now. He had to say something to make me turn round and look away from the table, so he said the first thing that came into his head. And then she—the woman—said that her husband had been on the ship. Why didn't I notice that? And Glenn dropped his cigarette into my glass. To make sure that no one else would drink it I suppose.'

'He also,' said Steve grimly, 'arranged for the disposal of the deck-hand. He was taking no chances. The chap was supposedly killed in a bar-room brawl: which was, oddly, enough, the reason why Miss Moon's staff, who were related to the widow, did not return on the day that Monica Ford was murdered and you were so neatly shoved over the battlements at Hilarion.'

Amanda shivered violently. 'But *why* Steve? Surely if—if I'd died here it would have been just as bad for him? Uncle Oswin would have come over then.'

'Would he? From all I've heard of him he doesn't sound like a man who would allow his niece, who was also his ward, to be buried in a place like this. It would have been the Derington Family Vault or nothing! Barton would only have had to cable your uncle that he was arranging to fly your corpse home in a coffin, pronto, and would he please meet? And it's my bet that your grief-stricken relative would have scrubbed the rest of his business schedule and taken the next plane to England, so that he could collect the dear-departed at London Airport, and lay on a suitable funeral. And if he *had* come here, he would have been in no state to start bothering about his wine business. That's for certain!

'If he'd come, it would only have been to collect the coffin from scratch, so that he could escort it home in person. Either way, he wouldn't have had the time or the inclination to start investigating the affairs of Mr Glennister Barton until he'd got your mortal remains parked in the family vault. And by that time, Barton would have been living it up in Buenos Aires or Montevideo, or wherever.'

'Yes, I see,' said Amanda with a shiver. You're right about the family vault; and about Uncle Oswin too. He'd never have left me here . . .'

'Exactly. I expect Barton was banking on that. But once you'd arrived in Cyprus—presumably to spy out the land—Barton could not risk letting you leave here alive. It was the time factor. He had to have those extra weeks, and the money involved was worth taking risks for. Any risks! He would have killed you and half a dozen others cheerfully for it.'

Amanda said: 'But why on earth should I have committed suicide? What possible reason could I——'

'Judging from statistics,' interrupted Steve impatiently, 'the average adolescent can decide to "End It All" for any number of footling reasons. Unrequited love coming high on the list—the "I can't live without him" syndrome. That would always have been a safe card to play, since it would have been difficult to disprove, once you were dead. After all, it even occurred fleetingly to me—and a lot less fleetingly to the police!—that you might have bumped off Julia Blaine in the hope of snaffling her husband. It was considered a possibility. And if you'd died of the same poison in that pub; it could have been written off as remorse!'

'Yes, you told me about the "possibility",' snapped Amanda, torn between indignation at remembered outrage, and annoyance at being classed as an 'average adolescent': 'But what about Monica? It wasn't possible for Glenn to have killed her. Not by any stretch of even *your* fertile imagination!'

'Oh yes it was. He saw her going into Miss Moon's that afternoon, and followed her in. She had come to see you.'

'But why? What did she want to see me for?'

'Because both she and Barton, as a result of your uncle's letter, had it firmly fixed in their heads that you were really here as a sort of private agent for him. And she had found out what Barton was up to.'

'But surely, she must have known before?'

'She'd probably always known or suspected that there was something pretty peculiar going on, but I think she deliberately shut her eyes to it and tried to pretend that it was merely a matter of smuggling a few cigarettes. Something on those lines. But that afternoon a case, supposedly containing wine, got broken, and as Barton was out, she opened it herself and realized what he was doing. A week earlier and she might still have looked the other way, for she was about as completely under Barton's thumb as a frustrated spinster can be. But her brother had just been murdered by Mau Mau terrorists—armed by Glenn Barton! It broke her up, and she rushed into Kyrenia to see you and spill the beans. And Barton strangled her.'

Amanda said: 'He can't have done, Steve! He can't possibly have done it. The police proved that he went straight from Hilarion to Nicosia.'

'He did. But he killed Monica Ford before he ever arrived at Hilarion.'

'But she was *warm!*'

'I know. That was what put us all out of step for a bit. He'd left her in front of the french windows, where the sun had been full on her from the time he killed her until just before it set. It had barely gone from the room when we got back; remember? Of course she was warm! It's never as easy as detective fiction would have you believe to fix the exact time of death. It depends on a good many things, and temperature has a lot to do with it. Glenn Barton had his wits about him, and made very good use of the fact that the sun would be on that bit of the room from roughly four fifteen onwards. He came on to Hilarion, mentioned having seen the woman, and provided himself with a nice alibi all round. And when he was telephoned for by the police—as he knew he would be—he arrived complete with that neat bit of evidence against his wife, and planted it as he came through the hall.'

'I knew it was Glenn who had done that,' said Anita Barton with a shudder. 'It couldn't have been anyone else. There were several of those flowers in the house. They were always coming off, and I'd left a lot of my stuff behind. He must have gone through my dressing-table drawers, and found one.'

'I imagined so,' said Steve. 'He then provided an affecting scene by registering sufficient horror at the sight of it to attract everyone's suspicious attention. And Amanda nearly spoilt the whole show by rushing into the breach like Florence Nightingale or Flora Macdonald, and claiming it as hers. However, just in case the police proved bat-witted enough to believe her, he took the precaution of ringing up Mrs Norman and spilling the beans under cover of a distracted plea that she should go and see you, Mrs Barton, and tell you to destroy the dress. He knew dam' well that she'd see you dead first, and also that she could be trusted to spread the story around the whole of Cyprus.'

Anita Barton said: 'He meant to get me hanged for murder!'

Steve shook his head. 'I don't think so. The last thing he wanted was a court case of that sort. He was working up to an artistic disappearing act, so that people would jump to the conclusion that you had lost your nerve and bolted. He worked round to that angle very nicely, and I added the last touch by ordering Amanda to write at once to her uncle. That tore it. If she had done so, and her uncle had arrived by return of post, the whole thing would have blown up in his face. I thought that threat would fetch him, and it did.'

Amanda stared at him, speechless, and Anita Barton said wearily: 'And I thought she was in it with him. That she'd fallen for him too, like Monica and all the other fools. I hit her over the head with that gun, and I thought I'd killed her. I'm sorry, Amanda. I knew he was trying to kill me, and I thought you were helping him.'

Amanda was not listening to her. She was clinging to the door handle of the car and looking at Steve:

'You mean you *knew* that he'd do something like this?' demanded Amanda breathlessly. 'You told me to write that letter just to make him—to make him . . .' Words appeared to fail her.

'I had to darling,' said Steve. 'We had to panic him into showing his hand. But if it's any consolation to you, it was quite the most unpleasant thing I've ever had to do. We'd have got him on the gun-running without it. But we might well have failed to pin him with murder. And we did at least go to a great deal of trouble to remove the bullets from any guns he possessed and replace them with blanks. Which wasn't as easy as it may sound. However, I will admit that I had left out of my calculations the possibility that Mrs Barton might crack you over the head with a blunt instrument—although I can sympathize with her point of view.'

Amanda stared at him for a long moment, her face white in the moonlight.

She said in a small, frozen voice: 'If you are thinking of driving us back, I think we'd all like to get home. Persis, are you ready?'

'And how!' said Persis. 'Anita honey, will you sit in front by the driver? And I guess it might be a good idea, when we get back, if you and I doubled up for the night just to keep each other company. We'll get a spare bed put up in my room and order up a bath of hot coffee and a quart of chloroform. This has been quite a party, and the sooner we sleep it off the better.'

Amanda got haughtily into the back of the car and said: 'Come on Persis!'

Persis closed the door on Anita Barton and looked at Steve Howard.

'Steve honey,' she inquired softly, 'how much am I offered to drive this car?'

Steve laughed.

'Persis honey,' he said, 'you will drive this car or else——!'

'Okay,' said Persis. 'It's a stick-up!'

Amanda attempted to descend but Steve was too quick for her. He slammed the door behind him and pulled her very roughly into his arms.

Amanda made a small, sobbing and unintelligible sound that was abruptly silenced, and presently said breathlessly: 'Steve, please——!'

'My heart,' said Mr Howard, 'shut up! You can keep the conversation for later. We are not alone.'

'Don't mind us,' said Persis cordially, starting up the car and backing it expertly on the sandy verge. 'Go right ahead and kiss her.'

'What do you think I'm doing?' inquired Steve with pardonable irritation.

Persis laughed, and having tactfully twisted the driving mirror until it faced the roof, headed the car down the long white moonlit road towards Kyrenia.

ABOUT THE AUTHOR

M.M. Kaye is the author of eight romantic thrillers, two historical novels and several children's books. She was born in India and spent much of her childhood and adult life there. After her education in England, she returned to India and married Goff Hamilton, an officer in Queen Victoria's Own Corps of Guides. Her husband's military assignments took them all over India as well as Egypt, Kenya, Germany, England, Northern Ireland and Scotland. She became world famous in 1978 with the publication of her monumental bestseller about India under the British Raj, *The Far Pavilions*. She is also the author of the bestselling *Shadow of the Moon* and *Trade Wind*.